DAYBREAK

FATE'S FORSAKEN SERIES

BOOK 4

Shae Ford

For Nana and Boompa; Mimama and Poppy
There was always a new adventure to be had, wasn't there?
Whether we trekked by machete or paintbrush —
it didn't matter to us
Your homes were the corners of our Kingdom

TABLE OF CONTENTS

PROLOGUE
The Earl's Fate

Devin stood alone at the mountains' top.

The world was cold and still. Snow poured so thickly from the clouds that if he paused, he could hear it: the earth tugging on their bellies while the air hissed across their backs. The heavy flakes wavered uncertainly. They spun like creatures with broken wings until they finally struck the ground, their fragile bodies shattering against unforgiving mounds of white.

They broke one after another, spilling across the remains of those who'd fallen just before. As all the little pieces of their crystal flesh rolled away, each made a distinct sound — its own tiny, final gasp.

Noise had become unbearable, of late.

Devin could hear everything, even the things he didn't want to hear. The whistling of the archmage's breath as he sucked air between his teeth, the way his steps dragged across the cold stone floor — the things he laughed about with the castle guards. These sounds haunted him to the edge of the Kingdom, to the crest of the mountains' top.

A ruined, frozen castle surrounded him. Devin didn't remember the journey. But if he closed his eyes tightly, he could see it: a broken memory of rounded walls and a shattered tower perched upon a hill of bright blue stone. There was a gap taken out of the back wall — as if the rest of the fortress had broken off and fallen into the sea below ...

The sea ...

Devin's mind cut from the memory of the frozen ruins and struck upon another. He saw swirling waves and mountains of ice set adrift among the blue. Though a part of him curled its toes at the distance between his body and the ground, another part cleaved to the memory — it welcomed the cold relief of the icy spray, relished the danger of gliding between the mountains' peaks.

It wasn't the sea that excited him so much as the thing that lay beyond it ... a warm shadow in the distance ... a refuge set atop the world that made both parts of him long to take flight ...

The sea, Devin thought again. He took a half step towards the shattered cliff ...

Concentrate, beast. Tell me what you've found.

Devin clutched his ears at the sudden burst of Ulric's voice inside his head. The archmage was always listening. All the words that Devin thought belonged to *him* — he'd made that very clear.

But Devin never had much time to think.

A strange darkness had come along with the sounds. It stood unflinching at the back of his mind, always coiled to strike. Sometimes its presence was nothing more than a dull throb — an annoyance he shoved aside. But other times, the darkness rose sharply.

It covered his eyes and trapped him in something that felt like sleep, except that when the darkness covered him, he *knew* he was asleep. His mind scratched and clawed against its hold. Hours might pass while Devin battled the darkness. Sometimes it would be days before he woke — and its hold was always strongest around the archmage.

He was often awake when Ulric entered the chamber. Sometimes he would even feel the pain of the first cut or burn. But after that, the darkness snapped its wings over his eyes. He knew no more until he woke, wounded and sore.

Devin knew the darkness must've been *his* doing: the dragon whose soul he'd fought with at the Braided Tree. Though they'd tried, neither of them had been able to defeat the other. Their battle crashed through the shadowed realm and into the world beyond. Now the dragon's grip on their bodies was just as strong as Devin's. Sometimes, it was even stronger.

There was no end to it, either. There was no hope that the darkness would ever relent. Devin could escape the dragon's hold no more than a man could escape his shadow.

He'd shoved Devin aside the moment they took flight. He'd carried them here. But the dragon didn't always understand what Ulric wanted from them. So he'd had no choice but to slink back and let Devin speak.

The fortress is ruined.

8

Devin picked his way across the snow. Behind him lay a broken tower. Its top had burst and its bricks were scattered across the field. The ruins spread in an arc throughout the courtyard.

Among the bits of brick were a number of strange mounds. Devin scraped the snow from the edge of the nearest one. His stomach twisted when he saw a hand lay beneath it — a human hand, perfectly preserved beneath a cask of ice.

There are bodies in the courtyard.

Whose bodies? There should be an emblem on the chest.

Devin didn't want to look for an emblem. He didn't want to scrape any deeper. But Ulric would not be ignored.

Search the body!

His voice stabbed Devin's ears with something that felt like the barbs of bees. Their insides swelled, screamed for relief. He swiped desperately at the snow beside the hand.

If there had been an emblem on the man's chest, it was gone now. There was nothing but a ragged hole — edged by the shattered remains of his ribs, stained with the dark red of his blood.

Devin's stomach lurched and his last meal came up behind it. He was still retching when Ulric's voice stung him again. He nearly tripped in his rush to get to the next mound.

It was much larger than the first. When he wiped the snow away, a monster's face startled him backwards.

Fur sprouted from its flesh in coarse, uneven patches. Fangs cut out from a mouth twisted in a snarl. The bridge of its nose was wrinkled in what could've been pain or shock. Its empty black eyes were frozen in death.

What do you see? Ulric demanded.

Monsters — like the ones in the dungeons. Some sort of cat, he added, scraping the snow from its pointed ears.

This monster sickened him more than the corpse. Devin had seen the creatures trapped in His Majesty's dungeons: their human halves had been nearly devoured by the animal. A curse twisted their bodies into horrible shapes ... the same curse Devin wore around his neck.

The iron collar had rubbed a raw circle into his flesh. If he ignored Ulric for too long, the collar would burn white-hot with his fury. He would threaten to boil Devin's blood and cook his innards. But though he feared the pain, he feared the change even more.

9

Devin's hand shook as he traced the curse's first mark: a line of scales that'd popped up down his nose. They'd burst through his flesh and bled weakly until they healed. The skin beside them was strangely hard. If he pressed down, he could feel another layer of scales growing beneath it.

Eventually, they would overtake him. They would twist his face and make his teeth grow long —

The emblem, Ulric snapped.

Though his hands shook badly, Devin forced himself to wipe the snow away. Tiny links of steel were embedded into the monster's flesh — as if the change had pressed against the armor, but couldn't break it away. So its skin had begun to grow over the edges of the breastplate.

Ulric cast a spell on Devin's clothes that allowed them to stretch with his shape. But tears had begun to appear along the seams of his tunic. There were holes in his boots: he could feel the wet of the snow leaking through them.

He tried not to wonder if his skin would wrap around his clothes the way this monster's had ... but he couldn't help it.

Carved into the shining metal plate — just above another tattered wound in the creature's gut — was the snarling head of a wolf.

Titus, Ulric mused when Devin described the emblem. *His army froze to death at the summit, then?*

No, they were ... slain.

Slain? How?

Devin tried not to look at the monster's wound, but his eyes seemed to have a mind of their own. *It looks like a fist went through his middle. It's —*

He retched again at the thought. Ulric's voice grew impatient.

Impossible. No one could punch through armor. If they are truly slain, then you'll search for Titus's body.

Please —

Now, *beast. His Majesty demands it.*

Devin didn't want to have to sift through all of the bodies. He didn't think he could stomach the sight of one more frozen wound. But if he didn't obey, Ulric would punish him.

10

He'd resigned himself to his fate when a strange feeling made him turn around. The feeling grew as he stared at the broken tower. It tugged on his bones, made him want to go closer.

This feeling was another thing that'd come with the dragon's soul. It pushed him along, sometimes. It showed him things he couldn't have possibly seen or heard — and it was never wrong. He'd learned to listen.

Devin dragged his feet through the snow, stepping carefully along the thick layer of ice that cloaked the summit. His blood boiled so hotly that he often had a difficult time falling asleep — even in the cool damp of the dungeons. The cold would've likely frozen any other man to the rocks.

But for Devin, it was a welcome relief.

He was near the rampart steps when a sudden gust of wind ripped through the still air. Bumps rose across his flesh where it touched; his bones trembled against it. The feeling that guided him towards the broken tower now whispered that those winds were meant for *him*. The mountains were speaking to him.

They roared that he wasn't welcome.

Find Titus!

Devin bared his teeth against the mountains' growl and forced himself to the top of the ramparts. He climbed through the shattered remains of the tower and onto a stretch of wall. There were so many chunks of tower scattered around that he almost didn't see the lone mound hidden near the edge of the ruins.

It was misshapen, buckled in at its middle. When Devin cleared the snow away, the face of a man gaped back. Though his mane of hair was tangled and his face twisted in shock, it matched the memory Ulric had given him — one of many thoughts that'd come with the curse. Even now, the words of a thousand captives swam inside his ears, behind his eyes.

Ulric's was just one of the voices that kept him awake.

Interesting … how did he die? Ulric said.

Devin cleared the snow at Titus's chest — the part that bent inwards so strangely. Though the ice shell was as clear as glass, it still took him a moment to realize what he saw.

One final blow had finished Earl Titus. It'd bent his breastplate, collapsed his chest. A nearly blackened puddle of blood ringed his corpse. Devin studied the mark for a moment, still not entirely sure. Then he stood.

When he placed a foot on Titus's chest, his boot slid perfectly into the mark.

There was no denying what had happened. As impossible as it seemed, someone had stomped Titus to death. But Devin knew Ulric would never believe it. *He was crushed.*

How?

A fallen rock. It landed straight on his middle.

Ulric's voice disappeared with a *whoosh*. He must've pulled out of the spell to speak to His Majesty. Devin knew he would only have a precious few moments before Ulric's voice returned — and he planned to make the most of it.

He climbed one jagged edge of the tower, the highest point he could reach. The thick fall of snow made things more difficult. But if he focused his gaze, he could see quite a ways down the mountain. Had it not been for the clouds, he bet he could've seen into the Kingdom.

There was a whole world beyond the fortress in Midlan: miles of land, thousands of faces, realms upon realms of sights. He remembered watching them drift through the Seer's scrying bowl. He'd longed to see them for himself.

But Devin would never get to walk among these lands. No, the King would keep him tethered to the skies and only bring him down when it suited his task. Perhaps, if he had enough little moments like these, he might be able to piece them together someday and pretend he'd seen it all ...

But he doubted it.

Devin was about to climb down when a spot of blue drew his eyes to the south. He thought it was only a crop of that strange stone, at first. But then it moved.

His eyes sharpened onto the creature's graceful, serpentine body — tracing its blue scales from its wide nostrils to the tip of its stout tail. Spines grew down its back. They didn't stand straight, but curved in arches. They sprouted from a line of white fur that started at its horns and stopped just short of its tail. Other mats of white curled from its chest and the bottom of its proud snout. But what surprised Devin most about the creature were its eyes.

They cut through the curtain of snow and fell upon him. The creature's black, slitted pupils widened as they roved across his face — and froze when they touched his stare.

It was like gazing into a pool of water, except the reflection he saw wasn't warped by the ripples or darkened by the earth. The eyes that met his were a pure unfettered blue. They were ... *Devin's* eyes ...

His mother's eyes ...

The creature's furry chest swelled and Devin nearly fell off his perch when a ghostly hum rose from its throat:

Welcome, flyer, it sang. Its song pierced the clouds, rode across the frozen wastes upon a wind of its own. *Welcome home.*

CHAPTER 1
THE WRATH OF THE KING

Winter's grip had begun to tighten. Snow lay thickly beneath the Grandforest's trees, the mark of an unreasonably cold and dreary turn. The lake had disappeared beneath a shield of ice. It would be ages before the wind could stir the water to ripple and wave once more. But though its hold was strong, the winter would eventually fade.

Countess D'Mere feared that the storm breaking upon her now might never end.

An impenetrable night draped over her castle: its face was torn of stars and the moon sulked behind it. The lake, usually alive and glittering at this hour, was nothing more than a sunken pit — a shadow so dark that it stood out from the rest.

But though the sky didn't offer so much as a ray of ghostly light, the world had lights of its own.

D'Mere glared at the fires that glowed in the village across the lake. There were enough to hem the water in an arch of flame. Tents packed Lakeshore's narrow streets and lined its dock. Cook fires flickered between the tops of the tents, winking from a distance.

Taunting her.

D'Mere drew the curtains tightly and paced to a second window. From here, she could see the courtyard and the castle's wide front gate. Her soldiers paced uncertainly across the ramparts — their helmets shining against the lights of other cook fires glowing just outside the walls.

Laughter rose in a swell to drift through the window. D'Mere clenched the ledge tightly as the noise reached her ears, grounding her palms against the stone until her arms began to shake.

Midlan patrols often camped at Lakeshore in the spring — but it was far from spring, and this was no patrol.

D'Mere's spies warned her a week ago that Midlan's army had begun to spill from its gates. She thought it odd that the King hadn't summoned her. Surely if Crevan meant to go to war with Titus, he would've called upon the forest for aid. In fact, she'd been counting on it.

Now that the other rulers were slain and the seas had ... refused, an offer of treaty, Crevan had nowhere else to turn. He would *have* to call upon D'Mere — and she would see to it that his army fell into Titus's trap.

But she discovered too late that she'd been fooled.

Her plan hadn't worked. She'd wagered far too much on Crevan's fury. She'd been certain that Titus's betrayal would drive him to the summit, where the elements and the wilds would devour his army. But Midlan wasn't going to the mountains at all.

No, Crevan planned to go to war with the *Kingdom*, to tighten the reins and bring every region back under his control. The battles would be bloody and quick. With the thrones of the Sovereign Five broken, there wasn't an army left that could stand against the wrath of the King — and D'Mere's army was no exception.

Crevan insisted that he'd sent his men into the Grandforest for her protection. The letter that'd arrived along with his army was dripping with concerns for her safety: what if the war spilled over into the Grandforest? What if militants marched upon his final ruler in revolt? Crevan wasn't prepared to take that chance.

But D'Mere knew it was all a lie. The soldiers camped far too thickly in the village, far too boldly before her gates. They questioned anyone who left and inspected every ware the merchants brought inside. D'Mere had a feeling that if she tried to leave, she would be locked away. And if she so much as twitched to fight, there were enough soldiers gathered in Lakeshore to slaughter every man, woman, and child twice over — and they would move at Crevan's nod.

She was being held prisoner, a captive in her own realm ...

A calloused hand wrapped around one of D'Mere's shaking arms. She knew its touch well enough to feel the question in its hold. "Crevan must've figured out about Titus's monsters. By spy or bird, his eyes have somehow reached the mountains' top. He knows that I've betrayed him. So he's trapped me here and left Titus to rot at the summit. That's all I can think of."

The hand tightened.

"No." D'Mere smirked, and her anger cooled. "No, Crevan won't kill me. He *fears* me. He knows a battle with the Grandforest would leave him sore, and he'd much rather take me alive. He'll trap me here until I give myself up."

The hand fell away, and D'Mere turned to glare at the young man beside her: a forest man with short-cropped hair and a slightly crooked nose. When his dark eyes roved to the lights beyond the castle gates, D'Mere shook her head.

"You'd be killed before you could do me any good, Left. Our moment will come — I promise it will," she said when his brows snapped low. "Just give me time."

They stood silently for a moment before Left reached for her again. His head turned expectantly to the door. A moment later, it opened.

D'Mere wasn't at all surprised when a second forest man stepped through — one who matched Left down to the angle of his crooked nose. The twins had always been connected strangely. They seemed able to sense each other's presence, seemed to know when the other had come to harm. They'd never once spoken a word.

But she supposed they didn't have to.

D'Mere frowned at Right. "What is it? You're supposed to be watching the village."

He stepped aside to let another man through.

Filth coated him so thickly that he left prints across the chamber floors. There was grime caked beneath his nails and in the creases of his arms. The hems of his trousers hung in tatters. His face was cloaked, but D'Mere knew from his plain black garb that he was one of her spies. There was a muted emblem in the clasp of his cloak — set so shallowly that only a certain angle of light would give its shape away.

When the man twisted to shut the door, the light caught it and she saw a burning sun upon the clasp. It seemed her agent from the desert had finally returned. She'd sent him away months ago to discover what had become of Baron Sahar — and for his sake, she hoped he'd discovered something useful.

"Well?" she snapped as he shuffled towards her.

The spy didn't answer. He stopped a few paces short and froze. His body swayed and his hands hung limply at his sides.

He staggered backwards when D'Mere shoved him. "Are you *drunk*? Answer me!"

The spy stood, wavering for such a long moment that D'Mere was about to have him locked away. She would wait to execute him when he was sober. But just before she could give the order, a voice whispered from beneath the spy's hood.

It gurgled inside his throat and came out in a strangled hiss: "I'm ... coming for you ... D'Mere."

Her chest tightened; her throat went dry. "What do you mean?"

The spy laughed — or rather, he tried to. But the noise sounded as if he choked on blood. His hand inched toward the dagger in his belt. "D'Mere ... D'Mere," he *tsk*ed. "You knew what the boy was ... didn't you? Convinced me to spare him ... left me to die. *Me*, your closest ally."

Ice snaked through her veins, growing colder as the voice continued. Left pulled on her arm, but her legs were too frozen to move.

"I want him ... need him for my army ... you owe me that much. And I mean ... to take what is owed. D'Mere ... D'Mere ..." The spy gripped the dagger's hilt as his voice crept into an eerie, gloating song: "I'm coming for you ... D'Mere."

The spy ripped the dagger free and lunged for her throat.

Instead, he met the tip of Left's sword.

Though the blade tore through his chest, the spy didn't seem to notice. He shoved himself further, drove the steel deeper. Blood gushed upon the floor. His hood fell away as he threw himself into one final heave, and D'Mere couldn't believe what she saw.

The dark was gone from his eyes, replaced by two deadened orbs of white. Wounds festered across his face — scratches and punctures that had never quite healed. She tried not to think about the brownish stains around his lips.

Left kicked the spy back and Right hurled him down by the cloak.

"Cut off the head," D'Mere whispered.

She barely heard the spy's gurgling screams or the swift fall of Right's sword. What little fear she'd felt was gone, vanished. Her mind was already set upon the game ahead.

When Left grabbed her shoulder, she pushed his hand away. "I'm fine. In fact, I think we may be able to use this to our advantage." D'Mere lifted the hems of her nightdress and stepped absently over the body upon the floor, careful not to dirty her slippers. "Come with me — both of you. There's much to be done."

****

"You've done this to yourself. This is what happens to little beasts who don't listen to their masters."

The grand room shook with Devin's anguished roar; the windows rattled. King Crevan stood with his back pressed against the door as the dragon rent the floor with his claws. Chips of stone sprayed up in a stinging wave behind him as he flailed.

Ulric stood a mere arm's reach from the dragon's monstrous snout. A length of silver chain was wrapped around his wrist. He pressed his thumb against one of its links, and it came to life with an angry red glow.

Devin flinched against every pulse of the chain's light. His body shook as Ulric's hand twisted, as he forced his great wings to shrink back inside his flesh. Human skin stretched over Devin's scales. Blood trickled from its edges as it grew — the rim of foam ahead of the tide.

But though he roared, Devin never blinked.

His burning yellow eyes stayed locked upon Ulric — even as his horns shrank and the spines atop his head gave way to a dark crop of hair. Soon the dragon was gone and a young man lay upon the floor in his place. His clothes were torn to rags. Blackened ridges of scales burst through his skin in places, the flesh red and swollen around them.

But though he'd been twisted into a human shape, he kept the dragon's eyes — and the hatred in his stare was enough to make Crevan's blood freeze to the bottom of his veins.

Ulric didn't seem to notice. In fact, he drank it in. "I think that's enough for today ... yes, you understand me now, don't you? The next time I call, I wager you'll come straight back." He twisted to snap his fingers at a pair of guards who'd been assigned to the grand room. They'd started out at Ulric's side — but wound up stuck very firmly against the back wall. "Lock him up with the others. I'll send word when I'm ready to continue."

The guards moved stiffly towards Devin. Neither seemed willing to touch him: they prodded him with the butts of their spears until he rose, and pushed him out by their points.

18

Crevan stepped aside to let them through, careful not to look Devin in the eyes as he passed. They reminded him of another gaze, another blazing hatred:

I'm going to teach you, Crevan. Let me show —

No. He shoved her voice aside and blinked hard against the memory, forcing it back. Even after her image faded, his skin crawled and his fists curled tightly. He told himself it was *anger* that burned in the pit of his stomach.

But it wasn't.

Ulric kept his back turned as the guards marched away. The moment they closed the door, he collapsed on hand and knee.

Sweat beaded up across his neck and wept in lines to the collar of his robes — dulling the golden threads with damp. His ears had grown abnormally large from all the years he'd spent listening to the thoughts of Crevan's beasts. Now they were stretched so thinly that they were almost transparent. The blue veins that webbed across their backs were clearly inflamed.

"That dragon's going to kill me, Your Majesty. Sometimes he obeys, other times his will is strong ... nearly too strong. I don't know how much longer I'll be able to control him," Ulric rasped. He held his wrist out to the side, and the silver chains wrapped around it almost seemed to squirm in the torchlight. "The impetus has grown too heavy. I can't bear it on my own."

It was always the same complaint, always the same ragged moan — and Crevan was growing tired of hearing it. "I've given you the run of my mages. Find someone else to carry the other chains."

"I've been trying, Your Majesty. But this is a *living* impetus. Its power grows with each new link. It feeds off the creatures it controls — and if a mage isn't strong enough to wield it, the chains will devour him." Ulric nodded to the front of the room, where a number of shriveled bones lay piled in a corner.

They'd tried several times to pass the links on to the other fortress mages: some who had more experience, others who were young and strong. But the chain had devoured each one.

It'd snaked up their bodies and coiled around them tightly. Crevan didn't look away the first time it happened. He'd watched the chain crush an older mage beneath it. The impetus had drained him of everything: his blood, his marrow, his innards. It'd soaked him up,

19

screaming, like water into a sponge. Then it'd slunk back to Ulric and wrapped around his arm, glowing in content.

"No, there's only one mage in the fortress who might be strong enough to bear it." Ulric's eyes dragged upwards. There were dark, heavy rings beneath them. "I await your order."

Crevan knew what he wanted. For whatever reason, Ulric was convinced that Argon was the only mage strong enough to carry the chains — which might solve their problem, if it were true.

But if it wasn't ...

"I won't risk my Seer. As long as the Dragongirl remains unbound —"

"The Seer is blind! What good is he to us —?"

"Silence," Crevan growled. The whole impetus came alive at his command, and Ulric's mouth snapped shut. "You forget, mage, that I could end you with a word. Do not interrupt me again."

Sweat slung off the archmage's chin as his head bobbed up and down.

"Good. I've taken care of D'Mere, but I'll need your mages for the chancellor's castle. I'd like all the councilmen burned alive in their chairs and the island sunk to the ocean's bottom. The people of the High Seas should never have any reason to believe they can survive on their own. Leave them with nothing — make sure they are never able to rebuild."

Ulric moaned as he nodded.

"As for the dragon," Crevan went on, "I believe the time has come —"

"Your Majesty?" a guard called from the door. He leaned around it carefully, as if he preferred to keep a few inches of oak between his chest and Crevan's sword. "It's the Seer, Your Majesty. He says he needs to speak with you."

"Send him in," Crevan growled.

The guard stepped aside and Argon shuffled quietly into the room. His head was bent low and nearly hidden by his long, gray beard. He was so thin and frail a thing that a single trip down the stairs might've left him in pieces — and he moved at a pace that made Crevan want to strangle him with his beard.

"What is it?" he snapped.

"Your Majesty," Argon whispered, his voice hardly a breath. "I have news."

"No he doesn't." Ulric lurched forward. "He knows he's useless. He's just trying to save his sk —"

"Silence!" Crevan glared until Ulric slunk back. Then he turned to Argon. "What news?"

The Seer raised his head, revealing the thick trail of blood matted into his beard. It'd run out from his nose and spilled down in falls. His nostrils were still swollen from the pain. "I've Seen something, Your Majesty ... a powerful vision."

Crevan could hardly breathe. "Tell me."

"The Dragongirl ..."

His stomach twisted; his blood froze again. "Yes, what about her? Speak up, Seer!"

Crevan grabbed Argon by the front of his robes and shook him hard. The Seer's eyes rolled back as if he clung to life. "Copperdock," he rasped. "I've Seen her in ... Copperdock."

Crevan shoved him aside. His legs shook as he stumbled towards the guard. "Sound the bells, have my army ready to march at dawn! I will fill the Kingdom with Midlan's fury. We'll stretch to every corner of the realm. *She will not escape*!"

He chased the guards out the door, bellowing at them long after they'd scattered down the hall. Then he spun to Argon. "Get in your tower, Seer. Do not sleep, do not blink. I want to know where she is at every moment. Do you understand?"

Argon's head sagged as he shuffled for the door. "Yes, Your Majesty."

Crevan grabbed Ulric and hurled him away. "Forget about the council. I'll send Greyson to deal with them once the ground has thawed. Wake the mages — all of them. Lead the swiftest to Copperdock and scatter the rest. I want eyes in every region. Do not return until you have her bound. And bring Devin along as well," he added, as a wild grin split his face. "I think it's time the Kingdom met my dragon."

CHAPTER 2
SOMETHING BROKEN

Morning light bounced off the pool of ocean trapped within the white cliffs of Gravy Bay. Ships sat anchored by their bottoms to the rocks beneath the waves. One lone vessel sailed across the pool — a tiny fishing boat guided on by two darkened forms of men.

Elena watched until the vessel slipped into the narrow crack between the jutting cliffs. Only when its end had disappeared did she dare to blink.

"Well, I suppose that settles it," Jake said from beside her.

They were alone, now. The whole rest of the wedding party had followed Kael's sprint down the hill and into the village square. A great fountain stood in the square's middle, surrounded by a mass of houses that were decorated strangely with statues and plunder.

The villagers' colorful garments formed what looked like an enormous puddle around the fountain. If she closed her eyes, Elena could hear the trill of a cheerful song floating up from where the pirates danced — celebrating the wedding of the Dragongirl and the Wright.

"They're going to go on like that all day," Jake murmured.

When she glanced at him, she saw the shadow of a smile played across his lips. The pale blue eyes behind his rounded spectacles glowed warmly in the rising sun.

"*And* it'll go on all night. Believe me — I've already survived one pirate wedding. We'd better join them, I suppose. Uncle Martin wanted me to turn the fountain's water into spirits." He frowned. "Though after what happened the last time, I can't imagine why ..."

He went on about skin turning purple and some misfortune involving a goat, but Elena wasn't listening. She watched his lips move through his words, watched his hands flex against the leathery grip of his too-tight gloves — *her* gloves. The ones she'd given him ...

The gloves he'd cared enough about to turn into his impetus.

By the time his eyes had traveled back to hers, she'd decided. Her mind was entirely made up. It was a certainty she'd been waiting months to feel — and if she didn't grasp it now, it might never come again.

There was no time to doubt.

Jake's story stopped abruptly when he saw how her brows had tightened above her mask. "What —?"

"Not a word, mage." Elena's heart squirmed when she pressed her hand against his mouth. "Not one word. Do you understand?"

He nodded, his eyes wide.

"Good. Now come with me."

She'd gotten used to his scent, but the raw magic inside his impetus still itched her badly. So she dragged him down the hill by the sleeve of his robes, instead.

"Where are we —?"

"No, not a word," she snapped as they reached the hill's base. Her heart thudded so viciously that it shook her smile.

Jake managed to hold his tongue until they'd pushed through the mansion's front door. "But what are you —?"

"*Shhh!*" Her finger trembled against his lips. "Hush. Just ... trust me for a moment, will you?"

He nodded, and she led him up the large spiral staircase — her breath quickening with every step.

Her chamber stood at the end of the hall, its door hidden well within the shadows. Warm light spilled from her window: it pooled upon the oaken floors and slid across her bed. Elena's heart was thudding wildly, now. She was certain she'd never felt it beat quite like this.

It was such a strange feeling, such a terrifying thrill — not even when she'd stared into the face of Death had her chest risen and fallen with such fury. She had to bite her lip to keep her heart from leaping out her throat as she dragged Jake inside.

She slammed the door behind them.

"Elena ..."

At last, Jake seemed to understand. His eyes didn't rove but locked onto hers — searching, questioning. With far more courage than she felt, Elena managed to growl: "I'm not going to tell you again, mage. Be quiet." She pulled her mask away slowly, let it fall to her chin. "Now ... take off your gloves."

23

He did. Jake grimaced as he tugged them free and set them on the small table beside her bed. Next came his spectacles. When he turned around, it was all she could do to keep her footing.

He stood blurry-eyed and powerless before her. His bare hands flexed nervously at his sides. And yet ... her legs felt like lead, her boots seemed welded to the floors. "Come here."

When he stepped within her reach, she caught him by the wrists. She pulled him in against her. A strange, heart-rending warmth spread out from his hands and across her waist, down her back. But though his hands moved, his eyes never left hers — and his gaze held her to her feet.

"Are you sure?" he whispered, hands pausing their climb. "You ... you're certain?"

Her heart was too high, her throat too swollen with warmth to answer. Instead, she grabbed him under the chin and pulled him down to meet her lips.

Oh, her head went light. Every pinprick of her flesh bunched together tightly in a swell of blood. She could taste the magic in him. It coated his tongue: not as bitter as she'd expected, but oddly ... sweet.

His hands rose and his thumbs dragged across the twin black daggers strapped to her arms — bold and unafraid. She'd lost count of how many throats they'd hewed. Slight and Shadow had sent hundreds of men to their graves. And yet, Jake handled them without fear.

A thrill rose up her spine, trembling as Jake drew each blade from its sheath and set them aside. Then his lips came back — firm, calm, and brave. Warmth trailed each pass of his hands, every dart of his tongue ...

Then quite suddenly, the warmth began to fade.

She felt it first at his lips: they brushed gently across her chin and left a cold line in their wake. The frost spread from his tongue and onto hers. It slid down her throat and into her middle. Icy patches formed beneath his hands. Everywhere he touched, he froze her.

Soon, she couldn't feel anything. Her skin eased and slipped back, hardening across her bones like a river's flesh against the winter. It dulled the pressure of Jake's hands. Her arms slid from around his shoulders and fell limply to her sides — suddenly too heavy to lift.

24

Jake's hands seemed to widen, to grow, to become impossibly strong. The pressure began to hurt her; the cold stung her lips —

No, she thought furiously. Elena squinched her eyes and tried to concentrate on the warmth she'd felt before — tried to remind herself that it was *Jake* who held her now. And Jake would never try to hurt her. But out of the dark came a face that wasn't Jake's at all.

Holthan's black eyes stared down at her, now. It was the biting pressure of *his* lips that she felt scraping down her throat, the painful grip of *his* hands. It was Holthan's horrible, gloating laugh that stung her ears ...

"Elena?"

All of the cold fled her body as Jake pulled away. Her eyes snapped open. They clung to his, trying desperately to forget the man who ruled her fears. But though she fought, a shadow of his face still hung before her.

"Are you all right, Elena?" Jake said again. He half-reached for her and drew back. "I don't want to hurt you."

"You aren't going to hurt me. I'm fine. Don't ... don't stop."

She rushed into his arms.

The cold rushed back.

Elena tried to fight it off. She was determined to shove Holthan away, to forget everything she'd known and begin something new. Nadine told her that she'd been wronged — that what Holthan had done to her wasn't love at all. She swore that *love* was different, and Elena knew she loved Jake. She was certain of it ...

So why did the cold still bite her flesh? Why couldn't she see him through Holthan's face?

"I can't," Jake gasped. He pulled back again and hurried to the bedside table. "I can't do this to you, Elena. I won't."

"You will," she snapped, the words bolstered by a sudden fear. Rage burned at the sides of her head as she watched him pull on his gloves. "You have to! I swear I'm ready for it. There's not a doubt in my mind that this is what I —"

"I can't," Jake said again, shoving the spectacles up the bridge of his nose. He wouldn't meet her eyes as he swept past her to the door.

When he opened it, Elena felt the whole earth fall out from beneath her.

"Fine. Go on, then! But don't you dare try to come back to me, mage," she yelled as he ducked into the hallway. "Don't *ever* come back!"

****

Days passed. The sun rose and fell. Its light gathered, pooled ... slid into the crack between the walls and floor ... plunged the world into darkness. Elena sat cross-legged in a corner of the room. Her eyes were open, but unseeing.

What'd happened with Jake was entirely her fault. She should've known that he would pull away at her slightest flinch. He was so careful, so kind. Had she held her ground against the memories, she might've woken that morning with him by her side — her heart flooded with warmth.

Instead, she battled the cold alone, fought on through endless nights ... and she was still no closer to forgetting.

Each time she tried to force him into the darkness, Holthan rose against her. Every horrible moment flashed behind her eyes — glancing her with a dagger's bite. She watched through a cold, blue film as he defeated her over and over again. Soon, it became clear that she would never overcome his laughter. She would never be able to shove his hands aside.

Holthan lived on to torment her, even through his death.

Elena still wasn't strong enough to stop him.

In a few of the darkest hours, she thought about telling Jake. Perhaps if he knew, he would understand that she needed him. Perhaps he would see that the warmth he'd given her might be the thing that melted the ice from her blood. Perhaps this would be just another battle they might face together ...

No.

No, with the rising sun came clarity: Jake could never love her if he knew the truth. He wouldn't look at her in the same way again. The woman he knew was strong, after all. The mask she wore was of a warrior who could not be beaten. But inside, she was a broken thing.

Nobody could love something broken.

It was that thought that finally dragged Elena to her feet. She wouldn't try to fight the cold any longer. She would simply cover it up, and perhaps time would eat its edge.

26

The mansion was alive that afternoon. Servants bustled here and there. She followed the pattern of their steps and slipped around them to avoid their eyes. Elena was little more than a plume of smoke, a breeze so slight that it hardly stirred the things it passed. She drifted through the crowd on the balls of her feet and took refuge among the shadows.

A manservant peeled from the main room and set a brisk pace down one of the hallways. Elena followed silently in his wake — using his broad shoulders as a shield against the eyes of passersby.

"What's all this confounded noise about?" a blustering voice called from up ahead. "No sooner does a man get his grand-nephew settled for a nap than the whole house erupts. It's a curse, I tell you — a *curse*!"

Elena slipped behind the manservant's right shoulder when she saw a frazzled crop of gray hair approaching. Of all the many bodies swarming around the mansion, the Uncle was the absolute last one she wanted to be caught by.

She had no choice but to pin herself against the wall when the manservant stopped abruptly. "There's trouble in Harborville, Mr. Martin. Captain Lysander's ordered an emergency sailing —"

A metal platter struck the polished stone floor in the main room, and the resulting *clang* woke the baby with a scream.

"Confound it all!" Uncle Martin swore. He bounced the blankets in his arms for a moment, but to no avail. "What in high tide are they doing with the silver? No — you come with me," he said when the manservant tried to escape. "You can explain it all on the way."

Elena kept herself close to the servant's right shoulder throughout his reluctant turn, slinking behind him as she would an opened door. The Uncle and the servant took off back towards the main room, and Elena ducked into a nearby chamber.

She was careful to breathe lightly as she entered. Her mask muted the stink of magic in the spell room, but she could still taste it. The fumes made the back of her throat itch and stung the sensitive flesh inside her nose.

Shelves lined with books, tables piled high with vials and instruments covered the room. She could barely see the floor for the mess. But it wasn't nearly as messy as she remembered it being — it wasn't as messy as it *ought* to have been.

The last time she'd been inside the spell room, rings of books covered the floor. There'd been various liquids inside the vials and bits of parchment strung all across the chamber, covered to their bottoms with strange symbols. Now the books sat neatly upon the shelves, the vials lay empty. There wasn't so much as a scrawled note in sight.

A small cot lay crammed against one corner of the room. She stepped over to it carefully, wondering why its blankets had been stripped and folded to the side. Then she spotted the tongue of a rucksack sticking out from beneath the cot.

It'd been packed. When Elena sifted through it, she found a cloak, a fresh change of clothes, and a couple of books — including a plain leather tome with no title.

She drew the plain book out and held it carefully. It was Jake's notebook — the thing he was always muttering over and scribbling in. Elena ran her thumb down its pages, watching as his words, numbers, and drawings flipped by. Some of it was written in the strange tongue of the mages.

She'd begun to flip through it a second time when a pair of shuffling steps echoed down the hall. She slid the journal back exactly where it'd been — wedged between two thicker tomes — before she kicked the rucksack beneath the cot. Elena had just enough time to walk to the other side of the room before Jake entered.

His robes scraped quietly across the floor as he ducked in, arms laden with what looked to be stashes of dried provisions. Elena watched from the shadows as he tried to make room for them in his already-bulging pack. She read the frustrated words that formed upon his lips, watched as his rounded spectacles slid further down his nose.

When they neared the tip, she stepped forward instinctively — afraid they might slide off and be broken. But Jake managed to catch them ... just as her shadow crossed the wall.

He whirled around so quickly that one foot caught against the heel of the other, and he sat down hard. "Blast it, Elena! You know I hate it when you do that." He sprang up from the cot. His face burned red as he tried to cram rations between the folds of his spare robes. "Why are you here? I thought you didn't want to see me again."

His voice cut across those words and scraped against the thing buried beneath them. "I've come to tell you I'm sorry for what I said. I didn't mean it ... I don't want you to leave."

Jake's hands slowed, but he didn't answer.

Elena stepped closer. "I was only a bit nervous."

"Is that all it was? *Nerves*?"

"Yes," she said evenly, trying to ignore the scoff in his voice.

There were so many things she wanted to say, so many things she *needed* to say ... so many things she couldn't tell him. They wove around inside her head as she glared at the back of his neck, trying to work them all out. In the end, she couldn't. So she grabbed him by the robes and turned him around.

His brows lowered over his spectacles at the question on her lips.

"Please, give me one more chance."

"I don't think it'll —"

"I love you."

The words were out of Elena's mouth before she could think to draw them in. Her chest lurched strangely at the end — the throes of some fear trying to escape. She crossed her arms and held it pinned; she tried to meet its curious gales of frost and fire with calm. But it was difficult.

Jake, and his peculiar, quiet gaze, undid her.

"Do you?" he said, his voice hushed.

"Yes."

His face was completely unreadable. Even the vein beneath his chin moved in a steady throb. Jake held her gaze for a moment more before he sighed. Then he slid his gloves from his hands and laid them carefully upon the cot.

Elena's heart thudded once, hard, when he stepped forward. Her arms fell from across her chest and she closed her eyes.

Be calm. You must *be calm*, she told herself when she felt his hands against her throat. Warmth bubbled up inside her middle and she clung to it desperately, hoping it would be enough to hold back the frost. *Jake is a kind man. You love him. You —*

No, the ice wouldn't let her. Memories of a dark set of eyes overtook her vision; a spine-raking laugh filled her ears. The softness of Jake's hand turned callused and hard. His grip became strangling. It snuffed out the warmth and left Elena frozen. But she fought to hide it.

Be calm. Don't move. Just ...

"You've gone cold again."

She opened her eyes when Jake took his hand away. Shock stole her breath for a moment before she remembered to hide it. "You're imagining things."

"No, I'm not. I can feel it. Your skin is like stone."

"It's only nerves," she growled, stepping into him. "Quit worrying about every little thing and love me. I won't stop you."

"That isn't what I want! That's the *least* of what I want. At the moment, there's only one thing in the whole Kingdom that concerns me."

"And what's that?"

"Your eyes," he said shortly, glaring as if she should know full well why he was angry with her. But she didn't.

"You can have those, too. Take whatever you want."

"No, that isn't ... " Jake was quiet for a moment before he grasped her hands. "When I look into your eyes, I see a monster."

Elena glared to hide her surprise. "You knew what I was from the beginning, mage. I've told you that I'm a killer. I've made no attempt to hide it."

Jake shook his head. "I don't mean you — I mean *me*. My reflection. You go cold when I touch you ... you close me out. I won't be the thing that frightens you. I would rather harm myself a thousand times over —"

"Please, you're —"

"Listen! No, *listen* to me," he shouted, clutching her hands. "I won't do it. Too many people have looked at me that way. I know fear when I see it — and I've lived as a monster, but no more. I know my magic must hurt you, and I ... I won't do it. I swear I won't touch you again."

He spun away from her and tugged his gloves on roughly. Elena watched, still half-frozen and in shock. "Where are you going?"

"To the plains. There's a ship leaving this afternoon. Brend promised I could stay for a while and study things, so that's what I mean to do. It'll help, I think, getting some time apart."

He swept past her, and she couldn't even turn to follow. The truth might stop him. One confession might bring him back, might possibly change everything ...

Then again, it might well *end* everything.

"Elena?"

30

When she finally managed to turn, Jake was standing in the doorway. A faint smile bent his lips as he pulled his eyes from the floor to meet her.

"I love you, as well. I always will. It was too much to ask of a whisperer to withstand a mage's touch ... but I thank you for trying."

He slipped out the door, then — taking every last shred of warmth away with him.

CHAPTER 3
LOVE WITHOUT FEAR

Darkness cloaked his eyes — impenetrable, at first. But it slowly began to soften. The dark gave way to a warm, golden light. The light crept from yellow, to orange, to a heated, furious red.

It was the red that woke him.

Kael groaned as the morning light glanced across his eyes — stinging at their fronts, aching across their backs. He slammed them shut once more and draped an arm over his face, absolutely determined to sleep until a decent hour …

Wait a moment.

The fog crept back. He braved the glare of the sun just long enough to peek out from beneath his arm and groaned when he saw that the hour *was* decent. Even through the chamber's one small window, he could see the sun had risen a good inch above the glittering waves. All of Copperdock would be about its chores by now.

Which meant that Kael was already late.

He tried to bolt up and very nearly snapped his neck. There was a strong arm clamped across his chest. It held him pinned to the bed — and it absolutely refused to budge.

"Kyleigh?"

She mumbled unintelligibly from beside him.

He'd learned the hard way not to try to force her awake. The first time he'd grabbed her by the arm, she woke up swinging — and he tumbled off the bed with a broken nose. So he'd had to come up with a trick to get free.

After a few moments of careful squirming, he was able to reach the back of her shoulder. He jabbed, flung his arm aside to avoid the wild swing of her fist, and managed to roll successfully onto the floor. "Get up, Kyleigh," he said as he tugged on his trousers. "Copperdock can't have its lady sleeping in all day. The sun's awake, so you might as well be."

Somewhere amid her muddled swears came a word that sounded suspiciously like *no*.

She was a tangled mess: wound up tightly among the blankets, pillow crushed between her arms and her raven locks held tamed only by a very clumsy pony's tail. It also looked as if she'd claimed one of Kael's shirts during the night — the one he'd stripped off the day before because it'd finally become too filthy.

He frowned when she shifted to clutch her pillow tighter and he saw the grimy streaks trailing behind her arms. "There are plenty of clean tunics lying around here, I'll have you know."

"Well, I like this one," she mumbled, grinning into her pillow. "It has your scent."

"*I* have my scent. And I'm lying right beside you. So there's no need —"

"Anything you leave on the floor is fair game, whisperer." Her eyes cracked open, and her lips bent into a smirk. "Now come back to bed."

No. He had to tell himself, very firmly, *no*. Flames danced behind the green of her eyes as they locked onto his. Her smirk spread into a grin that almost made him grin back. He swore he could see the memories drifting behind the flames, the shadow of the secret they'd shared ...

"No." He had to say it aloud. For some reason, his legs had started to drag him towards the bed. "You can stay here if you like, but I'm going to the docks. I swore to Shamus that I'd look after the repairs while he's away. And I mean to keep my word."

"Suit yourself."

He would. As a matter of fact, he was determined to get his boots on and head out immediately. Kael righted a chair that lay on its side in a corner of the room — and nearly toppled over before he remembered that it'd been broken.

The back was gone, having been snapped off and hurled to another end of the room. The book he'd been trying to read lay sprawled between the wall and the floor, while the bedside table had been knocked askew. Though their chambers were in a near-constant state of mess, it certainly wasn't the worse thing to have happened.

After their first night together, Kael woke to find the mattress in ruins and the bed's stuffing plastered across his every inch: stuck in his hair, against his skin, and wedged into places where no man should've ever had to find feathers. The bed's frame had been reduced to splinters — crushed, with its legs trapped beneath it.

He couldn't remember *exactly* what they'd done to cause such a mess, but he knew he didn't want to have to spend the day trying to seal all the broken pieces back together. So he'd decided to make them a frame of iron, instead.

Kael had shaped the metal beneath his hands, weaving an immovable pattern of slats beneath the mattress, twisting each of the four legs into spirals that occasionally bent, but never broke. The head wound high and the foot arched low. So far, it'd all held together.

But the rest of the chamber's furniture hadn't been so lucky.

Kael sat down carefully, easing forward as the chair groaned against his weight.

"The clouds are rolling in," Kyleigh murmured from the bed.

Her back arched as she stretched her arms above her. One of her bare feet stuck out from beneath the covers. Her toes curled and uncurled as she gazed out the window, smiling as the morning light drifted across her face and left a trail of pink behind.

All too soon, the light was gone — shadowed by a cloud's billowing chest. The bright fires in her eyes fell to embers. They smoldered as they lighted onto his.

"Weren't you in some sort of great rush to get to the docks?"

Kael realized that he'd been staring — stuck bent over, with his foot frozen halfway inside his boot. "I was — I *am*," he amended, when she raised a brow. He tore his eyes from her smile and crammed his foot purposefully into the boot.

It was the wrong one.

"I think I'll go for a fly today," Kyleigh mused, her gaze returning to the window.

Kael had known from the moment she mentioned the clouds that *flying* was precisely what she wanted to do. But he didn't like it. "Just be careful, will you?"

"I flew around the Kingdom for centuries without being discovered — I think I'll be able to manage a few more," she said wryly. Then she stretched her hands towards him and whispered: "But I don't think I'll be able to do anything unless you help me out of bed."

He was most certainly not going to do that. "I haven't got time for this, Kyleigh."

"For what?"

"You know very well what. If I come over there, it'll be another hour before I make it out the door — if I'm lucky," he added, glaring to keep the fires from rising up.

She rolled her eyes. "Oh please, I'm far too tired for any of that."

"You are?"

"Yes ... it isn't easy, trying to hold my own against a Wright."

The arch of her lips cut against the smooth pale of her cheeks. Red bloomed across her face. It spread down her neck as the fires within her eyes started to dance. The memories were there again, sliding behind the flames.

Kael supposed she had a point. "All right, fine — I'll help you up. But no mischief."

"None whatsoever," she promised.

But no sooner did he take her hands than the world spun and Kael's head struck the pillow. He was trapped: one of Kyleigh's legs draped across his middle while she wrapped his shoulders in her iron grip.

"Oh, I can't *believe* you fell for it again," she murmured into his ear.

He would have protested — he'd had every intention of protesting. But as if she could sense the words forming, Kyleigh's lips were there. They pressed against him, tied his tongue. When she finally released him, he found he no longer had the breath to protest.

He gripped her arm as her lips trailed across his jaw and teased the vein that throbbed in his neck. It gave him away every time. That line of his blood rushed close to the surface, howling as it burst into flame. His fingers dug into her arm; he tried to bring her closer. Her grip tightened across his chest, and her lips parted in a grin at the agonized pounding of his blood.

In one final attempt to see reason, he arched his neck away ... but she followed.

Her growling laughter trembled against his side as she dragged her teeth across that vein — stirring the fires with something that frightened and thrilled him all at once. It was dangerous to be trapped so tightly against her. His body should have tried to wriggle free, to escape the trailing pressure of her teeth.

But in that moment, his only worry was that she wasn't close enough. There were empty patches between her limbs and his, places where they didn't quite touch. He didn't want anything between them — not even the emptiness. So he grabbed her around the waist and pulled her onto his chest.

The fires roared. They lapped at the under-edges of his skin and brought his heart to life. Love with Kyleigh dragged him into a trance all its own: his heart pounded without mercy, his strength seemed to drop from limbs and into the depths of his blood — where it woke a strange, wild part of his soul.

This part of him never worried, it never thought. The wildness met Kyleigh's love without fear, and Kael never fought it.

Her grip tightened the moment the fires burned hot, as if she could sense the battle was about to begin. Their love was a never-ending war — a blaze of fury driven to anguish by their attacks. The world dropped away and the battle consumed them. Nothing was safe, once the fight had begun.

If they ever woke to find the castle torn down to its base, Kael wouldn't be the least bit surprised.

He held his ground as Kyleigh's lips returned. He let her lead him through their kisses — occasionally moving in a way that made her grin. In the moment before the wildness cloaked his eyes, his hand went to her throat. He traced the arch of her neck up to her chin. He wanted to see if her blood pounded as fiercely as his ...

It did.

Just when it looked as if the morning would be lost, a terrified scream startled them apart.

In the half-breath it took Kael to be surprised, Kyleigh had pinned him beneath her — one arm clamped protectively across his chest and her full weight planted on his middle. He heard a hiss and a shrilling hum as she ripped Harbinger from among the sheets and leveled the white blade at the door.

The maid standing in the archway screamed again and flung her arms protectively over her face. "Don't hurt me, Lady Kyleigh! I only came in to tidy things up a bit. Crumfeld said you'd gone, and that I was to sweep the broken bits of chair off the floor and change the sheets. I wouldn't have come in had I known you were still ... um, *here.*" She peeked through her hands at Kael before turning a tearful look onto Kyleigh. "Please don't lop off my head!"

"She's not going to hurt you," Kael promised. Then he glared up. "Didn't we agree not to keep any weaponry in the bed?"

36

Kyleigh shrugged. "Not that I recall."

"Really? Because I very clearly remember —"

"Tell Crumfeld we'll be along in a moment," Kyleigh growled, without taking her eyes off of Kael.

He knew that look, and realized this might be his last chance to escape. "No, there's no point in bothering Crumfeld. I'm on my way out." He scrambled from beneath Kyleigh and began searching through the shattered dresser for a clean tunic.

"Ah, I'll just come back when you've gone."

Kael turned in time to see the maid's eyes whip away from his back — and Kyleigh's glare followed her out the door.

"Humans," she muttered, shaking her head. "Always peeking around every corner and through every crack."

Kael didn't think that curiosity was an entirely human trait. He seemed to remember a certain halfdragon who loved to poke around. But it wasn't worth the argument. "I'm heading out."

"Wait — take this with you."

She slid out of bed and paced over to him, twisting the ring from her finger as she went. Its delicate white-gold band had been woven into the symbol of the Wright: an eye with three tiny triangles fanning from its top, three interlocking triangles at its base, and a small onyx stone carved into the black triangle at its middle.

It was a tiny thing, but the ring felt like stone in the palm of his hand. "How long will you be?"

She shrugged. "That all depends on how interesting the world looks today. It'll be nightfall, by the latest."

She couldn't wear the ring when she flew. It wasn't made of scales, which meant it couldn't hold her second shape. Still, the band felt oddly cold as he slid it into his pocket.

"Fine. I suppose I'll see you tonight."

"Kael?"

He turned at her growl and nearly choked when he saw how her eyes blazed.

"When I return, I plan to finish what I started," she warned with a grin.

******

Though Kael had promised to look after things while Shamus was gone, there wasn't much to do. Copperdock was always packed to its edges with ships needing repairs, and the shipbuilders could fix just about anything. They handled the merchants and dealt with the coin.

All Kael seemed to be good for was pretending to be the one in charge — and slipping in occasionally to fix the things they couldn't.

"The weld keeps cracking," one of the shipbuilders muttered, dragging a sleeve across the damp of his brow. "We've been at it for ages, now. Nothing will stick."

They were deep in the belly of a merchant's vessel, crouched in front of a beam that'd popped free of its bolt. Kael felt as if he had an old sock stuffed over his head: the air was impossibly thick and reeked of mold.

He knew by the way the beam warped upwards that a weld would never stay put. "I'm going to have to seal it to the wood. Keep a watch for me."

The shipbuilder crawled away while Kael slipped into a trance. As he concentrated, the wood of the beam and the iron of the bolt became like clay in his hands. He pushed the metal downwards and dragged the wood over its edge — leaving just enough of the rounded top exposed that the unknowing eye might think it was simply a little more hammered in than the others.

Kael worked quickly, and finished none-too-soon.

"All I'm eager in understanding is when we'll be able to sail off. You promised two days, and it's been two days. You've had plenty of time to get everything —"

"Done," Kael said as the merchant ducked in. He nodded to the shipbuilder. "Well done. I'm pleased with this."

"Thank you, Lord Kael."

"*You're* Lord Kael?" the merchant said skeptically, eyes scraping down Kael's frame. "Huh, not even a seas man."

Kael didn't have time to listen to another rant about how a lordship belonged to those who'd been born in the seas. He couldn't have cared less about being a lord — in fact, he thought the title fit him about as well as a bear fit in a longboat.

But it wasn't worth explaining. "You're all set here. Sail off whenever you're ready."

"Ah, and *after* you've paid," the shipbuilder added quickly.

Kael ducked out into the narrow corridor, but the merchant followed close. "Is Shamus coming back anytime soon?"

"I'm not sure. I haven't heard from him."

"Well, *I've* heard that things at the chancellor's castle have rather deteriorated," the merchant said smugly, as if the knowledge he possessed could've easily been traded in for a sack of gold. "They still haven't been able to decide on a new high chancellor, and rumor has it that the councilmen have started taking matters into their own hands."

Kael wasn't at all surprised. He'd hardly spent a week with Kyleigh when Lysander sailed into Copperdock — eyes wild and trousers aflame, going on about how one of the councilmen had trapped his beloved ship in Harborville.

"I *knew* I should've gone with them," he'd ranted. "It was supposed to be a quick round of trade — to the plains, the northern harbors, and back. All I wanted was a few days to spend with my wife and son. Now look at the mess we're in!"

Lysander had already enlisted Jonathan's help, hoping that if the plains threatened to stop sending supplies, the council would listen. But just to be safe, he'd taken Shamus along, as well.

"Their ships can't sail forever. They'll need repairs, eventually. If the council won't listen to their bellies, then perhaps they'll listen to their legs. There's room for one more," he'd added, nudging Kael with a look. "You could seal them up inside their blasted hall, flatten the stairs so they can't escape. I imagine things would get done rather quickly, if a Wright started pasting the council's boots to the floor."

If there was one thing he hated more than being a lord, it was the thought of getting into the middle of a merchant's squabble. Just hearing Thelred talk about the council's meetings made his eyes roll back — and he didn't trust himself not to set fire to the tables the minute things got dull.

So Kael had offered to stay behind and deal with the repairs, instead.

But even *that* was beginning to test him.

"It's the longest the seas have been without some sort of ruler," the merchant panted as he tried to follow Kael's bound up the stairs. "I'm interested to find out what will hap —"

"Yes, it sounds exciting," Kael said as he climbed onto the ship's deck. Every merchant who sailed into Copperdock had the same tale — and each one assumed that he was the first to tell it.

But he couldn't sit through another moaning story about how the seas weren't nearly as grand as they'd once been, or how the council was in trouble. There was a line of dark gray clouds gathering in the west. They'd travel quickly over the seas and break open the moment they struck land. Kael wagered he only had an hour or so left to work — and he wasn't going to waste it listening to rumors.

"*Exciting?*" the merchant scoffed behind him. "It's going to be a disaster! The council will gut itself at the rate things are headed. And where will we be then, eh? What's going to become of our people?"

Kael wasn't sure, but he was certain the council would find some way to work it all out. After all, there were far worse things than a few late shipments.

CHAPTER 4
BAD LUCK OR PIRACY

Night blanketed the seas. They'd left the calmer swells behind them about an hour before. Now the pirates sailed across a stretch of ocean that had been worn smooth — not by the wind, but by the silent war raging just beneath it.

The southern seas clashed against its northern head. Their waters ebbed in cold and warmth, each flattened by the battle. Though the waves looked calmer than ever from above, Captain Lysander could feel the war in the soles of his boots.

There were little tells in every groan, every slight shift off course. His hands wrapped tightly about the railing each time he felt them start to drift. The ship's sides creaked as the battle scraped across her belly. Wind wouldn't be much help against this sort of wave. No, the only thing that might save them from being dragged aside was the skill of their helmsman.

Shamus, master shipbuilder of Copperdock, was doing a fairly decent job of it. His thick arms swelled each time the seas pulled them an inch. He turned the wheel against the flow and his jaw went taut between his bushy sideburns.

But though he'd managed to keep them from being swept into the west, they still lagged well behind the others.

"I can't believe you let Perceval cut past us," Lysander muttered, glaring at the ship just ahead of them.

It'd passed them some time ago — after the crew had grown tired of crowding their sides and sending the pirates' bow through their wake. Lysander still glowered against the memory of their laughter. He was certain there wasn't anything worse than being passed by a merchant.

And over the course of the day, they'd been passed by all seventeen of them.

Lysander pounded his fist into the railing. "*Perceval*, by Gravy! Everybody knows he's got the slowest fleet in the seas. There's a reason they say that if you give the rest of them a day, you'd better give Perceval two — and he's left us in his wake!"

Shamus didn't seem at all concerned. "You've got some of the *toughest* vessels in the High Seas, not the fastest. Every captain likes to think his ship is best. But there's no such thing."

"What do you mean?"

"Well, would you rather have your fleet surviving storms or winning races?"

Lysander pursed his lips.

Shamus held out a hand. "And there's your answer."

"Still ... *Perceval.*" Lysander glared at the vessels ahead, the furthest no more than a dot on the horizon. "At this rate, that trinket-trolling scab will have Harborville laughing at us a good three days before we make berth."

"I would've stopped him if I could, but there's only so much give in her sails and guide to her rudder. She's a monster in the sides," Shamus added, peering over the rails. "You wouldn't have given me the helm if you didn't think I could steer her."

Lysander frowned. "No, I gave you the helm because it seemed to be the only way to keep you from leaping off."

"Aye, perhaps you're right about that. It's bad luck to board a ship you had a hand in building." Shamus pawed worriedly at his bushy sideburns while his other fist stayed white-knuckled upon the wheel. "Bad luck, indeed. No good's going to come of this, Captain — you mark my words."

Lysander didn't see how their luck could possibly get any worse.

They'd returned from the mountains to discover the whole region in turmoil. Chaucer had gone missing — a fact that Lysander found neither upsetting nor surprising. He'd been cad enough as a manager, and the chancellor's office had only given him room to grow. There'd likely been three different plots on his life before he'd even warmed the chair.

No, Chaucer was bound to have run off or been killed at some point. It was what had happened *after* that caused all the mess.

Without a high chancellor to rein them in, the council began writing its own rules. There were different writs and decrees pasted on the docks in every port, and a whole host of new taxes. Each one seemed to be designed for the sole purpose of capturing another merchant's fleet — and each time a ship was detained or a councilman got his wares confiscated, he'd write a new law to retaliate.

Things were starting to get a bit ridiculous. There were rules about how many barrels a ship could have on her deck and how tall the crates could be stacked. Ships with a mast over a certain height could only make port in certain places, and at least one merchant had ordered that they all be docked by the width of their sails. Colderoy would only allow ships to port between the hours of midnight and two bells.

But the worst, by far, was Alders.

"Twelve knot-lengths from the docks," Lysander muttered, his stormy eyes fixed upon the dark horizon. "That's all he said. No mention of what sort of knot, or how far apart they ought to be spaced. It isn't possible. How in high tide is anybody supposed to be able to measure *that*?"

"Eh, I think that might've been the point, Captain. He doesn't care if you can measure it. More broken laws is more gold for Alders." After a moment, Shamus inclined his head. "Not a bad way to make some extra coin, if you want my —"

"I don't," Lysander said shortly. He peeled his hands from the railing and clamped them smartly behind his back. "By the time we've paid all the blasted fees, we limp home with hardly enough coin to cover our wares. It's not worth it anymore. We can't go on like this."

"Well, you've tried all you can," Shamus offered. "If the council won't listen to the shipbuilders or the plains, then they're not likely to budge on much else. Maybe we're doing right, Captain, getting the merchants together like this." He waved a hand at the ships sliding further into the distance. "Alders can't ignore us if we pack up his harbors. And once we've freed your men, maybe it'll be best if we just cut our ties and drift on home."

Lysander shook his head, his mood growing darker by the moment. "We shouldn't have to *cut our ties*. A man ought to be able to sell his wares for a decent price and anchor however many knot-lengths from the dock as he blasted well pleases."

Shamus was quiet for a moment. His thick hands twisted nervously about the wheel. "Maybe we should've brought Miss Aerilyn along. She knows a thing or two about merchanting."

"I'd rather put a hole through my ship than drag my wife into this mess. She doesn't need anymore to —"

43

"Ahoy there, gents!" Jonathan called. He loped up the stairs, his boots thudding loudly against each step and a ridiculous grin plastered across his face.

If Lysander hadn't felt the night's exhaustion wearing on him before, he certainly did now. "Shouldn't you be getting some rest?"

Jonathan sighed. "I should be, but I can't."

"How about a swig of something strong, lad?" Shamus called. "That'll make you forget your troubles."

"So would a crack over the head," Lysander muttered.

Jonathan didn't seem to hear them. He dragged his feet across the deck and slumped miserably over the rails, his arms dangling above the waves.

"Seasick?" Shamus guessed.

"*Heart*sick," Jonathan moaned. "I've tried to sleep. But every time I shut my eyes, I see my sweet giantess."

Lysander frowned at him. "Really? I don't remember you being quite so mopey the last time we set sail."

"That was a *quest*, mate — we were marching out to clobber evil and set the mountains free." Jonathan's voice grew muffled as more of his body sagged over the rails. "It was worth the leaving because we were doing something right, and I knew Clairy would be proud. But this is just a load of talking and squabbling over coin. I don't think I could stand the sight of another powdered wig."

"Or another whiff of that musk," Shamus agreed, wrinkling his nose. "Half of the councilmen smell like they've drenched themselves to their collars."

Jonathan let out another heavy, moaning sigh. "I thought tossing my cap in with a load of pirates meant life would never be boring. But we haven't done any pirating in ages."

"Well, there hasn't been any need for it," Lysander said stiffly.

Jonathan's head swung up. "No need? Last I checked, we were sailing to the top nose of the Kingdom to rescue one of your ships from the paws of some over-stuffed merchant. And what did we pack to fight with? A mound of gold."

"We aren't *rescuing* them. They aren't in any danger." Lysander shifted his weight. "They couldn't afford Alders' docking tax, so he's just … holding them until he's paid."

"Aye, holding them to a tax he had no right to levy," Shamus muttered out the side of his mouth.

44

Lysander shot him a look. "The seas are just a bit frayed, at the moment. Once the council elects a new high chancellor, everything will be back in order."

Jonathan slung his body up with an exasperated huff. "I don't want things to be back in order — I want us to be proper pirates again! Sheath our mercy and draw our blades!"

He tore the cutlass from his belt and swung it in a series of wide, dramatic arcs — so wide and dramatic that Lysander had to leap back to avoid having the scruff nicked off his chin.

Shamus pounded a thick fist against the helm, eyes shining brightly. "Oh, imagine the look on old Alders' face when he sees us coming —"

"We aren't storming Harborville," Lysander said firmly. "I won't risk it."

"There's nothing to risk, mate. The council is so busy fighting each other that they'd never suspect it was us. I'll bet we could sack a dozen ships before they even thought to check their wake for pirates."

"The council has always been after our trade. It wouldn't take much to convince merchants to go to war over us, and I won't be the enemy that unites them. I haven't got the army to take on the seas."

"Midlan does," Shamus mumbled, glaring at the shadowy lands to their east. "The King can't be pleased about what happened to his Duke. I'm surprised he hasn't tried to throttle us already. A man like that can smell weakness a hundred miles out. If the seas don't get their problems settled, Crevan'll be coming to settle them for us. You mark my —"

"No, I'm all out of marks," Lysander jabbed a finger between Jonathan's eyes, "and I'm all out of patience. If I hear so much as a whisper about bad luck or piracy again, I'll toss you both in the brig. Understood?"

"Aye, Captain," they mumbled.

"Good." Lysander straightened the hem of his shirt roughly before he marched down the steps.

It was a long, quiet walk to the bow. Lysander passed the watchman on his way. He listened for the call of the bell behind him, timing each step with its strokes. Twelve. The very middle of the night. No sooner had the last echo faded than the deck shuddered beneath him.

The ship trembled for half a moment as she struck the choppy northern waves. She groaned, trying to get her footing. But her nose plunged ahead the moment she found her pace.

Lysander walked until the deck ended. There was an ache in his back. It stabbed between his shoulders and made him long to slouch against the railing. He wanted nothing more than to be able to sigh as Jonathan had, or worry aloud like Shamus. But there was plenty of worrying and sighing as it was.

What his men needed now was a strong back — and no matter how he ached, he was determined to stand tall.

A crest of rocks rose from the waters to the east. They would go on like that for miles, until the jagged shore finally gave way to a ring of sheer cliffs. He wagered they were still a week's sail from Harborville. It was agony, to be so far adrift while his men sat in prison. He would've given anything to be there with them.

There'd better not be a single sick or starving man among his dogs — and if anything had happened to *Anchorgloam*, Alders had better set sail before their bow crossed the harbor.

Lysander wouldn't need much of a wind to catch him.

"Perceval," he muttered, scowling at the vessel ahead if them. The lead ship had slipped out of sight, gliding into the shelter of the dark horizon — a curtain that hung down from the edge of the night and hid everything beyond.

The stars above him were shrouded. Still, Lysander watched for them out of habit. He couldn't help but try to find some bearing written in the skies, some idea of where this all might be headed. But there was none.

His hand slid from his belt loop and to the whittled hilt of his sword before falling limply to his side. He'd gone to turn away when a flash of something on the horizon turned him back.

A flare of light, a golden orb that burst to life before it flickered and died. Lysander turned just as the last of the light faded, but it was enough to bring him back to the railing. He leaned out as far as he could, his gaze locked unblinkingly upon the darkness and his mouth sealed shut.

Such a long moment passed that he nearly gave up his watch. It'd probably only been the flash of a storm, after all. The Valley and the northern forest still struggled against a long winter, and the storms that rose from this stretch of the seas were quiet and fierce.

Lysander leaned back, his lips pursed amid his scruff.

Then, quite suddenly, the light shone again.

It was closer this time. He watched its fall: from a thin streak in the clouds to a burst upon the seas. Lysander's hands froze to the railings. When the light came again, it illuminated the faintest shadow on the horizon — so small that it was difficult to distinguish its bow from its sails. But when the light faded, it didn't matter how clear the ship had been.

There was no mistaking that it was gone.

"What in high tide was that, Captain?" Shamus called from the helm.

Jonathan was already sprinting. He crashed in next to Lysander. White ringed the darks of his eyes as another bolt appeared. "Fire! It's falling straight out of the clouds."

The next streak fell close enough that it illuminated the lines of shock on his face. Ahead of them, the ships had begun to turn. Lanterns flared to life all across their decks. The sailors' cries were faint, but sharpened by panic. They worked the rigging and moved the sails as their helmsmen tried desperately to steer them towards the open sea.

"Fire from the clouds? That can't ..." Shamus's mouth parted into a wide O when a fresh bolt devoured one of the scrambling ships. "No time to wonder, I suppose. I'll turn us west —"

"No, east! We have to go east!" Lysander grabbed Jonathan by the back of his tunic and flung him for the stairs. "Wake the men. Shamus, work the lanterns. See if you can't get the others to follow us."

"But Captain, east'll send us on top of those rocks," Shamus sputtered as Lysander reached him. "We'll be wrecked!"

"Better wrecked with a chance to swim than burned with no chance at all. We can't hide on the seas. But if we can get close to land —"

"The lads can make a run for it. Aye, Captain. Sorry, my beauty." Shamus's hand fell heavily on the wheel before he jogged for the lantern.

The pirates woke to the resounding screech of Jonathan's fiddle. It carried through the hammocked chambers and startled the sleep from their eyes. They poured out across the deck, tugging on bits of clothing as they went.

47

Lysander took the helm, barking a stream of orders as he spun them towards the rocky shores: "Down to your tunics and trousers, dogs — no cloaks, no coats, nothing that'll drown you. Hang your blades across your shoulders and leave your arms free for swimming."

"What about the longboats, Captain?" one of them called.

"No boats!"

"But, Captain —"

A *whoosh* and a blast of light sent the pirates sprinting to the rails. The fire cast the shadows from their faces and drew horror across their eyes. They watched as a ship three ahead of them went down — moaning and crackling beneath the power of the flames, its flesh split open by a bright red swell of embers. A mix of steam and smoke billowed up as the waves dragged it under.

The pirates didn't need any more convincing:

"Aye, Captain — no boats!"

"Come on, mates! Help me clean out a few of these barrels," Jonathan said. He tipped one over and heads of cabbage came rolling from its top. "It'll all be burned up anyways, so we might as well have the barrels to float with."

The pirates leapt to help him while Lysander's eyes stayed locked upon the eastern shores. "Shamus?"

"No luck, Captain." The shipbuilder worked the latch of a signal lantern quickly, opening and closing its shutters in a pattern of lights. "They all think we're mad for cutting inland ... wait, here's one!"

The ship just ahead of them rocked so violently that it nearly tipped over as it swung east.

"Perceval," Lysander muttered as the ship out-paced them. It bounded up and over the waves in a desperate sprint while its crew held on tight.

The other ships paid their signal no heed. They split away and raced towards the open sea. Lysander grimaced when a fresh bolt of flame roared through the air behind him, but he kept his grip. "Move to the railings, dogs! Jump at my order and swim for your lives."

Sweat poured down his face; fire singed the air at his back. Screams rent the night as the last of the west-heading ships went down. Shamus stumbled from the lantern, his face ghostly pale. He dragged a hand through his hair and whispered:

"Fate ... poor souls."

"Could we reach them?" Lysander called, but Shamus shook his head.

"Reaching them wouldn't do a blasted thing Captain. The heat's in the water around the ship — I can see the bubbles popping up. Those poor lads are boiling alive. They'll be dead before we've turned around."

Lysander's lips pulled back from his teeth and he leaned against the helm. He shoved forward each time they struck a wave, as if he might be able to will them through. A loud *crack* to his left told him that Perceval's ship had just run aground. His shallower bottom carried him a greater distance inland. A few of his sailors had already paddled their way to shore.

Lysander watched the men duck into the woods — nothing more than shadows, at first. But then the details of the garments and faces became bright by a growing light in the clouds.

He watched as their dark gray bellies were boiled away, churned aside by a heat so fierce that he could feel it burning across his face. The light went nearly white before Lysander had to look away: it ached his eyes so badly that he feared he might be struck blind. He'd just managed to blink the dark patches aside when the light finally broke.

Flames spewed down upon Perceval's wrecked ship. Their roaring drowned the pirates' cries and a wave of heat dropped them to their knees. Lysander bared his teeth against a searing pain as the hot air scraped across the back of his neck. But he spun the wheel hard — aiming the ship's nose between two jagged spires of rock.

Even when Perceval's ship sank and the fires went dark, he held his course. The pirates dragged themselves to their feet only to drop once more and grip the rails.

"Captain?" Shamus said, eyes widening when he saw where Lysander was headed. "Captain!"

"Hold fast, men!" Lysander cried. "Jump the moment we've stopped and get yourselves to shore!"

Shamus crouched and wrapped his arms around the railing just as the ship reached the spires.

Her sides scraped as she charged through. The sound of her splitting flesh cracked through the air. Lysander managed to hold on until the ship's belly struck the rock. Then the force of the sudden stop threw him over the wheel.

"Jump, mates!"

The pirates followed Jonathan's wild, flailing plunge into the waters below. He wore a barrel like a dress, secured to his lanky frame by a coil of rope. The pirates clung to barrels and crates — any bit of wreckage they could salvage. Once they struck, they beat their legs through the violent waves towards a thin strip of shore.

Lysander lay alone upon the upper deck. He rolled over onto his back, gasping in pain. His stormy eyes fixed upon the sky above him; his chest went tight. The night was dark and silent, for now. But in a moment, the fires would come. His breaths deepened, his eyes closed ...

"That was the wildest bit of sailing I've ever seen! You're blasted lucky to be alive," Shamus bellowed as he grabbed Lysander under the arms.

"No — I swore a captain's oath, and I mean to go down with my ship!"

"Eh, you can go down with the next one," Shamus said as he hauled Lysander up. "Ready, Captain?"

"You can't —!"

But Shamus tipped backwards over the rails before he could protest further, plunging them both into the icy waves below.

Cold shocked him. Lysander held on with numbed hands as Shamus dragged him up for air. He tried to kick against the shove of the tide, but his legs were too stiff and the waves were too fierce. His head still spun from his fall.

Shamus fought hard. He barreled them through the first couple of swells and had crashed into a third when the sky erupted.

Light plunged down upon them — so thickly that Lysander could feel it pressing against his skin. Next came a wind that flattened the waves. It howled from the light's middle in a heat that burned his flesh like the sun. The waters around him began to warm.

All at once, the ice melted from his legs and Lysander's breath returned. He kicked wildly beside Shamus, trying to beat a path for shore. But they were too far out. The clouds roared and the heat drew steam from the waters' top.

"We're not going to make it," Lysander gasped as he fought. "We're going to be boiled alive!"

"Ha! Let them try!" Shamus bellowed, his gaze settled fearlessly upon the roiling fires above. "Even if they boil us, what a tale that'll be — oof!"

His words were cut short by a coil of rope slapping across his face.

"Grab on!" Jonathan called. He held onto the other end of the rope — a whole band of pirates lined up behind him. The second Lysander and Shamus grabbed on, they pulled.

The pirates tore them across the water and onto the shore a blink before the fires fell. They ran for the shadow of the trees, heads craning behind them to watch the flames devour the ship. She moaned piteously as the fire raced down her beams, chewed her sails to ashes. Lysander turned back in time to see her mast tilt and fall.

He went straight to his knees. "My ship … " He groaned as Jonathan dragged him up again. "You should've let me die."

Shamus snorted. "She was a beauty, Captain. But ships can be replaced. You've got far too much to live for."

CHAPTER 5
A WHISPER

Kael stayed up until late into the night, waiting for Kyleigh.

The storm that'd been threatening the village all afternoon finally broke. Now rain lashed the windows and the thunder grew along the breath of the wind.

Kyleigh loved flying through the storms. Nothing seemed to make her happier than cutting along the bursting clouds. But though Kael's heart muttered that all was well, his mind still worried.

When he tried to read, his eyes wouldn't focus on the page. They kept flicking to the window, turning back to the door. No amount of drawing or thinking could distract him. He quickly ran out of things to fix. Even when he paced, his hand kept trailing back into his pocket.

It was a stupid thing — he *knew* it was stupid. But for some reason, Kyleigh's ring sat heavily at its bottom. He swore he could feel the metal growing cold. It burned his skin through his trousers and after a while, his own ring started to cool.

The white-gold dragon coiled dully about his finger; its burst of onyx flame seemed darker now than ever. He knew it was only his mind playing tricks on him. If he allowed himself to sit and worry, there was no end to the ridiculous things he might dream up. Still, he couldn't stop it.

When his hand began to ache from the cold, he slid his ring off and stuffed it down next to Kyleigh's. Once she returned, all would be set right.

But he'd have to find some way to distract himself until then.

Kael was actually relieved when somebody knocked on the library door. "Come in. It's only me, Mandy," he called, when he saw how slowly the door crept open.

While the other maids burst in on them every chance they got, Mandy was always careful. She was a round-faced woman with a warm smile and a very firm grip.

"Good evening, Master Kael," she said as she entered. "Crumfeld just sent me along to make sure you've had your dinner. He didn't remember seeing you in the dining room or the kitchens."

Kael hadn't seen Crumfeld, either. It was strange because so much of Roost seemed completely reliant on its butler. They'd never once crossed paths. Soldiers and maids would pop up every once in a while to give him one of Crumfeld's messages — and occasionally, he would wander into a room that had clearly just been tidied.

But though he'd scoured every inch of the castle, Kael had yet to find him.

It seemed today would be no exception. "I got hungry earlier, so I ate in the village," Kael lied. The fact was that he'd completely forgotten about dinner. But he knew if he said as much, he'd just get dragged off to the kitchens.

"Very well. Just so long as you've eaten," Mandy said. Her eyes cut quickly across the room before coming back to his. A frown marred her cheery features. "Has Miss Kyleigh not returned?"

"No," Kael said with a sigh. "She's out playing in the blasted rain again."

He'd tried to keep the bitterness from his voice, he really had. But Mandy must've heard. She flashed him a smile that made his face burn horribly before returning to her frown. "Well, when she gets in, would you kindly let her know that I'm perfectly capable of handling my own affairs?"

"All right." Kael was almost afraid to ask it. But as he had nothing better to do, he thought he might as well. "What do you mean?"

"Gerald turns white as a ghost any time he sees me. He jogs off, sputtering about having to do one thing or another. And I know she's had a hand in it."

Though he'd been with them for a few weeks, Kael hadn't quite gotten used to the castle — and the various goings-on of its residents still made him a bit cross-eyed. But if he remembered correctly, *Gerald* was one of Roost's guards. He often manned the keep doors or patrolled the upper levels.

And sometime while Kyleigh had been away, he'd apparently taken a liking to Mandy.

"How can you be so sure it was Kyleigh's doing? Perhaps he's only nervous."

"Oh, I'm sure he is. I'd be nervous too if I'd been promised a head-first plummet from the clouds."

Well ... that certainly *sounded* like Kyleigh. "I'm sure she didn't mean it like that — but I'll speak to her," he added quickly, when Mandy raised her brows.

"Thank you," she said with a dip of her skirts. "It's been a fresh turn of the tide, having you here. She can get a bit fiery about this sort of thing."

She certainly could. Kael wasn't at all looking forward to have to try to reason with her, but he promised he would do his best.

Once Mandy had wandered off for the night, Kael went back to trying to find some way to stay busy. He rescued the fire from dying and then brought out the small chessboard he'd found tucked inside one the desk's drawers.

While much of Roost went bare, the library was packed full of things. Kael liked the narrow desk, and how it'd been arranged in a corner of the room that allowed him to watch the door and the window at once. He liked the cushioned chairs that'd been settled before the hearth, and the little table that sat between them.

Though the chairs were a bit more lavish than he would've liked, he found that draping bear pelts across their backs helped soften them up a bit. He'd also replaced the gold-threaded rug with one made up of the stitched-together hides of animals. And slowly, the library had begun to feel more like home.

Kael settled himself in one of the cushioned chairs and opened the board upon the table. Uncle Martin had insisted that chess was a game he could play on his own, but Kael had never quite gotten used to it. If he set up a convincing attack, he always knew exactly how to counter. Back and forth he'd battle until the game finally went stale.

No, he'd prefer to play with an opponent who kept him on his feet. He wished she would hurry up and fly home.

He was in the middle of trying to rescue his pawns from the queen's advance when he heard the creak of the library door. "It's about blasted time," he growled, trying to look severe. But it was no use.

Kyleigh's eyes were far too warm, her smile far too bright. Her raven hair was damp and dripping down the back of the shirt and trousers she'd nicked from one of his drawers. She'd obviously thrown them on in a hurry: one of the legs was rolled higher than the other, and the tail of the shirt hung out the back.

She clutched her blackened dragonscale armor to her chest as she entered. "It was brilliant out there tonight. You're lucky I came home at all."

His throat tightened as he watched her drop the armor onto the desk; his heart began to race. "What?" he croaked, even though when he saw how fiercely her gaze burned, he knew full well *what*.

"I warned you that I planned to finish what I started," she murmured as she sauntered towards him.

He sprang to his feet and caught her hands in his, bracing himself for the coiling strength that surged across her limbs. "One game," he pleaded, holding her back.

"No."

"You can't just keep beating me!"

"Apparently, I can," she said, thrusting forward. But just when it looked as if he would lose, she finally relented. "Fine. One game."

Something about the way she held him reminded him of the night before. The memories flared up behind the backs of his eyes and he pulled away quickly. "White or black?" he said, hoping Kyleigh hadn't noticed his look.

Though judging by the growl in her voice, she had: "White, of course."

It was difficult to concentrate with Kyleigh sitting across from him. He loved to watch how her eyes moved across the pieces. She kept her finger propped against her lips as she studied the board. But every once in a while, the edges of her mouth would slip into a smirk — usually just before she wreaked havoc on his pieces.

It took Kael ages to decide which way to turn, but Kyleigh moved in a blink. Soon, the numbers of his blackened army had dwindled considerably — and he honestly couldn't remember how half of them had been taken.

"How do you do it?" he grumbled, sliding his knight to a position he was certain wouldn't get him mauled.

Kyleigh didn't answer. When he looked up, she snared him in her gaze. "Do you really want to know?"

"Yes."

She raised a brow at the hesitation in his voice. Then she leaned forward, propped her elbows upon the table, and whispered:

"You'll need to watch me, then ... very, *very* closely. Are you watching?"

He was — or at least he *had* been. Something about the way her lips moved around her words made him forget what he was supposed to be doing. He stared until they bent, ever so slightly, into a triumphant smirk.

"You weren't watching closely."

"I was," he insisted, forcing his eyes away from her lips.

Her brows arced high. "Oh? Then what became of your poor knight?"

Kael looked down, and was shocked to see that his knight had vanished from the board — the knight he'd been certain was safe. No, he *had* been safe. There was no possible way any of Kyleigh's pieces could've gotten near him.

He glared at her.

She propped one fist pensively beneath her chin. "Well, whisperer? What have you got to say for yourself?"

He glanced across the table for his missing knight, while Kyleigh looked on with a mocking grin. But it wasn't until he thought to check the floor that he finally discovered it: his knight lay slain beneath Kyleigh's chair — along with a host of other blackened pieces.

He couldn't believe it. "You've been cheating this whole time, haven't you?"

"How *dare* you accuse me of cheating!" Kyleigh roared. She flung out her arm and hurled the table from between them.

And while Kael was still gaping at the scattered pieces, she tackled him.

****

With their game ruined, Kyleigh made good on her word. "It's not fair," she moaned, half-laughing. She buried her head against his neck before she punched him weakly in the chest. "It isn't fair at all."

Kael thought she'd been pretty *unfair*, herself.

While she trailed a slow line of kisses down his neck, he craned his head back to survey the damage — and groaned at what he saw.

One of the cushioned chairs had been completely torn apart. The other was missing a leg. Once the world stopped spinning, he could probably seal them back together. But there would be no salvaging the table: it'd toppled over and fallen into the hearth. Now it lay half-out of the fire, with the flames already eating their way down its legs.

Kyleigh reached up and shoved it the rest of the way in before the fire could leap onto the hide rug. "I'm afraid there'll be no returning from that."

Kael agreed. "I'll make a new one tomorrow." Sometime during the scuffle, one of the bear pelts had gotten trapped beneath him. It was missing a paw, but he still thought it ought do nicely.

"I'm not cold —"

"I don't care," Kael said firmly as he draped the hide over them. "Your people are always bursting into places without knocking. I'm not going to leave you stark naked on the floor for everybody to see."

"You're assuming they haven't already seen it?"

"Come off it, Kyleigh. You wouldn't wander around the castle naked ... would you?"

"I suppose you'll never know."

He wasn't sure he *wanted* to know. "Speaking of maids — Mandy was looking for you."

"Oh?"

"Yes. And she wasn't very happy."

"Well, I'm sorry to hear that. Goodnight."

She tried to roll away, but Kael grabbed her by the shoulder. "You can't keep threatening Gerald with a gruesome death every time he comes near her. It isn't fair."

"I didn't tell him not to come near her. I simply warned him not to hurt her."

Kael frowned. "He thinks you're going to drop him from the clouds."

"Well, I felt I ought to at least give him fair warning."

"*Well*, Mandy wants you to stop."

Kyleigh shrugged. "All right. Noted." Then she pulled out of his grasp and rolled aside, turning her back to him.

It took Kael a moment to realize that she hadn't exactly agreed. "Does that mean you'll stop?"

"I said it was *noted*," was her growling reply.

Though he should've been cross with her, Kael couldn't help but smile. This was one of the few times when her dragon half showed through.

Granted, there hadn't been much in the dragon books he'd found in the library. Most were simply legends. But there *had* been a passage about lady dragons, and how fiercely they guarded their nests. As protective as they were of their skies, the book had warned that it was nothing compared to the fury with which they would defend their brood.

With Roost very firmly under the shadow of her wings, Kyleigh must've felt the need to protect Mandy. And he couldn't fault her for it.

But he'd seen enough pictures of armies being roasted alive to know that Kyleigh *would* drop Gerald from the clouds if he ever hurt Mandy. He hoped it wouldn't come to that.

Kael wrapped himself around her carefully; he pulled her close. His arms dipped into the curves of her waist. He pressed his chest into her back until he could feel the steady beating of her heart. She fit against him perfectly. She made him whole.

Her breathing slowed to a murmur and her heart slowed to match. The hand she'd had clutched against his arm loosed its grip and trailed softly to the floor. Only when he was certain she'd fallen asleep did Kael dare to whisper:

"I love you, Kyleigh."

CHAPTER 6
THE RED WALL

Something startled Kael awake. The storm still growled outside the window, but the hearth fire had gone dark. Cool air glanced across his chest and his arms were empty. He heard the patter of feet and rushed to blink the sleep from his eyes.

Kyleigh was standing before the desk, tugging on her boots. She already wore her leggings and her jerkin hung open at her chest. Her hands moved in a blur as they sealed every buckle and clasp in a swift, practiced motion. Her eyes stayed fixed upon the window.

Even by the fire's embers, he could see that she was glaring.

"What is it?" Kael said hoarsely.

She didn't reply. She glanced at the desk for half a blink to snatch Harbinger up before her eyes flicked back to the window.

It took Kael several moments of digging through the shambles of the room before he finally came up with his trousers. They were ripped straight down the middle — torn beyond repair. He didn't remember what had happened, exactly ... but he could guess.

Fortunately, the pair Kyleigh had been wearing was still intact. He found the trousers beneath a pile of broken chair and slipped them on as quickly as he could. "What's out there?" he hissed as he worked the laces.

When she replied, her voice was hardly a whisper: "Something's happened ... something's wrong."

Her voice sounded strange — as if she spoke from sleep, though her eyes were opened. "Are you certain it wasn't a dream?"

She'd woken him before with worries that something was after them. She would spring from bed and go tearing off down the hall if he didn't stop her. While she was awake, she assured him that they were safe. But her heart must've felt differently in sleep.

"I think I'll go for a walk," Kyleigh said, backing away from the window.

Kael jogged over to take her place. He tried to peer through the warped lines of the glass and the steady, trickling path of the rain, but it was no use. Not even the guards' braziers had survived the wet. All he could see was darkness.

He turned at a creak of the door. "No, don't go out there — there's no point in it."

She stopped in the doorway and watched him from over her shoulder. "I feel I should. I'll feel better if I know for certain."

Kael sighed. "All right. Let me find my boots, and I'll ..."

His words trailed off as a bright orange glow filled the room. The arc of its edge stretched quickly across the broken furniture, growing more furiously bright until it touched his boots — launched into two separate corners of the room. Finally, the light flooded up the doorframe, to the ceiling ... and he saw every perfect line of Kyleigh's face twist in horror.

"Kael!"

He didn't have time to look back. He charged across the room and didn't stop — not even when the wall behind him exploded. He felt the pressure of the rattling *boom* against his ears, felt the wind shove him forward. He dove for Kyleigh at full tilt.

She clamped an arm across his back; his weight knocked her down. She managed to kick the door shut as they fell — only to have it ripped off its hinges a second later.

Kael's elbows bit the ground hard, but he managed not to flatten Kyleigh beneath him. He grunted when the door slapped across his back and nearly lost his grip when a shower of heavy bits of wall thudded on top of it. He likely would have been crushed to death, had Kyleigh not braced it with her hands.

"Go!" she grunted.

He slid out the gap between her arms and the door. Once he had his feet under him, he tore the rubble aside and pulled her free. "Are you —?"

Another explosion sounded overhead. The floor shook beneath them. Kyleigh's head whipped around at the noise of terrified screams. "You take the bottom floor — I'll take the top."

She tore off down the hallway, and Kael followed on her heels.

They split at the main room: Kyleigh charged down the passageway that would lead to the stairs while Kael tried to manage his way through a crush of castle folk.

They were red-eyed and half-dressed. Many of them were already wounded by debris. There were too many bodies packed inside the hall — and each and every one of them scrambled madly for the keep's one small door.

Kael was trying to shove his way through without hurting anybody when someone bellowed from behind him: "Make way! Let the Witchslayer get to the door!"

Gerald's voice rose above the panicked shouts. Several of the guards took up his cry. The castle folk parted out of his way. They shoved him on. When he reached the door, he saw it'd been caved in.

"Bloody trapped," Gerald hissed from behind him. "We'd better turn around and make for the back."

There wasn't time for that. The back led to a narrow walk that dangled over the edge of a cliff. Kael didn't think the villagers would be able to make it in the dark.

So he shoved his hands into the wall, molding the stone and mortar aside like clay. People began slipping through the hole the moment it was wide enough. He dragged its sides until the hole resembled something like the slit in an iron helmet.

"Keep moving," Gerald said as he urged the last of them outside. "Head straight for the village!"

"What's out there?" Kael panted. His head was still spinning from the shock, his ears still ringing from the blast. But he tried to force himself to be calm.

Gerald, on the other hand, looked as if he'd just lost a bucket's worth of blood. "I haven't got a clue! I was about to take my turn at the watch when the castle started blasting apart. We've been hit in the back and the shanks. Looks like forward's our only option."

Before Kael could wonder how on earth someone had managed to get behind Roost, a loud *clang* drew his eyes down the hallway towards the library.

A handful of guards tumbled out of the back room, running like Death snapped at their heels. White ringed their eyes and their arms swung madly at Gerald. "Move! Get out of here!"

Before he could ask, Kael saw it: a red light glowed softly in the doorway. It filled the castle from ceiling to floor, like a sheet of glass that changed its shape along the curves of the hall.

It blackened the guards' armor and made their flailing shadows look like wraiths. The man at the back of the sprint tripped over his boots. He managed to crawl a few paces, but the red light didn't slow. Kael was running to help when a thick, moldy tang struck his nose.

Magic.

In the second he realized this, the guard was overtaken. He screamed and writhed upon the ground as the red light scraped across him. Kael managed to grab his hand just as the spell enveloped them. He was so focused on holding his breath against the tang of magic that he moved the guard a foot before he realized that he was dragging a skeleton.

The magic had stripped the guard's skin away, peeling his flesh aside until all that remained was shining bone. Kael dropped him, and the guard's helmet rolled away — revealing a smooth, grinning skull.

"Run! Get out of the castle!"

Kael barely heard Gerald's cries. He was already focused on the hallway, searching for the source of the red light. Fury surged through his limbs. He didn't know what stood at the hallway's end — but if it had a heart, he would rip it out.

The noise around him vanished as he charged deeper into the light. Here, the world shimmered like sun across the waves and everything was doused in a haunting red. The smell of magic sickened him. It filled his mouth and spilled wetly down his throat.

There was only one thing the light didn't seem able to touch: a thin, shimmering figure that marched at its back. Its arms were raised and it held what looked like a staff between its hands.

The mage must've seen Kael coming. It stiffened, its limbs curled back and its mouth opened in what could've only been a shriek. But he couldn't hear it. He burst from the light and swung blindly through the darkness. His fist collided with something that gave way with a crunch. A body struck the ground.

Then came the smell of blood.

It burned the insides of his nose and swelled to cloud his vision — a thick, bitter stench that made bile rise up his throat. A roar burst from his chest as he lunged. His hands curled out like talons before him, feeling for the wet warmth of the blood. The mage shrieked again and tried to scramble away from him.

But he caught it around the throat.

Kael pressed down hard, eyes burning as his grip tightened. Soon, the blood would stop. Soon, the madness would fade ...

"Please!"

Through the fog that clouded his vision came a small, trembling voice. His roar shrank back from its wailing, confused. His grip loosened against the plea of hands much weaker than his. All at once, the madness slipped away.

Kael followed the shaking line of his arms to the end of his clenched fists — where a young girl stared up at him in terror. Her face was bloodied from his punches, her skin pale for the lack of air.

He let go of her throat with a lurch.

"Who are you?" was all he could think to say.

She was a young forest woman. Her rounded eyes were filled to the brim with tears. Kael followed the line of blood that dripped from her chin to the collar of her golden robes. His stomach churned when he saw the twisting black dragon sewed into its front — the crest of Midlan.

He was still battling against the shock when the girl reached to soothe her throat. There was an iron shackle clamped about her wrist — a shackle that glowed with a red, pulsing light.

He suddenly understood. "Here — no, I'm not going to hurt you. I swear you're safe." Kael pressed his thumbnail into the milky white film coating the shackle and peeled the spell away. The iron tore like parchment between his hands.

The moment the shackle fell, the young woman gasped — as if she'd been holding her breath for ages. Brightness returned to her eyes. But when she looked at Kael, white terror ringed them again.

"Don't worry, I won't touch you again. The King sent you here, didn't he? You're one of his mages. How many more of you are there?" he pressed, raising his voice to be heard over the noise of a fresh wave of explosions. The tower shook and the floor above them groaned. Kael took his eyes away for half a blink to make certain the beams weren't about to give way.

But when he glanced down, the mage girl was already gone.

He didn't have time to worry; he didn't even have time to swear. The moment she vanished, he heard the castle folks' panicked yells coming from behind him, and he turned on his heels.

The people who'd fled the main hall hadn't gotten very far: they were gathered in a crowd across the courtyard, beating desperately against its stubborn gate.

There was a withered knot near the middle of the left door. The lumps in the center of the knot gave it the look of a lopsided face —

one with mismatched eyes and a slightly squished nose. As the villagers pounded upon the door, the knot shrilled back:

"Stop it! Stop hitting me! I'm only trying to hel — ouch!"

Kael shoved his way through the crowd, already howling at Knotter: "Open up, you stupid apparition! We're under attack!"

"Don't you think I know that?" Knotter snapped in reply. "That's why I'm keeping you all locked up inside here, where you'll be safe —"

The thunder of a collapsing tower froze his words. Kael whipped around and for a moment, the whole kingdom went still.

The tower that held their chambers was collapsing. He watched the windows droop like saddened eyes, their lids heavy with flame. The balcony dropped in a gaping, horrified scream. The tower tilted and swayed, groaning as it fell.

Kael had taken a panicked leap forward when the roof suddenly burst open.

A large white dragon erupted from its top, an armful of castle folk pressed against her scaly chest. Her serpentine body darted upwards until it became lost among the clouds.

Spells of every color chased after her. They burst from the cliffs behind Roost and arced in from the village below. Kael knew that as long as Kyleigh stayed above the clouds, she would be safe.

He had to take care of the villagers. "Roost is finished, we have to move."

Knotter's jagged crack of a mouth twisted sharply. "No, *no*! It's worse out there. It's far worse —"

"Let us out, or a swear I'll rip the skin off of you!" Kael bellowed.

"All right, all right. But don't say I didn't warn you," Knotter huffed.

The castle gate swung open, and Kael blanched at what he saw.

It was a picture taken straight from his nightmares: walls of red charged towards Copperdock on either side, drifting hungrily through the spiny woods. They were the arms of some monster about to wrap everything up inside its deadly embrace. Dark shapes of people poured from the homes and shops, streaming for the docks. Their screams thickened the night. Ships were already beginning to make their way from the harbor.

There was only one thin sliver of earth untouched by the light — a mage's worth of clear space, the gap left by the young woman he'd freed. "Everybody stay close to me," Kael called behind him. "We're going to have to run for it."

Gerald balked for half a second before he sputtered: "To the docks! Quickly now, men!"

A handful of guards took off, charging to the lead while the castle folk followed. Servants hauled their children across their shoulders, the women picked up their skirts. They tore down the winding castle path and plunged into the haunted woods below.

Rain lashed them while the storm howled above. The red walls slid in on their either side. They rose as high as towers and ringed all of Copperdock in a thick, deadly spell — a horseshoe of flesh-rending light that cut them off from the rest of the Kingdom. The walls left them only one path of escape.

They had to reach the seas.

Kael urged the villagers on as he ran. The walls' eerie light darkened the shadows, deepened the terror across their faces. Not even the veins of lightning were enough to drive them back.

The smell — sweet mercy, the tang of magic was everywhere. Kael felt the madness begin to rise. His hands shook; his heart started to pound. He wanted nothing more than to plunge into the light and tear every last mage's head from his shoulders. But he knew that if he left, the villagers would be defenseless.

So he had no choice but to stay by their side.

He fell back the moment they reached the docks, waiting until the last servant made it through. The red light seemed to end where the docks began, which meant that everyone who'd managed to board a ship would be safe.

Unfortunately, all of the ships were well out to sea.

"Come back! Come back, blast you!" Gerald cried, waving as the nearest vessel slunk off into the waves. He grabbed Kael by the arm. "The merchants have taken off, and they've taken everything seaworthy with them. We'll have to go some other way."

There *was* no other way. Kael knew that if they stood at the docks for too long, the mages would overtake them. He spotted a small boat he thought might hold them all: a vessel that was little more than a deck and a sail. But it would have to do.

"Get them on board."

When he saw where Kael pointed, Gerald's mouth fell open. "Are you mad? That thing'll never get us through a storm—"

"We'll just have to try," Kael snapped impatiently. "We have no other choice."

Now that the red walls had reached the shoreline, they were starting to close in. They pressed together, sealing the narrow gap between them. The villagers would be one fireball from death once the mages saw them. Kael couldn't protect them all.

Their best chance was to head out to sea, to try to disappear inside the storm.

Gerald seemed to realize this. The guards herded everybody onto the deck while Kael took the wheel. A few of the men seemed to know enough to work the sails, and he was grateful for it. The storm winds filled them quickly and spat them out to sea.

Kael held his breath as they sailed — hoping to mercy that they were small enough to go unnoticed. When he chanced a look behind him, a number of blackened figures had appeared throughout the light.

They stood together in a perfect line, unmoving. As he watched, the man in the middle of the line stepped forward. He raised an arm to the clouds and another red light flared brightly from his fist.

Kael gripped the wheel. He was ready to turn from the spell's path, ready to spin them away, if he had to. But all at once, the light faded. The red disappeared from the shores. The blackened figures slipped back inside the walls.

And the world went eerily still.

CHAPTER 7
THE BLACK DRAGON

The night crushed them. Waves slapped against their sides and the wind tested their sails. Kael's grip tightened each time their mast moaned against the storm's breath.

He hoped to mercy it would hold.

Behind them, Copperdock had fallen silent. Kael couldn't look back: he was too focused on the waves ahead. But he watched the red light fade from the village through the reflections of the guards' widened eyes. They stared, their hands white-knuckled upon the weapons at their hips.

Gerald's mouth sagged beneath his helmet, and the darks of his eyes stretched to caverns. "What now?" he murmured.

Kael wasn't sure. The ships ahead of them seemed to know what they were doing, so he followed as closely as he could. The fury with which the rain struck the sea muddled the air. It formed a thick curtain that seemed to devour everything. Soon, he had to rely on flashes of lightning to catch a glimpse of the nearest vessel.

They'd sailed for hardly a few minutes when a roar startled them from above. Kael spun around and his heart lurched inside his chest when a white bolt *whoosh*ed behind them.

Kyleigh sped close to the water, stirring up a wave that rocked them. Spells of all colors shot out from the darkened shores. They bolted towards her, but she twisted and spun in a rabbit's pattern across the sky — avoiding them with ease.

She flew in a wide arc back towards the burning village before she shot into the streaming clouds. The mages followed her, flinging spells as they went.

She knows what she's doing, Kael told himself, even as his hands screamed to turn the wheel. *She knows what she's —*

"Help!"

A round of panicked splashing drew his eyes to where Kyleigh had flown past them, and he saw that a handful of villagers bobbed in her wake.

"Turn around and get us close," Gerald said, stepping to the rails.

The guards worked together, pulling three sopping maids and one rather small, wide-eyed man from the waves. Kael didn't recognize the man. He was trying to get a look at his face when a woman's relieved cry drew his eyes away.

"Oh, Gerald — I'm so glad you're safe!" Mandy said.

Gerald didn't seem to mind the fact that she was sopping wet. He held her close and smiled shakily. "You ... you are?"

"I thought you'd gone out to the watch. I thought for sure that you'd been killed! The whole time we were flying around, I should've fainted. But I couldn't even be worried over the height for worrying over you."

"I was worried over you, too. I'd been hoping to Fate that you made it onto one of those ships ..." Gerald went pale-faced when he saw Kael watching and tried to pull away.

"Don't worry — I won't tell," he promised.

Kael knew they'd been incredibly lucky. Not so long ago, he would've boiled over what the King had done to Copperdock. His fury might've driven him to the edge. But he'd seen far too much since then. He'd stared into too many lifeless faces and felt the ache of losing something far worse than a home.

He couldn't help but smile as he watched Gerald and Mandy speak, couldn't help but feel relief at the sight of so many people safe aboard the boat. Yes, Roost had been destroyed and the people run from their homes, but they were lucky. He'd seen what could happen when the King's eyes fell upon an unprotected village.

Kael would rather Copperdock be empty than full of bones.

The mages' spell blasts taunted him as he sailed, but he forced himself to look ahead. Kyleigh had outrun the King's men for years — and with the storm hanging above them so thickly, the mages weren't likely to catch her tonight. Once she returned, they would figure out how to answer Crevan.

But for now, he focused all of his thoughts on getting the villagers to safety.

They cut across the heaving swells, following in the wake of the larger ships. The breadth of their monstrous sails carried them away quickly, and it wasn't long before Kael could barely make out their shadows.

"Where are they headed?" he wondered.

"The chancellor's fortress," Gerald said, his mouth taut. "They'll be looking for answers ... and for the council's protection."

But it won't do them any good.

Those were the words that hung between them, the words that sat so heavily across their heads. Kael gripped the wheel tightly and tried to keep his frustration at bay.

He remembered the island fortress all too well — and he thought it was about the worst possible place for the whole of the seas to gather. If Gerald knew the villagers would flee to the chancellor's fortress, then it was likely Crevan knew it, as well.

There had to be a reason the mages hadn't blasted them from the waves ... had to be a reason Copperdock wasn't burned ...

Dark things swirled in the back of his mind. Half-formed plans drifted behind his eyes, but he couldn't focus with Kyleigh so far away. He found himself glancing back more and more often.

Gerald's hand clamped across his arm, startling him from his thoughts. "Do you hear that?"

Kael had been so intent on listening for Kyleigh's roars that he hadn't actually been paying attention. He looked up to where the clouds trembled softly overhead. "It's only thunder."

"Then why isn't it stopping?"

Hairs rose down the back of Kael's neck when he realized Gerald was right: the thunder hadn't stopped. If anything, it seemed to be growing.

Ahead of them, the last ship slipped out of their sight. It disappeared into the storm-muddled seas as the rumbling grew louder. A yellow orb appeared in the clouds above the fleeing ships. It cracked open like an eye and shone above the waves — illuminating the whole fleet before them.

Gerald peered at the orb, leaning over the bow. "What in Kingdom's —?"

Kael's heart shot up his throat as the rumbling burst into a roar. The orb erupted — a pillar of flame spilled from its middle and into the waves. A cluster of ships ahead of them was stricken with color. Kael swore he could make out every line of their planks, every flutter of their sails. And then they were gone — replaced by towering balls of flame.

Kael realized with a horror that stole his breath that he'd been right. There *was* a reason Crevan had spared them at the docks. He'd forced the villagers away from land and onto their boats, left them with no place to run.

He'd been sending them into a trap.

The deck erupted in swears and Gerald leapt backwards as the flames devoured the ships. "To the sails! Change course — change course!"

Kael spun the wheel around, cutting to the left. He watched in disbelief as the ruined ships glowed for a mere few seconds before the ocean sucked them down. Then just as suddenly as it'd appeared, the orb was gone — leaving them only with the slap of the waves and the steady thud of the rain.

Bells started to clang from the decks of the others ships. They spun on their hulls, stumbling like blind men through a lash of rain. One bell in particular began to grow loud: it started at their right and cut directly across their front.

"Hold on!" Kael bellowed as their tiny vessel met the ship's wake. "Hold —!"

There was a blast of searing heat and a burst of light. A pillar of flame struck the ship in front of them, wrapped its sails and rigging between its monstrous jaws. The ship was gone in a blink, dragged to a watery grave.

Kael's ears rang loudly in the silence left behind.

Mandy screamed.

"Get us out of here!" Gerald roared.

Kael was trying. But no matter where he steered them, the pillars of fire fell. They crashed into the seas in bolts all around them, reducing one ship after the next to flames. Boiling water slapped up under the force of the fire and rained down upon them in stinging waves.

The light was so blinding and the roar of its breath so furious that the most Kael could do was steer them towards the few black patches on the horizon — hoping the darkness meant a clear sky.

"Make way!" Gerald cried, thrusting a finger over Kael's shoulder. "There's one coming up on our heels. Make way, or she'll run us over!"

Kael heard the panicked groans of the ship behind them — heard the panicked shouts of its crew as they charged for the same black gap that he did. But he also felt the growing heat on the back of his neck, saw the tensed white of his knuckles illuminated against the ship's wheel as fire in the sky grew at his back.

He held his course.

The pillar fell and devoured the ship behind them. Wind roared from its flesh, the waves spouted from its fall in a powerful rush. The force of the wind and the waves crushed Kael against the wheel — it made Gerald stumble sideways and sent the rest of the crew directly to their rumps.

That blast of wind and crush of the waves propelled their little vessel forward. Its slender mast bowed as the sail filled it to tearing, but it didn't break. Kael held on tightly as the seas spat them away, aiming for the dark horizon.

The ship behind them sank with a crackling moan. Soon, the darkness returned and the world went silent.

"Mages!" Gerald gasped, pulling himself to his feet. His hands shook as he reached to help Mandy; his eyes stayed fixed upon the clouds. "Oh, I can't stand magic — can't they leave us alone for a blasted moment?"

Though worry marred her face, Mandy kept her voice calm. "Are we …? Do you think any of the other ships …?"

"I don't know," Kael managed to whisper over the yelps of his heart. "I don't know."

"A lucky thing we're small. Otherwise, we would've been … what's that?" Gerald leapt back and his hand flew to his sword.

Mandy's eyes followed the soft rumble overhead until it faded. "It was only the thunder," she said. But though the men on deck relaxed, Kael couldn't breathe.

He remembered all too well what the Witch of Wendelgrimm had done to the seas. The tempest she'd crafted from the wind and waves was a mark of how powerful magic could be. Though the Sovereign Five all had mages under their command, Kael had no doubt that Crevan had kept the best of the battlemages for himself — and he had no trouble believing they could call down fire from the skies.

71

The mage who'd raised his arm, the one whose fist had glowed so brightly, *he* must've been the one responsible for this. What Kael had hoped was merely surrender was actually the casting of a spell.

Now the fires were upon them.

Little hairs rose on the back of his neck as he listened for the rumble to come again. His companions' voices grew muffled. He squinted through the fat drops of rain that thudded across his brow, peering into the blackness above him. A flash of lighting revealed the feathered bottoms of the clouds, but nothing seemed amiss.

Thunder followed the lightning's flash. It rumbled overhead, sent tremors down the sail's ties and across the polished deck. As Kael watched, he realized the thunder hadn't trailed away.

It only grew louder.

"Kael!"

He saw it. He saw the orb of light appear in the clouds ahead of them even before Gerald cried out.

A blast of heated wind stopped their boat in its path. It shoved against the storm and trapped them between the gales. Screams cut above its bellow. The villagers fell to the ground and threw their arms over their faces, trying desperately to shield themselves from the heat.

Kael swore he could feel the topmost layer of his flesh being ripped away, becoming red and raw. His eyes streamed against the heat, ached from the light of the orb. Little glowing embers began to appear across the mast and sails. They flickered to life like torches upon a distant shore.

He knew he had to do something quickly. If he didn't, they would burst into flame. Rather than try to fight the force of the heated wind, he spun the wheel. He ripped them to the side and broke out of its path.

For a moment, the heat shrank back. Kael wrenched his head to the side and watched as the orb slid between the clouds. A deep rumbling shook his bones again. Then all at once, a pillar of yellow flame spewed down.

It crashed into the seas beside them and cut up the waves, tearing for their flank. Kael tried to turn them away, but the pillar moved too quickly. Its head ground into the seas, two great wings of water sprayed up as it roared to devour them. The light blinded him; the heat stole his breath.

He knew, in an instant that froze his blood against his bones, that they were trapped.

People screamed. A few of the servants scrambled below deck. Gerald held Mandy tightly against his chest, teeth bared against the red blisters that popped up across his face. Kael twisted the wheel so hard that one of the knobs snapped beneath his strength.

The fire was coming for them; the white light stabbed his eyes. Kael searched for a black patch on the horizon, but there was none.

Then, in the half-moment before the orb could burst, something remarkable happened: the heat faded and the light suddenly went out. The wind stopped and the seas fell silent. Soon all that remained was the murmur of the seas and the shadow of the storm.

The night crushed them once again.

****

Kyleigh soared through the clouds above Copperdock, her ears straining for the telltale *pop* of the mages' spells. These were the same mages Crevan always sent after her — the ones who could travel over land through short portals.

He'd learned the hard way that his armies and beasts had little chance against her. Any creature that flew within her reach would have its wings torn apart, and her flame would reduce anything on the ground to ashes.

No, this band of mages was the only chance Crevan had against her — and from the speed with which their portals popped, she knew something else must be driving them on.

They only moved that boldly when Ulric was among them.

It wasn't difficult to find the archmage. The portal that traveled furthest and popped the loudest was clearly Ulric's. Sometimes there would be a flash of light when he landed — a fireball that burst from his fist to devour a nearby home. He always made it a point to stomp back to Midlan, leveling as much as he could along the way.

But tonight, his journey would be short-lived.

Clouds whipped by as Kyleigh fell towards the ruins of a burning home. Ulric stood outside its door, his horrid grin fixed upon the blaze. She breathed in until the flap over her second set of lungs opened. There was a faint *click* inside her chest as the heat climbed her throat.

She held the flames trapped against her tongue as her fall carried her closer to Ulric. He saw her shadow dull the light of the blaze before him and spun. The chained impetus glowed against his arm and he disappeared in a lightning's flash of red — narrowly avoiding the blast of Kyleigh's flame.

"The Dragongirl! Stop her, you fools — bring her down!"

Kyleigh knew better than to linger. Her wings snapped open and she raised her chin, turning the force of her fall to a power that launched her into the refuge of the clouds. And not a moment too soon.

Faint red dots appeared along the earth beneath her as the mages' shackles burst to life. Their spells flew with more fury than thought, crazed by the ring of Ulric's furious command. Had they slowed to aim, they might have actually hit their mark. But as it was, their magic was more annoying than dangerous.

Kyleigh stayed out of their reach for most of the chase. She listened for the whistling of spells and spun to dodge the ones that came too close. All the while she moved, her eyes scanned the red dots.

Most were careful to bunch together. They knew she wouldn't risk coming too close, if they stayed in a group. But that was before tonight — before they'd destroyed her home and hurt her people. Kyleigh wasn't going to be careful, tonight.

She was going to make sure they knew her fury.

One mage strayed too far from his companions. She hovered over the spot where his shackle glowed. The breath of the storm held her aloft, pushing gently on the thin under-edges of her wings. She tilted them as she took a breath, shifting to catch the blusters of the storm.

The clouds hissed by. The rain thundered against her scales. Lightning flashed behind her, and the mage saw her shadow cross his boots. His face went white with terror.

A blast of Kyleigh's flames devoured his screams ... and his flesh.

Before the mage's bones had finished crumbling to ash, his companions fired back with a deadly hail of colored bolts. Kyleigh darted into the clouds and tore east — deeper into land and further from the shores. All she had to do was lead them away. As long as they were focused on her, Kael and the villagers would be safe.

Angry shouts pierced the storm. Kyleigh darted quickly out and up, gliding along a current of the wind. The mages saw her white wings appear and gave chase. It was too easy to fool them. Kyleigh dipped down every once in a while to give them a flash of her wings, and they tore off after her. Just a little bit further, and Kael would be safe.

Ulric's voice filled the air suddenly, as if he'd spoken from the storm: "Stop her, beast! Do not let her escape!"

Kyleigh sighed inwardly. Though she knew most had been crazed beyond saving, she didn't like to harm the shapechangers. She would much rather go back to roasting Ulric and his lot. But Crevan still hadn't learned.

Her ears twitched to catch the far-off beat of wings. They were coming from behind her. Kyleigh glanced down at the red dots one last time, marking them in her memory. Once she'd finished with this beast, she'd come back for Ulric.

And this time, she intended to hit her mark.

The wingbeats grew louder as Kyleigh turned — so loud that she expected a swarm of crows or hawks to come bursting from the clouds. The noise grew stronger by the moment, and soon she'd slowed to a hover. It was impossible ... she *knew* it was impossible. But the longer she listened, the more convinced she became:

The noise wasn't coming from a *swarm* of wings, but from a single, monstrous set.

Kyleigh climbed higher. She rose through the storm and circled as the noise grew beneath her, careful to stay quiet. Something moved through the clouds. They churned like water from the bow of a ship, helpless against the creature's edge. The churning stopped just beneath her; the beats became deeper as the creature paused.

With every stroke of its wings, the clouds were cast aside — until she could see the full, enormous body of the thing that hung within them.

He was a monster: a beast more than thrice her size with wings that bullied the storm. They flattened the bumps from its crest and tore a hole through its maw. The mass of scales and spines that covered his body were the color of a starless night. Kyleigh felt lost, staring into their depths.

But that was before she saw his eyes.

For a moment, the world stopped turning. She hung suspended in his gaze while her vision darkened around its edges — plunging her into a dream. She'd seen those eyes before. She'd felt the fury of that gaze in a shadowed stretch of her thoughts. There was a part of her that remembered them well.

Other things filled the corners of his gaze ... a softness the dragon in her remembered, a courage that framed her chest in steel. A strange feeling clawed at her as she watched him. She dropped a little closer, filled her lungs to call out ...

All at once, the dragon's eyes changed. Their blackened slits narrowed; the yellow flames inside them burned with hunger. His jaw cracked open, revealing a jagged cage of teeth. The collar around his neck flared brightly. Its glow matched the hunger within his eyes.

She didn't have time to think. Whoever the dragon had been before, Crevan owned him now. The curse controlled him. Kyleigh's flames turned to ice inside her chest, and she flew for her life.

His voice filled the air when he roared. The rumbling inside his chest warned her of his strength. His claws could crush her ribs as surely as his voice could rattle them. Panic seized her limbs when she heard the thunder of his wings. But though the human cringed, the dragon in her was calm.

Pictures flashed before her eyes — memories that were not her own. She saw those powerful horns crush other dragons beneath them, saw those teeth snap through flesh and bone. She watched those claws rake through lines of scales: they fluttered from the chests of his enemies in a rain of glowing ash.

His eyes came to her again — eyes she'd seen many times in her dreams. They were walls of yellow flame bolstered by fury, pressed against black, merciless slits ...

He is not all he seems, the dragon in her whispered. *He's strong, yes ... but only dangerous if he catches us.*

When Kyleigh chanced a look behind her, she saw the black dragon wasn't as close as she'd thought. In fact, he'd only just managed to turn around. His strength was frightening, but his girth slowed him down.

She would face him as the crow faced the hawk.

Kyleigh cut upwards. She looped back and shot behind the black dragon — sailing directly over his monstrous wings. A furious roar split the air and she couldn't help but grin at his cursing. Those were Crevan's words, *his* fury. But though the King deserved to have his skull crushed in, Kyleigh didn't want to harm the dragon.

Perhaps she could lead him into the desert, or find some obliging mountain to trap his great body against — any obstacle that might slow him down. She'd only just begun to plan when a blast of air spun her to the side.

The black dragon was right behind her.

Kyleigh shot downwards with a single, powerful beat. She tucked her wings against her sides and let the force of the earth whip her towards the black dragon. She darted past his scaly face and had to twist to avoid crashing into his wings. But at least she managed to get him angry.

His eyes shot towards her and his body twisted to follow. When he roared, it was all she could do to ignore the might of his voice: *Stop! Stop, she-dragon!*

His words made her heart tremble upon its strings. Ice climbed up her spine when she heard him gaining. She blinked against the panicked memories that flashed before her eyes: trees bent to breaking beneath the gales, smaller dragons batted aside.

Two powerful beats, and he was right behind her.

Kyleigh shot upwards and grimaced when she heard his fangs snap into the space she'd been just seconds before. She tore away in a book's corner of a turn, earning herself a few moments to breathe.

She slowed her pace and waited for him to come up behind her again before she tucked her wings and dropped — falling upside down between his monstrous arms to lash his belly with her claws. She shoved hard off his middle and towards the crashing waves.

He roared in annoyance, and she had to drop again to avoid a swat of his tail. *Stop, Dragongirl!*

She spun to watch as he raised his head — and nearly tumbled from the sky when she saw that his collar had burst into a white-hot blaze. His eyes sharpened against the burning. The black slits inside the walls of yellow widened in rage.

You will answer to me, Dragongirl! You ... will ... answer!

Kyleigh's blood went cold as the black dragon barreled down upon her. It was all she could do to avoid the deadly swipes of his claws. She cut from side-to-side — leading him south, then east, then north. Villages whipped beneath them. Lands passed in a blur. Kyleigh couldn't even pause long enough to be shocked, or to wonder how in Kingdom's name Crevan had managed to enslave a dragon. Her worries shrank back and she listened to her other instincts, to the oldest part of her soul ... the part of her that dreamt of dragons warring long ago.

She dropped from the sky and glided close to the seas. When the black dragon dove down to snatch her, she opened her wings as wide as they would stretch and let their span drive her to a halt. The black dragon couldn't stop: he sailed overhead and crashed among the waves.

A torrent of water spewed up where he landed; the noise of his great body crashing down quashed the thunder's roar. Kyleigh watched for a moment too long. Had she spun away quickly, she might've avoided the fall of his tail.

But instead, it coiled and slapped down as the dragon tried to free himself from the waves.

Its spines caught her in the side. The world spun as her body flew skyward. The insides of her head slapped hard against her skull. Pain seared her flesh, burned her eyes. Most of her scales held against the blow, but she felt blood welling out of a gash along her ribs.

Somehow, Kyleigh managed to get control of her wings. She climbed into the shelter of the clouds before the black dragon could pull himself free. She slipped into their thickest depth and forced herself to beat on through the pain.

As she flew away, she could hear the dragon's frustrated cries booming behind her:

He swore to find her ... and he swore her harm.

CHAPTER 8
THE LAST SCALES

"We — we're alive." Gerald raised his head slowly from the crooks of his arms. Though the skin across his cheeks was raw and the tip of his nose burnt to a bright red, it didn't stop him from laughing. "I can't believe we survived that! It's a bloody wonder, I tell you. I'm beginning to think no spell can kill me."

Mandy was far less pleased. Her fingers traced gingerly down her burns, and her eyes welled with tears. "Why is it always mages? What have we ever done to them?"

It wasn't only *mages*: it was the King's mages — and after seeing the way they'd taken off after Kyleigh, Kael could only imagine what she must've done to them.

But he thought better of saying it aloud. "We'll have time to figure it out later. Take the helm for a moment, Gerald," he called, waving him up. "Anybody who's got a burn, come straight to me. Don't just sit there and bear it."

They were all a bit singed — some worse than others. Raw streaks had appeared in the places their arms couldn't cover. A few sported bright red chins and at least one man had a very distinct X through the middle of his face. It was easy to tell which of them had peeked: raw lines crossed their eyes in a bandit's mask, and their brows had all but vanished.

Blisters dotted the backs of their hands and those who'd run out in their nightclothes had welts rising upon their feet. But there were plenty of unhurt patches of skin between the marks. Kael dragged the bits of flesh that weren't burned over the raw bits, sealing them. His stomach churned while he worked, but it wasn't the villagers' wounds that troubled him ...

It was *his*.

He could feel their eyes upon him, feel the questions forming on their lips. Their mouths fell open as they stared at the mask of red that crossed his features. But they never asked — and Kael didn't have an answer.

He'd never been hurt by magic before. He'd fallen through fire to gouge the Witch, sprinted through Finks's spells. Perhaps if he'd thought to conjure his dragonscale armor, he wouldn't have gotten burned. But he never imagined he would need it.

Now he realized just how close they'd come to death. He had no doubt that they would've been devoured to their bones, had that spout of fire reached the boat. It'd destroyed much larger ships than theirs. The winds that'd torn from the orb's middle cast enormous vessels into the waves.

But at the last moment, the fire spout had disappeared ... and that's what troubled him the most.

Perhaps they'd merely sailed beyond the spell's reach. Perhaps Kyleigh had managed to lure the King's mages away. But a strange feeling whispered that the truth was something far more sinister.

As he worked, Kyleigh's voice rang inside his ears: *The King always ... knew. It was like he knew where I'd be before I even knew it.*

It seemed like ages ago that they'd argued about flying into the Unforgivable Mountains. Kyleigh had insisted that it was too dangerous. She worried that the King might find them if she took to her wings so close to Midlan.

Kael had thought the whole thing a bit ridiculous. He didn't see how the King could've possibly known where Kyleigh would turn up — and he certainly didn't think Crevan would send his whole blasted army out to find her. But after what he'd just seen, he could imagine nothing else. He was beginning to believe it.

Midlan had come after them in the dead of night because the King knew Kyleigh would be there. He'd attacked Copperdock because he knew she would be desperate to protect it. He'd rained fire upon the ships knowing it would draw her out.

And the fact that it'd all gone silent could only mean ...

"Kyleigh." His stomach dropped and for half a breath; his worry froze him where he stood.

"Is that it, then? Am I healed?"

The villager's question drew Kael back to the present, and he knew he had to focus on what needed to be done. He had no time to worry. For now, he had to trust that Kyleigh knew what she was doing.

There were too many people depending on him.

"Yes, that's it. Is there anybody else?" he said.

"Just me," Gerald called from the helm.

But as Kael made his way over, something itched in the back of his memory. "Are you sure?" He looked around again. "I could've sworn there was one more ... a man we pulled from the water, I think."

"Well, what'd he look like?"

That was precisely the problem. Kael couldn't remember much of anything about him except that he'd been wide-eyed and dripping wet. But he was certain there'd been one more man.

"Someone go check below, will you?" Gerald barked.

A guard ducked into the ship's one tiny cabin for a moment before he returned, shaking his head.

Kael was about to go look for himself when a familiar roar sent him sprinting to the helm. "Kyleigh!"

She dipped from the clouds and swooped by, the blast from her wings filling their sails with a lurch. Kael waved madly. He yelled at her to come down. But she soared into the dark without a backwards glance.

He couldn't be sure, but it looked as if she was favoring her left wing.

Gerald squinted through the storm. "Where's she —?"

"She's going to see the pirates," Kael said as he shoved him from the helm. "She's going to Gravy Bay."

****

The night passed into a hazy afternoon. Once the relief of their survival had worn off, the sorrow crept in quickly. The villagers spent the night in a tight circle, worrying over loved ones on other ships — hoping they'd made it to safety.

"Fate help them," Mandy had murmured, time and time again. Though the night was black as pitch and the stars hidden behind a wall of clouds, she still seemed to know which way was home. Her chin turned towards Copperdock with every whispered hope: "Fate help them."

One by one, they dropped off — each falling into a fitful sleep. But Kael couldn't sleep. All of his concentration was bent on the next crest of waves, on reaching the distant edge of the horizon. And once they arrived in Gravy Bay, he wasted no time.

His worry was a creature all its own: it vaulted him over the ship's edge and into the crowd of pirates below. When it was clear he had no intention of stopping, they scattered from his path — bellowing questions at his back.

The hill to Gravy's mansion shrank beneath his feet. One of the maids saw him and managed to whip the door open just in time — otherwise, Kael might've gone straight through it. He charged to the back of the spiral staircase and saw, just as he'd suspected, that the trap door to the basement was opened. He rushed foot over fist, dropping down the last half of the ladder and to the earthen floor below.

Clang! *Clang*! *Clang*!

He followed the familiar song of Kyleigh's hammer, grimacing against the heat that billowed up from a glowing corner of the room.

Kyleigh was there, thrashing at her forge — and she wasn't alone. An old man with frazzled gray hair and a twirled mustache stood stubbornly at her side. He had his hands clamped over his ears and his cane tucked beneath his arm. Though his tunic was nearly transparent with sweat, he still managed to bellow over the hammer's fall:

"Do you have any idea how long it took me to climb down that blasted ladder? I feel I deserve an explanation! What in high tide has happened?"

"Midlan," she barked. "Crevan's found me. He sacked Copperdock last night, and it won't be long before he finds me again."

Uncle Martin's mouth fell open for a moment before he snapped it shut. "Well, I still think you're making a mistaking, taking off like this. Just stay here and —"

"I can't stay here, Martin. I can't *stay* anywhere. Don't you understand?" Her hammer came down all the more furiously. "I can't pause — not even for a breath. Wherever I go, I'll bring all of Midlan with me."

She slid whatever white-hot object she held between her tongs into a vat of water. The cloud of steam that billowed up from it was enough to stagger Uncle Martin backwards. Still, he kept on: "If you won't stay, then at least let our healers stitch you up."

Kyleigh shook her head. Though she wore her boots and breeches, she'd replaced her jerkin with a white tunic. Even from a distance, Kael could see the thin red line weeping through it.

"It'll mend on its own. A healer will take too long, and I haven't got time to waste. I've got to leave here before —"

"Before what?" Kael demanded.

Uncle Martin whirled around at the sound of his voice. "*There you are, Sir Wright! So good to* —"

"Before what, Kyleigh?" Kael said again, never taking his eyes from hers. "Before I find you?"

He knew by how the flames wavered beneath his stare that he'd guessed her plan. Still, she didn't blink. "You aren't coming with me."

"Like Death, I'm not."

A heavy silence followed his words. Kyleigh glowered from the forge and Kael glared back, fists clenched at his sides.

"Ah, I think I heard the cook calling for me a moment ago," Uncle Martin said. He backed away from them slowly. "What was that, Bimply? I'm needed in the kitchens?"

Kyleigh waited until Uncle Martin had gone before she snarled: "No. Not a chance."

"You can't stop me."

"I won't have to — you can't follow me."

She went to drag the cooled object from the vat, but Kael grabbed her arm. He slid his hand beneath her shirt and found where she was wounded. It was a deep gash — one that cut almost to the bone of her rib.

The mark of a mage's spell.

He tried to be gentle, but she still flinched when he traced its length. She bit her lip while he worked and raised her chin to the dusty arches above them. Kael kept his hand against her waist even after he'd sealed the wound shut. He pulled her close and whispered:

"I'll walk the whole blasted Kingdom on foot, if I have to. I'll follow your shadow from one end of the realm to the next."

Kyleigh said nothing. She twisted her arm from his grasp and pulled the object from the cooling vat. It slapped wetly onto the table beside them.

It was her jerkin. There was a large gash in its side — one that matched the wound on her ribs. Where the tear cut through, all of the scales were gone and those that remained were charred on their ends, as if they'd been burned away.

Kael had seen this happen once before, when Titus had managed to hit her with dragonsbane arrows — gold forged with mage blood capable of holding onto its magic for eternity. Charred holes had appeared in her armor where the arrows struck. Though he'd managed to stretch them closed, it left the scales weakened in three shining spots.

"You aren't coming with me," Kyleigh said firmly. "It's far too dangerous."

She pulled away before he could reply. Her tongs went into the fire again and returned with a small, white-hot plate about the size of a man's thumb. She drew more plates from the fire and laid them down the tear in her jerkin. The hammer fell viciously upon the line of plates. She forced them into the blackened scales, lashing until they'd completely flattened out. Then she took her hammer away.

Kael watched the heat leave the plates. As they cooled, they shrank. They dragged the black scales together until the tear was sealed. Her jerkin had a scar's line of white where the gash had been before, but at least it was whole.

"I don't have time to blacken it. But I don't suppose it matters, does it?"

Kael ran a hand across the finished edge. "Were those ... scales?"

"Yes. I have to keep them in the fire once they fall. Otherwise, they melt to ash. I kept a few of my scales here from the last time," Kyleigh said as she lowered the trough's lid, leaving only a thin line of yellow light behind.

"The last time, what?"

"The last time I molted. Dragons shed their scales once every hundred years. Those were the last of the ones I'd saved, and I've still got quite a few years left to go," she added with a sigh, glaring down at her armor. "I suppose I'll just have to be more careful."

She stripped the tunic away and slid into her jerkin. Kael went to help with the clasps, but she pulled out of his reach.

"I can't risk setting a whisperer's strength loose on my armor." Her lips bent into a smirk as her fingers ran expertly up the buckles and clasps. "You've already proven yourself to be rather ... impatient."

He was only impatient when he was trying to work things the *other* way. But before he could say as much, she'd swept past him — clasping Harbinger on as she went. "What will we do, now?"

"I've already said that I can't stay here."

"Yes, but you haven't mentioned where we're going."

"Kael ..." His name faded into a frustrated growl as she climbed up the ladder.

He followed, his mind whirring with thought. "We have to do something to get the King's attention. As long as Crevan's eyes are on us, the Kingdom will be safe."

"You aren't coming with me."

She climbed out into the main room and took off quickly down one of the long, winding halls. Kael had to trot to keep her pace. "If what you said is true, then Crevan will send his army the moment he spots us. They'll be more vulnerable, easier to pick off. I'll bet we could even lead them into tra —"

"You aren't coming with me!"

All at once, the world spun and Kael's back slammed hard against the wall. Kyleigh's arm held him pinned in an iron bar; her lips pulled back from her teeth in a snarl. Her eyes blazed with such fury that he almost forgot to breathe.

When she spoke again, her words were even — and dangerously quiet. "I brought this trouble upon myself. This is *my* task, mine alone. And while I'm away, you're going to stay here with the pirates. You're going to stay safe. Do you understand?"

Kael matched her glare. "You aren't alone anymore, Kyleigh. You can't just wing off whenever you please and expect me not to follow. I will always follow you," he said, pushing against her hold. "I will always find you."

"Not this time."

"Why is it when I don't want you following me, we're *tied together* —"

"That's completely different."

"— and when you don't want me following you, it's all fire and threats."

"I can't protect you!" Kyleigh roared. The wall groaned as she crushed his body against it, as if the pressure would somehow drive reason into his skull. "I can't protect you, up there. If I fall, you'll fall with me. Don't you understand?"

He *did* understand. He understood her perfectly. But it wasn't her words that jolted him so much as her eyes: though the fires shone, their blaze was sharp and desperate — the eyes of a wolf caught inside a trap.

If he kept arguing with her, she would only growl at him. He tried to think of something else. "If I let you go, I'll never see you again."

Her brows rose in surprise. She took a step back. "That isn't —"

"It's *exactly* what would happen. You can't fight Midlan on your own, and you won't risk dragging them back here. It doesn't matter if I'm standing in your shadow — there'll be miles between us. I still won't be able to reach you. We'll never see each other again, if you leave me now. So if that's what you want ..."

"No."

"Then trust me," Kael said. He peeled her arm from his chest and took her hands in his. "Trust that I'll be able to hold my own ... and I'll trust *you* not to drop me."

Her smile was reluctant and fleet. "This is it. Once we leave, there'll be no turning back."

"Until we sack Midlan and knock Crevan off his throne, you mean."

"What if we can't?" Her voice was hardly a whisper. When he rolled his eyes, she grabbed him under the chin. "I mean it, Kael. There's a very good chance that we'll be on the run for years. I need you to plan for the day when things go horribly wrong."

There was something in her stare that made him hesitate — the flicker of a warning in the dark, the starlight glancing off a dagger's blade. It made him wonder if perhaps there was something she wasn't telling him. He thought there might be something else to fear.

But the moment passed in a glint, and the darkness covered his worries. "Nothing's going to go wrong. We'll cross that river when we come to it," he said shortly, when he saw the argument in her glare. "Is there anything else?"

"Yes, and it's very important." Her grip tightened as her voice dropped to a growl: "I need you to swear, on everything you hold dear, that you'll stow your pig's head and blasted well listen to me — especially while we're in the air. Will you do as I say?"

"As much as I ever have," he said with a nod.

She groaned, half-laughing. Then she kissed him gently. "Come on, then. Let's find you something other than a pair of rumpled trousers to wear — the world's much cooler above the clouds."

After weeks of enduring the stuffy weather of the seas, he was looking forward to it.

Kyleigh led him down the hall to one of the empty chambers. There was a small dresser crammed beside one of the windows. They were looking through it for something that might fit when a slight cough drew their eyes back to the door.

It was so faint and unremarkable a sound that it took them several moments to turn. A man stood near the doorway. He wore a full set of black, salt-stained clothes and kept his hands clamped firmly behind his back. Between the length of his face and the way his stare dragged across them, Kael began to feel as if they were boring him ...

Kyleigh groaned loudly. "Hello, Crumfeld."

And at the same moment, Kael said: "Geist!"

CHAPTER 9
GOODBYES

"Geist?" Kyleigh passed a look between them. "Who's Geist?"

"I am." He peeled the mold off his face, revealing the plain, bored set of eyes that'd once focused long enough to map every square inch of the Duke's castle. "*Crumfeld* is little more than a character I devised to gain access to your Roost. I hope you aren't too terribly upset by it."

The drone of his voice made it sound as if he didn't care one way or the other. Kyleigh's lips parted for a moment. She squinted at him as if he was a rude message scrawled at the bottom of a page, and she was trying to decide whether or not to be offended. "What?"

It took a painful amount of seconds for Geist to turn to Kael — revealing the raw burn on the side of his neck.

All at once, he understood. "*You* were the servant! I knew there was someone else."

"Yes, it was me," he said, in what was possibly the least-exciting exclamation Kael had ever heard. "With the Duke toppled, I'd intended to make Roost my permanent home. I was rather taken with butlering, and the Dragongirl provided no end of entertainment. But," his expression stayed fixed as he sighed, "I knew the moment you arrived that *Crumfeld* was in very serious danger — I knew you would recognize me the moment you saw me. A fascinating talent, to be sure."

The flatness with which he spoke made Kael wonder if he actually knew the meaning of the word *fascinating*, or if he'd accidentally confused it with *ordinary*.

"I'd planned to tell you the truth, eventually. I suppose now is as good a time as any. I'd like you to heal me before you leave," he added, dragging a finger to point at his neck. "I can't have anything memorable about me, and a wound will always draw the eye."

Kyleigh frowned at him. "How did you know we were leaving?"

"Don't bother asking," Kael mumbled as he went to work. "He's full of secrets."

When he was finished, Geist straightened his coat hems. "Splendid. My ship leaves in an hour."

"You can't go sailing now — you'll be burned!" Kael said.

Geist's eyes slid dully over to Kyleigh. "Not as long as Midlan's sights are fixed elsewhere. Now that Roost is gone, I shall have to find a new castle to call home ... a rather taxing thought, to be sure. And the process itself is even more taxing. Good day."

He moved so slowly that it took Kael a moment to realize that he'd inched out the door. "Wait — where are you ...?"

The hallway was empty. Or at least it certainly *seemed* empty, but there was never any telling with Geist. Kael kicked the legs of a suspicious-looking armchair, just in case.

"I'll never understand him," he grumbled as he stepped back into the room.

Kyleigh pursed her lips. "I can't believe he actually made me miss Crumfeld. Here, put this on."

She flung a tunic at him and, in the second he was blinded, shoved him onto the bed. While he struggled to find the sleeves, she slid a pair of boots onto his feet. They were a bit too big, but it was better than having to go barefoot.

He'd gone to tuck his shirt in when he thought to check his pockets ... and found them horribly empty.

"Why are you pawing around like a —?"

"Nothing. It's stupid," Kael said shortly, even as his stomach burned.

He'd left the rings inside the pocket of his other trousers — the ones that'd been torn nearly in half by Kyleigh's attack. They were probably melted together somewhere in the ruins of Roost ... along with the bow she'd given him, and the dragonscale gauntlets she'd made ...

Though it stung him to think about all he'd lost, he knew it would do him no good to fret over it. *They were only things*, he reminded himself. *You still have what's most important.*

"Where are we off to?"

"The kitchens. We won't be landing for a while, and I can't have your stomach growling in my ears all the way to Midlan. What if we get hit because I can't hear the spells over the rumbling?" Kyleigh's eyes slid up from the laces. "I'm sure you'd feel awful about it the whole fall down."

"I'm not sure I would," he said at her grin.

But in the end, it did him no good to argue.

They slipped into the Bay's grand dining room unnoticed. The afternoon sky had again become clouded by a storm: it dulled the shine of the great window that overlooked the water below, and sent the tiny fishing boats scrambling to their docks.

Fortunately, there was a lunch waiting on the dining room table.

*Un*fortunately, the table was already occupied.

"Hello, hello! Come in and join our feast," Uncle Martin called from the table's head. There was a grin on his face and what looked suspiciously like a large number of cookie crumbs scattered throughout his mustache. In his arms he held a tiny, wailing bundle.

Kyleigh moved so quickly that Kael hardly saw it: one moment she was standing beside him and the next, she'd plucked baby Dante from Uncle Martin's arms.

"Hello, you," she whispered, grinning as she held him aloft. "I hope you haven't been too fussy for your poor old Uncle."

"He starts wailing the moment he wakes and doesn't pause for so much as a breath. But the moment a woman gets a hold of him," he clamped his hand in a fist, "silence. He's all giggles and grins. Yes, I know what you're up to," he said severely, when Dante's wide blue eyes appeared from over Kyleigh's shoulder. "Enjoy it while you can, you little villain — sobbing won't get you anywhere with the ladies in few short years. Then you'll be just as lost as the rest of us."

While Kyleigh snuggled Dante, Uncle Martin went back to shoveling in cookies at his usual alarming rate. Kael took the opportunity to fill his pockets with bits of cheese and dried meats. He stuffed two fistfuls of provisions down and grabbed some bread to eat on the way.

He'd gone to tell Kyleigh that he was packed when she suddenly gasped. "What have you got there?" She unclenched Dante's tiny fist and drew a small gold earring from between his fingers, *tsk*ing with mock severity. "I think you've got some explaining to do, little one. Whose is this?"

Uncle Martin looked up from his cookie long enough to frown. "It must be Clairy's. She came along with Jonathan a little while back.

Then after he went off with Lysander, she stayed here. It's turned out to be a good thing, too. I don't know what little Dante and I would do without her."

"Where's Aerilyn?" Kael wondered.

It was the wrong thing to say.

Uncle Martin's cookie fell onto the table. As it rolled between the plates and onto the floor, Kael saw it wasn't just any cookie: it was a ginger cookie with extra sugar on top — Uncle Martin's favorite.

And Kael knew that nothing short of a disaster could've possibly made him lose his grip.

"Kingdom if I know!" Uncle Martin cried. "All my children have left me — scattering into the wind, fleeing in every direction. My son is arguing with merchants at the chancellor's castle, my nephew took off to rescue one of his blasted ships. I can't even tell you how they're all getting on because that silly little bird-boy —"

"Eveningwing."

"— hasn't been by in ages. Elena might still be around here somewhere, but even if she is, I'll never be able to find her!" Uncle Martin's head sagged with a heavy moan. "Oh, but it's gotten worse. It's gotten so much *worse*."

"How?" Kael said carefully.

Uncle Martin just moaned and shook his head for a moment. When he finally spoke, he sounded close to tears: "Even with the others gone, I thought I would always have Aerilyn. *She'll never leave me*, I said to myself. Then not two mornings after everybody else scattered, I woke to discover that my favorite niece-in-law had slipped away in the dead of night — heading for the Grandforest, no less! It's enough to make a poor old man's heart seize up, I tell you, having to rise each day and wander an empty house!"

Kyleigh glanced down at Dante — whose eyes were falling heavy with sleep. "That doesn't sound at all like Aerilyn. Did she happen to say why?"

"Oh, some rubbish about righting wrongs and saving the seas," he muttered as he ground another ginger cookie absently into the tablecloth. "She wrote it all out, but I don't remember the details. That girl always speaks in riddles — it's her one and only flaw."

Worry bent Kyleigh's lips into a frown, and Kael began to feel it. "Can we have a look at the letter?"

"I burned it."

"Oh, for mercy's sake."

"I'm a very passionate man," Uncle Martin said defensively. "Once I'd read that letter, I knew I couldn't stand to read it again. So I tossed it —"

"*Mr. Martin!*"

They all jumped at the indignant cry. A plump woman with rosy cheeks burst in from the kitchens. She'd replaced her usual apron with a light coat, and wore a broad hat over her tight knot of hair. There was a small basket hanging from her hand — and she brandished it at Uncle Martin like a sword.

"Would you kindly stop grinding your lunch into my good cloths? They're stained enough as it is ..." Her words trailed away as her eyes narrowed upon the crumbs. "Is that a cookie?"

Uncle Martin's shoulders straightened. "So what if it is, Bimply?"

"You know you aren't supposed to have sweets, Mr. Martin. They're not good for your — no, never mind it. Not today." Mrs. Bimply straightened her hat and marched abruptly for the door.

Uncle Martin nearly toppled his chair in his rush to stand. "Where are you going?"

"I'm going out!"

"*Out?*" he said, as if he'd never heard that word spoken before.

Mrs. Bimply spun in the doorway. "Yes, I'm going out. Harold's promised to take me sailing. We're going to catch some fish and have a lovely picnic on his boat."

"Harold? Harold the *blacksmith*?" Uncle Martin sputtered. "But — but what about the cooking?"

"There's a giantess in my kitchens, Mr. Martin. A *giantess*. I think she's got things well in hand. I'll be back late. Good day to you all," she added, curtsying as she swept out the door.

Uncle Martin stared after her with the look of a man who'd just taken a boot to the breeches. "It's all falling apart, I tell you. My whole life is crumbling before my very eyes," he moaned as he slumped down into his chair.

Kyleigh patted him on the shoulder. "Cheer up, Martin. It'll all come back around. And in the meantime, you'll have this little pickpocket to keep you company."

Amazingly, Dante had managed to fall asleep through the racket. Kyleigh place him gently into Uncle Martin's arms — and set Clairy's earring on the table beside him.

"Yes, I suppose you're right," Uncle Martin whispered, grinning down. "All of these things just follow a pattern, don't they?"

Kyleigh slipped back, grabbing Kael around the wrist as she went. He followed her out the door, glancing behind him one last time … and the realization finally struck.

They might not ever come back to Gravy Bay. As long as the King could find Kyleigh, they wouldn't be able to come back. They couldn't risk the lives of their friends. The same emptiness he'd felt when they'd set out for the Mountains pressed down upon him again.

Only this time, it felt more … permanent.

As they made their way down the hall, Kyleigh's hand slipped from his wrist to wind her fingers in his. "After all the goodbyes I've said, you'd think I would've gotten used to it," she whispered, her eyes hard. "But it always hurts just the same."

****

They wound their way through the mansion's passageways and up several flights of stairs — each narrower and more impossibly twisted than the last. When they reached a room so bare and filled with dust that Kael's eyes began to water at the sight of it, he thought for certain they'd reached the end.

"What's up here?"

Kyleigh glanced at him from over her shoulder. "It looks like quite a bit of dust and nothing to me."

The ceiling was so low that it scraped the top of Kyleigh's head. Kael had to hunch to follow her. "Well, then why are we here?"

"Patience," she growled.

"What —?"

Kael's words were cut short as Kyleigh rammed the side of her fist into the planks above them. A hatch sprung open where she struck — and sent a shower of dust down the back of his neck.

He tried to shake it off before it could trickle down his shirt, but wound up smacking his head against the low ceiling, instead. "Well, you could've at least warned me!" he cried, groaning as he felt a line of grit slide down his shirt. "It would have taken you no time — it isn't funny!"

"Yes it is! It's *always* funny."

He felt a reluctant grin tugging at the corners of his lips at the sound of her laughter. So he shoved her out of the way and climbed from the hatch — prepared to march purposefully down whatever twisting hallway awaited them next.

Instead, his toes curled inside his boots.

He stood at the mansion's top: a flat section of the roof where the breath of the wind felt more powerful than ever. The Bay stretched out beneath him — a bowl of ocean turned dull by the thick clouds above it. The only things taller than he stood now were the white cliffs that ringed the village.

"What do you think?" Kyleigh called from behind him. She'd pulled herself over the ledge and was dusting the grime from her armor when she saw the look on his face. She laughed again. "It's not too late, whisperer — you can always turn back."

Kael quickly hid his shock with a scowl. "I'm not going anywhere."

"All right, then."

Kyleigh stretched her arms over her head, bending herself in a curve that made him lose track of his feet ...

"Kael?"

"What?"

"I said you're going to want to step back."

He knew there was no point in trying to hide it: a blind man could've seen the burn on his face. "Well, you shouldn't do such distracting things if you don't want people to gape."

"I don't mind your gaping. I like the way you look at me," she added, with a smile that set his skin ablaze.

He watched in amazement as Kyleigh transformed. Her limbs grew long and her neck bent into a graceful arc. The black of her armor stretched into the lines between her scales to reveal the pure white beneath it. Wings unfurled from her shoulders. Even paced back, he had to duck to avoid getting swept off the roof as she flexed them.

A dragon now crouched in the spot where Kyleigh had been standing only moments before. Her scales were snow-white, her eyes a fiery green. The dry, rasping sound of her dagger claws scraping against the shingles was the only sound for miles.

Well, besides the worried thuds of Kael's heart.

"All right," he said when she tilted her wing back. He followed the line of her eyes and saw she meant for him to climb onto her shoulders. The warmth beneath her scales made the pads of his fingers tingle as he braced himself against her side. He raised one leg hesitantly. "Should I ...? Or is it like this? I don't want to — oof!"

He managed to grab onto one of her spines as she nudged him up — the only thing that kept him from falling off her back. No sooner had he gotten settled than faint pictures began sliding behind his eyes. He realized Kyleigh was trying to talk to him, to show him something.

As he focused, he saw other hands grasping onto one of her spines. There were other legs sliding into place — wedged securely against a line of her ribs. Kael followed their instruction carefully. "This is what you did with Setheran, isn't it? When you flew him into the mount —? Yes, I know," he said, when she showed him what would happen if he didn't mind the spine near his rump. "I know things could get crushed. You don't have to show it so ... clearly."

Her rumbling laughter brought such a wave of heat under her scales that Kael had to rise up to avoid getting singed.

Once he'd insisted for the third time that he was ready, she raised her wings. Kael clamped his legs down upon her ribs as she leaned over the edge and he saw the fantastic drop awaiting them. He held on tighter to her spines, so tight that his hands began to sweat. When he loosened his grip, his stomach lurched and screamed that he wasn't holding on tightly enough — which made his hands sweat all the more.

Her low growl came out as a question.

"Just get it over with," he groaned.

And with another rumbling, singeing laugh, Kyleigh fell headfirst into oblivion.

The roar of the air filled his ears as they dropped from the roof. He had to squint his eyes as the wind beat across them. They were halfway down before he realized that his stomach hadn't followed: he was certain it was still lying on the roof somewhere, leaving him with this strange, panicked emptiness that kept trying to force its way out his throat.

Kyleigh bolted down; the glittering waters rose to meet her. And just when Kael thought they might crash into the waves, her great wings opened into a soar.

He held on tightly as she carried them into the clouds. They left Gravy Bay far beneath them and burst into a world that was rife with white and silence. Here, the land swelled in drifts that sat thickly side-by-side. It reminded him of the snowy banks that crowned the mountains ...

"Where are we going?" he said, forcing those memories aside.

His heart throbbed again when her vision struck him: miles of land held pinned by monstrous walls, trapped beneath the gaze of dark, leering towers. He saw the gold-tinged horde gathered across the ramparts, heard the thunder of its undefeated steps.

"Midlan?" he gasped, pulling away. "You can't be serious — the King will see you!"

Isn't that the point?

He jumped. The way her voice filled his head made it sound as if she spoke directly into his ear. "You ought to warn me before you do that."

How am I supposed to warn you that I'm about to speak, exactly?

He didn't know. As long as they touched, the healer in him allowed him to see whatever she chose to show him: thoughts, memories, even words. Though Kyleigh's thoughts always came to him clearly, he often had a difficult time sharing things with her.

Even now, his mind moved in a thousand directions. There was the anger over what'd happened to Copperdock, the frustration of not knowing what would happen next — all covered over by great, billowing clouds of worry that muddled all of his thoughts.

When he tried to show her what he was thinking, she replied with a frustrated grunt. *Ugh, you're going too fast. Just say it aloud, will you? It's starting to make me dizzy.*

"Why risk going to Midlan? Why don't we just go after one of his patrols, something a bit smaller?"

She shook her horned head. *That's not good enough. Crevan destroyed my home, so I'm going to breathe fire on his. It's only fair.*

"No, it's also mad," Kael insisted.

Her back swelled with a heated sigh. *Nobody's attacked Midlan since the Whispering War. The guard there is lazy. Trust me — we'll be* able to make Crevan angrier in five minutes torching Midlan than we would in five weeks of killing patrols.

"And why do we want him angry, exactly?"

Because if he's angry, he'll follow us anywhere. I know what I'm doing, she added with a growl. *I've been causing trouble long before you were born.*

He supposed he didn't exactly have a choice. It wasn't as if he could force her to turn one way or another. So instead of arguing, he spent the rest of the journey trying to get his thoughts in order.

No matter what Kyleigh said about Midlan, he wouldn't believe it. He wouldn't give in. He wasn't going to spend his life in hiding. Crevan would have a weakness, just as all of the other rulers had. He could be beaten — but first, Kael had to come up with a plan.

****

It was near dusk before Kyleigh finally began drifting downwards. When Kael assured her that he was ready, she dropped from the clouds.

He'd only ever read of Midlan: it was the King's region, the impenetrable fortress that whisperers had built long ago. But there weren't nearly enough words in the Kingdom's tongue to do it justice.

From above, the fortress of Midlan looked like a great eye. The eight outer walls that hemmed the land were the rounded whites. Four middle walls created a diamond-shaped iris, with tips that stretched to touch the north, south, east, and western most faces of the outer eight.

Within the diamond iris sat the inner wall: a perfectly rounded pupil that kissed the middles of the iris and left only four small triangles of land between them. And within the pupil rose the King's castle — a monster of towers and ramparts stacked one above the other, until the whole thing looked like the jagged face of uncut onyx.

It was only when Kyleigh let out a low roar that Kael managed to peel his eyes away. His heart hammered in his throat as he tightened his grip, and his palms sweat all the more furiously. He understood now why the fortress of Midlan had never been defeated.

Even with the height making it smaller, it seemed too vast to conquer.

97

Wind howled across his ears as Kyleigh dove, tilting to slide in a wide arc before the outer walls as she fell. The force of her body pulling against the wind nearly plucked Kael off her back. He had to put every ounce of his concentration into holding on as she went after the King's soldiers.

The air whistled too loudly across his ears to hear them, but he could see the soldiers' helmets twist back in fright, see their fingers jabbing towards them — see the light glinting off their armor as they fought to escape the ramparts.

Heat swelled in such a furious wave across Kyleigh's back that it went straight though the flimsy material of Kael's breeches. He had to conjure his dragonscale armor to keep his flesh from getting burned. No sooner had he managed to focus the armor into place than a blinding yellow flare burst from Kyleigh's mouth and struck the ramparts.

Kael couldn't help himself: he grinned as he watched a whole clump of soldiers tumble off the wall, their armor melted around their blackened bones. The warrior in him rose, trembling with excitement at the noise of battle.

"For Copperdock!" he howled.

Kyleigh answered with a roar that sent a pair of soldiers tumbling down the stairs. More of her fire bolts fell. There was a handful of soldiers crouched at the top of one of the outer towers. When Kael pointed them out, Kyleigh reduced them to cinders.

Though they managed to wreak a fair bit of havoc, their battle was short-lived. A mage hobbled up the stairs behind a fresh company of soldiers. He had a long gray beard and held a black orb in the palm of his hand. When his eyes found Kyleigh, the shackle around his wrist lit up with a furious glow.

"Mage!" Kael warned.

Kyleigh twisted away from him and began beating a path towards the clouds. Kael held tightly as she twisted and turned, watching behind him for the blast of the mage's spell.

The black orb now hovered above his palm, shining with a sickening green light. The mage's eyes tightened on Kyleigh's back as they slipped into the clouds, and Kael knew the battle wasn't over, yet.

A moment later, a high-pitched whistling pierced his ears. Kael leaned over just as a flash of green light appeared beneath them. The black orb sat at its head, and a deadly looking spell trailed in a bolt behind it.

Kael didn't have time to think. He held on with his legs and swung his body across Kyleigh's ribs, catching the spell in the middle of his back. The orb *thunk*ed hard against his armor and the spell itched him madly. But it seemed to lose its power the moment it struck him: the orb fell away and plummeted like a rock to the world below.

"I'm fine," Kael insisted when Kyleigh groaned. His hands shook badly as he righted himself. With the orb gone, he realized how close they'd come to falling. "Just get us out of here, will you?"

She did. Kyleigh darted along the path of the wind, tucking and raising her wings — moving as swiftly as a fish beneath the waves. It'd always been a marvel to watch, but it was even more exciting to feel. After a while, he began to see the things she saw. He began to sense when she would drop and turn, began to feel for the patterns of the wind.

"Where are we going now?"

The swamp would be the easiest place. It's nearby, and the soldiers don't know it very well. Their armor sinks them nicely, she added with a growling laugh.

"They'll figure it out, eventually — or they'll just give up."

Yes ... but then I'll go ruffle them again.

"So we'll just be on the run forever, then?"

I warned you, she reminded him. *You said yourself that if we left, we'd never come back. We can't fight Midlan on our own.*

"Then I suppose we'll need some help," Kael said, thinking aloud.

Something had begun to take shape in the back of his mind. He liked the idea of leading Midlan into a trap — but he wanted to make sure it was a trap Crevan's army couldn't escape. There was a corner of the realm where his mages would be useless, where his army would stand no chance ...

No, Kyleigh said firmly, just as he pieced it all together. *I know what you're thinking, and it'll never work. Fighting Titus to save the mountains is one thing, but they would never go to war with the King.*

Kael thought that *never* was an awfully long time — far longer than he cared to wait. "I can convince them."

Nobody *could convince them. Fate herself would have to ride into their midst on a white horse before they'd consider it — and even then they wouldn't listen. It's a complete waste of time.*

"We'll never know unless we ask. If you're right, I'll never argue with you again," he swore when she snarled. "I'll shut my mouth and go wherever you take me. Just give me this one thing, this one chance. Please," he added, when she bristled.

The fire that'd been growing steadily beneath her scales slowly cooled. *Fine,* she muttered after a moment. *I'll take you into the Valley. But I'm warning you, whisperer: the wildmen will never go to war with their King.*

CHAPTER 10
A SHIELD

The Grandforest was quieter than Elena remembered it being.

Trees stretched over the road and draped their shadows across the top of her head. Only the faintest glimmers of sunlight made it through their branches. The air hung thickly, still damp from a morning rain. There wasn't any wind, and the brush hardly stirred. But Elena didn't mind it. She'd always welcomed the silence.

Braver carried her down the twists in the beaten road, his pace rocking her gently. His reins sat loosely between Elena's fingers. There was no need to hold them tight: she knew he would stay his course. The dapple-gray horse wouldn't twitch from the road unless she pulled him away.

And Elena knew better than to do that.

Her eyes cut across the undergrowth as Braver plodded along. She searched in the shadows beneath the shrubs and in the scant patches of earth not covered by thorns. She knew the Countess's agents were watching.

D'Mere's eyes were everywhere. The ship Elena had taken from the Bay didn't lead straight into Oakloft, but anchored at a small village to the south. She'd known D'Mere's men would be searching. They'd be at every major port in the forest, watching the ramps of each boat that crept into the harbor. So Elena chose to travel through the Grandforest on horseback, instead — hoping it would delay the Countess's attention.

But she was wrong.

One patch of thorns was slightly mangled at its edge. Elena's eyes sharpened upon its wounds, took note of how flatly its spines were bent. The crushed portion formed a shape that was rounded at either end and narrow in the middle — the mark of a creature she didn't care to meet.

She'd known the Countess would find her out eventually ... Elena just hadn't expected her to pick up the trail so quickly.

More marks dotted the undergrowth ahead as other agents joined the first — and this was only the beginning. They would gather reinforcements from every village they passed. But no number of men would do them any good.

Elena carried a shield across her back that would freeze D'Mere's hand upon her dagger. She could ride straight to the edge of Lakeshore, if she wished. The Countess could do nothing to stop her.

No matter how many of them there were or how furious they became, Elena would be safe. Her shield would protect her. Yes, the Countess could do no more than watch as she crept closer to the walls of her castle. It was a near-perfect plan.

The only real problem was how often her shield wanted to chat.

"Have you noticed how odd everyone's been acting?"

The whisper broke the calm. It itched Elena's ear. She tried to ignore it.

But Aerilyn wouldn't be silenced. "All of the inns are closed, all of the windows are shuttered. No one will speak to us. If we have one more door slammed in our faces, I think my ears will rattle off my head."

Elena wished *her* ears would rattle off. Aerilyn hadn't stopped talking since sunrise: she tittered about how lovely the forest was, went on about how she'd missed it. Every time they happened upon some half-budded plant, she'd gasp that it was the most beautiful she'd ever seen. It'd gotten to the point that Elena cringed each time she saw a flower.

And her chattering showed no signs of ending.

"Surely you've noticed it," Aerilyn went on, her grip tightening around Elena's waist. "Isn't it odd how the villages close up when they see us coming? Or how the stables are empty but every tavern is mysteriously full? You practically had to twist that shopkeeper's arm just to get him to sell us provisions."

"Yes ... practically."

She flinched when Aerilyn gasped in her ear. "*Elena* — you didn't!"

"If it helps you sleep."

"Oh, I can't believe you," Aerilyn hissed. Her arms clamped around Elena's middle in what was likely meant to be a threat, but she hardly felt it. "Keep riding around snapping everybody's elbows across your knee, and the village guard will lock us away."

That thought made Elena's blood rise to a boil. It bubbled against the cold shell of her skin and for a moment, she felt half-alive. "They can try."

"They will," Aerilyn warned, "and we don't have time for it. We've got to reach the Countess before Lysander gets us all killed ..."

She babbled on, but Elena didn't hear her. It seemed like ages ago that Aerilyn had come bursting into her chambers, blathering on about how the seas were at the edge of a war.

According to the councilmen, the high chancellor had simply disappeared during one of their meetings — never to be seen or heard from again. There were rumors that'd he'd been murdered, and something about a bag of severed heads. Elena hadn't exactly paid attention to the details.

But at some point amid her blubbering, Aerilyn had mentioned something about it all being the Countess's fault — and that if she had the chance, she'd march straight to Lakeshore and make certain D'Mere was dealt with.

She hadn't had the means to escape from beneath the Uncle's watchful stare, nor the skill to make it through the forest on her own. But Elena did.

And she'd been only too happy to help.

****

Leaving the main roads had a price. Not long after they'd slipped into the woods, Elena began to see things: shadows drifting through the undergrowth around them, their footsteps quick and expertly hushed. Forest people could become nearly invisible if they wished, so that not even the best-trained eyes could spot them.

Elena just happened to know what to look for.

She felt the agents' grip tightening upon her. There were more of them, now. They grew more confident as their numbers swelled. Soon, they might have enough to give her trouble.

A pair of steps crunched in the shadows to her left — so faint it might've been mistaken for a brush of the wind. They followed boldly beside her for a moment before Elena reached to touch one of the slender daggers strapped to her arm.

She twisted her hand about Slight's hilt, turned her chin towards Aerilyn. The merchant's daughter chattered on, unaware that her life had just become a part of a deadly bargain.

The footsteps slowed. When Elena began to draw Slight from his sheath, they faded back entirely — slipping to a less-threatening distance.

It was only a very small victory. Elena was locked in a furious chess match with the Countess, one that could only end in death. She was careful to keep Aerilyn close at every moment — close enough that any arrow that went through her chest would pierce the merchant's daughter, as well. It was her only chance to reach Lakeshore alive.

And she *would* reach it, before the end. They might both very well wind up dead ... but Elena swore D'Mere's body would strike the ground first.

So she was patient. No matter how Aerilyn grated against her nerves, she forced herself to be calm.

The merchant's daughter chattered endlessly during the day and at night, she sobbed. Elena only allowed herself a few minutes of sleep every hour. Even then, she slept so lightly that the rustle of an owl's feathers would've woken her — and the further they went from the seas, the less sleep she got.

Each time she managed to drift off, the sharp noise of Aerilyn's sniffling jolted her awake.

"What in Kingdom's name are you whimpering about?" Elena growled.

"I'm not whimpering," Aerilyn said thickly from beside her. "I miss them. I miss them so much I can hardly stand it."

"Who?"

"Lysander and Dante. I'm worried sick over them."

Had she not been so exhausted, Elena might've fought the urge to roll her eyes. "Your husband is off squabbling over coin in Harborville. The only thing he's likely to die of is boredom. And I'm sure the child is fine."

"How could you possibly be *sure*?" she huffed. "What if he's hungry?"

"He has a whole village of nurses looking after him — and you left him in the care of a giantess. You'll be lucky if he fits in his crib once she's done with him."

"Well, what if he's ill?"

"Then I'm sure the Uncle will send his ships out in every direction to get what he needs. He'll empty his coffers, if he has to."

"But what if he misses me?" Aerilyn took in a shuddering breath. "What if he … forgets me?"

"He's an infant," Elena said evenly. "He can't even remember if his napkin's on or not, let alone who his mother is. The important thing is that you're alive. You mean to return. You'll be back before he even starts to care."

She rolled away from Aerilyn, glaring against the things that swarmed inside her chest. The merchant's daughter had no idea how bitter life could be. Not all infants were cared for. Not all were loved. There were some who grew up without their mothers.

And at least one had taken a mother who tried to slip a dagger between her ribs.

She slept little that night. At dawn, they saddled Braver and set out again. They were only a few days from Lakeshore, now. The trails Elena followed were as familiar to her as the soles of her boots. While Braver plodded along, she thought carefully about what she would do to Countess D'Mere — or at least, she tried to.

"What's rattling back there?" she snapped, when the noise broke her concentration.

For some reason, Aerilyn wore two quivers: the one that hung from her belt contained plain arrows, while the arrows on her back had fletching that was bright red. Combined with the bulk of her bow, she was a constant, rattling mess — and today's rattling was more obnoxious than usual.

"We've been riding for ages. My whole bottom half is numb. I simply adjusted my quivers a bit to keep the rest of me from aching."

"Why do you even need those things?"

Aerilyn paused. "Well, I brought one along to hunt with. But since you refuse to let me off this blasted animal until nightfall, I haven't been able to use it."

Elena doubted she *could* use it. "What about the other one?"

"This one is for … trouble," she said, tugging on the strap across her chest.

"What sort of trouble?"

"The sort we need to end quickly. Jake enchanted it for me, if that tells you anything."

A strange numbness filled Elena's limbs, swelling in the echo of his name. All the edges of her mind fled backwards. They sunk down to her memories and pooled, leaving her mind without its strength.

"Elena?"

She blinked the memories back when Aerilyn grabbed her shoulders. Her lungs gasped as if she'd just woken from a nightmare. She still wasn't entirely sure if she stood in the real world, or the realm of dreams.

"Don't touch me," she snapped, shrugging Aerilyn away.

"You were tipping over! You nearly fell off. If I hadn't grabbed you —"

"Don't *touch* me."

Elena punched out every word, careful to give them each their own bite. Things were frightening enough as it was. She didn't need Aerilyn pawing at her the rest of the way to Lakeshore. What she needed was a distraction — a taste of blood to bring her focus back.

Their numbers weren't overwhelming quite yet. The Countess's agents could do with some thinning.

Braver snorted when she pulled him to a halt. "All right, I think we've gone far enough for one day."

Aerilyn's brows arched high. "We have? But it's hardly afternoon."

"You were just complaining about being in the saddle. Now you don't have to be." Elena slid down and held out her hands. "Let's move, lady merchant."

Aerilyn glowered at her. "I thought you didn't want me touching you."

Elena moved her hands to Braver's straps. "You can climb down on your own, or you can fall off with the saddle. It's entirely up to you."

Aerilyn swung her leg around and dismounted on the other side — but not before she'd shot Elena an icy glare.

She hardly noticed. Aerilyn's look wasn't nearly as potent as her mother's.

"Well, if we're stopping for the day, then I'm going on a hunt. I'm sick of dried meat and stale biscuits."

Elena shrugged, careful to keep her eyes away. "I couldn't care less what you do, lady merchant."

"Stop calling me that."

"Then stop behaving like every little inconvenience marks the end of your perfect world."

Aerilyn spun around mid-stomp and cried: "I never liked you, Elena —"

"I'm shocked."

"— but I loved you for Jake. I was prepared to ignore how horrible you are because you made him happy. But now you've broken his heart and chased him away, and no matter what I do, you insist on being horrid." She un-slung her bow and leveled its blunt end at Elena's face. "I've been traveling these roads since I was a child. I know how to get to Lakeshore. I don't need your help, and I certainly don't need your blades."

Elena flung the saddle onto the ground — or rather, she told herself that she had. The truth was that her limbs had gone so numb she thought she might've simply dropped it. "Then why did you beg me to come with you, if I'm such a horrible person?"

"I asked because I thought ... I *hoped* I could change your mind about Jake." Aerilyn's mouth wavered, but her chin jutted out defiantly. "I know what it's like to be uncertain about love. I was uncertain about Lysander, at first. But then a very dear friend showed me the truth — he showed me all the goodness behind the pirate, and I've felt silly every day since for thumbing my nose at him in the first place.

"It seems obvious now, but there was a time when I wasn't sure. Had my dear friend not pushed me, I don't know that I would've ever seen it." She lowered her bow, but her chin stayed sharp. "I'd hoped to be that friend for you, Elena. But now I've changed my mind — I don't want you to see the good in Jake. I don't want you to believe, even for a moment, that you deserve him."

She'd gone to stomp away when Elena thought of something. "Aerilyn — wait."

"What?"

"If you insist on playing hunter," she held out the reins, "why don't you make yourself useful and find Braver something to drink?"

She snatched the reins and stormed away. As she led him into the thicket, Elena could hear her ranting to the poor horse about all the many flaws of his mistress.

While they marched off, Elena got ready. Her fingers slid down her bandolier of throwing knives, dragging across each of the seven hilts. Slight and Shadow were strapped to her upper arms. Their smooth, blackened pommels reassured her as she touched them. They calmed her nerves and chased the numbness back — bringing her limbs alive with her mind's strength.

If she closed her eyes, she could hear them better: the many pairs of footsteps heading her way. They moved fractions at a time, careful not to stir a single twig or leaf. But their silence gave them away.

Elena could feel the pressure of their focus upon her chest, her back — against the thick vein beneath her throat. They might as well have lunged for her, the way their eyes grabbed. But though they ringed the entire clearing, her heart kept a calm, steady beat.

"All right, gentlemen," she called into the trees. "Let's get this over with."

CHAPTER 11
THE MERCHANT'S DAUGHTER

Aerilyn's mood didn't improve.

She'd finally lost her temper. After days of putting up with Elena's constant grumping and snide remarks, she found she could no longer hold it in — and the moment she'd dragged Braver into the woods, the words came spilling out.

"I can't believe her! No one could possibly be so horrid — a *witch* would've blushed at the things she's said. What Jake could ever see in such a woman is completely beyond me."

Beside her, Braver watched with his large, brown-eyed stare.

Aerilyn frowned at him. "You're decent enough, for a horse. What do you see in her, then?" she asked as she led him to the edge of a trickling stream. "What isn't she telling me?"

Braver dipped his mouth into the waters, grasping at them with his lips. Aerilyn watched for a moment. She brushed the dirt from the short hairs on his neck, and found the warmth beneath his skin to be rather soothing.

In any case, it reminded her that there were more important things to worry about.

"I suppose it doesn't matter," she said, thinking. "We'll be at Lakeshore in a few days' time. Once I've convinced the Countess to speak to the King on our behalf, the seas will be saved. And we can put all this behind ... behind ..."

No, it wasn't any good. Her worries had been building up, pressing against the back of her eyes. She'd managed to keep them pinned behind a wall of other things — other worries that she'd convinced herself were far more important. But now that Elena wasn't around to attack her for it, she found she had no defense.

"I don't know what to do! What *am* I going to do? I've got no chance at all. I can't stop the King. There's going to be a war ..."

Aerilyn pressed the hem of her tunic against her eyes, hoping it would staunch the flow of tears. But it didn't. There were too many of them, each one was too full. They would spill out until they'd run their course.

Nobody would listen to her. Everyone she'd spoken to was convinced that the trouble in the seas was nothing more than a merchant's squabble, that the election of a new high chancellor would solve everything. They seemed to think that Chaucer had simply run away, or that the council had quietly deposed him.

Nobody believed the rumor that the heads of Midlan's soldiers had been stuffed into a bag, or that the servants had seen the castle guards dumping their corpses off the bridge — the council swore that the King's envoy had left of their own accord. Nobody believed the Countess had anything at all to do with it.

But Aerilyn knew very well what D'Mere was capable of ... and she didn't doubt it for a moment.

Still, Lysander couldn't be convinced. He thought all of their problems ended with the council's bickering. Even Thelred didn't believe her — and he'd blasted well *seen* D'Mere at the castle! He'd heard how she threatened them.

"It doesn't make any sense," he'd snapped at her. "She's stood by Crevan all this time. He's got every last shred of power. Why in Kingdom's name would she suddenly turn against him?"

Aerilyn hadn't been able to answer them, and so they'd sailed off: Thelred to the chancellor's castle, and Lysander to Harborville — leaving her with no choice but to turn to Elena.

As miserable as that forest woman made the air around her, Aerilyn needed her help. She had to reach Lakeshore alive ... and Elena was her best chance.

Braver stood patiently while Aerilyn crumpled down beside him. His ears twitched at the noise of her sobs before he bent to nibble at the tufts of grass near her boots.

It was strange, but having a good cry about something always seemed to clear her mind — like the sunlight after a rain. She didn't know why she put it off, why she sat around in the haze. For it was in the moments she felt the lowest that she heard her father's voice:

Dry those tears, my darling. Feeling sorry for yourself doesn't help anybody else — and there are plenty of people who deserve to cry more than you.

Aerilyn's chest shuddered as she took a deep breath; the bottom of her tunic was positively soaked from her tears. But she knew her father was right — he'd always been right. There were women in the Kingdom who'd lost their children and husbands, who would never have the chance to see them again.

Aerilyn was apart from those she loved, yes. But she hadn't lost anything. In fact, she had a chance to *save* everything. If she couldn't convince the Countess to help the seas, there would be more death, more tears. She had no choice but to save it.

But she would need Elena's help.

Braver seemed to be enjoying himself, so rather than dragging him back through the thicket, she hung his reins upon a tree. "I'll be back in a moment. Try to stay out of trouble, will you?"

The grass at his nose flattened against his snort.

The undergrowth was horribly spiny. She supposed she hadn't noticed it before because she'd been so furious. But now she had to pick her way through briar and thorn, lifting her boots to her knees in some places just to inch across.

Her quivers kept getting snagged, her bow kept lodging its end into every tangle of roots she passed. Aerilyn finally slung the blasted thing from her shoulder and held it above her head. She was a half-dozen paces from the clearing when she heard the noise of someone screaming.

It was a man: he shrieked as if he'd just been badly hurt, and the terror in his voice made Aerilyn take a lurching step forward. But at the last moment, she forced herself to stop.

You don't know what's on the other side of those shrubs, she thought, trying to stay calm even as the screams grew more desperate. *Take a good look before you jump out into the open.*

Slowly, she crouched and slid forward, clenching her teeth against the screams. There were other, fainter sounds coming from the clearing: grunts and thuds, and the clanging of steel.

When Aerilyn found a hole to watch through, she had to clamp a hand over her mouth to keep from gasping at what she saw.

It was Elena — Elena against a horde of men. They swarmed so closely around her that Aerilyn could only catch a few glimpses here and there: the fall of her black daggers, the spray of red behind them; the armored heel of her boot thrust from the swarm, knocking one of the men to the ground with a yelp.

Elena slid among her attackers like a shadow, moving so fluidly that she seemed to be doing nothing more than whipping her hands past them or tapping her fists against their throats. Yet, their bodies fell at an alarming rate.

In the few moments Aerilyn watched, the horde thinned considerably. Men would come charging into the center and a half-second later, stumble straight out the other side — a desperate grip on their spurting throats. She caught a full look at Elena's body when she rolled herself over a man's shoulder ... and flinched when three arrows thudded into his chest.

Elena held the man's body up like a shield as she charged towards the place where the arrows had come from. The horde followed close behind her — but not closely enough to save the archers.

The man who screamed now crouched alone where the circle had been. He clutched a bloodied hand to his chest and shrieked at the little objects scattered across the ground around him.

Aerilyn hoped they weren't fingers. Oh, she hoped to the seas that they weren't fingers. But when the man raised his hand out before him and she saw that all but his thumb was missing, she knew that was *precisely* what they were.

His eyes were crazed and white around their edges. As he leapt to his feet and came charging towards her, Aerilyn saw the crest emblazoned upon his tunic. Even through the blood, she could make out the twisted oak tree of the Grandforest — the mark of Countess D'Mere.

These men must be her agents. But then why were they attacking Elena? She'd thought ... no, she'd been *certain* ...

A hollow *thud* broke Aerilyn from her shock. One of the black daggers dropped the wounded man mere paces from the clearing's edge, buried to its hilt inside his back. Elena cut through what little remained of the horde and stepped across their bodies — not so much as a drop of red upon her armor.

She'd reached the middle of the clearing when a noise stopped her short.

An archer stepped out of the bushes on her left. His bow was drawn, his hand steady. One of his eyes was already locked upon Elena's chest.

Even from a distance, Aerilyn heard her heavy sigh. Elena looked at the archer as if he'd just said something stupid — no more concerned with his arrow than a slight hurled from across the room.

Her hand went to her bandolier and Aerilyn flinched, expecting a dagger to go bursting through the archer's chest at any moment. But it didn't.

For some reason, Elena wasn't moving — not even when the archer tugged his arrow back its full length did she flinch. The dark brows above her mask, usually so sharp and taut, fell slack. Her hand dropped from her chest and the black dagger she carried fell from the other.

The arrow flew.

Elena stood still.

Aerilyn felt a scream tear from her throat. She watched in horror as Elena fell to her knees — gaping at the arrow that hung from her chest.

The archer laughed. He flung his bow aside and drew the dagger from his belt. "The Countess wants you skinned alive. She wants your hide for her floors. Where should I start, eh? At the ankles … or the wrists?"

Something fierce came over Aerilyn. She watched that archer stalk towards Elena and didn't remember even getting to her feet. She was vaguely aware of the fletching beneath her chin, and just remembered to brace herself for the blast.

Still, when the arrow struck and the archer's body exploded, the force knocked her off her feet.

"Elena?" Her ears rang so badly that she couldn't hear if she'd actually *said* her name — perhaps she'd only thought it. The ringing made her head spin too terribly to concentrate. She knew better than to fire at such close range. A normal arrow would've done her just as well.

Why hadn't she just taken a moment to *think* before she shot?

Slowly, Aerilyn pulled herself from the brush and stumbled into the clearing. There was little more than a blackened smudge where the archer had stood. She tried not to look at it too closely, tried not to wonder about all the charred bits scattered around its edges. Instead, she kept her eyes fixed upon Elena.

The forest woman had managed to prop herself up on one elbow. Her other hand was wrapped absently around the shaft that hung from her chest, just below her shoulder. Aerilyn knew by the way her dark brows rose above her mask that she must be in pain.

"Elena! Oh, does it hurt terribly? Are you all r —?"

113

"*What* in the bloody under-realm was that?" Elena howled. There were charred bits of archer stuck to her face and in the loose strands of her hair. When she twisted to look at Aerilyn, shock ringed the darks of her eyes.

"Well, I did warn you — I told you those arrows were for dealing trouble."

"*Dealing* with it? Is this what *dealing* means to you?" Elena flopped onto her back, turning her shock upon the high arches of the trees. "You could've missed. I could've been blown into a thousand pieces."

Aerilyn thought she was being slightly ridiculous. "He shot you! What was I supposed to do? Just stand back and let him skin you? And my aim is excellent, I'll have you know. I make it a point to practice at least once a week."

Elena groaned.

Aerilyn frowned at her before she turned to the wound. Blood welled at the arrow's base, but she didn't think there was *too* much blood — not enough to cost Elena her life, surely. Still, the skin above her mask had gone frightfully pale, and she seemed to be breathing quite a bit more heavily than usual.

"Are you ...? Will you live, do you think?"

Elena looked at her as if that was the stupidest question she'd ever heard — which assured her more than anything. "Yes. I'm going to live. That idiot missed my heart."

"I should hope he did. Why didn't you move?"

Elena didn't answer. Her scowl turned dark. "Just be careful when you pull it out, all right? I don't want the head to get loose —"

"You want *me* to pull it out?" Aerilyn's stomach lurched when she nodded. The tips of her fingers went numb.

"There was poison on the arrow — no, it's not that kind of poison," Elena snapped in the middle of her gasp. "This poison only affects whisperers. It takes my strength away, for a while. I don't trust myself to pull it out cleanly. So ... you'll have to do it."

****

Elena was surprised at how quickly she agreed. She was surprised about a lot of things, actually: the confidence with which Aerilyn had drawn her bow, the straight flight of her arrow — the

114

bone-rattling blast that'd followed. But what surprised her most was the fact that she seemed completely unbothered by it all.

The look in Aerilyn's eyes as she gripped the arrow was so calm that it was almost … unsettling.

A blinding pain, a jolt that made her cry out and brimmed her eyes with tears, and the arrow was gone. Elena lay very still as the ferocity of her wound clogged her ears. She heard the sound of ripping fabric, then felt such a burst of agony inside her wound that she had to shut her eyes just to stay conscious.

Slowly, her flesh stopped screaming. The pressure of Aerilyn's hands dulled the pain to a steady thud. "I wish Kael were here. He'd have this sealed up in no time."

"Well, he isn't. So we're going to have to wrap it in something else."

She heard the sound of more ripping fabric beneath Aerilyn's muttering. "I told you we should've packed some binding."

"If it'd been left up to you, we would've packed half the mansion. Why did you come back?" Elena said, cutting off whatever indignant reply Aerilyn had at the ready. "I thought you were off playing hunter."

"Well, I … all that ended rather quickly when I heard the yelling and clanging coming from over here. And I wasn't playing — I really *do* know how to hunt. Turn over."

Elena sat up and tried to be still while Aerilyn fumbled her way through the wrapping. "You're going to have to bind my arm to my chest."

"Is it broken?"

"No," Elena tried to speak slowly, "but if you don't brace it, the wound's likely to tear. Wrap it beneath my elbow. You're going to have to make it tight —"

"You need stitching," Aerilyn growled, pressing the fabric against the wound. "Pinewatch isn't too far from here, and we have an excellent healer."

Elena's pain numbed with her dread. "No. Not there. I told you I didn't want to stop in and spend days sitting around while you chat with your people," she said when Aerilyn frowned.

"We haven't exactly got a choice, have we? Pinewatch is the closest village … and I don't think you want to stop in at Lakeshore for a healer."

She stood and wiped her hands across her trousers. There was so much material missing from the hem of her tunic that an arch of her skin showed out its bottom. "Why wouldn't I want to go to Lakeshore?"

"I know who you are, Elena. She doesn't bring you out often, but I've seen you in the Countess's court. It would take more than a mask to fool me," Aerilyn added wryly. "When you first showed up in the plains, I thought D'Mere might've … sent you to look after me. Even when you went away, I always assumed you were somewhere close by. I planned to confront her about it when we reached Lakeshore. I planned to tell her that all of her games were at an end — that you'd already told me everything and were willing to speak about it before the King.

"I know the sort of work you must've done for her," Aerilyn went on, careful to keep her eyes from Elena. "After seeing the way you handle those blades, it isn't difficult to imagine. And I thought the Countess would be so desperate to keep you that she'd listen to whatever I had to say. But you don't work for her anymore, do you?"

There was a flash of cold behind her smirk. Though the ice wasn't meant for Elena, she still felt its bite.

Aerilyn gazed over her shoulder at the bodies scattered around them; her grim smile never wavered. "D'Mere might've sent you after me in the beginning — to watch me or bring me back to the Grandforest, I'll never know. But whatever she sent you to do, it looks as if you've had a change of heart."

She wound her fingers tightly in what remained of her tunic and bit down on her lip.

Elena knew what was about to happen. "Don't. Please don't —"

"And even though you knew she would kill you, you were still willing to take me!" Aerilyn cried. "You've been so brave while I've done nothing but hurt you. *I'm* the horrible one. I've been so busy turning my nose up at you that I couldn't see what all you've done — for my friends, for the Kingdom … for me." Tears streamed from her eyes and left wet trails down her cheeks. "I know she must have forced you to do some terrible things, but I want you to know that I don't care anymore. Whatever you were before, it doesn't matter. It's obvious now that you love us. And I'm … I'm going to try harder to deserve it."

Elena managed to keep her face calm — but inwardly, she sighed in relief. Aerilyn had been so close to guessing the truth. She'd come right to the doorway and stopped just before she reached it. While she was a bit surprised that the merchant's daughter had been hoping to use her against the Countess, it didn't change anything.

Elena would keep to her plan.

"There's no point in sobbing over it. Let's just get to Lakeshore — I know another way in," she said when she saw the argument on Aerilyn's face. "The Countess won't know we're there until it's too late."

"But what about your wound? I don't want you suffering the whole —"

"I've suffered worse." Slowly, she dragged herself to her feet, wincing against the way her skin pulled on her wound. "Help me find the rest of my throwing knives, will you? Two are stuck in those corpses over there."

Aerilyn wrinkled her nose, but did as she was told — with a great deal of squealing.

CHAPTER 12
NEW THANEHOLD

Even after nightfall, Kael's blood didn't cool. He listened to the rhythm of Kyleigh's wings as they rose and fell, as she carried them towards the mountains. But his eyes stayed fixed on the clouds below.

There were breaks every now and then, darkened gaps between the rifts that the stars couldn't touch. Kael wasn't quite sure what he searched for: a glimpse of torchlight, the flash of a spell — any sign that Midlan was following them. He hoped it was. He hoped Crevan sent the full force of his army into the Valley.

If they passed through the Cleft, they weren't likely to return.

The warrior in him began to stir with this thought. It cleaved to the memories of what they'd done at Midlan and howled for more. Kael's muscles tensed at the faded bursts of the mages' spells, the echoes of the soldiers' worried cries. The night air glanced across his teeth as he broke into an involuntary grin at the memory of Kyleigh's fire — the ferocity of its heat, the danger wrought in each bright yellow line of flame ...

A low, rumbling growl cut through his thoughts. The scales across Kyleigh's back bunched together as her muscles coiled.

Kael realized that she must've been able to see the things he saw, to feel the wonder radiating through his grip. He knew he shouldn't spur her on, but the wildness of his heart won out over the warning of his mind. So he placed his hands very firmly against her back and let one thought rise to the front of his mind — words that gave a name to all the fiery, prideful things that burst within him:

You were magnificent.

She growled again, and this time a longing note trembled at the end of her voice.

Somehow, he managed to be reasonable. "We can't land now — we have to at least make it past the Cleft. I'm not going to be responsible for you getting hexed."

118

She rumbled her reluctant agreement and flew on, heading towards the mountains.

A few moments later, they arrived in the Valley. The clouds were so dense and gray that Kael couldn't see beneath them, but he knew by the change in the wind that they'd crossed into the shadow of the mountains.

The air had grown colder — stiff with the long winter held pinned inside the mountains' peaks. Jagged spires rose to pierce the clouds ahead of them, and Kael's heart thudded unexpectedly at the sight.

The King's Cleft — the narrow mountain pass between Midlan and the Valley — was packed with snow. White filled the long vein from its back to its end. Though the end nearest to Midlan had begun to melt, the snow still climbed nearly to its lip.

As Kyleigh flew them beneath the clouds, little white flakes drifted across Kael's face — leaving cold, wet trails behind them. Winter still clung to the Valley. With any luck, it would hold a little while longer.

A small castle sat at the Valley's start, just inside the mouth of the Cleft. It was perched atop a slight hill of jagged rock. Kael couldn't help but marvel at how stout its walls had become, and how high its towers had grown. An outer wall ringed the castle and its hill. He smiled when he saw faint lights winking from the windows of the many stone houses settled within it.

It seemed the wildmen had been hard at work rebuilding the fortress of Thanehold from the ruins of the Earl's old castle.

Kael was so busy marveling at the thickness of the outer wall that he didn't notice Kyleigh coming in for a landing. She struck the ground on all fours — and the sudden halt sent him sailing over her left wing.

He saw the ground hurtling towards him and managed to catch himself on his shoulder. He rolled across the snow-covered earth, ears burning with a mix of slush and Kyleigh's rumbling laughter. "Well, maybe next time you won't drop out of the sky like a blasted rock!"

By the time he'd pulled himself to his feet, she was already human. "That was a perfectly good landing, I'll have you know," she said, rolling her shoulders back. "Had I dropped out of the sky, you would've felt it. Now ... wasn't there something you wanted to tell me?"

"Not that I recall," he said as he began marching for Thanehold's front. He looked for a gate, but didn't see one. From end to end, the whole thing seemed to be nothing more than a line of solid rock.

Kyleigh jogged to catch up. "I believe you were in the middle of telling me something … something about my being magnificent."

"That doesn't sound like something I'd say."

"You very clearly thought it."

"It was a *fleeting* thought," he said off-handedly, gazing down the wall. He wondered if the entrance might be further down. Perhaps more towards the Valley. "And if I've already said it, why should I have to say it again?"

"Perhaps I'd like to hear you say it aloud." Her hand clamped around his arm; she pulled him against her. "Go on, then … tell me I'm magnificent."

Mercy's sake, the way her voice growled across his ears sent warmth rushing down his spine — where it pooled in the soles of his boots. It would've started to melt the snow straight out from beneath him, had a strange noise not broken them apart.

It was a chalky, grating sort of noise — the sound of two rocks being scraped together. Kael spun back to the wall and watched with a grin as a small section of it began to ripple before his eyes. Several sets of hands appeared beneath it. They bent and peeled the wall aside like a curtain, forming a perfect arch.

He'd barely had a chance to wave at the craftsmen who grinned in the doorway when a red-striped bolt erupted from between them.

"Kael!"

A boy dressed head to toe in furs crashed into him, knocking him onto his back with surprising force. "Hello, Griffith," Kael said.

Had it not been for the thin stripe of hair that grew down his scalp, Kael didn't think he would've recognized him: the wildmen's black, swirling paint was gone from Griffith's face. The boy who grinned down at him now had pale skin and a band of freckles so rowdy that they seemed to dance across his nose.

"I knew you'd come back — I knew it," Griffith said excitedly. He sprang to his feet and plucked Kael up by the wrist. Then he went to Kyleigh. "Gwen says she'd rather have to sit on ice for a thousand winters than ever have to speak to you again, but I know that just means she's missed you." He punched her playfully in the arm.

120

Kyleigh laughed.

Kael groaned inwardly. Somehow, he'd forgotten about how difficult Gwen could be. But he imagined it would all come back to him quickly.

Griffith led them through the arch in the wall and into the little stone village beyond. The craftsmen grinned and slapped Kael hard in the back as he passed through. A chorus of howls sounded above him, and he saw a group of warriors gathered along the ramparts.

They brandished their swords and cried, "Wolfstomp!" through their grins.

Kael gave them a quick wave before he ducked his head. He didn't like the pressure of having all of their eyes upon him.

Kyleigh watched with interest as the craftsmen molded the wall back into place, dragging the arch downwards until it was smooth and solid once again. "Sorry for all of the trouble. We would've come in through the gate —"

"Gate?" Griffith scoffed. "There's no gate. Why put in a gate when our craftsmen can lift the walls? It would only weaken our fortress."

Kyleigh's brows arced high. "That's actually rather brilliant."

"Thanks ... it was my idea," Griffith said with a slight smile. "Now come on — Gwen will be furious with me if I don't take you to her straight away."

As they followed Griffith through the new Thanehold, Kael couldn't help but be impressed. The wildmen's houses were squat and rounded, their walls made of solid stone. The thatching along their roofs bunched up at the middle to make way for thin tendrils of smoke. He was surprised to smell the heavy perfume of meats and spices wafting through the air.

"Are the wildmen not having dinner at the castle?" he said.

Griffith's freckles bunched with his grimace. "No ... we've stopped."

"What about your caddocs?" Kyleigh pressed.

"That's stopped, too. Gwen says there's no point in it anymore." He sighed heavily, and his hand slipped into his pocket. A moment later, Kael saw the glint of a rounded blue stone rolling between his fingers. "She's been moping all winter. I don't think she's lifted her axe in weeks."

Kyleigh looked more than a little concerned. "*Weeks?*"

121

"I know — it's bad," Griffith muttered. His eyes wandered up to her hopefully. "Maybe you could pester her a bit? Get her stomping again?"

"Well, it'll be quite a task ... but I suppose someone ought to do it," Kyleigh said with a sigh.

Kael had only to see the way the fires danced in her eyes to know that she was planning mischief. "You shouldn't fight her. She might hurt you."

"Nonsense," Kyleigh said lightly. "It's all in good fun."

She slapped him hard in the rump before he could protest — much to the amusement of several nearby warriors.

"Get her back!" one of them cried over her companions' howling laughter. She swung her hand through the air in front of her. "Go on, then — give her a smack!"

Kael was most certainly not going to do that — or any of the other things the warriors bellowed after him. Instead he set a very brisk pace for the castle, hoping the chill air might somehow soothe the burn in his face.

There were more craftsmen waiting for him at the keep's walls. They lifted an arch and pounded him heartily on the back as he ducked through. Beyond the wall was a small courtyard. Several images had been molded onto the cobblestones at their feet.

It was like a bird's view of a war. Kael recognized the painted forms of wildmen charging all around — battling monsters that looked like dragons with furry chests and no wings. They were wynns: the monsters that lived at the mountain's top and fought with the wildmen for centuries. He recognized the cool, frozen slits of the largest wynn's eyes and knew it had to be Berwyn — their King.

He was so entranced by the stony battle beneath his feet that he nearly ran smack into the man standing at the keep door. "What are you doing here, Marked One?"

Kael recognized the haughty voice before he even met the strange, glowing eyes of Silas. The halfcat was dressed in what looked like the pelts of wolves — with two of their great furry backs draped across either shoulder and sewn into the leather of his jerkin. But though he was far more clothed than Kael had ever seen him, his feet were still bare.

"What business do you have in my village?" he growled again.

"I'm here to see Gwen."

The short crop of his dark hair seemed to stand on end for a moment; the glow in his eyes turned fierce. "No — you can't see her."

"Why not?"

"You'll only make things worse, you stupid human." His eyes scraped down him haughtily. "You are always making things worse."

"What do you —?"

"Hello, cat."

Silas's eyes went wide at the sight of Kyleigh striding through courtyard. He darted past Kael, waving his arms in desperate arcs. "No — go away, Dragoness! Your scaly face will only make her angry."

"Nonsense. I'm sure she'll be thrilled to see me."

"You know she will not be *thrilled*," he growled through bared teeth. "You're just here to cause trouble. And I won't let you trouble my Thane."

"Is that so?" Kyleigh crouched, and her hands curled into claws as a daring smile parted her lips. "Then why don't you try to stop me?"

Much to Kael's surprise, Silas charged her with a roar. His body moved from a sprint into a fantastic leap, twisting in midair. His powerful limbs shortened and fur burst down his back. In less time than it took for Kael to breathe in, a great mountain cat had erupted from the jerkin and pounced onto Kyleigh.

She rolled to avoid his grasping claws and thrust her heels beneath his chest — sending him flying with a terrified yowl. He landed with his feet already beneath him and whirled around to charge again.

But instead of turning to face him, Kyleigh dove straight for the jerkin.

Silas ground to a halt.

"What have we here? Is the great King of all beasts worried about losing his human clothes?" she teased when he growled, holding the jerkin aloft.

Silas's muscles bunched atop his shoulders; his great claws scraped menacingly against the cobblestone.

Kyleigh shrugged. "Well, I suppose you should've thought of that before you leapt out of them." Then with a grin and a powerful heave, she tossed his clothes straight over the wall. "Come on, you," she said as she trotted by, grabbing Kael around the arm.

Silas roared at their backs, but Kyleigh only laughed.

"Oh, open the wall for him," Griffith hollered through his grin.

After the things Griffith told him and the way Silas behaved, Kael was beginning to get concerned. Gwen had never been the most reasonable of wildwomen, but now he feared things might've actually gotten worse.

And he shuddered to think of what a *less* reasonable Gwen might look like.

By the time they stopped outside the throne room doors, Kael's heart had inched its way up his throat. "What am I going to find in there, Griffith?"

The boy's hand paused upon the latch. When he looked up, his eyes were strange: hard around their edges, soft and helpless in the middles. "Just … try to understand, will you? She's lost all she knows."

"We'll speak with her," Kyleigh assured him, her stare already burning its way through the door. "Leave it to us."

This seemed to calm Griffith more than anything Kael could've thought of. He pulled the door open with a quick tug.

Kael stepped in first, his eyes searching the edges of the room for trouble. His lungs lost their breath when he saw that the oaken panels along the wall had been set and restored. There weren't bookshelves ringing the walls anymore. Instead, the shelves had been replaced by hooks, and settled onto the hooks were the wildmen's dragonsbane weapons.

They glittered in the dancing light of the hearth fire — swords, spears, and axes. Just a few months ago, most of these weapons had been melted into collars and hung about the throats of the Earl's beasts. The craftsmen must've labored over each piece, reshaping them into the proud weapons of their ancestors. Though they no longer warred with the wynns, the wildmen had found a place for their ancient swords.

Kael thought the room suited them rather well.

Set into the stone above the panels were the heads of Gwen's prized beasts. Badgers, foxes, wolves, and bears snarled down at him in a ring. The craftsmen had set their mouths and bared their teeth — leaving each one looking as if it was letting out a roar.

But though the weapons and the beasts were certainly remarkable, it was the floor that stopped Kael short.

It seemed like ages ago that the craftsmen had uncovered the Wright's eye carved into the castle's floor. There'd been so much dust and grit, the room around it so ruined that the eye itself hadn't really stood out. But under the craftsmen's care, it'd become the centerpiece.

Each of the crisscrossing lines had been polished and painted to a shine, forming three triangles on top, three interlocking triangles on the bottom, and one blackened triangle in the very center — the pupil of the Wright's eye.

He was so focused on the shining center of the eye that he hardly glanced at the wide table situated on a shallow platform at the back of the room — and consequently, he didn't notice the woman sprawled in the chair behind that table until her words slid across him:

"Well ... what have we here?"

Kael tore his eyes away from the floor and the hair on the back of his neck stood on end as Gwen's sharp eyes locked onto his. The swirling lines of her paint were gone — replaced by pale skin and freckles. Her lips were such a light shade of pink that had it not been for the shadows cast by their arches, he didn't think he would have seen them. But though the bareness of her face made her look less menacing, it didn't make her smirk any less annoying.

"Hello, Gwen," he said evenly.

He jumped when her heels slammed onto the tabletop.

She traced the arches of her lips carefully with the tip of one finger, her stare never breaking from his. Her finger dragged a slow line down her jaw until it settled beneath her chin. "You've finally come to your senses, have you?" she murmured, and her smirk broke into a sharp grin. "I knew you'd come to them eventually. You've decided to accept my offer."

Kael's face began to burn for an entirely different reason. "Wh —? No, I haven't!"

"You have. Why else would you come storming into my throne room? And in the dead of night, no less." Her eyes glinted. She slung her legs off the table and her boots struck the floor. "Your passions have carried you across land and sea. There's no other possible explanation."

Kael stepped back when she began clomping towards him. "No, that's not — I'm not going to marry you, Gwen. I'm already married! And we're very happy, thank you."

"*We're?*"

"Yes. We ..." Kael reached out beside him, but Kyleigh wasn't there. The doorway was dark and empty. He was completely alone with Gwen. By the time he realized that he'd been tricked, it was too late.

She was already upon him.

"You knew this would happen one day." Her fingers wound tightly into the fabric of his shirt; her grin made his blood burn and boil all at once. "There's no shame in it."

"For the last bloody time, I'm not —"

"— at all interested in the bearish advances of a lady Thane," Kyleigh finished as she strode through the door. "Though it *has* been rather amusing to watch."

Kael didn't even have a chance to yell at her before Gwen hurled him aside with a roar. "*You!*"

She lunged, but Kyleigh managed to avoid her fist with a graceful step. Gwen spun and her foot came down upon Kyleigh's heel, trying to pin her. But she must have forgotten about the deadly spurs that stuck out from the dragonscale boots.

Gwen burst out with something that was halfway between a yelp and a swear before she snatched one of the golden spears off the wall and limped after Kyleigh — her every other step leaving a red, wet spot behind her.

"I swore that if you ever came back here, I'd put a hole between your eyes!"

"Lucky for me your aim is terrible," Kyleigh retorted as she slipped behind the table.

Gwen hurled the spear with a snarl.

Kyleigh ducked.

Kael groaned when the weapon thudded into the oak paneling, splintering its polished flesh. "There's no need to go throwing things —"

"Argh!"

Gwen vaulted over the tabletop, hands curled for Kyleigh's throat. Instead, Kyleigh tilted the table and caught Gwen against it like a shield. The Thane flopped helplessly onto the floor. Kyleigh flipped the table on top of her before darting away, laughing as the Thane's fist crashed through its top.

She ripped the table aside, clawing out from beneath the ruins like the Witch's army had done at Wendelgrimm. Bits of table splintered between her trembling fists and her face boiled red as she roared.

Kael tried to step into her path, but she shoved him aside — following Kyleigh out the door.

There were some muffled swears, the thud of fists, and then a crash. When he charged out into the hallway, he saw both women had burst through the keep doors, splintering them from their latches.

They were tangled in the drifts: a mass of limbs and flying fists — grappling, landing blows. Snow matted Gwen's furs and caked the edges between Kyleigh's scales. Wildmen seemed to pour in from every corner of the courtyard. They beat their chests and roared for their Thane. But though the wildmen urged her on, Gwen was quickly losing ground.

Kyleigh had already pinned her on her back. She wrestled Gwen's arms beneath her knees and leaned forward to avoid the flail of her legs. Then slowly, her hands wrapped around Gwen's throat.

The wildmen's cheers grew louder; their pounding became more desperate. They tried to will Gwen to her feet with their song — tried to goad their Thane into fighting back.

She dug her nails into Kyleigh's legs but couldn't pierce the scales of her armor. Her boots flailed though empty air. Finally, the edge of her eyes dulled. It went out like a candle's flame and her fierce snarl went soft. Even when Kyleigh took her hands away, Gwen lay limp and defeated beneath her.

The courtyard fell silent. Griffith stepped in front of Kael ever so slightly, just enough to eclipse his shoulder with his sword arm. He followed the line of the boy's eyes back to where Gwen lay and tried to be patient.

The two women held each other's gazes: Gwen's shielded, Kyleigh's searching. After what seemed like an age, Kyleigh reached out and prodded Gwen hard in the chest.

She didn't move.

"Blazes ... you really *are* in trouble, aren't you?" Kyleigh murmured.

Gwen shrugged. Her head cast to the side and she grumbled something that Kael couldn't hear under her breath.

Kyleigh leaned forward, her palms thudding into the ground on either side of Gwen's face. "Well, that's a shame. I didn't want it to end like this — not after you barely put up a fight. But I suppose there's no point in us waiting around Thanehold." She popped onto her feet with a sigh. "Come on, Kael. I'm afraid the wildmen can't help us."

Though she made a great show of marching towards the wall, he thought he caught a glimpse of her smirk as she turned away. Kael only managed to take half a step before Griffith snatched him around the arm.

"Wait — help with what?" He raised his voice to shout at Kyleigh: "What have you gotten into, pest?"

"Nothing I can't get out of," she said with a shrug. "But it just so happens that it was something I thought might interest you lot."

"What is it?" Griffith pressed. Curiosity stained his features by this point, and Kael suddenly figured out what Kyleigh was up to.

He had to try very hard not to smile as he ruffled Griffith's stripe of hair. "Don't worry about it. We were wrong to come here. Gwen's in no state to be battling anyth —"

"Battle?" The Thane sat up immediately. Flecks of snow wound through her fiery crop of hair. "What battle?"

"Never mind it," Kyleigh insisted with an impatient wave of her hand.

Kael nodded in agreement. "Yes, it's far too dangerous — even for the wildmen."

That did it.

Gwen leapt to her feet with a roar. Snow fell from the bristled ends of her furs as she stomped for Kael. When she grabbed him by the shirt, he saw the edge had come back to her eyes. She wore the same fierce snarl she'd had when she met Titus's army at the summit.

And when she spoke, he was actually glad to hear the sharpness ring in her voice: "Tell me what you know, mutt. If there's a battle within a thousand miles of Thanehold, the wildmen will have a part in it."

CHAPTER 13
THE TALES OF A HALFCAT

"No."

The word bounced off the throne room walls, slid across the ceiling and down to the floor, where it ground against Kael's ears.

"No," Gwen said again. She'd fallen silent the moment they began to speak, and her gaze sharpened by the minute. Kael swore she hadn't blinked.

Still, he couldn't believe her answer. "You aren't going to help us? The King ran off our entire village!" he said when she shook her head. "He sank dozens of ships, sent a hundred innocent men to their graves —"

"Innocent? I think not." Gwen leaned back in her chair. Her boots squeaked as she shifted her heels against the tabletop. "The pest has troubled the wildmen for years, and I'm not at all surprised to hear that she's been troubling the King. But while *we* are content to simply chase her away, I imagine a crime against Midlan would not be so easily forgiven — and those who hide an outlaw from the crown are no better than traitors, themselves. Whatever happened to your village was a punishment well-deserved, I'm sure."

It was only the knowing that Gwen wanted him to lose his temper that kept Kael's voice even. "The King hates whisperers. He's murdered hundreds of us, and if he finds a whole nest in the Valley —"

"Lies," Silas purred. "Why would a King who sent his Marked Ones on a sacred task suddenly turn against them?"

"It's not the same King," Kael said through his teeth. "The wildmen were sent to the mountains centuries ago. There have been dozens of Kings since then."

Silas inclined his head, eyes already aglow with triumph. "Still, I'm sure they've kept the tale alive. A task of such importance would not be so easily forgotten."

"An excellent point," Gwen murmured, smirking.

Beside her, Silas stood with his hands behind his back, chin raised to an obnoxious height. He watched Kyleigh through the bottoms of his lids — and judging by the way she glowered back, it was all she could do to keep from wiping the smug look off his face.

But she said nothing in reply. Though a span of silence passed when she could have spoken up, she didn't. Kael could only hope it was because she had some sort of plan.

Still, he wasn't giving up. "What about Titus? He was one of the King's rulers, and you certainly had no problem crushing him."

"Titus was a traitor," Gwen said with a wave of her hand. "He wanted the mountains for himself."

"Once he got to the top, perhaps he *did* decide to keep them," Kael allowed. "But who do you think sent him to the mountains in the first place? Do you really think Crevan would've sat by while Titus's army tromped through his lands? I've seen the power of Midlan, and believe me — no army could make it into the Valley without the King's permission."

"Really? I seem to remember your pirates climbing to the summit with no trouble at all," she retorted.

"Well, they came in by sea," Kael said, thinking. "Titus didn't have that option."

"I should think no path would be closed to one of the King's rulers," Silas mused.

Gwen nodded. "Yes, I believe you're right. This reeks of the pest's mischief," she said, turning her glare upon Kyleigh. "The King won't stop until he has her in chains ... and anyone who helps her will pay the price. The wildmen aren't traitors," she added, eyes narrowing as she balanced a finger against her chin. "But we're grateful for what you did at the summit — and as a show of our gratitude, I *won't* skin you alive and pass your hide onto the King. I'll even let you stay the night, if you wish." Her boots clomped to the floor and she rose from her seat. "But you're to be gone by morning, pest. Silas will show you to your chambers."

"My Thane," he said with a slight bow. Then he jerked his chin at Kyleigh. "Follow me, dragoness."

She did — so closely that she must've trampled on his heel. Kael heard him yowling from the hallway.

But he didn't follow. He stood before Gwen, matching her glare with one of his own. All the furious things he wanted to say wriggled dangerously on the edge of his tongue. She was being a fool. He wanted to say it with the full force of his lungs, to yell so loudly that it would pound against her ears each time she stepped into the room:

You are a fool.

But he knew by the way she smirked at him that yelling would get them nowhere. She *wanted* him to yell. She wanted him to fight. So instead of losing his temper, he forced himself to stay calm.

"I hope you're right, Gwen. I hope Titus was a traitor. Midlan saw us fly this way. I wager they'll be in the Valley by week's end … imagine how angry the King will be if he finds out the wildmen slaughtered a *loyal* ruler."

The edge of her stare faltered as his words sank in; the line of her mouth seemed to harden. And for one fleeting moment, Kael thought he might've gotten through.

"Get out," she barked. "I don't want to see you in my presence again."

Kael threw in a bow as he left — and had to step aside quickly when Gwen threw her chair.

He couldn't even enjoy the sound of it shattering against the wall, or her trail of furious swears. He was far too angry to laugh … and it wasn't only Gwen he was angry with.

It was near dawn, now. The castle's slitted windows breathed cold air across his neck. Occasionally, a particularly strong gust would bring a flurry of snowflakes in with it. They swirled as they entered, dancing gleefully along the hidden trails of the wind. But their dance was short-lived.

The castle's warmth devoured them quickly, and they disappeared before they struck the ground.

Though his eyes watched snowflakes, his mind saw other things: towers of flame and smoke, ships dragged into the depths, the blackened shapes of men who'd stood upon their decks for only a few seconds before the fire devoured them — their bones crumbling before they even touched the waves.

He was so lost in his thoughts that he nearly ran smack into Silas. "In here, Marked One," he hissed, watching as Kael climbed the last in a set of narrow stairs. "You will sleep until morning … then you will be gone."

His exit was made far less haughty by the way he limped. Silas inched down the stairs, favoring his left foot, while Kael went inside the chamber.

It was larger than he'd expected it to be: the bed's posts twisted over his head, and the mattress was probably wide enough to fit three people. There were heads on the walls and furs upon the floor. The hearth was grand enough to have fit an armchair and a table inside of it quite comfortably, and the heat it spilled into the room chased the cold from the stone floors.

Three windows graced the far wall, rounded on their tops. Kyleigh had the middle one shoved open. She leaned against its sill, eyes closed to the breath of the wind.

"I warned you," she murmured as he shut the door. "I told you the wildmen would never fight against the King."

Kael had known before they even turned towards Thanehold that convincing the wildmen would be difficult. They believed the King had charged their ancestors with the task of chasing all the monsters from the Valley — and even though their battle would have to wait until the mountains healed, he had no doubt Gwen's great grand-devils would go marching after the wynns the moment they got the chance.

No, he'd known the wildmen would fight him. In fact, he was surprised they'd even been allowed to stay the night.

That wasn't what he was angry about.

"We'll have to lead the King away from here, I suppose. Then we'll head to the swamps."

"Why?"

Kyleigh's eyes cracked opened. The fires within them were unassumingly calm. "It's the one place in the realm I know better than the mountains. As long as we're in the swamps, we'll be safe."

"So you aren't planning to leave me there while you go off to fight Midlan? I'm not an idiot," he said when she blinked. "I know what you're doing."

"Then you must know that I'm only doing what's best."

"I don't want to spend the rest of my life in hiding, Kyleigh —"

"Then perhaps you shouldn't have left the Bay," she growled, the fires spouting up. "I told you this was the way things would be."

"No, things don't *have* to be this way. We could convince the wildmen to join us — I had a plan! But you didn't help me. You just

132

stood there and let Gwen say whatever she wanted. You never meant to help me, did you?" he said, piecing it all together. "You'd rather us cower in the swamps for the rest of our lives than to ever have to risk facing Midlan."

It was the only possible explanation, but he still regretted it the moment the words left his mouth. He waited for Kyleigh's anger to burn him, or her tears to lash his heart. For half a second, he was trapped in the silence — imagining what horrible, hurtful thing would come of his words.

But her expression never changed. She remained unreadable and calm, as if he'd done nothing more than remark about the weather. It was as if he hadn't said a word. It was as if she didn't care.

And for some reason, that stung him worst of all.

"Perhaps we should sleep on it and decide what to do in the morning." Kyleigh kicked off her spurred boots, hung Harbinger across the back of a nearby chair and slipped beneath the covers — still dressed in full armor. "Good night."

Kael didn't reply. He didn't want to sleep. There was too much to do, too many worries packed inside his head. He was so furious with Kyleigh that he thought he might've been able to kick through the wall.

They wouldn't need the morning to decide: his mind was already made up. He wouldn't leave Thanehold until he convinced the wildmen to fight with them. No other force in the realm stood a chance against Crevan and his mages.

The wildmen were their only chance at living freely — and he would fight for it.

Kael stayed out of bed for as long as he could. He paced, trying to work through the tangle of his thoughts. He kept the hearth fire roaring. But no matter how furious he was with her, his eyes kept drifting back to Kyleigh.

She was turned away from him; her shoulders rose and fell with her steady breaths. She'd gone to bed in such a hurry that her hair was still tied in a pony's tail. After a moment of watching her sleep, Kael realized nothing was worth this — there was nothing he felt or worried over that was worth going to bed angry about.

Especially when he was lucky enough to have the world lying right beside him.

He slid in next to her, careful not to stir her from her dreams. He slipped her hair free of its bonds and pressed against her as tightly as he dared. Almost immediately, his heart calmed. Things didn't seem so desperate. And after a moment, his eyes began to get heavy.

"I love you, Kyleigh," he said before sleep could take him.

He was convinced he would always love her — even if his plan failed and they wound up having to live in hiding. It wouldn't be so bad, as long as he had her by his side.

But it didn't matter how he felt. The things he thought to himself must not have mattered a whit. For when Kael woke the next morning, he woke alone.

Kyleigh was gone.

****

The world outside was magnificent.

Oh, how the skies chilled him — oh, how the mountains roared. Great bursts of wind raced down from their spiny tops and swirled inside the Valley's heart. Their power sharpened his eyes and brought new life to his flesh. His blood raced twice as fast. But the most interesting things of all were the little messages hidden inside the wind.

They whispered of change: the winds would stay here for a while, they would bellow through the Valley and try to rip the snow from its hills. These were the last breaths of winter — the cold's dying gasps. The struggle at this change of the seasons was always fiercest. But spring, with her gentle warmth and cloak of green, would eventually win out.

The scent of roasting meats drifted in from the village behind him. He turned his head to follow the sweet trail of a deer's flesh as it whipped beneath his nose.

There weren't many things the humans were good for, but the way they prepared their food was magic. The meat sang beneath their hands — and that was almost worth all their weakness.

Silas paced through the drifts. His weight sank him to his elbows, but the span of his paws kept him from touching the bottom. It was dawn: the quiet hour of the morning when all of the little, scratching things felt safest. They believed the hour too gray for predators, the light too feeble for a hunter's eyes.

But Silas's powers were far greater than the common cat's.

He paused as the wind blew across his ears — bringing with it the noise of frantic chewing. He followed the sounds, his nostrils flared to catch the first scent of blood.

A rabbit was crouched at the base of a shrub. The wind had worn a slight dip into the drifts, revealing its withered bark. Silas sank until his chin brushed the snow before him. His eyes settled upon the rabbit and held him tightly.

The rabbit stripped away at the shrub and crushed the bark between his flat teeth. He thought his white fur was shelter enough. For a moment, he seemed unaware of the eyes upon him.

But then all at once, he froze.

This was the game between predator and prey: both of their bodies were coiled, both prepared for the chase. Silas watched the rabbit's whiskers bunch against his nose. The rabbit sat still as a rock, set to bolt at even the slightest twitch.

Silas waited a moment more, relishing the pause before the hunt. Then he charged.

His powerful limbs barreled him through the snow. Stinging waves of white flew up from the rabbit's feet. He darted to the left, to the right, to the left again. But Silas knew better than to stay on his heels. When the rabbit cut right, he was ready for it. He was already there.

And the chase ended just as suddenly as it'd begun.

There was a red stain on the rabbit's neck from where Silas's jaws had crushed him. But the rest of his fur was untarnished. His coat was especially thick to guard him from the winter — and his flesh would be tender.

Yes, he would make an excellent gift.

Silas turned back towards the village. The great stone den hung in the shelter of the mountains. Sheer, jagged cliffs crowned it like the spines of a deer's horns, their flesh adorned with snow.

The dragoness was gone. Silas had woken to the news ... though he was disappointed that she hadn't taken the Marked One with her. He'd been in the kitchens at first light, stuffing a pack with food for his journey. The air around him was clouded and hot.

Silas had lingered in the doorway for a moment, reveling in the fury that wafted from the Marked One's flesh. He deserved his bitterness. How *dare* he think he could return here to bark orders at their Thane. How dare he speak to her in such a way. She would not bend; she would not be bullied.

The Marked One brought nothing but trouble with him. Yes, he deserved his anger.

Silas had only managed to take a few paces towards the great den when a familiar scent struck his nose. It was hot and dry — the smell of a stone beneath the summer's heat. There was sweetness to it that made his tongue curl between his teeth.

His jaws froze against the rabbit. His head turned to a set of cliffs beside the village and his eyes sharpened. There, just visible between two faces, was a small hole. It was so slight an opening that the shadows nearly hid it from view. But Silas wasn't fooled.

No ... it isn't possible.

But even as he thought this, his legs carried him towards the cliffs. He would search them once, just to make sure he was only imagining things. And then he would return to the den.

There wasn't a thing that rose from the ground that Silas couldn't climb. Even the cliffs hid a secret path. He held the rabbit tightly as his powerful body sprang him from one jut to the next, careful not to crush its little bones.

In a few short minutes, he'd climbed his way up. The scent had only grown sharper: the sweetness behind the muggy heat was far too strong. It sickened him. Still, he wasn't prepared to believe it.

Silas slid through the crack, into the blackened mouth of a cave. It was much larger than he'd expected it to be. As his eyes adjusted to the dark, he saw that the ceilings were as tall as a tree, the floor easily the width of a pond. But for all that, Silas didn't blink.

No, it was the thing lurking at the back of the room that finally dropped the rabbit from his mouth.

"What are you doing in my lands, dragoness?" he said after he'd hurriedly donned his human skin. This flesh was not as strong against the cold. His bare feet began to ache almost immediately. But he was far too angry to care. "I warned you to be gone by morning."

"Is it morning already?" He could see the little fires dancing in her eyes from across the cave. The way her lips bent at him was a taunt worse than a roar.

"The Thane said you were to leave at first light."

"If I ever start caring about what Gwen says, I want you to slap me," she retorted, and the taunting bend only grew more severe.

A pool gathered deeper within the chamber: he could smell its sweet waters from where he stood. There were several deer laying on the ground about her. The scent of their flesh made Silas's middle growl in protest. But it was odd. "Why have you killed so many? You can't make a den here, dragoness. You're supposed to *leave*," he snarled. "Your presence will only bring the swordbearers upon us."

"You understood all of that, did you? Yes. If I stay, the King will come for me."

"Then leave!"

"I will ... but I've got to do something for Kael, first." Her eyes slid over to the rabbit. "What a handsome creature. Who's he for?"

"That's none of your concern — because it isn't for anybody," Silas added quickly. His face burned as if the sun had bit it, even though he stood in the dark. The dragoness's stupid smile was all to blame.

Fortunately, she went back to cleaning her kills. "If I were to tell you something, would you keep it a secret?"

Silas had no intention of keeping any of her secrets. After the way she'd defied him, he should do nothing for her. Still ... he couldn't help but wonder what her secret might be. It itched him like blades of grass beneath his nose.

He couldn't help it. "Certainly, dragoness," he purred.

Her story was far more interesting than he'd been expecting. Even when he moved deeper into the cave, bumps still rose across his skin — as if the wind had bitten him.

"Another dragon? *More* of your kind? And why did you keep this from your mate?" he asked when she nodded. "These wild humans love to hunt the dragons. One word, and they would have knocked him from the skies."

"I know that."

"Then why didn't you speak?"

"I don't want him dead. I ... remember him, somehow. I think there's a part of me that cared for him, and I don't want to see him killed."

She twisted her fingers through her hair — hair as black as the shadows. Her lips had fallen from their taunt. Silas didn't know what those gestures meant. But he understood her words.

And he thought she deserved no less.

"I warned you, dragoness. When you first told me of your feelings for the Marked One, I warned you it was Abomination."

She shook her head. "This has nothing to do with that."

"Doesn't it?"

Her eyes wandered up to him. Uncertainty thrived within her stare.

"The ritual changes us," he said. "My kind never keep their mates for long, of course. But when I roamed the mountains as a beast, there was *one* lioness I liked better than all the others. She was a powerful thing — a fearsome hunter. I admired her strength ... and she bore me several litters.

"After I was called to bond with this human," Silas scraped a hand down his bare chest, "I was determined to find my lioness once more. I escaped my captors before they could curse me and began the long journey to the mountains. I even forsook an offering to join the other shapechangers, so great was my passion. But when I finally returned, nothing was the same."

It had been a raw wound, once. But now Silas watched the memories with a clear vision of what they'd meant. "Through my mixed eyes, the fearsome lioness who'd once thrilled me was no more than a common beast — a creature too simple to be a match for the thing I'd become. I remember thinking this as I watched her stalk through the wilderness, and I did not go to her. Instead, I let her be.

"The Marked One may thrill your human half, but the dragoness longs for something greater. You desire a mate who knows your mind *and* your wings. That is why to bond with anything less than your own kind is Abomination."

Her face twisted suddenly; her eyes grew bright with anger. She knew the truth. She knew he was right, whether she wanted to admit it or not. The great dragoness who thought she was *always* right had just been shown how wrong she was.

Silas couldn't help himself: he laughed when she got to her feet. "You've brought this upon yourself, dragoness," he called as she stalked to the cave's mouth. "It would be better to leave the Marked One now rather than cause him further pain. Humans have such a tendency to get attached to their mates."

The dragoness stopped just before the cave's opening and spun around. Her arms were crossed over her chest — a feeble human attempt to guard a thing she knew was weakness. "I love Kael. He's my match in every way — nothing will ever change that. But I've walked the earth for hundreds of years and have never come across another halfdragon. I want to speak with him, to free him from the curse, if I can. No matter what he's done, I think there's … goodness, in him. I *feel* he's good. But there's no way Kael or the wildmen will ever understand this. I need to capture him, myself. And while I'm away, our humans must be ready to battle the rest of Midlan." Her lips bent again, and her eyes flared brightly. "That's why I'm going to need your help, Silas."

Hairs rose down the back of his neck. He suddenly felt as if a chasm had opened behind him and the dragoness stood in his only path of escape. Still, he forced himself to be calm. "I would rather die than help you."

"I'm afraid you've got no choice, kitten. The King's army is already on its way. Kael can talk until his lungs turn purple, but Gwen will never listen. There's only one voice in Thanehold that can reach her, only one creature whose instincts she trusts. And if he were to suddenly go missing … well, I think that would be a greater warning than any amount of words."

Silas's mouth went dry. He sprang to his feet and tore for the opening, screaming: "No, dragoness!"

But it was too late. Her second form burst from her human skin and her great, scaly girth blocked the hole — sealing him inside the cave.

CHAPTER 14
A CARE FOR WORDS

Kael couldn't believe it. He knew Kyleigh wasn't pleased with him, but he'd never expected her to run off in the middle of the night. He thought they were going to talk about things, for mercy's sake!

Well, whatever she had planned wasn't going to work: he was determined to find her.

The castle was quieter than it'd been the night before, but there were still plenty of wildmen up and about. Several of them greeted him on his way to the kitchens. He could do no more than nod in reply. He was afraid if he opened his mouth to say *good morning*, all of his frustration would come spilling out. And he doubted if even Thanehold's walls were strong enough to hold them in.

At least the kitchens were empty. There was a sack tossed against one of the walls. It had a handful of goose feathers stuck to its bottom, but he didn't mind. Kael dug through the cabinets and baskets until he found enough provisions to last him the week — pointedly ignoring the shadow that lurked in the doorway.

He didn't have to turn to know it was Silas: he swore he could feel the halfcat's haughty eyes pressing upon him. "I'll be out in a moment," Kael said shortly.

"Good ... and what about the dragoness?" Silas purred.

"She's already gone."

"Excellent."

He must not have heard the edge in Kael's voice — or he wouldn't have thought for a moment that it was *excellent*. He'd turned around to say as much, but found the doorway empty.

By the time he'd marched from the keep, Kael was entirely fed up with people disappearing. So he supposed he might've had it coming when Griffith dropped from a balcony and nearly scared the skin off of him.

"Are you going on a hunt? Can I come along?"

Kael had to stuff his heart back down his throat before he could mutter: "No, I'm not going on a hunt. I'm leaving."

"For good?" Griffith's eyes went wide. "But you can't leave — you've only just got here! What will I tell Baird?"

Kael had tried rather hard to *forget* about Baird. He didn't think he had the patience to sit through an episode of the beggar-bard's ranting. "I'm sure he'll understand. He probably doesn't even know I'm here."

Griffith snorted. "Please. He knew the moment you set foot inside the castle. *What's that I hear? Is that the mighty tread of Kael the Wright?* I had to put a guard outside your room just to keep him from barging in."

Had Kael not been so caught up in his thoughts, he might've laughed at Griffith's act. He had to admit that the way he'd slung his hands about was certainly like the beggar-bard. But he didn't have time.

"Kyleigh's left me. I'm afraid if I don't find her, she'll do herself harm. I can't stay."

Griffith didn't look the least bit concerned. "Oh, she's always flying off to one place or another. That's a dragon's way: they're solitary creatures, mostly. The wynns live scattered in caves all across their peak." His mouth split into a wide grin. "It's only when Gwen starts cracking skulls that they swarm together."

He was wrong. Kael had read *Tales of Scales* four times through, and he knew that dragons might've lived alone at first. But once they'd chosen mates, they were supposed to be inseparable. Still, he didn't think Griffith would understand.

"I'll speak to Baird next time, I promise. But right now, I've got to get moving."

Before Kael had even reached the keep walls, there were three craftsmen scrambling to peel the stone back for him. It was hard to tell who they were without their paint. But he thought he might've recognized their smiles. They molded the stone into an archway — and winter came storming in.

The way the wind beat him as he passed through the arch made him feel as if he was perched a mile in the sky, about to leap from a dragon's back. It ripped around in unreliable patterns. He was bent into it at one moment, only to stumble sideways the next.

Griffith followed him stubbornly — one thin arm braced over his eyes like a shield. "I wish you didn't have to go!" he shouted over the gales.

"I wish that too," Kael said back. A wave of snow came roaring towards them, bolstered by the wind. He turned his head away and shut his eyes as the little icy flakes lashed his skin.

"When will you be back?"

"I'm not sure, Griff."

"Well, if you're going to leave, then you might as well take this with you."

Kael turned when Griffith latched onto the back of his tunic and pressed some object into his hand. It was a dragonsbane dagger — a weapon with a curved, golden blade and a hilt carved from bone. He turned it over, marveling at its weight and the little hairline swirls of red inside the blade.

"Only wildmen are supposed to carry our sacred weapons. But the craftsmen scraped a little gold from each one and found enough to make you a dagger. Gwen would be furious if she knew," Griffith added, pressing a finger against his mouth.

Kael couldn't help but smile as he tucked the dagger into his belt. "I'll take good care of it. Maybe once I find Kyleigh, I can convince her to —"

"Wolfstomp!"

He turned to wave absently at a warrior perched atop the keep's ramparts, and saw her eyes were set upon something in the distance. "What is it?"

"I see lights! They're coming from the other side of the Cleft. I thought it was only a storm at first." She shook her head. "But I don't think lightning comes in so many colors."

It didn't.

Kael forgot his task. The sack of provisions fell from his hand as he went charging for the rampart steps — Griffith latched firmly to the hem of his tunic. The stone was icy. He nearly busted his chin trying to scramble to the top. But somehow, his legs carried him to the rampart walls.

Clouds hung thickly over the Valley, all the way to the edge of the Cleft. Kael strained his eyes beyond the snow-filled pass to the lights in the distance. He could see why the warrior had thought it was a storm: the way they flashed and burst through the clouds certainly *looked* like lightning. But he knew for a fact that lightning never flashed purple or red.

And he was certain the bolts didn't send up monstrous waves of snow behind them when they struck.

"It's the King's mages," Kael said. His lungs tightened so forcefully across the words that he could hardly get them out. "They're blasting their way through the snow in the Cleft. They're marching for the Valley."

Griffith's mouth parted into an O beneath his band of freckles. "Do you think he's coming to question us about the pest?"

"I doubt it."

As Griffith spoke, he wound the blue marble tightly between his fingers, and his eyes went dark. "Well, he won't hurt us. We've done nothing wrong."

It didn't work that way. Garron the Shrewd had done nothing wrong, but the King's beasts still ripped him to shreds. The giants, the villagers of Copperdock, the children in Harborville — even the wildmen had done nothing to deserve the horrors they'd suffered. But they'd suffered them all the same.

And the chances of any of that changing were about the same as the sun coming out.

Kael knew he couldn't leave the wildmen on their own — not with Midlan barreling down upon them. Gwen had made it very clear she had no intention of fighting the King. If she clomped out to meet Crevan's men unarmed, they'd lop off her head.

At least with Midlan's eyes turned on the Valley, Kyleigh would be safe. It was only the knowing she wouldn't be blasted from the skies that gave him the strength to hold his ground. He would stay to help the wildmen — whether they wanted it or not.

"Gwen needs to see this," Kael said quietly. "She needs to know what she's up against."

After a moment, Griffith peeled away. Kael and the warrior stood together silently, watching as the lights swelled and burst inside the clouds. Wave after wave of white sprayed up from where they struck — and he knew that if they could see the explosions from such a distance, they must be impossibly large.

Midlan was making good time.

It wasn't long before Gwen clomped her way up the stairs behind him. "Still here, mutt? And what about the pest?"

143

"Gone," Kael managed to say.

Gwen shrugged. "Well, as long as *she* isn't here, I suppose there's no harm in letting you stay — as long as you don't annoy me."

He watched carefully when the warrior pointed to where the lights burst. But if Gwen was worried, she didn't show it.

"When the King arrives, we'll tell him that the pest has moved on. That'll be the end of it." She twisted to look the other direction, out where the Valley stretched. All of the concern that *should've* been on her face at the sight of the King's army suddenly appeared. "Has anyone seen my cat?"

"He left at first light, Thane. I'm sure he was going on a hunt," the warrior said without taking her eyes from the Cleft.

Gwen's frown deepened. "Yes ... but he's usually come back by now."

Kael didn't see how a cat was anywhere near as important as an army. "He'll come back on his own. Right now you ought to be getting ready for a fight — wake the village, get the warriors on their feet!" he cried at her look. "Midlan's breathing on our doorstep, for mercy's sake!"

"I know what I'm doing," Gwen said icily. She glanced over her shoulder. "Griffith? Take the mutt inside the castle. I can't have him running around stirring up panic across the village. He's not to set one foot outside until this business with the King is taken care of. Understood?"

"Yes, Thane." Griffith waved him forward. "Come on."

Kael went — but only because he could see the worry on Griffith's face. The blue marble rolled between his fingers as they walked back to the castle doors. Never once did it halt its path.

And Kael saw a tiny bit of hope.

When they stood outside the castle doors, Griffith stopped. "Have you ever met the King?"

"Not exactly," Kael admitted.

"Do you think he's a good man?"

A clear and resounding *no* was the obvious answer. As far as Kael could see, there wasn't a single redeeming thing the King had done for the realm. He was no better than Titus — worse, actually, because it was Crevan who'd given Titus his power in the first place.

"I may not have met the King, but I've met his rulers," Kael said carefully. "And I can tell you that each and every one was impossibly

144

cruel to his people. I can't imagine that a good man would've given such an awful bunch their thrones, or let them keep their power for long."

Griffith was silent. He stared at the sky above the ramparts. The marble stopped at his palm, and he clamped down upon it tightly. "Well, I suppose we'll find out in a few days."

"I'm not sure it'll take them that long," Kael said, hoping it might prod him in the right direction. He'd learned the hard way that arguing with the wildmen only made things take twice as long — and they didn't have twice as long to wait.

In fact, he doubted if they had even *half* as long.

"You should go speak to Baird. You're going to be stuck inside the castle anyways, so you might as well," Griffith added, smiling heavily as he turned. "I'm sure he has all sorts of interesting things to tell you."

****

Kael put it off as long as he could. But after three hours of pacing through the castle, trying not to rip the mortar from between the stones, he finally gave in. At least if he spoke to Baird, he was very likely to have his mind put on something else — and he wasn't disappointed.

One of the wildmen led him to Baird's chambers: a large, sprawling room that took up a full corner of the castle. He wasn't surprised to find that most of the walls were filled with shelves. Granted, there weren't very many books — and Baird's small collection of treasures only made the shelves seem emptier. There was a whole wall of windows and a set of narrow doors between them, leading to a balcony outside.

Perhaps the one thing he didn't expect to find inside the chamber was a flock of birds.

No sooner had he closed the door behind him than a dove crashed into the side of his head. It obviously hadn't been expecting someone to come through the door. The dove beat its wings in a clumsy panic, trying desperately to get away from him. Kael finally had to duck to avoid getting bruised.

There were nests in every conceivable place: along the shelves, atop the windowsills, inside the torch sconces. A crowd of finches had claimed the protruding row of stone above the hearth, which he didn't think would be particularly comfortable, if there was ever a fire. The dove that'd nearly beat him senseless had a nest settled directly atop the desk — and the way its little black eyes squinted at him made Kael feel as if *he* was the one doing something odd.

"Baird?" he called, almost dreading the answer.

Feathers flew and Kael jumped when the balcony doors slammed open.

An older man with short-cropped hair and a set of bandages wrapped over the top of his face burst through the doorway. He grinned through his beard as he waved to the chair on Kael's left.

"Ah, I *knew* I heard you enter! No other soul in the Kingdom could possibly match your steps. Come closer, young man," he said, waving again. "I should like to greet you as a friend."

Kael had been expecting a clasp of the hand, or perhaps a slap on the back. Instead, he got a full-fledged embrace. He grimaced when Baird squeezed him tightly — partly because the closeness was a bit uncomfortable, but mostly because he worried for any birds that might be nesting inside his billowing fur robes.

"They keep me company, and *I* keep them warm," Baird explained when he asked. "Seed is difficult to find in the winter, but the wildmen have their ways. My friends' little bellies glow with a fire's warmth when fed."

"All right, but couldn't you feed them just as well from the balcony?"

"I tried that for a while," Baird admitted. "But when one wakes to the sweet little pleas of chilly feet and frozen beaks … one's resolve melts quickly."

The streaks running down his shelves weren't likely to melt so quickly — if they melted at all. But before Kael could say as much, Baird tugged him forward.

"Follow me, young man. We're very nearly finished."

There was a little table outside, and a couple of stocky chairs. A wildwoman sat in one of them. She wore her fiery hair in a braid that draped over her shoulder. There was a quill in one of her hands and a stack of parchment pinned beneath her elbow, no doubt in an attempt to keep the pages from being swept by the wind.

The wildwoman watched the snow swirling across the fields beneath them with eyes that were a deep, listless blue. When she saw

146

Kael approaching, she knocked the snow out of the other chair with a swipe of her hand. "You might as well sit. This is going to take a while."

"Nonsense! We're near the end."

"We've been *near the end* since yesterday," she retorted with a flick of her quill.

"Yes, well, there's simply no guessing how long so grand a story will take. You must tell it until it's finished. Now, where were we ...?"

Baird felt along the table until he found the balcony's edge. He leaned over the railing and faced out at the Valley — as if he were staring pensively into the distance.

Kael hardly glanced at him before he went back to squinting at the wildwoman. He hadn't realized how much he'd relied on their paint to tell their faces apart. Without the unique swirls and dots adorning their features, it was like all of Thanehold had been replaced with strangers.

But those eyes ...

"Lydia?" he guessed.

Her smile broke into a grin. "You remember!"

"Of course I remember." Kael had spent so many hours with that band of craftsmen that he didn't think he'd ever forget them — even if it took him a moment without their paint. "How have you be — ?"

"Ahem, if you please?" Baird called from the rails.

Lydia rolled her eyes at him before she went back to the parchment.

"I remember it was a warm summer day — a day at the height of summer, in fact," Baird began. "It was only by the mercy of strangers that I arrived at Midlan unscathed ... well, *mostly* unscathed. If you will remember, dear reader, I had to gouge my own eyes out in chapter twelve.

"So how did I know it was summer, you ask? Well, because it was hot! And it wasn't a lovely dry heat, either. No — this was that dreadful, sticky sort of heat. It was as if a dragon crouched above the fortress and panted damp clouds of breath upon our heads. Made me wish the fire would fall and be done with it, to be honest. One blistering bolt is a greater relief than a slow summer's boil ..."

Baird rambled on, but Kael wasn't listening.

Something squirmed in the back of his head, maddened him with its whispers. For a moment, Thanehold disappeared: he stood aboard the fisherman's vessel once more and his eyes watched the glowing orb grow in the sky above him. There was a flash of heat, a burst of wind —

"Drat and blast it!" Baird cried. His brows fell over the top of his bandages as he spun around and hissed at the doors: "What happens next?"

Kael wasn't sure. But there were more important matters to worry about. The thing in the back of his head stabbed at him with its muffled warnings. He wished he could hear what it said.

The vision darkened and the whispers evaporated, leaving him more frustrated than ever.

"What is it, young man? I can hardly think with your sighs blasting through my ears like a giant's cough," Baird grumbled.

His sigh hadn't *blasted* anywhere. He'd barely made a sound. "Midlan's at the Cleft. They're marching for the Valley."

"Is that all?" Baird snorted before he could nod. "The rebel whisperers had Midlan on its heels towards the end of the War — and that was without a true Wright at their lead. I can only imagine what will become of the King, should he choose to meet *you* in battle."

"If I had the wildmen, things would be simple," Kael agreed. When he glanced at Lydia, he saw she'd gone back to staring at the fields. Still, he spoke quietly: "Gwen won't listen to me. She won't fight. I can't do it on my own."

"Nonsense. You've got the Swordmaiden by your side. And I hear she's *always* by your side," Baird added with a wide grin. "More and more often, each and every day —"

"Kyleigh's gone," Kael said shortly.

Baird's grin vanished. "Well, then I suppose you're on your own."

"I know that."

"And you haven't got the slightest chance against Midlan on your own —"

"I know!" Kael said sharply. "I know I've got no chance. I don't need you barking at me about it."

"*You're* the one who's barking." Baird swept a knobby hand to his thin chest. "*I'm* merely trying to help."

Kael tugged roughly on his curls, trying to think through the flames that whipped behind his eyes. "If I had a month to wear her down, Gwen might see reason. But I haven't got a month, this time." An idea suddenly came to him. "What if you were to ... convince her for me?"

"Hmm." Baird scratched at the scruff on his chin. "An interesting idea. What would you have me say, exactly?"

"I don't know. Whatever it is you say to whisper people in line."

Baird gasped as if he'd just found a troll stashed in one of his pockets. "No, young man. Oh dear, oh me — *no*." He waved his hands frantically before him. "Do you not remember what I said? The man who holds the whole realm captive upon his tongue must be *careful* with his gifts. I would never use those powers upon a friend. I would use them only if I had no other choice."

"Well, we haven't got another choice," Kael said evenly. "If Gwen doesn't listen, she'll be killed."

Baird pursed his lips. "Words can be powerful, yes. But they can also be frightfully vague. If I told the Thane to obey everything you commanded, you might in jest send her walking off a cliff!"

Kael wasn't so sure it would've been *in jest*. But he could see Baird's point. "What if you told her to only obey the serious things I said?"

"How is she to know whether or not you're serious? My words move feet, young man. They can't read minds."

"Well, then have her obey only *one* command — whichever one I give her first."

Baird threw his hands up with such vigor that he nearly tumbled off the balcony. "Which one would you give her? If you said *go fight the King*, she would march out straight away — barehanded and lost in a trance. Her eyes would be so fixed upon Midlan that she would pay the land no heed. I wager she would drown in the first river that snaked across her path. *No*, young man," he said again. "Words are powerful and dangerous things — much better suited to the ears of my enemies."

Kael was about to argue when Baird slapped his hands against the sides of his head and cried:

"Stop it! For the sake of all that's still good in the realm, would you kindly stop that racket?"

At first, Kael had no idea what he was talking about. It was only when Lydia stopped drumming her fingers against the table that he noticed there'd been any noise in the first place.

As the silence crept in, he realized it'd been the tapping of her fingers that'd made his blood run hot, made everything seem more desperate. Even after she stopped, his heart beat after it.

"Sorry. I can't help myself," she said with a sheepish grin.

Baird frowned at the air above her left shoulder. "Be that as it may, you were assigned to finish my book. Where did we leave off?"

Kael glanced at the pages between Lydia's arms and saw that Baird's words had trailed into scribbles back at *a warm summer's day*. Instead, an elaborate drawing filled the pages of his story — one in which the beggar-bard was so covered in birds that Kael could hardly make out his bandages.

Lydia reddened at his grin and turned the page over quickly. "I think we ought to end here for the day —"

"But the day's only just begun," Baird sputtered. His chin followed the rustling of the papers as she hurried for the balcony doors. "We were about to get to the exciting bit!"

"And in a few months, I'm sure we'll get there."

"Blasted girl," Baird growled when she slammed the door. He felt around for Lydia's empty chair and plopped into it with an exasperated sigh. "When I asked for a scribe, I expected to get a young person who actually *cared* for words. I've been through fourteen different scribes and not a one's shown any interest — but I'd take them all back in an instant to have this one gone.

"If it's not the tapping, then it's the whistling or the humming." Baird groaned into his knobby hands. "I swear she'll be the death of me."

Even if Baird could've seen his smile, Kael doubted if he could have held it in. It seemed the beggar-bard had finally met his match.

"It's a great relief to speak with someone who understands," Baird said after a moment. "A Wright knows the power of words better than anyone. He sees them wholly, in their entire form. He understands them so well that a word passing before his eyes shall forever be remembered."

Kael was caught off-guard by his smile. "What do you mean, I can see their entire form?"

"All those who read are searching — they seek to fill the empty portions of their souls. A warrior feels a word's power inside his chest. A craftsman sees its beauty reflected behind his eyes. And in a line's calm repose, a healer finds his courage. But a Wright ... well, a Wright can hear all of their meanings. He knows them to their full extent." Baird smiled. "And so he does not soon forget."

Something about what he'd said made Kael feel uneasy. "I don't think —"

"Ah, and speaking of words ..." Baird began digging through his robes with gusto. Out came a handful of seed, bits of string, and something that looked suspiciously like a wadded-up handkerchief. Finally, he slapped a sealed envelope upon the table and declared: "I want you to keep this for me, young man. I don't trust it, here. There are too many wandering eyes about, too many curious young gazes. They don't understand the danger ... but you do."

He certainly did.

Kael's stomach bunched into a knot as he stared down at the familiar, twisting seal of Midlan. The dragon's tiny eye seemed locked upon him — daring him to turn the envelope onto its front. But if he did, and if he read the words scrawled across it, the whispercraft would overtake him. It would steal his legs and march him straight for Midlan.

His fate would be the same as all of the other whisperers at the end of the War.

"I'm not keeping that for you."

"Just stick it inside your pocket —"

"I'm not sticking it anywhere."

"— and you'll forget it soon enough."

"No, Baird," Kael said sharply. "It's too dangerous. Just burn it and be done."

He sputtered indignantly. "But it's one of my treasures!"

"It's evil, is what it is," Kael growled.

The beggar-bard's face hung so piteously that he couldn't bring himself to tear it to pieces ... at least not in front of Baird.

"Fine. I'll take it," he muttered, stuffing the envelope into the pocket of his breeches.

Baird's wide grin returned. "Thank you, young man! Look after it well."

He had no intention of looking after it. The moment he was out of range of Baird's ears, he'd toss it in the hearth. But at that moment, there were far more pressing matters at hand. Kael turned to watch the spells flashing in the distance ...

And he *did* forget.

CHAPTER 15
MIDLAN'S ARMY

Kael tried to spend the rest of the day working out some sort of plan to convince the wildmen to fight, but it was difficult. Baird's voice rang inside his head every few moments: *words are powerful and dangerous things ... all those who read are searching — they seek to fill the empty portions of their souls.*

It was annoying, at first. It seemed as if every time he took a step in the right direction, those words pulled him back. They grated against his ears with such obnoxious force that it drove him to grind his teeth. But though he tried to shove them aside, he couldn't.

And it wasn't long before he began to listen.

There had to be a reason his mind kept coming back to what Baird had said. There was a message inside the words he was missing, a loose thread he had to follow. Kael found the thought's end and gave it a sharp tug. He traced its path through a tangle of muddle pictures until he finally stopped at Griffith.

It was a memory of the day the wildmen arrived at the Earl's old castle — the day he'd passed his favorite book onto Griffith. He remembered how his had been lost between the pages of the *Atlas of the Adventurer*, how he'd hardly seemed able to put it down. Now Kael realized that Griffith had read so intently because he'd been searching for something — searching for the answer to the question in his heart:

How will I know which paths to take? How will I know what's best for my people?

Those were the questions he'd asked in the moment before Kael handed him the *Atlas*. Those were the worries that plagued him, the answer he searched for. But the stories Griffith had read seemed to calm him. It made Kael wonder if perhaps Baird had been wrong.

Perhaps there *was* a wildman in Thanehold who heeded the power of words.

It was a risk, but he knew he didn't have time to beat the wildmen into listening. Convincing Griffith might be his only chance — and he thought he might've known just how to do it.

Kael spent the rest of the day hunched over a blank sheet of parchment, trying to bring it to life. He didn't have Baird's voice, or Setheran's powerful tone. No, all he could do was tell the truth.

As he wrote, he drew each line in desperation. He fed his worry into every page. He told the story of a village that'd been unprepared — defenseless against an army of wolves that'd torn it apart with iron teeth. Everything he felt ran from the tip of his quill. The words he used were pounded out in anger, sharpened by despair.

His eyes burned by the time he'd finished — whether from exhaustion or fury, he wasn't sure. But he knew that if even one line struck the worry in Griffith's eyes, the wildmen would be prepared.

Once he'd finished, Kael sealed his story up and passed it on to one of the warriors to be delivered. He didn't want Griffith to see him. The story would speak for itself.

After a day had dragged by and Kael heard nothing, he began to fear that he'd made a mistake. He spent his time with Baird and Lydia, letting their ceaseless spats distract him from his worries — fighting against all the little fibers of his soul that screamed for him to do *something*. In the short breaths between their arguments, he watched the spell-lights in the distance.

They grew brighter by the hour. Soon he could hear the far-off rumble of the hills of snow giving way. Their white flesh blasted upwards in a tower's spire beneath every spell, snow that had sat undisturbed for so long that it'd hardened into a near-impenetrable vein of ice. He hoped it would hold for a few days longer.

But at the rate things were going, he doubted it.

That night, he woke to wild chirping and the panicked flapping of wings. Kael hadn't been eager to go back to the chambers he'd shared with Kyleigh. Instead, he'd fallen into a fitful sleep on Baird's floor. Now every bird in the chamber tore from their nests and threw themselves against the balcony doors. Their feet scratched against the wood and they swirled about the room in a frantic spiral.

Baird tumbled out of bed and chased them around — tromping on Kael's hand and knocking over furniture as he went. "No, little things! The winds are too strong. You'll be torn apart if you venture out — oof!"

154

He tripped over his night robe and would've crashed straight into the wall, had Kael not grabbed him around the arm. "They aren't going anywhere. You're likely to break something if you keep running about. Stay here," Kael said firmly as he began making his way towards the window. "I'll see what's happened."

By the time he'd fought his way through the cloud of birds, the rumbling had stopped. Kael stared into the darkness for what seemed like an eternity before he saw the hundreds of orange lights.

They were torches — each carried by a soldier of Midlan. He watched, breathless, as the torches moved toward the end of the Cleft. For one heart-stopping moment, he feared they might've burst through. But they stopped just before they reached the end.

Spells lit up the night and the rumbling continued as the mages went back to hacking away at the last remaining stretch of ice.

"What is it, young man? What do you see?"

"They've just collapsed a huge bit of the pass," Kael said, piecing it together. "They're nearly out."

"Good. All of this blasting is starting to give me a headache. The sooner they get through, the sooner you can silence them."

Kael's mouth went dry even as his palms began to sweat. He didn't think he'd be able to silence anybody — not without the wildmen's help. His knees locked together and his legs shook as he spun for the door. He'd been foolish to think words would do anything. He'd wasted too much time. If he left now, perhaps he'd be able to beat some sense into Gwen before it was too late.

He was reaching for the door when the knob turned. He leapt back when Griffith stepped in.

There was a suit of armor wrapped in one of his arms. Kael's letter hung from his hand — so read that tiny holes had been worn into its creases. But Kael hardly noticed any of that. From the moment he stepped inside, Kael's eyes locked upon the boy's face.

Black paint adorned his features once more.

"She's going to fight," he breathed.

Griffith's head tilted to the side. "She's *prepared* to fight, if need be."

"Oh, there'll be a fight," Baird called. In spite of having been told to stay put, he somehow managed to shuffle his way over to latch himself onto Kael's arm. "Promise me something, young man — promise me that you'll deal swiftly with his mages. They're a crafty lot.

If you leave them to sit and think, they'll fester into a rot. They chew the legs out from under you before you even realize what's happened."

"I don't think I'll have any say in it," Kael said, turning back to Griffith. "I doubt Gwen's going to let me out of here."

"She won't," Griffith said with a nod. "The craftsmen are useless in the wind, so she's only using the warriors — and she says she doesn't need your help for that. In fact, you're not to come within a mile of them, understood? You're to stay right here. Gwen'll skin me if I let you out." The armor fell from his grip and struck the ground with a *clang*. The helmet rolled to a stop at Kael's feet. "So it's best if she doesn't see you."

****

Dawn came quietly. A red sky swelled behind the mountains and bled upon the white at their feet. Creatures rose from the snow as they marched — beasts with hundreds of limbs and countless tiny claws. They tore through the wildmen's ranks, howling as the wind brought them to life.

Kael watched the creatures' dance through the slits in his iron helmet. Their flesh collided with his body and the sound was like a roomful of glass shattering against his skull: it filled his ears with a near-constant hiss that stifled everything else.

The wind had beaten the drifts for days. Now they filled the Valley in high, uneven waves. Sometimes the snow hardly came to Kael's ankles, but other times he sank to his knees.

There wasn't much space between the castle and the Cleft. When Kael chanced a look behind him, he could see the black patterns on the faces of the guards who watched them from the ramparts. The head that barely rose above them was Griffith's. If the Cleft's mouth was even a half-mile from Thanehold, it would be a near thing.

Gwen marched straight to the last remaining wall of ice. Its crags were swollen and blue. Spells crashed behind it. The colors that swelled and burst inside its flesh made it look as if the evening sky was trying to fight its way out.

A particularly loud blast made the wall groan. It shed a few monstrous scales of ice — some twice the size of a man. But Gwen never flinched.

One of her fists was clenched around the strap of a rounded shield and from the other hung a double-headed steel axe. The way the wind blasted across her wild crop of hair made it look as if flames spouted from her head. She turned as another enormous chunk of ice shattered upon the ground to her left — revealing the sharp edge scowl.

Kael stood just a few rows behind her. Gwen's gaze cut over the top of his head to the wind-blasted fields behind him, and he stood perfectly still. Her eyes tightened upon something in the distance. Her bluish-black lips twisted in a grimace. Only when she turned back to the wall did he chance a look behind him.

As far as he could see, the fields were empty. He didn't know what she'd been looking for — and he didn't have time to wonder.

The warriors on his either side kept glancing in his direction. He could feel the pressure of their eyes as they scraped across him, roving from deep within their helmets. But he looked pointedly ahead.

He remembered what Geist had said about how strange it was that Kael was able to see through disguises that'd fool so many. He wasn't sure if the talent was his alone, or if it was something all whisperers shared — but he wasn't willing to test it. Kael convinced himself that any little movement might give him away, and he stood perfectly still.

A sudden calm drew his eyes to the center of the wall. The spells ceased, the air fell silent. For a long moment, all Kael could hear was the ice as it hissed across his armor and his own heavy breaths.

"Maybe they've given up," a warrior beside him whispered.

Kael knew full well they hadn't given up. The animal in him bared its teeth as hairs rose down the back of his neck. He wasn't at all surprised when a red light appeared behind the ice.

It grew quickly, trembling as it swelled. Every inch seemed to bring it closer to bursting. A high-pitched whistle rent the air as the light grew: the more it trembled, the higher the whistling climbed. Soon, the wall began to shake.

Scales of ice broke free and crashed into the ground. The warriors fell back, cursing. They clapped hands to the sides of their helmets; their ranks went from even lines to a clustered, swearing mass. Even Gwen paced a step back, hand tightened around the hilt of her axe.

Then all at once, the wall exploded.

157

Boulders of ice flew over their heads and into the field beyond. The warriors raised their shields against the deadly wave that blasted from the Cleft's mouth. Kael's arm shook against the unexpected force as ice struck his shield. One of the jagged shards splintered the wood above his wrist and stopped mere inches from his face.

Gwen swatted at the ice shards, meeting their force with the spiked front of her shield. A particularly large chunk of ice screamed for her middle, but she hardly glanced at it. She batted it aside absently while her eyes stayed fixed upon the Cleft.

Kael crouched with the other warriors, their shields raised in a protective roof until the last of the ice fell. When he dared to look, he saw an army gathered inside the Cleft.

Hundreds of soldiers stood before them — their gold-tinged armor reddened by the dawn, the twisting black dragons upon their chests coiled for battle. They filled the pass to its jagged walls and waited in perfect, unwavering lines. Their bodies were so still, the vents of their helmets so fixed that for a moment, Kael thought they might be statues.

Then a man at the head of the line barked an order and the front ranks broke apart. They peeled into an archway, feet pounding in an unbroken rhythm and spears clamped across their chests. From between their ranks marched a dozen mages.

Their robes matched the soldiers: gold, with dragons adorning their chests. Even from a distance, Kael could see the red glow of the shackles upon their wrists. His eyes scanned across their faces quickly. But to his relief, there weren't any children among them.

He supposed Crevan had sent his best.

One mage marched fearlessly at their lead. He was a desert man with a clean-shaven head. The open-mouthed grin he wore was all teeth and no shape — the grin of a polished skull. Kael couldn't help but stare at his large, overgrown ears. They were stretched to near-transparency; blue veins crisscrossed down their arches.

The remnants of the red spell coiled in wisps about the mage's fingers. A length of chain wrapped around his arm. Perhaps it was the dawn light toying with him, but Kael swore the chains seemed to squirm across his wrist ... as if it was a creature that moved of its own accord.

The lead mage marched until he stood hardly fifty paces from Gwen, and then he stopped.

Not a sound stirred from the ranks of Midlan; the wildmen stayed remarkably still. The hiss of snow blustering against their breastplates was the only noise between them.

Gwen took a step forward, turning so the lead mage could see her axe. "Are you from the King?" she called.

"I'm Ulric, his archmage." The desert man's eyes squinched at their bottoms as they dragged across Gwen's fur armor. "I'd heard that bandits had taken over the Earl's castle ... though I must admit, I didn't expect you to be so *hideous.*"

Gwen's knuckles went white about the axe even as her neck burned red. "We aren't bandits. The King sent our ancestors to cleanse the mountains long ago. This land is ours by right."

Kael knew by how her words snapped at their ends that she was doing everything in her power to keep from burying her axe in Ulric's skull.

But instead of backing away, his manic grin grew wider. "Yes, I'm sure it is," he called, as if he were merely appeasing a child's demands. "But as delightful as this little talk has been, I'm afraid we have business to attend to. Give us the Dragongirl, and I promise no harm will come to you. We'll even let you keep the castle."

Kael didn't believe it, not even for a moment. The King hadn't sent an army into the Valley for Kyleigh — not when he knew that their swords wouldn't be any good against her scales. No, the *mages* were here for Kyleigh.

The army was here for the wildmen.

CHAPTER 16
A FIERY BATTLE

"The pest is gone," Gwen said with a wave of her hand. "We haven't seen her for months."

As she spoke, Kael drew the sword at his hip. He wished he had his bow. Ulric stood within his range — and he thought an arrow between the eyes would've done him some good.

"Well, that *is* regrettable. We rather hoped we would find her here." Ulric's dark eyes roved to the walls of Thanehold — and his grin stretched even wider. "Still ... it seems a shame to drag an army all the way from Midlan and not have it used."

Ulric raised his fist, and Kael knew what was coming. Fear jolted him forward. It swelled inside his muscles, brought strength to his limbs. His eyes sharpened upon Ulric's face and he threw the first thing he could think of — the only thing he had in his hand.

It was an impossible throw. The sword bolted from his hand and flew with an arrow's speed for Ulric — no more than a gray blur against the white earth. White ringed the archmage's eyes and for the second the sword flew, Kael thought he had him.

But one of the other mages saw it coming.

His spell struck the sword and sent it to the ground in a thousand glittering pieces. The wildmen stepped in behind Kael and hurled more bolts, but it was too late. The mages' shock lasted a mere half-blink. They raised their daggers and swords, their hands adorned with gauntlets and silver rings, and an identical blue spell blossomed from their ends.

The spells melded where they touched until it filled the Cleft's mouth. It made Midlan's army shimmer and wave, as if it stood behind an enormous bubble. The various weapons the wildmen hurled at Ulric shattered helplessly against its rounded front.

Kael knew they wouldn't be able to throw anything through the shield. They had to reach Ulric before the fires came. But he only managed to take a single step.

160

A gust of wind tore through the Cleft. It scraped across the soldiers first — stumbling them forward despite their heavy armor, tugging at their pikes and stirring the links of their mail into a clanging song. It whipped against the blue spell and stirred ripples from its front. Then it whipped across the mages' robes, striking Ulric last.

Though the wind roared so furiously that it seemed about to punch a hole through the spell, Ulric's open-mouthed grin never faltered — and his dark eyes stayed fixed on Kael.

The wind rose to a thunderous bellow, growing into a powerful storm. It burst from the clouds in unnatural gusts: knocking them backwards at one moment, dragging them forward the next.

Most of the wildmen were caught off-guard by the strange pattern of the wind. They rolled helplessly towards Thanehold, armor clattering through the snow. A handful managed to wedge themselves against rocks while their strength adjusted.

Even Gwen was struggling. She fell to her knees and wedged her shield against the lip of a rock, holding on tightly as the wind tried to beat her away.

Only Kael managed to keep his feet. He remembered the power of these winds — the gales that'd turned entire flaming vessels onto their sides. His legs braced against the push he knew would come, his muscles tightened to hold him steady.

While the warrior in him planted its feet, the craftsman went to work. Kael watched through his mind's eye as blackened scales popped up across his skin. They covered his every inch, from the top of his head to the bottoms of his feet. He braced himself against the heat he knew would come and shouted to the warriors behind him:

"Let go! Get out of the way!"

"No, hold your ground!" Gwen roared from ahead of him. She twisted to glare over her shoulder, her voice sharp with fury. "Don't give in, keep fight —!"

All at once, light broke above the Cleft.

Something like the afternoon sun erupted before them: an orb that burned with enough fury to chew a hole through the clouds. The snow turned a blinding white beneath it. Kael shielded his eyes against the stabbing light and watched from beneath the crook of his arm as black spots appeared across the ground in front of him.

161

Not even the mountains' winter could withstand the power of the light. It stripped the ice from the rocks and shoved the cold aside. Snow boiled and rolled away from the orb like molten steel; the hiss of rising steam filled the air beneath the storm's thunderous voice.

Shock stole Kael's breath and for half a moment, he felt a blast of heat slip through the hairline cracks in his armor. He fought against his doubt, fought to seal the cracks before his armor burst and the heat consumed him. He dragged his eyes from the blinding orb to focus, and saw that Gwen hadn't budged.

Her head was twisted aside, her teeth bared against the heat. But even when the light brightened and she cried out in pain, she clung stubbornly to the rock — determined not to let the wind cast her aside.

Kael forgot his worry, forgot his doubt. "Let go!" he bellowed, his heart thumping in panic. "Let *go*, for mercy's sake!"

But no matter how he roared, she couldn't hear him.

Flames had begun to boil inside the clouds. The orb was near to bursting. Kael fought against the ripping winds and the growing heat, against the knee-high weeping of the snow. He grabbed the furred back of Gwen's tunic just as the light erupted, blinding him. His warrior strength surged, bolstered by his panic. In the last seconds before the fires came, he wrenched Gwen from the ground and charged blindly out of the light's path — running as far as he could.

No sooner had they escaped than the fire rained down.

Flames as high and vast as the trees spouted from the earth behind him. They wrought all the ground they touched in a furious golden light, while everything around them fell to shadow. Kael held Gwen beneath him as the fires roared; her body shook with angry howls.

Though the scales of his armor kept his flesh from burning, Kael could still feel the heat. It was more a presence than anything: a serpent that lay coiled about him, its muscles poised to tighten. He knew that if his concentration wavered for even a moment, the heat would strangle them both. So he fought against it and held on tightly.

Just when he thought Gwen wouldn't last another moment, the fires abated.

The flames whipped away and died with a hiss against the frozen air. The winds that blew across them now were from the mountains — not the strange gusts of Ulric's spell. They carried the

162

smoke away, stirring up a monstrous cloud of ash from the charred earth behind them.

Kael's eyes still ached from the light. He watched as the shadows ahead of him became men and mages, as the archmage came into focus and as his dark eyes dragged from the sky and back onto Kael.

Sweat drenched his face and left a dark ring around the collar of his robes. When he saw Kael lived, the open-mouthed grin he wore slipped into a snarl. He raised his fist again, arm shaking with the effort —

"No!"

The cry didn't come from Ulric, but from Gwen. She shoved Kael away with such surprising force that he rolled to the side. She scrambled to her feet and took a few halting steps towards the charred land behind them before she fell to her knees. She collapsed as if she'd taken an arrow to the gut, and Kael thought she might be wounded.

He fell in beside her. There were raw, red burns across her face — gaps in her swirling paint, spots where a layer of her skin had peeled away. But as he reached for her wounds, she threw her fist into the side of his helmet and screamed:

"No!"

She struck him again, but he hardly felt it. The only thing he seemed able to feel was his gut as it plunged from his middle — evaporating before it struck the ground.

A circle of black stretched before them, a ring that'd obviously been meant to destroy the wildmen's front line. Though most had been swept backwards by the force of the wind, a few of the warriors had managed to hold their ground.

Now their bones lay in twisted heaps ... charred black as night.

"No ..." Gwen's voice was strangled, cracked in anguish. Her eyes were sharp with a mix of fury and pain. She dragged her fingers across her wounds and the rest of her skin turned as raw as her burns.

The warriors who'd been tossed aside by the wind had regained their footing. They came rushing through the cloud of ash at the sound of her cries. Their faces hardened at the sight of their companions' bodies. Anger boiled in their eyes.

Kael didn't have to grasp their hands to feel their fury, to hear the wild shrieking of their hearts. He saw it in their eyes, felt it in their stares. It washed over him in a furious, awakening heat; it added to his own molten rage. And by the time Kael turned, he was furious enough to shake the mountains.

Ulric must've seen the death scrawled in the dark of his eyes: his face turned ashen. He raised his fist higher and shouted words that Kael couldn't hear — he couldn't hear them because he was roaring, pouring all of his anger into a howl.

The cry that ripped from his throat grew — carried upwards and bolstered by the wildmen who crashed in behind him.

Ulric nearly tripped over his robes in his rush to get behind the soldiers. He ran between their ranks with his fist still raised, screaming: "Attack! Fight them, you fools!"

A block of soldiers stepped forward — Midlan seemed to think that was all they would need. The soldiers marched through the blue shield and its shimmering flesh clung wetly to their armor as they passed. The first rows dropped to one knee and raised their pikes, aiming for the wildmen's chests. Archers readied their arrows behind them. They moved swiftly, helmets turned upon the small pack of charging men.

Kael's boots thundered beneath him. He never once glanced at the deadly, glinting tips of the pikes but kept his eyes focused upon the soldier in front of him. The shaft of his weapon rested gently — lazily, even — between his armored fists. It wasn't until Kael was within ten paces that his grip tightened. His helmet dropped, and Kael imagined the soldier probably grinned when he realized the wildmen weren't going to stop. He likely thought the battle would be over by midday. But he was wrong.

It would be over much sooner than that.

Kael heard the screech of metal as the pike's tip shattered across his chest, saw the soldier's eyes widen through the slits of his helmet, illuminated briefly by a touch of the rising sun. Then there was wet, warmth — a scarlet wave that churned over his arm as the soldier's head rolled aside, hewed by the sharpened edges of his scales.

The warriors knocked the pikes aside with their shields, swatting the weapons away without ever breaking stride. They

164

dodged arrows with ease, swung their blades in relentless arcs for the soldiers' heads and chests.

When their swords broke, they swung their fists.

Kael had ripped his way to the middle of the horde when a burst of strange, muffled words came from the mages. Three of them stood together, sweat dripping off their chins as they struggled to hold the blue shield in place. But the rest had fallen back.

Now they cast a spell from behind the wall of soldiers. A thunderhead swelled over the ranks of Midlan, its rumbling edges bolstered by the mages' strange words. In mere seconds, it'd swelled to darken the sky above the Cleft. Seconds later, a torrent of blue-green lightning fell from the clouds.

It struck the earth with a crackling fury — cleft the hills and the rocks with its bolts. What little remained of Midlan's front ranks were melted inside their armor. But though the ground blackened and sank beneath their boots, the wildmen were unharmed.

Their battle slowed for a moment as the mothy tang of the spell washed over them. They blinked furiously, their eyes streamed against it. Even through the scales and his iron helmet, Kael could smell it — and he knew the wildmen could, as well.

Red filled his vision as the warrior in him roared. He saw only bits of things: the shield's blue flesh parting around his body, the blood pounding inside the mages' throats — the dark lines of fear that wreathed their eyes when he raised his fists ...

Bodies fell beneath his arms; wet warmth spattered across his face. The three mages that'd been left with the shield were now no more a worry than the rocks beneath his feet — and the scent of their blood drove the wildmen's strength to madness.

Gwen fell in beside him. She charged with her shield braced against her shoulder, knocking a whole row of soldiers onto their backs. Her axe split their helmets and her boots clomped down upon their chests. The crazed strength that filled every wire of her limbs sunk into Kael as she ground in beside him. She plastered herself to his shoulder, and he matched her blow for blow.

It wasn't long before he realized they were no longer battling Midlan: they warred with each other. Each tried to outfight the other — each tried to be the first to reach Ulric.

Each wanted to be the one to rip the ridging from his throat.

The army was just a spiny, gold-tinged wall in their path.

"Come back!"

The cry was faint at first — merely a scream that skittered across the tops of the soldiers' helmets. But the next time it came, Kael heard the magic in the command as Ulric's spell drove it to thunder:

"Come back! Come back and finish them, beast!"

Kael slowed; Gwen shoved past him. Blades shattered across his scales as Midlan tried to bring him down. A tidal wave of wildmen charged by and swept the soldiers back, but he hardly noticed:

Kael watched the skies.

Beast?

Something wriggled inside his head — the same nagging fear that'd clawed at him as he listened to Baird's story. It was impossible. He'd *told* himself it was impossible. Even now, he didn't want to believe it. But his feet seemed to have a mind of their own.

Kael raced back for the fields between the Cleft and Thanehold, to where the deep rumble of a storm had begun. As he watched, the clouds began to churn aside. They were little more than wisps of smoke against the thing that glided through them — the monster that brought the roaring winds.

Gales stirred the ash into an even thicker cloud. It rose and rushed for him, crashing over his body in the way the seas struck the rocks. The little flecks of ash hissed across his armor; charred bones crumbled and rolled past his boots.

From deep within the cloud of ash rose an enormous shadow.

It was the coming of a second storm — a second wave that darkened the skies. Kael felt as if he stood alone in the middle of the seas: there was a ship crashing towards him, its hull towering above the waves.

The way the earth trembled and shook as the shadow came to rest made Kael feel as if he stood atop the swells. He bent his knees against the jolting and managed to keep his feet. The shadow stopped mere paces before him, and the earth stopped its trembling. Behind him, the wildmen still howled and hacked their way through the King's men. But where Kael stood, in this cloud of ash between the earth and the monstrous shadow, the world was eerily quiet.

He felt it in his toes when the earth began to shake again. It seemed to quiver, moaning, until it finally gave way to a hum. The song was so low that Kael more felt than heard it — an utterance that rattled his chest and made the vein in his neck trill like bowstring. It pressed down upon him, put strain on his knees. Just when he thought he could bear the weight no longer, the song fell silent.

"What are you waiting for?" Ulric screamed, his voice crackling above them. "Kill him! Kill him now!"

The clang of a giant's sword rent the air and a glowing red line carved its way across the closest bit of shadow. It crackled like flame and screeched until Kael thought his ears might burst. Then quite suddenly, it stopped.

Two fires roared to life before him — two molten cores of flame. They burned with such a piercing yellow light that Kael felt their heat stabbing in the backs of his eyes. He looked at their middles, trying to find relief from the light.

Instead, he found something that stopped his breath.

Black crevices opened up in the middle of each eye — bottomless cracks hemmed on either side by dancing flame. They shone like the surface of a quiet pond: Kael saw himself gaping back in their reflection. The cracks narrowed to cut out his fists, his shoulders, until only his face and chest remained ...

Oh, no.

Oh, *no*.

Even when the cloud of ash parted around its curved horns and smoldering muzzle, even when its entire scaly head slid forward to within an arm's reach of his face, Kael couldn't believe it. He couldn't quite grasp it.

Somehow, a monstrous black dragon stood before him.

Then he saw the glowing collar around its neck and knew, with a realization that made ice crust along the tips of his fingers, what this meant — what it meant for this battle, for the wildmen ...

What it meant for the Kingdom.

"Kill him!"

Kael wasn't afraid of the dragon's flame: he'd once reached inside Kyleigh's fires and never felt the heat. He knew the dragonscale armor could protect him. So he planted his feet and prepared himself as the dragon's jaw cracked open.

A molten red tongue whipped lazily between teeth the size of pike blades, but no fire blossomed behind it. Kael's hair stood on end as the dragon's breath pressed against him and he realized that its mouth was coming closer: not to burn, but to feast — to crush, devour, or swallow entirely whole. Kael didn't know which it would be, but it didn't matter.

If he wanted to live, he had to move.

Kael threw himself to the ground, gasping when the dragon's chin scraped across him. The pointed scales at its base dragged down his back. A large chunk of his armor broke away, peeled aside by something stronger.

He tried not to panic. He scrambled away on hand and knee until he could pull himself back to his feet, all of his concentration bent on repairing his armor.

The dragon's head rose behind him. Its shadow eclipsed his boots even after Kael tried to dart away. It was simply too massive, its reach too great.

"Kill him! *Kill him!*"

Ulric's voice grew frenzied as the dragon's head snapped down. Kael felt the air hiss away from its chin, felt the pressure of its breath upon the back of his neck. He threw himself again, made one final, desperate lunge —

The screech of steel, an earth-rattling roar and the dragon's shadow jerked away. Kael flipped over in time to see the monster arch its neck towards the sky. An enraged hum made the pebbles on the earth beside him bounce in panic. The dragon hummed again and this time, a white bolt fell from the sky in answer — knocking its great head aside with a roar that made Kael's heart pound in answer.

It was Kyleigh.

CHAPTER 17
DEVIN AND THE DRAGON

You dare to strike me, she-dragon? You dare to fight?

The scales across Kyleigh's back bunched together tightly at the power in his voice. She'd been stuck inside that cave for what seemed like an eternity, waiting for the black dragon to appear.

Her ears still rang with the memories of Silas's yowling threats. He'd roared at her until he went hoarse, slapped her scales until he bruised his paws. But her plan had worked: Gwen had been troubled enough by Silas's disappearance that she'd readied the wildmen for battle.

Now they beat against Midlan with a fury unmatched by anything she'd ever seen. The wildmen in the Cleft were so maddened by the fight that they didn't seem to notice the enormous black dragon crouched behind them.

But the warriors in Thanehold had certainly noticed.

She turned her back on the black dragon, sailing in a wide arc along the path of the wind. As she prepared to fall, she saw that the warriors had abandoned the ramparts and rushed inside the keep. She wagered they would return in a few moments — armed with their dragonsbane weapons.

She had to move quickly.

A part of her cringed as she plummeted from the clouds. It begged her not to fight the black dragon, screamed that she would be crushed in an instant if she struck him again. His eyes were already fixed upon her — she didn't have to fight him.

But Kyleigh didn't listen.

Her wings folded tightly at her sides as she plunged towards the earth. The sky screamed past her; the wind shrieked inside her ears. Though the black dragon grew larger every second, she hardly glanced at him: all the power of her eyes was locked upon that stubborn man from the mountains.

Kael was all right. He was covered in gore from battle and ash from his dive, but he wasn't wounded. The slits in his helmet were turned towards her. She strained to hear the words he shouted, tried to etch his every detail into her mind.

In the second before she struck, Kyleigh's gaze shot to the black dragon. She had to move quickly — not because she feared the wildmen would kill him ... but because she wanted to kill him, herself.

Her claws snapped open; she aimed for his head. And as she struck, a furious song burst from her throat: *Harm my mate, and you answer to me!*

The black dragon growled as her claws glanced his face.

Kyleigh swore. Her wings burst open and she beat them for the clouds. A ringing pain ran from the tips of her claws and through the bones of her hands. She felt as if she'd just slung her fist into a castle wall.

It all came back to her in a rush. The black dragon's scales were far too thick: he was built for war, armored enough to be able to defend his lands against other males. The teeth and claws he wielded were powerful enough to rip through anything.

That's what her dragon half had been screaming about. It wasn't that he didn't deserve to be beaten — it was that she *couldn't* beat him.

"Stop her, beast! Stop the Dragongirl!"

Kyleigh couldn't even pause to grin at Ulric's panicked screams. Spells burst upwards into the clouds: she heard them whistling towards her and dodged them with ease. But the one thing she couldn't dodge was that great, black beast of a dragon. And in half a moment, he'd burst through the clouds.

Her scales bunched again as he spewed flame across her. His breath was a final warning: a promise that if she didn't turn away now, he would slaughter her. She waited until the bright yellow had raged across her vision before she fired back.

Flames burst from her lungs and roared up her throat. They spilled past her tongue and directly into his burning eyes. It was a good shot — and she knew by how he roared that it would cost her dearly.

So she flew for the mountains.

The jagged peaks were difficult to navigate even on clearer days. With the clouds hanging so low across their tops, she hoped the black dragon would have a difficult time catching her. If she was lucky, he might even strike a cliff face and end this whole mess of a fight.

She wove in and out of the peaks, his breath boiling on her tail. His great wings turned him slowly, but he was clever: he seemed able to sense which peak she would go around next, seemed to know which path she would take to reach it. Soon his great head had eclipsed her tail and she knew it was only a matter of time before he clamped down. In a panic, she headed straight for a crack between the peaks.

Its walls were so narrow that she nearly got stuck between them. She folded her wings tightly and scrambled across the last hundred paces of wall before she plunged out of the other side and into the air beyond —

A darkened flash, a searing pain, a force so strong it knocked her off her wings. Kyleigh tumbled from the sky, bouncing and crashing along the gushing vein of a waterfall — blinded by a mix of frosted water and her own fiery blood. She opened her wings and landed clumsily in the shallow edge of an icy pool. The clouds were gray and silent above her, but she knew the black dragon was coming.

Her face stung badly. She didn't know how much of it was left, but she didn't have time to worry.

A ledge protruded from beneath the spray of the falls. She dragged herself into her human form and stumbled towards it on two legs — through the frozen wet and into the dark relief of a shallow cave.

Though the waters roared inside her ears, she still breathed too loudly. Harbinger's song was hushed as she drew him from his sheath. He sat firmly in her grip and his smooth weight calmed her. Blood slid down her nose and off her chin as she waited. It struck the frozen water on the floor and disappeared into a cloud of steam, hissing as it cooled.

Her breath caught inside her throat as the sky went dark for a moment. The black dragon's mighty wings made the pines screech just outside the cave. But Kyleigh didn't move.

Long minutes passed when she did nothing more than stand and listen. She strained to hear above the bellowing of the falls, tried to sift through the nearly-overpowering scent of her blood to catch even the slightest hint of the dragon's coming. He would find her — of that, she was certain. Her dragon half whispered it was only a matter of moments, now. It urged her to be brave.

So when she saw his shadow approaching a second time, she set her feet and prepared to meet him.

A man's form slithered in behind the falls. His figure seemed to tremble as he approached — the thousands of rushing droplets that spewed from the rocks gave his head and shoulders the dancing life of flame. He towered above her, standing easily at a giant's height. The shadow paused just outside, silent as a wraith behind the curtain of water.

Waiting.

A red line bloomed across his throat. His collar glowed and hissed like the noise of a sword's blade grating against stone. Then he moved.

Icy water rushed across his body in a torrent: it forced his head downward and flattened his dark crop of hair against his face. Crystal veins snaked down his bare shoulders and chest. They bumped across the lines carved into his middle — lines topped by thin ridges of blackened scales.

More scales covered his knees and the tops of his toes. She traced them upwards back to his fingers, and saw the full backs of his hands were entirely covered in a shield of shining black. Deadly spurs twisted up from his elbows.

His chin hung against his chest and a shadow cloaked his face — one that seemed to be made darker by his collar's molten glow. His breaths were deep and practiced. They rumbled inside his chest as if he'd drawn them in for a thousand years, until the labor had worn his innards smooth.

The air between them sharpened. He was going to attack.

Kyleigh swung Harbinger for his middle, prepared to fight to her death. But his hand shot out and grasped her wrist in a vice. He slammed her against the wall so forcefully that Harbinger fell from her grasp. The stone behind her knuckles broke with a crack.

He was going to kill her. He was going to crush her where she stood —Kyleigh felt this warning tremble along every string of his muscle, heard it in the collar's screech. Still, she fought.

Her fist collided with his middle. She struck him again and again, hoping to stumble him backwards — but he never so much as twitched. Even when she swung for his chin, his head never moved. She stomped on his toes.

Nothing.

His grip only tightened ... the warning grew fiercer. Pain wracked her wound and made the insides of her ears go hot. Her fist struck him feebly, now. She doubted if he even felt it.

Then all at once, the trembling stopped. The warning grew faint.

Though the collar still glowed about his neck, the anger was gone — whooshing like air through an opened door. And in the silence it left behind, he drew a ragged breath.

"This pain the spellweavers bring upon me ... it's nearly unbearable," he rumbled. The hand that held her wrist to the wall trembled slightly, and he leaned against her. "I bear it only because I know a much greater pain."

His fingers snaked about her wrist. His grip wasn't strangling. If anything, the way he held her seemed almost ... desperate. It was as if he feared to let her go.

When he spoke again, his voice was hollow: "But had I known that to suffer in this way would bring me to your side once more, I would have suffered it sooner. I would have taken on this weaker flesh long ago. I would have borne my humiliation with pride. There's not a shred of my soul I wouldn't have gladly torn away to see you again, my heart."

Kyleigh froze.

Dark memories glided behind her eyes and drifted away, their meanings hidden well within their shadowy flesh. There was a reason the black dragon seemed so familiar, why his voice made pictures flash inside her head.

A part of her had known him, once ... and perhaps it'd even loved him ...

Deep inside the quiet black of her memories, something stirred. It drifted from the waves and wriggled tentatively towards the shore, but Kyleigh shoved it back.

She didn't care about who this dragon was, or who he might've been. It didn't matter what her two souls had done before: their pasts *belonged* in the depths. No, this new life was the only thing that concerned her now. The things she'd done as *Kyleigh* were the things that deserved the light.

Nothing else mattered.

A low, hissing moan escaped the halfdragon's throat. Then slowly, his chin lifted from his chest. Shadows fled his eyes — revealing a pair of burning yellow orbs set beneath his brows. Black scales bumped down the bridge of his nose. They stretched from the bottom of his lower lip to cross his chin.

"My bond, my heart ..."

His eyes wrapped around hers, consuming her with their blaze. Her spine stiffened as his fingers wrapped around her other wrist. He held her arms against the cave's wall and crouched to her height.

Kyleigh's eyes brimmed with tears as the pressure of his body made blood pound behind her wounds. Her head swam with it. All feeling left her legs as the pain became too much. In seconds, the darkness would consume her. She would be unconscious, helpless ...

"What have I done to you?"

His gasp startled her. The pressure of his body relented and his hands opened, releasing her.

"The spellweaver's curse did this." Flames swelled inside his eyes as they scraped menacingly across the ruins of her face. "He made me hurt you. He — *argh!*" The halfdragon ripped furiously at his collar, but the molten iron didn't give way ... and he didn't stop. Not even when sweat ran down his face and his eyes went glassy with pain.

"Stop — stop it!" Kyleigh didn't know what had come over her. After how he'd gone after Kael, the halfdragon deserved to be hurt. Still, there was something about his voice, his words ... she couldn't help but pity him. "You can't break it like that. The curse is too strong. You'll only hurt yourself."

He stopped at the pressure of her hands against his scaly arms. He peeled his fingers from the collar and scowled at their pads. "The spellweaver will pay for this," he growled after a moment. "He thinks I'll bring you to him ... but we will make him *pay.*" He spat that last word, and then his eyes went back to her face. "I cannot let you suffer. I cannot see you hurt ..."

"Don't touch me," Kyleigh growled. She tried to knock his hands away, but he was too strong. His human body was as unrelenting as his scales. He was going to crush her skull, squeeze the life from her throat. She bared her teeth as his fingers clutched her chin —

174

A gasp, a roar of pain, and the pressure was gone. The halfdragon stumbled backwards and fell to his knees. He grasped his hand before his face. Her blood hissed and boiled on the tips of his fingers. He stared in disbelief at the little bubbles that popped along the scarlet stain before his chin dragged up to hers.

His eyes were wrought with pain — the purest, most unshadowed anguish she'd ever seen. The collar burned his throat; her blood boiled his flesh. Angry welts covered his face from where she'd struck him. But for all that, he'd never grimaced.

This pain, though ... this seemed to break him.

"My heart?" He choked on the words, brows creasing to frame the agony that filled his stare.

Kyleigh said nothing. She snatched Harbinger from the ground, never once taking her eyes from the halfdragon — and he never once took his eyes from hers. Not even when she'd pressed the tip of the blade against his throat did his stare waver.

Instead, he roared.

Red singed his flesh for a moment. Flames sputtered weakly inside his gaze. His chin fell back to his chest and he roared again. He seemed to forget Kyleigh was there: he roared at the mountains, at the skies — at something larger and greater than anything that might walk the earth. She'd begun to fear that he would lunge for her again and raised Harbinger high.

"Gah! Ah!" His roar rose in pitch; his rumbling voice gave way to the cries of a young man. The halfdragon dove aside and plunged his hand into a puddle on the cave floor.

Steam rose in a hissing cloud. His other hand shook as he wiped the cooled blood from his fingers. Kyleigh watched, not daring to breathe, as the red of his collar flickered and went out — becoming cool iron once more.

"What was that? What happened?" the halfdragon said, still in the voice of a young man. He rushed to his feet, cradling his wounded hand against his chest. His chin swung to Kyleigh and her stomach flipped when she saw how his eyes had changed.

The flames and the yellow were gone from them, replaced by a stark blue.

He looked as startled as she did. He seemed to forget his hand as he took a half step towards her. "You ... you're like me, aren't you?"

A gasping laugh burst from his throat and before Kyleigh could move, he'd grabbed her hand.

He smiled at her, and she was shocked to see relieved tears brimming along the crease of his eyes. He clutched her fingers tightly to his palm — as if he'd have thrown his arms around her in an instant. "I thought I was all alone! I thought I was the only one left. But here you are, sister." He smiled widely, squeezed her hand tight. "Here you are."

Kyleigh didn't know what to say. Her face had swollen so horribly around her wounds that her head felt like one enormous, throbbing mess. The young man's face blurred at each throb, his curious smile slipping in and out of focus.

The dragon in him was an old and tired thing — a spirit full of strength and pain. But this young man seemed the opposite of him in every way: his eyes were light in spite of his wounds, he clutched her as if they'd been friends for ages. And as much as she'd wanted to slaughter the dragon ... she couldn't wish this boy any harm.

"I'm Devin." He bent to a less formidable height. "Who are you?"

She focused through the pain long enough to mumble: "Kyleigh."

"Kyleigh ..." His eyes brightened for a moment. Then they fell dark. "What happened to your face, Kyleigh?"

When she didn't answer, he scowled.

"It was *him*, wasn't it? He's always hurting people — I hate him! I want him out!" His hand tore from hers and went to his head. He tugged on the dark crop of his hair, as if he might somehow be able to rip the dragon from his skull. "How do you stand it? How do you stand having them in there — hurting everybody, ruining everything? How do I ...? Oh, no."

A weak red light began to glow inside his collar. He stumbled away from her, grimacing and clutching his throat.

"Oh, it's happening again! I can hear the voices." Devin bit his lip hard and grabbed the blistered tips of his fingers with his good hand. He squeezed until the color fled his face and tears rolled down his cheeks. But under his pain, the collar's light went out.

Kyleigh knew what was happening. She might not have cared for the dragon, but there was something about this boy that made her heart lurch. "Wait — don't leave!" She struggled forward as Devin bent to duck out the cave's mouth. "I can help you!"

"No, you can't. No one can. I've done too many horrible things. I've hurt far too many people. My only chance is to get as far away from that mage as possible. I have to run ..." The stark blue sharpened suddenly as he focused on something behind his eyes. "I know where to go ... I see it in my dreams, sometimes. They can't follow me there. I'll be safe." He smiled hard. "And you'll be safe too, sister."

It happened too quickly. Kyleigh hardly had a chance to protest before he threw his arms about her and whispered:

"Goodbye."

CHAPTER 18
A DIFFERENT ENDING

Kael watched as she fell like an arrow from the sky. A blast of wind, a streak of ash, and Kyleigh was gone — darting back into the thick maw of the clouds.

The black dragon's wings snapped open and sent out a violent burst of air. Its wicked yellow eyes burned into the spot where Kyleigh had disappeared; its collar screeched like a pot coming to boil. Its powerful limbs coiled beneath its rumbling chest.

There was no time to think. Kael grabbed the dragonsbane dagger from his belt — the only weapon he had that might possibly reach the black dragon in time. He took his aim just as its great wings unfurled, blinding him with a haze of ash. No sooner had he managed to lock onto one of the dragon's eyes than its wings snapped violently down.

The blast knocked Kael's body aside. He rolled backwards in a wave of overturned earth, holding the dagger out to keep from accidentally skewering himself. His armor clanked as the world spun by. Somehow, he managed to latch onto the surface of a jagged rock and stop the earth from spinning. He held on tightly as the wave of grit and rock crashed over him. Only when the winds had passed did he dare to open his eyes.

"Find the Dragongirl! Bring her to me!"

Ulric's voice boomed through the air above the Cleft, and Kael suddenly understood. The silver chains around the archmage's wrist had called the dragon down. It was tied to his voice, as Titus's beasts had been tied to his will.

The black dragon was gone: he'd vaulted his great body miles above the clouds, and Kael knew he had no hope of reaching him. But Kyleigh was impossibly fast. She'd been nothing more than a blur when she fell to strike the dragon. He knew she could outrun him easily.

And while she ran, Kael would take care of Ulric.

He tore to his feet and pounded his way across the earth to the mouth of the Cleft — where the wildmen still warred with Midlan. There were too many bodies in the way. He couldn't see any of the mages through the writhing mass of armor and fur, but he knew they would be somewhere near the back of the ranks — if they hadn't already fled.

The soldiers of Midlan weren't giving up the fight. They pressed tightly against the wildmen, bracing their companions' bodies up like a wall. It would only earn them a few moments more: the wildmen would soon hack their way through.

Kael was close enough to see the patterns across the wildmen's flesh when the Cleft suddenly began to shake. The warriors' charge slowed as they tried to hold their footing on the bouncing earth. They gaped down, but the real danger was above them.

"Get out!" Kael roared when he saw how the walls of the Cleft shook. "Get out, or you'll be crushed!"

The wildmen followed his shouts and saw the danger. They left the battle behind and tore for the fields. Two of them dragged Gwen out by the arms. Her boots flailed wildly and an impressive trail of curses streamed from her mouth. She'd beaten the soldiers so severely that her axe's blades were bent beyond recognition.

With the help of two more warriors, the wildmen managed to carry her away — and not a moment too soon.

Kael watched in horror as the Cleft's walls collapsed. Monstrous boulders cracked from their tops and stormed downwards — dragging sheets of stone along with them. The noise was every bit as deafening as the chaos inside a tempest's heart: he swore the rumbling lasted a full minute. He couldn't hear the soldiers' screams, couldn't see the terror upon their faces. But the way their armored bodies flailed at the last told him everything.

In a moment, the army was gone. Silence descended upon the Valley — silence, and a ghostly cloud of earth. Kael was still gaping at it when he heard the thunder of steps behind him.

The warriors that'd been left to guard Thanehold came pouring out. They carried armfuls of golden weapons that they passed around the others. One of them tossed a golden axe to Gwen.

She threw the bent remains of her weapon aside and caught it with a snarl. Dark spatters of blood adorned the swirling lines of her paint. Even from several paces back, he could smell the death wafting from her.

"We'll gut the dragon," Gwen promised the wildmen darkly. "But first, I want that mage's head!"

She hurled her shield with such force that it splintered against the rocks. The warriors howled at the noise of its shattering and tore back for the Cleft. They ripped stones from the fallen pile, cast boulders aside. Kael was about to go after them when a wild yell made him jump.

"No, my Thane! There is danger behind those rocks!"

Silas burst from the snow and into the charred circle — bare, except for the flopping corpse of a white rabbit that he had clamped to his front. His eyes were wide, their glow sharp and wild. The earth must've still been hot: the way he leapt gingerly from one foot to the next made it look as if he danced a madman's jig.

But though he was obviously in pain, he still managed to hop his way to Gwen. "The King's swordbearers wait behind it — *ow!* They've come to — *oh!* — to harm you!"

"We've already dealt with the soldiers," Gwen said, shoving him towards Thanehold. "Get out of here before you hurt yourself, c —"

"No, there's more," Silas insisted. The rabbit's limbs flailed piteously as he hopped back to within a hand's breadth of Gwen. The motion likely would've snapped its neck, had it not already been so thoroughly stiff with death. "The King has sent his dragon, and — *yow!* — and his shamans! You must turn back, my Thane. You mustn't chase them. There will be nothing but fire and death if you follow."

Gwen grabbed Silas by the shoulders and flung him away. "Get back to the castle —"

"But it's true!"

"I *know* it's true!" The muscles in Gwen's arms swelled and Silas turned white as the rabbit's fur when she lifted his body from the ground. "I've seen the King's dragon, I've battled his mages! His fire has already devoured my warriors. And if you cared even a whit about us, you wouldn't have run away. You would've warned me sooner."

Her voice tightened over those final words. The rage in her glare was frayed, dissolving at its edges into something that made Silas's eyes go dim.

"I *do* care. I tried to reach you, my Thane," he whimpered. "But the dragoness trapped me — she stuffed me inside a cave and blocked it with her great scaly rump. Ask the Marked One!" He held the rabbit in one hand and used the other to thrust an accusing finger at Kael. "He can tell you the truth! I'm certain he was a part of her plan."

He'd actually known nothing about it — and the fact that Silas seemed to know everything before he did burned him all the more. But before he could even think to be furious, Gwen was upon him.

She ripped the helmet from his head. Her face turned scarlet. "*You!*"

"Yes, it's me," Kael said sharply. "And if it hadn't *been* for me, you'd be de —"

The screech of iron cut over the top of his words. Gwen ripped the helmet down its middle as if it were no more difficult a feat than shredding parchment.

Kael had to move quickly to avoid getting struck by its jagged halves.

"You lied to me — you *tricked* me!"

"I saved your sorry arse!"

"The pest used me," she hissed, turning her glare to the sky. "This was all just a part of her mischief. She brought Midlan here. She used the wildmen to fight him while she slipped away."

"No, this was my idea," Kael said sharply. "If you would've just listened to me in the first place, none of this would have —"

"*You* did this?" Her eyes burned when he nodded; her lips peeled back from her teeth in a snarl that might've frightened a wolf. Behind her, Silas quickly dropped into his lion form and darted out of reach.

Kael tried to speak calmly. "We didn't use you. This wasn't about *slipping away* — it was about putting a stop to Midlan. Why would Crevan send an army after Kyleigh when he knows that their swords would be no use? Think about it, Gwen," he said when her face burned redder. "The King never meant to simply capture her and leave. He planned to take the Valley the same way he's taken the seas. Crevan's lost his grip on the Kingdom, and he means to get it back."

For half a breath, her glare wavered. Kael stood still — as if to move even an inch would undo what little ground he'd gained. But in the end, it didn't matter.

"Wildmen died today," Gwen said, her words deathly quiet. "They've left their wives without husbands and children without mothers. They are friends I'll never see again ... and it's all because of you."

Her words stung him for half a moment before he realized that she was wrong.

No, this wasn't his fault. He'd done everything he could to help the wildmen. If Gwen had stopped scoffing at him long enough to listen, they might've had a decent plan. They never would've marched straight out into the open. When he told the warriors to let go, *she* was the one who'd ordered them to hold their ground. Had she only listened, they might still be alive.

The weight of their blood belonged to Gwen, and Gwen alone. He had every right to yell this at her, to throw it all back into her face. But when he saw the glass that covered her eyes and the raw, red anguish behind it, he found he didn't have the heart to say these things aloud.

She already knew it.

"I'm not your enemy," Kael said quietly. "I've been trying to help you, for mercy's sake! Don't you understand? The King isn't going to stop — he'll call his army down upon every hold across the realm, he'll send his dragon to turn their bones to ash. The wildmen are the only people who have any chance against him. You're the only ones who can stop him. The Kingdom needs your help."

"The Kingdom's forgotten us. I owe it nothing. You've done enough, mutt," she added, turned back for the Cleft. "I don't want to see your face in my lands again."

It was the excitement of battle that was making her snarl at him — it had to be. Nobody in her right mind could've possibly thought the King's fight would end here. She couldn't honestly believe this was his fault.

But there was no room left to be calm. Kael's frustration had finally boiled to the top of his head. He could hold it back no longer: "You're a fool, Gwen. In fact, I don't think I've ever met anybody so ridiculous. The King's going to come back to Thanehold — and next time, his army will be ready to fight the whisperers."

She said nothing. She never so much as turned. Kael wanted nothing more than to march as far as he could in the other direction, but Ulric was behind those rocks.

And he had to be stopped.

No sooner had Kael begun to jog than a familiar roar drew his gaze to the clouds. Kyleigh swooped down in front of him, landing with such force that the wind coming off her wings nearly knocked him backwards. But shock kept him on his feet.

Large cuts split her face — from the side of her forehead and across the bridge of her nose, down to the tip of her chin. The green of her eyes was muted and glassy with pain. Kael didn't even remember moving: the next thing he knew, his hands were upon her face.

Her words burst inside his head: *No, there's no time.*

"It'll only take a moment. I can't let you —"

I'll be fine. We have a chance to stop him, Kyleigh said, the fires in her eyes rising against the pain. *The dragon's curse is weakened. If we can reach him, we can put an end to this. But we have to go* now.

Kael wanted her nowhere near the black dragon. He'd felt how easily it'd torn through his scales. The wounds on Kyleigh's face were the marks of its claws, and he had a feeling the dragon had been responsible for the tear in her armor, as well.

No, there had to be a better way. He turned back to the Cleft. "Ulric is on the other side of those rocks. If you can get me close, I can kill him."

Ulric is gone — I've already looked. He never stays for long, once the tide turns. I'll bet he slithered off the moment he felt the curse weaken. Believe me, I'd like nothing more than to gut him. Her snout twisted in what could've only been an expression of contempt. *But he's too quick.*

She lowered her wing, waiting for him to climb on. But Kael couldn't. "This is madness, Kyleigh. We've got no chance at all against that dragon — it'll tear us from the skies!"

His curse is weakened, she said again, as if that utterance should've done everything to assure him. *I know he won't harm us.*

"How could you possibly know that?"

I can sense it, she growled. *The King's curse maddens its victims — it makes them do horrible things. Don't you remember what it did to Jake?*

Yes, Kael remembered. They would've lost a very dear friend, had they not set him free. But then again ... Jake had never carved lines down Kyleigh's face. If he had, that story might've had a different ending.

183

"All right," Kael said after a moment.

By the time he'd pulled himself onto her back, his mind was already made up. Perhaps she was right: perhaps the dragon really *was* harmless. But if it wasn't, if its claws curled or one of its wicked eyes so much as twitched towards Kyleigh, he would put a dagger straight through the middle of its blackened slit.

The dragon wouldn't get another chance to harm her.

CHAPTER 19
THE VOICE OF THE MOUNTAINS

Griffith watched the pest as she thudded into the charred field. The man who ran up to her must've been Kael. They talked for a moment, their heads close. Griffith squinted through the clouds of whipping snow as they spoke. He tried to see what they were saying.

After a moment, Kael climbed onto the pest's back. She took off with a burst of her wings and turned her head towards the ramparts. For a moment, Griffith thought they might be coming back.

He slung his arm at them and his lungs filled with a howl. But they didn't stop. The pest tore over Thanehold and beat for the mountains.

Griffith watched until the clouds swallowed them up, frowning.

"Where are they going?" one of the craftsmen hollered at him. With the warriors gone, a few of the bravest had inched their way up the rampart steps. Now they stood clustered beside him, their thin arms clinging to the walls as the winds beat against their frail bodies.

Behind him, a large crowd gathered in the village square. Most of the craftsmen waited beneath the safety of the walls, along with the folk from downmountain. All of their faces were turned expectantly towards Griffith.

"I don't know where the pest has gone, but it looks as if our Thane is making good time." He turned back to the Cleft and couldn't contain his grin as he watched the warriors cast a hill of boulders aside. "The wildmen will have Midlan split wide by evening."

Cheers sounded behind him, and Griffith allowed himself a sigh of relief.

It'd been a difficult fight. When he closed his eyes, he could still see the pillar of fire that'd erupted from the clouds. His chest froze and his stomach dropped. All the while the fires raged, he didn't take a single breath. But Kael had kept Gwen safe. He'd thrown her from the fire's path.

Griffith just wished the others had been so lucky.

185

The longer the warriors dug, the tighter he gripped his sword. He longed to charge in beside them. Heat surged through his limbs at the thought of joining their ranks. But Gwen had ordered him to stay put — and he knew he had to listen.

Still, his hand twisted tightly about his sword as he paced, his jaw set tight. Every inch of him was coiled and bunched — ready to spring over the ramparts at a moment's trouble.

"One day it'll be you leading the charge, young Griff," a craftsman called from where he clutched one of the iron braziers. Though the wind tried to rip him away, his mouth still split in a knowing grin. "Just a bit more height on those legs, a bit more bulk on those arms, and you'll be set for crushing skulls."

"I'm set *now*," Griffith insisted.

He thrust his sword in a wide arc, but the craftsmen only laughed. A few tussled his stripe of hair as he strode by them.

Several moments passed with Griffith swinging absently at the ground before a loud whistle pierced the air beneath him:

"Make way — make *way*, blast you!" Baird cried. A pair of downmountain folk led him gently through the crowd. Even though everyone moved out of his way, he still barked like mad. "I heard the crashing of the earth, felt the touch of a strange wind. The wretched shrieks of mages filled my poor old ears. But now silence cloaks the battlefield. Tell me, young Griffith," he called when he reached the bottom of the rampart stairs. "Are the mages defeated? Have their spells been silenced?"

"Not yet. But as soon as our Thane breaks through those rocks, they will be."

More cheers followed his words. Hard smiles covered the wildmen's faces.

Only Baird seemed upset. "No, he promised me! Kael the Wright swore he would silence the mages at the very first. They can't be left to sit, they can't be left to think — that's precisely how mages become trouble!"

"He's cracked," one of the craftsmen muttered. "If he'd seen how Gwen dealt with that first line, he wouldn't be worried. There's hardly a smudge left of them."

Griffith agreed. Still, he knew how wild Baird could get. "I'm sure they've run off by now," he said carefully.

"Run off?" Baird sputtered. "No, they won't run off — they *can't* run off. The King will keep them here. He won't bear so great a slight. He won't bear it, I tell you! Oh, he'll think of something." Baird's hands twisted into the front of his robes. His head turned to the ground and his voice sounded as if he spoke to someone else: "He'll think of something, won't he? Yes, Crevan *always* thinks of something ..."

Though most of what Baird said was nonsense, he spoke so grandly that many of the downmountain folk had taken him for some sort of wise man. Muttering filled the courtyard at his words; smiles fell into frowns.

As he watched them, Griffith's middle began to squirm.

"We must stop the mages, young Griffith! We mustn't delay," Baird cried.

"We'll have them stopped soon enough. There's no point in worrying over it," a craftsman shot back.

An argument erupted. Their voices sounded like screams inside Griffith's ears: the words sharpened until they lost their meaning, the voices melted into a pile of mush.

Soon, his head rang so fiercely that he could no longer tell who spoke. The screams swirled around his ears until they plunged inside his head — where they erupted into a storm.

Can't do anything ... must *do something ... the Thane needs ... skin our hides if we go ... must go ... be killed ... we'll* all *be killed ... he'll think of something ... always thinks of ...*

The screams dulled and the voices began to quiet. Griffith ran his fingers across the smooth surface of his marble — an orb made of stone-ice from the summit. Its flesh cooled his burning ears. He rolled it between his fingers, trying to untangle the knot of voices inside his head.

Every dip and turn followed the path of a different voice. He traced each one carefully, pulling it apart from the next until he could hear them all. But through the crowd inside his ears, one calm utterance rose above the rest:

"You must trust me, young Griffith. The wildmen need our help."

When he opened his eyes, he saw that Baird stood within an arm's reach. He'd crawled his way up the frozen steps. His knobby hand reached out. The pads of his fingers were worn as smooth as stone.

"I can stop the mages ... but I lack the strength to battle the winds, to cross these frozen lands. You must lead me out," he pleaded, his bandaged face lined with deep cracks. "I need your strength."

The bard's words calmed him: they cooled his heart like the stone-ice cooled his flesh — ringing clearly above the others. Griffith always followed the clearest voice. The words that struck him loudest would lead him onto the best path.

The marble just helped him see it.

"Keep watch from the ramparts —"

"But, Thane-child —"

"I'll be back before you have time to worry," Griffith said firmly.

He sheathed his sword and took Baird by one of his knobby arms. The bard's hands latched onto him tightly. Griffith tried to ignore the muttering as he marched through the crowd. The downmountain folk sounded relieved, but the craftsmen thought him a fool.

Still, Griffith kept his chin high. He tried to walk the way Gwen did: straight-shouldered and with heavy steps. "Craftsmen, let us out," he demanded when they reached the wall.

They obeyed — though several grumbled as they worked.

The craftsmen peeled the wall away, careful to stand to the side as winter came blasting in. Baird's hands dug in tightly as the wind tried to knock his body away. Griffith braced him with an arm and bent his head against the gales.

It was an angry wind, the last breath of winter — the time that Thane Evan had called the Wailing Week. He remembered how winter used to shake the summit with its dying gasps. It'd blown so fiercely that Thane Evan had ordered them all to stay inside the walls during the Wailing. But here, the cold's fury wasn't nearly as fierce.

Griffith dropped his shoulder into it, dragging Baird along. He grinned when he felt the angry winds give way.

It was only when the walls had closed behind them and they'd marched halfway across the frozen field that Griffith's heart began to pound. Something like webs of ice snaked their way up his legs. Gwen really *would* be furious with him for leaving.

Even from a distance, he could see how she stalked back and forth before the pile of rocks inside the Cleft. He could tell by how much snow sprayed up from her boots that she was furious — and she hadn't even seen him yet.

He could only imagine how much angrier she'd be when she caught him dragging a blind man through the wind ...

"Courage," Baird called, as if he could sense how Griffith's chin twisted back. "You must trust me as you've never trusted another soul. My words must be your anchor, your mighty sword. I cannot stop you, should you choose to turn back. But the whole fate of your people rests squarely upon your shoulders. Are you prepared to carry it?"

"Yes," Griffith said, though his throat tightened around the word.

The way Baird gripped his arm assured him. He clung to Griffith as if to let go would send him rolling across the fields and smack into the castle walls. Surely he wouldn't have risked stepping out if there wasn't any danger.

Surely he was doing what was right.

"Courage now, young Griffith," Baird called again. "No matter what you hear or what you see, you must carry me towards the fight. You must be my strength. We must not turn back."

Griffith nodded and plunged ahead.

They were a hundred paces from the Cleft when he heard it: a mass of voices twisted together, chanting along the path of the wind. The voices grew sharper, louder. Their strange words grated against Griffith's ears.

"Courage," Baird bellowed. "Courage!"

Griffith ground his teeth against the magic and pressed on, pulling Baird close behind him. A shadow covered his boots, scraped across his head. Then all at once, he felt the earth tremble. Swears erupted inside the Cleft. The warriors closest to the wall toppled over; the rest struggled to keep their balance.

A monster rose from the drifts before him — a beast with its flesh made from the rocky earth. Snow rolled from its back in a mist. Its head burst from the ground and charged towards them, crashing through the warriors as if they were no more trouble than dust.

Griffith grabbed Baird as the monster charged towards them. The way the earth shook beneath its coming made him realize that the mound they saw was merely the monster's head — the rest of its body was far beneath the surface.

He ran as far as he could and held Baird tightly as the monster passed. The earth jolted him, made his vision bounce and ached his head. Still, he managed to keep his footing until the monster was little more than a rumble in the distance.

"What was —?"

"Closer! Bring me closer!"

Griffith marched a few paces more before panicked screams filled the air behind him. He turned and saw with a jolt that the monster hadn't disappeared: its great head struck against Thanehold.

The rocky mound of its head was pressed against the outer walls while its body kicked the earth beneath the village. Their walls shook, their towers swayed. Above them, the cliffs seemed about to collapse: massive sheets of rock cracked and fell from the mountain's flesh, shattering just outside the castle. White clouds raced down from the snow at its top.

As more rock broke from its base, the cliff top leaned dangerously over Thanehold. The screams were swallowed up for a moment as the mountain groaned. It crushed the whole castle beneath its shadow. Griffith had known warriors who were killed by much smaller rockslides. If those cliffs fell upon Thanehold, the castle and everyone in it would be crushed.

His heart slammed as he watched several tiny figures fall from the ramparts — thrown from their posts by the castle's shaking. He kept waiting for the walls to open, for people to start coming out. But if the warriors in the Cleft couldn't even hold their footing, he knew the craftsmen had no chance.

They were trapped.

A band of warriors peeled from the Cleft and charged for the field. Silas led them with a roar, snow churning up from the beat of his powerful legs. Gwen sprinted close behind him. Her eyes widened at the sight of Griffith and her voice went sharp:

"Get back to the castle! You can reach it — get our people out!"

Her words frightened him; the panic in her eyes froze his legs.

Then Baird's hands bit forcefully into his arm. "No, we haven't the time, we mustn't stop — we must reach the mages! Bring me closer!"

Gwen's face burned red. The golden axe hissed as she cut it through the air. "Run!"

Every part of him wanted to turn back for Thanehold. The cliffs screamed, the castle groaned. In moments, his people would be crushed to death beneath the rocks. Griffith turned ...

"Press on!" Baird cried from behind him. "Courage! *Courage*!"

Ahead, Gwen lashed him with a furious howl. The warriors began to scream:

"What are you doing?"

"Your people need you!"

"Come on, Griff — *run*!"

Their voices hurt his ears. He didn't know what to do. Silas charged by and the warriors burned him with their glares. Gwen was growing steadily larger. He could see the fury wrought in each line of her eyes, felt his limbs begin to shrink beneath it.

There were too many glares, too many screams. They danced before him and shook his head with the force of that monster's flesh. Even Baird's voice was lost to it. Snow stung his eyes. He reached blindly for the marble.

As it rolled between his fingers, one word cut through the fog: *Courage.*

"Get back to the Cleft — move the stones," Griffith bellowed.

The warriors at the front paid him no heed. He numbed his ears to Gwen's roar and the others' furious swears and locked eyes with the warriors who charged behind them.

Their legs froze for a moment, unsure.

"Move the stones," he said again. "We have to stop the mages!"

That seemed to do it. They spun and fell back upon the shattered wall, their hands moving more furiously than before — their strength bolstered by panic.

For half a moment, Griffith moved surely through the drifts. He dragged Baird behind him and kept his eyes fixed upon the warriors' work. But then the rumbling didn't stop. The screams only grew louder. The mountains began to howl.

When Griffith looked back, he saw the cliffs were only moments from breaking. Everything would be gone in an instant — crushed to death beneath the fall. It didn't matter how furiously the warriors worked: there was still a hill of stone between them and the mages.

The realization stuck him like a boulder across his back. Griffith crumbled to his knees. "We'll never reach the mages! We'll never stop them."

His throat twisted and tears brimmed inside his eyes. He'd been a fool to go marching out here. He'd been such a fool.

Baird's frail hands pulled desperately on his arms, but it was his words that brought Griffith back to his feet: "We don't need to *reach* them. We'll slay them without the fist or sword. Courage, young Griffith!" he bellowed over the rising storm. "Steel your legs and carry me on."

They were too far to save Thanehold, too far to stop the mages. And so Griffith had no choice but to do as he was told — begging Fate for mercy at every step.

Three paces, the three longest moments of his life, and then Baird roared:

"*Silence, mages! I am the voice of the mountains, the great refuge against all spells. Your powers whither beneath my shadow.*"

His words burst inside Griffith's ears — a loud boom of a summer storm, more forceful than a river. It thrust his legs forward and bolstered his strength. He bared his teeth, his legs charged hot by the power in Baird's words.

"*Your voices are swallowed up by my mighty winds. See how I carry them away? See how your magic rolls like water from my sides? You have no power here.*"

At first, Griffith thought he was only imagining it. But soon it became too clear to doubt: the mages' voices shrank beneath Baird's words. The cliffs slowed their trembling.

But as the earth stilled, it was the bard who began to shake. It was as if he'd taken the whole spell upon himself, as if that stone monster had rammed through his skin.

Griffith slowed for half a pace before Baird rasped:

"No, don't stop! No matter what, you mustn't stop."

So Griffith didn't. He dragged Baird against his side, all but carrying him into the Cleft. His eyes stayed fixed upon the rock wall in front of them. He pushed at the warriors with his gaze, silently begging them to dig on.

"*My peaks fall down upon your bodies, worms,*" Baird cried. "*They bend defiantly from your spells. You feel my voice inside your bones — your blood freezes against my spirit. You knew from the moment you stepped beneath my shadow that you would not live to see the setting ... setting of ...*"

Baird clutched desperately at Griffith's arm. His legs shook too badly to move. When he turned, Griffith saw with a shock that he was bleeding. Scarlet tears rolled from beneath his bandages, gushed from inside his ears. They stained the edges of his beard.

Griffith knew what was happening — he'd seen this once before. "No —!"

"You *must*! We've nearly got them, young Griffith. We're nearly ... but I can't ... can't do this alone." Baird's knobby fingers went taut across his arm. He bared his teeth in a defiant grin. "Courage, now ... *courage*."

It took every ounce of Griffith's courage to move. He scooped Baird into his arms and marched for the Cleft. The earth stopped its trembling, but only because Baird shook. The warriors had begun to beat the hill aside with their fists; the sound of Baird's chant stoked their strength to frenzy.

Gray light burst through from the other side — the faintest glimpse of hope. They were nearly there.

Though Baird couldn't see it, he must've sensed that they were close. Griffith lunged ahead when the bard roared: "*Yes, you knew from the moment you stepped beneath my shadow that you would not live to see the setting of the sun. Your spirits quake against this truth. You see Death coming towards you, now — his great sword leveled at your throats!*"

The warriors threw their bodies against the last line of rock. They burst through and went after the few remaining soldiers that waited on the other side.

Even as his limbs swelled beneath the power in Baird's voice, hot tears streamed down Griffith's face. He felt the wet warmth of Baird's blood against his chest. As he stepped through the rubble and into the battle beyond, he kept his eyes fixed upon the robed men cowering behind the soldiers' backs.

Their faces were masks of terror. Their hands coiled about their throats and they screamed as Baird's words raked across their ears.

The warriors clobbered the soldiers away. They left him a straight path through the fight. As they neared the end, Baird laughed through the blood that coated his lips and howled: "*Death comes for you now, mages! He strikes your spirits into the depths with a mighty roar:* You are dust!"

Griffith gasped as the mages' bodies burst. Their skin ripped back from their skulls as if they'd been caught inside a pillar of flame.

Their bones blackened, cracked, and crumbled — their robes fell emptily upon the ash.

The sounds of battle rushed inside Griffith's ears. His chest swelled with a howl as he watched the warriors crush the remaining soldiers beneath their fists. "We got them, Baird! We ..."

But the words trailed away when he looked down and saw the beggar-bard's face resting gently against his chest. One of his knobby hands still lay atop Griffith's arm, though the grip was gone from his fingers.

Red stained the bandages over his eyes. It darkened his hollow cheeks and colored the slight gray of his beard. But the blood was the only mark of his pain: the rest of his face was smooth with sleep, his lips bent ever so slightly upwards ... parted in a smile.

Griffith sat down hard. He pulled the bard into his lap and pressed an ear against his chest. Through the fading noise of the battle and the warriors' excited howls, he heard the tiniest murmur of life ...

The smallest, faintest *thud*.

CHAPTER 20
PERSUASION

Far beneath the fortress of Midlan, the King's prisoners had awoken. Howls tore through the chambers; screams thickened the air. They rent the mortar with their claws and threw their monstrous bodies upon the iron doors.

Argon the Seer leaned against the dampened wall of a chamber much larger than the rest. His swollen hands gripped the sides of a scrying bowl; his head fell so low that its water soaked the tip of his beard. A moment ago, the basin had rocked under the force of his vision. It'd been alive with swirling colors, voices, the noise of battle and flame. Now, there was only silence ...

A silence that frightened him more than the monsters' wails.

"What's happening?" Crevan growled. His stony eyes roved as he paced, flicking to follow every thrash and scream. His knuckles were white about the hilt of his sword.

Argon couldn't think to reply. His vision wavered beneath the lingering power of what he'd Seen. His head throbbed. Blood dripped from his nose and fell one drop at a time into the bowl, stirring its waters and coloring its ripples once more.

He would've preferred all of his blood to fall. He longed for a more permanent ring of silence ...

"I asked you a question, Seer."

Crevan wrenched his chin up by his beard, forcing Argon from his trance. "They can hear it, Your Majesty."

"Hear what?"

"The battle." Argon blinked against the wavering colors, hoping to still the throb inside his skull. "They listen through the mages' ears as the battle rages on. They feast upon its fury."

As far as Argon knew, Crevan had never actually set foot inside the dungeons. It was obvious by how he bared his teeth against the noise that he found it unsettling. "Tell them to quiet."

195

"I can't, Your Majesty. Their minds are gone," he said, when Crevan's grip tightened. "Your beasts don't understand that the things they hear are miles away. They believe themselves to be *in* the battle, a part of the fight."

This didn't seem to calm him. If anything, the King's anger only grew. He whirled around to a large man who haunted the chamber's doorway — a man so bruised and scraped that his body seemed lopsided, a man with more scar than skin.

"Silence them, beastkeeper! Silence them, or I will."

The lump above the beastkeeper's one good eye rose to nearly brush the uneven sprouts of his hair. The crack of his mouth fell in worry — revealing a half-row of broken teeth.

Once he'd thumped from the room, Crevan spun back to Argon. "Show me again."

He didn't have the strength to draw the vision. He was certain the effort would kill him. But the shackle upon his arm flared to life at the King's voice. It understood the command and burned so angrily that Argon had no choice but to obey.

The scrying bowl crushed against his knees. The soldiers had carried it from the tower and into Devin's cell at the King's command. Something dark had overtaken the boy — some spirit that made him violent and angry. This spirit raged above the soldiers' strength and even beyond the beastkeeper's control. Though Ulric managed to keep him from erupting into his dragon's form while he raged, his strength was still terrible.

Dark stains covered the floor near the chamber's entrance — the prints of the soldiers who hadn't escaped him in time.

But for whatever reason, the visions in Argon's bowl seemed to calm him. This new spirit was as entranced by the magic as Devin had been. So Crevan had ordered Argon to stay in the dungeons day and night, hardly ever out of Devin's reach.

The visions had so weakened him that Argon felt trapped beneath the basin. He wasn't sure he could've lifted it to save his life. There was nothing to do but obey the King's command.

He dropped his Seeing stone into the basin's middle. Its marbled black surface began to spin violently, carrying the stone in a circle around the basin's edge. As the stone rolled, the waters swirled. Colors leaked from its edges and came together in the middle, forming a picture.

A field of snow loomed out of the darkness. Wind stirred its flesh — a wind too great for Crevan's birds, but not strong enough to dull Argon's gaze. He Saw the bandit army gathering in the field. The woman at their lead carried an axe and a rounded shield. A strange mass of paint swirled across her features.

Argon held on tightly as Devin tore from the snow-filled pass. This was the part of the vision that shook him most: Devin's fires would consume the woman. Her army would retreat inside the castle's walls, where the mages would call the mountains down upon them — bringing every last bandit to a swift and violent end.

He braced himself as the fires grew inside the cloud, as the bandit woman's face was stricken white with fear. But in the second before the fires fell, the image suddenly went dark.

It was as if the future blinked: a moment of black, and the image reappeared.

Only this time, everything had changed.

Something ripped across Midlan's army — a shadow that tore through its magic and churned its steel aside. Bodies fell hewed in its wake. Blood coated the ground where the shadow passed.

The bandit woman and her army followed in its wake. They battled feverishly against sword and spell, widening the hole the shadow had left behind. Nothing the soldiers did seemed to stop them. It was as if they warred against the mountains, themselves ...

Argon gasped when the vision suddenly changed. The shadow wrapped itself around his throat and dragged him from the clouds. Another flash of darkness, and Argon had fallen into the thick of the fight.

He stood in the soldiers' ranks, helpless as the shadow crashed towards him. Bits of steel whipped past his eyes in a gold-tinged cloud. Hot spatters of blood stung his face. But worse than all of that was the noise — the roar the shadow loosed as it neared shook him to his bones. His spirit cringed and tightened against his marrow.

The ground came closer as Argon's legs collapsed beneath him. He pressed his hands against his ears and watched from the tops of his eyes as the shadow burst through the last rank. It dragged the darkness in behind it — a seething, impenetrable cloud ...

"Gah!"

Argon was so desperate to escape the cloud that he pulled himself from the vision. His head slammed hard against the dampened wall.

****

"It's impossible! It's *not possible!*"

Crevan's voice cut across his ears. Argon struggled to pull himself from the dark, struggled to make sense of all the screaming.

Ulric was there, though his voice sounded ... strange. His words barely slid out between ragged breaths: "I wouldn't have believed it, had I not seen it for my —"

"They were *bandits*!" Crevan roared. "Nothing more than an aimless pack of savages. You had every advantage. And you still lost!"

The chains upon Ulric's wrist began to shriek with the King's fury. Even through the cloud that muddled his head, Argon caught the hiss of its power.

"Please, Your Majesty!" Ulric yelped. "They weren't bandits — you *know* they weren't. Only one race in the Kingdom could've withstood our spells."

"No, it isn't possible!"

"I didn't believe it either! But after what happened, there's no mistaking what they were."

Crevan roared again. There was a sharp *clang* as he slung his sword against the wall. Argon's eyes snapped open in time to see the two halves of its blade strike the ground.

The King's face was crimson with fury. He gripped the black dragon sewn onto his tunic, as if he meant to rip it from his chest. After a moment, his growling ceased. He spoke with deadly calm: "You let my mages die, you led a full branch of my army to its slaughter. You've lost my dragon —"

"He'll return, Your Majesty," Ulric whimpered. He fell to his knees and clutched his wrist out in front of him as the chained impetus burned. "He was wounded in his fight with the Dragongirl. Physical pain weakens the curse for a moment, makes its prisoners flee. But I can feel its hold returning," he added when Crevan stomped towards him. "His presence is growing stronger. He won't be able to resist my commands for long."

"Good."

With that single utterance, the shackle's blaze went out. Ulric crumpled in relief — and Crevan's eyes slid over to Argon.

There was nothing in them but the edge of steel: the cold promise that he would be dealt with … and dealt with swiftly. "You lied to me, Seer. You can't tell me that you didn't know those bandits were whisperers. You must've Seen their powers. You've failed me for the last time —"

"Your Majesty?"

Crevan dragged his glare from Argon and fixed it upon the door, to where a steward had appeared. Unlike most of Crevan's stewards, he didn't hide behind the doorway but stood boldly beneath its arch. He kept shoulders squared and his back straight — no doubt in an attempt to distract from the fact that he was a good head shorter than any of them.

"What?" Crevan snapped.

"I apologize for the interruption, Your Majesty. But I wanted to let you know that the Grandforest patrols have been reached and are ready to march upon Lakeshore at your command."

Crevan's glare slipped back. He squinted as if he'd just heard a secret whispered in a foreign tongue.

The steward raised his brows. He glanced at Argon and Ulric before he slipped up next to Crevan, favoring his right leg in a limp. "I'm sorry, Your Majesty. I should've been clearer." He dropped his voice in a whisper that Argon had to strain to hear. "You told me — in the strictest confidence — that you wished to have the Countess brought to Midlan. Something about her having a weapon that might help us deal with the trouble in the Valley, a weapon she isn't likely to give up without some sort of, ah," he cast his eyes around him again and whispered something that sounded like *persuasion*.

Argon began to wonder just how long he'd been out.

Crevan, for his part, brightened immediately. His glower melted into a most unsettling grin. "Yes, very good. Give the order — and I want her brought in *alive*," he added with a snarl. "D'Mere will be no good to me dead."

"Of course, Your Majesty. I'll see that it is done." The steward bowed deeply before he limped from the room.

When Crevan turned back, Argon feared the steward's interruption had only bought him a little more time. But the King's anger seemed gone, and his eyes were alive with thought. "I'm going to give you one last chance, Seer. Watch for the Dragongirl. Tell me everything you See. I need to know when she'll cross the Kingdom's shores ... and I want to know *where*."

This was strange news: Argon had never known the Dragongirl to leave the Kingdom. Though he wondered where she'd gone, he knew better than to ask. For now, he would be content in the knowing that Crevan's eye was turned elsewhere. "Yes, Your Majesty."

The King stared at the wall above Argon's head for a moment. His hand traced the jagged scar that cut through his beard — and his eyes turned dark as the dungeon's innards.

"Once I have the Countess, the problem in the Valley will end swiftly," he said, turning to Ulric. "I want your mages prepared to move the moment Argon knows where the Dragongirl will be."

The archmage's jaw went tight. His glare cut to where Argon lay. But in the end, he nodded.

"Good. And what about the prisoner from Copperdock? Has he spoken?"

"He hasn't shut up," Ulric growled. "He blathers on day and night about how we'll all be sorry. But he hasn't said anything useful, if that's what you mean."

"Then why don't you kill him?"

"I've tried," Ulric said evenly, the fury in his scowl dulled by exhaustion. "Spells don't work, swords are useless. I've got him sunk inside a vat of water even as we speak. If that doesn't kill him, I'll have no choice but to lock him up somewhere and hope the worms do the rest."

"Do whatever it takes. If he won't talk, then he's of no use to me," Crevan said off-handedly. He took a few stomping paces towards the door before he paused. "In the meantime, I want you to gather the birds. Send them to the Endless Plains — to *threaten*, not destroy. They can kill a few of the giants, if they wish. But I'll need the rest."

"For what?"

"To work the soil, of course. We haven't had a shipment since Gilderick disappeared. If I'm going to reclaim the Kingdom, my army must be fed."

"But, Your Majesty — my grip is faint enough as it is," Ulric said, pawing at his ears. "I can barely control that dragon with the mages hanging from my wrist, let alone a flock of birds —"

"Your problems don't concern me. You'll do as I command."

The chains glowed hot with these words, and Ulric had no choice but to nod. He dragged himself to his feet and shuffled from the room.

"Watch for her, Seer," Crevan growled as he went to follow. "Your every vision, every thought, and every dream had better be about the Dragongirl."

"Yes, Your Majes ..." Argon reached for his Seeing stone, but his arm locked up. A searing pain traveled along his tendons and bone — the path of a molten finger not to be ignored.

Tell the King the truth. Tell him what he needs to know.

Argon was no warrior, and he wasn't a young man, either. He crumbled quickly beneath the pain. "There's a great power in the Endless Plains — I've Seen it."

Crevan froze in the doorway. "What sort of power?"

"I do not know, Your Majesty. In my visions it was a murderous storm that tore the wings from your beasts. Only by the mages' spells was it at last made silent."

Crevan scowled, though the fall of his brows was more brooding than angry. "Very well, have Ulric send some of the mages along — but I want them back at their posts the moment the giants are taken care of. I won't risk letting the Dragongirl slip past me again."

Ripples fanned across the basin's waters when Crevan slammed the door, trembling under the force.

Argon lay heavily upon the cold stone floor and buried his face inside his hands. The silence broke him: not long ago, he'd been safe inside his tower, warmed by the chatter of young mages, the noise of their work, the odd blast of a mis-formed spell.

But now all of that was gone, as well.

Crevan had ripped the young mages away not long after he'd taken Devin. Now they were scattered all across the Kingdom, forced into the ranks of the battlemages. Fury stung Argon's flesh when he thought of the horror their young eyes had seen, of the terror they were being forced to witness. The realm suffered beneath Crevan's rule. But at least the young ones had been safe.

Now the Kingdom was at war once again, and he'd called out the power of every mage.

Argon's nails bit into his skin as he clutched the sides of his head. Oh, he wished desperately to be a stronger man — to have the strength to resist the pain, or the freedom to end it. But she would never let him. No, he was doomed to serve her until Death closed his eyes.

"Why?" Argon whispered into the cold. "I've done everything she's asked for. I've kept to her plan. Why is she doing this to me?"

"You've been chasing your *own* visions," a sly, crackling voice answered. "You've done only the tasks that served your purpose, and you've ignored the rest. The King will never triumph without your visions ... so she's sent me to make certain you listen."

Argon lifted his head and glared at the figure standing in one of the chamber's corners — the charred skeleton of a man clad in ragged, singed robes. It stood with one boney hand tucked behind its back. The sharp tips of its fingers clicked and scraped together dryly as it closed its fist. The other hand was poised in front of it, stretched towards a trail of stinking water that dripped from the ceiling.

Molten cords of marrow filled the cracks in its skull. Flame spouted in a line from its base around to its front in a perfect, fiery crown. The flames wavered when it turned its head and fixed Argon with the burning coal of one eye. "You are bound to her service, Seer. It is a burden of being one of the chosen."

Argon never asked for the Sight — he'd been born with it. He would've plucked out his eyes if he thought that would end the visions. "She's making a mistake! Crevan is a madman. Killing the Dragongirl won't change that. He'll plunge the Kingdom into darkness, before the end."

"She cares nothing for the Dragongirl," the Firecrowned King hissed.

It stretched its skeletal hand into the dripping water. The corners of its frozen grin seemed to sharpen as the drops struck its bone: the moisture hissed and spat, obscuring its face in a cloud of steam.

Argon felt his shackle begin to burn with the King's command. He felt another vision pressing against the backs of his eyes, fighting its way towards the surface. "Please, specter ... if there's any human left in you at all, you'll —"

"There isn't, and I won't. Fate doesn't make mistakes," the Firecrowned King whispered. "All of her plans are perfect. The realm must be led back into glory, the King must secure the throne, my eternal crown must be given." Its head swiveled upon its spiney neck to trap Argon within the fires of its grin. "There's only one force she can't control, only one shadow she cannot see. He alone has the power to undo everything. You've seen for yourself the will he holds against her. The realm can't be left at the mercy of this mortal whelp. No," it hissed, coals flaring into spouts of yellow flame. "The Forsaken One must ... be ... *stopped.*"

CHAPTER 21
WARMTH AND SILENCE

They flew over the Valley and between the mountains' peaks. The air was so thick with angry, frosted clouds that Kael couldn't see where they were going. He cringed every time Kyleigh turned her wings and waited for the *whoosh* of something enormous passing them by: cliffs and the spiny tops of trees, the misty gush of the falls. She tilted sideways at one point, and he clung on for his life.

Kael had begun to suspect that she was doing it on purpose. But it wasn't until he nearly got his head scraped off beneath a jagged arch of stone that he knew for sure.

"It's not funny," he insisted over her rumbling laugh. "I could've been very seriously mangled."

Oh, you had plenty of room, she replied.

"Yes, *after* I ducked. How much further do we have to go?" he went on before she could retort.

I'm not sure.

Kael would've thrown his hands up in exasperation, had he not had such a firm grip on her spines. "How can you not be sure? I thought you knew where the dragon was going."

I do know where he's going, she said testily. *I'm just not sure how long it'll take to get there.*

They'd been flying long enough that Kael was certain they were about to run out of map. The only thing left was the summit. When he said as much, she laughed again.

The world doesn't end at your mountains, Kael.

Before he could ask her what she meant, they were falling. He flattened himself against her back as the force of the earth tried to rip him free. His knees clamped against her sides and he clung so tightly to her spines that his fingers began to ache.

After a few weightless moments, her wings burst open — smacking Kael's head against her back. He peeled his face from her scales, fully intending to scold her. But the sight beneath him froze the words to his lips.

The mountains loomed far behind them, their tops lost within an impenetrable army of clouds. Before them stretched something he'd never seen: an ocean the color of the purest blue.

Frosted white crests topped each of its waves. Chunks of ice drifted across them — many larger than a ship. But there were a few so enormous that he thought the whole of Tinnark could've settled upon their tops. Some were jagged, with spines that made them look like the spires of the Unforgivable Mountains. One stretched so far that for a moment, he was convinced they'd stumbled across a new land.

He could hardly believe it when they passed its end.

"The northern seas," he said, his voice a whisper. "But this *is* where the Kingdom ends ... isn't it?"

No, there's a land beyond this one, Kyleigh insisted.

"You've seen it?"

Yes. Well, I suppose it's more accurate to say that I've dreamt *of it.*

Kael couldn't believe what he was hearing. "Oh, for mercy's sake. We've got to turn back. If we leave now —"

I'm not going anywhere. I know Devin went this way. Now might be our only chance to catch him without Ulric's hand around his throat.

"Devin?" Kael was slightly disappointed. "That's a ridiculous name for a dragon."

What were you expecting his name to be? Great-One? Fire-Breath?

"Anything would've been better than *Devin*. I'm not even afraid of him anymore."

Kyleigh's laugh faded after a moment. When she spoke again, her voice came softly: *He's not only a dragon. If I show you something, will you promise to not to be angry?*

"What makes me angry is *not* knowing there's a dragon after us, in the first place. I'm still furious with you about that. Why didn't you just tell me?" he said at her pause. "I could've warned the wildmen. They could've carried their dragonsbane —"

I didn't want him to be killed.

Kael couldn't believe what he was hearing. "So you'd rather kill the wildmen?"

Even if I'd told them the truth, do you think they would've listened? she growled against his ears. *Did Gwen listen when you told her Midlan was coming, or when you warned her about the King's attack? Did she listen when the mages were blasting their way through the Cleft?*

No, she hadn't. Not even when the clouds were boiling and Kael yelled for her to move did she listen. She'd clung to her stubborn will until the moment the fires fell — and had he not shoved her away, she would've been turned to ashes.

Kyleigh was probably right about the wildmen: she could've drawn the dragon's picture out for Gwen, and the Thane would've ignored her until the last. But even for all that, there was one thing Kael didn't understand, one thing that troubled him greatly.

One thing that burned him worse than all the rest.

"Why didn't you tell me?" he said again.

I didn't think you'd understand. I was curious. I was desperate to speak with him. You don't know what it's like to be alone, to be the last of your kind, she said, her voice imploring. *And I thought if I had a chance to save him, I would. But then he went after you, and I hated him for it. I planned to kill him. But then we spoke ... and I ... now I don't want to hurt him.*

Kale's head was spinning. "So you were curious, and then you wanted to kill him, and now you know you *can't* kill him. What in Kingdom's name —?"

Let me show you.

He sat very still as her memory rose before his eyes: he saw a young man standing with his back to the spray of the falls. His body was stretched and warped — his flesh a mix of skin and scales.

The young man's eyes raged yellow, at first. They were the dragon's eyes, and his voice was every bit as harsh as his roar. Then his lids closed and his eyes turned blue. Kael hardly listened when he spoke again: he was frozen by the young man's stare, trapped against the shadow of something else.

He swore he'd seen those eyes before ...

Now do you understand why I can't kill him? There's more to him than dragon. There's a part of him that's good — just like Jake, and Eveningwing, Kyleigh said.

Kael blinked as she pulled the memory away and the cold breath of the skies filled his lungs. "Yes," he said after a moment. "I understand."

This seemed to please her. There was a bit more lift in her wings as she carried them between the caps of ice. But Kael hardly noticed.

Something had begun to worm its way inside his heart — a feeling with countless spiny limbs. There was venom in its touch: little burning patches flared up wherever it squirmed. They grew together and swelled until the venom began to rise in his throat. Even after Kael forced it down, he could still feel it hissing inside his chest.

Perhaps Kyleigh was right: perhaps there truly *was* more to the dragon than he'd seen. If he'd known for certain that the black dragon wouldn't harm her, he'd release him without a second thought. He would've given her anything she asked for.

But he didn't know it for certain — and the black dragon had already harmed Kyleigh twice. He'd felt the strength in his scales, the power of his breath. No matter how much Kyleigh wanted to see him free, Kael wasn't sure he could do it.

He would've given his life for her without a second thought … but he wouldn't let her risk her own. He would protect her for as long as he drew breath — no matter what it took.

****

Night fell upon them quickly. At this edge of the world, the sun didn't set: it plummeted beneath the horizon. The red streak it left behind was their only light for hours. Soon, even that began to fade.

The darkness was unsettling. A thin swath of clouds muted the starlight and gave the waves beneath them a strange glow. Instead of settling upon its top, the light sank beneath it — warping the sea from the inside out, turning the pure blue into a sickly green.

Kael couldn't help but be reminded of the Tempest: the color of the waves, the eerie silence that hung in the air around them — it all reminded him of that monstrous storm. Though the northern seas lay still, he couldn't help but worry.

"Can you see anything?" he said to Kyleigh. His voice barely rose above the beating of her wings. He couldn't bring himself to speak any louder. He felt as if the sky above them watched.

As if it waited.

I can see well enough. We aren't in any danger, Kyleigh assured him.

"We've been going for a while. Aren't you tired?"

Not particularly. The wind's doing most of the work.

"Still, I think we ought to land somewhere and wait until dawn. Just to be safe."

I love your imagination, Kael. It has a way of making things ... exciting, she said, with a growl that matched the sudden wave of heat that coursed across her flesh. *But if I hear one more comment about how you don't like the way the moonlight hits the water, I swear I'll give you a closer look.*

"Don't bother. If we go on for much longer, I wager we'll both be getting a closer look. You can't fly forever," he insisted.

Her sigh filled his head in a heated cloud. *There's nowhere to land but on the ice caps — and I don't think you'd fancy that.*

She drew up an image: one of him curled inside his bedroll, snoring and unaware until he suddenly snapped through the ice. It was completely ridiculous, and he was still cross with her.

But that didn't stop him from smiling. "I like to think I'd be able to feel it melting *before* I fell in. And I don't snore like that."

You do, sometimes ... especially if the moon is bright.

She drew up other things — things linked to the memories of his snoring that had nothing to do with sleep ... things that made heat spread across his face and down his neck. "Yes, well, you'd fall through the ice first," he said testily. "Your skin is hotter than mine."

Her memories broke against her rumbling laugh. Kael had to come up on his rump as a swell of heat pressed against her scales. But it was better than having to watch the things she showed him.

He didn't like to look at himself through her eyes.

They sailed on for a few quiet minutes before Kyleigh showed him something else. He saw himself grasping the black dragon's collar and ripping it free. But the image was blurred at its edges — a question. If Kyleigh distracted the dragon, did Kael think he could free him?

"Maybe. But it'll be dangerous," he said, careful to keep the other things he felt pressed far behind his words.

Had this been a wolf or even a bear under the King's spell, he would've freed it without a moment's thought. If a wolf or a bear turned savage, he could handle it easily. But not even Kyleigh could stop the halfdragon if he came after them again.

Kael's blood bubbled hotly when she turned to watch a gap in the clouds and he saw the jagged cut across her muzzle. The scaly bridge of her brow was swollen taut. No matter how she rolled her eyes, he knew she must be in pain. No matter how much she swore she could handle herself, he wouldn't listen. Even if she were willing to put herself in danger, Kael wouldn't let her.

Not a thing in the Kingdom or to the edge of the map was worth Kyleigh's life — and that went doubly for the black dragon.

No ... Kael had no intention of risking her life to set the dragon free. His hand twitched to where the dragonsbane dagger lay sheathed inside his belt. If he got a clear shot, he would take it.

"How much further do we have to go?" he said after a moment, trying to cover his thoughts before they swelled too close to the surface.

I'm not sure. But I know Devin went this way, and this feels ...

Her words faded as her thoughts flicked to something else. "What if he's turned around?" Kael said after a moment.

He hasn't.

"He might've."

No, I'm fairly certain he hasn't.

"We've been flying all day and haven't caught a single glimpse. So maybe —oof!"

His stomach leapt up his throat as Kyleigh plunged downward. He thought she was only doing it to shut him up when a gust of wind ripped across his body, nearly snatching him from her back.

A familiar noise sank into the air above them: a deep, rumbling hum. Kael twisted his head upwards and saw the black dragon's enormous shadow pass overhead, silent as the darkened belly of a cloud.

Be very still, Kyleigh warned as she turned. *I'm going to bring us closer.*

She climbed into a tight loop and shot off after the black dragon. The speed made the air howl inside Kael's ears. He couldn't even hear his own breaths. They followed the dragon's trail for nearly a full minute, but he was careful to stay inside the clouds — and the dark of his scales hid him well.

After a moment, Kyleigh had no choice but to drop back down. Kael felt as if they'd fallen into a pit. The clouds hung around them so thickly that after a moment, he forgot about the stars. He was certain there'd never been any light at all.

Even Kyleigh seemed hesitant. Her wingbeats weren't nearly as confident as they'd been before.

Kael's skin had begun to crawl when he caught something out of the corner of his eye: a bright red glow, a steady pulse that stained the clouds around it pink.

His collar is glowing again, he thought, and he knew by how her ears pinned back that the words must've burst inside her head. *We have to get away before he sees — are you mad?*

But Kyleigh didn't stop. Her long neck twisted around and her body followed. She moved slowly towards the red glow, keeping a steady distance. Kael jumped when she suddenly burst into song.

Kyleigh's hum was low, but much softer than the black dragon's. It was the noise of a distant wind, of a breeze across a chimney's top. When the black dragon boomed in reply, she hummed again.

Kael thought furiously: *This is a horrible idea. Please don't —*

I know what I'm doing.

He'll tear you from the skies!

No he won't — because you're going to stop him. Get ready.

Before he could think to protest, the black dragon turned. The glow of its collar grew larger and brighter with every second. Kyleigh's wings tensed, preparing to throw her body into a tight loop.

Kael reached for his dagger.

Clouds parted around the black dragon's spiny muzzle. Kael caught a glimpse of his burning eyes, his jagged fangs — of the storm of golden flame brewing between them. Kyleigh dropped from the clouds. Wind screeched through his ears and his eyes streamed as she cut beneath the black dragon's belly.

Get ready! she cried.

The force of her loop flattened Kael against her back. His head screamed as it tried to hold on to consciousness. The veins inside his neck were about to burst from his skin when the pressure finally stopped.

The world was upside-down; the black dragon was beneath them. He paused, confused, watching as they sailed over his back. At the height of Kyleigh's loop, the earth stood still. They were suspended, weightless for a breath.

And they were directly above the black dragon's head.

Now, Kael! Break the collar!

He could've done it. All he had to do was drop from Kyleigh and onto the black dragon's neck. His hands could've torn through the collar in an instant — and the warrior in him howled for the chance. But in the split second he had to decide, the dragon's eyes told him everything.

They flared up the moment they found Kael. Every vein within them swelled, trembling as they made way for a rush of seething yellow. The flame between the dragon's jaws began to spill past his teeth; his shock had given way to fury. A breath of air filled his mighty lungs.

In that moment, Kael knew that if he set the black dragon free, he would tear them both to pieces. There wasn't an ounce of mercy within those eyes — there was only rage.

He raised the golden dagger and his every muscle tensed to throw, adjusting to its weight. His eyes locked upon one of the blackened slits and he focused, prepared to send the blade hurling through its middle …

Kyleigh's voice rang inside his head, but he couldn't hear what she said. Time slowed. His arm was already coming forward when the dragon's pupil collapsed: its points shrank into its center and as it widened, blue burst into the yellow.

It doused the fire, cooled the rage. The flames fell dark between his jaws. Fear and confusion filled these eyes. They made Kael's throat twist tight. He doubted slightly, just as his arm came forward.

And it was that single doubt that saved the dragon's life.

The golden dagger flew wide of its mark. The tip glanced the scales beside the dragon's eye and skittered off, glinting as it fell into the darkness. A thin spatter of blood trailed its path. It hissed as its fires struck the cold night air and made the dragon roar.

His voice was weaker than it'd been before — more shocked than angry. Those blue eyes widened as they flicked from Kael to the sky ahead. Then his great body twisted around. The black dragon shot back towards the Kingdom, pounding the clouds aside with the panicked strokes of his wings.

Kael grit his teeth when the second half of Kyleigh's loop flattened him again — followed closely by a torrent of her furious swears. *What in blazes were you thinking? You could've killed him!*

"That was the plan," Kael said back. The memory of the dragon's panicked stare hung behind his eyes for a moment before he shoved it away. "I won't set him free. I won't risk loosing him on the Kingdom. He's a monster, Kyleigh —!"

He is not a monster!

Her thoughts burned hot between his ears, bolstered by a roar. Kael held on with all of his might as she whipped around and went tearing off after the black dragon's trail — swearing with every beat of her wings.

She was mad! It was completely and utterly insane, to go chasing after the dragon — especially since they'd very nearly been scorched. When he said as much, she replied with something that could've made a pirate blush.

"Fine! Go on, then," Kael said back. "I'd love another crack at him."

What if I cracked your skull on an ice cap, whisperer? Would you love that?

"You wouldn't —"

I most certainly would.

Finally, Kael had reached his wit's end. "What in Kingdom's name has gotten into you? You're being completely —"

All at once, Kyleigh's body flipped upside-down, and Kael wasn't ready for it. He felt the pull on the insides of his ears as the world spun; his lungs slammed against his ribs. She moved with more force than ever before, and it caught him by surprise.

The spines jerked from his grasp and his legs clamped down upon the empty air. Wind tore at him, tried to rip his face from his flesh. The weight of his armor sent him plummeting at a speed he was sure his bones couldn't withstand. Somehow, Kael managed to twist his body around to catch one look at Kyleigh before the clouds swallowed her up.

She was nothing more than a shadow behind the clouds: a creature with wings spread wide and claws bared for the fight. Her body twisted onto its back just in time to meet the fall of a second creature. When they struck, the noise split the air like a thunderclap. Kyleigh's furious roar clashed with another.

In half a second, Kael had fallen too far. All he could see now was the bottom of a starless night — and the glowing ocean awaited him with opened jaws.

All of his muscles tensed as the warrior in him braced for the fall. He could do nothing to stop himself from striking the waves, and he couldn't bear to look. Kael shut his eyes, teeth clenched together as the wind tried to rip him apart ...

In the instant before his body struck, a pair of claws wrapped around him. He tensed to keep their grip from shattering his ribs and held on tightly as Kyleigh swooped him upwards.

"What happened? What was that?" Kael said, his heart still screaming.

Before she could reply, a chorus of hums filled the air above them. There were three different voices: one carried a steady tone while the other two fell above and below it. Together, they formed a perfect song.

A gap broke within the clouds, and Kael saw them: monstrous, winged shadows circling tightly overhead. They moved like wraiths caught between the worlds of the living and the dead — beings that paid no heed to the earth's laws.

"*More* dragons?" Kael hissed.

Kyleigh didn't reply. Her tail curled tightly beneath her and slowly, she turned — moving away from the Kingdom's shores and deeper into the shadowed sea beyond.

The dragons circled hungrily. Their song had risen to such a height that Kael's ears began to ring. Just when he feared they would burst, another voice silenced them.

It crackled across the other three, the labor of a storm about to break. Kael was expecting the resounding *boom* at its end, but it still made him jump — and it drove the other three voices into silence.

"What's happening?" was all he could manage to say. His heart was crammed so tightly against the floor of its cage that he could barely feel it beating

And that was before Kyleigh's thought filled his ears with a heavy sigh:

We've been captured.

****

213

Kael couldn't believe it. By this point, he was entirely fed up with being captured — and they had absolutely no time for it. "Whatever you did to them, just apologize. Maybe they'll let us go."

I didn't do anything — honestly, she said when he twisted to frown at her.

It was difficult to sound severe while he dangled from her claws, but he glared and tried his best: "I doubt that very seriously. I don't think you could put a toe across any border without stirring up some sort of trouble."

She inclined her head. *True. But I've never been across their borders. I've only* dreamt *of it.*

"Well, what if you only *thought* you were dreaming? What if you sleep-flew over here and wreaked all sorts of havoc — it isn't funny!" he snapped over her rumbling laughs. "We're in enough trouble as it is. We don't have time to be anybody's prisoners."

You can't accuse a woman of sleep-flying and expect her not to laugh. Dragons are rather protective of their territories, she said when she saw the words forming upon his lips. *I'm sure that's all this is. We crossed into their skies without permission, and they're going to make us land and sulk on the ground for a few days. Once we've been sufficiently shamed, I'm sure they'll let us go.*

Kael hoped she was right.

But at the same time, he doubted it.

The dark of the clouds and the howling winds eventually broke — giving way to an endless sky. Countless orbs of light filled the space above them. There were so many worlds stretched across the night that there was hardly a patch of black between them. The ice caps thinned a bit — no longer the massive islands they'd been before, but shards of glass balanced atop the sea. Their flesh seemed to wink at the sky as the waves rocked them.

And the stars winked back.

The dragons' song above them rose and fell in blusters: it grew so slowly that Kael could feel the chilled bumps rising across his arms before his ears even caught the song. The dragons' voices would swell to fill the air, trembling with such force at their height that Kael's limbs sagged beneath them. But just when he began to fear that his bones would crack, the song faded — slipping back like the tide from the shore.

Kyleigh's wingbeats stiffened each time the dragons sang, and Kael knew it had nothing to do with the cold. The next time the song came, he pressed his hands against her scales and concentrated on listening for their voices.

The song struck Kyleigh's ears and their words trailed like ghosts beneath the tremors: *Fly on, halved one … fly to the Motherlands … do not stop.*

When he tried to ask Kyleigh what the Motherlands were, his mind struck a wall. She was keeping him out on purpose. There was something she didn't want him to hear, something she didn't want him to know. Now when he tried to listen, the dragon's song was as cryptic as it'd been before.

He didn't know what she was hiding, but he knew it would do him no good to argue with her now. He would wait until they'd landed.

A great, black mountain rose from the sea before them. The mountain was a hole carved from the starry horizon — a shadow that seemed untouched by the world. It was as if every pale strand of starlight had died upon its shores. Kael doubted if even the sun could warm it.

The crackling thunder came again. The dragons' shadows peeled off the back of his neck, and Kael watched as they pulled ahead. Their great wings carried them swiftly onward, until the mountain's shadow swallowed them.

He was so busy watching them that he didn't notice another shadow coming until it'd already passed. It flew much higher than the others: drifting slowly across the stars, swerving on monstrous wings in a pattern that made him dizzy to watch. It followed in the path of the other three, disappearing into the shadowed land.

A space of rolling hills surrounded the mountain — a whole region's worth. Kyleigh didn't carry them far beyond the shore. No sooner was there earth beneath their feet than she landed. Kael slid off her back and into a patch of stringy, knee-high grass. He was surprised to find grass this far north, and even more surprised at how soft it was. But there was little time to wonder.

"What's going on, Kyleigh?" he said as she slid into her human form. "You've obviously done something to make the dragons angry. And I have a right to …"

His words trailed away when she turned to the stars, and he saw the deep, jagged wound that scraped across her face. It carved through her skin and marred her features. Had it not been for the blaze in her one un-swollen eye, he didn't think he would've recognized her.

"Come here."

She stood surprisingly still while he healed her. The black dragon's claws had carved gouges into her flesh. He had to seal her skin from its root. Inside the deepest cut, he healed a crack that scraped across her cheekbone. But though her wounds were horrible, she'd still been lucky.

"If he'd gotten you across the throat, you'd be dead. You *do* realize that, don't you?"

She said nothing. Her eyes stayed locked upon his, their fires unnaturally calm.

Kael's hands fell to his sides. He held her gaze, hoping she might be able to see everything he felt — all of the fear, all of the worry ... all of the things he couldn't quite put into words.

He hoped she understood why he couldn't free the black dragon. He hoped she could see that he would do anything to protect her.

"I couldn't risk it. It wasn't worth —"

Her lips pressed against his, silencing them. She clutched the back of his neck and brought him in closer; she wrapped her other arm about his waist.

Through the heat that flooded beneath his skin, Kael thought to be surprised. He was certain she'd be furious with him for trying to kill the black dragon, or angry about being captured — or already planning some daring escape. There was no anger or worry in her touch, but there was ... something.

He wrapped his arms around her and held her close, trying to figure out what it was that had her pressed against him — that made her touch so firm and desperate. Her hand slipped down his neck and across his chest. A calmness washed over him, spurred on by her touch. It doused his fear and snuffed his worries out. Soon there was nothing left but warmth and silence.

When she pulled away, there was something strange in her look — something out of place. But before he could figure out what it was, she spoke:

"I know things seem a bit grim right now, but we'll sort it out. Trust me."

Kael felt his head bob up and down. He *did* trust her — he trusted her completely. He hardly noticed the fall of her smile as she slid back into his arms.

Things suddenly didn't seem so grim.

CHAPTER 22
WITCHCRAFT

The night passed quickly, nothing more than black slivers between the patchwork of her dreams. There were a few restless minutes when Elena feared that Aerilyn might get them lost. It wasn't difficult to imagine that she might wake to find herself several miles from where they meant to go. But the mindrot left her with little choice.

A pale dawn gave way to early morning. The exhaustion drained from Elena's limbs, replaced by the cold nothingness she'd come so accustomed to over the past several weeks. She remembered how the cold had wrapped around her in the second the arrow flew, how it made everything else seem small. In that moment, she'd felt as if she had nowhere else to go.

She'd felt as if the world was at an end — and she'd seen no reason to move.

Now, she was beginning to regret it.

Despite Aerilyn's attempts to bind it, the wound beneath her shoulder had swollen considerably. Elena swore she could feel it growing by the minute, festering against the little pieces of grit and splinters the arrow had left behind. Soon she could feel her heartbeats radiating from its middle: their tremors shook her stomach, her ribs. They climbed up her throat to pound inside her head.

The world shook so fiercely after a while that Elena had no choice but to close her eyes. She leaned heavily against the back of Aerilyn's shoulder as Braver plodded on, clinging to the faint sounds of the woods.

Finally, she woke to a gasp.

"What ...?" Elena couldn't finish the question. She breathed in a lungful of thick, blackened air and wound up choking on her words.

Aerilyn's hand was clamped tightly around her wrist. She kicked Braver into a trot and Elena tried to stay conscious as the world bounced past her. Tall, spiny trees stood over their heads. The ground beneath them was littered in stone. Clouds of smoke hung so thickly between the trees that it turned the land beyond to haze.

It wasn't until Aerilyn led them to the crest of a hill that Elena realized where they were.

She saw the mouth of a large, glittering lake stretched out before them. And her heart froze inside her chest. "What are you doing? Get back — they'll see us!"

She lunged for the reins and nearly toppled when the movement swirled her vision. Aerilyn's grip tightened around her arm. "We aren't in any danger. I don't think there's anyone left to see us."

Her voice was oddly quiet. Elena blinked against the pain and followed her gaze across the lake, where she found the source of the smoke.

A black cloud thickened the air above the village. The gates were smashed; the walls still glowed with embers. Charred skeletons were all that remained of the shops and homes. A pile of corpses lay at the water's edge. Their gold-tinged armor glinted weakly through the haze as it caught the morning light.

"Midlan," Aerilyn breathed. "The King must've attacked Lakeshore ... but why? What could he possibly have to gain by killing D'Mere?"

Elena wasn't sure. After all the plotting she'd done, the Countess more than deserved to be sacked. But she doubted if the King had ever found about her plan: all of the evidence of her betrayal now lay frozen at the mountains' top — where Crevan would never find it.

Though Elena tried to concentrate, her pain was too great. Her vision blurred with every throb of her wound. The castle sat below them — empty, with charred rings around the sockets of its windows. More gold-tinged bodies lay scattered before its gates.

Something had burst through the doors and snapped the monstrous beam at its middle. Smoke wept from the collapsed portions of the roof. D'Mere's guards lay dead throughout the courtyard ... but there weren't as many bodies as she thought there would be. In fact, only a handful seemed to have come out to face Midlan at all.

It was ... strange ...

"You need a healer."

Aerilyn's voice cut sharply across her ears. Elena blinked through the darkness and struggled to fix her eyes upon the shore. "No, I'm fine. We ought to get as far away from here ... there could be others ..."

"I'm taking you to Pinewatch."

"No ... please ..."

"We're going to get you a healer, and that's final," she said as she turned Braver from the hill. "It'll do you absolutely no good to argue."

Elena's eyes swam with the motion of the turn. Braver passed a gap in the trees and for one brief moment, she caught a glimpse of the castle's shores.

They were littered with bodies, dozens upon dozens of them — each swollen taut against the sun. Village men and castle guards lay beside others: men from the desert and the seas. But one corpse among them made Elena's blood run cold.

It washed up against some wooded debris and rocked with the slap of the waves. Though its face was pressed into the sand, she knew from its size and its crop of stark white hair that it had to be a giant. She was *certain* of it.

Pain closed her eyes and dulled the edges of her mind. Still, the giant's body hung before her as the darkness rushed in, rocking back and forth against the shores of her memory ... haunting her with its warning.

****

By the time Elena woke, it was nearly evening. Her eyes opened to the noise of another gasp, and she found herself on the outskirts of Pinewatch.

She'd traveled this road so often that she would've known it by its bumps and dips — which turned out to be a very good thing, because the village itself was unrecognizable.

Pinewatch had grown since the last she'd seen it. They were a mile from where the heart of the village stood and Braver was already picking his way through people. Most lived in tents, but several had half-built homes on the land beside them. The noise of hammers filled the air. The smells of cook fires and resin hung thickly in the pockets between houses.

Aerilyn's pace slowed as she gazed around the tented village. "There are so many of them. What are they all doing here?"

She nudged Braver towards the sound of haggling. Elena slid forward and held on tightly to the saddle when Aerilyn jumped down. She dragged the reins to the edge of the village, where several merchants had set up camps.

Aerilyn cut a straight line to one man in particular: a merchant Elena recognized immediately as a fletcher from the southern forest. She kept her head down as Aerilyn dragged Braver over to him.

"What are you doing in my village, Foster?"

"Bleeding coin," he snapped as he tied a package for one of his customers. No sooner had he bound one set of goods than a woman stepped up with another.

Aerilyn pursed her lips as her eyes cut down the line of people waiting for his help. "Really? It looks as if you're doing rather well."

"Things are selling, if that's what you mean. But the price to set up a trade in Pinewatch is thrice what it used to be. I can barely keep my tunic at the rate that blasted cook is charging," Foster moaned, and his eyes slid over to the coin the woman had set on the counter.

At his look, she begrudgingly set a few more.

"Thank you, madam! You've helped a poor old shopkeeper stay open a few days more," Foster called after her. Then he slipped Aerilyn a wink.

She didn't look at all amused. "Horatio's charging threefold for caravans to set up shop? And you're paying it?" she said incredulously when Foster nodded. "Why?"

"Witchcraft, mostly."

She narrowed her eyes at him. "Have you been drinking again?"

"I haven't had a drop in almost twenty years, not since I saw that ghost," he swore, eyes flicking about him — as if he expected some wraith to coming crawling out of the woods at any moment. But he recovered quickly. "Rumor has it that you've been off adventuring in the seas, Miss Aerilyn. I just spoke to a man who said he saw you in the high chancellor's court. Been making some friends, have you? And here I thought you'd given up on trade."

"Never mind what I've been doing," Aerilyn said coolly. "What's this I hear about witchcraft?"

Foster leaned back, frowning. "That blasted cook has come up with something — some sauce he puts on everything down at his

221

tavern. The mercenaries can't seem to get enough of it. If they happen to come through here on a job, then they come back once they're finished. Most have set up shop."

"Why should that make any difference? It's not as if you're being forced to follow them."

"Well in a way, I am." Foster traced a swollen finger across the counter between them. His voice dropped low. "Midlan's been awful busy this spring. Forest folk have started to disappear. The Countess hasn't been seen in ages — word is that she's under siege. Surely you've heard the rumors by now."

"I've heard some things, yes," Aerilyn said, her jaw tight.

"Then you'll understand that people have started to worry. They're looking for protection now more than ever. The common man can't afford to hire a blade, but he knows that a mercenary will defend his own home. So the blades have settled here for the food, the people have all followed the blades, and now we poor merchants have no choice but to follow the people."

Aerilyn narrowed her eyes at Foster before she led Braver away. Her shoulders bent forward and her eyes stayed fixed up the hill. As they reached the heart of Pinewatch, she smiled at the villagers' greetings. They were just as busy, working just as hard as always, but they swarmed Aerilyn she moment they spotted her.

Elena tried not to breathe as the villagers crowded in around them. They didn't stop Aerilyn but walked with her up the hill. Several of them embraced her. She bent to hug the children who tugged on her sleeves. She called each of them by name.

The two boys who always seemed to be hovering around Garron's home shoved through to greet her — shouting at the tops of their lungs:

"Oi, Aerilyn! You've come back!" the youngest boy called. He flung an elbow at his brother. "See? I told you she'd come back to us."

"I never said she wasn't coming back!" the elder boy insisted.

They spoke at a level that made the blacksmith's dog howl at the end of its chain, but Aerilyn swooped both brothers under her arms. "Have you been taking bets against me, Chaney?"

The elder boy shook his head vigorously and jabbed an accusing finger at his brother. "Claude's just telling tales."

"I am not! You said —"

"Enough, boys. I've got plenty of kisses for both of you."

Claude squealed and tried to run, but not before Aerilyn managed to plant her lips on the top of his head. Chaney didn't put up near as much of a fight — and his skin burned where she'd kissed him.

As they neared the house at the top of the hill, the villagers' words turned solemn. Tears flooded Aerilyn's eyes. One of the men took the reins from her hands so that the women could comfort her. Several of them cried as they spoke about Garron. They assured her all was well, and that the village was healing.

Elena thought she would've been less frightened if the villagers had charged them with their swords. She would've preferred anything to this cloud of tears and smiles, and somber words — even the bite of another arrow.

"Be careful with my friend," Aerilyn called when they reached the stables. "She's wounded."

"I'll get the healer!" the Claude declared.

Chaney sprinted ahead of him. "Not if I get there first!"

Dust tore up from their heels as the brothers galloped away, but Elena didn't get a chance to watch them. One of the men pulled her from the saddle and directly into his arms.

"I'm fine. I can walk," Elena insisted.

The man shook his head. "Miss Aerilyn says you're wounded. It'd be best for you to just lie still."

She felt foolish lying like an infant in his arms. But it was better than having to march along in the crowd.

They were a stone's throw from Garron's simple house when the front door burst open. "Aerilyn!"

She squealed and ran for the man who lumbered towards them, a man with enough girth to have easily been spotted as a cook. Aerilyn didn't slow at the sweat plastering his face, or at the sauce-covered ladle he brandished like a sword. She crashed full-force into his belly, buried her face in the folds of his badly-stained apron, and cried:

"Oh, Horatio — you have no idea how I've missed you!"

He wrapped his arms around her, nearly swallowing her in his girth. "I've missed you too, dear girl. Things haven't been quite the same without you."

"Nothing's the same! I go away for a year and come back to all of this ... where are they going?" She peeled her head from Horatio's chest as a large group of men tromped through the crowd. They hailed

223

Horatio with waves and grins before inviting themselves inside the house. "Are they friends of yours?" Aerilyn said, frowning after them.

Horatio scratched at his tuft of hair. Elena's head swam as the man who held her shifted uncomfortably.

"Ah, they're customers, actually. Business has been going rather well — so well in fact that we've had to make a few adjustments." Horatio waved his ladle downhill. "The tavern's much too small to fit everyone, and it's nearly impossible to do any building during the winter. So we started serving them out of the house."

"Well, winter's over," Aerilyn said hotly. When another man stopped to scrape his boots off on the steps, she brushed past Horatio and marched purposely for the house. He trailed behind her with a string of apologies.

The man who carried Elena followed them uncertainly.

"You know how father loved this house."

"I do, Miss Aerilyn."

"I don't think he would want strangers traipsing in at all hours."

"I'm sure you're right."

"And furthermore ..."

Aerilyn's words trailed away as they stepped inside and a deafening noise accosted them: a mix of laughter, clattering plates, and the many shouts for second helpings — all settled atop the steady rumble of a house packed with voices.

Small tables lined the hallway. They were hardly large enough to seat two, but some had three or four men gathered around them. Swords hung from their belts and many had weatherworn shields draped across the backs of their chairs. The men slid aside so Horatio could fit through. Several reached up to slap his thick shoulders as he passed.

Ahead of them, Aerilyn's pace quickened. She cut between chairs and darted into the first room she came to. Elena groaned when she heard an ear-piercing squeal.

"Just set me down here, will you?"

"Are you sure, miss?" the forest man said.

"I don't think you want to stay around for this."

It was clear by how quickly he set her down that he didn't. By the time Elena made it into the room, Aerilyn was already in tears.

She recognized the tiny space as Garron's office. Though there was a long table crammed into it now, his desk and chair still sat against the wall. Aerilyn's chin cut from the desk, across the patrons who gaped at her sobbing, and to the portrait that hung above the mantle.

It was a painting of Garron astride his horse. Elena recognized his stern expression and feathered cap immediately. The painting hadn't been there the last time she'd visited, but it was very well done. She didn't understand what there possibly was to be upset about.

Aerilyn tore from the room before she could ask and rushed down the hall, wailing the whole way.

"It's only temporary!" Horatio called after her. "As soon as we've got the tavern finished, we'll ... gah!" He threw his hands up when Aerilyn disappeared into the stairwell. His shoulders bunched in anticipation of the resounding *slam* of her door.

Elena didn't have time for this. The day was already lost, and her shoulder was beginning to ache down to her fingertips. "I'll talk to her. And send that healer up the moment he gets here, will you?"

Horatio frowned at her for a moment, his eyes combing across her glare. Finally, he nodded. "Yes, very well."

Elena swept between the tables and chairs with ease. She doubted if half of the men even saw her. They were buried up to their beards in plates piled high with assortments of meat slathered in a bright red sauce. All conversation stopped the moment their plates hit the table. They only paused to breathe or take a drink from their tankards.

The stairway was dark and narrow. Elena passed through it quickly. People wandered down the hallway upstairs, as well. Some were patrons who'd obviously stayed the night, but most were maids. They watched curiously as Elena strode by.

Even if she hadn't already known which room was Aerilyn's, it would've been obvious by the yelling. A middle-aged woman stood outside her door, pleading with her to open it.

"You can't stay locked away forever, Miss Aerilyn." She frowned as some inscrutable string of words came through the door. "Horatio never meant to upset you. This all came upon us so quickly — he was only trying to do what was best for the village!"

"Why don't you bring us some tea, Alice?"

The maid whirled around like she'd taken a shock. Her eyes narrowed onto Elena's mask. "Who are you? How did you know my name?"

"I'm a friend of Aerilyn's ... and I know plenty more than your name, Alice." Elena held those words menacingly, as if she knew her every secret. In truth, she'd overheard her name once while ... investigating, for the Countess. "Tea. I believe Aerilyn prefers the sort that tastes like blackberries."

Alice stiffened, but did as she was told. Elena counted her steps as she marched down the stairs — fully aware that the other maids were watching her intently from the end of the hall. "Aerilyn? Can I come in?"

"No! I've already said that I don't want to talk. And I don't want tea. I just want everybody in this house to leave me alone for five blasted minutes!"

"Very well. I suppose if you insist ..."

Elena drove her heel into the latch and the door burst open, taking a good chunk of the frame away with it. The maids screamed at the noise — screamed again when Elena glared at them. They practically tripped over their skirts trying to be the first down the stairs.

"Go away!" Aerilyn cried, hurling a pillow at the doorway.

Elena hurled it back. The pillow smacked Aerilyn in the chest and knocked her flat onto the bed. "Stop crying. You're behaving like a child."

She looked as if she'd just been slapped across the face. "This is my father's home! It's all I have left of him. It isn't childish to want things to stay as he left them."

"Do you plan to move back here?" Elena said, fighting through the pounding of her head.

"Well ..."

"Do you plan to leave your mansion in the seas, pack up your husband and son, and drag them all into the forest?"

"No, I don't. But that doesn't mean things have to change so horribly."

She had no idea. Her life was warm and sickly-sweet. Aerilyn had never tasted a single drop of the Kingdom's bitterness — the stale bread so much of the realm lived on.

Still, Elena tried to speak calmly. "The rest of the forest is struggling. Shops have closed, people are scared. It's becoming more likely with every passing day that Crevan will attack the seas — and his army will march through the forest to get there." She waved a hand behind her. "But in Pinewatch, the people are safe. Your cook's blasted sauce has drawn so many mercenaries in that I wager nothing short of *Midlan* would be able to take them.

"You've been incredibly fortunate, Aerilyn. Many villages haven't fared as well as yours. Think of Lakeshore," she added, her throat tightening at the end. "A house you'll never use again is a small price for your people's safety."

Aerilyn fell silent. Her face burned and she looked away.

"Ah, did someone call for a healer?"

A slight forest man had appeared in the doorway behind them — and judging by how wide his eyes were, he'd heard quite a bit.

"She's got a nasty arrow wound," Aerilyn said, pointing to Elena. "You can work here. I'm going to speak to Horatio." Then she slid off the bed, straightened her tunic, and marched out the door.

****

By the time the healer finished sewing her up, the tavern had been filled for the evening. Aerilyn still hadn't returned, and Elena wasn't hungry. So she lay down on the bed and tried not to undo the healer's work.

She still couldn't believe what had happened to Lakeshore. Some moments, she was certain it'd all been a nightmare — a vision drawn in feverish sleep. But the longer she thought about it, the more real it became.

D'Mere was ... dead. She had to be. There was no way Crevan would've let her escape. All the things she'd meant to say to her were now stuck inside her chest, swirling against her ribs — trapped for all eternity. She thought she would've been relieved by the Countess's death. It was what she'd wanted, after all.

But for some reason, it left a bitter taste in her mouth.

When the noise downstairs finally died, Elena ventured back into the tavern.

The door was closed, the windows shuttered, and all the candles lit. The maids were just finishing up their mopping. They quickly scattered at the sight of Elena.

She followed the sound of voices down the hall into Garron's office. Aerilyn and Horatio were seated across from each other at the long table. She took sips from a cup of tea and he drank deeply from a goblet. Both were food-stained and lathered with sweat.

"I never realized tavern work was so positively brutal. Is it like this every night?" Aerilyn said.

"Yes," Horatio replied, after a particularly long swig of his drink. "Good gracious, yes! Men start clomping in the moment we've opened and don't leave until we've kicked them out. Hired blades do well for themselves, these days. They've got coin to spend, and they eat like an army."

Aerilyn's eyes widened. "How could you possibly have enough to feed them?"

"I don't," Horatio admitted gravely. "They've drained us of nearly every morsel. I'm going to have to start taking apples instead of coin if we're going to make it to autumn. Foster goes into the Valley, occasionally. Perhaps he could bring me something back."

Aerilyn nearly choked on her tea. "You can't let the merchants know you're running out — they'll swindle you! They're furious enough as it is. Do you have any idea what an apple will cost if you tell them you're running low?"

Horatio pursed his lips, and his eyes slid away. "Really? They're furious with me?"

"You've got them by their purse strings. They have no choice but to pay what they're told." A smile bent her lips as she added: "Papa would be thrilled."

Horatio chuckled. "He would be, wouldn't he? I like to imagine that he's grinning about all this, somewhere across the river ..." He blinked quickly. "But if I don't find some apples soon, he'll be furious. Oh, I wish that boy hadn't used so many apples in his recipe! But I suppose I shouldn't complain, should I? That sauce is the closest thing to *magic* an average cook could hope to wield ..."

While Horatio ranted on, Aerilyn looked down and bit her lip. She fiddled with the handle of her teacup. She did everything but offer up the obvious solution: the plains were thick with apples nearly every month of the year. Lysander could've had Pinewatch's stock refilled in a fortnight.

The fact that Aerilyn said nothing about this could only mean ...

"I can't believe it. Please tell me you've told him," Elena said.

They both jumped.

Horatio grasped his chest. "How long have you been standing there? You're liable to kill a man, bursting out like that!"

"I know." Elena sat next to Aerilyn — and pointedly ignored her glare. "Have you told him?"

"Elena!"

"You haven't? Oh, dear." Elena glanced up at Horatio. "I have a feeling this is about to get interesting."

He couldn't see her smile through her mask, and it was obvious by the way his eyes had widened that he was worried. "What's interesting? What haven't you told me?"

"It's nothing. We can discuss it in the morning," Aerilyn said quickly. "Goodnight."

Elena grabbed her around the arm before she could escape and pulled her back down into the chair. "The longer you put it off, the more it's going to sting. Are you ashamed?"

"No!"

"Then just tell him."

Aerilyn gave her a scathing look before she turned back to Horatio. "Well, while I was away, something happened."

"What sort of something?" Horatio leaned forward. His eyes searched. "Were you injured?"

"No."

"Attacked? Because Kyleigh swore —"

"No, no! It was nothing like that. It was something ... good. Marvelous, really." Aerilyn took a deep, wavering breath. "I've fallen in love."

Horatio looked as if he'd just had the wind knocked out of him. His eyes flicked between them as he leaned back in his chair. "Love ...? Are you sure?"

Aerilyn nodded. "With all of my heart. I've never been so impossibly happy."

After another moment of staring, Horatio leaned forward. He took Aerilyn's hand — and inexplicably, he took Elena's, as well. She was trying to figure out what was happening when he smiled and said:

"Well, I'll admit this wasn't at all what I'd been expecting. But I suppose the heart wants what the heart wants. And as long as you're happy —"

"No." Aerilyn shook her head and very firmly said *no* again. In the second it took her to peel her hand away, her face had already turned crimson.

Horatio looked more perplexed than ever. Had Elena's shoulder not been aching so badly, she might've laughed. But her pain made her impatient. "What Aerilyn's trying to say is that she's taken a husband — and you'd be lucky to have me, by the way," she added with a glare.

Aerilyn rolled her eyes.

Meanwhile, all of the color had fled Horatio's ruddy cheeks. "A husband? What husband?"

"He's a seas man —"

"*Elena!*"

"— and also a pirate captain." She let her words hang in the air for a moment: Aerilyn watched through her fingers as a wild, dangerous purple spread across Horatio's face. "There. Now that we've got that out of the way, I hope we can —"

"A pirate captain?" Horatio roared. "A *pirate* captain?"

"He doesn't pirate anymore! He runs an honest trade," Aerilyn yelled back.

Horatio's girth lurched the table forward as he sprang to his feet. "Outlaws don't change! Men who have the taste of blood on their tongues will never be anything more than —"

"He's not a savage! Don't even say it." Aerilyn's chair clattered onto its back when she stood. "He's an honest, decent man. And I happen to love him."

Elena slipped away from the table as quietly as she could. Had she known a trip to Pinewatch would be so dangerous, she would've died in the woods rather than let Aerilyn drag her here.

The yelling carried on in a never-ending stream behind her as she paced towards the room's one small window. It was blacker than a cave's mouth outside, but her eyes adjusted to the darkness quickly. After a moment, she smiled.

It seemed that Fate had given her a chance at the Countess, after all.

CHAPTER 23
ANOTHER ARMY

Countess D'Mere watched from beneath the hood of her cowl as the last of the house's patrons stumbled out the door. There were tears in her clothes and bits of bramble lodged in the knot of her hair. A bruise swelled across her ribs. It bit her with a fresh sting as she shifted her weight.

A mere few days ago, she'd been safe inside her castle — confident in her plan. Another army was coming after her. Someone else wanted her blood. But she hadn't worried. In fact, it'd given her the opportunity she needed to escape. While Midlan clashed against this other force, she'd planned to slip away quietly.

They would cross the lake and disappear into the woods beyond the village. The other army would perish against the strength of Midlan, and Crevan would assume she'd been killed in the fight. D'Mere had seen to it that the castle burned, wiping away any hope of finding her body. She'd thought it was the perfect plan.

But, she was wrong.

Nothing could've prepared her for the night when the other army struck. She'd underestimated its force: the army devoured Lakeshore in minutes, dragged it into a burning oblivion. Then it charged along the shore and slammed against the castle.

She'd never seen such cruelty, such a deranged lust for gore. They'd used their fists, their heels ... their teeth. She'd seen her own shock reflected in Midlan's eyes as it sprinted for the gates, felt the desperation in the pounding as it tried to force its way inside.

But the moment the soldiers' backs were turned, the other army fell upon them ... it tore their bodies apart like wolves ...

It was only by sheer luck that D'Mere and the twins had managed to escape. They burned the castle, but these new enemies weren't fooled — and they pursued her.

Several of her agents had fallen into this army's hold. They were men who knew the forest better than the tops of their boots.

They knew which paths to watch, which roads to block. But worst of all, they knew how to track her.

They'd been locked in a desperate chase around the forest, trying to stay one step ahead of their pursuers — trying to get out. But the army had them hemmed to within a few miles of Lakeshore's smoldering ruins. It forced them to run in a circle, and the circle was growing smaller by the hour.

Even now, D'Mere swore she could hear their footsteps dragging through the darkness. Their heavy breaths scraped across her ears; their hollow eyes peeled the night away ...

Left gripped her arm.

"No, not yet," D'Mere whispered, her gaze upon the windows. Darkened figures bustled past them, wielding mops and brooms. "Once things quiet down a bit, we'll begin."

They'd arrived at Pinewatch in the early afternoon. It was an incredible risk to linger in one place for so long. But after days of getting nowhere, D'Mere realized they had little choice.

There was a chance they might be able to break the army's line and escape the forest, but they needed supplies. She'd stashed a few bottles of poison in Garron's house long ago — in case he was ever under attack. But he'd never needed them.

And with Garron gone, this place was nothing more than a house inside some worthless village. She no longer cared if it was protected.

They'd slept for a few hours in the woods outside the house, waiting for the cover of night. D'Mere thought it best to slip in unnoticed. She didn't want news of her survival leaking out to Crevan: *one* army on her trail was more than enough. But even if her supplies were still there and everything went according to plan, they might not make it out of the forest alive. Their enemies were far too close.

Then, just as the sun began to fall, she'd noticed something ... intriguing. It was something that might slow the army down, something that — in the proper light — might possibly draw its attention away.

An unexpected gift.

At last, the lanterns dimmed and the servants stored their mops. D'Mere waited a moment longer. "Are you prepared, Right?"

The young forest man nodded. There was a nasty bruise swelling over one of his eyes and the golden crest upon his tunic was torn. But the blood that spattered his sleeves wasn't his own.

D'Mere pursed her lips as she drew a small envelope from the pocket of her breeches. "Mix this in with the leaves. Remember, it's the tin with the blackberries. Make sure you aren't spotted."

He disappeared into the darkness, calm and silent as a wraith.

"Find us a fresh set of mounts," D'Mere said to Left as she crawled from the shrubs. "I'll meet you upstairs."

She stepped to the front door alone, her cowl drawn over her eyes. Something moaned behind her and she nearly jumped before she realized it was only the wind. The bruise on her ribs throbbed to life as her heart began to pound.

Finally, D'Mere's limbs thawed enough to push on the door. The latch was undone. She stepped inside to the sounds of an argument: the cook blustered about something, and Aerilyn shrilled back. There wasn't time for it. There wasn't nearly enough time. But D'Mere slowed to listen.

"I never should've let you go off on your own!" the cook cried. "This whole mess is entirely my fault. You were far too young, you knew far too little. Had I kept you at home, that pirate never would've snared you."

"He didn't snare me — I chose him!" Aerilyn said back. "I love him!"

"No, you only *think* you love him. I know how these roguish fellows work. They'll say whatever it takes to get around your skirts —"

"Ugh!"

"— and then they sail off at the grayest hour of the dawn, never to be seen or heard from again. I've known far too many bright-eyed young women who've fallen into their trap," the cook railed on, ignoring Aerilyn's protests. "Now one of them's gotten to you. He's ruined you!"

D'Mere glanced into the office as she passed and saw them glaring daggers at each other from across a long, food-stained table. Once she'd slipped by, she set her eyes down the hall —

"We have a son," Aerilyn burst out.

D'Mere paused.

"A son?" There was a loud *thud* as the cook's girth struck the seat of his chair. "You ... you've become a mother?"

"I have. And it kills me every moment I'm away from him. But there are far greater things happening in the Kingdom — horrible things that no one around here seems to understand. I came to the forest because I thought I could help the seas. I haven't come for your blessing, and I don't need your lectures. Lysander is a good man, Horatio," Aerilyn said severely. "He cares for his people, and he cares for me. I have to practically force him to leave my side. Goodnight."

D'Mere took a few rushed steps down the hall.

"Wait — please!" The cook's chair scraped the ground and his steps thudded quickly towards the door. He reached Aerilyn just as she was about to cross the doorway. D'Mere caught a glimpse of her shadow as she turned.

"What?"

"It's a difficult thing, learning the little girl I've looked after for so long has become a woman. I can't imagine you as a wife or a mother when you're still a child in my eyes. Just ... just give me a moment to let it all sink in." The floors creaked as he shifted his weight. "I'll have one of the girls make us a fresh pot of tea. Then you're going to tell me everything ..."

D'Mere was gone before the cook lumbered through the doorway. She darted up the narrow flight of stairs and down the hall to a room she knew well. It'd been her room once, for a brief season many years ago. She was pleased that Garron had given it to Aerilyn.

The door opened to the dimly-lit chamber beyond. One lantern glowed on the bedside table. All of the other lights had been put out. The room still reeked of their muted wicks.

D'Mere didn't bother to close the door behind her. She drew her cowl back and paced straight to the window, where she leaned out into the night. Though the air was cool, a cold sweat filmed her throat. She had to close her eyes against the forest's pitted stare, against the moaning of the wind. As long as they were open, they would try to trick her into thinking she saw other things: soulless bodies dragging through the brush, hollow gazes turned unblinkingly upon her face.

Her arms began to shake the longer she stood in the window. Nearly every part of her screamed to draw the curtains and step back inside ... except for one.

234

Cords of a dark, quiet something snaked their way through her veins. It was soothing — the caress of an old enemy easing its way into her blood. Though most of her shrank back beneath its spell, there was a part of her that loved the darkness ... and it woke with a moan.

This other woman grinned at the danger. She no longer felt like a carcass hanging above a pack of wolves, but counted herself among them. D'Mere was the fiercest wolf, the most cunning of them all. The others would cower against her strength.

In a matter of moments, the scout would find her. There was no chance he would miss. She was raised among the trees with a lantern glowing at her back — a beacon for her enemies. D'Mere couldn't have made herself anymore of a target.

And she wasn't disappointed.

The scout's signal drifted through the woods: the faintest call, the screech of an owl. The others would be close behind. Now all D'Mere had to do was make sure they stayed.

She drew the curtains tightly closed and paced back, smiling when the door creaked shut behind her. Soft, practiced footsteps paced across the floor. D'Mere knew that tread. She'd been listening for it.

"That was clever, using my daughter to get through the forest unscathed. Though I suppose I shouldn't be surprised. You've always been the clever one. And how is my Aerilyn?"

"Not a thing like you," Elena snarled. "She would be ashamed if she knew the truth."

"Yes ... which is why we never told her."

"I don't know how you did it, Countess. I don't know how you escaped Crevan or survived long enough to make it here. I don't know what you're doing in Aerilyn's room, but I don't care." There was the faintest hiss of a dagger sliding free. "I'm just glad we're going to have the chance to ... settle things."

D'Mere smiled when Elena came to a stop at her back. "You're finally going to do it, are you?"

"Give me one reason why I shouldn't."

"You should. You have every right to slaughter me where I stand ... but you can't do it."

"The only problem I'll have is figuring out how best to kill you."

235

D'Mere sighed at the pressure of a dagger's tip against her back. It stuck tightly to her skin, but went no further. The blade didn't plunge through her flesh or draw a line of her blood — and it wasn't like Elena to hesitate.

This was going to be far too easy. "Go on ... kill me."

The dagger pressed tighter, pushed her flesh nearly to breaking.

D'Mere laughed. "Don't go soft on me now, girl. I thought you were a killer."

"I am."

"No, you're a disappointment."

D'Mere spun, slapping the blade aside. Elena's dark eyes burned above her mask; her brows were fixed in a glare. But her twin daggers hung loosely from her hands.

She still clung to it, then — this hope she'd held onto since she was a child. Elena's eyes turned up to her now in the same way they always had. She watched D'Mere through their tops as if, at any moment, she might dissolve the wall between them and draw her close.

But it would never happen. This hope she held onto was nothing more than a dream — and over time, it'd become her chain. It was the very chain D'Mere had used to bind her. There was no longer any pointing pretending. Elena was of no use to her. In fact, she'd stopped being useful a long while ago.

It was time her chains were broken.

"I expected so much more from you, Elena. You could have been so much more — you have within your grasp all the power of Death, perfected." D'Mere spoke softly, careful to hold her eyes. "But you're too weak to wield it."

Her brows cinched together even as her glare wavered. "I'm not weak."

"Look at you," D'Mere hissed. "You've spared a woman who's tried to have you killed half a dozen times, who heard your screams and did nothing to stop them. Yes, I know why you hated Holthan."

D'Mere took a step forward when Elena stumbled back. She'd lost her grip: her scowl was gone, replaced by a mix of hurt and shock. Now it was D'Mere who held the dagger ... and she would show no mercy.

"You ... knew?"

"Of course I knew. Not a whisper passes through my castle that I don't hear. I'd hoped that you would kill him for it. I would've been proud, had you killed him. But I suppose you loved him too much —"

"I didn't love him! I hated him!" Elena screamed.

D'Mere smirked as she watched her knuckles go white about the twin daggers. "No, you loved him, Elena. The only people you love are the ones who've hurt you. You can't seem to help it. Do you want to know what I think?" D'Mere stepped into her. She wound her fingers through the dark waves of Elena's hair and whispered: "I think you love to be hurt because it suits you ... you know that you deserve it."

"I don't ..."

"You do, child." D'Mere kissed her softly on the cheek. "You do. Think of all the things you've done, all of the horrible, merciless things. This is Fate's way of bringing about your reckoning."

"I only did what you told me to do."

"Yes, you've been my loyal pet for many years. You hunted those I sent you after, you killed as I commanded. But even the best dog sometimes suffers a kick from its master. You deserve no better."

Elena stumbled backwards, her brows creased in aguish above her mask, the steel in her eyes finally broken. "Is that really what you think of me? Then why did you choose me?" she snapped at D'Mere's nod.

"Choose you? I never *chose* you. Taking you in was merely a matter of convenience. There were several families of whisperers staying at the inn that night, all of them bound for Midlan. I took the five infants because I knew you would grow to be loyal. You would know nothing else. And I was fortunate: four of you turned out to be warriors, but the fifth ... well, he wasn't of any use to me."

"So you killed him," Elena spat.

"Had I not stolen you away, Crevan would've dashed your heads against the floors of Midlan. You ought to thank me for preserving your life for as long as I did." A smile bent D'Mere's lips as the truth crashed over Elena, pushing her back another step. "Even after all of this, you're still searching for a reason not to kill me. In spite of all I've done to you, there's a small, pathetic part that still loves me."

Elena's eyes creased above her mask. "You never cared for me at all, did you?"

"I'm not your mother," D'Mere said coldly. She cupped Elena's chin, forced her to meet her eyes. "And you should be grateful for that. Mothers abandon, mothers die." She smirked and added at a whisper: "Yours certainly did."

That time, D'Mere pushed a bit too far.

Elena broke. Her daggers fell to the ground and she knocked D'Mere's hand away with a snarl. The window rattled as she shoved her against it — one hand clamped around her throat.

Elena's eyes burned darkly. They stretched as D'Mere's head began to pound, covering the world in shadow. Her hands went numb. She tried to reach for her dagger, but Elena's elbow was pressed against her chest — trapping the blade beneath it.

Elena's voice swam from the darkness, chilling her with its calm: "I've wasted my life playing your games, D'Mere. Now you're going to play one of mine. I'm going to squeeze until you scream that you're sorry. Then, I'll give you a little air. We're going to go on like this until you've apologized for every betrayal, every lie. I'm going to make sure you're sorry for every time Holthan tortured me. Your last breath will be wasted in a scream —"

Thud.

D'Mere sank to the floor when the pressure relented. She crouched as the world swam, trying to blink the darkness from her eyes. Elena's body lay at her boots, having been driven down by the pommel of Left's sword.

"I'm fine," D'Mere snapped at his look. She spoke hoarsely; her throat nearly sealed shut by Elena's grip. "She'd better be alive."

Left nodded.

"Good. Take her to an empty room — and make sure she has her weapons. If Aerilyn's to have any chance at all, she'll need them."

Left slid the twin daggers into the sheaths on Elena's arms and then scooped her body off the floor. He carried her easily through the doorway. D'Mere lost track of his muffled steps almost as soon as he'd gone.

All was going well. D'Mere drew the cowl over her eyes once more. She made certain it covered the rising bruise on her neck, and listened carefully for Aerilyn. Her steps sounded down the hall not a moment later: heavier than usual.

Right had finished his task, then. The rest would be easy.

Aerilyn's golden brown hair hung loose around her shoulders. Her boots were muddy, her breeches stained. And for whatever reason, the entire bottom half of her tunic had been torn away.

She stumbled into the room and froze mid-yawn when she saw D'Mere. "Countess! You ... you're alive."

"I am," D'Mere said coolly. She wasn't certain what Aerilyn knew, and she was determined not to say too much. "I've had a trying few days, girl. You must know that I can't stay for long — I couldn't bear it if something were to happen to Pinewatch."

Aerilyn's eyes squinched at their bottoms. "What have you done? Why is Midlan after you?"

"What have I done? I stood against the King. I refused to help him wage war with the Kingdom, and so he made an example out of me. Things are changing swiftly, Aerilyn. I fear the seas may be next ... so I've come to warn you."

"*You* were the one who started the trouble in the seas. I know it was you," Aerilyn said, the vehemence in her voice dulled by a heavy yawn. She seemed to be struggling to hold her glare. "Chaucer disappearing, a bag of heads ..."

"Nothing more than a series of nasty rumors. The council failed to negotiate a treaty with the King and, rather than face the wrath of their people, they put the blame on me."

Aerilyn's body swayed with her blink. "Well, that certainly ... *seems* like something the council would do."

"And it's precisely what they did," D'Mere said calmly. She stepped over to Aerilyn and wound her fingers through her hair — tying it into a knot that matched her own.

"But it ... it isn't fair. It's not fair for you to ... take the blame ..."

Aerilyn looked about to tip over. D'Mere grabbed her shoulders tightly. "Nothing's fair about the council's games. The lesser men band together against the strong until all that's left is weakness. But weak men can't bear the weight of rule for long. That's how all regions fall. The High Seas will soon belong to Crevan."

Aerilyn's eyes had fallen shut while D'Mere spoke, but she slowly forced them open. They were perilously red. "It's all been for nothing, then. I came all this way because I hoped you would speak to the King on our behalf, I hoped you might be able to get us a treaty. But if the council's turned its back on you ... if Crevan ... oh!" Her head slung forward into D'Mere's shoulder. "I don't know — know what to do!"

She held Aerilyn carefully, lips pursed against her sobs. There would be no saving the seas. Midlan had likely begun its march upon the council, if it hadn't already reached the gates. But the King's wrath would be a mercy compared to the force that stalked D'Mere.

Its soldiers never tired, they never stopped. A handful of them had even tried to swim after her boat. She'd turned to watch as the twins rowed for the middle of the lake, her skin tightened against their screams.

They were terrified of the water. Their arms flailed and they rent the night with blood-chilling shrieks. Still, they marched on — until the water covered their heads and stilled their flailing in death.

Even if D'Mere *did* manage to escape the Grandforest alive, they would follow her across the Kingdom. Their pursuit would be as relentless as the sun's journey across the skies. They would never slow, they would never stop ...

Aerilyn slumped hard against her chest, reminding her of the task at hand. D'Mere shook her awake. "Why don't you open the window, my dear? A breath of cool night air might help sharpen your eyes."

While Aerilyn stumbled over to the window, D'Mere slunk back. She was careful to hang in the shadows of the doorway when Aerilyn drew the curtains aside.

"Is there any way you might consider speaking to the council?" Aerilyn murmured as she leaned against the sill. "I know you can't do much ... but if people ... knew the truth ..."

D'Mere had been listening so intently to the scout's excited call that she almost didn't hear. "The council? What good would that ...?"

She stopped. An idea crept up to her as she thought about the chancellor's island fortress. She wouldn't be able to outrun her enemies, but she might be able to stop them — once the council was out of the way, of course.

"Yes. I'll leave at once," D'Mere promised.

"Thank you."

Aerilyn leaned into the night and breathed deeply. Her weariness made her vulnerable. It was difficult not to imagine her as a child. When she turned from the window and wandered sleepily to her bed, D'Mere almost regretted everything ...

Almost.

CHAPTER 24
A CAGE

Elena woke with a curse.

She'd been a fool to listen to the Countess, to allow her to speak at all. She would've done better to carve a line across her throat and spare herself the trouble. Instead, she'd fallen straight into another of D'Mere's games — one in which she enraged Elena to the point that she'd dropped her guard.

Now her skull throbbed and her heart stung horribly. As she lay still in the darkened room, trying to blink back the film of her pain, D'Mere's words coated her tongue in some bitter truth:

The only people you love are the ones who've hurt you ... it suits you.

As much as Elena hated to admit it, the Countess was right. She'd spent her entire life believing that she deserved what she'd been given. It made her torment easier to accept. She supposed there was a certain amount of comfort in the thought that all was as it should be.

But at some point, her comfort had become her cage.

D'Mere taunted her from outside the door while Holthan sat heavily upon its top. The world beyond was dark: there was no guarantee that she wouldn't be hurt again, once she left. She'd accepted the cruelty and the games out of fear, nothing more. Uncertainty jammed the door's only latch.

Perhaps she would never know if she deserved any goodness in her life. But she knew for certain that staying locked away would only leave her open to more cruelties, other torments. The sorts of people drawn to the cries of a caged woman were exactly the sorts who would stand upon its top. Her pain would never end, as long as she believed herself to be broken.

Though the Countess's words had been meant to hurt her, they'd unwittingly drawn the veil aside. Now Elena could see how she'd been trapped. She had to try to forget the lies she'd told herself. She had to leave the cage behind. There was no hope in comfort.

Walking into the uncertainty was her only chance of finding Jake.

Only after her pain had dulled did Elena think to be shocked that she was still living. The Countess had her pinned and unconscious. Why hadn't she slit her throat?

She was feeling along the ridges of her neck, wondering if it *had* been slit, when something hit her: perhaps she was still alive because the Countess hadn't been after *her*.

Perhaps ...

Aerilyn.

Elena jumped to her feet, squinting when the ache in her head sloshed forward and struck the backs of her eyes. The hallway seemed to tilt as she struggled to hold her footing. By the time she'd reached Aerilyn's bed, she'd managed to get her focus back.

But it didn't stay for long.

"Aerilyn?"

She was lying in the darkened chamber atop her sheets, unmoving. Elena pressed her ear against Aerilyn's chest and was relieved to hear the slow, steady *thud* of her heart. But she didn't stir — not even when Elena shook her did she do anything more than sleep.

The Countess must've drugged her ... again. It seemed like she preferred to put Aerilyn to sleep rather than have to talk to her. But why would she have come to Pinewatch if she hadn't meant to talk to Aerilyn? If she hadn't meant to kill Elena? Why would she have risked staying so close to Lakeshore?

One thing Elena had learned over the years was that the Countess never did anything without a purpose. Sometimes it didn't make sense until after the hammer had fallen, but she knew to look closely.

The window was opened a crack. A cool breeze swept in while Elena was thinking, stirring her from her thoughts. She'd stepped over to close it, annoyed, when a strange sound caught her attention.

It was the noise of heavy footsteps dragging through the grass — of snapping twigs and stones kicked aside. It was the sound of an army that wasn't even bothering to cover its march. And it was heading directly towards them.

Elena's vision sharpened, but the shadows that draped down from the monstrous pines were too thick for her eyes. Still, she could tell by how the shadows writhed between the pale gaps that there was a large company of men heading towards them.

Garron's house was practically defenseless. There were a few mercenaries staying at the house, but most camped in the village below. Elena couldn't face an army on her own. She had to think of something quickly.

Perhaps she might be able to frighten it away.

Aerilyn's bow stood in a corner of the room, propped between its quivers. Elena grabbed the one with the exploding arrows and draped it over her shoulder. The magic in it was so strong that it seeped through her armor. Her skin came alive where it touched: it gathered in itching bunches and protested her every move.

For all of her training, Elena had never fired an arrow. She hated archery, hated the guesswork of aiming, the nearly dozen steps that had to be perfected in order for the arrow to fly true. She loathed the possibility that, even with a perfect draw, one shift in the direction of the wind could knock an arrow completely off its course.

She preferred the weight of something more predictable.

Her fingers curled when she reached back to draw an arrow. Memories of Jake flooded her as she readied the bow. She could feel him in this spell, see him behind her eyes. Her mind was so focused on him that her strength wavered for a fraction of a second at the height of her draw — and the arrow slipped free.

It fell well short of its mark. The head struck the base of a pine just outside the window and exploded. Flames ate quickly through the tree, bolstered by its sap. With a huge chunk already blasted out of its base, it only took a moment for the fire to weaken it.

Elena heard the tree groan, saw its spiny branches come closer. She jammed the bow over her shoulders and hauled Aerilyn's body into her arms. The hallway shrank with her sprint. She thought she was prepared for the tree to strike the house, but the resounding *crash* still jolted her.

Doors swung open. Men cursed at the sight of the flames devouring the floor beneath them. Elena knew they would all go sprinting for the front door, and she planned to be well ahead.

She held Aerilyn tightly against her chest as she tore down the stairs. Horatio stumbled from his chambers, eyes wild and the wooden ladle already clutched in his hands.

"What was that confounded noise about? What's happening up there?"

"The house in on fire, and we're under attack," Elena called as she shoved past him. "Follow me if you want to live!"

She threw her shoulder into the front door and broke it off its latch. The cook's panting erupted into swears when he saw the horde waiting for them outside.

Blackened figures stood silently before them, their edges barely illuminated by the flames rising from the house. They stood so impossibly still that Elena almost didn't see them. Some of the shadows were the size of men — some were much larger. They looked almost like ... giants.

Something tugged on her memory: the image of a body washed up from the lake ...

Elena froze as the fires grew and cast a light across the nearest man's face. He was a desert man. His deadened, milky-white gaze fell from hers and dropped onto Aerilyn. His mouth opened, and he let out a shriek.

Maids, servants, and mercenaries tumbled out of the house behind them. Torches were beginning to flare up down in the village — no doubt awakened by the noise. One of the mercenaries shoved past Elena. He wore little more than his underthings and the sword at his hip.

"All right, who needs a gutting?" He bellowed at the frozen army. A handful of his comrades clustered around him, weapons drawn.

The man at their lead didn't answer. His eyes never moved from Aerilyn. They widened, he shrieked again — and this time, the others joined them.

Elena tore away as they charged, sprinting for the woods. The mercenaries swelled in behind her and cut the deadmen off. Their swords fell in skilled arcs. They fought angrily. But the horde never stopped.

The man at their lead swiped an arm at a mercenary's blade — only to have it hewed at the wrist. He didn't cry out. He didn't so much as grimace. His mouth hung slack and his dead eyes stayed locked onto Aerilyn. Even when a second mercenary swiped off his head, his body lumbered a few paces more before it collapsed.

A string of curses flew from Elena's lips as the deadmen broke through the mercenaries' line. She was well into the trees but could hear their footsteps pounding behind her. A swell of men from the village tore into their flank and slowed the deadmen further. But they would never stop.

Elena had seen the corpses of men who looked like this before, after their battle in the Endless Plains. And she suddenly understood why the Countess had come to Pinewatch, and why there'd been so many dead Midlan soldiers at Lakeshore. It wasn't the *King* she feared: it was Gilderick.

Lord Gilderick's army of deadmen was coming after her.

Even though it made sense, Elena couldn't believe it. That horrible witch of a woman! Was there nothing she wouldn't do to survive? She'd used her own daughter as bait — she'd thrown Aerilyn into Gilderick's jaws and put all of Pinewatch in danger.

The crash of Garron's roof caving in sounded off in the distance, but the noise of battle was growing fainter. Perhaps the mercenaries had been able to hold the deadmen off —

"Argh!"

Elena saw the shadow out of the corner of her eyes and managed to dart away just in time to avoid the swipe of a deadman's arm. It was a forest man. An involuntary gasp raked Elena's throat when she saw his face.

She knew this man. He was one of the guards at D'Mere's castle. His eyes hadn't given over to death quite yet. They were still dark, but vacant. His tongue lolled as he moaned:

"El-na ... El-na."

He was trying to speak her name. That must've been what he was saying. She slowed for a moment, a breath to listen. And it cost her dearly.

A pair of monstrous hands ripped Aerilyn from her arms just as a monstrous fist collided with her ribs. Elena steeled herself against the shock of a second blow and tore Slight and Shadow from their scabbards.

She managed to bury them in the back of the giant who had Aerilyn before the second flung her away. The world spun as she rolled onto her shoulder, but she quickly found her feet. Elena knew the giant wouldn't go down easily. His throat was far out of reach. His stride was too long. It would do her no good to run.

She would have one chance at finishing him — and she'd be lucky to get it.

When he barreled towards her, she matched his charge. Elena drove Slight downward, burying him deep in the giant's thick chest. She pulled herself up by the dagger's grip before his arms could wrap around her and swung Shadow for his throat.

Blood poured from his wound in arcs and torrents. The giant fought on even as his body slowed. Elena ripped her daggers free and tried to dart away when the giant's arm struck her in the back.

He swatted her down and she fell hard upon her stomach — but somehow managed to scramble away before his body could crush her.

She had to find Aerilyn.

Following the other giant's trail wasn't difficult. His heavy steps left tears through the foliage; the wounds in his back made the brush tops shine with gore. After a few moments of panicked sprinting, she saw them: two giants and the forest man crouched in the path ahead of her. While the forest man stared listlessly at the trees above him, the giants' heads stayed down.

The wounded giant was bent over Aerilyn. The other held ... something else.

Elena couldn't be sure, but she thought she saw a pair of emaciated legs dangling from them. She'd set her eyes upon the wounded giant when a slimy voice burst out:

"Fools — this isn't the Countess! She's slipped past us again. All isn't lost, however ... this pretty little thing knows where she's headed. Move, all of you! No, leave that here. Her body isn't any use to me."

Elena crouched low and stayed perfectly still while the giants and the forest man tore away. Once they were gone, she sprinted for Aerilyn.

The merchant's daughter lay still in the grass, her eyes gazing upwards. They seemed so distant, so transfixed by something that hovered in a world just beyond them. Elena knew that look. She'd seen it before. And her heart plummeted from such a surprising distance that she felt it shatter at the bottom.

"Aerilyn!" She grabbed the sides of her face and pulled her head from the ground. She tried to get her to move, to blink. But she wouldn't. She ... couldn't.

Elena didn't even feel the tears begin to fall. It was only when she pressed Aerilyn against her that she felt the wetness staining the leather of her mask. She had no idea where those tears had come from — no idea that she actually *cared*. She couldn't even remember when she'd started caring. But she supposed, somewhere along the way ...

This was her fault. Elena realized it with a second bitter coating of truth. She never should've led Aerilyn from the seas. This was entirely, completely, her ...

A pair of arms wrapped tentatively around her shoulders, and Elena pulled back so suddenly that she nearly strained her neck. "Aerilyn?"

She blinked as her gaze slid to Elena. "Why did you wake me ...?" She frowned. The sleep faded back as her eyes focused upon the trees. "And why are we outside? I could've sworn I fell asleep in my room ..."

"You did."

Her eyes went sharp, and her grip tightened. "The Countess! She was here."

Elena sighed heavily — too relieved to worry over the mess that awaited them in Pinewatch. "Yes, she certainly was."

****

"What do you mean, she *poisoned* me?" Aerilyn gasped as they fought their way through the woods.

It'd been a trying number of minutes. Elena told her what little she knew about the attack, but didn't have nearly enough answers to suit Aerilyn. She didn't know what the Countess had planned, or why Gilderick was after her in the first place. They'd always been close allies. She suspected Gilderick was even a bit fond of D'Mere ...

Well, as fond as a soulless bag of bones could be of anything.

"But why would she ...?" Aerilyn gasped and snatched Elena around the arm. "She's been doing it for years, hasn't she? Every time she would come to visit, I would get so sleepy that Papa would have to carry me to bed. I thought it was just the excitement of having the Countess over to visit."

"Maybe it was," Elena said, hoping that would be the end of it.

But it wasn't.

"I wonder how she did it? The servants always handled the tea, and she was nowhere near me tonight."

"She probably had someone do it for her," Elena said absently. She bared her teeth against Aerilyn's indignant squeal.

"That's it! She had one of her agents sneak into the kitchens and slip it in. Oh, that horrible, awful ..."

All at once, Elena's neck arched back as Aerilyn snatched a large handful of her hair. "What —?"

"Did *you* ever drug me, Elena?"

"I would nev — ow! I *rarely* drugged you," she amended, when Aerilyn twisted her hair.

"Why would she knock me out? Am I really that unbearable?"

Elena thought quickly. "No, it's just that she and Garron always had a lot to talk about, a lot of merchant talk. And she knew you would be bored with it."

That wasn't at all what their meetings had been about. But if Aerilyn never noticed the Countess's room being left untouched, then she supposed she didn't need to know anything further.

By the time they returned, Garron's home was awash in flame. Billows of smoke seeped from its ruins and drifted down into the village, hazing its lanterns and lights.

Elena had been expecting the weeping of an age when they arrived, but Aerilyn was strangely quiet. Her chin jutted out defiantly at the smoldering ruins before she went to Horatio's side.

The cook sat atop a fallen tree near the forest's edge. Gathered around him were the maids and menservants, the kitchen help and the stable boys. All eyes were turned upon the fiery remains of their home.

Loss deepened the shadows on their faces.

Aerilyn wrapped her arms as far as she could reach about Horatio and pressed her cheek against his thick shoulder. Elena kept to the shadows and tried to listen from a distance.

"I'm sorry, dear girl. I'm so terribly sorry."

"It isn't your fault. I brought this trouble here," Aerilyn muttered into his shirtsleeve. Her arms tightened, and she bit her lip. "I've done things, Horatio. I've been a part of all sorts of trouble."

"Things like toppling the Duke? I'm not as slow as my gait," Horatio said when she looked up in surprise. "The news of Reginald's fall reached the forest only days after your letter. I had a feeling your new friends might've been behind it. I told Garron from the beginning that I didn't think they'd come from the Earl. They're far too strange a pair not to be trouble."

"They are, indeed." Aerilyn's slight smile faded quickly into a frown. "Well, no matter what we've done, it doesn't mean much to us now. Midlan is marching on the council and the seas haven't got the army to stop it. The whole Kingdom is falling apart." She sighed into his arm. "Papa was always telling me to bargain only with the coin I carried. I should've listened to him."

Horatio said nothing in reply. The mercenaries and village men were returning from the woods. Their chests rose and fell heavily from their sprint. Their hair was matted with sweat, and their nightclothes stained with blood.

They slowed as they reached the burning house. Their faces were taut and angry. One of the mercenaries and a burly man Elena recognized as the village blacksmith walked far behind the others, obviously deep in talk.

Elena tried to listen over the crackling of the house:

"... I don't know. I've not seen anything like it before, I swear," the mercenary said. "Sure, there were rumors of folk disappearing in the southern woods. But there's always rumors. You learn not to listen."

The blacksmith carried a thick sword. He turned it over, frowning at the dark wet that covered its blade. "Did you see their eyes?"

"Like corpses," the mercenary said with a nod. "They kept running, too. No matter how much of them we lopped off — if they had the legs to move, they did."

"And if they didn't, they crawled." The blacksmith's chin dragged up to the burning house. "Desert men, plains folk ... our own people."

"Do you think it's some sort of plague?"

"Could be. Maybe the barbarians bit them."

While they went on about all the things it could've been, Horatio and Aerilyn were silent. The cook's eyes reflected the flames like mirrors — each tendril recast perfectly in the dark of his gaze. Aerilyn's seemed to take the fires in.

She seemed able to feel their heat from a distance.

"Perhaps you have more coin to bargain with than you realize," Horatio murmured as the men headed towards them.

Aerilyn frowned at his smile. "What do you mean?"

"The seas might find an ally, yet." His shoulders slumped and he made a great show of sighing as the men drew even with him. "I'm sorry, boys — but I'm afraid that's it. The fire's just taken out the last of my supplies and destroyed my tavern. I have nothing left to cook with."

"You could rebuild it," Foster called as he limped his way up the road. Judging by how his scant patch of hair stood on end, he must've just rolled out of bed. "We've paid you enough coin to build that thing twice over."

"It's all burned up."

"Coin doesn't burn."

"Well, it's melted, then. The copper's run into the silver, and the gold's run into that. We'd probably have to scrape out every grain of wood just to get half of it back. And I'm far too old to bother with all that. No," Horatio sighed again, "it's hardly worth the trouble. I'd rather just shutter the whole thing and live off of what I have left."

"What if we got your coin back?" a mercenary called. He turned to his companions. "One of the fellows I cut down had the Countess's mark on his chest. I'll bet a month's wages she had something to do with all this."

"Nothing goes wrong in the forest that the Countess hasn't had a hand in. She probably couldn't stand to have all of her merchants setting up shop over here," a villager added.

The rumbling grew to a heated growl among the men. Elena had begun to wonder if they were about to take off when Foster stepped in.

"I know what you're all thinking," he said, casting a severe look around them, "and it'll never work. The Countess won't listen to reason."

A mercenary towards the back of the crowd raised his sword. "We're not going to *reason* with her — we're going to get our tavern back!"

Cheers filled the air. Weapons rose high.

Horatio thumped a meaty fist against his chest and thundered: "Recompense! We'll be paid back one way or another."

"To Lakeshore!" a villager cried.

251

"No — wait!" The crowd fell silent and all eyes turned to Aerilyn. "Ah, it's just ... I have it on very good authority that Countess D'Mere is heading for the seas."

There was a moment's pause. Then:

"To the seas!"

The crowd made its way towards the village, Foster calling gleefully in its wake: "Don't forget to refill your quivers on your way out, lads. Foster's has the finest quality arrows in the realm!"

The two brothers darted into the crowd. They brandished wooden swords and bellowed *recompense* at every step.

Horatio took off after them. "Oh no, you don't! This is mercenary work. The only place you boys are going is straight home to your pap!"

While everybody else trailed away, Aerilyn stayed behind. "Elena," she said after a moment, "how did a burning pine tree wind up half inside my house?"

"The wind caught it."

"Elena ..."

"All right, I missed." She pulled the bow off from around her shoulders and handed the quiver back — relieved not to have the itch of magic on her anymore. "I'm sorry I crushed your home."

Aerilyn held the quiver thoughtfully. "Don't be. I suspect the noise woke the villagers. It certainly woke the mercenaries." She smiled slightly. "And now, against all odds, we're bringing an army to the seas."

"Is this how all wars start?" Elena wondered, glaring down the hill.

Aerilyn smiled wryly. "Over baked chicken? I doubt it. But at least they're on *our* side of things — and they're fighting for free, I might add. Do you have any idea how much it would cost to hire them all?"

Elena shook her head, glad her mask could hide her smirk. "I suppose you have a point, lady merchant."

CHAPTER 25
RUA

Kael fell asleep thinking it'd all been a dream — that he'd only *imagined* they'd been captured and led into a strange land. The dragons' shadows muddled the things he saw; their hums were the ebb and flow of his dreams.

When the sun rose that morning, a thin mist covered the land. They'd slept at the world's edge: on a bed of stringy grass and with the northern seas crashing behind them. Kyleigh slept soundly, no doubt still exhausted from the day before ...

Something flitted behind Kael's eyes. It was the shadow of a distant memory, a mere brush of noise and heat. The things inside the darkness swirled all around his mind. When he reached for them, they shoved him back.

Fine. The shadows could keep their secrets. He was certain nothing they might tell him would be worth getting upset over. In fact, he didn't think he *could* be upset.

He held Kyleigh for a moment longer, grinning as each heavy breath pressed her against him. There was very little that could've drawn him from her side ... but the strange land behind the mist was calling, and soon he could hold his curiosity back no longer.

A crest of hills sheltered them from the land beyond. Their sides were so steep that Kael had to pull himself along by fistfuls of grass just to make it to the top. Trees crowned the hills. Their trunks were thick enough that he felt ridiculous standing beside them. A half-dozen giants would've likely had a difficult time linking hands around the nearest one.

Though their tops were squat, the reach of their branches was great — so great that several of the trees had grown into their neighbors. Had it not been for their trunks, he didn't think he would've been able to tell one from the next. The ground beneath their shadows was bald from a lack of sun, and damp from a heavy morning dew.

By the time Kael had reached the forest's edge, the sun had begun to climb.

The mist shrank beneath its warmth. Each tendril weakened under the sun's gaze and melted into the earth. A jagged outcrop of stone appeared on his left, heavily shadowed by an arch of trees. There was a field of grass just beyond the shadows' reach: each blade grew tall enough to brush his knees. At his boots, the hill ended just as steeply as it'd begun.

He stood at the edge of a new world — one that not even the *Atlas* had spoken of. It was a region filled with deep valleys and crowned by sharp, rolling hills. The great mountain in the middle of the island wasn't the only one: high peaks sprouted from the land as thickly as the trees, their gray flesh draped in curtains of leafy green. They stretched on until the distance blurred them and melded their tops to the sky.

The air was as cold here as it'd been in the Unforgivable Mountains: Kael's breath came out in white puffs. But unlike the mountains, this land seemed to be at peace with the cold, content with the weather. The thick grass and enormous trees thrived — not in spite of the frost, but because of it.

A breeze swept over him as he thought this. It plummeted down the hill, scraping its wings across each blade and brook in a whistling song. And the fields sang back.

With the sun rising, he could see the rivers that wept from the mountains and the great lakes shining inside the valleys' maws. Creatures dotted the fields below — too distant to see clearly, but odd enough to make him wonder.

He began to pace as more of the land's shadows were melted away, as the light revealed more of its secrets. The moment Kyleigh woke, he wanted to go adventuring. He wanted to see every inch of this land, explore its every crevice ...

A rumbling sound cut over his thoughts. The jagged hill on his left was beginning to shake. Rocks crumbled from its sides and its top swayed dangerously towards the valley.

Kael was too startled to run. He backed away slowly, watching as the hill wavered and squirmed.

All at once, a pair of lights flared up inside the shadow — two glowing sets of eyes with blackened slits in their middles. Kael realized with a jolt that this wasn't a hill at all: it was a dragon. An absolute monster of a beast.

Kael's hand went to his sword and he gripped it tightly, prepared to plunge it through the middle of those eyes if the dragon attacked.

But it didn't.

A crackling hum filled the air between them. It wasn't a voice he knew, but it was ... familiar. The hum was broken up in short bursts; the yellow eyes creased in what could've only been amusement as they roved to his sword.

The dragon was laughing at him.

Before Kael could think to be insulted, its enormous head snaked from the darkness. The dragon's scales were a deep crimson. Its horns were short and thick. Spines ran from the tip of its snout across the middle of its head and down the back of its neck, each one growing a bit larger than the next.

The dragon's eyes were slightly rounded — which made its stare seem more curious than severe. Its serpentine neck twisted, carrying its head all around Kael's body. Those yellow eyes dragged across him and as it sang, its hum rose in interest.

Kael didn't know what the dragon wanted, but he was fairly certain it meant him no harm — and he was *completely* certain that he was tired of its hot breath blasting across his rump.

He supposed there was nothing for it. "Hello?"

The dragon stopped. Its ears twitched and its head cocked to the side.

When Kael tried to reach for its face, it pulled back — so sharply that its horns crashed into the branches above them and sent a mess of twigs and leaves raining down upon Kael's head. "I'm not going to hurt you, you silly beast! Just hold still."

The dragon would have none of it. When Kael tried to inch closer, one of its limbs scraped out of the darkness and shoved him back. Each of its claws came almost to Kael's knees.

He managed to grab one before slid away and thought, as loudly as he dared: *Hello?*

The dragon stopped squirming; the hum died in its throat. It stared at him for a moment, the black slits widening upon his face. Then something rumbled deep inside the dragon's chest. It rose up its throat, trembling louder as it climbed.

Kael had begun to concentrate on his dragonscale armor, fearing a blast of flame, when the dragon's voice struck his ears:

Hello, human. His voice was decidedly male. The way he rasped and hissed across his words reminded Kael of the crackling of flame. *I've not spoken to a human before ... then again, I've never worked up the courage to touch one.*

Kael couldn't help himself. The idea that a dragon might be afraid to touch him made him grin.

The dragon's eyes narrowed upon his face. *Do not bare your teeth at me unless you mean it, human. I don't wish to flatten your pale, fleshy body into the dust ... but I will if you continue to threaten me.*

"Oh, so you can giggle at me, but I'm not even allowed to *smile* at you? Is that how it works?"

You did a silly thing, reaching for so dull and frail a weapon. It doesn't have the fire to best me — and you may smile, as long as your mouth stays closed. Dragons do not giggle, he added, narrowing his eyes. *At most, we chortle.*

For a creature who'd never spoken to a human, he certainly knew a lot of their words. When Kael said as much, the dragon sighed — with such force and heat that he had to latch onto his claw just to keep from being swept backwards.

When I was young, my wings carried me across every sea, into the heart of each realm. Humans must be Fate's favorite creatures — they live nearly everywhere. I've always found their words ... amusing. They make such interesting sounds. I wished to learn them all. His eyes drifted from Kael and he boomed: *I* wished *to learn them all ...* them *all ... them* all —

"All right, that's enough," Kael growled, his ears ringing from the dragon's voice. "There's no need to try them out every blasted way. The words mean the same no matter how you make them sound."

Do they? Then why do they have so many different *sounds?*

"I'm not sure. But it doesn't matter. I'm Kael," he said, hoping to change the subject. "What do you call yourself?"

Rua, the dragon said. His eyes drifted away again and his scaly lips bent into what could've only been a smile. *My name is Rua ...* Rua *... R —*

"I've got it," Kael said evenly. He thought he might've preferred Rua's breath to his voice — the stench of charred flesh and all. "What do you call this place?"

Ah, these are the Motherlands, the first realm Fate ever stitched together. She is beautiful, is she not? Rua bent his head down to Kael's, blasting him with another hot breath. *You can see her care in the mountains' peaks, her smile in every river's bend. She loves these lands the most, I think.*

"Does she?"

Yes. The Westlands are dangerous and the Wildlands are fierce. But these are the —

"Wait a moment — you've been to the Westlands?" When Rua nodded, Kael forgot about being annoyed with him. "What were they like? What did you see?"

Rua's eyes widened. *It is a dangerous realm, even for a dragon. There are creatures in the Westlands you could not imagine — beasts made of ice and flame. The very mountains rise to do the wizards' bidding.*

"Wizards?" Kael breathed.

Oh yes, great *wizards. Their spells are so powerful that they swell to cover the sea and sky around them in a poisonous smog. No man or beast can survive it.*

"How did you get through, then?"

Rua inclined his head. *Well, once every century, a strange wind blows through the Westlands.*

"A wind?" Kael said skeptically.

A strange *wind*, Rua corrected him. *It blows for a time ... not very long a time, but still — time enough. And while the wind blows, it keeps the smog away. I crossed the Westland's shores with my chest full of thrill, but I left with a bit less.*

He stretched forward, revealing a blackened, shining scar upon the heavy plates of his chest. The scar was longer than Kael's arm. It split the scales it crossed between, leaving a charred cleft in its wake.

Kael was about to ask him more about the wizards when Kyleigh strode up behind him. Her pace quickened at the sight of Rua. But if she thought it odd to find a dragon hidden inside the woods, she didn't say it.

In fact, she hardly glanced at him before she grabbed Kael around the arm and pulled him away. "Come on. Let's find some breakfast."

Rua's hum crackled after them. Kael couldn't hear its meaning, but Kyleigh seemed to understand. She whirled around and said testily: "We're going on a hunt — if hunting is *allowed*, that is."

Rua sang again, his stare boring down.

Kyleigh's fingers tightened around Kael's arm for a moment, so quickly that he wasn't sure he'd felt it. "Well, I don't have your answer. So I can either starve to death while I wait for it to come to me, or I can stay alive long enough to find it. Your choice." She glared at his hum and rather tersely replied: "Brilliant."

"What does he want to know?" Kael asked as she dragged him away. He didn't like to see Kyleigh upset, and it was clear by how she drove her heels into the ground that she was far from happy.

"Never mind it," she growled.

Kael glanced over his shoulder and saw Rua watching them intently. His great eyes never so much as twitched from Kyleigh's back. "Do you know him?"

"No, but we spoke a bit last night."

His memories of the last few hours were far from clear, but Kael still thought he would've remembered meeting Rua. "Where was I?"

"Asleep. Look …"

Kyleigh dragged him behind a tree, out of the line of Rua's gaze. She wound her fingers through his curls and brought him close. Her touch soothed him. Whatever he'd been about to say died upon his lips …

Wait a moment — what *had* he been about to say? He couldn't remember.

Kyleigh's voice made him forget.

"Rua needs my help with something. But it's a task only I can do, all right? I promise I'll work quickly." She kissed him on the chin. "It'll do you no good to worry over it."

All Kael could think to do was nod. His head was so light that he wasn't sure if he could've found anything to worry about. A smile tugged at the corners of his mouth. He wanted to see Kyleigh smile back. There was something in her eyes that didn't seem quite right, and he thought a smile might make them brighter.

But her smile never quite seemed to reach them.

****

Kyleigh carried him a little ways from the shore and into one of the valleys.

Strange creatures grazed in a herd along the shadows of the hills. Their fur was every bit as thick and stringy as the grass. They looked like mountain goats: the herd's leader had massive horns that curled down his back and wide, gasping nostrils. But the creatures' legs were stocky, and their gaits seemed to carry them more in a series of tiny hops than a walk.

Kael followed Kyleigh into the shelter of a nearby clump of trees. They snuck to the edge of the shadows and watched the creatures graze.

"I wonder how they'll taste?" Kyleigh murmured from beside him. Though most of her attention was focused on the goat creatures, she kept an arm draped absently across his shoulder. Her hold tightened when he grinned. "What are you smiling about?"

"I've never seen you on a hunt before. I suppose I'm a little excited."

She brightened considerably at this, and her eyes looked a bit more familiar. "Which one should I go after?"

There was an old bull near the back of the herd. His horns were short and cracked, and his shoulders stuck out in two sharp hills — crowning either side of his spine. While the rest of the herd moved briskly from tuft to tuft, the old bull spent so long chewing one mouthful that Kael had to wonder if he'd forgotten how to swallow.

"I think we ought to put that one out of his misery."

Kyleigh pursed her lips. "Blazes, look at him shuffle around. I can practically hear the creaking. But the old ones *are* softer on the teeth … all right, then," she said after a moment. "I suppose it'll be ancient goat for breakfast."

She ruffled his curls before darting off into the woods.

Kael couldn't sit still. He paced back and forth beneath the trees, keeping his eyes on the old bull — waiting for the moment when Kyleigh would come plummeting from the clouds.

And he wasn't disappointed.

Her shadow started small but swelled across the herd like an inkblot until it'd grown into a monster. The creatures' ears shot up and their stocky legs bunched beneath them. Their leader nagged his herd to move with a throaty bellow, but it was too late.

Kyleigh's shadow swelled over the old bull and before he even had a chance to raise his head, she'd struck.

Kael heard the snap of his neck and watched as the old bull went still. The rest of the herd panicked and bounded away. Their stubby legs launched them surprisingly high — well over the roof of a Tinnarkian home. He could feel the *thud* of their bounds as the goat creatures followed their leader in a panicked mass over the hills, into the leafy crags of a nearby mountain.

Kael watched until they were little more than dots in the distance, amazed at how high they'd leapt. It wasn't until Kyleigh roared at him that he looked away and began climbing down the hill.

Everything about the Motherlands land seemed a bit ... off. He supposed it must've been the way the hills rolled and the mountains leaned that made it difficult to measure the distance, and the goat creatures wound up being far larger than he'd thought.

Though the bull Kyleigh had trounced was certainly ancient, he was also a monster — thicker than Kael was tall and easily large enough to sate a dragon's hunger.

Kyleigh stripped off a chunk of the bull's hide, and Kael could hardly believe how solid it was. He went to inspect it the moment she tossed it away and saw that it was nearly as thick as the width of his hand. He imagined the hide would make some rather sturdy leather.

And his fingers itched to try it.

"Which bit do you want?" Kyleigh called.

Kael had been so busy making plans for the hide that he'd forgotten about breakfast. "I'm not particular. Whatever you ... oh, for mercy's sake," he grumbled, when he saw just how much blood was matted into her hair. "You'd better find yourself a river to jump in."

"Surely it isn't that bad."

"You know very well how bad it is," he said when she grinned. "And I'm not sleeping next to you if you smell like death."

She breathed in deeply. "There's water nearby ... though I'll probably need help with the washing," she added with a wink.

Her look wasn't lost on him. And after the way she'd just fallen from the sky, he would've liked nothing better than to *help her wash*. But there was a problem. "I can't — not with him staring at us."

Kael thrust a thumb behind him, where he could feel Rua's eyes on the back of his head. The dragon had followed them out and now lay sprawled across the top of a hill, watching. He didn't know exactly how far a dragon's eyes could reach, but he knew from what Kyleigh had been able to see that they were well within his range.

"Privacy is a human thing. He won't be bothered by it."

Kyleigh sauntered up to him and pressed her lips against his. Kael hardly noticed. He couldn't even think to be mad about Kyleigh's very bloody kiss with Rua's eyes boring into his face — let alone focus long enough to kiss her back.

He finally had no choice but to push her away. "I can't. I can't go on with him gaping at me."

He expected her to laugh at him, or do something to make him deeply regret it. Instead, her face twisted sharply. Her brows fell low and her eyes blazed as she hissed: "Then you're the only creature on this blasted island who cares a whit. Now which part do you want?"

"Any of it is fine," Kael said carefully, stepping back.

She marched to the carcass and wrenched a full, stocky leg away with her bare hands.

CHAPTER 26
WEE MOUNTAIN MICE

While most of the Kingdom was just beginning to shed its frost, the Endless Plains was already warm with spring. New blades had begun to sprout beneath the deadened waves of grass. The soil had been churned back and seeded. For the next few days, the giants would be hard at work on their roofs and windows — readying their stout homes for the fierce spring rain.

Declan's roof was nearly finished. There were a few thin bits in need of patching, but they'd still be there in the evening. For now, there were far more important matters at hand.

He stood barefooted inside the horses' pen, his trousers rolled up to the knee. A small army of redheaded children gathered on his either side. They held bits of apple in their hands and giggled when the horses tried to steal them with their grasping lips.

Only one child seemed anything but pleased.

"No!" she squealed when Declan hoisted her off the ground. "No, they bite!"

"They aren't going to bite you, Marion. Horses don't eat wee mountain mice — they're far too gamey. You're not getting down without at least *trying* to feed one," he added when she began to squirm. "So you might as well sit still."

She stopped with a huff. He put a wedge of apple in her hands, and Marion gripped it like it was the last hold in a crumbling wall. "Only a small one," she pleaded.

"I can't promise you it'll be small. The horses choose who they come to."

She craned her head back, and the glare she gave him made the freckles across her nose bunch together.

Declan had to fight hard not to smile. "Keep snarling like that, and you're likely to draw a lion out of the grass. Would you rather feed a lion?"

Marion shook her head in terror, slinging her red curls about.

"Well then, you'd better put on a grin. Here comes one," he said, dropping his voice to a whisper.

A young gelding had been standing nearby, watching in interest. He snuck forward a hoof at a time, his shining black eyes fixed upon the apple. His thick neck stretched out as far as it could reach; his lips grasped.

But the moment Marion felt his hot breath upon her hands, she let out with a scream that rang Declan's ears and sent the horse bolting back.

"What in all clods was that? The poor wee thing only wants a bite of apple. He's *not* going to nip you," Declan insisted at her worried blubbers. "Here, let me prove it."

He'd been trying since the day they came home to get Marion near the horses. None of the other children seemed frightened of them — and it was a good thing, too. Declan was going to need help getting the foals trained to the saddle, and it might be nice to have helpers who could actually *ride* them, for once.

But Marion had been nothing but terrified of the horses from the first moment she saw them. There wasn't a child in clan Horseman who'd ever feared his trade. And it wasn't going to start with Declan's lot. He'd make friends of them, yet.

Declan took a wedge of apple from his pocket and held it between his teeth. The gelding crept up and grasped it away, ears perking as he chomped.

"See? He may not have much in the way of manners, but he isn't going to hurt you. Give it a try."

Marion thrust her apple out and shut her eyes tightly, wrinkling the freckles on her nose once more. She squirmed when the gelding took his first bite. But it wasn't long before her worry faded into an open-mouthed grin. "His nose is soft!"

"Of course it's soft. The rest of him is soft, so why wouldn't his clodded nose be?" Declan set her down among the other children and stepped back slowly, careful not to spook either gelding or girl. "You stay close to your brothers, now. Be sure not to get under foot."

Once she'd promised to mind, Declan set out.

He climbed over the fence and headed into the open land that stretched beyond his home. The Prince's castle was there before him, as it'd always been. Its rounded walls and towers seemed to dance along the ripples of the afternoon sun. But as grandly as the castle stood, it wasn't anything compared to the view behind him.

When Titus marched through the plains, his mages flattened the house Callan had built. But Declan drew it up from its roots.

Oh, he'd certainly had help: the house was barely started when he left for the mountains. But by the time he'd returned, the Prince and his men had finished it up nicely.

Brend had spent the better part of the week marching through the holds near the castle, helping with the fences and roofs. He was bound to come home at any day. Declan didn't think there was another ruler across the six regions that would've dirtied his shirtsleeves like Brend did. He doubted if any Lord or King had ever stooped to lay a brick.

That was the grand thing about their Prince: even at a stoop, he'd stand head and shoulders above the rest.

Declan walked backwards for a few steps, grinning at the house. The walls and windows were just as he remembered them; a garland of wildflowers hung across the front door. Little wisps of smoke still trailed from the chimney — the gasps of the fire he'd set for breakfast.

It was a grand thing, to have it all built again. He'd thought he would spend the rest of his days in the quiet and the calm, tending to his lands. Never in all the moon's passings could he have guessed that he'd have so many little creatures to share it with.

The walls nearly groaned when they were all packed in together, and there was never such a thing as quiet or calm. But he wouldn't have had it any other way. A home could always be stretched out a bit further, after all.

Declan tore his eyes from the house and back to fields. Jake was sitting hunched upon a rock before the Prince's castle, that book of his sprawled open across his knees. He scratched a lump of charcoal against the parchment in such a string that Declan thought he must be writing something brilliant.

But when he glanced over for a look, he didn't see any of the shapes he recognized. Instead of sitting in neat little lines, the scribbles flew all across the page. He wasn't certain what Jake was at, but he supposed there must've been a reason behind it.

Jake was one of those men who always seemed to have a reason.

"Is that the tongue of the mages I've been hearing about?"

Declan tried to ask it quietly, but Jake still jumped — and the line he'd been weaving shot across the page. "Ah, no. I was just … sketching."

"Sketching what?" Declan turned his head to the side, trying to figure it out. "The wind?"

"It was supposed to be the Prince's castle," Jake said, frowning as he pushed his spectacles up his nose. "But it doesn't looks as if I got there, does it?"

Declan plopped down beside the rock. "Eh, I'm sure you were getting around to it."

"You're just being nice."

"I'm happy, is all. The fields are mostly planted, the horses mostly foaled — and I've got plenty of wee hands to help. There's no grander thing for a giant, than to have his lands cared for. Things are good. They're finally good." Declan glanced over at the scribbles again. "Yeh, that doesn't look a thing like a castle."

Jake clapped his book shut. "Well, the clouds keep … shifting. I can't get a good view."

Declan frowned up at the sky. "What are you talking about? There's not a wisp of white up there — not even the shifty sort.

"There was a moment ago."

"I haven't seen a cloud since dawn."

"They were there," Jake insisted. "They've been up there all day, casting shadows over my — oh, blast it all!"

The lump of charcoal he'd been holding suddenly glowed hot. It burst into ashes and scattered all across the front of his book. He shook it out in front of him quickly, swiping at the little red embers. But they still managed to leave burns on the leather.

While Jake swatted and swore, Declan watched silently. There were lines on the mage's face that he hadn't seen in a long while — the troubling sort of lines, the little creases that made him look worn. Yet, he'd been all bright and grins a month ago. The last time Declan had seen him so ragged, it'd been after they'd won back the plains.

He remembered it well because Jake had been frowning on a night when everybody else was nothing but cheery. Now all of those lines were back again. They'd turned up when he did — in the middle of the night and without so much as a warning …

It made Declan wonder if Nadine had been right. "It's the clouds casting shadows, eh? Are you sure it's not that glare of yours?"

Jake looked up from where he'd been scowling at his gloves. "I wasn't glaring — I was concentrating."

"Well, you haven't stopped *concentrating* since you got here."

"Perhaps I've got a lot to think about."

"Yeh, maybe that's it." Declan scraped a hand through his stubbled crop of hair and looked straight out at the waving horizon. "Or maybe you're just missing someone."

"Even if I am, I'd rather not talk about it."

Declan understood. He'd rather not have to ask, to be honest. But Nadine had been so sure about it that he felt sick *not* asking. "All right, suit yourself," he grunted.

The afternoon had started damply and only promised to get damper as the day wore on. Something about the early spring always thickened the air. But once they'd had their first rain, it'd cool off nicely.

Perhaps the damp was just the sky groaning, working its way to spring.

Laughter filled the air behind them. Declan glanced over his shoulder and saw another handful of children gathered in the field beside the pens. They walked in a perfect line behind a desert woman who barely stood over their heads.

Declan had been through lash and storm. He'd fought battles with mages, beasts, and bloodtraitors. But he'd never been more nervous than the day he brought Nadine home.

He swore his heart didn't stop pounding the whole time they walked. The closer they got, the more he worried that she wouldn't like it. Whitebone was a great deal sandier, after all. The way she spoke of her little mountain farm made him feel like nothing in the plains would ever be grand enough, or green enough.

But it turned out that he'd worried over nothing: Nadine fit the plains like the moon fit the stars — and she glowed every bit as brightly.

There was a satchel across the front of her red dress, now. The silver links that weighted its hem were dulled with the crust of earth; she'd removed her bangles and rings. While she paced down the tilled rows, she used the butt of her silver spear to press holes into the soil.

The smallest of the children wandered close beside her. They reached into her satchel and put seed wherever she pointed. Some of the older children carried satchels of their own — and walked with staves that had clumsy points carved into their tops.

Nadine said something that made the children giggle. She was always making them laugh — even when she was supposed to be scolding them, she still brought out their grins.

Declan couldn't help but smile when the noise of their laughter drifted across the emptiness between them. But something crushed the smile just as suddenly as it'd appeared: a little gap in his roof that let the rain come in. "Don't scowl over it too much. There's not a man alive who understands womenfolk."

Jake snorted. "You seem to understand them pretty well. I don't think I've ever seen Nadine so happy."

"Yeh, she's happy. Maybe it'll be better just to leave it at that. Maybe we'd only be clodding it up, the other way."

"What other way?"

Declan looked down. Perhaps Jake might be able to help him — but he didn't want the whole plains knowing about it. He wound his fingers through the dead bits of grass and pulled them up by their withered roots, trying to think of a clever way to ask it.

"You've spent time with Nadine's folk, haven't you?"

"The mots? Oh, yes." Jake propped a fist beneath his chin and nearly smiled at the red mountains that rose against the southern sky. "They're a fascinating people. I'd very much like to visit them again."

"Do they do anything … strange? Anything we wouldn't do here?"

Jake pursed his lips. "Well, they honor the earth more than the sun — which is strange for desert folk. They've managed to fit the whole of their society inside three different colors … five, if you include the Grandmot and her Dawn. But that's a complication all in itself —"

"What about the normal sorts of things?" Declan interrupted, before Jake could give him the full history of it.

"Normal things?"

"Yeh, like eating or sleeping or … marriage?"

Jake's eyes pierced him from over the top of his spectacles. He stared for such a long moment that Declan began to worry that perhaps he hadn't been clever enough. But if the mage suspected anything, he didn't show it.

"The mots eat and sleep like anybody else. They marry like anybody else, but the asking *is* a bit different."

That was exactly what Declan needed know. He stared at the ground again. "And how is the asking any different?"

"The women are usually responsible for it."

"Well, what if she never asks?" Declan growled, digging his fist into the dirt. "And what if when *he* asks, all she ever says is that she'd only disappoint him? And how in the clodded summer breeze is he supposed to know what that means, eh? What's he supposed to be disappointed about? Her smile, her laugh? The way the sunlight touches her skin? Maybe his heart isn't *supposed* to swell up and burst when she dances. But what if it does? What's the rule for *that*?"

Declan hadn't meant for it to all come spilling out. But now that it had, he supposed there wasn't any point in sobbing over it. He'd held it in for so long that it felt better to finally say it.

"That's rather, ah … specific." Jake's robes scratched against the rocks as he shifted his weight. "I'm not sure the mots have a law for that — in fact, I doubt if anybody does."

"They ought to make one," Declan growled again. "I tell you, mage — you come up with a potion that protects a man from a woman's spell, and there'll be a line outside your clodded cavern."

"My cavern?" Jake frowned. "Where do you think mages live?"

Declan thought it was obvious. "In holes, mostly. Dark places where you can whisper secrets and read dusty books."

Jake's mouth fell open for a moment before he snapped it shut. "I'm going in."

"For a man who came here to study the plains, you've spent a lot of time indoors," Declan called.

Jake didn't answer. Declan watched from over his shoulder as the mage shuffled across the open land and ducked inside the heavy front door.

Nadine and the children had finished their planting and were on their way back. The children peeled off to join their siblings with the horses, and Nadine went straight for Declan.

He ducked his head as she drew close. "It'll never work, mite. Clan Horseman's soil isn't good for anything but galloping and grass-growing."

Nadine leaned against her spear, one hand propped upon her hip. "Perhaps that is because you do not tend to it. Not all earth is made perfectly — but with a little work, it can be made *good*." She jerked her chin at the house. "Did you speak with him?"

"I did."

"And?"

"He didn't admit to it."

"Why not?"

Declan went back to plucking grass as a bothersome heat spread down his neck. "We wound up talking about … something else."

Nadine pursed her lips. "I suppose I will have to speak with him, then."

"No, you'll only make things worse."

"How does speaking about something painful make it worse?" She flung a hand into the air. "If I were wounded, I would want it bound!"

Declan would've smiled at her, but he knew it'd only make her angry. "You can't keep picking at him. Magefolk are a clever lot. Jake'll figure it out. Now quit stomping your feet and come sit beside me."

"I will not sit — there is too much that must be done."

"And it'll all get done. There's plenty of spring left to do everything. But right now the sun's shining, the breeze is cool, and there's not a single weeping mouse in sight." He tugged playfully on the mailed hem of her skirt. "Enjoy it for a moment."

She tried to swat his hand away, but he only laughed. Finally, she seemed to give up. "You are a fool," she muttered as she plunked down beside him.

Her dark hair had grown long, and was bound every hand's length with a silver clasp. It fell across her shoulder as she bent to lay her spear in front of her, and the sun shone down its length.

They were quiet for a moment, listening to the horses' snorts and the laughter of the children. Then Nadine broke their silence with a heavy sigh. "I wish I could speak to Elena. I am certain there must be a reason she would turn him away."

"Maybe he caught fire to her lips. You can't force it," Declan muttered when Nadine glared. "You've got to let these things work themselves out."

"Sometimes *these things* need some prodding," she insisted. "If I knew her reason, perhaps I could help."

"Maybe she doesn't know her reason."

Nadine snorted. "Every woman knows her reason."

"Really? Then what's yours?"

Declan didn't look away when Nadine fell silent. If she wouldn't have him, then he would at least have an answer. "I have already told you —"

"You haven't told me a clodded thing. All you've said is that I would be disappointed, which is the silliest thing I've ever heard."

Nadine glared. Her chin rose defiantly. "I was married once before. Did you know that?"

No, he hadn't known that. But he was only surprised for about as long as it took to draw a breath. "That doesn't make me any difference."

"Well, would it be *different* if I told you he was killed in battle?"

Nadine's eyes shone furiously, now. But Declan didn't flinch. Instead, he leaned forward and took her hand in his. His thick fingers covered her to the wrist, but he held her gently. "Is that all it is? You won't love me because you're afraid I'll —?"

"No, that is not all it is!" she said vehemently, pulling out of his grasp. "There is another thing, something that shames me. You must trust me when I say you would only be disappointed."

Declan was about to say something else when Marion came sprinting up to them. She threw herself in Declan's lap and laughed as she pointed skywards. "Look at the birds!"

"What birds?" Declan frowned as he squinted up. "You aren't telling stories again, are you?"

"They're flying," she insisted through her giggles as Declan tickled her. "Look at the birds!"

"You're just being a silly wee mouse —"

"No, she is right." Nadine got to her feet quickly, her gaze fixed upon the sky. "I can see them."

They were blackened pinpricks in the distance — a flock of birds flying so high that they looked more like a cloud of gnats. The birds circled aimlessly at first. But as Declan watched, their circles began to creep them closer.

They hovered above the Prince's castle and grew larger with every pass. It was strange for them to be gathering there. He was certain there weren't any crops inside the castle walls. There wasn't anything at all that might've interested birds.

It was too strange a thing to ignore.

"Get the children inside," Declan said. He put Marion into Nadine's arms and leapt from the ground. "Don't step one foot out from under that roof."

"What is it?" she called as he charged away.

But Declan didn't answer.

Something grew inside his chest as he ran: a black cloud that filled him to the skin with worry. The birds were still a castle's height above the walls, but their bodies were growing larger by the second.

And by the time they landed, they'd be monsters.

CHAPTER 27
TO THE GATES OF MIDLAN

The sea of dried grass shrank beneath Declan's stride. His feet thundered in a furious beat. Sweat drenched his tunic and his lungs were tight with strain. But he never stopped. The closer the birds came, the faster he ran.

They were crows — he knew from their glossy black feathers that they *must* be crows. But he'd never known crows to stay so quiet. Not a caw or squawk sounded among them. He swore not a wing beat harshly.

When the crows came a tower's reach from the walls, he could see large gaps between their feathers. Patches of dark, swollen skin popped up across their bodies. The flesh of their wings was stretched so thinly that he could see the sun glowing through.

Some of them had strange-looking legs. Instead of keeping them braced against their tails, the legs dangled freely. The way they kicked beneath the wings made them look as if they were running. It was almost ... human.

Declan didn't have time to wonder. He didn't have the breath to fear. A fresh surge of strength burst through his limbs when he realized what those creatures were.

He was nearly to the castle walls when a soldier came up the rampart stairs. He moved slowly, and didn't seem to notice the horde closing in above him.

Declan swung his arms and bellowed: "Monsters! Beat the drums — call the guard!"

His helmet craned upwards and he nearly startled himself off the wall when he saw what Declan was pointing at. The soldier turned on his heel and went sprinting for the drum tower. He was nearly at the doors when the glint of his armor dulled, covered over by a monstrous black shadow.

272

It happened too quickly for Declan to follow: from somewhere among the crows dropped another sort of beast. It was a tawny bolt with blackened eyes and a great, curved beak — a hawk.

Its talons swung out as it struck, crushing the giant as if he wasn't anything more than a rabbit. Declan heard the crunch of the soldier's armor as the talons dug in. The last thing he saw was the monster's wicked beak: it flashed down and returned with an arc of red.

Declan roared. Black flooded his vision until all that was left was a narrow strip of light. The monster's eyes swelled inside the strip — growing, burning, taunting.

He was going to rip them out.

He was going to *rip them out*!

The hawk monster matched his roars with a screech. Its wings burst open and its black, maddened eyes locked upon Declan's. A lion woke inside his chest: it stretched its mighty limbs to his fingers and toes. It filled his lungs with its roar. The lion grew until his skin could barely hold its strength. It would split him down the middle if he didn't calm it quickly.

And there was only one way to sate such a beast.

He grabbed the hawk's talons the moment they slid into his vision. Its struggling only swelled his limbs, made his blood burn hotter. The lion roared as it smelled the monster's fear. Declan slung the hawk's body against the ground. He shattered its bones and drove its flesh into the dust.

But the lion didn't calm.

No ... it wanted more.

Crows fell upon him, drawn to the hawk's dying screech. Declan's vision blackened against their caws. Soon he could no longer see the battle before him ...

But he could feel it.

Bones snapped against his fists. Flesh gave way beneath his hands. He crushed them, he stomped them. A warm, sticky cloud wrapped around his body. Its tendrils scraped down his back and across his chest — maddening him with its hold.

Then all at once, the flesh and bones were gone.

His fists pounded against something that didn't fight him back. It didn't scream. No matter how hard he struck, it only made one sound:

Thunk ... thunk ... thunk ...

Cold crusted over his body. It seized his limbs and stole the roar from his chest. Declan tumbled out of the blackness and back to solid earth.

A strange blue light covered everything. It gave the blood on his knuckles a purplish sort of shine. His breaths came out like smoke. When he dragged his chin from the dirt, he saw he'd been trapped beneath some sort of window.

It arched over him — a stone's top of blue glass that shimmered and froze the air. Its sides were frosted up. Declan crawled over to the nearest one. There were dark smears beneath the frost. He could make out the clear marks of his fists.

His tunic was soaked in sweat and gore, but there was a clean patch on his elbow. He scrubbed a hole into the frost and stared out at the shimmering world beyond.

What he saw brought the lion roaring back.

Jake stood beside the window. One of his hands was stretched out towards Declan, his glove pulsing in time with the blue window's light. He raised the other at the coming horde: a storm of screeching crows.

They were a wave of talons and beaks, a mass of murderous eyes. Declan's rage swelled up again. He beat the window with his fists. But it never shook, it never budged.

The crows had come to within an arm's reach of Jake when a light erupted from his hand. Declan heard a low *boom* and the crows' bodies went flying backwards. The ground beneath him trembled. Most of the monsters simply tumbled away and clawed themselves back into a panicked flight. But those closest to Jake burst into tiny shreds of black.

No sooner had the crows gone than the world beyond lit up with a fury of colorful bolts. They flashed so brightly that Declan's eyes began to ache. Jake slowly disappeared inside the storm of colors until all Declan could see was his fingers — the hand that held the blue window tightly.

Declan didn't know what was happening. There was a constant noise outside: the crashes and rolls of a thunder that never seemed to stop. He wouldn't be any good trapped beneath the window. "Let me out, you clodded mage! Let me out!"

Slowly, the flashing stopped and the colors faded back. Declan jumped when Jake's body fell against the window. His face was twisted, pained. Sweat stained the glass where his skin touched. There were red lines coiled all around his chest, neck, and limbs. But he still managed to keep one hand lifted towards the window.

Jake's eyes were closing. His teeth were bared as if he stood beneath the lash.

Declan threw his fist against the glass in a panic, and the noise seemed to wake him. He shook his head at Declan's cries and sank to his knees.

Men strode out of the clouded world beyond. Each one had a red line gripped in his fist. They tugged on their holds, dragging Jake further onto the ground. And Declan realized they must be mages.

"Kill him," one of the mages grunted, his voice ragged with strain. He jerked his head at a mage beside him — one who stood smaller than the rest. "You do it. Your ropes are too weak to do us any good."

"I can't," the smaller mage pleaded. His voice was that of a child. But when a red line appeared upon the boy's wrist, he stepped forward.

Declan could see his face: he was a seas boy hardly over the age of ten. Though the other mages howled at him, he held his staff stubbornly to his chest — his eyes burning into Jake's. Soon his arms began to shake badly. Then his whole body shook. He bit down so hard upon his lip that the skin around it turned white.

Jake pulled himself up into a sit. But his face was so drenched that his spectacles slid off the end of his nose. He didn't seem to notice when they struck the ground. He didn't lean to pick them up.

"Do it," Jake grunted through his teeth. "It's not worth the pain — you can't fight it."

"No!"

The boy jumped backwards at Declan's roar. "I don't want to! Please," he twisted to the mage who'd given the command, his body trembling so badly that he could hardly keep his feet, "please don't make me."

"It's good for you, lout. The more you do it, the easier it gets. Now quit your sobbing and kill the battlemage!"

"One explosion spell to my head," Jake whispered. "One quick blast, and I won't feel a thing. You'll never have to see my face — it'll be easier if you don't have to see it." He glanced at Declan from over his shoulder. "Once I'm dead —"

"No! You're not dying!"

"— the shield will break. You'll have to run for the castle."

"I'm not running anywhere, you clodded mage! I'm going to rip their slimy guts out through their gullets! I'm going to snap their necks across my knee! I'll — I'll — argh!"

Declan dug his hands beneath the window's lip and tried to wrench it from the ground. He begged for the darkness, for the strength he needed to throw it aside. But every time the lion raised its head, a blast of cold wind knocked it down.

"Do it!" the mage hissed again. He turned his glare onto Declan. "I'm looking forward to shutting that one's mouth."

The boy's shackle went from red to a burning white. Tears streamed down his face as his legs dragged him forward a half-pace at a time. His body shook so badly that his staff wavered as he pointed it at Jake's face. It swept from left to right, a dangerous light growing at its end, until it finally halted — aimed directly between his eyes.

Jake said something, but Declan couldn't hear it over his roars. He threw his body into the window. His shoulders bruised and his head rang fiercely; his knuckles were so torn that he could no longer feel the pain. But no matter how he fought, the window held — and the boy's spell grew brighter.

A blistering orb wavered at the staff's end. It screeched as it grew, a terrible power building up behind it. Then all at once, the light went out.

"Stop!" the boy cried. He threw his staff away and his body collapsed upon the ground. His limbs coiled and his head rose as if someone gripped him by the roots of the hair. His eyes were strangely empty as he spoke: "Don't kill that battlemage — he might be useful. Bring him back to me."

One of the mages who held Jake's ropes looked as if he'd just been slapped. "He's too dangerous, Ulric! We can barely hold him down —"

"Bring him to me!" the boy screamed.

All around the circle, the mages' shackles lit up red. Even the crows' collars glowed hot. They'd gathered boldly behind the mages as soon as Jake was bound. But the second the red light bloomed across their throats, they took off in a thick, startled cloud. A number of hawks swooped into the space the crows had left behind. They clawed impatiently at the ground and shattered the air with their screeches.

Finally, it seemed as though the mages had no choice.

"Hold your spells. Do *not* let him loose," the lead mage barked.

They held their impetuses towards Jake while they struggled to mount the hawks one-handed. The boy managed to drag himself to his staff before a hawk wrapped its talons around him. It took off with a swoop of its wings and a blast of earth.

Declan had stopped fighting the moment the boy screamed. But when a hawk moved to grab Jake, the darkness began to cover his eyes once more.

He tried to yell. He wanted to tell Jake to get onto his feet and fight back. But the lion wouldn't let him. Instead of words, maddened roars tore from his lips. The world was growing smaller and hazed.

Jake lay unmoving upon the ground — collapsed beneath the weight of the red spells. All of his strength seemed to be bent upon the hand that held the blue window: it trembled against the pull of the ropes, but didn't fall. Declan's fury rose with every twitch of his fingers. The lion grew stronger.

A cool voice came from somewhere beyond the madness — the warning of the lead mage: "Tell your Prince that Midlan requires supplies. Give His Majesty what is owed, or he'll send his army back to destroy your pitiful region. You've been warned, giant."

The hawk that held Jake crushed him with its weight and bent its twisted face down to screech inside his ear. He cried out, twisting against the pain. In the last moment before he was taken, Jake's eyes dragged over to Declan.

And the lion overcame him.

******

Emptiness stretched beneath him. The world was dim and silent. Declan lay upon the edge of sleep. His mind wavered on the wall between a pale blue light and the infinite black beyond. One strong wind might send him over the edge. He couldn't wait for the winds to blow, wouldn't leave his fate to chance.

Declan leaned forward and braced himself for the fall.

His chin struck the earth as his body jolted. The pale blue light gave way to shimmering, frosted glass. A monstrous shadow stood just outside: a beast with dozens of tiny hands, all of them pressed and clawing against the window.

Blood coated his every inch. There wasn't a patch of his hide that didn't sting him. It took several moments for Declan to wipe the frost away, and the smears of blood away from that.

The shadowed monster burst out with an army of tiny voices. Its hands beat upon the glass where Declan's arm swept by. But it wasn't until he'd managed to clear a patch away that he saw the monster's faces — all of them freckled, smiling and pressed just as tightly against the glass as they would fit.

Their little fists pounded into the window; their voices rang out in a chorus:

"Nadine! Nadine!"

She crammed in among them and her face lit up with relief. "You are awake! Are you hurt? Where is —?"

"What in all clods happened?" a new voice bellowed. Brend gathered a clump of children in his lanky arms and set them aside, squeezing into the narrow gap left behind. His brows rose to nearly touch his spikey crop of hair at the sight of Declan. "I was only gone to help the Grovers a few days — hardly enough time to fuss over. But when I come back, Darrah's crying, one of my guards has gotten himself ripped to pieces, and my General's been magicked to the ground! Everybody's going on about a flock of giant crows, but nobody knows where they came fr —"

"Midlan," Declan grunted. He squinted against the throb in his head and pressed his face against the cold glass. "The King sent crows … and mages. Jake fought them off, but they … they took him."

Nadine gasped, and the children erupted into a mass of questions.

"What happened?"

"Who took him?"

"Where's Jake?"

The last question came from Marion. She had Jake's spectacles clutched in her hands and held them out to Nadine — as if the offering would somehow bring him back.

But it wouldn't.

278

Nadine took the spectacles from her and gave her hand to the eldest boy. "Take your brothers and sisters home, Thomas. We will be there in a moment."

Declan couldn't bear to meet their eyes, to see their faces. He leaned heavily against the window and stared at the blood-soaked ground at his knees. Only once they'd marched out of earshot did he dare to speak.

"Jake held the monsters off of me ... he saved my clodded life. And they took him for it. I couldn't ... I couldn't stop them!"

He slung his fist into the frosted glass and the jolt of pain shocked him. There were gashes down his arms, punctures in his flesh. His tunic had been torn to rags.

A sudden heat pressed inside his wounds and made him wince. He looked up in time to see the blue shield disappearing — melting like frost against summer winds. Nadine gasped again when the last of the shield faded and she saw the reach of his wounds.

"Bring me ointment and bindings," she said sharply.

Declan realized that a whole company of giants stood behind Brend. They'd been kicking through the twisted pile of hawks and crows, their mouths agape. Two of them split away at Nadine's command and went sprinting for the castle.

Her hands grasped his face, but Declan hardly felt it. His heart was too sore to feel it. The memories of Jake's face, of his body twisted in pain — they jabbed him each time they passed. And Declan's failure echoed inside his head:

I couldn't stop them, I couldn't —

"Cowards!" Brend roared, jabbing a thick finger at the sky. "You thin-blooded clods! Swooping in here while the Prince is away, murdering his guard, terrorizing his wife and babe? Do you feel powerful now, Your Majesty?"

"*Shhh!*" Nadine hissed, but his words brought Declan back. They dragged him from the pit and numbed his wounds with focus.

Brend stomped to crouch before Declan, and the determined edge in his stare steeled him. "What'd that yellow King want from us, eh? Or did he just come to shed blood?"

"He wants supplies. If we don't send them, he'll send his mages."

Brend's mouth went taut. They both knew what that meant.

But Nadine didn't seem to understand. "We cannot fight them. It would be best to give the King what he wants for now, and perhaps with the help of our friends —"

"No, there'll be no helping us, wee mot," Brend grumbled. His hands twined into a single, trembling fist. "If we bow to his orders once, he'll be back again. Things are going to be just like they were before — only this time, we'll be slaving under *Crevan's* whips."

The realization tightened Declan's chest. He thought of the home behind him and all of the little creatures living beneath its roof. There were so many lives balanced upon his shoulders, so many strings tied to his heart. They'd trusted in his strength.

And now, his strength had failed.

"We've got time to get the women and children out. Send them to the seas —"

"No! We are not giving up," Nadine said vehemently, cutting over the top of him. "Send word to our friends. They cannot help us if we do not ask."

"The pirates?" Brend sorted. "Their region's so muddled I doubt they could find time to lace their boots, let alone fight with us. Besides, they wouldn't be any good against the mages."

Nadine ignored him. Her grip tightened upon Declan's face and her brows fell in desperate lines. "The wildmen could help us. You have seen what they can do."

"They're on the other side of the Kingdom. We'd never reach them before —"

"Enough!" Nadine cried furiously. "Do not waste your breath with all of these reasons when it is clear that you mean to give in. If you want to labor for the King, then you are free to do so. Not even Fate can lead men who refuse to take a step."

"She's a blister, that one," Brend muttered as he watched Nadine march away. "Small, but she knows just where to sting you."

Declan said nothing. Nadine had Jake's spectacles clenched in her hand. They glinted each time she swung her fists — a tiny spark of light just bright enough to make him blink.

Brend thumped onto the ground beside him, and the other giants followed suit. "What are you thinking, General? I can always tell when you've had a thought."

Declan cast a glance around them. For so long, he'd seen nothing but their smiles and brightened eyes. He'd nearly forgotten how they used to be: hollowed and sunken in, their stares dulled with hunger — the mere husks of giants.

Now with the King's command, some of those lines had begun to come back. Weary shadows stretched across their faces; their shoulders fell slack. The life they'd had under Gilderick was no life at all.

Declan would rather have his eyes closed for good than sunken in.

"*All men are mighty, when they know they're bound to win. It's when a man's made small that you see him for what he truly is.* That's something Callan used to tell me," Declan said, thinking. "It took me a long while to figure out that he wasn't talking about my *legs* — he was talking about the things in life that drive a man down, and whether or not he decides to get back onto his feet.

"Our lands were taken from us, our families torn apart and slain. There wasn't a homestead left standing, by the time Titus finished his march. We were made small. We were driven low until we had dirt ground between our teeth. But we got back up, didn't we?"

They grunted in agreement.

Brend thumped his chest.

Declan breathed deeply. "Now the King's come to drive us back down. He means to make us small. I can't taste the dirt again," he whispered, grinding his teeth. "And I can't run. I can't stand the thought of my plains sitting empty any more than I could bear another lash ... besides that, there's a wee mage in Midlan who saved my life. I can't have a debt like that stand between us."

Declan dragged himself to his feet, grimacing as his flesh pulled against his wounds. "I'm marching to the gates of Midlan, to whatever death awaits me there."

"And you won't be alone," Brend said, springing up beside him. "I'm coming along."

Declan shoved him aside. "No, you won't. The giants need you."

"What do they need a Prince for if they've got no lands?" Brend said, shoving him back. "If all goes well for the plains and badly for me, then they'll still have a wee Princess to look after them. That's the grand thing about children," he added with a wink. Then he waved at the other giants, who'd sprung to their feet behind him. "Gather your armor and sharpen your scythes. We'll march at dawn."

The shadows left their faces and their eyes grew bright once more. The giants followed Brend into the castle, beating their fists against their chests.

Declan turned and nearly stumbled backwards when he saw Nadine standing right behind him. She wore the fiercest smile. "I knew you would not give in — I knew you would fight."

"Did you?" Declan said. "Because it sounded an awful lot like a scolding."

She wound her fingers through the rags of his shirt, careful of his wounds. Her eyes shone as she spoke: "Sometimes I must speak harshly to get my words through your stone head ... what is that?"

Drums boomed from the castle tower: one deep thump, two quick taps.

Nadine let go of him and paced away, moving in the direction of the Red Spine.

It was an unlucky thing. Declan fully intended to pummel whichever soldier had decided to beat the drums. When he twisted to frown at the castle, a guard caught him with a wave: "General! Look!"

He followed the tip of the guard's scythe to the crack in the Red Spine — the one that led into the desert. A large number of tiny people were filtering their way through it. They wore red and carried silver spears. Declan didn't even have a chance to be shocked before Nadine cried out.

She took a few rushed steps towards them, shouting at the tops of her lungs in strange, sing-song words. The man at the head of the line hollered back, hand raised in a fist.

Nadine gasped.

Declan rushed in beside her. "What is it? What are they saying?"

A fierce grin split her face. She grabbed him by the front of his tunic and her dark eyes shone brightly as she said: "Grandmot Hessa has sent her warriors to the plains. She has dreamed of a great light breaking across our realm — a banner carried by scythe and spear. The giants will break the shadows' hold," her hands tightened, "and the mots will fight beside them."

CHAPTER 28
A Horrible Dream

The days in the Motherlands seemed to drag longer than anywhere else — and Kael quickly ran out of things to do.

It only took him a few hours to figure out how to tan the old bull's hide into leather. He whispered his hands into a burning heat and worked until the skin was dried and flat. The trousers he'd made were a little lopsided, with one of the legs slightly longer than the other. But he thought it was a decent first try. In any case, he was glad to be able to peel off his stained clothes and heavy armor.

He couldn't remember what had happened to his clothes to make them stained, or why he'd been wearing armor in the first place. There was a haze over his memories that made a cloud of everything. His head throbbed so viciously each time he tried to peer through it that he eventually gave up.

Even if he couldn't remember everything, he didn't worry about it. His head kept telling him that nothing beyond the haze was worth troubling himself over.

The mountains and valleys stretched so endlessly into the distance that Kael had begun to wonder if they touched the shores of another sea — one so far north that its waves were frozen in a shell of ice. But though his eyes couldn't quite reach their ends, he would never get to see all the wonders the Motherlands kept hidden:

The dragons had far too many rules.

Kyleigh spent much of the day either hunting or flying about. Sometimes she would bring Kael along, but often times she didn't. He wasn't sure what she might have to do that he couldn't be a part of — and anytime he asked, she would simply glare and say that her task was something she had to *figure out for herself.*

It was frustrating enough, not being able to help her. But Kyleigh's absence meant that Kael was often stuck at the shore alone, trapped beneath Rua's suffocating gaze.

The dragon had a near-endless list of things that Kael wasn't allowed to do. Thus far he'd been scolded for traveling too far inland, and getting too close to the seas. He also got snapped at for just generally *wandering out of sight.*

That particular day, and after a particularly damp night, Kael pulled himself up the hills into the canopy of the forest — looking for someplace to start making camp. He didn't know how long Kyleigh's task would take her, but he knew for certain that he didn't want to spend another dew-soaked night upon the ground.

Rua sprawled across the hill's ledge while he searched, sunning his great crimson body atop the rocks. His scales only seemed to darken in the sun — as if the light dried the fresh red into a dull, crusted black. The dragon lay so still that Kael thought he'd gone to sleep. But the moment he found a promising place to start, Rua's eyes snapped open.

His head snaked into the trees and he planted his wet, steaming nostrils in the middle of Kael's bare chest. *I know what you're doing, human. These are my lands, and I won't have you building one of your human roosts in my woods. Your homes are nothing like the beauty of the trees — they are ugly little squares with pointy tops.*

"What if I give it a rounded top?" Kael said, turning his head from the damp heat of Rua's breath.

The dragon didn't seem to notice that Kael was inching away from him. In fact, he moved his snout up a bit — pressing its entire sticky front to the side of Kael's face. *No. It isn't polite to try to nest in another male's lands. And by* it isn't polite*, I mean that I would tear the cords from your throat, were you a dragon. The only reason you have even been allowed to set foot here is because I am generous.*

"And the only reason I haven't left is because I don't have the wings to get away from you," Kael muttered. Sweat had begun to bead up across his chest, and the curls of his hair were all but straightened out.

He held his breath when Rua said: *Hmm, even if you had wings, they would be too small to outpace me.* His eyes darted away and his voice crept into a whisper. *Why* don't *humans have wings? You only have half the legs of other creatures, and the legs you do have are pitifully frail. It seems to me that you must always be getting chased down and eaten — and yet, there are so many of you.*

284

Kael had honestly never given it much thought. "I suppose we must taste horrible."

Rua's blasting laugh knocked him off his feet. Before he had a chance to sit up, the dragon stuck his nose against his middle — pinning him to the earth. *My mother used to tell me that humans are poisonous. Is that true?* he rasped, eyes narrowing upon Kael's face. *Are you poisonous?*

"Yes. Very," he said quickly. "One bite will kill you."

You are not even a bite ... After a moment, Rua sighed. *Still, I do not think you would be worth the stomachache. No nests, human. If you do not wish to be rained on, you may sleep beneath the trees — and the earth is warm enough to shelter your skin from the cold.*

The ground in the Motherlands *was* strangely warm. Kael would often lie awake while Kyleigh slept fitfully beside him, feeling for the ebb and flow of the heat. It was as if the land was a creature all its own — as if the peaks were its spines, the hills were its flesh, and the great mountain in the middle was its rearing head.

If all that were true, then the fires that churned beneath the earth had to be the island's pulse. The pattern was too steady, the warmth too deep for it to have been anything else. But he still didn't see why they should have to sleep out in the open.

He was about to argue when Rua raised his head above the trees and craned it to the south. He stared for such a long moment that Kael got curious. One of the trees had limbs that drooped down to his reach, and he climbed them quickly.

The valley danced before him. Its long bed of grass waved beneath the icy wind, like the feathers of some monstrous bird ruffled against the cold. There was only one large, rounded section of grass that didn't move — a patch wedged beneath the body of a glittering purple dragon.

This dragon was quite a bit smaller than Rua. Its body was long and lean, and its horns grew straight from the top if its head. The spines across its face were so small at their points that they looked like needles.

Rua's voice crackled over the trees and into the valley below. The purple dragon raised its head at the sound and answered in a softer groan.

Before Kael could ask, Rua stuck his wet nose against his knee — so roughly that he nearly toppled off the branch. *Once the halved one has done what we've asked, you will leave the Motherlands. And you will never return.*

That was fine by Kael. He wasn't at all interested in living in a place where he was forced to spend his nights crouching beneath the trees. Still, he was curious. "What have you asked Kyleigh to do, exactly? And who is *we?*"

I cannot tell you what she has been told to do. She asked in earnest that I keep it from you, and so I shall.

Kael had to concentrate to keep his voice even. "Yes, well, she's known for keeping secrets — to the point that she gets herself into trouble. She's miserable," he said, watching as the dragon's eyes twitched uncertainly. "I've never seen her so unhappy. I only want to help."

Kyleigh hadn't been herself, of late — a fact that exhausted him more than all of Rua's laws put together. It wasn't like her to disappear all day. When she finally did come back, she was careful to keep her eyes cast down. She hardly looked at him any more, let alone touched him. And when he tried to reach out to her, she would back away like there were barbs growing from the tips of his fingers.

Then one night, a thin line of earth appeared between them. Now it had stretched to nearly a hand's width. He wasn't certain she would've returned to him at all, had Rua not forbade her to go flying at night. It made Kael sick to think she was miserable, but his prodding only seemed to make things worse. He wasn't sure what to do.

If Rua would simply tell him what her task was, he might be able to help. But the dragon flatly refused.

She asked in earnest *that we keep it from you. We cannot ignore a request asked in earnest.*

"Who's *we?*" Kael said again, hoping there might be someone a little less ridiculous on the island to deal with.

My mate, Rua replied. His great chest swelled with the word, stretching the blackened scar across its middle.

Kael leaned around him, to where the glittering purple dragon lay sprawled in the grass below. "Is that her?"

Her? Rua's eyes bulged from their sockets. *Are you blind, human? That isn't a* her. *That is Corcra — a friend from the north. You would know my mate if you saw her,* he added with a rumbling growl. *There would be no doubt.*

286

"All right," Kael said slowly. He was fully aware of how Rua's sharp teeth pressed against his leg, and couldn't forget how the dragon had mentioned he was less than a bite. He tried to speak carefully. "Who is Corcra?"

He lives with his mate inside the great caverns to the north, in a land that is always evening. I've not seen him for a hundred years, but my daughters have been spreading word throughout every roost that there is a halved one and a human living here. So he has come to see —

"Wait a moment. You have daughters?" Kael said.

Yes. The words came out somewhere between a growl and a groan, and Rua's yellow eyes rolled back. *I fear their chattering will end me, human, if time does not end me first. Normally, I would not have allowed Corcra into my lands*, he went on, his stare roving back to the valley. *But he flew in respectfully, so I could not deny him a glimpse.*

"How does one fly respectfully, exactly?" Kael wondered.

Rua looked at him as if he was stupid. *By slowing one's wings and dropping beneath the clouds, of course. Height is everything to a dragon. The further in the air you are, the more power behind your fall. So a male who wishes me harm will fly in above my head, while one who wishes me respect needs no such advantage.*

Though he hated to admit it, Kael supposed it made sense. "Is that how your daughters traveled around, then? Flying respectfully?"

Rua's laugh rumbled inside his chest. *No, human. A* daughter *is a female — females do not battle for skies or lands*, he said when he saw Kael's confusion. *They are not a threat to us, and so they may fly wherever they wish.*

Kael was still trying to wrap his head around it all when Rua crushed his spines tighter against his knee, bruising him again.

I must go now, human. Corcra will look after you while I am away, and you would do well to stay beneath his eyes. Rua's voice dropped to a crackling growl as he added: *If not, he will slip beneath your belly and spill your guts upon the ground. I have seen far greater beasts than* you *fall dead before him.*

A chill raced up Kael's spine. He kept a wary eye on the purple dragon, who'd crept from the grass and now rolled contentedly in an obliging patch of thorny shrubs. "Where are you going?"

To see my mate, he murmured, eyes brightening. *The ache in my chest has grown unbearable. Her heart calls to me, and I must answer it.*

****

Days crawled by, and things only became worse.

Corcra wasn't at all interested in speaking with him. Any time Kael got close, he would take to his wings and circle the sky — and he could circle for hours, using the gusts of wind to hold his slender frame aloft. Kael stared at him for nearly a full day once, hoping Corcra would eventually tire and come down. But he never did.

Kyleigh returned far less frequently. She left at dawn and would glide in with the last remaining shreds of light, her brows dropped low over her eyes.

Kael watched her stomp in from a distance, once. He couldn't help but notice how she walked — like there was a weight upon her back and stones tied to her feet. Dark lines hung beneath her eyes and dragged at the corners of her mouth. Her stare, when it finally returned from some shadowed trail of thought, was hollow and vacant.

The fires were gone, and all that remained was an ashen shell of green.

When she saw him watching, her face went smooth and her stare returned to the ground. But it was too late. Kael had already decided that he'd had enough.

"All right, Kyleigh," he said, snatching her around the shoulders. "I can't stand this anymore. Tell me what's going on with the dragons. What has Rua asked you to do? Whatever it is, I'm certain I can —"

"You can't," she snarled, glaring over his shoulder. "You can't help me. I'll figure it out on my own."

"No, you won't. You've been at it for days and all you've managed to do is snap at me. You're getting darker by the minute, and we're running out of time ..."

His words trailed away as something in the back of his mind woke with a jolt. Pictures slid behind his eyes for a moment, dulled and gray at their edges. A wave of heat coursed over his flesh; he heard voices and screams.

"What did you say?" Kyleigh whispered.

Her question broke him from his trance, thrust the pictures aside. When he blinked, he saw she was staring at him very intently — as if she could see the pictures, as well.

288

"I said we're running out of time." Voices drifted through his mind for a moment, carried softly by the wind. "I'm not sure why, but I feel like there's something we ought to be doing, someplace we ought to be ... but we can't get there unless you ..."

Kyleigh placed a hand against his throat. Her fingers splayed across his neck and her thumb pressed very firmly against his chin. A soothing warmth stretched out from where she touched. It slipped inside his veins and Kael shut his eyes as the warmth numbed him to his toes. But it lasted only a moment.

When he looked up, Kyleigh's face had changed.

It happened in a blink, a breath. Flames swelled inside her stare — not as bright as they'd once been, but driven to a sharpness that must've pained her. Her brows clamped down and her mouth twisted in what could've only been agony. Her look was too furious, her face too pale for it have been anything else.

Kael's heart leapt up his throat. He lunged for her instinctively, prepared to do whatever it took to stop her from hurting. But she shoved him away with a roar.

"Leave it alone, Kael! For once in your life, just leave it blasted well alone!"

She left him, then — marching into the woods, where the trees' shadows draped across her blackened armor until she slowly disappeared.

Kael stood alone in the darkness for a long moment, trying to make some sense out of what had happened. But it didn't make any sense at all. He had no idea why she was angry with him. All he'd wanted to do was help her, to try to stop her pain if he could.

Perhaps she was right: perhaps he really ought to leave it alone.

When a few hours dragged by and Kyleigh still hadn't returned, Kael fell into a restless sleep. Things clawed at him from the darkness. They were hurt and angry things. More than once, a pulse of heat from deep within the earth dragged him from his sleep. He woke feeling sick, the warmth too much for his stomach.

It was in the hour when the night air was coolest that he finally relaxed enough to dream ... and it was a horrible dream.

He dreamt that he stood in the Unforgivable Mountains once more. Snow blustered so thickly about him that he couldn't see what lay ahead. Still, he walked very purposely onward, picking his way down the slopes and across the frozen lands.

Every once in a while, he heard a cry on the wind:

... finish it ... finish what we started ...

The voice was so faint that Kael wasn't sure he'd heard it. When he turned, the world behind him was too shrouded to tell if someone followed. His legs kept moving even as he watched, as if they were determined to carry him down. And after a moment, his eyes turned back to the frozen path ahead.

... finish it, lad ...

The voice had grown louder. He was certain he'd heard it, this time. Kael twisted against the march of his legs and stared intently at the thick curtain of snow behind him. It swirled, pulsing against the tug of the wind. He stared until his eyes ached from the strain, but the voice didn't come again.

He was about to turn away when something inside the blusters began to take shape: the stocky figure of a man limping through the snow. The man's pace was short and halting. He seemed to more stumble than walk. Though the ground was treacherous, he kept one arm clamped against his chest — nursing it as if it were broken.

Kael tried to turn back, but his legs wouldn't let him. They marched on at a steady pace even as the man behind him stumbled and fell. The snow stormed in as Kael outdistanced him. Everything he tried to yell was torn aside by the wind.

In the moment before the man could be lost behind the next rising hill, he raised his arm. His hand was gone, hewed from his wrist. A torrent of blood wept thickly from its ragged nub. The bright red somehow cut through the winter and seemed to glow as he cried:

You finish it, lad! Finish what we started!

Kael cried out when the man collapsed. He grabbed his knees and tried to force his legs to turn, but they kept marching on. Behind him, the man's blood became a river: it ran down the slope and washed over Kael's boots. The blood pooled in a mirror before him, and he saw images swirling inside the red.

A black dragon fell from the skies, wildmen clashed against a gilded army. Villagers screamed, fires churned the seas aside — a castle moaned as it crumbled to the ground.

Kael leapt away from the cackling of a horrible, grinning skull, and the shock jolted him from his sleep. He woke with the sun blaring above him.

And he remembered everything.

CHAPTER 29
HIS-RUA

"Kyleigh!"

Kael roared her name into the sky, the trees. He searched throughout the forest and hardly paused for a breath. He didn't know if it was a trick or a curse, or some ridiculous brand of dragon magic.

But he knew for certain this was all her doing.

No man simply lost his memories. It was no coincidence that he numbed every time she touched him. He should've known when his mind went soggy that there was something odd happening. There had to be a reason his head had been so muddled the past ... however long it'd been.

Blast it all, he wasn't even sure how long they'd been trapped in the Motherlands. The whole Kingdom could've fallen apart by now.

They had to get out.

Kyleigh was nowhere to be found. Either she was still sulking from the night before, or she'd heard him cursing at the trees. But it didn't matter where she hid: he was determined to find her.

After a few hours of combing through the woods, he thought she might've gone back to camp. There wasn't any sign of her beneath their tree. His filthy clothes and armor sat untouched upon the scant pile of their belongings. He marched out from the woods to the cliffs that overlooked the valley, hoping to catch some sight of her there.

Instead, he found Rua.

The red dragon was curled atop his usual hill, so unmoving that Kael might've mistaken him for its jagged crest, had the sunlight not revealed his scales.

Rage carried him over the valley and up the side of the hill. His warrior strength pulled him swiftly across the earth, cutting through the mile between them in a handful of minutes. He thought of nothing as he ran — every bit of him was focused on finding out what the dragons wanted.

Rua's red body seemed to swell as Kael drew closer. With his limbs sprawled and his wings unfurled, he capped the entire hill. Kael climbed as far up the slope as he could without coming within reach of Rua's spiny muzzle. He focused on donning his dragonscale armor with one half of his mind — while the other tried not to think about the fact that what he was about to do might get him eaten.

"All right, this has gone on long enough," Kael shouted, even though he knew the dragon could've heard him at a whisper. "The Kingdom is in danger. There are far too many people depending on us for you to keep us here. Either tell me what you want, or let us go."

For a long moment, Rua did nothing. His great head stayed tucked beneath his wing and his breathing rumbled as if he was lost in a deep sleep. Kael was trying to decide whether or not to risk kicking him in the claw when the dragon raised his head.

At first, Kael thought he might've been mistaken. The dragon who glared at him now didn't look a thing like Rua. Sharpness creased his brows and brought his teeth from his lips. His eyes roared inside their sockets. The scales across his muzzle burned red-hot: they flared in warning as his spiny face darkened, glowing like embers.

Kael stepped backwards when the dragon's great voice crackled inside his chest — the noise of a tree splitting into two. But he forced himself to be calm, holding tightly to the image of his dragonscale armor.

"I don't care how big you are. I don't care if you're cross. I'll do whatever it takes to get off this blasted island — even if it means stepping over your corpse."

The angry red glow that'd begun at Rua's muzzle spread the length of his face. It climbed down his throat and swelled into a furnace in his chest — turning everything but the blackened scar into the face of a furnace.

Sparks spewed from his nose; flames hissed from his snout. Still, Kael didn't move. He couldn't imagine that the dragon who'd spent hours shouting silly words into his head could possibly be angry enough to scorch him. He wasn't entirely sure that Rua could even *get* angry.

But before he could think to be surprised, the dragon attacked.

A world wrought in blinding gold descended upon him. It took all of Kael's concentration to ignore the pounding of his heart and cling to the scales of his armor — the only protection he had left. He dropped to the ground and threw his arms over his head. He bared his teeth against the pain he knew would come, waited for the moment when his skin would begin peeling from his bones.

But it never came.

The heat was there — he could feel it pressing against the shell of his armor, devouring the ground beneath him. It roared across his ears, but didn't burn. Slowly, he opened his eyes and stared in wonder at the golden world around him. Shapes twisted in and out of the fire: men, trees, beasts, and monsters. Winged creatures, their paths cut from flame, waged battles above him.

It took a great deal of concentration to keep from getting knocked backwards as the fire roared across him. He heard the dragon's crackling voice twined among the flames. He steeled his legs and tried not to think about the fact that what little remained of his clothes was being burned away. After what seemed like an age, Rua's fire abated.

Kael glared through the smoke at him and didn't flinch — not even when the dragon's glowing eyes rolled down the entire bare length of him. The fires within them *whoosh*ed out as the yellows widened. His ears bolted up and his spiny mouth snapped shut.

It was as panicked a look as Kael had ever seen on a dragon. And he wasn't about to let it go to waste. "Release us, or I swear by the sky above me that I'll kill you."

He took a step forward, and Rua snapped back. His great claws gouged pits into the earth. The sudden rise of his wings toppled a nearby tree. He shot into the air — crumbling the whole backside of the hill in his haste to escape.

The sudden blast of Rua's wings knocked him off his feet. But Kael pulled himself up quickly. "That's right — fly off!" he howled at the dragon's back, the surge of his strength pulling him to his toes. "Come near us again, and I'll flatten you!"

****

It was done. He was certain Rua wouldn't be back.

Kael jogged into camp and pulled on his stained clothes and armor. He gathered their things and waited at the edge of the woods for Kyleigh's return. Though he was still furious with her for whatever it was she'd done to him, there would be time to argue about it later.

294

For now, they had to leave the Motherlands while the way was clear.

It wasn't long before the beat of a familiar set of wings drew his eyes skywards. Kyleigh dipped from the clouds and drifted towards him. He forgot about being angry with her: they were finally free. He raised a fist as he charged to meet her.

His excitement was short-lived.

Another dragon swooped in behind Kyleigh. It was only slightly larger than her, and covered in snow-white scales. His stomach lurched when Kyleigh struck the ground before him. The second white dragon glided in behind her and landed softly upon the grass. Its yellow eyes watched without blinking.

Kael didn't know what to think. His gaze never shifted from the second white dragon — not even when Kyleigh blasted her hot breath through his curls. He reached distractedly for her muzzle.

What in blazes have you been doing?

"What have *I* been doing? What have *you* been doing?" He grabbed her around the horns and stood on his toes to glare at her. "What did you do to me?" he hissed.

I didn't do anything to you.

"Come off it, Kyleigh. I know you hexed me, or something. I've been wandering around here like an idiot for Kingdom knows how long while you've been off visiting ..." he waved a hand at the white dragon, who watched curiously from over Kyleigh's shoulder, "your family?"

She is not *my family,* was her vehement reply. *This is His-Rua. She's been sent here because you've been pestering her mate with what he seems to think is magic ... and now, he's afraid to come near you.*

There was the slightest tinge of amusement in Kyleigh's voice and for a moment, her eyes brightened. Kael was still trying to piece it all together. He craned to look at the white dragon, who'd inched closer — her ears perked for his voice.

Kael realized he would have to speak carefully. He tried to shove his thoughts into some sort of order. *This is Rua's mate?*

Yes.

And she actually calls herself His-Rua?

It's a dragon thing, Kyleigh said with an impatient sigh. *The females take the names of their males. But that's not important. Why would Rua think you have magic?*

Kael couldn't help but grin as he thought about the look on the red dragon's face, how he'd torn up the hillside in his haste to get away. *He tried to torch me. But it didn't exactly work out for him.*

Kyleigh's eyes brightened again, and Kael forgot to be angry. He was just happy that she seemed to be coming back to herself.

I'd very much like to hear more about that later. But for now, I'm afraid we have to leave.

They're tossing us out of the Motherlands?

No, unfortunately. The darkness returned to her glare. *We've been summoned for a scolding, I think. But as Rua's afraid to come to us, we've got to go to him. Oh ... and it's probably best if he goes on thinking you're a mage,* she added with a sideways look. *He made such a fool of himself that I imagine he'll kill you, if he ever learns the truth.*

****

The land rolled beneath them as they followed the white dragon into Rua's domain.

It was obvious she was in no hurry to get there. His-Rua dipped and looped her way towards the great mountain in the middle of the island. She followed the gusts of wind that swirled around them, letting them fill her wings and carry her along. She seemed content to ride them to wherever they blew — even if that meant flitting several miles to the east or west.

And much to Kael's annoyance, Kyleigh was happy to follow her.

The white dragon hummed as she drifted further from the mountain. Her voice was soft and high, like a whistle that trailed the wind. Kael figured that since he was stuck a mile in the air with nothing else to do, he might as well listen.

He flattened his palms against Kyleigh's scales and concentrated. The white dragon's song became strange words in Kyleigh's mind, and Kael heard their meaning trail behind them:

What do you think of our Motherlands?

Beautiful, Kyleigh sang back. *I've never seen such a sky.*

Fate knew the reach of our wings, the depth of our hearts, the span of our eyes ... The white dragon tucked her wings and arched back, looping behind them. *So she gave us a land we would never tire of loving.*

296

They flew side-by-side, now. Had Kyleigh tilted a hand's breadth to her left, the tips of their wings would've touched. Kael glanced over and saw the white dragon was watching him intently.

Her scaly face was smooth: there wasn't a snarl upon her lips or a bend in her brows. The slits in her eyes were wide and unguarded. Had she been human, he might've thought she looked … kind.

But she wasn't human. And so far, he hadn't had much luck with dragons.

What do you call this one?

Kael, Kyleigh said — and he couldn't help but notice how her blood warmed with the word.

A Kael *that you have taken for a mate.*

How did you know? Kyleigh said, her song made uncertain by surprise.

The white dragon's muzzle twisted upwards. *We argued about it for many nights. Rua is still not convinced, but I have seen the truth. You carry him on your back without shame. Only valtas can turn what is humiliating into something proud. It makes us all into joyful fools.*

"Valtas?" That was the only thing the dragon had spoken that didn't weave itself into a word Kael knew.

How far does the land go? Kyleigh said, pointedly ignoring his question.

To the next horizon — days and days of flight. There was a time when we filled it to its edges, when not a breadth of land went unclaimed. But, wisps of flame curled out from her nostrils as she sighed, *now our Motherlands are empty.*

Her bright yellow eyes slid from Kael's face over his shoulder, to where they sharpened upon something in the distance. When he turned, all he could see was the great mountain in the center of the island — a silent, purplish shadow crowned by thin white clouds. Its sides had been worn smooth by the icy gusts. But there was one place where the rock seemed broken.

A cave, one no taller than a man's height, leered at him from between the crags. There was a darkness behind it that tugged upon his heart and iced his skin. Were the mountain to split open down its middle, he wouldn't be surprised if a thousand wraiths came pouring from its top.

He was almost certain that something glowered at him from just within the cave's leering mouth.

When he finally tore his eyes from the mountain, he saw that His-Rua watched him. The gusts off her wings blew his curls back in absent beats. The black slits in the center of her eyes narrowed. They swept across his face from side to side — twin blades leveled at his flesh.

Just when Kael's skin began to crawl, she looked away.

Come ... Rua is waiting.

She whirled from her path and plunged towards the earth below. Kael left his stomach behind as Kyleigh followed.

He was more than a bit relieved to have the great mountain behind him. For a moment, he'd been afraid that was where they were going. But His-Rua didn't lead them too close. In fact, she seemed to give it a wide berth.

The white dragon flew purposefully north, and it wasn't long before he saw where they were headed.

A range of mountains burst from the land in front of them. Its sides were jagged, but its tops were flat and even — like a set of teeth stacked one behind the other, climbing until they scraped the under-edges of the sky.

The mountains' flesh reminded him of the Red Spine: a hundred crimson shades swirled across it in a pattern of lines, each bleeding into the next. They cast shadows across the flats, cut boldly down the curves. Kael's hands itched as his eyes traced the patterns' march across the mountains. But that wasn't the most interesting thing about them.

Holes peppered the mountains' sides. They were perfectly carved: arches that spanned beneath the flat tops and formed something that looked like a web of bridges. Some of the arches were so thin at their crests that he thought even the slightest weight might snap them at the middle.

And yet, many sported pairs of full-grown dragons.

Kael saw the glittering purple dragon first. He was perched near the mountain's middle, his slender body curled about that of a much larger white dragon. Her horned head rested atop her foreclaws, while his lay across her back.

Corcra, and His-Corcra, His-Rua sang, gazing down at them. *They have come to see you for themselves ... and Rua has allowed it.*

The purple dragon and his mate never blinked. Both sets of yellow eyes rolled to follow Kyleigh as she passed, but neither head lifted.

Other pairs dotted the mountains. There was a pale orange dragon and one the color of moss — both tangled around the stark white bodies of their mates.

"Are all female dragons white?" Kael asked.

To all but their bonds, His-Rua sang in reply.

They passed a green dragon, a silver dragon, and one with scales like the sea before a storm. They watched calmly as His-Rua sang each of their names and told of how far they'd come. Kael was still trying to grasp it all. He'd had no idea that there were dragons living so close to the Kingdom, or that they came in such an astonishing number of colors.

No two are the same, the white dragon said when Kyleigh relayed his thoughts. *Once, there were as many colors as there were wonders in the land ...*

Her words trailed into another fiery sigh, and she turned her wings upwards.

The sun had fallen so that it was almost even with the mountains' top: a stretch of flat rock that climbed into a jagged hill large enough to hold a village. A cluster of white dragons were gathered at its far edge. At least one of them was tall and sturdy, while another was quite small. It was difficult to count them when they were tangled all together. But as His-Rua approached, she sang:

Daughters!

And three horned heads popped up to greet her.

Mother!

Mother, you've returned!

Is that him, Mother? Have you brought the magic one?

Kael recognized the noise of their voices even before Rua's crackling grunt boomed them into silence: these were the dragons that'd swarmed over them in the northern seas.

He watched in disbelief as the mountain's jagged crest shifted. An enormous horned head peeled back from where it'd been tucked and Rua's familiar gaze swept over him. For a moment, the darkness and the fury seemed gone from his stare.

Then a shadow crossed his face.

Another dragon circled the sky above Rua's head. His thick body was covered in blue-black scales, and the under edges of his wings turned almost purple as he crossed over the sun. The horns that curved behind his ears seemed a bit too large for his head: his long neck had to snap in a whip's motion just to lift them.

Gorm, one of the unmated, His-Rua said as she cut sharply aside. *Follow me, halved one. We must give Rua his space.*

Though she spoke calmly, the other dragons moved as if they'd been jolted by a shock: they clambered under arches and hid in the depths of caves. The three daughters crammed themselves behind a boulder, all of their eyes fixed warily upon Rua.

The scales across his muzzle began to glow as he watched Gorm circle. He roared in warning, snapped open his monstrous wings. But the blue-black dragon didn't flinch. In fact, he tucked his wings and fell into a dive.

Gorm dropped like an arrow's bolt. Flames spewed out the sides of his mouth in wet tendrils as he fell; the weight of his horns dragged his great body to a perilous speed. In the half-blink before he reached Rua, he swung his claws out before him. Each of their dagger points was aimed for Rua's eyes. He bellowed as if he meant to gouge them out, meant to snap his neck.

Rua still hadn't budged. For a moment, Kael thought he might be crushed. He gripped Kyleigh's spines and braced himself for the moment when the dragons' bodies would collide.

At the last second, Rua swung his head forward. It fell like a hammer on the back of Gorm's neck, rent the air with a crash so loud and sharp that it stung Kael's ears. And he won the battle with a single blow.

Gorm slammed into the cliffs beneath him, launched by Rua's head and dragged down by the weight of his horns. Chunks of stone spewed up behind him as he tumbled from one arch the next. His claws scrabbled madly as he tried to regain his footing. In the end, he didn't stop until he reached the mountains' bottom — a tangle of wings and limbs buried beneath a pile of rocks.

Rua glared as Gorm dug his way free, scales burning across his face. The blue-black dragon grumbled back, but seemed to think better of going after him a second time. Rua scowled until Gorm slunk beneath one of the arches. Then he looked away.

Kael clenched Kyleigh's spines tightly. Scales popped up across his skin and his warrior half sharpened, ready for trouble. But the red dragon's gaze hardly touched him before they drifted to follow His-Rua.

My-Rua, he boomed.

One of his great wings unfurled, revealing a gap of rock by his side. The white dragon slipped into it gracefully. He bent to press his muzzle against her scaly cheek. His great head dwarfed hers easily.

Kael was so busy watching them that he didn't realize Kyleigh was about to stop. She landed hard on the small peak beneath Rua, and the jolt sent Kael rolling across her shoulder. His legs broke into a stumbling run the moment his feet touched the ground — the only thing that saved him from scraping his chin.

Rua's crackling voice shook the ground beneath his boots. Kael rushed over to Kyleigh and pressed his hand against her flank, trying to listen.

... will not wear that skin in my presence. It is a mockery of one who was dear to me.

"What's he talking about?" he hissed as Kyleigh slipped into her human skin.

The fires in her eyes whipped about as she stared at the red dragon. "Nothing. He's mad."

You do not understand the depths of my anger, Rua rumbled back — though Kael was fairly certain she'd meant the *other* sort of madness. *You live only because I wish you to know how you've hurt us. I wish you to remember everything you've done, so that the stain of your cowardly act may never fade from your eyes.*

"So says the dragon who sent his mate after us. You ought to think twice before crying coward," Kael said back, his blood burning hot. "Were you too afraid to come face me yourself? Didn't want another scar, did you?"

Molten scales flared to life across Rua's muzzle. His wings snapped open with enough force to roll several rocks off the side of the cliff. *I will face you now, human! I will tear your face from your skull —! No*, his eyes widened and he pulled back from His-Rua suddenly. *No, my heart. It will hurt you.*

Then hold it carefully. Do not let it overcome you, she growled.

His great head dipped in a nod, and the fire in his face went out. *I sent My-Rua to you because I knew you would not harm her. We*

301

males only quarrel with each other. But now she has led you here, into a mountain filled with males. If I fall to your magic, they will have you torn apart before you cast again.

Kael felt the weight of their glowing eyes upon him: the dragons down the mountain rumbled their warnings while Rua's daughters peered tentatively over the boulder. Even if he'd *had* magic, he didn't like his chances.

Kyleigh's hand tightened around his. "Look, I honestly can't remember what I've done to you. There's much about my life — my lives — that's lost to me. It often happens during the … change."

Kael stayed still. She was admitting this to him as much as she was to Rua. Though she'd never said it aloud, he'd already guessed.

"The thing you asked of me … it's gone, faded away. I can't remember, and keeping me trapped on this island isn't going to help."

It might come back in time, Rua growled.

Kyleigh set her jaw tightly, though her voice was strained: "Whatever I've done, I'm sorry for it. I can't offer you any more than that. There's a war in our homelands, and our companions need us."

Men are always at war, Rua muttered, without an ounce of concern. His monstrous head tilted to the side. *What do you wish, My-Rua? Ask, and it shall be yours.*

Kael felt his mouth drop open. The white dragon watched him intently — and he couldn't help but think that her eyes weren't nearly as kind as they'd been before.

Something dangerous burst within them for a moment. Her muscles coiled and swelled. Kael took a half step forward. He wasn't sure what he would do if His-Rua charged, but she would have to go through him to get to Kyleigh. Fortunately, that didn't happen.

Rua pressed his muzzle into her cheek, and the fires went out. Her eyes were wide and calm once more when she replied: *For the halved one to remember what she has done would be punishment enough. When she comes to us with both of her names, we'll lead her to them. Then she will be free to go.*

You've heard my mate. Do not step back into my presence until you remember.

The crackling in Rua's voice had grown into a steady growl. When his eyes snapped open, Kael's breath caught in his throat.

His-Rua hadn't calmed. Her fury was still there, every flame still burning bright — but they burned inside Rua's eyes now. It was *his* muscles that coiled, *his* teeth that bared. And when he spoke again, his voice shook the mountains:

> *Leave us — now!*

CHAPTER 30
SHIPWRECKED

They were only a few miles outside of Harborville, now. And it couldn't have come at a better time.

The moment Lysander gave the order to halt, Shamus plunked down hard. There were blisters on the sides of his feet and holes worn into the creases of his boots. Though pebbles had been rattling around their soles for days, he was afraid to take them off.

He didn't want to think about what his skin might look like underneath.

"Seas men weren't made for hiking around," he grumbled as he sat. The ache dropped from his legs and went to pound at the tips of his toes. He groaned against it.

They'd spent several clouded days and long, damp nights trekking through the spiny woods along the shore. The air only got colder the further they went. The pirates' hair and clothes were salt-crusted, their boots squeaked as they dragged their bodies across the hills. Not a one of them said much of anything: they sat down atop rocks and bits of fallen trees, mumbling curses as they peeled off their boots.

Lysander marched away from them and went to stand beside Shamus. He glared at the horizon like it'd cheated him. "It's been days, now. There hasn't been so much as a flash of light or a wisp of flame behind us."

"Isn't that a good thing, Captain?"

"Perhaps," he whispered, his mouth gone taut. "Whatever was after us has obviously given up ... but it's still out there. I get chills just thinking about where it might be going next. Scout ahead, dogs," he called behind him. "I think we've gone far enough, for today. See if you can't find us somewhere with fewer blasted rocks to make camp."

The pirates shuffled off with a muttering of *ayes*.

Shamus knew all too well what'd been after them. It'd started to haunt him the moment he saw the flames. He waited until the pirates had wandered out of earshot before he growled: "It was those blasted mages again — I know it was. They're always tearing across the seas, dragging decent men to early graves. My bones start trembling any time there's a mage around."

"Perhaps if they'd started trembling sooner, I'd still have my ship," Lysander muttered.

"Just because you're bitter about the Witch doesn't mean every mage in the Kingdom decided to drop spells on our heads." Jonathan's dark hair was wilder than usual: stiff with salt and poking up at every angle. "What could the mages possibly want with us?"

"If they can make a storm pop up out of nothing, then they can call down fire from the sky," Shamus insisted. "Whoever it was is probably trying to trap us inland. Oh, I don't want to be a fish again! I can feel the scales coming back ..."

Jonathan rolled his eyes while Shamus scratched at the sudden itch that'd sprung up across his arms. "No one's going to turn us into fish. It was probably some fiery boulder launched from shore. Two treetops says it was Alders trying to make more coin off of us."

"It was mages, I tell you! Listen to you, gabbing on about flaming catapults when it was very *clearly* magic! And they don't need a reason to spell anybody, I'll have you know. They just hex and curse wherever they ple —"

"I'm a coward!" Lysander wailed — so suddenly that Jonathan leapt back with a yelp. "I'm a spineless, shipless coward! I can't go into Harborville like this. What will my dogs think of me? How could anybody ever listen to a captain with no ship?"

"Hold on there — you've still got a ship. We've just got to march ourselves into Harborville and get her back." Shamus tried to be gentle with it, but Lysander seemed beyond consoling.

"I don't deserve to sail her! I've got no right ... I should've just drowned and been done with it." He sank down upon the nearest rock, burying his face in his arms.

"Poor Captain," Shamus whispered.

Jonathan frowned as a noise that sounded suspiciously like blubbering emanated from the crooks of Lysander's arms. "I don't know, mate. Maybe the rules are there for a reason."

"Don't be a codpiece about it. The poor man lost half his heart in that fire."

"And *all* of his marbles," Jonathan muttered under his breath.

Shamus glared at him before he crouched beside Lysander. "I know you're hurting, Captain. But we're not far from Harborville. It'll be a day's walk at most. There'll be a ship and a crew waiting for you —"

"Yes, one I can't do anything about. All of my gold is melted and sunk at the bottom of the seas. If we set foot in Harborville, we'll be at Alders' mercy."

"If only there was some way to rescue it *without* paying for it," Jonathan whispered loudly as he turned to stare into the distance. "Hmm, there's a word for this. It's right on the tip of my —"

"You aren't helping things," Shamus growled. He clapped one thick hand on Lysander's shoulder, jolting him mid-blubber. "I'm sure Alders will be reasonable once he hears what's happened. He'll never get his coin if he keeps us locked away. And that doesn't seem like a very sensible thing for a merchant. What do you say we straighten up and have a chat with him, Captain?"

Lysander raised his head. He dragged a filthy sleeve across his eyes and muttered: "Very well. I suppose we don't have much choice, do we? Perceval and his lot are probably already at Harborville, spreading nasty rumors. We might as well —"

"Captain!" One of the pirates bounded over the craggy rocks, eyes wild and sword in hand. "You'd better come quick, Captain. Things are about to get thick."

Lysander followed him at a run. Jonathan loped behind him and Shamus tried to keep up. The running jostled his poor feet so badly that he wound up moving at more a hop than anything. But at least he managed to keep his pace.

They tore through the thorny brush and out into an open stretch of shore. The cliffs beside them dropped straight into the seas. Another outcrop of woods lay ahead. The pirates stood in an arch near the shore's edge, blades drawn and glinting at the trees.

By the time Shamus followed Lysander to the front of the line, he was out of breath — otherwise he might've sworn at the sight that lay before them.

A company of stony-eyed soldiers were gathered at the edge of the woods. They wore gold-tinged armor and kept their spears leveled at the pirates. The man at their lead held a thick set of chains in his hand, chains that linked to the shackles of the merchant beside him.

Shamus recognized Perceval immediately. There weren't many fellows with eyes that stuck out like a frog's, and they only got wider at the sight of Lysander. He thrust a stubby finger at them and shrieked: "There he is! That's their leader. I told you there was a band of outlaws roaming around. My crew and I are nothing but honest merchants," he went on, pleading with the man who held his chains. "If you let us go, we'll be no trouble at all ... or if you could just let *me* go —"

"Shut it."

A robed man slunk out of the crowd and stood on Perceval's other side. He kept one hand draped against the twisting black dragon etched into his robes, and in the other he clutched a slender dagger.

"So these are the pirates, are they? Well, they certainly don't look like much," he mused, his gaze sweeping across them. "Nevertheless, I'm afraid you're going to have to come with us. His Majesty has commanded that all outlaws be questioned, and summarily executed."

Shamus didn't like the sound of that. "I'll bet it has more to do with red-hot pokers than actual questions," he muttered out the side of his mouth.

"Or finger clamps," Jonathan added. "Or thumb screws."

"They won't be taking us anywhere," Lysander growled. He drew his sword and its strange, patch-worked blade glinted dangerously in the sunlight. "I carry the Lass of Sam Gravy — we can't be beaten!"

The robed man looked about to reply. But Perceval's squealing cut over the top of his words.

"I'm not an outlaw, and I won't be treated like one! I demand to be released." His eyes seemed about to pop as he tugged against the soldier's grip. "Let me g — ah!"

The robed man tapped the dagger against Perceval's chest, and the whole thing caved in with a sickening crunch — as if some great beast had gone and stomped him with its heel. Red leaked from between Perceval's lips. The soldier didn't even look as his body crumpled: he simply opened his hand and let the chains fall with the corpse.

The mage, on the other hand, grinned down at it.

"How do you like our odds now, Captain?" Jonathan said stiffly.

Lysander's face went taut. "Not nearly as well."

****

"I told you it was mages!" Shamus fumed. He rattled the irons clamped around his wrist in Jonathan's face. "Any strange happenings, anything goes amiss, and it's always a mage's doing."

"You're lucky my arms went numb an hour ago, or I'd swat you," Jonathan retorted. While the rest of the pirates sat miserably in their chains, the fiddler hung upside down by the clamps around his ankles.

"I warned you not to fight," Lysander muttered.

Jonathan twisted to glare at him. "Well, somebody had to put up a fight! And since you were too busy moping, I thought I'd do it. You'd better find your gall, Captain," he added vehemently. "You saw what they did to Percy. It won't be long before they start busting up our ribs one at a time."

"Mages," Shamus hissed. A sudden chill shook him to his bones.

Lysander, on the other hand, didn't do much of anything. It wasn't like him to let Jonathan have the last word. But he slumped against the wall and stared at the ceiling like none of that mattered anymore. There wasn't so much as a spark in his eyes.

His stare was as worn and dull as the soles of their boots.

Granted, there wasn't much to smile about. From what Shamus could gather, it sounded as if Midlan had marched into Harborville a couple of weeks ago. Alders must've given it up without much of a fight: the shops and houses were all intact, and most of the villagers stayed on as slaves. They'd hardly glanced up from their chores when the pirates tromped in — which made Shamus think they weren't the first ship to be captured.

But oddly enough, there wasn't a sign of *Anchorgloam*, or any of the other vessels that'd been trapped at the docks. Shamus didn't like to think about it, but he wagered Midlan had already gotten to them. They'd be halfway to the chancellor's island castle, if that were the case. The seas would carry the King's army much faster than any march across land.

And they'd be out for blood.

"We'll get there, Captain," Shamus said, though he wasn't certain anymore. "I know it all seems a bit grim right now, but we'll

308

figure a way out of here. There's no one I'd rather be locked up with than a whole band of pirates. I wager you lads have gotten ..."

He stopped when a pair of heavy footsteps rattled dust from the ceiling. A creaky trap door snapped open above them, flooding the room with light.

"All right, who's first?"

"Do the tree rat," a soldier growled, crouching to fix the slits of his helmet onto Jonathan. There was a bloodied rag wrapped around one of his hands, and he held it gingerly against his chest. "That whelp nearly bit my finger off."

"And I'd do it again!" the fiddler declared. "If I were you, I'd find myself a thick pair of gloves and drop my visor."

"No, there's no point in questioning him. He's a madman," Lysander called when the soldier stormed down the ladder.

His helmet swung around. "Is that so? Then maybe I ought to pound some answers out of *you*."

Lysander shrugged. "There's absolutely no point in that. The King already knows everything, I'm sure — about what happened to Reginald, where Gilderick is, how the Baron's castle got blown to bits. I'm sure he's even figured out about Titus, by now."

The soldier dragged Lysander to his feet by his tunic. "You know an awful lot, pirate."

"I suppose I listen awful well."

"Is that it?" The soldier's voice dropped to a dangerous level. "Or did you have a hand in all this?"

Lysander grinned widely. "All of what?"

The soldier glared a moment more before he hurled Lysander to the ladder. "March. We'll have you singing by sunrise."

The soldier at the top of the ladder dragged Lysander by his tunic, while the man behind him drove him up with a knee. There was some laughter as the trapdoor slammed, then a meaty *thud* — followed by a gasp.

"We've got to do something," Shamus said as the footsteps went out the door.

"Right. Well, I'd hoped it wouldn't come to this, but I suppose we've got no other choice." Jonathan twisted to lock eyes with Shamus. "You're going to have to get my lucky lockpick."

Shamus was more than a little surprised. He thought for certain that Midlan had taken all of Jonathan's picks. They'd spent a good deal of the afternoon digging them out of his coat pockets and from patches on his sleeves. He'd had so many wedged beneath his boot buckles that they'd finally just tossed them off the cliffs.

"Most people don't think to check your boots," Jonathan insisted when Shamus asked. "But I've got one more stashed away — tucked in a place I knew they wouldn't search."

His grimace made Shamus leaned back. "And where is that, exactly?"

"Someplace no man would ever look."

"Oh, for the love of seas and serpents, lad!"

Jonathan twisted around, "I need your help. It's sewn in right between my —"

"I know where it's sewn!" Shamus cut in. "And you can forget it. I'm not reaching in under there."

By now, all eyes were upon them. The pirates were beginning to snicker.

"You've got to, mate." Jonathan's face was serious. "I'd do it myself, but I've been hanging upside down for so long that my arms are too numb to split the thread."

"You *are* the only one who can reach him," one of the pirates called.

Shamus glared at him.

"C'mon, mate — Lysander needs us. If it was you getting the stuffing punched out of your gut, he'd do whatever it took to spring you."

The snickering grew into full-out laughter, at this. A few of the pirates whistled.

Meanwhile, Shamus's face burned so hot that he could hardly think. "No, there's no point in it! Midlan's out there, and we haven't got enough blades to face them. Even if we manage our way out of these chains, we'll still be trapped."

Jonathan sighed. "You heard the mage: they're going to kill us all, anyways. And I don't know about you lot, but I'd rather die with a blade in my hands than at the end of a chain."

There was a rumble of agreement.

"So what do you say, mates? Are we going to hang around here and let our captain have all the fun, or are we going to get out and take a few of those tinheads with us?"

The pirates roared in answer. They grinned and thumped their fists against their burly chests.

Jonathan swung back to Shamus. "It's all up to you, mate."

"All right, fine. I'll get your blasted pick," he snapped. "But if you utter one word about this — and I mean it, fiddler — I'll cast your bones into the hull of my next ship."

"No worries, mate. Your secret is safe with me," Jonathan said.

But the way he grinned said otherwise.

CHAPTER 31

LOWLANDERS

"You're running out of time, pirate," the mage hissed.

The floor danced before Lysander's eyes. Wet warmth coated his lips and ran down his chin. He spat it away, watching as the blood soaked into the grain at his knees.

His lip had been busted at the middle. Though it stung him horribly, he forced himself to grin. "No, *you're* the one running out of time — and options, I might add. You've burned me, shocked me, split me. What do you plan to do next? Skin me?"

The mage smiled. "No ... we're going to hang you. We're going to leave your body dangling there for the next man we question — and I'm certain we'll get through to him much quicker."

Lysander's grin faltered. His stomach bunched into a knot as his throat suddenly went dry. "What do you mean, *the next man*? There is no next man. I've already told you that all of my original crew perished in a tempest on our way back from the mountains. These men don't know anything."

"Do you honestly expect me to believe that?"

"Well, it was a monster of a tempest. We never saw it coming."

"I've had the pleasure of torturing dozens of men in His Majesty's name," the mage said, eyes trailing around the darkened room. "A moment with you, and I knew you'd never utter a word about what happened to the Sovereign Five — even if you do know the truth, you aren't giving it up."

Lysander glared. "Why did you keep me here for so long, then?"

"To give us time to finish the gallows, of course." The door opened, and the mage nodded to the man behind it. "Perfect. Right on schedule."

Two sets of hands clamped around Lysander's arms, pressing painfully against the raw burns the mage's spells had left behind. But he hardly noticed — all of his worries turned elsewhere. "You're wasting your breath. They'll never talk to you!"

"Oh, one of them will," the mage assured him as he followed with a smirk. "There's always one."

A muted red sky hung over Harborville — the last faint shred of a dying light. Soldiers milled about the village square, spears propped over their shoulders. They'd taken the houses for barracks and seized the shops. Makeshift camps filled the alleyways, packed to their seams with guards.

Lysander balked when they reached the heart of the square.

Bodies already littered the area around him. The sunken remains of men hung from stocks, several pairs of legs dangled from iron cages. A damp wind blew across it, waking the stench of rot and decay. The noise of the guards' march startled the carrion birds from their feast. They took off in a flurry of indignant squawks but stayed circling overhead — each of their mirror-black eyes fixed eagerly upon Lysander.

He soon forgot about the reek and his stomach heaved against something else. The gallows steps became like a mountain before his eyes: they stretched and wavered at their tops, shrouded by a haze. He ground his heels into the cobblestone and shoved back against the guards. For one crazed moment, he clung to where he stood.

He knew that if his boots left the ground, they would never return — but dangle for an age inside the ruins of Harborville, his ribs a nest for carrion birds ...

"This is my favorite part. I rather like to watch them struggle."

The mage's voice swam inside his ears, carried in by the echo of the guards' laughter. And in that moment, Lysander came to his senses.

His heels struck the stairs hard. His legs shook slightly when he reached the gallows' top. But by the time he turned to face the square, he'd locked them tight. Nothing would sag his shoulders or drop his chin — not even when he felt the noose scrape down his neck did he flinch. It pressed hard upon the bone above his chest until the hangman cinched it tight about his throat.

The mage slid to the front of the platform and propped his elbows on the floor before Lysander's boots, watching in interest. "Any last words, pirate?"

Lysander kept his eyes on the red horizon, and a thought pulled a smile from his lips. "My father was hanged ... and I plan to bear it with a grin, as he did."

The hangman crammed a sack over his head, dulling the mage's laughter. Lysander's middle bunched tightly as he prepared himself for the fall. He sucked in panicked breaths, heaving against the moldy reek of the sack.

"On my count, hangman. Let's see how long those legs twitch —"

Something like the shriek of a falling tree cut over the top of his words. Lysander jumped at the sound — and judging by the wave of rattling and swears, quite a few soldiers jumped as well.

"They've kicked in the front gate!" someone cried from behind him. He gasped and choked, his words jostled by his sprint. "They kicked it in! Knocked it off its bloody hinges!"

"What do you mean, they kicked it in?" the mage shouted back. "No one could've possibly kicked in that gate. It weighs more than —"

Screams filled the air where the gate had fallen. Lysander didn't know what was happening, and he didn't have time to wonder. This might be his only chance to escape.

He twisted against his bonds. If he could only see how they'd been tied, he might be able to squirm free. That blasted sack was in the way. He slung his head about, trying wriggle it off. But it felt as if the hangman had knotted it behind his neck.

The screams were fading fast. Lysander didn't know what had come bursting through the gates, but he knew the soldiers of Midlan weren't easily rattled. For the army to be shrieking the way it was, it must've been something horrible — and he had no intention of being around when it reached the square.

"Form ranks, hold your ground," the mage cried. "I don't care what sort of devilry comes around the corner — the first man who twitches will have his legs lopped off at the knee!"

Sweat poured down Lysander's face and his head went light from the strain of trying to breathe the thickened air. Somehow, he managed to get one cord of the knot undone. He held it carefully, trying to lead it through another tangle ...

"Blast it all!" he shouted when the end fell.

"Silence, pirate. I'll deal with you just as soon as I'm finished here," the mage snapped.

Lysander was about to retort when a chorus of howls drowned his voice.

314

It was a frightening thing — the call of a beast so bloodthirsty and powerful that not even Midlan stood a chance against it. And it made Lysander grin.

"I'd start running if I were you," he warned.

His grin only widened when he heard the mage's boots tromp up the steps. He flinched away from what he knew was the searing tip of the dagger. But the rope only stretched so far. When he reached its end, the mage pressed the red-hot metal tighter against his ribs.

"What do you know?" he hissed.

The dagger burned through Lysander's tunic and stung his flesh. He gasped against the pain, but still managed to hold his grin. "You'll see ... don't want to spoil ... the surprise."

Something hissed across the mage's dagger, the start of a spell. Lysander had bared his teeth against what he knew would be a singeing pain when the noise came to a halt.

Everything had gone quiet: the soldiers' screams, the rattling of their gold-tinged armor. Even the howling ended. When Lysander strained his ears, he thought he could hear the faintest march of steps — an army of feet clad in soft boots led by a pair that clomped its heels into the cobblestone.

The mage laughed. "Mountain rats. They fight like savages, so you'd better kill them quickly. I'll take care of the leader," he said as he thumped down the stairs. Then he raised his voice: "You've made a deadly mistake, trespassing on His Majesty's land — and you'll be made to pay for it."

"I'll tell you exactly what I told the men at the gate: I don't carry coin. So you can either step aside, or we'll cut through your middle," a woman's voice replied. "It makes me no difference."

"Oh, good Gravy," Lysander muttered through his grin. "If that's who I think it is, you'd better let her through."

"Shut it, pirate," the mage snapped. Then he yelled again: "The King's servants yield to no one, least of all a swarm of mountain rats."

With a roar, he loosed his spell. Lysander heard it hiss through the air, heard the *whoosh* as it struck a body on the other side of the square. And for half a moment, there was silence once again.

Then the mage began to scream. "Whisperers! Move — get out of my way!"

Another spell blasted up as the mage tried to escape. It knocked out the gallows' front legs and the platform rocked forward, sending Lysander to his knees. Bits of armor clanged onto the ground all around him. Howls pierced the air.

He listened to the mage's panicked steps as he tried to race away. There was the sound of some object ripping through the air, a woman's furious cry, and then a fleshy *thunk* brought the mage's sprint to a halt.

The battle ended quickly: the howling warriors silenced Midlan with a bone-crushing attack, laughing as they fought. Lysander grimaced when he heard another *thunk* from where the mage's body had fallen.

"I hate mages," the woman growled. "The only way to kill them is to cut off their heads."

"Wisdom indeed, my Thane," a man purred in reply.

"How many times have I got to tell you, Silas? I'm not —"

"Actually, mages die in as many ways as anybody else," Lysander called. The floor beneath him creaked dangerously as the broken gallows shifted. One wrong move, and he might fall through. "Ah, would you mind cutting me free?"

He flinched when something struck the rope above him, and the sudden slack dropped him onto his face.

"Be careful, Lydia," the woman said as she clomped up the stairs. "We don't know what's under there."

"Don't you remember me?"

"Well ..." her voice came a mere inch from his nose, "you do sound a bit familiar."

"It's me — Captain Lysander."

"The pirate?"

"Yes. Now if you'll kindly take this sack off my head —"

"You didn't mean to wear it?"

"No! Why would I put a sack over my head?"

"I don't understand anything you lowlanders do. It's been one strange sight after the next since we left the mountains."

Lysander blinked when the sack was torn away, and he found himself staring into the face of a wildwoman. Paint adorned her features and stained her lips. Her short crop of bright red hair seemed to almost stand on end as her eyes wandered over him.

"What are you doing here, pirate?"

"Well, it's a rather long —"

"Taste blood, tinheads!"

"Aye — hold on, Captain! We're coming to set you free!"

The pirates' furious charge ended abruptly when they nearly collided with the wildmen. From the looks of things, they'd managed to raid the armory: they'd retrieved their cutlasses — and quite a few other weapons, besides.

Jonathan's bare feet slapped to a stop, and his mouth fell open. "Pig's feathers ... what are you lot doing here?"

The wildmen hailed him with grins and bloodied weapons.

Shamus, on the other hand, looked far less pleased. "I can't believe it. A few moments more, and these fellows would've sprung us. Now I've got no pride and a memory I can't put back."

"Oh, quit your moaning. It wasn't all that —"

The wildmen erupted in laughter when Jonathan turned — revealing the torn-out seat of his breeches.

Gwen rolled her eyes. "Lowlanders," she muttered.

****

Apparently, Midlan hadn't quite managed to capture the ships that'd been stuck at the docks. "Some of the fisherfolk took off with them," one of the villagers said when Lysander asked. "They were out before dawn and saw Midlan coming over the hill. So they grabbed as many ships as they could manage and sunk the rest. Left all of us merchants here to rot."

Lysander tried not to think about the fact that *Anchorgloam* might well be sunk. Instead, he focused himself on trying to find the pirates.

They found Perceval's men locked inside a blacksmith's shop, along with a few merchants from the Valley. There was a company of soldiers hiding inside a row of tents — and the wildmen dealt with them handily. Lysander had started to lose hope when he heard Jonathan yelling from one of the jewelry shops.

"Hello, mates! How about a bit of fresh air, eh?"

A familiar chorus of cheers sent Lysander running. He slapped the pirates on their backs as they climbed out of the cellar. Several of them had full pockets, and they jingled suspiciously as they walked.

"We didn't know how long we'd be caged in, so we thought we might as well do a bit of looting on the way down. A bad idea, locking pirates up in a jeweler's shop," one of them said with a wink.

Lysander wasn't the least bit surprised. "I'm just glad you're all —"

"Well, it's about blasted time!" a man cried from behind him.

Lysander turned and was more than a little shocked to see Alders crawling out of the cellar — and he was more than a little furious when he saw what he wore. "Is that one of our tunics?"

"It's all right, Captain. We agreed to hide him, and he agreed to call our ships back the moment we escaped. They've got a signal worked out with the fisherfolk."

Lysander found that rather hard to believe. "You'd better not be lying, Alders."

He glared as he stood. "I'm not. Do you think this is the first time Harborville's been invaded? Where do you think the bandits go, once they've been kicked out of Crow's Cross? The ships are in a cove not far from here. They'll return at my signal."

Lysander grabbed Alders around the tunic and thrust him out the door with a growl. "Then you'd better get signaling."

The pirates seemed thrilled to see the their companions from the mountains. They dug into their pockets and fished out handfuls of jewels, which they passed around the wildmen.

Gwen frowned at the necklace Jonathan pressed into her hand: a golden chain with a teardrop ruby hanging from its middle. She held it out as if it might bite her. "What's this for?"

"What do you mean, what's it for? It's your share of the loot," he said, nudging her with an elbow.

She wrinkled her nose at it. "But what do I do with *loot*?"

"Wear it, trade it, give it to somebody else — it's yours to use however you want," Jonathan called as he loped away.

Gwen glared at it a moment longer before she held it out to Silas. "Here. Do something with this."

"Yes, my Thane."

"I'm not a Thane anymore," she growled as he took it.

Lysander couldn't hide his surprise. "You're not?"

"No. My brother's better suited to rule our people. He's far wiser than me. I only wish I'd seen it sooner." Her face went dark for a moment before she straightened up. "I've agreed to stay on as his Warchief, though. He gave me a small army and sent me to find the Wright — we need his help."

At a snap of her fingers, Silas drew a small, worn book from the pocket of his breeches. Lysander recognized it immediately as the book Kael used to read. "Where did you —?"

"We know he lives here," Gwen said, pointing at the map. "We just don't know how to get there."

"That's my village. I'll be happy to show you the way, lass," Shamus called.

"Yes, as soon as we're done at the chancellor's castle, we'll take you straight to Copperdock," Lysander said. He didn't even bother to hide his grin: with the wildmen's help, things with the council might just work out.

Silas edged in next to Gwen. "Shall I let your wild ones know, my Thane?"

"Yes." She grabbed him roughly by the collar. "And I'm not going to tell you again, cat. Don't call me a Thane."

Silas didn't look at all concerned. As his glowing eyes swept across her face, they seemed to trace every dip and swirl of her paint. His hands slid up and when they'd gone, he'd somehow clasped the teardrop necklace around her throat.

Gwen frowned as he slipped away, a curious red arched behind her paint. "What are you looking at, pirate?" she said when she caught Lysander watching.

He thought it best to feign indifference. "Nothing. Nothing at all. I was just wondering when those blasted ships are going to come in."

He snatched Alders by the hair as he tried to slink away and twisted hard. "Ah! Any moment, now — they'll be in at any moment!" he cried.

"They'd better be. There's a full village here that's willing to look the other way if the captain decides to gut you," Shamus warned.

Fortunately for Alders, the ships came in a few moments later. The pirates lit the torches along the docks and watched as the ships' lanterns drifted closer to harbor. When Lysander saw *Anchorgloam* sailing in at their head, his relief nearly sank him to his knees.

"There you are, Captain! I knew she'd be all right. No one could put a hole through such a beauty," Shamus said cheerily, slapping a thick arm across his back.

But though the docks were well-lit, the ships came to a halt just outside of the harbor. Alders swore when he saw their anchors drop. "What are you doing? Sail in, blast you!"

"No, Alders. We've had enough." A large fisherman stood upon *Anchorgloam*'s bow. His arms crossed over his thick chest and even from a distance, Lysander could see him glaring in the lantern light. "You starved us as a manager, swindled us a merchant. We swore that if we ever got the chance to better our lot, we would. You can either step down, or watch as we sail off with your fleet."

"All right, then. Go," Alders scoffed. "You won't get far without supplies — and Midlan's likely to scoop you up the moment you weigh anchor."

"We'll stick to the islands. They can't get us if we don't go inland. And there's enough supplies on this ship to last us a long while," he added, slapping a thick hand across *Anchorgloam*'s rails.

Normally, Lysander would've been all for Alders losing everything. But there was a problem. "That isn't his fleet — that's my ship!"

The fisherman's eyes disappeared beneath his scowl. "You're a merchant too, aren't you? I'm sure you're no better than the rest of them."

"The council will hear of this! You won't get far. There'll be an army waiting for you at every port between here and Whitebone. They'll lock you away!" Alders insisted.

The fisherman smiled. "I wonder how they're going to hear about it without your ships? I wouldn't try going across land, after what you've done to Midlan."

They went on arguing, but Lysander wasn't listening. He stripped off his tunic and kicked his boots away. There wasn't a chance he was going to let the fishermen take off with *Anchorgloam*. Even if he had to swim for a hundred miles in her wake —

"No, Captain! You'll never catch them," Shamus said. When Lysander fought his grip, the pirates swarmed in around him.

"Let me go!"

"You're going to get yourself killed!"

"I don't care!"

A young boy appeared next to the fisherman, drawn up by the noise of the pirates' fight. He grinned as he watched them haul Lysander onto the docks. The fisherman laughed.

"Think this is funny, do you?" Lysander bellowed at them. "I hope someone sails off with the thing you love someday — and I hope I'm there to see it!"

"Oh, I'm sure you'll claw your way back into riches. You merchants always seem to find some poor, honest throat to stand on."

"He isn't a merchant — he's a pirate," Jonathan bellowed, striding to the front of the docks. "And if you steal his ship, he'll hunt you down and deal with you in a *pirate's* way: a slow skinning and a quick drop to the sharks."

While the fisherman rolled his eyes, the boy gaped at Jonathan. He tugged roughly on the fisherman's tunic and seemed unable to look away. There was so much distance between them that Lysander couldn't hear what he said. But when he pointed to Jonathan, the fisherman's scowl softened.

Soon his face had changed completely. Though his voice still carried, it wasn't nearly as sharp as it'd been before. "My son says he knows you, forest man. Said you came through here with a merchant's caravan back when Reginald had us living like thieves ... said you and another lad fed him. He says you got the whole caravan passing out its wares."

Jonathan shifted uncomfortably. "Well, it was Kael's idea, really. He was the one who started it —"

"I don't care about any of that. Those rations got us through the roughest months we ever lived." The fisherman's face went tight around his eyes and for a moment, his mouth twisted. Then he raised an arm and jabbed a finger at Jonathan's face. "*You* ... you can come aboard."

He took a hesitant step forward. "What about my friends?"

"They can come, too. I'll send the boats."

"No, *no*! They still haven't paid my docking fees!" Alders howled over the pirates' cheers. When the fisherman shrugged, he latched onto Lysander. "The laws are there for a reason! It'd be bloody anarchy if every man simply went around doing as he pleased. The High Seas would crumble. If you let them sail off with my ships, you'll be no better than a —"

"Pirate?" Lysander said with a grin. He peeled Alders' hands aside, twisting them at the wrist. "I've tried playing merchant with you lot, but I'm afraid I'm just not patient enough for it. There's only one thing I know how to do, and I do it rather well. If it's freedom you're after, look no further," he called to the fisherman. "We pirates split our loot in equal shares."

The fisherman raised his fist with a grin. "Then welcome to your new fleet, Captain."

"The council *will* hear of this!" Alders shrieked. "Just wait until the other merchants find out what you've done. They'll have you hanged for this! *Hanged*!"

Gwen pressed a thumb against her forehead as his screaming continued. She bared her teeth against the noise — and her scowl grew more dangerous with every passing second. Finally, she seemed able to take it no longer. "Silas? This man annoys me. Do something about it."

"Yes, my Thane." He bowed deeply before spinning on his heel and launching his fist into Alders' jaw.

The merchant toppled off the docks with a yelp and fell heavily into the water below. He splashed around for a moment before he managed to grab onto the dock's edge. But when he tried to pull himself free, Gwen shoved him back under with a thrust of her heel.

"Lowlanders," she growled again.

CHAPTER 32
HOLLOWFANG

Kael tried to focus on keeping his mind clear as they flew back to camp. His fight with Rua had gotten them into deeper trouble: now Kyleigh was only allowed to wear her dragon skin if they were summoned to the red mountains. As long as they were at camp, she had to be human.

They weren't likely to be summoned again until they found His-Rua's answer. The only problem was that neither of them had any clue what that answer might be.

Gorm was following them. Kael could feel his shadow pressing down upon the top of his skull. He'd been sent as a punishment for going after Rua: if any dragon was going to get blasted away by a spell, the others all agreed that it ought to be Gorm.

His eyes would be upon them every hour of the day and night. They would have no rest and not a moment's peace. Dark thoughts clouded the back of Kael's mind, but he managed to keep them from leaking to where Kyleigh could hear them. He tried to keep his heart calm.

He held them back until the moment they landed. Once he'd slipped off her shoulders and taken a few steps away, the darkness flooded in.

"What are you thinking?"

Kyleigh's voice rose above his thoughts, as it always did. "Nothing."

"Come off it. I can tell when you're thinking about something —"

"Don't." He moved before she could touch him. "Stop it — stop coddling me. I know you've been putting it all on yourself. That's the only reason I haven't ripped my hair out, isn't it?" he said, thinking back to the strange fury that'd burned inside Rua's eyes.

It was only after he'd touched His-Rua that fire had sprouted across his muzzle. *She* was the one who was furious with Kyleigh. He knew that dragons could share pain. He supposed it wasn't too much of a stretch to think they could share emotions, as well ...

He only wished he'd seen it sooner.

"You've been taking my worry away so that I won't have to feel it. You make everything seem less than what it is. I can't let you do it anymore."

"I'm only trying to help."

"Well, it isn't helpful!" he snapped. His fists shook as the realizations washed over him, nearly drowning him inside their fury. "I've been moonstruck for days because of it — I've been loping around the island like an idiot. And if you keep it up, you're going to make yourself sick."

"*You're* making me sick! I can't stand it when you're so gloomy. Yes, it hurts for a while," she said when she saw the argument in his eyes. "But a larger part of me feels better knowing you don't have to carry it all on your own. At least things aren't completely miserable, this way."

"I work best when I'm miserable. If you keep making me lightheaded, I won't be able to think," Kael said firmly. He tore his eyes away from her and tried to focus on getting his thoughts in order. "His-Rua wants your names ... your shapechanger name?"

Kyleigh turned her glare upon the sea — towards the darkening sky. Storm winds brushed the hair from across her eyes, and he could see them glowing clearly. "She wants the names of my souls, my two halves."

That stirred Kael's memory. It seemed like an eternity ago that he'd been trapped inside the Endless Plains, working with Eveningwing to bury the body of one of Lord Gilderick's mages. But he still remembered clearly what the halfhawk had told him:

All shapechangers are bonded souls — one human and one animal. It's our binding that allows us to take each other's shapes. The boy I bonded with is still here ... we protect each other. I know the secrets of the earth and he knows the words of men ...

Kael pulled himself from his thoughts, slowly piecing it together. "She wants the names you had before you became a shapechanger — the name of the woman and the dragon. You don't remember them?"

She rolled her eyes. "Of course I remember them. We're just stuck at the edge of the Fate-forsaken world for the joy of it."

324

"Kyleigh," he growled, "I'm only trying to help."

Her fingers twisted tightly in her pony's tail. She turned so he couldn't read her eyes. "I know. I just ... I hate this part of it. I hate that I can't remember — and at the same moment, I'm not sure I want to."

"Well, you're going to have to remember some of it. What's the first thing you recall?"

"It won't help —"

"Try."

Kyleigh shook her head. "The furthest I can reach is to Hollowfang."

"One of the halfwolves?"

"The first alpha I remember — Bloodfang's thrice great grandsire."

Kael remembered. She'd spoken of him once before, just after he'd told her about Bloodfang's death. Bile still rose in his throat at the thought, but Kael forced it away. If there were any clues in her story, he had to find them. He had to concentrate.

"What do you remember about him?"

Kyleigh held out her hand without turning. "See for yourself."

Kael hesitated. "Only memories, all right?"

"Only memories," she promised.

He wound his fingers through hers and closed his eyes as the image rose up:

A young man's face filled his vision — a forest man. He was bare-chested and had lithe features. His dark eyes peered sharply from beneath the crop of his hair.

"Emberfang?"

His voice was muffled. A black curtain fell over Kyleigh's memory as she closed her eyes. There was a *thud*, a scraping sound across her ears.

"You must wake, child." The young man's voice hissed through the darkness. "We're not ready to have you leave us."

These words lifted the black curtain. The young man's dark eyes came into focus — along with the eyes of a dozen others gathered around him. They clustered in a ring above Kyleigh. A thick ceiling of leaves hung over their heads.

The young man's hands were on her ears. It was their roughness that'd caused the scraping sound. Kael could just see the blurred tip of his thumb as he traced a circle beneath her eye. The dark-skinned people behind him leaned forward. Many of their mouths hung agape.

"Hollowfang ..."

He bared his teeth in a wolfish grin when Kyleigh spoke his name. "I'm pleased you remember. That was a brave thing you did for us. Though I'm afraid we will never be able to repay you for your treasure."

"What ... brave thing?"

Hollowfang turned his head ever so slightly when the people behind him began to whisper.

Their tittering stopped immediately. "You protected your family. You gave up everything for your pack. You've been a good wolf, Emberfang. I'm proud to call you *sister*."

His eyes lingered upon hers. His thumbs ran beneath them again. "What is it?"

"Nothing worth the trouble," Hollow fang insisted. His hands slid down to her shoulders. "Come, now — we must hunt hard before the winter ..."

Kael stumbled forward when Kyleigh pulled away. "That's it. I can't remember what I did. I haven't got a clue what he meant about a treasure. Hollowfang would never tell me," she added. Her voice was harsh, though her eyes stayed distant. "He said the darkness was a gift — that it'd brought me peace. He didn't want to take my happiness away."

"But you remember some things," Kael insisted, stepping closer. He reached to grasp her arm, but thought better of it. Once they'd found the answer to His-Rua's question, he could hold her again. But until then, he had to be careful. "You said you remembered the way across the northern seas. There has to be a memory somewhere —"

"I have dreams sometimes ... just bits of things, really," Kyleigh whispered. Her gaze slid further. "There are hordes of men beneath me. I hear screams as they run from my flame. Their bodies are so small, so helpless ... it seems a shame to harm them. But harming them is the only way to draw the others out."

Her voice had dropped to a growl; her body stood frozen upon the shore. Kael was afraid to breathe. A long moment passed before he found his voice: "What others?"

"Dragons." Her lips pulled back from her teeth in a snarl. Her fingers ground against her armor. "My people are dying, and these other dragons have something to do with it. They are smaller than me, but fierce. Their males share the sky without trouble, their females are mixed among them. They fight as one creature — their strength swelled tenfold by their numbers. But though they're fearless warriors, it's their eyes that trouble me most ..."

Only a hair's breadth of space separated them, now. Kael was trapped somewhere between fire and the open sea: too entranced by the flames to move, to afraid of the waters to flee. "What's wrong with their eyes?" he whispered.

Kyleigh grimaced. "They're blue." She blinked, and her gaze returned. "I know it's not terribly helpful, but that's what I dream."

After hearing her speak, after seeing the way she watched those memories, there was no doubt in his mind that what Kyleigh had said was true. He believed there was a dragon's soul within her — a soul that'd warred with men, that'd fought against these other dragons. He knew her memories weren't lost, but simply buried somewhere deep inside her mind ...

And he thought he knew how to get them.

"Do you remember what I said to you, that morning in the mountains?"

He didn't have to say anything more than that. She knew what morning he spoke of — the only dawn that mattered. Kyleigh tore her eyes from the sea and onto his, where they warmed. "You asked me to be brave."

He took her hands and stared into the very center of her eyes, prepared to lose himself inside their depth — prepared to fall into a world he'd hoped he would never have to walk again ... into a world he feared.

"I need you to be brave one more time, Kyleigh," he whispered as the Motherlands slipped away. "I need you to trust me ..."

CHAPTER 33
A DRAGON'S FURY

The first thing Kael was aware of was the floor beneath his stomach. It was cold, uneven — stone. He didn't want to open his eyes, didn't what to see where he'd wound up. His ears cringed against the silence.

For in this world, silence could mean trouble.

He opened his eyes slowly, not at all certain about what he would find. Though the stone floor was cold, the hallway in front of him was full of light. Beams washed down from the ceiling: slits carved out from where the top met the wall, spaced only a few hand-lengths apart. Kael knew the slits were fitted with narrow panes of glass — glass so refined that there was hardly a ripple across any of them.

He knew this because he'd made each pane and set them in, himself.

This was a hallway in Roost, *their* hallway — the passage that led to their chambers. Its sides were turned towards each face of the sun: one set of windows caught the dawn light, and the other caught the evening. The glass made the passageway much hotter than the rest of the castle, but Kyleigh loved the light.

He remembered how she'd grinned when she saw what he'd done; he knew by how her hands had tightened around his that she was thrilled. But he never could've guessed that the hallway meant so much to her — enough to shape the passages of her mind.

Tapestries lined the walls to their ends. They covered the stone from bottom to top. Kael's heart raced as he stepped over to the nearest one. He recognized the scene immediately: they were back in Tinnark, sitting at one of the hospital's bloodstained tables.

The image had been woven as if he looked out through Kyleigh's eyes, and he saw himself seated across from her. An involuntary smile pulled at Kael's lips as he watched himself glare down at the bowl of stew between his arms — and he could practically smell its charred broth.

It was a small tapestry tucked between grander ones, a strange thing for her to treasure. And yet it sat alongside some of their greatest adventures: the tempest, the Witch, the day they'd freed the giants.

Kael walked slowly when he came to her memories of Whitebone desert. His toes curled at the lumpy flesh and grasping teeth of the creatures that must've been the *minceworms* she'd told him about. A picture of Silas and Elena made him laugh, but the next cut his laughter short.

It was a memory of Nadine — crouched, with her arms wrapped tightly about the shoulders of a little girl. Even through the thread, he could read the agony on their faces.

He walked quickly after that. Seeing Nadine's face reminded him of what would happen if Midlan took back the realm — it reminded him that everything would be undone. The Kingdom would be exactly as it'd been before: full of people living from one day to the next without hope.

The last time he'd seen Nadine, she'd been standing next to Declan on the back of a ship bound for the Endless Plains — an entire horde of red-headed children from the mountains surrounding her. That was the face he wanted to remember: the one that seemed stuck in a glowing smile.

And so he focused himself on the task at hand.

It wasn't long before he no longer recognized the images in Kyleigh's mind. He supposed it was because he'd slipped beyond the time he knew her. He was near the middle of the hall when something caught his eye: a wall-height marvel of colored thread, each woven tightly against the next into a beautiful, swirling pattern ...

Kael blinked, but nothing changed. Though the colors and the pattern were beautiful, they were ... nonsense. They formed no picture, made no words. If he stepped back, he thought he could almost see something beginning to take shape within the pattern.

But when he squinted, it was lost.

Everything in the next half of the passageway was the same. They drew his eyes and brightened his heart at first glance, but he stepped back, frustrated. Even the few trinkets he found stacked atop the shelves had their pieces scrambled until he couldn't tell what they were. It was all a remarkable, jumbled mess.

Each door was different, from the color of its paint to the grain of its wood. Some of their handles were rusted, some were brazen, others were simple iron rings. There was one that had nothing but a series of bolts all down its side, and Kael thought it looked important.

He slid each bolt away, listening after every click for the rumble of something dangerous inside: *Beware the monsters of Fear and Doubt, for they will devour everything.*

He didn't like having Ben Deathtreader's voice inside his head — especially now that he knew Deathtreader was the one who'd caused the Whispering War, who led the rebel army into battle against the Kingdom. He liked it no more than he would've liked Gilderick's slimy voice inside his head.

But Deathtreader's *Dreadful Journeys* had taught him all he knew about mind-walking — and if Kael wanted to stay alive, he had no choice but to listen.

When the last bolt sprang free, he paused a moment more. There was nothing but silence behind the door. He opened it a crack, just enough to see what lay beyond. There wasn't much.

Water covered the floor: he could hear it slapping gently against the bottom of the doorframe. Light from the passageway spilt in, illuminating its ripples. They popped up here and there — many disappeared before he had the chance to get a decent look at them. But the ones he did manage to see were as scrambled as the tapestries. The ripples were just more frustrating, half-pictures warped by the water's flesh.

They played across the stone above him in a mirage of ghostly shadows. Whispers glanced his ears, swelling along the lines of light that grew, sharpened. He could almost see the pictures, almost hear the words. And then just as suddenly as it'd appeared, the ghostly light was gone.

He was beginning to understand why Kyleigh was upset. This wasn't at all like the emptiness of Brend's mind: the rooms were full, there was plenty of light. But nothing was quite as it should've been. It wasn't clear, it didn't make sense. He was sorry for all the times he'd rolled his eyes when she said she couldn't remember.

If he ever made it back to the present, he would apologize.

Kael closed the door and did back its bolts. He had a feeling he would find confusion behind every door, and he had no idea how to set it all straight.

"Hello?" he called into the passageway, hoping someone might answer.

The Secrets called back. He recognized their screeching voices as they tried to lead him to one door or the next, but their words were just as scrambled as everything else. Kael was so lost that he couldn't even be lured to his death.

His frustration grew with every step. The hallway seemed to stretch forever. At last, he came to its end. He recognized the stairway in front of him immediately: the series of winding steps that — in the present — would've led him to the chambers he shared with Kyleigh.

He had no idea where these steps might lead him in her mind. If he traveled too far, he might accidentally go too deep and wind up inside her heart, or perhaps even the house of her soul — her Inner Sanctum. So as he climbed the steps, he was determined not to go too far. Even if the hallway continued, he wouldn't press on. He would simply open their chamber door and be done with it.

The floor *did* continue at the top of the stairs — much further than it did in the present. There was an entire second floor that stretched on into darkness. Kael wondered what might lie beyond the door he knew ... but in the same breath, he hoped he wouldn't have to find out.

Their chamber door was small and rounded at its top. He turned its familiar handle without bothering to listen for what lay behind it — convinced that it would be just as empty as the rest.

But he was wrong.

Hello, my love.

Kael nearly fell out the way he came. He hadn't been expecting to come nose-to-muzzle with a great, white dragon — and his surprise knocked him off his feet.

"Ah, hello?" was all he could think to say.

The dragon's face was so close that its burning green eyes filled his vision. Her pupils were slitted — not rounded like Kyleigh's. But other than that, this dragon looked exactly like her second skin. And that was the only thing that kept him from panicking when the dragon's teeth clamped around his boot.

For all her size, she was surprisingly gentle. Kael tried not to squirm as she dragged him through the doorway. *I heard you calling for me, but I couldn't answer. I knew you would come to me on your own. I knew you'd find me.*

"Really? I wasn't sure I would. It's … strange, here," Kael said as the dragon leaned over him again.

Her eyes closed when he pressed a hand against her face. The white scales were smooth and warm. She leaned heavily against his palm. *You've always been so kind to me, no matter what shape I wear. Few humans tolerated me. Some feared me. Most hated me. They saw the other half of my soul as Abomination — a corruption of the thing they hold most dear.*

"What thing is that?" Kael wondered.

One of her eyes cracked open. *Beauty*, she murmured. *All humans love beauty. They long for what pleases their eyes, waste their short years searching for this faint pleasure — all the while unaware that were they to reach out, these beautiful things would crumble to dust beneath their hands. Beauty is as passing and frail as humans. Perhaps that is why they seek it out. Even* you *are vulnerable to it.*

Kael's face burned as the dragon's eye closed once again. "I do think you're beautiful," he admitted quietly.

It was something he would've never said aloud to Kyleigh's human half. For some reason, he'd always been more comfortable talking to the dragon. Though he knew Kyleigh loved him, a small part of him worried that if he told her how beautiful she was, if he tried to speak the words his spirit whispered when she kissed him — if he dared to tell her that she held him completely captive by the strings of his heart …

Well, he was afraid she might think him silly for it.

The day I revealed my second half to you, I knew my soul would break if you hated me, the dragon rumbled. *It was the most terrifying moment of my life, the most perilous height I've ever climbed. My heart lay exposed and beating at your feet. But …* the dragon's eyes opened slowly, *you did not crush it. You treated me no differently than you had before. And for that, I will be forever grateful.*

Kael didn't know what to say. Kyleigh had never spoken to him like that.

They often talked late into the night — about their battles, their adventures. He loved her stories about the Whispering War; she loved to ask him questions about life in the mountains. In the short season they'd been together without any sort of trouble hanging over their heads, he felt he'd learned a lot about her.

Now he realized there was a whole other side of her he hadn't even spoken to yet — the side she hid behind her laughter and her grins. This was the part of her she guarded, this dragon half that spoke so deeply ... the part of her that was every bit as vulnerable as him.

Now, you've come here for a reason, have you not?

"Yes," Kael said — trying to focus on the task at hand even though there were at least a hundred questions bouncing around inside his head. "You don't happen to know your old name, do you? The name you had before you bonded?"

The dragon shook her head. *The only names known to me are Emberfang and Kyleigh. Though the human leads us, I am always here. We've been one creature for as long as I can remember. But ... there is a way to find your answer.*

"How?"

The dragon gave him a long look. Then she bent and snagged his boot again. Kael held onto his middle as the dragon lifted him over her shoulder — as if that might somehow keep his innards from sloshing. She turned slowly, though the room was stretched inside Kyleigh's mind to the point that three dragons could've moved about it easily.

Perhaps it was reluctance that dragged her claws.

Behind the dragon loomed a great stone wall. Kael followed it upwards and saw it disappear into darkness — as if the ceiling was so high that not even the light could reach it. Hanging upside down from his boot meant he had to crane his neck backwards to see the floor. He was trying to focus through the swinging of the room when he noticed the windows.

In the present, their chamber had only one window. But in Kyleigh's mind, there were two. They were small and identically plain. Badly-worn shutters clamped tightly over their mouths. Iron latches held them shut, and from each latch hung a fist-sized lock.

These are our pasts, the dragon murmured as she set him down. *They've been shut away since the beginning of my memory, and I have been their guardian. You'll find every answer you seek beyond these portals.*

Kael crept over to them, his heart racing.

This wall reminded him of the one he'd destroyed inside his Inner Sanctum — the wall that'd held his Fear. Was that what lay behind these windows? Was Kyleigh afraid to learn her past?

"How do I open them?" Kael said.

The locks will fall open in your hands, my love. There is nothing I have, nothing I am or might someday be that I would deny you.

There was a considerable amount of heaviness in the dragon's voice. When Kael turned, he saw her eyes were fixed unblinkingly upon the windows. "What's going to happen when I open them?"

I'm ... not sure. Neither of us remembers what became of our pasts. There's no way to know what you might see beyond them. Her foreclaws scraped against the floor as she tucked them beneath her, and her eyes slid back up to Kael's. *But if you throw them open, we will remember. And I ... that troubles me.*

"You're afraid that if you remember who you were before, you won't be *Kyleigh* anymore," Kael guessed, searching through the worry in the dragon's eyes. "You're afraid the truth might change you."

She nodded. *Perhaps for the better ... perhaps not. But you must open them, my love. This is the only way.*

Kael thought carefully. "What if I only opened them a bit — just enough to look inside, but not enough to let anything out?"

The dragon's scaly lips twisted into a smile. *You could try.*

Trying was his only option. He doubted there was a room inside Kyleigh's head that would've made more sense than this one. And if the dragon said looking through the windows was the only way, then he believed it.

The woman might've been a bit mischievous, but he trusted the dragon completely.

Kael stepped up to the left window first. It rattled when he reached for it, as if a great wind roared behind it. No sooner had he touched the lock than it fell open inside his hand.

The bolt thudded hard against the shutters as the wind roared. He could practically hear the iron groaning to hold its own against the gales. Kael braced himself against one shutter and planted his elbow firmly atop the pane of the other. He slid the bolt back fractions at a time — his warrior half swelling to match each thrust of the wind.

When the bolt slid free, he let the shutter push his arm back. It opened just enough to form a hairline crack into the world beyond, and Kael peered through it carefully.

****

Fire burst across his eyes — furious tongues of yellow flame. They blinded him, enraged him. He slung one of his claws into the heart of the fire and bared his teeth as they tore across flesh.

He tucked his wings and fell in the direction of an agonized screech. A small white dragon was bolting towards the earth — towards the high walls of an enormous city. Its spires glowed with the evening light. Every pale brick was stricken with the sun's fire: it roiled inside a cradle of green, the whole thing made molten by dusk.

Anger burst inside his chest at the thought and his great wings beat against his sides, ripping him towards the white dragon.

Her head slung around and her strange, blue eyes widened with fear. The mark of his claws were drawn in scarlet lines across her chest. "Please — enough!"

These words meant nothing to Kael. There was no *enough*. Nothing would ever be *enough*. These monsters would never stop slaughtering his people. They'd slaughtered dragons for hundreds of years without mercy, without any thought. Not even when the hatching grounds fell cold did the Halved Ones stop their killing.

Now when he slept, he dreamt of the end of dragonkind.

No, they would find no mercy from him.

Kael dug his claws into the dragon's back. The wind's howl filled his ears as he plummeted from the sky like a rock. He slammed the white dragon's body into the earth, reveling in the snap of her bones.

Her blood poured across his claws — each drop broiling with her inner flame. It slid into the cracks between his scales and seared the flesh beneath them. His eyes blurred against the pain, but he forced himself to dig in, to snap more of her bones and draw more of her blood.

Kyleigh's voice filled his chest and burst with angry words: "Give up your hatching grounds, Halved One! Tell me where they are, and I will kill you quickly."

335

Angry screeching filled the air above him. Kael could feel the shadows of his enemies falling towards him, swarming to save their companion from his grasp. They would rip his flesh from its bone and his heart from its cage. They would tear him apart so swiftly with the force of their numbers that he would have no chance to fight back.

But he didn't care.

Let them come.

"... don't know ... hatching grounds ..." the Halved One whimpered from beneath him. "We don't ... don't ..."

"Argh!" Kael thrust forward with all of his weight and snapped the Halved One's neck. He dragged his claws against the dirt to staunch the burning of her blood.

The shadow of the swarm was falling upon him: females, males of every color — they wore the skins of those he'd lost. They made a mockery of his friends. He could see the fury wrought in each blue line of their eyes, but he felt no fear.

There was only rage.

The sky between them disappeared as he charged into battle. They had the force of the earth behind them. The Halved Ones would pummel him in a swarm and thrust his body into the ground. They would snap his neck just as he'd done to their companion.

Still, Kael's pace never slowed. He would crash straight into their middle and drag as many as he could against his belly. Their corpses would break his fall —

A roar pierced the clouds, shook the skies. Kael's wings beat with a new speed as a monstrous black dragon burst through the Halved Ones' swarm. His claws hewed their wings. Their throats split against his jagged teeth. With one powerful swipe of his tail, he flung their shattered bodies from the skies.

But there were more.

A strange sound came from the molten city: the clang of metal forced into the shell of a song. Kael had come to hate the noise, and to fear it. This sound meant the Halved Ones' Great Swarm was coming — led by a human who wielded a terrible fire.

"Flee, the battle is lost!"

Kael's ears hardened against the black dragon's voice. A blinding white light had appeared inside the city's middle. It bounced with the sprint of the man who carried it. Even from a distance, Kael

336

could see his eyes were set upon him — and his mind clouded with the thought of blood.

Thousands spilled from the city behind the man who carried the light, twisting and bursting into their stolen skins. The man leapt astride the largest Halved One and the Great Swarm followed the blinding arc of the fire he carried.

Let them come!

Kael wanted nothing more than to slaughter every last one ...

"My heart's bond!"

The words tore Kael's eyes from the Great Swarm and to the black dragon hovering above him. He saw all of his pain, all of his anguish reflected inside the dragon's eyes. Blood burned between the cracks of his scales. His once-proud head sank low with exhaustion. He knew the weight of Kael's pain. He'd entrusted it to him, asked him to bear it wisely.

But this time, he'd failed.

He remembered it, now: the black dragon's anger had carried him across the seas into the heart of the Wildlands. It'd driven him to start a battle he couldn't win.

"Please, my heart — I couldn't bear it if you were slain even a moment before I. There will be a time to fight the Halved Ones. But for today, the battle is lost."

The world turned and the molten city disappeared as Kael followed the black dragon into the sky. The Halved Ones were quick in battle, but the span of their wings was far too short. Their human halves weakened and shrank the dragon. It wasn't long before Kael had out-distanced them.

His vision swelled with the ice-capped seas; his ears filled with the beating of the black dragon's wings. The fires of the anger he'd carried suddenly went out. Sorrow waited beneath it.

"Our nests are empty, our hatching grounds have gone cold. If we cannot stop the Halved Ones, they will destroy the few of us who remain. I fear our time is nearly at its end."

"I fear that too, my heart," the black dragon said from beside her. His great voice hardly rose above the murmur of the wind. "But then I remember that Fate wove our souls from nothing, that she bid our Motherlands rise from the sea. I think she would not have bothered to give us life if she planned to let others steal it away."

A heavy sigh filled Kael's chest. "And yet, they steal it. We could have stopped the Halved Ones. But this human who carries flame ... he will never stop. I see it in his eyes."

"With enough time, the Halved Ones will fall, My-Dorcha. As for the human ..." the yellow of the black dragon's eyes flared brightly, "I will see to it that he stops."

CHAPTER 34
A WOMAN'S SORROW

The vision fled him with a *whoosh*, slamming the shutter tightly. Kael did back its bolts before the next vision could throw them open.

His hands shook as he snapped the lock into place. Something tore at his flesh, pressed down upon his shoulders. It dragged him to his knees. Kael felt as if he wore a cloak made of iron: it hung from his back and turned his skin to ice. But the feeling within him was worse.

Needles jabbed his innards; daggers cut his bone. His blood bubbled and shrank inside his veins, drying to a thick, blackened crust. Flames gnawed through his every rift and lapped furiously at his marrow. Kael wrapped his arms around his chest and squeezed them together tightly.

Desperation bent his back and anger ravaged him from within, but behind all that was fear — the fear that he would be crushed, devoured. It was *fear* that stole his strength and gave him over to the darkness. He had to stop it, had to thaw the spines of ice growing up his back before they reached his head —

My love!

"No!"

Kael threw himself against the wall just as the white dragon lunged for him. He couldn't let Kyleigh touch him. He couldn't let her feel these horrible things. If she felt them, she might remember — and the memories would consume her.

"Don't touch me," he pleaded, when the dragon crept forward. "Please, just … just talk to me. Tell me everything's going to be all right."

It was a foolish thing to ask — Kael knew this. But he thought that perhaps if he were to focus on something else, he might not have to think about the fact that he was being eaten from the inside out. He trusted the dragon not to laugh.

Whatever it is, you can defeat it. There's not an enemy you've faced that you haven't found some way to overcome, not a battle you've started that you haven't won, the dragon said.

It was the confidence in her voice that steadied him more than the words. Her belief in him cooled the anger, tore the desperation aside. It melted his fear.

Kyleigh had seen more of the world than he could ever hope to. If she believed in him, he thought it must be true. "Thank you," he muttered as the last of the anger went out.

The dragon's fiery green eyes swelled in his vision as she bent her face to his. The flames sputtered in uncertain arcs. *What did you ... see?*

Kael wasn't sure what to say. He didn't want to think about the black dragon — the dragon who'd called Kyleigh his *heart's bond* ... the dragon he was almost entirely certain now lived inside the body of the shapechanger bound to the King. Just the thought of it made him bare his teeth.

He was afraid to say anything about what he'd seen. Even the smallest detail might undo the window's lock. One wrong word could release her memory and cause the past to come flooding in. If that happened, she would have to bear that horrible anger and desperation once more. He couldn't take that chance.

Instead, he forced himself to smile and say: "I saw a dragon who loved deeply and battled without fear. You have nothing to be ashamed of."

More of your kindness. The dragon tilted her head, and her fiery eyes narrowed. *Sometimes I think you are too kind. But this is merely a strand of thought flowing down the river. My love runs too fiercely to let it sink in.*

That was something Kyleigh never would have said. He couldn't believe her two halves were so completely different. Slowly, Kael got to his feet. "All right ... one more window."

You discovered my name? What is it? the dragon said at his nod.

"I can't tell you — not here. Not so close to this wall."

No sooner had he spoken than the shutters rattled hard.

Kael took a deep breath. "I'll tell you the moment I'm ... out."

The dragon inclined her head. *That's probably for the best. Be careful.*

Kael knew he had to be careful. He was prepared for the shutters' push, and his warrior half swelled against it. But this time, the metal bolt was strangely hot. He pulled his sleeve over his hand and slid it back quickly. Then he pressed his ear against the worn oak, listening for what lay beyond.

Instead of wind, he heard screams.

Kael's heart was thudding before he even cracked the shutter open and plunged into the scene beyond ...

****

Darkness — a damp shroud soaked in orange light.

Footsteps thudded into the earth all around him. The ghosts of screams crawled down the base of his skull — present, but not entirely full. Blurred shadows darted through the soaked orange edges. The fires were so bright that he couldn't watch them for long. They hurt him. The pain shut his eyes ...

A woman's startled gasp dragged him from the darkness: "Fate! Oh, thank Fate."

When he opened his eyes, the woman's face was a hand's breadth from his. The glow of flame warmed her pale skin, painted shadows across her features. Her raven hair had fallen from its bonds and flowed into the darkness. Her stark blue eyes were fierce and bold — a warrior's eyes.

Kyleigh's voice slid between his lips as he moaned: "Ryane ...?"

"I'm here."

The world swam as the woman pulled him up. She dragged him against her chest. The arms that wrapped around his middle were as hard as coils of iron, but they held him gently.

"Fate," Ryane whispered again, her voice strangely tight. "How did you survive it? How could you have possibly ...?"

His lips were pressed against her shoulder; he could taste the smoke staining the material of her jerkin. He mumbled when he spoke, hoping she wouldn't be able hear him: "I was looking out the window —"

"I told you not to look!"

"Had I not, I would've been blasted away with the others!" he growled, lifting his head to glare at her. "When that bloody spell hit us, it knocked me out the window —"

341

"Don't swear. You know Mother hated your swearing," Ryane said sharply. Then she hauled him up by his elbows and grabbed his hand. "Can you run?"

"I think so."

"Good. We haven't got much time."

She dragged him into the darkness. A ruined city grew out of the shadows: the pale remains of statues and buildings wrapped in coils of flame. Windows spewed cinders upon his head. Smoke scratched his lungs.

There were people everywhere. They filled the streets and ran as if Death snapped at their heels. Their skin was as pale as the walls of their city, their hair black as dusk. The fear that ringed their blue eyes sank down to Kael's knees. The worry that marred their features chilled his blood — and he was almost certain they were heading the wrong way.

"Where are we going?" he gasped as Ryane dragged him forward.

"The shaman says our time has come. We must flee the city or be destroyed."

A horrible, icy something lurched against his lungs. "But I thought the flyers were picking the spellweavers off! You said it was only a matter time before they —"

"They've brought out a new magic, tonight. Spells are flying from every hand, swinging from every fist. They've brought down three flyers already. Our shaman says he can't protect us against the magic this army wields — its power is too great."

Ryane turned slightly to avoid the charge of the crowd, and he saw the slender, glinting blade clutched in her hand. "The flyers will guard our escape for as long as they can, but Draegoth is lost. All of the groundlings must flee."

"Then why aren't we running for the gates?" Kael gasped. A cloud of smoke burned his eyes and made them stream. When he wiped the blurriness aside, he saw where they were headed. He tugged hard on Ryane's hand. "The *relic*? Is that where you're taking us?"

"I promised Father —"

"Father is dead, and he wouldn't want you to join him!"

"You don't know what he'd want. You don't remember our parents like I do," Ryane said harshly.

342

His palm went cold in her grip. "But what about the curse? You'll be burned to nothing if you try to take it!"

"I won't let it fall into the hands of these people. They've destroyed all in their path — imagine what they might do with the relic. I swore to guard it in Father's place, just as his father swore before him. If I burn, then so be it."

Ryane's teeth were bared against the words. She pulled Kael closer behind her as they broke through the last surge of people and into the burning ruins beyond.

A statue loomed before them — the pale statue of a sword wrapped in intricate coils of flame. The sword stood in the middle of the flame upon its tip, tucked inside a plain leather scabbard. Streaks of black fanned out across its rounded hilt and charred grip, but the orb on its pommel still shone.

His heart leapt up his throat as Ryane climbed the steps towards the carved wisps of flame. "Please, don't —"

"I must," she said firmly. She slid her sword into its sheath and her fingers coiled about the relic's charred grip. "If the curse destroys me, you have to carry the relic away from here — as far as you can. You must be its guardian."

Before Kael could stop her, Ryane tugged on the blade.

He heard the *clink* of the rounded hilt as it struck the stone top of the flames, but it didn't come free. Ryane pulled again. She crouched and tugged hard, lending every bunched muscle in her arms to the effort. But the blade didn't move. It was stuck inside the statue.

Kael's legs carried him up the steps and he slid his hands beneath Ryane's. "It's a puzzle," he said when she tried to stop him. "You can't just pull it free. You have to work it out."

"How do you know?"

"I ... might've heard the shaman talking about it with his mate. It was dark out and I was bored," he said quickly, when he saw her scolding look. "You can't expect me to sit around all day *and* all night —"

"Search the city! Find the monsters!"

Ryane's hair whipped across her neck as she turned. Her blade was out before she'd taken half a step towards the alley. "Work it out, then — but don't pull it free," she called as she sprinted away. "I'll be the one to take the curse."

Kael's hands shook as he stared down at the flames. The coils nearly touched at their tops. From the side, it looked like a tangled mess. But if he stood on his toes and looked straight down, he could see that the gaps between their tops formed a maze.

Ryane cried out as she met a small company of soldiers in battle. They were men clad in armor that shone like gold — soldiers of the man who called himself *King*. They hefted swords that shone as brightly as their armor, and carried shields crusted in gold.

They were strong, but Ryane was quick: she cut inside their ranks and punished them with her speed. Kael's hands paused as he watched her do battle. His eyes were entranced by the arcs of her blade, the dance of her feet. She was never silent — laughing when they missed her, grunting as she swung. Her voice rose and fell along the fury of her attack, like a song ...

"Hurry!"

"I'm trying!" Kael said, forcing his eyes back to the relic.

He dragged the grip quickly through the maze of flame-tops. More than once, he had to turn its edge in order to slide the scabbard between cracks. But it was coming free. There was only one turn left to get through.

"Have you got it?"

Ryane was charging towards him. A pile of gold-tinged bodies lay in a scattered mess behind her. Delicate spatters of blood crisscrossed her features, and her hair whipped with her sprint. Her eyes — Fate, her eyes were fiercer than they'd ever been before. And in that moment, Kael realized their people needed Ryane's strength far more than they needed him.

He shut his eyes against her scream and pulled the relic free.

He waited for the pain, for the fires the shaman had spoken of to burst from the relic and consume him, but they didn't. No sooner had he allowed himself a breath did Ryane tear the sword from his hands.

There was a loud *thunk* as she gripped his face. "Are you hurt?"

"No."

"Are you sure?"

"Fairly." His eyes slid from hers to where the relic lay upon the ground. "I can't believe you just tossed it like that. You'll be lucky if its ghost doesn't rise up and set fire to your arse —"

344

"That mouth!" Ryane growled. She kissed him swiftly, then pulled him onto his feet. No sooner had she slung the relic's belt across her shoulders than another company of soldiers burst in from the blazing streets.

Their helmets swung from the pile of their slain companions to where Ryane and Kael stood beside the statue. Their leader raised his sword. "Monsters — over there!"

Ryane ripped Kael towards a narrow passageway, one nearly gutted by the flames. A yelp escaped his throat when they turned a corner and nearly ran flat into a man sprinting towards them. He ground his heels and his eyes widened in recognition.

"Ryane! They've swarmed the gates. We have to get to the northern w — gah!"

He lurched forward as if he'd been shoved. Three golden barbs ripped through his chest, their tips soaked in red. He dug his sword into the ground to keep his feet. The skin on his face went taut.

"Archers … go!" he spat through the dark wet that coated his lips. Then he swung around and broke into a stumbling run towards the men crouched at the end of the street.

They drew back on their bows at the rise of their leader's sword.

Ryane tore him away, but Kael still heard the sickening *thud* of their volley striking true.

They sprinted through a maze of burning houses towards the northern walls. The heat singed the flesh on Kael's face; he shut his eyes against the stinging of the smoke and forced his legs to pound on through the ache. Still, he wasn't strong enough.

He fell hard on his knees and Ryane jerked him back to his feet. "Just a little further, we're almost to the walls —"

"Pick it up, you louts! The monsters can't be far ahead."

Ryane bared her teeth in the direction of the shouts and scooped Kael up around his waist. She carried him the last length of the street and stopped at the foot of the city's wall. It stood at three times the height of a man. Its pale sides looked smooth from a distance, but there were plenty of cracks. Kael had climbed to its top many times before.

"Go, I'll follow," Ryane gasped.

Kael scrambled into the nearest foothold and pulled himself up — his limbs charged by fear as the soldiers' shouting grew close.

Ryane climbed behind him, urging him on. But as he neared the top, his arms began to hurt. The run had exhausted him. His arms shook, sweat slickened his grip. The ground spun beneath him and he feared he might fall.

"Keep going, we're nearly there!"

"I can't!"

"You *can*." Ryane shoved him hard in the rump, hoisting him into the next foothold. "Go! Keep — ah!"

The world stopped. The thud of an arrow piercing flesh was the only sound he heard. Kael felt the scream in his chest when he looked down and saw the barb hanging from Ryane's leg.

"No, don't kill them! The King's offered a price for the women." One of the soldiers knocked an archer forward with a thrust of his boot. "Now get up there and bring them down."

"Riona ... Riona ..."

Kael tore his eyes away from the archer who climbed up after them and onto Ryane.

Pain filmed her eyes, but they burned through it furiously. "You've got to run," she whispered. "Protect the relic."

Time seemed to turn back on itself as she lifted the relic's belt from her shoulder and hung it across his neck. Ryane's lips peeled back from her teeth in a snarl when the archer grabbed her ankle, but she thrust forward.

She pushed as far as her arm could reach, more forcefully than Kael could bear ... and he tipped over the edge.

He was still screaming when he struck the water below and its cold, dark flesh devoured him ...

****

Kael gasped when the vision left him. His arms ached badly. He was barely able to make his fingers work long enough to bolt the window shut before he melted onto the stone floor.

Tears rolled down his face unchecked. They burst from the depths and poured out in frozen streams — horrible, heavy things that struck the floor like lead when they dripped from his chin. They weighed him down, dragged his face to the cold stone beneath him. He sobbed until the mortar ran thick with his tears.

346

"My sister," he gasped to a new flood of anguish. "No ... my sister ..."

Let me help you, my love, the white dragon pleaded.

Kael's chin ground against the floor as he shook his head. Kyleigh's sorrow was leaving him slowly. If he could bare it a moment more, this horrible loss he felt would fade — just as the dragon's anger had.

But he would never forget her story.

CHAPTER 35
FAMILIAR WOUNDS

"... suppose I've got to trust you, haven't I? Though I wish you'd just tell me what you're up to."

The silence and the darkness left him. Kael dragged in a shuddering breath when the storm winds blew across him. Its frozen moan startled the fog from his mind, and he slipped back into the present.

Kyleigh watched him curiously. Behind her, the clouds formed a looming shadow across the horizon. The storm's blue-black light darkened her pale flesh, but somehow made the red of her lips more vibrant. Her eyes came to life in the gathering darkness: the hour when the world began to fade was the hour in which her fires burned brightest. They met the tempest's fury with a danger all their own.

"Kael? Are you all right?"

The first drops of rain began to fall. They poured so thickly that he knew he must be soaked, but he couldn't feel it. The cold and the damp couldn't touch him: half of his mind still clung to the other world. He listened to the music of the rain as it struck Kyleigh's armor — their hands twined together, his eyes wrapped in hers.

He took a half-step closer. All of the things he wanted to say, all of the things he'd felt and seen hung in a vapor before his eyes. If even a hint of the woman's sorrow or the dragon's anger flickered inside her gaze, all of these new, frightening things would come pouring out.

They would wash away the wall between them — a wall he'd had no idea existed before now. He would drag her in against him until their wounds touched, until the unscathed portions faced the world while the raw, aching gashes pressed together. He knew their wounds would never heal entirely.

But as long as they held each other close, their hearts would be whole.

He waited, breathless — searching for the sputter of flame that meant Kyleigh's guard had fallen. Even if she couldn't remember everything, perhaps she could see that he'd surrendered. Perhaps his vulnerability would draw the dragon out ...

But it didn't.

"What is it?" Kyleigh arched a brow. A drop of rain slipped from its curve, down her nose, and to her lips.

Kael brushed it away before he leaned in to kiss her gently. "I know your names."

"What? How could you ...?"

She dropped his hands and backed away. He looked at her through the hair that the rain had plastered against his forehead, as if its strands might somehow lessen the look of horror upon her face. But they didn't.

The way Kyleigh glared made him feel like the worst sort of villain. His spirit shrank back and his temper rose in defiance. "You know very well it was the only way."

"You could have asked me! You could've at least warned me before you crawled inside my ..." She gripped the side of her head. Her knuckles went white and she spun away from him.

Kael knew what was coming. At any moment, she would burst into her wings and tear off into the skies. She would spend every hour until dawn hiding from him — as she always did when she was furious. But Kael wasn't going to let her run any longer.

Two steps into her sprint, and he'd already tackled her.

They landed heavily upon the grass. Kael caught most of the force of their fall on his elbow. Kyleigh arched away from him with a growl. She grabbed his wrists and pressed the spurs of her boots against his legs in warning, but he didn't budge.

"I know you won't hurt me."

She struggled for a while longer and Kael held on tightly. When she finally went still, he eased his grip.

It was a mistake.

The pouring rain slickened Kyleigh's armor. No sooner had he relaxed than she tore from his arms with a burst of strength. He lunged for her, and he didn't see her fist. In fact, he didn't realize that she'd swung for him until he'd already gotten his breath knocked out.

He managed to catch her around the shoulders as she scrambled away. Kyleigh twisted again, and it was only by sheer luck that he caught her neck as she spun around. Soon they were stuck: crouched in the grass with the rain beating down upon them — his face squashed against the scales on her back, her head trapped very firmly beneath his arm.

And neither of them would budge an inch.

"Let me go!"

"No, you're going to stay here and talk to me!"

"What are we going to talk about, Kael? The fact that you just spent Fate knows how many hours digging around inside my head without even *asking* first?"

"Well, had I asked, would you have let me?"

"No!" Kyleigh roared. "No, I wouldn't have blasted let you!"

"Then you left me no ch —! Stop it," he warned, when he felt her body swelling to take its second shape. "Don't — Kyleigh!"

He jerked his head back when spines grew out of her armor, stretching the blackened scales until the stark white appeared beneath them. He grabbed the horns that curved out of her scalp and held onto them tightly.

His warrior's strength swelled until he could feel it pressing against the edges of his skin. It filled the cords of his muscles until they became parchment-thin. Though he swore the blood was about to erupt from his veins, he managed to hold his ground. He forced his feet to stay glued to the earth and forced everything else to hold on to Kyleigh.

Her furious roar burst the insides of his ears; her wings beat him with gales made sharp by an icy lash of rain. She pressed her bared fangs against his forehead so that he could feel their dagger points — and the flames that churned behind them.

"I don't care!" Kael shouted over her growling. "Burn me if you like, but I'm not letting you go. It's too dangerous. Rua will kill you if he sees you like this. And I ..." Kael grit his teeth against the memory, but he thought the black dragon's words might be the only way to staunch her anger. "I couldn't bear it if you died even a moment before me. Please ... I couldn't bear it."

Her growling stopped immediately. Kael's grip loosened as she shrank back into her human skin. He let her drag him down into the sopping grass, let her arms wrap about his shoulders and pressed his face against her chest. That's what he told himself, at least.

The truth was that he'd had no idea how the mind-walking had exhausted him. Add to that his battle with a dragon, and Kael could barely hold his eyes open.

It helped when Kyleigh kissed the top of his head. The fires that began at his scalp raced down the back of his neck and warmed him against the slowing rain. The skies trilled more frequently than the drops came down. It fell at hardly a drizzle, now. He supposed they ought to find someplace dry to sleep.

"I'm sorry," Kyleigh whispered. Her arms tightened about him — as if she clung to the edge of everything. "I was just ..."

"Worried?"

"Terrified," she admitted. "Scared out of my wits. But if you haven't thrown yourself into the sea by now, I suppose I must not have been too horrible."

"I would never throw myself into the sea. You know I can't swim."

Her laughter warmed him every bit as much as her kiss. She squeezed him again.

A long moment passed when they didn't speak. Kael waited until her heart slowed to its usual steady thud before he spoke again: "I don't suppose you'd want to know what I —?"

"Never," she said firmly. "There was a time when I might've wanted to hear it, but that was before all this. I know where I belong, now. And that's enough."

Kael sighed and wrapped his arms around her waist. There would be a time to worry about the things he'd seen. But for now, he was simply happy to be back at her side. "That's probably for the best. There was nothing much in there but some cobwebs, and a bit of dust —"

"Shut it," she said, half-laughing.

He grinned when she slapped his arm. Then he lifted his head so he could meet her eyes. "I love you, Kyleigh. Nothing will ever change that."

She kissed him on the chin. "I know."

Kael waited, wondering if she would finally say it — on her own and unprovoked. But then her hand slipped beneath the collar of his shirt and bumped across the scars that scraped down his right shoulder. Her fingers traced the four lines down to their ends ... and they fit against them perfectly.

Her smile slipped into a frown. "I wish you'd erase this."

"Why?"

"I don't like being reminded that I hurt you."

"We hurt each other," he whispered. "But that night was the start of everything. I don't want to forget it."

He'd bent to kiss her when a monstrous shadow crossed over their heads. Kael looked up and groaned when he saw that Gorm had made himself comfortable on the hill just above them.

His face burned when the dragon's yellow gaze scraped across their tangled bodies, but Kyleigh hardly flinched. She arched her head back and snarled: "Do you mind?"

Judging by the way the dragon settled his wings about him, he minded very little.

"He's just going to sit there and stare at us all night, isn't he?" Kael muttered.

Kyleigh shrugged. "Probably. But I'm not sure he can help it ... dragons are rather curious creatures."

"I'm certain he could help it. He's just being nosy." Kael rolled away and lay down beside her — close enough that their shoulders touched. "It's not as if you go around watching everybody."

She gave him a wicked grin. "Perhaps ... then again, perhaps I'm just very rarely spotted."

CHAPTER 36
A SECRET STORY

It'd been days since Rua first called them to the red mountains — and Kael spent the long hours of each one trying desperately to be patient.

He was beginning to understand Kyleigh, now. The time he'd spent with her dragon half opened his eyes: he believed her when she said she couldn't bear to see him hurt. What she'd done to him wasn't a selfish thing. It wasn't even a part of her mischief.

No, it was a desperate attempt to save him.

They truly *were* tied together. He understood now that his worry made her miserable. The darkness that plagued his thoughts must've stung her as meanly as it stung him. Kyleigh must've been able to feel his anger, his frustration. But worst of all, she must've sensed the hopelessness he felt — the wave that rose in the back of his mind, growing taller and fiercer with each passing day.

And if he couldn't push it aside, it would drown them both.

So Kael tried to keep his worries at bay. He shoved the Kingdom to the back of his mind and tried to stay busy. For now, he would focus himself on the task at hand ... and hope to mercy that his companions were safe.

Finally, the morning came when Gorm called them into the skies. He flew out ahead, leading them back towards the arched red mountains of Rua's domain. Kael could practically hear the glee in his brassy voice as he told the others of their coming. The morning light drew the blue from his darkened scales as he wove in towards the mountains.

He came so close to the summit that the muscles in Kyleigh's back bunched together in anticipation of another fight. But at the last moment, Gorm seemed to think better of taunting Rua: he bolted down to the rocks at the mountains' bottom and sulked while Kyleigh flew on.

"There are more of them," Kael said. He peered around her horns and swore there were nearly a dozen more pairs of dragons perched atop the mountains' arches. Their yellow eyes traced Kyleigh's path unblinkingly. "What could they possibly be waiting for?"

They're probably hoping I'll be executed — slowly, and with a great deal of screaming.

"Don't even joke about that," Kael growled.

Kyleigh's scales warmed with her rumbling laughter. *I told you: dragons are curious. They might never have a chance to see such odd, two-legged creatures again.*

Kael hoped curiosity was all it was ...

But he doubted it.

The moment they landed, Rua's daughters came scrambling out from odd corners of the summit — tittering as they rushed to huddle beside their parents:

They're back already?

Do they have the answer, Father?

If they don't, will you kill them?

No, don't kill them! They're funny little th —

Rua's grunt jolted the earth with such force that Kael might've toppled over, had he not braced himself against Kyleigh's wing.

Silence, daughters. Let your father deal with the humans, His-Rua answered in a whistling song. She lay between his massive arms, glowing with the sunlight.

Rua's chin rested gently atop her back. He kept his eyes shut as Kyleigh slipped into her human form. *Come closer,* he rumbled.

"Absolutely not," she said.

Kael couldn't have agreed more. "We've done what you asked. We have the names."

Speak them.

Kyleigh's fingers tightened around his arm. "My human name was Riona."

And the dragon?

"His-Dorcha."

If Kyleigh felt strangely about having been a dragon's mate, she didn't show it. Kael had expected her to grimace, or to roll her eyes — or perhaps even mutter some insult under her breath. Instead, she'd done nothing more than shrug.

Which wasn't like Kyleigh, at all.

Even now, her face was smooth and her eyes calm as she waited for Rua's answer. Kael was more worried about His-Rua. He thought he saw the edges of her teeth for a moment, but then her snarl vanished as quickly as it'd come.

Instead, it was Rua whose scaly lips peeled back. *You will not speak that name, halved one! You do not deserve to speak it.*

"All right, we won't speak it again." Kael was growing tired of all this. Now, with the Kingdom closer than ever, his patience hung on by a thread. "We've done everything you've asked. I think it's time you let us go."

No, there is one more thing you must do. Rua's eyes cracked open, and Kael swore he could feel the heat that burned within them. *You will follow me. You will see with your own eyes what you've done to us. You will feel the full burden of your betrayal, so that it may never be done again.* Then *you may leave.*

******

Rua led them south. They flew past the great mountain in the middle of the island and into a new land beyond. Kael grimaced as they crossed beneath the mountain's shadow — but he wasn't sure why. The cave he'd noticed before stared after him again. There was an eeriness about it, a spirit that chilled him to his bones.

If Death had a heart, he likely would've kept it inside that cave.

But though the mountain troubled him, Kael felt ... drawn to it, somehow. He could hardly look away. He craned his neck around to watch it as Kyleigh flew, trying desperately to figure out what it was about the mountain that made him itch. He was still watching when His-Rua dipped in behind them.

Her fiery gaze settled upon his without fear. The black slits carved among the flames widened, seemed to be trying to speak. But their meaning was swept away from him — lost like words upon the wind.

Just beyond the mountain's shadow stood a ring of sharp hills. From above, it looked like the gaping mouth of a minceworm: their tops were jagged, and an iron gray. The hills sloped inward at such an angle that they draped the valley within them in a thick, black shadow.

Kael wagered the only time it saw any light was when the sun stood directly above it.

Rua landed with an earth-rumbling *thud* atop the hills. His great claws wrapped around their jagged crests, holding him in place. Kyleigh landed beside him, while His-Rua landed far behind. Kael was sure to stand where he could keep both dragons in the corner of his eyes.

He didn't trust either of them.

"Where are we?" Kyleigh whispered, once she'd donned her human skin. Her dark brows furrowed as she drifted up the hill. When Kael grabbed her hand, she held it absently.

You remember it. Surely you must dream of it, Rua grunted. The shadow of his massive head swept over them as he turned to gaze into the valley. *A she-dragon's nest is as dear a thing as her fledglings, as her heart. It holds a happiness too great for her spirit to bear.*

Kyleigh's glare deepened. "Well, I don't remember it."

Kael couldn't be sure, but he thought he saw a tinge of red cross her face. "It's all right if you remember. I understand —"

"I don't," she insisted, though the way she bared her teeth said otherwise. When she turned to Rua, her voice was harsh: "What do you want from me, dragon? Just tell me what I have to do, and let's get on with it."

Rua took so long to blink that Kael had to wonder if he was being slow on purpose. *All you must do is step over to the edge ... and look.*

"Fine."

Kael stumbled forward as Kyleigh dragged him up the hill. Her grip was impossibly tight. He had to scramble to keep her pace. Once she'd marched her way to the edge, she stopped. "What am I looking at? What did you bloody well want me to see?"

She came to the edge no more than a pace before him. It only took a breath for Kael to reach her side. But by the time he did, everything had changed.

Kyleigh still scowled. Her teeth were still bared. Her fingers nearly crushed him in their grip. She was absolutely livid in every place, save for one: her eyes.

Flames whipped dangerously within them. Their anger was locked in a desperate battle against another force — a force that rose from the embers and swelled. This second force met the fire's rage with a depth that covered it to its sputtering top. Then, when her eyes could bear the rise no longer, they closed ...

And tears rolled down her cheeks.

It all happened too quickly. Kael didn't know what'd caused her tears, but he knew he wanted them to stop. He couldn't bear to see her cry. "What is it?"

She didn't answer. Instead, she tore her hand from his and stumbled backwards. Her face went white.

Kael knew it had something to do with the shadowed valley. He ran as close to the edge as he dared, but the darkness was far too thick. He couldn't see what it was that frightened her. "What's happening? What's down th —? Kyleigh!"

It was too late. She collapsed before he could reach her; her face was stark with pain. She had both hands clamped tightly over her mouth — desperate to stop the gasping screams trapped behind them.

Kael ran for her. He heard the sound of claws scraping against the stone, saw the white blur barreling down upon him. But he didn't stop. He dropped his shoulder and matched His-Rua's charge.

His muscles coiled as their bodies struck. The warrior in him planted its feet and tried to shove her away from Kyleigh. He'd gained an inch when the world suddenly turned upon its head.

"Put me down!" he roared as Rua lifted him by his boots. "Get away from her — don't touch her!"

But Rua only raised him higher, and Kyleigh got further away. She'd fallen to her knees. Her hands were braced against the ground as if it took all of her strength to keep from collapsing onto her chest.

His-Rua leaned over her shoulder, blocking her from Kael's sight. The dragon's whistling song filled the air — but he couldn't understand it. The only thing he understood was Kyleigh when she screamed:

"I don't want to — let me go!"

His-Rua came up on her hindquarters. Her powerful foreclaws were clamped around Kyleigh's arms. Her wings burst open in a spray of grit, and Kael swung up with a roar.

He drove his fists into Rua's snout and the dragon's mouth fell open in surprise. Wind howled in his ears as he plummeted towards His-Rua. The warrior in him fixed its gaze upon her throat —

Rua's massive claw snatched him out of the air. The insides of his head slammed against his skull and for half a blink, the world went dark.

When Kael's vision returned, Kyleigh and His-Rua were gone. A shock arced across his ribs as Rua's massive claw slammed into his back, driving him belly-first into the rock. The red dragon's palm spanned the length of his middle. Its scales were impossibly rough: they felt like shards of glass and scraped his flesh with even the slightest turn.

Rua had given him less than an inch to breathe. Slowly, Kael managed to lift his head just in time to see His-Rua dip into the valley — Kyleigh hanging from her arms.

Kael forgot his pain. His twisted onto his back and didn't flinch when Rua's scales cut deep lines across his armor. His head was caught between two of Rua's talons, but his arms were free. He clutched the tops of the claws. He wedged his fingers between the scales until he could press them against the hot flesh beneath.

Sleep, he thought furiously, concentrating as he glared into the yellow of Rua's eyes. *Sleep, you stupid dragon. Sleep ...*

He focused for nearly a full minute — pushing every memory of sleep he had into Rua's flesh. But the red dragon's body was far too large. He never so much as blinked, and it wasn't long before Kael's head began to feel light from the effort.

These words you speak are ... strange, Rua said quietly, his head tilting to the side. *There is such* fire *in them.*

"Let me go. If you harm Kyleigh, I swear I'll —"

Calm yourself, human. Your mate is not in danger. My-Rua has been waiting many years for this day. She has been waiting for the halved one to understand. She wishes to speak to her, to lay old wounds to rest. Nothing more. Rua settled his head upon his claw, bringing his heated snout to within an inch of Kael's face. *Perhaps you and I should speak as well.*

"What could we possibly have to talk about?"

I could tell you a story.

"I'm sick of your stories, Rua. I'm sick of this whole blasted island!" He slammed his fist into Rua's claw, but the dragon hardly blinked.

A shame. I was going to tell you a story about your mate — a secret story she would not want you to hear.

358

His lips pulled back in a toothy grin when Kael froze. "Really? Did you ... know her, before?"

I met her only once. But it was a fiery meeting. Would you care to hear it? Very well, he said when Kael nodded. *Many, many years ago —*

"Wait a moment." Kael had an idea. He tightened his grip on Rua's claw. "Why don't you *show* me the story?"

How would I do that?

"Think of it exactly as you see it in your head, everything you can remember. I'll be able to see what you think — it's, ah, magic."

Rua's eyes widened. *It will not hurt me, will it?*

"No. I promise it won't hurt."

After a moment, Rua blasted him with a heated sigh. *Very well. I shall* think *my story, then ...*

A vision flickered to life before Kael's eyes: the hazy image of a group of forest children. They were half-naked and huddled beneath a thick black shadow. Their mouths hung open as they stared up at him — he could read the terror etched into their eyes.

The shadow moved as a growl drew his vision downwards. A pack of wolves stood between Kael and the children. Their fangs were pulled taut above their teeth, hair bristled down their backs. Their sharp eyes glinted murderously.

A massive red claw rose above the wolves and the children, darkening the shadow. The wolves' growling grew louder; the children began to sob.

"Stop!"

He knew before Rua's head turned that it was Kyleigh who'd spoken. Her hair was wild and unkempt. Dirt stained the bits of her flesh that weren't covered in a rough garb of animal skins. There was a sword strapped to her hip, but it wasn't Harbinger. Kael hardly got a glimpse of its pommel before she turned away.

When Rua's gaze tightened upon her eyes, Kael's shock nearly shoved him from the vision: all of the green was gone from them, and in their place were a dragon's eyes — black slits wreathed in yellow flame.

"I know why you're here, dragon. I know you've come to punish this human for breaking our treaty." The black slits widened as they drifted over to the wolves. "Destroy us, if you must. But please ... spare these creatures and their fledglings."

The thunder of Rua's reply flattened the wolves' ears and made the children wail. But Kyleigh never flinched.

Instead, her eyes closed tightly. "Please, listen to ... he'll never listen," she growled suddenly. When her eyes snapped open, they were human eyes — orbs as clear and blue as the frozen seas. Her hand wrapped tightly around the hilt of her sword. "You aren't listening, dragon. So I'm going to explain this in a way you'll understand: harm my pack, and I'll send your soul screaming into the under-realm."

She ripped the sword free: a thick weapon with a blade that burned white-hot. The vision — and the forest — shook as Rua staggered backwards. His gaze fixed upon the sword, how its blade seemed to churn within the confines of its edges — how the ferocity of the heat boiling from its heart made it seem almost ... liquid.

When Kyleigh swung the blade into the flesh of a nearby tree, white fire burst from the sword. Rua's eyes clamped shut against its blinding light. Kael heard a *thud* in the darkness. When Rua's eyes peeled open, he saw that the tree lay on its side — burned mercilessly through its hundred years of rings by the blade Kyleigh now brandished at his face.

Sweat poured from her head and down her chin. The heat of the sword burned red into her cheeks, but she made no move to sheath it. "Leave us, or I'll swing for your throat."

Rua's voice rumbled. His claw came down upon the earth between them in defiance. Kyleigh swung her blade aside and an arc of molten liquid spewed from its edges, burning into the skin of the rock beneath her.

"Very well, dragon. You've chosen death — no!" Her body convulsed. Her eyes slammed shut again and opened yellow. "He'll kill the little ones before you have a chance to slay him. Let me speak to him. Why do you want to hurt us so badly?" she said, looking up to Rua. "Why do you wish to harm those we love?"

She held the sword out beside her, frowning as Rua grumbled something under his breath.

"My mate was a passionate soul. His temper often shook our Motherlands — but he was strong enough to bear it. Our daughter is not as strong," Kyleigh whispered. "She needs your strength, dragon. She needs your calm. It is ... difficult, I understand. And even *I* have fallen to the binding power of the valtas. But you must try to bear her anger wisely, as I often did for Dorcha."

Rua's claw ground into the earth as he growled something back.

Kyleigh's shoulders rose and fell. "What's been done to me cannot be undone. The human and I are one ... and what pains her will pain me, as well. However angry my daughter might be with the human, I do not think she would wish me harm."

Rua's stare cut back to the wolves. It sharpened upon their throats.

"Please, listen ..." Kyleigh blinked, and her eyes were blue. She slid the sword back into its sheath and her hands went to her belt. Slowly, she undid its clasp. "I'm sorry I broke your treaty, dragon. I thought if I were stronger, I might be able to free my sister. But by the time I woke, the world I knew was gone. The draega are gone. All of the other flyers have vanished. I have no idea where to find them. There's nothing I can do against the King's mages. My story is at its end. So, if you must take something ..."

She shook her head. The dragon's eyes were back, widening. "No, human — not your relic ..." The blue returned: "I must. He wants some sort of payment ... but it's all you have of your people ... my people are lost ... no, not lost ..."

Her eyes flicked between yellow and blue so quickly that it was impossible to tell which half of her was speaking. Then they slammed shut — tightly. Kyleigh's hands froze upon her belt and she stumbled backwards. Rua's vision was locked unblinkingly upon her face.

When her lids burst open, her eyes were no longer blue or yellow — but a pure, fiery green. She sank to her knees, as if she'd been exhausted. She seemed to be fighting to stay awake.

"No, not lost," she murmured again, her gaze sliding over to the wolves. "My people have merely changed. I've found a new home, a new nest. They've given me all the life I thought I'd lost. Here, dragon." She pushed the sword as her body crumpled to the ground, sliding it towards Rua. "Take the relic, if you want — in payment for what I've done. Without its power ... and without the draega ... there's no reason the dragons should ever ... fear again."

Kael let go.

He knew what happened next: Kyleigh would wake to Hollowfang — who would tell her that she'd done a great thing for the

361

wolves. That sword was the treasure she'd given up for them, the fire His-Dorcha feared, the thing Riona called a *relic*. Only it wasn't just any relic ...

It was the sword of Sir Gorigan.

CHAPTER 37
THE VALTAS

Rua became nothing more than a red blur as Kael pieced it all together. "Daybreak," he whispered, still not daring to believe it. "The sword she gave you was Daybreak, wasn't it?"

Yes, the great fire of the halved ones, placed into my claws. A fair payment, I thought. Molten red singed Rua's muzzle as he glared. *But then Dorcha was taken from us suddenly, and we began to think the payment was not so fair. When his halved body sailed into our Motherlands, his might corrupted by a human soul, we knew it was entirely false. Your-Kael lied to us: the halved ones survived their fall, and they have begun to steal our souls once more.*

My-Rua wanted them dead, he went on. And as he spoke, the red scales across his muzzle started to cool. *But I knew to kill the halved ones would only start another war.* They are short-lived things, *I told her. The humans must simply be reminded. I took My-Rua's fury and held it away from her, so that she could see the things I saw. Though I admit I have not always held it wisely,* he added with a tilt of his head, *I did keep My-Rua from tearing Your-Kael's chest apart. And that, little human, is a thing to smile about.*

Kael was still too confused to smile. He dug through Rua's story, trying to remember everything Kyleigh had said. "She called Your-Rua her daughter."

Yes, my mate is the fledging of Dorcha and His-Dorcha.

"The halved ones are really these *draega.*"

And the ancient guardians of the Wildlands, yes.

"And you hid Daybreak ...?"

In our ... Rua stopped. He blew an indignant breath across Kael's face. *Very clever, human. But even if I told you where it was, you could never reach it. The blade lies in the dark and the cold, forgotten ... along with all the other dead things.*

More riddles. Kael lay back and glared up at the sky, his mind still churning with thought.

Rua leaned in. *I know our anger must seem strange to you —*

"*Strange* doesn't even begin to describe it," Kael moaned.

— but the draega harmed us greatly. Until we met and forged our treaty, they did not understand how their rituals hurt us. They broke us into pieces. They destroyed our hearts. The draega killed the mated, human. And we do not kill the mated unless we have no other choice.

"Well, I very distinctly remember you blasting me with fire."

For that, you must forgive me, Rua said, a surprising amount of heaviness in his voice. *We had been watching you for many days, and we all agreed that you were merely hatchmates.*

Kael wasn't entirely certain what a hatchmate was — but he could guess. "You thought Kyleigh was my sister?" His face burned when Rua nodded. "How could you have possibly thought that? You saw us kissing!"

Rua's head tilted again. *The odd thing you did with your mouths? That is a ... mating practice, for humans?*

"Very much so."

Ah. We all agreed you were merely exchanging food.

"I don't care what you all agreed on!" Kael snapped, his face burning furiously. "That's not what we were doing."

Rua's eyes slid away. *It seems a shame to keep the mating at your mouths when there is so much your bodies could —*

"No, enough!" Kael shouted. More than anything, he didn't want to be forced to listen to a dragon's speech on mating — especially when that speech would be ringing inside his head. Even if he could've reached his ears to cover them, it wouldn't have helped. It was entirely unfair.

Rua didn't seem bothered by his outburst. In fact, his enormous head bent closer — blocking every last ray of light with its spiny girth. *There is something I have been meaning to ask you, human. It is something that has vexed me from the moment I first watched you.*

"As long as it isn't a question about mating," Kael said. He swore he felt the tug on the roots of his hair when Rua breathed in.

I cannot promise it has nothing to do with mating. Your practices are very strange. But I'll ask it anyways. One of his great eyes shut and opened. *What does that mean?*

Kael had no idea what he was talking about. "What does what mean?"

This. When his eye closed and shut again, Kael realized what he was trying to do.

"It's a wink."

A wink? I see. It is something that requires a great amount of skill, is it not? To close one eye before the other? I have been practicing for days — ever since I saw your mate do it to you. Tell me, human: what is the meaning of a wink?

There were countless meanings, and Kael had no interest in explaining them all to Rua. But he remembered the wink he was talking about: "She does that to annoy me — especially when she mentions something she knows will make me uncomfortable."

Strange that she would like to tease you. Stranger still that you seem to enjoy it. But I suppose every pairing is different. Had I known you shared the valtas, I never would have tried to harm you. It seemed impossible, you understand, for a halved one to bond with a human. But once I discovered you had magic, it all makes sense.

"How so?"

Rua inclined his head. *The Wildlands are not as they used to be. Mages have taken it over. It is far too dangerous a place for a dragon. But Your-Kael chose you as her soul's protector because you can* wield *the magic. She has no need to fear the power her mate possesses.*

Kael supposed that made sense — even though he didn't actually have any magic, he could still protect her from it. "Rua ... what is the valtas?"

You don't know?

"Kyleigh wouldn't tell me."

Rua gave him a long look before his neck bent upwards and his spiny chin pointed towards the sun. *I think this is a question better answered with the eyes than the mouth. The sun is high — you should be able to see them, now.*

"See who?"

Rua's chin dipped until the spines hovered an inch before Kael's face. His monstrous head filled every corner of his vision. *If I remove my claw, you must stay by my side. You must not go into the valley. Our mates need this moment alone.*

Only after Kael had sworn to behave did Rua release him. No sooner had he gotten to his feet than Rua's foreclaw wrapped around his middle.

You move so slowly, human, he growled as he carried Kael to the ledge beside him — which he thought was rather odd, given the fact that the dragons seemed to take their lives one century at a time.

But before he could say as much, Rua set him down.

Look, he whispered, nodding towards the valley. *There lies everything you need to know about the valtas.*

Thick clouds rolled across the sky above them. The reflections of their darkened bottoms glided across the hills, fitting against every curve and crag — drifting through the grass like creatures beneath the waves.

The spans of light between them illuminated the valley trapped within the jagged hills. Its bottom was covered in what appeared to be black sand. Ripples coursed along the sand and the sunlight made the grains sparkle. But there was one place inside the valley that the light couldn't seem to reach.

Kael thought they were the husks of blackened trees at first: branches stripped of leaves and trunks burned of their bark. They were piled together in a tangle against one of the jagged walls. They seemed to grow darker as the sunlight touched them — the shadows bleeding into every line of gray until they became entirely black.

Kael followed a ray of light across the trunk of a particularly knobby tree to the tangled roots at its base ...

Wait a moment.

Two roots curved proudly from the tangle, identical to their points. An enormous hole, almost perfectly rounded, punched its way through the middle of them. But it wasn't until Kael saw the full set of sharp, glittered teeth at the tangle's end that he realized he was looking at a dragon's skull.

What he'd thought to be trees were the sloped bones of his ribs, the thin threads of his wings. His claws still shone at the end of his skeletal feet. Kyleigh was crouched before them — and each one was half the size of her body.

She kept a hand pressed against the earth while the other clung to her face. After a moment, she reached out and touched the sand between the black dragon's claws. It was a light, ashen gray. She gripped it tightly in her fist and brought it against her chest.

Kael didn't understand what that meant. He looked to His-Rua, but got little help. The white dragon waited some distance behind

Kyleigh. Though Kael couldn't see the dragon's face, she lay calmly enough.

"Where is the valtas?" Kael said after a moment. He'd searched, but hadn't been able to see anything beyond the dragon's bones.

Rua slid one claw reluctantly towards him, just close enough to reach. *This* is *valtas, human. These are the bones of Dorcha, lying as he died — still protecting the ashes of His-Dorcha. The shamans of the Wildlands used their rituals to steal souls from animals. They would bind these souls to their own, to increase their lives and powers.*

Most creatures know nothing beyond their food and dens. They take mates for a moment. Being chosen to bind with a human would have been an honor — a chance to live as never before. But for the dragons, it was a curse. The fires of Rua's gaze slunk back as he stared at Dorcha's bones. *When the shaman of the dragon — the draega — performed his ritual, it would kill one of us. Our bodies would die and our souls would leave the Motherlands to join with the human Fate had chosen as our bond, never to return. Sometimes it was an unmated, but often it wasn't.*

To be torn from one's mate is to die while the body lives on — to be forced to breathe air with no smell, eat flesh with no taste ... to rot forever in a world turned dim and gray. It is cruel, what the draega did to us. Rua's scales clinked together as he twisted his neck to meet Kael's face. His eyes burned in earnest. *Dorcha was a powerful dragon. He fought with such terrible rage that no male would dare to cross his valley on wing. His hatchmates swore he carried flame inside his heart instead of his lungs.*

But on the day he lost His-Dorcha, his power left him. Her soul went beyond the Motherlands, and Dorcha was too broken to follow. Instead, he lay atop her bones until they turned to dust. Then he gathered the dust beneath him so that not even one grain would be carried away by the wind. The sky churned and time moved on ... but Dorcha's fire was already gone. His body wasted away, untouched by the dawn or the night ... until his soul was called to cross the frozen seas.

Kael couldn't think to draw breath. Rua's words echoed inside his heart. This wasn't only a matter of feelings or pain. Kyleigh shared ... everything, with him. They were bonded down to the threads of their lives. If he were to die, she would waste away, as Dorcha had.

And Kael *would* die.

Now he understood her completely. He knew why she sobbed. It wasn't her past that'd drawn out her tears: it was her future. *This future — this reflection of the truth that awaited her at the end of Kael's life.*

The valtas isn't always tragic. It brings great meaning to our lives, as well, Rua went on, clearly oblivious to the fact that Kael's heart had ground to a complete and utter stop. *Our mates make us better. They make us whole. Tell me, human: what color is My-Rua?*

It was a silly question, but Kael would've done anything to take his eyes from the dragons' bones. "She's white."

Rua blinked slowly. *To you she is, because she is not your heart's bond. But when I look at her, I see red — fiery scales that spark at her every twist and turn. She shines in all the places I am dull. But it is more than her scales that I love. Before I met My-Rua, I was an aimless thing,* he said with a groan. *My heart had no purpose, my wings carried me in wide arcs all around the world. But My-Rua had her father's fire, though she was far too small to bear it.*

I am told her fire often got her into trouble. But I am big enough, strong enough to carry all of the passion her heart can't hold. That is why the valtas brought us together, he said, his scaly lips twisting ever so slightly upwards. *It knows the things we lack and brings us mates who make us whole. And when we were newly mated, My-Rua brought a warm fire to my life. But after her mother, His-Dorcha, was taken from us so cruelly ... the flames turned furious.*

This is the other side of the valtas: to share in joy and in sorrow. I have been carrying her anger many years, and I have not always borne it well, Rua admitted gravely. *But even so, I would rather carry a thousand years of her sorrow than spend a moment alive without her. She is My-Rua because she is me, my most perfect self. I would be lost without her. Tell me, human* ... His thorny snout came closer. Impossibly close. *What color is Your-Kael?*

"Her name is Kyleigh. And she's exactly as you see her," Kael muttered. It was difficult to listen to Rua talk about the valtas and not feel cheated. This was just one more place where they didn't quite match.

No matter how much he loved her, it would never amount to this. He could never care for Kyleigh the way she cared for him.

Nothing he did would ever compare to the valtas.

CHAPTER 38
THE LAST RAT

There was no end to it. Even if Thelred sat for a hundred years, he was certain not a thing would change. Oh, the chair might crumble out from beneath him, and the seas might rise over his boots. The Kingdom itself might very well be gone.

But even after a hundred years of chaos and decay, the council would still be at war.

It'd all begun to fall apart shortly after their last meeting. Thelred wasn't entirely sure what had happened, and the rumors made uncovering the truth all the more difficult. Some of the councilmen claimed that Chaucer had been deposed, while others insisted he'd merely resigned.

There were some nasty stories involving Countess D'Mere, as well — most of which had to do with poisonings or beheadings. But though the grisly details made them difficult to forget, Thelred tried not to give them a second thought. The rumors about the Countess were too outlandish to have been considered truthful. He had a feeling their only intent was to distract the High Seas from the corruption in its ports.

But even if they couldn't agree on anything else, all of the councilmen swore upon their trades that they'd settled a treaty with Midlan. Thelred had comforted himself with this thought. For the last several weeks, knowing that the seas were safe had kept him from losing his mind while the council dragged on.

Now, even that one small relief had been taken from him. He felt as if he was a moment from hurling a chair across the room.

"Quiet, please! Would you please be *quiet!*" a councilman at the head table barked.

Makeshift camps littered the back of the council's chambers. The villagers had arrived a little more than a week ago, packed aboard a small group of vessels that'd limped in from Copperdock — the last handful of a spell-ravaged fleet. They'd spent days edging down the

369

coastline towards the chancellor's castle, afraid to sail too far or stay out too long.

Now that they'd finally made it to safety, they weren't going to be shoved aside. They'd set up camp in the council's chambers: there were bedrolls wedged into the aisles and children running wild absolutely everywhere. But the noise they made was nothing compared to the shipbuilders' fury.

"We'll quiet down when you answer Midlan!" one of them cried. He cradled a screaming infant against his chest while he thrust a finger at the head table. "You told us the council settled things with the King. You promised that there wouldn't be a war."

"We have, and there won't be," another councilman replied without turning.

His words called up another wave of indignant roars:

"Then why have we been run from our homes?"

"Why did mages burn half of our ships and roast innocent men alive?"

"And why in the bloody seas did they have the King's mark on their chests, eh? Last I checked, folks with treaties don't attack each other."

"Hearsay and speculation," another councilman blustered over the villagers' cries. He was a dumpy man with a thick mustache that bore stains at the tips of its bristles — the remnants of whatever pastry he'd just devoured.

He'd failed as a chancellor and had been a large part of why Duke Reginald was sacked in the first place. But Colderoy must've been better at politicking than anybody realized: somehow, against all conceivable odds, he'd managed to wriggle his way back up to the head table.

Now he stared at the shipbuilders from over the top of his mustache. Even if there *was* a shred of mercy in his eyes, they were far too dim to show it. "The council has heard your concerns and, once we'phe appointed a new high chancellor, we intend to giphe it our full attention," he said, dragging each word through his bristles. "But I'm afraid camping here won't do you people any good. You're going to haphe to giphe us time, and space to work —"

"Where should they go?" Thelred snapped. He was on his feet before he realized that his anger had reached its end. His wooden leg creaked loudly in the now-silent hall. The leather guard pinched the flesh at the base of his knee. But he hardly felt it. "Does the council *intend* to help them settle somewhere else? Do you plan to find them work? Do you plan to feed them?"

Colderoy blinked and his chin wobbled as he glanced around him. All of the council shared the same look — as if none of those things had ever once crossed their minds. "I'm certain they'll do just fine on their own."

"No, they won't. Not all men have their food set out in front of them. Most have to work for it. If these people don't work, they don't eat."

"Then perhaps they should go back to their trades."

Thelred tried to keep his voice calm. Even after all he'd heard, the council's idiocy still managed to shock him. "Have you not been listening? They haven't got a thing to go home to —"

"Yes, according to *them*," Colderoy huffed. "But the council can take no action unless these stories turn out to be true. We must haphe proof."

"Well, then perhaps one of you ought to send a ship to investigate."

For a long moment, the hall fell deathly quiet. The councilmen sat like stone in their chairs, while the shipbuilder's eyes burned upon them.

Thelred laughed — the only thing that kept him from slinging his fist into the tabletop. "What are you all afraid of? It's not as if a little *hearsay and speculation* could possibly burn your ships to ash."

Colderoy raised his brows. "Oh? Then why don't you send one of yours?"

"Because the first got trapped in Harborville when the council *started* arguing — and while the council *continues* to argue, the second had no choice but to go retrieve the first. Perhaps I could send for a third," Thelred mused, "but as that would require one of you to grow a spine thick enough to launch a messenger ship into waters that you insist are *not* ruled over by fire-wielding mages, I doubt it'll ever happen."

A steady rumble built up behind him. He could almost feel the villagers standing straighter, hear the resolve in the way their arms tightened across their chests.

Colderoy's beady eyes flicked over them worriedly.

"You don't even have to go, councilman," Thelred added. "Simply hand over a ship, and I'll captain it myself."

"Any man who'd let a cripple guide his ship *deserves* to have it sunk," Colderoy scoffed, drawing a round of laughter from the other councilmen.

But Thelred didn't care. He knew he had them trapped. "Well if you aren't going to send anyone to investigate, then I suppose you've got no choice. The shipbuilders will be settling here, under the council's protection — as is the right of all citizens of the High Seas." He nodded to Colderoy, who glowered from his chair. "Now that we've got that settled, I suggest we get back to work. Dig your hands out of your pockets and put them to good use, councilman."

Thunder echoed his words. The shipbuilders made their demands at a level that drowned out anything the council might've said.

After a few unsuccessful moments of trying to scold them through his mustache, Colderoy finally gave up. He hauled himself from his chair and squinted his dim little eyes at Thelred before waddling off down the hall.

The councilmen followed quickly. They tried to stay ahead of the shipbuilders — who swarmed behind them in an angry rush. The guards blocked the archway and fended them off with the butts of their spears.

Thelred wasn't looking forward to fighting his way through the crowd, but he didn't have a choice. It was late. There would be another daylong meeting tomorrow. His leg burned so furiously that he knew he needed to put it up for a while — especially if he wanted any hope of making it down before lunch.

And the only way to his chambers was through that arch.

He'd just reached the back of the crowd when one of the shipbuilders saw him. "Make way! Clear *out*, you lot! Let our councilman through."

They parted at his bellowing and cheered Thelred as he passed. "I'll do whatever I can," he promised over the noise. "The council can't toss you out. You'll have a home in the castle for as long as you wish."

The guards dragged him through the last swell and into the hallway beyond. Thelred began the long journey to his chambers, his leg aching worse than ever. All of the days he'd spent sitting around had pushed his blood to the end of his knee — pressuring the nub from behind. The leather cap of his wooden leg pressured it even more. Thelred thought he might be able keep time by the throbbing.

Though the council was well aware of his leg, they'd assigned him chambers at the top of the castle — more than likely with the hope that he would eventually become too exhausted to travel down for meetings. But he refused to let them win.

He groaned to think of all the ridiculous laws they might pass if he wasn't there to stop them.

Thelred was dripping sweat by the time he reached the third floor landing. Part of it was the damp heat of the evening, but mostly it was from the strain. He had to pause outside the door to catch his breath.

No sooner had he managed to work the latch than the door sprung open from the other side, stumbling him forward. Eveningwing managed to catch him before he fell, but Thelred was no less startled.

"Where in high tide have you been?" he snapped as the boy helped him over to the bed. "You were supposed to go to the Bay and come straight back."

"I meant to. But I got distracted."

That wasn't at all surprising. A winged creature should've been able to cross from one end of the Kingdom to the other in no time at all, but Eveningwing always seemed to take forever. On this particular occasion, he'd left just before the ships from Copperdock came hobbling in. So Thelred had been trapped in the chaos for weeks with no way out.

"Well, I hope you enjoyed yourself, because we've got a mounds of work to do. I'm up to my neck in trouble —"

"I've been to Copperdock," Eveningwing blurted. His trousers were only half-laced and completely crooked. He pawed nervously at the grayish feathers that sprouted from his elbows as he spoke. "I just wanted to stop for a day — to see Kyleigh and her Kael. But ..."

"It was burned?" Thelred guessed.

Eveningwing shook his head. "The castle was. But the village was just ... empty. It looked strange. I searched for Kyleigh and her Kael — but I didn't find them. They were gone."

Thelred grimaced as he bent to untie the straps on his leg. His mind was racing, but he knew how excitable Eveningwing could get. He didn't need him to go bursting out the window before they'd had a chance to come up with a plan. "Were there any soldiers in Copperdock? *Swordbearers*," he growled, when Eveningwing's head tilted to the side.

"No. Not that I saw." He leapt onto the bed when Thelred went silent, and pressed in uncomfortably close beside him. "What does this mean?"

"How should I know?"

"I know you know." The pupils in his strange yellow eyes narrowed into points. "That's your *I-know-something* face."

"The King's found out about Kyleigh, again. He's sent Midlan after her — that's only a guess," Thelred said quickly, when Eveningwing lurched for the window. "I don't know for certain. But if that's the case, it's a good thing."

Eveningwing leaned closer. His voice dropped to a whisper. "The King's chasing our friend. And it's a good thing?"

"Yes. It means that Crevan will be so focused on Kyleigh that he'll leave the seas alone. She knows what she's doing." He grabbed Eveningwing around the arm when he lurched again. "She kept Midlan off our backs for years, and I have no doubt that she'll be able to do it again. Flying off after her won't be any help at all. Do you understand me, hawk?"

His eyes flicked to the window before he nodded stiffly.

"Good. Kyleigh's given us a chance, here. We'd be fools to waste it. We have to get the seas together while Midlan is distracted, but I can't do it on my own. Did you manage ...?" Thelred couldn't say it. His face burned and his stomach turned sour at the very thought. His ears began to ring in anticipation of the squealing and the incessant *I told you so*'s, but he knew he had no choice. "Did you manage to convince Aerilyn to come out here? I've spent weeks with the council and haven't moved them an inch. She's the only one who knows how to talk to these blasted people."

"I went to the Bay."

"And?"

"She wasn't there."

"What? Are you sure?" Thelred slumped when the boy nodded. "Where could she have possibly ...? And what about the child?"

"The giantess had him. She said all was well." Eveningwing seemed about to say something else, but his eyes cut away suddenly, and he bit his lip.

Thelred didn't have time for this. "What is it?"

"I spoke to the Uncle —"

"Oh, good gravy."

"— and he says he's angry with you for leaving him there to wither all by himself."

"Yes, I'm sure he is. But did he happen to tell you anything useful? Does he know where Aerilyn's gone?"

Eveningwing's hands twisted in his lap. "He told me not to tell you. He says it will only get her into trouble with the captain."

"She's already in trouble," Thelred said evenly. "Lysander ordered her to stay put. But instead, she's wandered off to do Kingdom knows what. That's mutiny. Just tell me where she's gone, and perhaps Lysander can find her before she gets into *real* trouble."

Eveningwing's face twisted around the words for nearly a full minute before he finally burst out: "Aerilyn and the masked woman went to the forest!"

Thelred sat back. "What in Kingdom's name are they doing there?"

"She wants to speak to the Countess."

It wasn't possible. No one could've *possibly* been that stupid — not even Aerilyn. He'd blasted well told her from the beginning that it wasn't possible for the Countess to have been involved with any of the trouble in the seas. It wouldn't make sense for her to betray Crevan. She had no stake in their fight. The council was only using her for a distraction.

But apparently, Aerilyn hadn't listened. "Is she mad? She'll be killed! None of this would've happened if Lysander had just ... go find him!" Thelred thrust Eveningwing off the bed with the heel of his boot. "Lysander should've been back days ago. Go find out what's taking him so long, and bring him straight here. No more distractions, no more wandering off. I don't know how much longer I'll be able to keep this up. I'm at my wit's end."

Eveningwing nodded hurriedly and shrank into his feathers. He bolted out the window and disappeared into the night.

Thelred fell back the moment he was gone.

He felt as if the seas had just collapsed and the rubble fallen across his chest. The pressure shortened his breath and made his leg pound all the harder. If he'd had the strength, he would've flung that wooden crutch out the window. He would've liked nothing better than to have it gone.

His leg was just another reminder that he was trapped — stuck on an island while the Kingdom fell apart.

******

Thelred woke at dawn, his stomach churning. He slid from bed and limped down to the main floor, steeling himself against the fact that he would have to nod to everybody who wished him a good morning — and there would be dozens. The soldiers would already be well into their pacing and the servants about their chores.

When he managed to go the whole length of the hallway without coming across so much as a maid, he considered it good luck. There weren't any servants hauling bulky items up the stairs, or any crowds to push through. He made it to the end of the next passage without a single door flying open in his face.

But by the time he reached the council's chambers, his mood had begun to darken. What he'd thought was only luck had grown into a cold and empty silence. None of the lanterns were lit and the hearth fire had burned out. The chairs sat like stone and the tables cast hollow shadows across the floor — as if they'd always been empty.

Thelred stood for several long moments, his ears straining for any noise that meant he wasn't alone. He'd just steeled himself to walk across the empty room when the sound of footsteps caught his attention.

It was so light and practiced a tread that he likely wouldn't have heard it, had he not been listening so desperately. Thelred spun in the direction of the sound and saw a darkened figure slip down one of the hallways.

He followed as closely as he dared, grimacing against every creak and groan of his blasted leg. The man moved like a shadow down the hall. A mop and bucket hung from his hands and a strong, weedy scent wafted out behind him. Something that looked like resin glistened across his sleeves.

It's only one of the servants, Thelred told himself as the man ducked into the kitchens. *Perhaps it's earlier than you thought. Perhaps they're all still asleep.*

376

He clenched his fists at his sides and pushed through the kitchen door.

The man was waiting for him on the other side, standing a mere hand's breadth from his chest — a forest man with a short crop of hair. There were bruises on his face and his lip was busted open. Thelred might not have recognized him, had it not been for his slightly crooked nose …

Or that horrible, dead-eyed stare.

"Oh, for the love of — *omft*!"

Thelred stumbled backwards when the forest man's head collided with his chin. He was still reeling from the blow when someone else kicked him onto his knees — a second man with bruises and an identically crooked nose.

No sooner did the world stop spinning than the second twin wrenched his head back by the roots of his hair, forcing him to lock eyes with the woman who sat at the kitchen table.

There were bramble scratches on her face and leaves tangled in her hair. A tattered woodsman's garb replaced her elegant gown. But her eyes hadn't lost a single shard of their cold.

And she turned their full power onto Thelred.

"Hello, pirate."

"D'Mere," he spat. Blood coated his mouth and his lips were still numb from the twin's blow, but he forced the words out. "What in Kingdom's name are you doing here? The council —"

"Is gone. All of them. Every … last … one."

Slowly, she got to her feet. There was a pair of rucksacks upon the table. One of their mouths was opened, revealing a number of large bottles tucked inside. Thelred was trying to get a good look at them when D'Mere stepped into his path.

"What do you mean, the council is gone? What did you do to them?"

"*Do* to them? I saved them. Midlan is on its way — they'll be here by evening." D'Mere glanced out the window as she spoke, and the pale dawn revealed the shadows beneath her eyes. "Crevan's gone mad, you see. He burned Lakeshore, destroyed my castle. We barely escaped with our lives.

"He's coming for the seas next, and it'll all be the same: more burning and destruction, more innocent souls cast into death. I came here in the hopes that the council might listen to wisdom … and for once, it did." She turned back to him, her gaze colder than ever. "When Midlan arrives, everybody inside this castle will suffer a traitor's death. The council knows this — and rather than face Crevan in battle, they've decided to flee. They set sail last night, in fact."

Thelred couldn't grasp it. He didn't want to believe her. "You're lying," he growled, baring his teeth as the twin's grip tightened upon his hair. "The seas have a treaty with Midlan."

D'Mere rolled her eyes at him. "If that were true, the council would have no reason to run. There's nothing wrong with your *eyes*, pirate," she added, glancing down at his leg. "You should've been able to see that the ship was on fire. You shouldn't have waited for the rats to flee before you started to worry. Now, you're the only one left — the last rat in the chancellor's castle."

She wasn't lying. Thelred had only to look around him to know that the castle was empty. There was no way D'Mere could've slain them all, or sunk each of their ships. So the only explanation was that they *had* sailed away. They'd poured from the castle and slipped off into the night.

And they'd left him behind to rot.

Thelred supposed he shouldn't have been surprised. It wasn't as if he'd made any friends in the council. Still, it was a cad's move — even for Colderoy. "What about the villagers?"

"They're gone, as well. I made sure the council took them aboard. As long as they insist on playing *ruler*, they ought to at least be responsible for their people. Now, if there are no more questions ..." D'Mere reached behind her and drew a long, slender dagger from her belt. "I believe the last time we met, I promised to carve your face from your skull if I ever saw you again."

Thelred tried to ignore the murder in her look — but when the dagger's tip pressed against his chin, it was difficult. "If Midlan's coming, why are you still here? Why didn't you run with the others?"

"I suppose I *could* run. I could live the rest of my life in some forgotten corner of the Kingdom, flinching at every shadow and breath of the wind. But living isn't all that important to me anymore. It hasn't been for a while. No, Crevan's ruined me. He's taken everything from me — and I intend to ruin him back. I don't think I could live with myself, if I didn't try."

Her stare hardened as the dagger bit through his flesh. Thelred gasped against the pain: it stung him at first, spreading across his skin

378

in thousands of tiny thorns. But the knife didn't twitch again, and soon the pain dulled.

He knew without even catching the edge of her smirk that D'Mere was going to skin him slowly.

The twin wrapped one arm around his neck and planted the other atop his head, leaving his face exposed. His knee crushed Thelred's hands against his back while D'Mere's twisted about the knife. She turned it ever so slightly — just enough to awaken another horrible sting.

There was no point in fighting her. Thelred knew this. He was alone in a castle, stuck at the middle of an island — his only escape a mile-long bridge. Even if he managed to free himself from the twin's hold or avoid D'Mere's knife, there was no way he'd be able to outrun them.

"I'm going to peel off your mouth, first. So if there's anything you'd like to say ...?"

Thelred scowled at her. His words slid out from between his teeth with surprising force: "I don't care what you do to me. Skin me, if you like. But you'd better stop him, D'Mere. You'd better keep Crevan out of the seas."

She smiled at this; she dug a fraction more into his flesh. Her eyes traced the lines of blood that ran from his wound and down the dagger's blade. Something crossed her face in a bright red swell — some longing that carved a frozen path down Thelred's neck.

Then all at once, she relented.

D'Mere paced back to the table and sat down hard. Her eyes closed for a moment as she brushed a loose strand of hair from her dampened brow. Deep breaths shook her arm as she waved to the chair beside her.

"Please ... join me," she said hoarsely.

Thelred didn't get a chance to answer.

One of the twins pulled him onto his feet while the other kicked out his chair. They shoved him down and stuffed a cloth into his hand. He pressed it warily against his chin. "You aren't going to kill me?"

"No."

She offered him no further explanation, and the way she stared chilled him to his bones. "I'm warning you, D'Mere —"

"No, I'm warning *you*." Her voice went hard and her eyes turned cold. "Whatever you may think of me, whatever lies or rumors the council might have you believe, listening to me is your only chance of survival now. You will die unless you do exactly as I say."

He didn't know if she meant that Midlan would kill him, or if she intended to kill him herself. But for the moment, he had no choice. "Fine," he muttered. His eyes went back to the rucksacks, to the many sealed bottles stuffed into their mouths. "What's in there?"

"Poison," D'Mere said lightly. She drew a bottle out and held it up to the window. The liquid within it glowed an orange-red. "For the tips of our arrows and the edges of our swords. A single drop in a man's blood, and he'll be dead within hours. Midlan's in for quite a shock, I think."

CHAPTER 39
A Short-Lived Victory

It turned out that Thelred wasn't alone, after all. One of the twins found a number of guards passed out inside the dungeons — lulled to sleep by the contents of their tankards, scattered all across the card table and the floor.

Once D'Mere explained to them that they'd been abandoned by the council and were now very thoroughly trapped, it was amazing how quickly they sobered up. The twins marched them into the courtyard and stood watch while they practiced fighting — occasionally stepping in to slap them across their helmets for bad form.

Thelred wasn't at all impressed with the guards. Judging by the hesitance behind their blows and the sheer number of arrows that completely missed their marks, he wagered none of them had ever done any real fighting. They'd likely been given their spears for the sole purpose of stalking around the castle, *looking* formidable.

Still, with the gates shored and the bridge keeping their enemies trapped in one spot, he thought they had a decent chance of surviving for a few days.

Then Midlan marched in.

Several hundred soldiers entered the village at sunset. Thelred watched from the other end of the bridge as they took over the houses and let themselves into the shops. A line of carts packed the streets, each piled to its top with rations and gear.

They'd prepared for a siege.

While most of Midlan spent the evening either sleeping or buried deep in their cups, one man separated himself from the rest. He was obviously a seas man: he stripped down to his trousers and dove into the waves first thing, spear in hand. He swam beside the mile-long bridge and did his hunting just out of bow range — Thelred knew, because he'd sent an arrow at him the moment he came close.

"Greyson," D'Mere whispered. She smirked when the man shot them a rude gesture. "One of Midlan's more dangerous captains."

Thelred readied another arrow. "You know him?"

"I make it a point to know a little about all of Crevan's leaders. There are other seas men he could've chosen — I rather wish he would've sent anybody else." D'Mere sighed, and her smile slipped into a frown. "Greyson doesn't make mistakes. He's frustratingly thorough. The fact that Crevan sent him to the chancellor's castle means he wants it taken over, not destroyed."

Thelred supposed that made sense. Crevan would likely appoint another grubbing ruler the moment he captured the seas, and the island castle was too enviable a fortress to pass up. The rule would probably go to this *Greyson* fellow ... if he survived.

Thelred raised the bow over his head and drew back as he brought it down. He leveled the arrow straight between Greyson's eyes, but it fell well short.

"You have a strange draw," D'Mere said, glaring after his shot. "Perhaps that's why you keep missing."

"There's nothing wrong with my draw. I've been shooting this way since I was a child, and I've hit plenty," he added, before she could retort. "I'm only missing because that scab is floating out of range."

"Just make sure you have it sorted out before tomorrow. In order for the poison to work, it has to actually hit something."

Thelred glared at her smirk. "I know how to fight. Perhaps you ought to worry about your own men, D'Mere."

"I'll do that. And please," she said as he marched away, "call me Olivia."

That was the last in a long list of things he wanted to call her. But somehow, he managed to hold his tongue. All he had to do was suffer her presence for a few more days. If he could survive that long, the pirates would do the rest. They couldn't be far from the castle, now. They would turn up at any moment.

He was sure of it.

****

A red sun rose the next morning. The wind blew at his back, howling from the Westlands. Waves slapped against the island's jagged rocks in a near constant roar. Thelred thought for certain that he would be the first to the ramparts, but D'Mere was already there.

"No mages. That's … unusual," she whispered when Thelred approached. Her eyes sharpened upon the gathering crowd in the village: Midlan was preparing to cross the bridge. "Ready your archers, pirate. I'll gather the spearmen."

Thelred didn't know how she could've possibly seen from that distance, but he didn't question it. For now, his only task was to survive the morning — and it would be far from easy.

Most of the remaining guards were spearmen. They gathered on the ramparts with D'Mere and the twin she called *Left*. Only a few guards seemed to be any good at archery — and even then, Fate might have to intervene if they wanted any chance of hitting their marks.

The guards stood in a crooked line in the courtyard, waiting to file into the towers at his order. Half would go with Thelred into the southern tower, and the others would follow Right into the northern. At least Right was decent with the bow: after a few minutes of practice, he'd been able to fire arrows that thudded into the target every time.

As for the rest of them … well, Thelred just hoped their hands were steadier than their nerves.

"Chins up, dogs," he barked as he approached. "I need you all to —"

One of the guards heaved over the top of his words, spilling his breakfast across the stone. Another followed him, and a third became so violently ill that he collapsed upon his knees. The last man didn't raise his visor in time: he wound up spewing sick through the vents of his helmet while the others watched in open-mouthed shock.

That was precisely the moment when Thelred realized they were all going to die.

"Is everybody finished?" he growled. "Get it out, now. If things go well, we're going to be stuck inside those towers until dusk. I don't want to have to wade through the sick to reach the windows. Tighten your laces and let's get climbing."

The men slumped off into opposite directions. Thelred followed well behind his guards. By the time he'd finished climbing his way to the top of the tower, his leg ached and the grip of his bow was damp with sweat. It was going to be a long, miserable day.

A few slit windows ringed the walls — their only portals to the outside world. At least there was a breeze sweeping in to lessen the stench of sweat and nerves. That was one less discomfort Thelred would have to manage.

Three of the windows gave them a fairly decent view of the bridge. Thelred lined the guards up behind them, and took the front spot at the middle. "The first man will fire while the man behind him nocks. Once you've taken your shot, step to the back of the line and start nocking. Make every arrow count — and be careful," he added, glaring at them. "The Countess has tipped the heads with poison. If you get nicked, you'll die just as quickly as the tinheads."

They nodded — and took an inordinate amount of time to nock their first arrows.

Thelred couldn't bear to watch them fumble. If he had to witness one more arrow bouncing off its string, he'd start kicking shins. Instead, he turned his attention to the army below.

Most of the troops stayed behind while a small portion made its way across the bridge. It was wide enough to hold two wagons side-by-side, and sturdy enough to bear the weight of merchants' caravans. So as much as Thelred might've wished for it, hoping the bridge would collapse and drag the soldiers to their deaths wouldn't do him any good.

Midlan's front ranks were comprised of a group of heavily armored men. They lined either side of a battering ram: a weapon the size of a stout tree with an iron-capped head. Behind the ram marched several rows of archers. Thelred couldn't help but notice how they stood in perfect ranks. There wasn't a shaking hand or an arch of sick among them.

At the very back of the line was a company of swordsmen. They shifted restlessly, the slits in their helmets fixed upon the ramparts. Thelred knew by how intently they watched that the swordsmen were eager for a fight. If that lot made it through the gates, the siege would end quickly.

Greyson lurked in the middle of it all. He was mounted atop a horse, fully armored. He stripped his helmet away and addressed them with a grin. "Good morning, Countess."

D'Mere leaned against the rampart walls, inspecting the head of her spear. "You're making a mistake, Greyson," she called without bothering to look up. "You'll find nothing but death behind these gates."

"Really? I haven't heard very many footsteps on your side of things — and I've got ears like a fox." He turned his helmet over in his hands, gazing at her through the fall of his hair. "Your little trick at Lakeshore is going to cost you. There's a bounty on your head large enough to change any man's fortunes. I'm so pleased that I came across you first. Still, it would be a shame to put such beauty to the sword. Perhaps you'd like the chance to speak with the King, yourself? To plead for your traitorous life? Open the gates for me, my dear, and I'll give you that chance ... eventually."

Laughter billowed up across the bridge. The soldiers' shouts and whistles stifled D'Mere's reply. She glared down as they taunted her, but made no move to silence them.

Thelred wasn't sure if he could hold his place much longer. The way Greyson spoke, how he sat above everybody else and lorded over them with a smirk — all reminded him of Duke Reginald. He knew how the seas had suffered beneath Reginald's rule. And there was no doubt in his mind that Greyson would be worse.

When he grew tired of laughing at them, Greyson waved the soldiers forward and galloped from the bridge — moving back into the safety of the village.

A crooked rail marked the edge of Thelred's range. He'd managed to land arrows near it several times in practice. So the moment the battering ram's nose crossed it, he pulled back and fired.

It landed harmlessly between two soldiers and skittered off the bridge.

Thelred swore. When the guard behind him tried to step forward, he elbowed him back. "Move!"

"But you said —"

"I want another go."

Thelred fired again and this time, he struck true. The arrow thudded into the top of a soldier's forearm, biting through his mail. He yelped and dropped his hold on the ram — and yelped again when one of his companions ripped the arrow free.

Thelred couldn't stop his grin. "Ha! Got him."

"In the *arm*," someone muttered.

Thelred slapped him across the helmet. "It doesn't matter — he'll be a dead man before long. All you have to do is nick them, and the Countess's poison will do the rest. Now come on!" He grabbed the man behind him and slung him towards the window. "Give them a taste of their own blood, dogs!"

Their shots were weak at first. Many bounced off the top of the bridge or plunked into the waves. But Thelred wasn't going to give up. He'd never thought he would have the chance to go into battle again. This wasn't the sea, but it was a blasted good second — and he planned to make the most of it.

When a guard finally landed a shot through a soldier's foot, Thelred laughed. "There you go, lads! That one'll be limping his way to the river before midday. Nock another round, you sorry bunch of dogs," he yelled as he aimed. "I'm going to give this next scab something to think about."

He did — and while the soldier screamed, the tower erupted in cheers.

A few moments later, the ram struck the door with sound that brought their celebration to an end. They'd shored the bottom of the gates with stone and used the ripped-off tops of the benches for extra planks. The rubble was piled so high that it nearly covered the latch. Thelred kept telling himself that the gates would hold.

But with every *boom* of the ram's iron nose, it became more difficult to believe.

Midlan's archers began to fire back. Thelred held them off for as long as he could, ordering his men to the windows between volleys. But soon Midlan struck so fierce a rhythm that there was hardly a pause between arrows: they clattered against the walls and flew through the windows, forcing the guards away from their posts.

Thelred knew that with every second the archers went unchallenged, they would gain ground. It wouldn't be long before they'd be able to hit the ramparts.

He lunged for one of the far windows and saw that D'Mere was wreaking havoc on the men who worked the battering ram. The guards sprang up at her command and let loose a deadly hail of spears. Their bolts did far more damage than arrows: nearly every soldier they hit wound up too mangled to fight on.

Though the guards held their own, the twins were responsible for much of the damage. Thelred watched as Left pinned soldiers to the ground with quick, practiced throws. Some of the arrows flying from the other tower were particularly well aimed: they hit the soldiers in their gold-tinged helmets nearly every time.

But no matter how bravely they fought, they were simply outnumbered. More soldiers charged in to take the places of those who'd fallen. They carried fresh quivers for the archers and dumped the corpses off the bridge — along with several men who weren't quite dead, but simply too wounded to run.

With the towers pinned, the archers turned their attention to the ramparts. Two spearmen fell to their arrows — struck dead before they had the chance to scream. Soon their volleys grew so relentless that D'Mere and her guards had no choice but to flee. They rushed down the stairs and disappeared into the courtyard, sprinting out of Thelred's sight.

"Should we follow them?" one of his guards said.

It was too late for that. With the ramparts emptied, the archers went after the towers. There was hardly a missed shot among them. Arrows spewed through the windows and peppered the doorway beyond. The only safe place was along the wall beneath the windows. Thelred knew they'd have to be worse than daft to try to run for the door.

Unfortunately, there were more than a few daft men among them.

"We're going to get slaughtered, standing around like this!" one of the guards cried. His eyes were so wild that they practically bulged from his helmet.

"I wouldn't turn my back on those windows, not for all the gold in the realm," another said. He flinched as a bolt clattered off the sill above him. "We'll be drowned in arrows before nightfall!"

"They'll be *in* by nightfall! I'd rather just take an arrow to the back and be done." Before Thelred could stop him, the wild-eyed guard peeled from the wall and tore for the archway.

An arrow buried itself between his shoulders just as he reached the door. Thelred tried not to listen to the fleshy *thud* of his corpse flopping down the stairs, but it was difficult.

They were trapped inside that tower for what felt like an age: cramped beneath the windows, grimacing against every jolt of the ram upon the door. Thelred listened for a signal from the courtyard — any sign that D'Mere and her guards still fought. But he couldn't hear a thing over the noise of Midlan's battle. When he chanced a look, he saw that no arrows flew from the northern tower.

He swore under his breath.

Thelred had been a fool to trust D'Mere. It'd been well over an hour, and Midlan still fought. There'd probably never been any poison on the arrows to begin with. She'd already escaped the King's clutches once — sacrificing her own people in the flames, no doubt. What would keep her from doing it again?

By the time Greyson broke through the gates, D'Mere would be gone. Thelred didn't know how she would manage it. He didn't see how there could possibly be another way off the island. But if there was one, D'Mere would find it.

Thelred had simply been left for bait ...

"Fall back!" a man screamed, jolting him from his rage. "Get away from the gates — she's bloody cursed us!"

Thelred twisted around and peered carefully over the sill. A guard pressed in behind him, craning to see over his head.

Midlan was in a panic. The archers tore for the village, scattering like insects from the light. They stomped over the bodies of their companions in the rush to get away. Some convulsed in the middle of their running and fell — clutching at a graze or scratch. Their bodies flailed wildly, limbs kicking out in every direction. They screamed as if their heads were doused in flame.

The men who worked the battering ram faired worse. Half of them were already twitching upon the ground. The others tried their best to haul the ram back to shore, but only made it a few paces before the second wave dropped beneath the poison. The ram's nose thudded into the bridge, crushing a few hapless men beneath it — while the rest broke into a terrified sprint.

Thelred watched their mad charge across the bridge — laughing each time another soldier fell to his wounds. "Look at them run! What did I tell you, dogs? Follow me," he called over the guards' relieved howls. "Let's twist the knife."

His pain vanished as he hobbled down the stairs. D'Mere and her guards were already in the courtyard, moving stones from the gate. Thelred watched in amazement as Right hefted a rock the size of a man over his shoulders. Left ripped nails from the planks with his bare hands.

D'Mere nodded as Thelred approached. There was a hairline scratch across her cheek. The bright red line matched the color of her lips. "An arrow graze," she said, when he asked. "Left managed to throw me out of the way, or it might've been much worse. I was thinking we ought to toss the ram."

That was precisely what Thelred had been thinking, though he wasn't about to admit it. "The nose should sink it nicely. If we leave the corpses —"

"It'll make Greyson's next attack all the more difficult. It's a shame our paths didn't cross sooner, pirate," D'Mere said with a smirk. "We work well together."

She turned away, then — leaving Thelred with an uncomfortable twist inside his gut. He knew full well what the Countess had done to earn her throne, and to keep it. Her poison had just crippled a horde of the best-trained soldiers in the realm. She'd sent them screaming like maids from a mouse, which he couldn't help but find ... impressive.

That feeling troubled him greatly. His gut twisted more when they opened the gates and he got his first look at what D'Mere's poison had done: the corpses bled from the eyes and foamed from the mouth. D'Mere hardly glanced down as she strode towards the ram — but Thelred couldn't look away.

The guards must've had a difficult time looking away, as well. No sooner had they stepped outside than one of them was already heaving his guts over the rails.

"Oh, I hate to think what it'll be like when the sun stokes the smell from them," D'Mere called, her voice tinged with amusement. "Let's get to work, gentlemen."

Right and Left did most of the work. The twins stood on either end of the ram while the rest of them struggled at its middle. Even D'Mere took a spot along its girth.

"There's no need to trouble yourself. I wouldn't want you to crack that peg," she said when Thelred crouched beside her.

He shook his head firmly. "I worked for this just as hard as anybody else. I want my part of the celebration."

She gave him a long, inscrutable look — one that made him almost wish for the ice. Then she shrugged. "Very well. On my count, then ..."

They lifted with everything, each man lending what remained of his strength to the effort. They managed to toss the ram into the sea and only broke a few feet of railing in the process. The guards cheered as they watched the ram get dragged into the depths by the weight of its iron nose, but D'Mere was silent.

She'd turned her eyes upon the shore, and her smile vanished. "They're already moving," she whispered when Thelred stepped in beside her.

He'd known their victory would be short-lived. Still, he felt they ought to have gotten at least a day to celebrate. But Greyson wasted no time: lines of soldiers rushed among the slender woods around the village, moving at his command.

Thelred squinted, but lost them the moment they ducked into the trees. "What happens next?"

"They'll build catapults," D'Mere said quietly, her eyes distant. And she needed to say no more.

A catapult could fire from well outside an arrow's range, and it couldn't be poisoned.

Their victory would be even shorter-lived than he'd thought.

CHAPTER 40
OLIVIA

Boulders cracked the walls and rattled the gates. They fell in inconsistent patterns, breaking the silence whenever they least expected it. At every fall, they listened: all ears turned and the taut line of each mouth was a silent plea for the keep doors to hold.

The towers were broken, some of the upper rooms had been smashed in. Thelred spent three nights upon the floor in the council's chambers. Night froze the stones and day tormented him with a sweltering heat.

In a matter of hours, Greyson's catapults had forced them to retreat. His shots landed wide of their marks, at first. They crashed harmlessly into the sea. The soldiers he sent to ram the gates fell beneath their arrows and spears. But then quite suddenly, the catapults found their aim.

Thelred remembered when the first boulder crashed through: the splinters of rock that'd burst from the walls tore his shirt and left deep cuts across his face. Two guards had been trapped beneath the boulder. One died instantly, crushed to death. The other got caught by the legs.

They'd tried desperately to free him. The guards heaved against the boulder and Thelred's wooden leg cracked with the effort. But the rock was wedged tightly against the hole it'd left in the wall. They couldn't move it. D'Mere and her twins had already fallen back — chased away by the rocks that thudded into the courtyard.

More boulders fell. When Thelred saw a catapult turn in their direction, he'd had no choice but to order his men to retreat. The guard was still screaming as they tore down the stairs.

He screamed until a second boulder exploded into the tower ... silencing him.

Now, those screams echoed inside Thelred's skull. He woke with a start each time a boulder landed. He scanned the room, convinced for a moment that someone else had been crushed — that

Greyson had finally broken into the keep. Blow after blow shook the floors and rattled their nerves. But against all possibility, they survived.

The guards spent most of their time in a worried clump. They nursed their wounds and moaned about how they were doomed to die.

Thelred knew things were desperate. For the first couple of days, he'd listened for the bells — the familiar call of *Anchorgloam* as she sailed in to free them. But as the hours dragged through days and nights without so much as a ringing in the distance, he'd slowly given up. If the pirates hadn't come by now, they never would.

Perhaps the same fire that'd chased the shipbuilders from their homes had fallen upon pirates. That was the only possible explanation — the only reason he could think of that Lysander would ever leave him to die. They'd been through too much, shared in far too many ill-conceived adventures. He'd always thought that they would face the final battle together ...

But Fate must've thought differently.

Thelred knew he would go mad if he dwelled upon the pirates. He felt as if he was already an hour from *mad*, as it was. So rather than brood, he tried to play.

There was a small piano in the council's chambers — one of Countess D'Mere's gifts to the seas. Thelred played it for hours at a time. He let the notes wash over him, let the songs blanket his mind. For the time the piano sang, he escaped the crumbling walls and lost himself to the music ...

"You play rather well, pirate," D'Mere said quietly. She'd crept up beside him while he focused. Her eyes roved across the piano's keys for a moment before she waved to the bench. "May I?"

"If you must," Thelred grumbled as he slid over. He tried not to flinch when she sat down beside him, but it was difficult. "I'm not going to teach you."

She raised her brows. "Teach me what?"

"How to play. Every woman who comes over here wants to learn the piano. But all they wind up doing is wasting my time."

"How so?"

"They don't listen, for one thing. When they're not giggling, they're asking ridiculous questions. And they touch my hands."

"How awful of them," D'Mere said dryly.

392

He glared at her. "It *is* awful. I don't like to be touched. How in Kingdom's name am I supposed to teach them anything if I can't move my fingers? It's an absolute waste of my time."

"Perhaps it's not the *piano* they're interested in."

She sounded exactly like Lysander. He swore up and down that Thelred had a way with women — and if that were true, he would gladly give it up. "They're far more trouble than they're worth, always mooning over everything or crying about something. They're too noisy." He tapped the piano's keys. "This is the only sound I enjoy. Why is that so difficult for everybody to understand?"

D'Mere shrugged. "Perhaps you'll find someone who enjoys it as much as you do."

"Oh? Have you ever found someone who enjoys *killing* as much as you?" Thelred snapped. Had he not been so exhausted, he might've thought to regret his words. But he didn't — and it wasn't as if his fate could get any worse.

D'Mere laughed before she turned to him and whispered coldly: "No, I haven't."

Thelred tried to lean away from her … but she followed. Something glanced across her eyes as she came closer, an authority that froze him to the bench. Her hand slid beneath his chin and her thumb brushed against his wound — the mark her dagger had left behind.

Her lips were warmer than he thought they would be. He'd been expecting them to feel scaly and cold, like a serpent's flesh. But they moved against him softly. Her touch was gentle, her presence completely changed. For the moment she kissed him, it was easy to forget she was *D'Mere*.

For a single, heart-pounding moment, she felt like … someone else.

"What was that for?" he said when she released him.

D'Mere's eyes tightened at their bottoms; the ice returned. "Nothing. You reminded me of someone, is all."

"Someone you loved?"

"No," she laughed again, "I wouldn't say I *loved* him. I wouldn't cheapen it like that. But he was the only person I ever met who was truly good. Not everyone is content with what they are," she added with a distant look. "Some of us long for what we wish to be … for what we can't be."

For the first time in days, Thelred didn't notice the crashing of the boulders or the thudding of the ram. The world fell quiet as he tried to understand her. "What happened to him?"

She didn't answer. She stared at the walls as if she could see through them.

"D'Mere?"

"He died, of course. All good men die. And how many times have I got to tell you to call me Olivia?" she growled. "Countess D'Mere is gone."

Thelred was about to ask her what she meant. But in the moment he paused, he realized something … strange. He wasn't just imagining things: the world really *had* gone quiet. The ram didn't beat and the floor stopped shaking.

The guards dragged themselves up and stared down the hall — as if they expected to hear the keep doors rattle again at any moment. But they didn't.

"Go," Thelred said when they turned to him. "Get closer and see if you can hear what's happening."

No sooner had they gone than the twins appeared. Left had his sword drawn and Right wore a quiver across his back. There was a bow gripped in his hand. His fingers traced the fletching of a nocked arrow — one that had a drenched piece of rag tied around its head.

They didn't speak a word, but D'Mere must've been able to read them. "They're here? Good," she said when they nodded. "Remember, there's no guarantee that he's crossed with them. I don't think we'll be that lucky. So don't fire unless you're certain you see him — and I mean it," she barked at Right. "Killing his army won't do us any good. He'll just raise another one. We've got to stop *him*."

Right grabbed her arm, brows tight above his eyes.

She jerked from his grasp. "If his army takes me, you'll just have to follow. Don't try to fight them and whatever you do, don't let him see you. Your moment will come." She turned to Left. "I need you to lock me inside the chancellor's office — make it look convincing. Then you've got to find someplace to hide …"

Thelred didn't have time to wonder what she had planned. If Greyson was about to break through the doors, he had to warn the guards.

He limped for the hallway — only to be nearly flattened when someone else charged out the other side.

"Thelred!" the guard gasped, righting him before he could fall backwards. "You —"

"No, don't worry about me. Get everybody away from the doors. Midlan is about to break through!"

"I don't think so, sir. I don't think they're going anywhere. Midlan's screaming," he whispered, his eyes ringed starkly. "They sound like a monster's just washed into the harbor."

Thelred couldn't contain his grin. He couldn't believe he'd ever doubted. If Midlan was screaming, it was because the pirates had set upon them. They'd be free by evening. "Wake everybody — have them ready to fight. We'll push back from our side."

The guards did as they were told. When they reached the doors, Thelred heard the screams for himself. There was the thudding of panicked footsteps across the bridge, the screech of steel against armor — the occasional *splash* as a body tumbled over the rails. But beneath all that rose a noise that stopped his heart.

It was a sound he recognized: a mash of roars, grunts, and gurgling cries drawn sharply against the dawn. They were sounds no man in his right mind could make — the call of monsters with deadened eyes. He'd heard them once before, back in Gilderick's castle.

Not even the agony of his severed leg had been able to dull the horror of their maddened shrieks. They'd filled the floors to their mortar and the walls to their seams. Thelred lay frozen upon a musty bed while Lysander watched through a cracked door.

"I've never heard a giant make a sound like that," he'd whispered.

It was only after the battle was won that Kael told them about the Fallows — Gilderick's army of soulless men who obeyed every fleeting thought his mind possessed. They'd carried him off into Whitebone, that day. The giants hadn't been able to stop him.

And now, it seemed that he'd returned.

"Get away from the gates!" Thelred cried, just as the world beyond went still.

There was a half-moment when the guards froze and the shrieking fell silent — when Thelred's breath sounded as if it could fill the entire castle. Then all at once, Gilderick struck the gates.

It was a single, resounding *boom* — the noise of his entire army throwing itself against the door at once. Cracks bloomed from the marks the ram had left behind. They raced from the gate's bottom to its top, splitting wider with every passing second.

Bones crunched against the wood; red oozed from between the cracks. The hinges groaned in agony and the great plank that held the doors sealed began to moan.

"Get back!" Thelred said again, shoving the nearest guard towards the hall. "Get *back!*"

His yelling seemed to startle them from their shock. They tore away and began sprinting for the main room. Thelred followed at a hop, bellowing orders over the top of the gate's protests:

"Get to the upper levels! Barricade yourselves in and don't come ou —"

Boom!

The doors gave way and Thelred watched, horrified, as an army of soulless men tumbled inside. The ones closest to the gates had been crushed to death beneath the force of the others' push: a bloody mash of giants, desert folk and forest men. A wave of gold-tinged soldiers poured in behind them. But though they still bore the King's crest, these soldiers were no longer a part of Midlan.

They stomped over the top of their companions' shattered bodies — their stark white eyes peeled open, their lungs filled with shrieks.

Thelred didn't remember starting to run. He forgot to be careful with his leg and tore for the stairs. The last of the guards had just made it around the corner. If he fought, they might have time to hide.

He spun at the foot of the stairs and drew his cutlass. A desert man lurched at him. Festering wounds marred his features. He bared his teeth like a wolf, his overgrown nails stretched for Thelred's face.

He didn't seem to notice when the cutlass bit through his middle. In fact, he pulled the blade in deeper — clawing for Thelred's throat. The sword was lodged between the Fallows' ribs. He had no choice but to try to kick him away.

In the second it took him to force the desert man off his sword, his wooden leg bore the full weight of his body — and it was too much. The wood cracked again, and Thelred stumbled to the side. A giant swiped him away as if he was no more a threat than a gnat.

The wind left his lungs and the world shook when the cobblestones bit his head. More footsteps thumped towards him. He knew if he didn't move, he would be trampled. Thelred dragged himself beneath the stairs — digging his fingers into the mortar lines, trying to blink through the blood that ran into his eyes.

Pain seared his ribs, a fire that burned down his side and stabbed him with every breath. Black smudges swelled across his vision and tried to drag him into the darkness. But he fought them away.

The Fallows were searching for something. They slung the tables aside and ripped the chairs apart. Thelred bit down hard upon his lip when they reached the piano. Had his ribs not been screaming, he might've been sick at its cries for mercy. He might've groaned along with its final notes.

It wasn't long before Gilderick's army found the guards. He heard the shattering of a door above him and the Fallows' excited shrieks. His lungs burst when the guards cried out. From his throat erupted an inhuman sound. His fury swelled so mercilessly against his ribs that the black spots overtook him.

For a moment, he was blind — a sightless creature, its limbs twisted about its body in pain. His ears felt as if they'd been poured full of some warm liquid. Something churned within them and forced all noise into a high-pitched ringing. He thought the liquid might be his soul trying to claw its way out, the sound of its final cries. And his fear jolted him back into the present.

Someone gripped his hair. His vision was blurry at first but sharpened quickly upon a set of deadened eyes.

The eyes belonged to Greyson. All of the taunt was gone from his features. His mouth hung open and his tongue lolled as he twisted Thelred's head by the roots of his hair. The stark orbs pitted inside his skull sloshed from one side to the next — as if he could only see from their edges.

"No," a calm, slimy voice hissed from just beyond the reach of Thelred's vision. "This one's maimed. He isn't worth the trouble. Find the Countess!" the voice cried suddenly. "Drag her from whatever hole she's hiding and *bring her to me!*"

His command shocked the Fallows into frenzy. They burst in every direction and trampled anything that got in their way. Greyson shoved Thelred down, and his head struck the cobblestone with a hollow thud.

"She's here — she *must* be here!"

Thelred tried to be calm. He twisted his head ever so slightly and saw a giant crouched beside him. The giant's skin was so filthy that it'd become the color of dirt. His white mat of hair had yellowed. The few teeth left inside his gaping mouth were rotted — little more than blackened chips clinging to swollen gums.

But the most frightening thing about him was the creature he held in his arms.

A pair of emaciated legs hung from the crook of one elbow, and a greasy mop of lank hair draped down from the other. The hair clung limply to the sides of a man's face — a man so thin, and with eyes so dark and glistening that it could have been none other than Lord Gilderick, himself.

"Find her!" he shrieked again, stoking the Fallows into a rage. "Tear the castle apart, if you have to. Do not stop until she's found."

All at once, the noise in the hallway burst into a roar. Every Fallow spun from his work and tore off towards the chancellor's office. Some leapt from the balcony: Thelred's stomach swam when he heard the sickening *crunch* of their legs snapping and their ankles giving way. But they lurched on with bones sticking out of their flesh, their deadened eyes fixed upon the hallway.

It wasn't long before they found D'Mere. There was the sound of another door bursting loose, some excited shrieks. Then Thelred's blood chilled at her scream: "No! I told you to hide, you foolish child! *I told you to hide!*"

But Left must not have listened.

Thelred grit his teeth against the frenzied shrieks and the noise of steel biting flesh. Left must've fought hard: when the Fallows returned, many of them bore the marks of his sword. One staggered under the loss of blood before his body crumpled, dead, in the middle of the floor.

They dragged D'Mere in by her arms, but Left never returned ... and Thelred had a feeling he never would.

Though D'Mere looked uninjured, her face was like stone.

"Yes, bring her to me," Gilderick said, reaching out with a set of spidery fingers. "Bring her —"

"No!" D'Mere cried.

Her eyes shot to the balcony and she screamed for him to turn back, but Right didn't listen. He flung his bow and arrow aside, drew his sword and leapt from the rails. He landed atop one of the men who held D'Mere, snapping his neck. His teeth were bared and his eyes shone with fury as he sliced through the man who held her other arm.

"Kill him! Don't let the Countess escape!"

Right had D'Mere around the waist. He managed to sprint a few steps before the Fallows descended upon him. He swung until he lost his sword in the body of a giant, and then he swung his fists. He kept himself between the Fallows and D'Mere — snapping necks, breaking teeth, shattering bones. He fought like a wild animal for a few gut-wrenching seconds before the army overtook him.

"No!" D'Mere cried again as they dragged him down. Though she snarled, her eyes shone like glass. Thelred watched her lips twist to form the words: *You fool ... you fool.*

The Fallows raised their fists, balled like hammers above their heads, and brought them down in a deadly rhythm. They seemed to pound for an eternity. Thelred couldn't close his eyes, he couldn't cover his ears. The wet noise of flesh meeting stone overtook every other sound in the hall; the dark red puddle that seeped from between the flailing bodies engulfed his vision.

When Right's boots stopped twitching, Gilderick waved the Fallows aside. "Enough. That whelp won't trouble us again. Now ..." his black eyes slid to where D'Mere had collapsed, "bring me the Countess."

Thelred didn't know what was about to happen, but he knew he could do nothing to stop it. His wooden leg was shattered and useless. He would be dashed to bits the second he rose. He was trapped once again, forced to watch while Gilderick carried out whatever horrible torture he had planned.

D'Mere, for her part, didn't look the least bit concerned. She stared Gilderick down as the Fallows dragged her closer, her eyes burning and her fists clenched to white. There was anger on her face, perhaps even hatred. But one thing he'd expected to see wasn't there at all:

There was no surprise.

All at once, Thelred realized what was happening. Her words twisted inside his head and the truth spilled out before him. D'Mere wasn't surprised because she'd known that the Fallows were coming. Gilderick was the *him* they had to stop. And after seeing the way he'd devoured Greyson's army, Thelred understood why.

If Gilderick escaped the island, his rule would be worse than any Duke or King: he would consume the entire realm with his madness.

Thelred sank back, his heart pounding. He knew he had to lie still. He couldn't catch Gilderick's attention. No matter what happened, he had to stay conscious. He had to survive just a little while longer. The Kingdom had to be warned.

But when the Fallows dragged D'Mere into Gilderick's reach, it was all he could do to stay calm.

One of them shoved D'Mere onto her knees, while another wrenched her head up by the roots of her golden-brown hair.

"Open your eyes, Countess," Gilderick hissed. "Open them!"

She didn't flinch under his screams. If anything, her shoulders straightened.

"Fine." Gilderick's voice went deadly quiet. "If you won't open them, then I'll peel them open myself. Bring me closer."

The giant who cradled him leaned forward. One of Gilderick's spidery hands reached out —

"Gah!"

It happened so fast Thelred almost didn't see it: D'Mere ripped a dagger from beneath her collar and lunged for Gilderick. The Fallows shrieked at his cry and clutched their arms. The one who held D'Mere struck her hard in the side of the head.

Thelred had to bite his lip when her body fell limply to the floor. He choked on his screams, let his fury pound inside his skull. *Don't move*, he thought to himself. *Don't move, don't —*

"Don't kill her, you fools!" Gilderick moaned. The spidery hand shook as it reached out, stained with red. "She missed — I'm barely scratched. Now get her up, get her up quickly! Hurry, before her light fades."

A desert man pulled D'Mere up by her hair and brought her face to Gilderick's. Her features were hidden — drowned in a dark, sticky red. Thelred watched her hand for any small movement, any twitch of life.

But he saw none.

After a second of gazing into her eyes, Gilderick laughed. "That's it? That's all it is? Well then, that should be simple enough."

D'Mere moaned softly. Thelred couldn't hear what she said, but it made Gilderick's lips twist into a horrifying grin.

400

"No, Countess. That whelp destroyed me — he stole everything from me. While I was lost inside the desert, rotting beneath the sun, there was only one thought that kept me alive: that I would either have his mind, or have him dead. Your marvelous poison will make all of that possible. Once my army wields the mindrot, it won't be stopped. I couldn't have done it without you." His hand reached out and brushed down her darkened lips, mixing her blood with his own. "I didn't want to kill you, dear Olivia. It's a shame you chose to fight me ... then again, you've always been a bit too soft for my tastes."

Gilderick snapped his fingers, and the Fallows took off. They charged in a horde for the front gates. Thelred waited until they'd gone before he dragged himself to D'Mere.

Over bodies, across stone, through slick blood until he reached her. He pulled her head from the floor; he wiped the red from her face with his sleeve. Thelred stared into her eyes, not entirely certain of what he expected to see — but he knew he hadn't been expecting to feel their emptiness reflected inside his chest ...

Or the quiet snap of something deep within him breaking.

"D'Mere?" he whispered.

Her eyes widened at the sound of his voice. "Thel ... red?"

"Yes, I'm here. What do I need to do? How do I stop Gilderick?"

Her lips moved, but he couldn't make out what she said. Thelred had to lean over her before he could hear the whispered words:

"Get ... the torch ..."

Thelred followed her glare to the sconces upon the wall, where the torches sputtered weakly.

"The ... arrow ..." One of her bloodied hands twisted into his tunic. Her eyes sharpened behind the film of her pain. "The bridge ..."

All at once, Thelred understood: the mop and bucket, the rag coated in resin ...

"Burn the bridge. You've rigged it to burn." He gripped her hand when she nodded. "I'll do it. I swear I'll burn Gilderick alive."

Her eyes fell shut, then. Thelred had to bare his teeth against a sudden swell of pain — a pain that crashed against his wounds and threatened to drag him under. She was leaving him. He could already feel the cold stirring in the tips of her fingers ...

And he couldn't bear to watch.

"I hope you find him, Olivia. I hope to Fate you'll cross." He pressed his lips against hers and set her body down gently. After a heavy breath, he dragged himself to his feet.

Thelred limped to the sconces first and grabbed a torch from the wall. Then he began the long journey up the stairs.

He used his sword for a cane and leaned heavily upon the banisters, holding the torch out beside him. His ribs stabbed so mercilessly that he was out of breath by the time he reached Right's bow.

There was still an arrow nocked onto its string: a single bolt with its head bound in rag. Thelred slung the bow over his shoulder and kept the arrow clenched between his teeth as he fought his way up the stairs.

Every step was a battle — a race against the grains' fall from the glass. He had to reach the ramparts before Gilderick's army made it across the bridge. He had to stop them. Pain shook his leg; his vision was more black than color. But he forced himself on.

Morning light drenched his flesh as he pushed through the door to the castle's roof. It washed down his neck, warmed his skin, dulled the pain. The bodies scattered across the bridge were slowing the Fallows' escape. They moved clumsily, tripping over limbs and flopping onto the ground. They hadn't managed to go very far. He could hear Gilderick shrieking at them:

"Move, you worthless corpses! Step *around* it. Don't try to —"

A giant tripped on the body of a soldier and flipped over the rails. He landed with a heavy *plunk* into the waves below — drawing a fresh round of curses from Gilderick.

Thelred didn't know why he was so desperate, at first. He followed the line of Fallows' deadened eyes and his heart lurched when saw a fleet of boats moving towards the island. They were mostly fishing boats — and rickety ones, at that. He could practically hear them groaning against every wave that struck their sides. But from the bow of the lead ship came a familiar cry.

Eveningwing burst from the deck and swooped towards him, screeching — and the noise must've caught Gilderick's attention.

"Look — on the ramparts! Kill him! *Bring him down!*"

Thelred's blood froze when every last deadened eye turned upon him. The Fallows scooped up whatever they could find to throw while Thelred tried desperately to light his arrow. The ships were still

402

a ways out. Gilderick would be gone by the time they reached land. Thelred couldn't let him escape.

Eveningwing was coming closer, oblivious to the danger. Thelred's arms shook as he drew the arrow back. His ribs screamed in agony. His leg, blast his leg! It trembled with such fury that he more leaned against the wall than stood.

Objects flew past him: spears, swords, and rubble. A chunk of rock struck him hard in the shoulder, jolting him. But he forced himself to stand. He would not move. He would not be shaken. He was going to end Gilderick. He would end him for the Kingdom's sake …

… and for Olivia.

CHAPTER 41
A MONTH IN THE BRIG

"I'm going as fast as I can, Captain!" Shamus insisted. He gripped the wheel and swore at the sails. They fluttered against the push of a weak breeze — hardly enough to move them a length. "There's no blasted wind today! I can't do aught without the wind!"

"Keep trying!" Lysander barked.

He was pressed in at the front of the helm, half his body stretched over the rails and his eyes locked upon the madness at the chancellor's castle. The pirates and the wildmen were clustered at the bow in a knot that might've flipped a lesser ship. But *Anchorgloam's* weight held her down — and far more than Lysander would've liked.

"What is it? What do you see? Blast it all," he muttered when Eveningwing screeched back. He twisted to Silas, who was crammed in beside him. "Can you understand what he's saying?"

"I do not speak bird," was his hissing reply. He closed his glowing eyes, and his head tilted back. "Perhaps if the sun wasn't blinding me, I could see more. But I smell ..." His nostrils flared widely. "I smell ... blood."

"Blood?"

Lysander straightened so suddenly that he nearly lost his balance. He might very well have tumbled overboard, had Gwen not grabbed him by the belt. "Human blood?" she asked as she righted him.

"Yes, and a great deal of it."

Lysander spun to Shamus, his hair standing up like a madman's. "Hurry! Can't you move any faster?"

"I can't give any more than the wind gives me!"

"Perhaps what we need is a bit of music to —"

"*No!*"

Jonathan stuffed his fiddle away quickly at the noise of their collective roar. "All right, fine. No need to shout. I just thought a song might lighten things up a bit."

Lysander looked about to reply when a cloud drifted over the sun, blocking its light. Silas's glowing eyes cut across the bridge. "There's an army — they're running for the castle gates."

Lysander's face went white. "Do you see anyone else? Anyone in the castle?"

"I don't — wait a moment." Silas moved down the railing, shooing Lysander out of his way. Gwen stuck close behind him. "Look! I see someone."

They followed the line of his finger to the lone man upon the castle. His shoulders were just visible over the top of the wall. With the sun blocked, it was too dark to see anything else about him. He was nothing more than a shadow.

"He carries something … I can't tell what it is. The men on the bridge are throwing things at him. They are trying to knock him down," Silas said, his chin cutting away. "He'll be killed if he keeps showing his head.

Eveningwing's screeches came in sharp, panicked bursts — growing fainter as he beat his way towards the castle.

A ghostly white overtook Lysander's features. His words seemed stuck inside his throat.

A second later, Silas pointed again. "A bow! That's what the man carries." His head swung around to Gwen. "Why would an army fear an arrow?"

She didn't get a chance to answer. The moment the man drew the bow above his head, Lysander cried: "I know that draw! Thelred — get down! Get down, you fool!"

He yelled, he beat his fists against the railings. The pirates crushed in at the bow and lent their voices to his cries. But no matter how they screamed at him, Thelred didn't duck. He held his ground and loosed a single bolt down upon the army.

And all at once, the bridge exploded.

A burst of orange-blue flame engulfed it with a roar that shook the air between them. The fires devoured everything. Flaming bodies spilled from the bridge. In a matter of seconds, the whole thing buckled and collapsed — dragging what was left of the army down with it.

But though the noise shook their tallest mast, Lysander hardly glanced at the flames. He grabbed Silas roughly by the back of his shirt. "What happened? Where's Thelred? Do you see him?"

405

"The smoke is too thick — I'm trying!" he yowled, when Lysander snatched the top of his hair.

Gwen finally had to pull him away, but the captain wouldn't be calmed.

"Go faster! Tilt the sails, trap every last gust of wind."

Though his voice broke across his orders, the pirates had never moved faster. They scrambled to their work.

By the time they reached the castle, Lysander looked near to splitting. He leapt from the rails and into the choppy water below. He hauled his dripping body up the rocks and scrambled through the castle's front gates.

"Hold on, Captain — wait for us! You don't know what's in there," Shamus yelled. But Lysander didn't stop. He disappeared into the thick black smoke that trailed from the ruins, moving at a dead sprint.

Shamus signaled for the rest of the boats to make their way to the village before addressing the crew. "I just need a couple of men to row — the rest of you wait here. I don't know what we'll find in there, but it could be trouble. Bring some of your people along," he said to Gwen. "Just in case things get thick."

By the time they'd made it through the front door, Lysander was nowhere in sight. The once-grand room in the middle of the castle was destroyed: its chairs broken, its tables smashed. Bodies and gore littered the cobblestone.

Gwen glared around the wreckage, eyes sharp behind her paint. "What in Fate's name happened?" she whispered after a moment.

"I'm not sure, my Thane." Silas crouched before one of the bodies and jabbed its head with his fingers. "These men have the look of those long-dead, but not the smell of them. It's strange."

Shamus knew full well what these men were — and more troubling than that, he knew who they belonged to. No amount of grog could've drowned the memories of the Endless Plains. There was a darkness in Gilderick's realm the likes of which he'd never seen.

Now, that darkness had found its way here. Why? He wasn't sure. But just the thought of it chilled him.

"Search the chambers," Gwen said quietly. "See if anyone survived."

A handful of wildmen peeled off to follow Silas. They stayed close together as they went, and their legs carried them stiffly.

There was an arc of bodies upon the grand room floors. They were mostly those dead-looking fellows, though they found one that was crushed beyond telling — and another that chilled Shamus again.

"Tide take me," he whispered.

He was careful as he pulled the body of a woman off the floor. The woman's head was smashed, her golden-brown waves stained with red, her features frozen in the soft embrace of death.

Still, Shamus could hardly breathe. "Countess D'Mere?"

Gwen crouched beside him. "I'm sorry. Was she your friend?"

"No, I didn't know her well." He pressed two fingers against her neck, but only the cold answered him. "It's just strange, is all — to see someone you knew sprawled out like this. No matter who they were in life, you can't help but feel a bit ... sorry for them, in death."

Gwen reached over and closed D'Mere's eyes, her mouth drawn tightly. "Come on, shipbuilder. Let's find the captain."

Before they'd even made it out the rampart doors, they heard Lysander yelling:

"You should've listened to me, Red! I told you to bloody well duck. I told you to get down. You followed my orders every day for eight years — you never once ignored me. And this is the day you chose to turn. You should have listened!"

Those last words came out as a scream — a cry that broke across the waves and sent Shamus into a run. Gwen followed so closely behind that she nearly flattened him when he stopped.

Thelred lay still in Lysander's arms. A gash split the front of his head and spilled down his face. It blackened at his eyes, as if they'd been sealed shut by the gore. A bloodied spear lay beside him — its head matched the hole in the top of his shoulder. The wooden leg was shattered, nothing more than a handful of splinters at the base of his knee.

His clothes were torn; his flesh was bruised and swollen. Lysander screamed at him, but his face stayed fixed, and still.

Horribly, terribly still ...

"Oh, Fate," Shamus whispered. "I'm sorry, Captain. I'm so sorry."

"What are you sorry about?" Lysander snapped. His eyes burned and veins bulged from his neck. "He can hear me. He knows what I'm saying — don't you, Red? You're in an under-realm's worth of trouble."

"Captain, he can't —"

"Shut up!" Lysander cried. He held Thelred tighter as Shamus crouched, as if he feared his body would be taken away. "You don't know him like I do. You don't know anything at all."

He was right about that. Shamus had no clue what to say. When he looked to Gwen for help, he saw she'd wandered off. Eveningwing was perched upon the rampart walls. His eyes were squinched at their bottoms and his feathers ruffled miserably. He stepped onto Gwen's arm when she offered, and she carried him away.

It was probably for the best. Shamus didn't think a young fellow should have to see a thing like this.

"You should've listened," Lysander moaned again. His voice climbed when he pressed his face into Thelred's bloodied hair. "You should have listened to me, you idiot! Now you've given me no choice — I'm going to lock you in the brig for a month! Do you hear me, Red? A *month!*"

He'd turned the corner, now. Shamus knew if he didn't do something quick, the captain would drive himself mad. He'd reached to pull him away when a hand rose between them. It was bloodstained and bruised; it trembled as it held up its fingers.

And then a voice rasped:

"Two ... weeks ..."

Shamus nearly fell backwards when Thelred opened his eyes. "Seas and serpents!"

"I told you," Lysander said as his glare melted into to relief. "I told you he could hear me. He was just trying to knock a little time off his punishment ... and it worked." He laughed and clutched Thelred's hand tightly. "Fine — two weeks."

****

There'd been more to the castle siege than they realized. Thelred talked the whole trip to the village, but Shamus still didn't understand it. Countess D'Mere, Lord Gilderick, and Midlan had collided — all over some sort of poison. The army that went down with the bridge was Gilderick's. Thelred swore they'd all been killed: either by fire or sea.

But almost all of the bodies strewn throughout the village belonged to Midlan.

"Tide take me," Shamus said again at the sight of the battle.

Corpses clad in gold-tinged armor were scattered across the street and all along the alleyways. They coated the shop floors. It looked as if a stormwind had burst from the skies and torn them all to pieces. Midlan lay scattered and broken around them.

The pirates and fisherfolk had begun piling the bodies up to burn. But the wildmen's arrival sped things up — well, mostly. The craftsmen seemed taken with the armor's color, and reluctant to toss it away.

"This is good steel. We could make all sorts of things out of this," one of them said, as he crushed a gauntlet with his bare hands. The metal crumpled between his fingers like parchment. He passed a grin around the others. "We should keep some of it — just in case."

Lysander frowned at them. "You already have rocks from the Valley, and all of those blasted shells you found in Harborville. There's no way you'll be able to make something out of all of it."

"They can keep whatever they can carry," Gwen said, waving a hand at them. "Those are the rules."

Shamus watched in amazement as the craftsmen went about gleefully packing things into the warriors' rucksacks — crushing whole plates of armor into balls to make them fit. "They'll be dragging their boots, trying to haul all of those bits and baubles around."

The swirling lines of Gwen's paint creased together with her sharp grin. "My warriors will run out of *space* before they run out of strength."

There wasn't a true healer among them, but one of the fisherfolk knew enough about herbs and stitching to patch Thelred up. The worst mark on him was the gash across his face — but, thanks to a few tankards of pirate grog, Thelred didn't seem to feel a thing.

"Do you remember Greenblood?" he said, his words already getting a bit slurred.

Lysander had gotten a tankard of his own — in what he'd sworn was merely a showing of moral support. Now, he nearly choked on his laugh. "Of course I remember! It took us weeks to find a route through all of those bothersome islands. There were supposed to be mountains of gold locked up inside their middle."

"Never saw so much as a glittering speck," Thelred lamented. His chin fell to his chest — and the sudden jerk snapped the fisherman's needle from his string.

"Stop fidgeting," he grunted as he tied it on again.

"But we found something far better, didn't we?" Lysander said with a grin.

Jonathan — who'd very quickly insisted that *two* moral supporters were far better than one — swung up from his tankard in interest. "What was it?"

"The biggest cellar we've ever seen! Shelves upon shelves of dark, dusty bottles just waiting to be cracked." Thelred swooped an arm out to the side in a gesture that toppled him over — and broke the string again.

The fisherman cursed as he righted him. "If he wants it sealed properly, he's going to have to hold *still*."

"It'll all work out, I'm sure," Lysander said with an impatient wave. He smiled at his cousin's uncharacteristically silly grin. "Tell him what we did with it, Red."

"Stuffed as many bottles that would fit down our trousers and in our coat pockets, grabbed another armful apiece and ran like mad."

"What?" Jonathan looked more concerned now than when he'd been hanging upside down. "You left the rest behind? Why didn't you pack it all in your ship?"

Thelred leaned forward to answer — nearly popping the string again. But all at once, his face fell. He whipped around to Lysander, his brows bent in confusion. "Yeah, why didn't we?"

By this point, the captain looked close to bursting. His grin could've split into laughter at any moment. He propped a hand against his mouth and whispered loudly: "You were in prison."

"Because I was in prison," Thelred said, whipping back to Jonathan. He didn't seem to notice when the needle popped out of the fisherman's hand and *thwap*ed him in the side of the face.

Jonathan's brows rose high. "Really? What'd they lock you up for?"

"Fraternizing with a manager's daughter. He wasn't at all pleased to find her wrapped around a pirate — locked him away and swore he'd ship him off to Reginald the next morning for a swift execution."

"That was your fault," Thelred insisted, thrusting a finger at Lysander. "You were the one who spent half the night chasing that blasted woman."

"Yes, but *you* were the one who caught her," Lysander said with a wink.

Thelred's frown went slightly muddled, as if he wasn't sure whether or not he should actually be indignant. "Well, I only caught her because she threw herself at me."

"Women love him," Lysander explained with a loud whisper. "There must be something about a man with a scowl. I'll never understand it."

"It's the mystery of it all, mate. And I'm sure that hard-set jaw doesn't hurt things, either." Jonathan pinched Thelred's chin. He tried to swat the fiddler's hand away, but wound up knocking the fisherman aside, instead.

"If I have to tell you to hold still one more t —"

"If I hadn't caught her, she would've fallen off the roof!" Thelred shouted over the fisherman's rant.

"The roof?" Jonathan wagged his brows. "A bit of starlight, a summer's breeze. I don't know, mate — that sounds awfully romantic to me."

Thelred lunged for him. "It was *not* roman —!"

"Enough! I can't do anything while you're squirming about." The fisherman shoved him back and snapped his fingers at a passing wildwoman. "Come here and hold him still, will you? Don't let his head move an inch."

The wildwoman wore her red hair in a short braid across her shoulder, and her paint made it look like a monster's claw had scraped across her face. She paused — and gave Thelred a long look. "All right," she said finally.

Though he slurred his protests, the wildwoman sat behind him and pulled him straight against her chest. She kept one hand beneath his chin and wound the other through his hair.

"I don't need coddling," he grouched.

She smiled at his glare. "I'm not coddling you — this is how you hold a man when you mean to slit his throat." Her finger brushed along the ridges of his neck. "See? Just like this."

Thelred's glare sharpened. "Try anything like that, and I'll gut you, savage."

411

She laughed … and held him tighter.

Jonathan gaped at them from over his tankard. *What's happening?* he mouthed to Lysander.

"Magic," he said back, grinning as he shook his head. "Pure, untarnished magic."

At that moment, Gwen happened by. Her gaze narrowed upon the wildwoman. "Don't even think about it, Lydia. He's taken enough of a beating already."

"Yes, Warchief," she mumbled.

"I'm going to take a walk around the edge of the village," Gwen said, after another pointed glare at Lydia. "My wildmen should behave while I'm gone — if not, I'll clobber them when I get back."

"Mind if I come along with you, lass?" Shamus said, getting to his feet. "My legs could use a stretch. They've gone stiff."

Her brows rose for a moment — so slightly that he wasn't sure he'd actually seen it. Then they snapped back down. "Fine."

She set a brisk pace for the woods outside the village. Gwen walked like she had rocks sewn into the heels of her boots: they clomped so loudly that men several paces away moved aside, as if they'd thought she was right behind him.

Shamus didn't notice her being quiet until the noise of the village fell off. Then his ears began to ring. "Lovely night, isn't it?"

She frowned at the setting sun. "It's not night yet."

"All right — evening, then," Shamus amended. "What do you think of the seas?"

"It's hot."

"Aye, some days it is. But there's most always a cool wind blowing from somewhere — you've just got to know which way to turn your head."

"I'd rather have the cold all around me."

Shamus chuckled. "Well, the only way you're likely to find that around here is if you strip down to nothing."

"I'd planned to," she said smoothly. "Then you asked to come along."

Shamus couldn't tell if she was joking or not. Fortunately, Silas turned up before he had to think of something to say.

He swept out from the brush, wearing his lion skin and with a large rabbit clamped between his jaws. He dropped his kill at Gwen's boots. The rumbling in Silas's throat grew to a contented growl when she reached down to scratch his ears.

All at once, Silas's head turned and he slunk forward. He began pacing back and forth, eyes shining on the woods in front of them ... and there was suddenly nothing at all content about his growl.

After a moment, lights began popping up through the trees — faint little orange spots.

"Torchlight," Gwen muttered. She snapped her fingers sharply. "Get to the village — warn the others."

For half a moment, Shamus thought she'd been talking to him. Then a wildman dropped from the trees before him and broke into a soft-footed sprint down the road. "How long had he been up there?"

Gwen shrugged. "Never mind that. You ought to follow him."

Shamus wasn't going anywhere. He'd tried to keep it tucked back, because he knew they had a lot more to worry over than Copperdock — and Thelred swore the shipbuilders had made it to safety. But when he saw those torches flickering, his blood started to boil. "No lass, I'm staying put. If it's the monsters who set fire to my village, then I'll see them pay for it."

She rolled her eyes but said no more. Her hand twisted tightly about her axe.

The torches were still a ways off when Silas's growling broke into a roar. As startling as the noise was, the black figure that sprang from the brush was even more so. It dodged Silas's pounce and swiped the fall of Gwen's axe aside with its blade.

"Honestly, it's so easy. I don't know why you even bother," the figure said — after it'd somehow appeared behind Shamus.

He leapt back into Gwen, who didn't seem to notice. Her eyes scraped down the masked woman in front of them. "The hiding one," she said after a moment. Her axe went back into her belt. "Good to see you, Elena."

Shamus was still trying to swallow his heart. "You nearly scared us to death, lass! There's trouble coming our way, so you'd better get ready."

"Trouble?" Elena followed the tip of his sword to the glowing lights behind them. "Hmm, well I can tell you now that a sword isn't going to do you any good. She won't be stopped."

Elena drifted back into the shadows and Silas sprawled out at Gwen's feet, not so much as a line of concern upon his face. Shamus

413

was still trying to figure it all out when one of the torches broke away from the rest.

A thunder of hooves, a moment when the dark of the trees blocked everything, and then a familiar face came around the corner.

"Aerilyn?" Shamus called. She had her curls tied up and rode a dapple gray horse better than he'd ever expected her to. He wasn't sure it even *was* Aerilyn until she let loose with that unmistakable squeal.

"Shamus! Oh, it's so good to see you. I've been worried sick about you — about all of you." She slid from the horse's back and jumped into his arms, nearly winding him with the force.

"What are you doing all the way out here, lass? I thought you were supposed to be keeping the mansion held together."

"The mansion can hold itself," she said, easing from his chest. "There are things happening in the Kingdom — horrible things. We've come to help."

The horse didn't seem to notice the full-grown mountain lion sprawled in the middle of his path. In fact, he seemed more interested in a nearby patch of green than anything else. Even when Silas hissed at him, he did nothing more but flatten his ears and snort in reply. Then he plodded off to find his dinner.

"What a strange creature," Gwen murmured.

"You have no ... oh." Aerilyn's eyes went wide. She looked at Gwen in her strange paint and furs as if she was a griffin peeking its head from the clouds. "You must be the wildwoman."

"Gwen."

"I'm Aerilyn."

"Yes, I'd gathered as much," Gwen said with a slight smile. "Your captain hasn't stopped going on about you from the moment we joined him. I would've gladly kicked him overboard, had we not needed his skills."

"That sounds like him," Aerilyn agreed. "Where is he, by the w—?"

"Come on, dogs! Send those tinheads back to Midlan with cuts across their arses and blisters on their feet!"

Lysander and Jonathan burst from the undergrowth with their swords drawn and the tankards still in their hands. They roared as they crashed through, battle in their eyes. Thelred stumbled in behind him. His stitches were only half-finished and the needle dangled at the side of his head. A whole troop of pirates and wildmen bounded in behind them.

But they ground their heels when Lysander stopped short.

"Aerilyn?" he whispered, eyes wide.

Shamus could tell by how she glared that he ought to get out from between them. He stepped carefully aside — giving her a clean shot.

"Yes, Lysander. I'm here." Her eyes cut from his to the tankard he held out like a shield. "What is that?"

He quickly tossed the whole thing into the woods. "Ah, nothing."

"I thought we agreed you wouldn't stagger around like a drunkard anymore."

"Yes, well, I thought *we* agreed you were going to stay at home with our son."

"He's in excellent hands and perfectly safe — which is more than I can say for you."

Lysander licked his lips. He staggered backwards, eyes struggling to focus as Aerilyn stepped closer. "Now, now, I know you must be upset with me, but there's really no need to —"

"What in Kingdom's name is going on up there? We're nearly at the village. Why have we stopped?"

A rather large forest man bustled out from between the trees, took one look at the mess of pirates and wildmen scattered before him, and his wooden ladle froze mid-swing.

"This is my dear friend, Horatio," Aerilyn said, waving to him.

"Hello, mate!" Jonathan called cheerily.

"Oh, good lord," Horatio muttered. Then his dark eyes drifted across the others. "Are these your … ah, companions?"

"Yes. The men with red on their shirts are my pirates."

They cheered and swung their blades in greeting.

"The ones with painted faces are the wildmen."

They raised their weapons as well — and handily out-howled the pirates.

Aerilyn grinned at them before she turned her smile to Lysander. She wrapped her hands about his arm and dragged him forward. When she spoke, her words were a mix of exasperation and relief: "And this drunken, ragged mess of a man is my husband, Captain Lysander."

"Is he?" Horatio pursed his lips as his gaze cut down the length of him. "I practically raised this young woman. Did you know that?"

"Ah ..." Lysander squinted at him as if they stood a hundred miles apart. "No."

Horatio rolled his eyes. Then he snatched Lysander and pulled him under his arm. "Come with me — we're going to have a talk."

"All right. What sort of talk?"

"The talk her father would've had with you if he were still here to do it — the talk where I explain, in great and painful detail, what will happen to you if you ever treat my Aerilyn like anything less than the wonder she is."

"But I already think she's wonderf —"

"It doesn't matter. We're still going to talk."

"We'll save a tankard for you, mate," Jonathan called as Horatio dragged Lysander towards the village. His grin slipped into a serious look. "He's going to need one. The talk Brend gave me still burns my ears, when I think about it."

Aerilyn rolled her eyes at him. Behind her, a large mob of forest men clambered in. Some drove carts, others walked along on foot. They were dressed in well-worn, mismatched sets of armor.

"The village is straight through here, gentlemen. I'm sure the others will show you the way," Aerilyn said, waving them forward.

Shamus was more than a little impressed by how she handled them — and he was even more impressed by how many there were. "Where'd you find all these lads?"

Aerilyn shrugged. "It's a long story. But that's not important. Right now, we have to get ready. I have reason to believe that Countess D'Mere fled this way, and she's bringing all manner of trouble along with her."

"She was already here, lass. And *trouble* is the least of it. Come with me," Shamus said with a sigh. "I'll explain it all on the way."

CHAPTER 42
A MAD PLAN

Kael lost track of how long Kyleigh and His-Rua stayed inside the valley. Their *moment* stretched into hours, and then into days. He would climb to the top of the hills for a look each afternoon, when the sun shone into the valley.

And each time he saw them, Kyleigh and His-Rua had crept closer together — until they sat side-by-side, gazing at the bones of Dorcha.

He didn't know how much time they planned to spend in the valley: weeks, months, years — it no longer mattered. The rocks at Kael's feet were covered in half-finished plans. He'd scratched his thoughts into them, hoping that having the question written out might somehow reveal the answer. But the sketch he'd drawn of Midlan sat undefeated. The black dragon circled its courtyards, unchallenged. All of his ideas withered against its walls.

Though it should've crushed him to be so far from stopping Crevan, it didn't. In fact, he hardly felt it when his plans fell into ruin — for all of these worries were small compared to the thing that haunted him now.

Even if they saved the Kingdom and went on to live happily, it would only be for a short while. Kyleigh's life would stretch long after he'd gone. She might live in misery for a thousand years once he'd turned to dust, a slave to the love of the dragons — this *valtas* that they all seemed to think made their lives worth living.

But to Kael, it felt like a curse.

Perhaps there was a way to stop Midlan, but he couldn't pause to think of it. His mind turned back to Kyleigh at every few moments. There were ways a whisperer could live forever. His grandfather, Amos, was a powerful healer who'd managed to stretch his life over hundreds of years. But Kael didn't have a gift for healing.

His powers leaned towards craft — and though he'd managed to do some impossible things, it was only because he'd been able to convince himself that they *were* possible. Kael needed a reason to live forever. He had to convince himself, somehow.

But every time he started to think, his mind hit a wall. He remembered the warning Gwen had given him in the mountains:

You're the mutt who couldn't topple a tree because you thought its roots went too deep. What reason could you possibly find to convince your heart to beat forever?

That was precisely his problem. He could find no reason. The longer he thought about it, the more impossible it seemed. Kael might've very well gone mad brooding over it, had it not been for Rua's prattling.

The red dragon seemed quite taken with his own voice: he hardly stopped talking for a moment. If Kael tried to move away, Rua would simply reach out a little further until they touched again. Kael would've had to climb down the hill to avoid his reach — and even then, he still would've been well within range of his tail.

As long as he spoke normally, Kael could ignore him. It was when Rua began booming odd words into his thoughts that he reached his wit's end.

"All right, that's enough," he said, jerking his arm away.

Rua's claw screeched against the rock as he slid it against Kael's leg. *Enough what?*

"You know very well what. Stop yelling things in my head."

I like the way my voice sounds in this tongue. And in your head is the only way I can hear it. There are so many strange words — words I have not heard in ages. Listen, he took a deep breath, then boomed: *Fishmonger.*

Kael grit his teeth against the rattling of his ears. "What am I listening for, exactly?"

It is an odd word, is it not? He was quiet for a moment. *Battle! Now* there *is a word with fire.*

"No, fire's much quieter." Kael slid away again, determined to have a moment to think …

Buttercup! Rua's laugh crackled through the air and the hills shook when he slapped his tail against them. *Buttercup! What a silly noise that makes.*

Kael would've given anything to have even an ounce of magic in his hand. If ever a creature needed a good hexing, it was Rua.

Fortunately for him, Kyleigh and His-Rua returned before Kael could think up a way to clobber him through his scales. When Rua saw them coming, he quickly drew his arm away and filled the air with a crackling song.

Kael was just glad to see that Kyleigh's eyes were dry.

She ran to him the moment His-Rua set her down. He held her tightly while she kissed him and tried not to think about valtas, or the Kingdom — or any of the hundred worries that nagged at the back of his head. He wouldn't force her to endure his pain.

He didn't want her to have to carry him, not even for a moment.

"Is everything all right?" Kael said when she released him.

She frowned. "Of course it is."

"Well, I only ask because you seemed fairly upset —"

"It was just a shock, is all," Kyleigh said with a shrug. "I wasn't expecting to find a dragon's grave down there."

Not just any dragon's grave — *the grave of your soul and her mate*, Kael thought to himself. She was still trying to keep secrets from him. He pulled away before she could feel his frustration and turned to the dragons. "Is that it, then? Are we free to go?"

The whistle of His-Rua's voice rode the air lightly while she watched him — then her gaze sharpened upon Kyleigh.

"Yes. We're free to go," she translated.

But the way she glared back at the white dragon made Kael think there might've been a little more to it. He looked up at Rua — who suddenly seemed very interested in the pattern of the clouds. It was as if he *hadn't* just spent several days yelling things into Kael's head, or telling him everything he knew about the valtas.

"They're going to watch us from here and make sure we get on our way. I don't expect we'll ever come back," Kyleigh added. Her gaze swept across the rolling hills and jagged mountains one last time before she clapped him upon the shoulder. "Are you ready?"

No, he wasn't ready. The trouble in the Kingdom hung over him like a tempest. Its clouds bellowed and spat lightning onto his path. Its cold rain washed down his neck. But he knew there was no avoiding it.

"Yes. Let's go."

Kyleigh slipped into her dragon skin, and Kael tried to push the tempest aside as he climbed onto her back.

Make for the seas, halved one. Do not stop, do not turn. Our mercy is a gift ... it would be foolish to cast it aside.

Rua's warning came to him through Kyleigh's thoughts — softer than when he spoke directly, but somehow more menacing than before. Kael turned just enough to glance at the pair of dragons who crouched behind them. Rua had his mate tucked against his side, his eyes closed in content.

Kyleigh's wings rose and Kael held on tightly as her body lurched into the air. They flew for hardly a moment before Kyleigh's voice came inside his head: *What are we going to do about the Kingdom? Have you got a plan?*

No, he didn't have a plan. Kael scowled to keep his frustration from coming too close to the surface. He stared at the great mountain as they passed, wishing for its chill. The cave leered at him from between the crags. He thought its cold stare might take his mind off of things. He thought it might give him something else to ...

Wait a moment.

A memory woke as he gaped at the mountain. Voices rose in his head:

... our hatching grounds have gone cold ...

... now our Motherlands are empty.

... even if I told you where it was, you could never reach it. Rua's eyes blazed in his memory, pounding force behind his words. *The blade lies in the dark and the cold, forgotten ... along with all the other dead things.*

"Kyleigh?"

Yes?

"What if I told you the dragons had a powerful weapon — one that might end the war with Midlan?"

I'd say that couldn't possibly be true. Then, after you insisted that it *was* true, she added before he could retort, *I'd say we ought to ... borrow it, for a bit.*

The cave was coming closer. They were almost even with its mouth. "All right. But what if I told you it would be dangerous?"

How dangerous?

"Exceptionally so."

Well, I'd be a little less intrigued —

"And what if I told you that if we go to all this trouble, the weapon might not even be there?"

420

I'd say you were mad. Kyleigh sighed heavily. Her head turned so that he could just see the blazing edge of her eye. *But if you think it'll give us any chance at all against Crevan, I'm willing to try. It's not as if our odds could get any worse.*

Kael smiled — half in relief, and half to keep his throat from clamping down upon his next words: "Turn right. Head for the mountain."

Kyleigh's wings stuttered mid-beat. *The mountain?* No, we're still far too close to Rua. He'll tear us to pieces —

"No, he won't. There's a cave inside the rocks. Do you see it?"

She followed the line of his finger and groaned. *Kael —*

"Go!" he yelled, twisting to look behind him. Even from a distance, Rua's eyes stood out against the shadowed hills. They settled like daggers upon Kael's face —and he could feel the warning carved inside their every molten vein. "You have to go, Kyleigh! You have to go *now!*"

There was a considerable amount of defiance in her roar as she turned to glare at him — but her fury died in her throat when Rua snapped open his monstrous wings.

His warning ripped through the air the moment they pulled off-course. It echoed all around the hills and the crags, sharpening as His-Rua joined in. Kael could feel their fury on the back of his neck when Kyleigh landed. She plopped him none-too-gently upon the ground and shoved him towards the cave's mouth with her horns.

She pushed him through the darkness towards the back of the cave. When the walls grew too narrow, she had no choice but to get into her human skin. Her hands took the place of her horns and her yells cut against the rock as she forced him on.

Kael was still trying to adjust to the darkness. "Is this the right w —?"

"We've only got one way, and we'll follow it until it ends," Kyleigh snapped.

He stumbled under a thrust of her hands. "Being angry at me isn't going to solve anything —"

"Shut it and move! If we don't get out of this tunnel, we're ..." Her words trailed into an impressive string of swears.

"Wh —? Oof!" Kael bounced off the solid rock wall in front of him and into Kyleigh — who promptly shoved him back. "That isn't helpful!"

She pounded the meat of her fist against the wall with a furious snarl. "You'd better start digging, whisperer!"

Kael thought she might've been overreacting a bit. "Calm down, will you? They can't reach us in here."

"They won't have to."

The dangerous quiet in her voice unsettled him, and he went straight to work.

The rock bent like clay beneath his hands. If he concentrated on letting his vision soak into the wall's flesh, he found he could peel entire strips off at a time. But he'd only just started to make some ground when Rua's voice startled him.

It burst through the cave in a howling wind — one that filled the deepest corner of the mountain with heat and shook the grit from the walls. Kael knew by the way his song crashed through the tunnel that it was their final warning: come out or be destroyed.

Kyleigh pressed in behind him. "Hurry!"

"I'm trying!" Kael gasped. He scraped as fast as his mind would let him, but there seemed to be no end. His hands ripped through layer after layer of frozen earth. No matter how much of the rock he pushed aside, there was always more.

Rua's voice came again — quieter, this time. Kael thought that perhaps he'd given up when he heard a sharp, whistling reply.

"What are they saying?"

Kyleigh's hand twisted in the back of his shirt. "Well, I suppose the good news is they've decided not to torch us — they don't think fire will kill you."

Kael was almost too afraid to ask: "What's the bad?"

Before Kyleigh could answer, the cave rocked with a *boom*.

A giant's footsteps thudded against the cave: rhythmic quakes that came one after the other in a furious barrage. Kael remembered how Rua had shaken the hills with a slap of his tail just hours before. He had no doubt that was what the dragons were doing now.

They would beat their tails against the mountain until the cave collapsed — crushing them beneath it.

Kael had so much of his mind bent on digging that he couldn't brace himself in time: the tremors slammed his head against the wall and dragged him to his knees. Kyleigh jerked him up by the elbows and wedged her shoulder into his back.

"Keep digging — I'll hold you!"

With Kyleigh bracing him, Kael put every last ounce of his will into digging. His hands clawed their way through the rock as the cave shook fiercely. Kyleigh held one arm above them, trying to shield him from the bits of stone that broke from the ceiling. The cave moaned and trembled on in the space between blows.

Soon much larger rocks would fall — and not even Kyleigh would be able to stop them. But Kael didn't give up. He bared his teeth and moved the rock aside. He clung to his focus even as the world crumbled around him.

Finally, he made it through.

Kael lurched forward when his hand burst through the rock and into the open air beyond. "I see the other side!"

"So do I!" Kyleigh snapped back.

That wasn't exactly what he'd meant. But with the tunnel groaning the way it was, it was difficult to argue. "I'm almost there. Just a little more —"

"No time!"

Kyleigh wrapped her arms around his middle and threw herself against the wall, shattering the thin layer of rock that remained. Kael clenched his eyes shut as they fell into the darkness beyond — hoping they wouldn't fall far. By the time they struck the ground, the cave had collapsed with a thunderous moan.

Kael's stomach was lodged somewhere between his throat and his chest. He heard Kyleigh scramble to her feet beside him. She crouched over him, the worry on her face illuminated by a pale beam of light.

"Are you hurt?"

"I'm fine, I prom — ow!"

She punched him straight in the middle of the chest. "If I cared for you even an ounce less, I would kill you — you stupid, stubborn mountain boy!"

Kael tried not to move. If he so much as flinched, he thought her glare might very well melt his flesh. "I have a plan," he said defensively.

She swiped a hand around them. "Well, if your plan was to infuriate the dragons and get us stuck in the middle of a Fate-forsaken mountain, it worked. There'll be no wiggling our way out of this one. We've got a dagger fitted so far up our ..."

Her words trailed away and the anger on her face melted into surprise as she gaped at something behind him. "What is it?"

She reached absently for his hands and pulled him onto his feet, her eyes still fixed on what lay behind him. When Kael turned, he saw she had every right to be surprised.

They stood inside what had to be the heart of the mountain: an enormous cave that stretched to either end of Kael's vision. Its walls were smooth and glistening with damp. Smaller caves peppered their sides, and the shadows of their mouths looked like dragon scales.

Each layer of stone flowed into the other — cascading from the top to the floor like the swirls of a river's flesh. The walls and spires of Thanehold could've fit inside it quite comfortably. He didn't think his eyes would've been able to reach the ceiling at all, had it not been for the cracks.

Thin branches of light crisscrossed over the top of the ceiling and shed their rays into the chamber below. They shone like stars in the darkness, and covered the world beneath them in a blanket of ghostly light.

Kael dragged his eyes from the ceiling and saw that the cave's floor was covered in strange mounds. Most were about the size of a child, but some sat taller than Kael. The mounds lay like stones in a frozen river — smooth orbs with ripples breaking all around them. They were spaced a few man length's apart, and covered the floor from one end to the next.

Kyleigh was already kneeling before the closest mound: an orb that stretched the length of her torso. Her eyes closed as she pressed her ear against it. After a moment, she raised her head. "Cold," she whispered, her lips drawn taut.

Kael had been about to ask her what she meant. But when he came up beside her and saw the unmistakable shape of the mound, he figured it out for himself.

"Dragon's eggs," he whispered. He'd guessed these were the *hatching grounds* His-Dorcha had spoken about. But it still surprised him. He supposed he hadn't really ever expected to be standing inside of them.

Kyleigh seemed entranced by the eggs. She moved silently between them, her mouth parted in shock. "They need a tremendous amount of heat to hatch. Once they're laid, dragons carry them to someplace warm ... they come from miles and miles away, from every corner …" She kept one hand on the egg as her eyes swept around the room. Her other hand touched the floor. "I know what this is."

"You mean, you remember it?" Kael said carefully.

She shook her head. "Just dreams — just bits of things. But I've seen a place like this before, deep inside the Motlands. This was once a fire lake."

Kael remembered the story well. Kyleigh and the mots had once chased an army of trolls to their fiery deaths inside a molten lake. He'd had a difficult time believing such a thing could exist beneath the earth. But the ground in the Motherlands had always felt strangely warm. And when he pressed a hand against the blackened floor, he swore it didn't feel as cold as the rest.

"It's crusted over," he thought aloud. "Why haven't the dragons fixed it?"

Kyleigh pointed to the ceiling. "Even before it grew shut, that opening was much too small for a full-grown dragon. I'm sure they knew their hatching grounds were going cold, but they couldn't do anything to stop it."

Kael's gut twisted at those words. Part of him didn't think it was a bad thing that there were fewer dragons around. But part of him felt something else — an echo of what Kyleigh's dragon soul had said in her memories. He couldn't be sure, but he thought he might've seen a trace of that anguish in Kyleigh's stare for a moment. But just as suddenly as it'd appeared, it was gone.

She got to her feet. "All right, where's this weapon you were telling me about?"

"I'm not entirely sure, but it's got to be around here somewhere," Kael said carefully. He stepped away from her and began to weave a path through the eggs.

She followed closely. "Well, what does it look like?"

"It's, ah … small."

"What color is it?"

"I don't know. White, I think." With so many eggs lying about, casting shadows across the floor, he realized they could spend days hunting through the cavern without any luck. There had to be an easier way to find the sword. "Are you sure the dragons can't fit in here?"

"I'm almost certain. I don't think they'd simply let their hatching grounds go cold."

"Then how do they get the eggs in?"

Kyleigh pointed upwards. "They drop them. Their shells are hard as stone. Once they're grown, it still takes weeks of clawing for a hatchling to make its way out. I don't think an egg can even be cracked from the outside."

Kael focused on the largest gap of light in the ceiling and traced its rays down to the floor. If Rua had dropped Daybreak into the mountain, it would likely be around that spot. He nearly tripped over a half-submerged egg in his rush to get to the ray's end.

He searched along every brightened patch, between all of the surrounding eggs. He was certain the sword had fallen somewhere close. But the longer he searched, and the more empty ground he came across, the colder the room seemed to get.

What if he'd misunderstood?

... what if Rua had tricked him?

Soon the light turned brazen and began to fade into evening. Kyleigh was right: they were trapped. Even if Rua and His-Rua had flown away, they would be spotted the moment Kyleigh took to her wings. With so many dragons gathered at the red mountains, it was too much to hope that they wouldn't be spotted.

And he doubted if even Daybreak would be able to protect them from the ensuing swarm.

It had been a foolish thing, to drag Kyleigh here. He'd been so focused on defeating Crevan, on reaching the end of *something* that he hadn't paid attention to the step in front of him. They were about to go tumbling to their deaths, and it was entirely his faul —

"What's this?"

Kyleigh had her back turned to him, so he couldn't see what it was that she held. "What does it look like?"

Her hands dragged against something smooth. "Just some shoddy old sword —"

"Don't!" Kael leapt to his feet and grabbed her hands before she could draw the blade. She said something, but he couldn't hear her. He could barely even breathe.

From its rounded pommel across its charred grip, through the nicks in its belt and all along the cracks in its leather scabbard — this blade looked exactly like the one in Kyleigh and Rua's memories. There was no doubt the sword they'd found was Daybreak, the blade forged from a ray of the burning sun.

The sword of Sir Gorigan, himself.

CHAPTER 43
The Hatching Grounds

"Are you all right, Kael? You look as if you're about to faint."

Kyleigh waved a hand in front of his face, jarring him from his thoughts. "I might faint," he croaked. "I just very well might."

"I know we're not in the best of places, but we'll find a way out."

"Yes ... sure ..."

"Kael." She wrenched his head back by the roots of his hair, forcing him to meet her frown. "Why do I feel as if you aren't listening?"

He tried to pull himself out of his shock, but it was difficult. "I'm sorry, I just ... realized I'd never actually expected to find it."

Kyleigh followed his eyes to the sword and said incredulously. "Is this what you dragged us in here for? A crusted old sword? Brilliant."

He grabbed her wrists before she could toss it away. "No — it isn't just any sword. It's Daybreak. The blade of Sir Gorigan the Dragonslayer," he said when she raised a brow.

All at once, Kyleigh's face fell calm — a deadly, seething sort of calm. The air between them went still and when the last of Kael's words had echoed off its dampened walls, the cavern fell utterly silent.

"I'm going to do it, this time. I'm honestly going to kill you."

"But it's true — this is the sword of Sir Gorigan!"

"It's only a story! Sir Gorigan is nothing more than a character flitting across a few pages in your moth-eaten picture book."

Kael met her glare with one of his own. For a moment, he thought about telling her that he knew the truth: he knew that she'd carried Daybreak from her village and given it up to save the wolves. But the longer he watched her, the more he came to realize that her anger was ... real.

She didn't remember it. She didn't remember anything about Daybreak. But if he were to tell her what he knew, the memories might come back.

Kael still felt her sorrow. His memories of Ryane were as raw now as the day he'd first seen them. They'd left a piece of something inside his head, something sharp that ground against the backs of his eyes and stung them. Her agony was still there, lying in wait beneath the thinnest film of his resolve.

He couldn't do it. He couldn't tell her what he knew. He couldn't let Kyleigh remember that sorrow.

No, Ryane was a wound he would carry for her.

"Just trust me, will you?" he said at last.

"Let's see it, then." Kyleigh shoved the sword into his hands. "Draw it. I'm eager to see the blade that was forged from a ray of the sun."

Kael didn't think that was such a good idea. He remembered the way Daybreak had shone so brightly in the heart of the white city, how Kyleigh's dragon soul had feared it. He remembered when she'd drawn it in the forest and how, even at an arm's length, the heat singed her flesh.

He told himself he was only being careful. But in truth, he was more than a little afraid to draw it. "Look, I don't know if it's the real sword or not. Rua and I talked while you were in the valley. He said a bit too much — he mentioned there was a powerful weapon hidden inside the mountain. I thought if we could find it, then perhaps we might have a chance to save the Kingdom. That's all."

Kyleigh's glare slipped back. She wrapped a hand around his wrist. "I'm sorry. You were only trying to think of something, and it's not as if I've been much help."

"No, you're right. I did a stupid thing, trapping us here." He stared glumly at Daybreak as the realization crawled down his neck. "There's no way out. The moment the dragons see us, they'll swarm — and I don't think even the knight's blade will be able to stop them all."

Kyleigh took her hand away and crossed her arms over her chest. Her eyes swept the room; her brows furrowed together tightly. When she turned and began pacing away, Kael could hold his curiosity back no longer.

"What is it?"

429

"I'm thinking there might be a way out of here, after all. Stand back," she said before he could get too close. Then she drew up her hood, raised her leg, and brought her heel crashing into the floor.

Kael shielded his eyes against the burst of light as the floor cracked open. A blast of heat thickened the air and stole his breath. He nearly fell when Kyleigh stumbled into him.

"Fate, that's hot!" she gasped. There was a raw, red burn on the side of her face where the steam had cut beneath her hood. She touched it gingerly. "Perhaps that wasn't such a good idea."

Kael was far less calm. "It was a horrible idea! You knew there was fire under here. What in Kingdom's name were you trying to do? Burrow out?" Kael shoved Daybreak into her hands and went to work on her burn.

Kyleigh's eyes roved across the ceiling as he tried to drag a fresh layer of skin across the raw bits. "Well, stomping on it isn't going to work. But if we could think of a way to break the floor open, I bet some of these eggs would hatch." She pointed to one of the largest. "That one over there would likely bust open with just a spark —"

"Wait a moment — you *want* the eggs to hatch?" When she nodded, Kael lost what little was left of his patience. "Are you mad? You want *more* of these winged terrors chasing after us?"

She grabbed the sides of his face and brought him in close. "The dragons have been without their hatching grounds for hundreds of years. They have no young — their race is dying. They're broken and desperate. I swear to you that if they see even a wisp of flame come out the top of this mountain, they're going to forget all about us."

It was a good plan — better than anything Kael had thought of. But still, he worried. "Are you sure?"

"They would give up anything to have their young. A nest isn't complete without them."

He couldn't help but notice how her eyes tightened with those words, how the fires dulled and the glow slunk back. She let him go and looked away quickly, but the damage had already been done.

Kael couldn't give her a full nest ... but he could give her this.

He slung Daybreak's belt across her shoulder. "Here. Take this and get into one of those caves. I'll break the floors."

"You can't — the heat will melt you."

"No, it won't." He tugged her hood down over her eyes. "There aren't any gaps in *my* armor."

430

After a bit of a struggle, Kyleigh finally relented. He watched as she climbed effortlessly up the slick walls and into one of the caves. "It smells like fresh air," she insisted when Kael groaned about how narrow it was.

He just hoped she was right.

The crack Kyleigh's boot had left in the floor was so thin that he didn't think he would've been able to see it, had the cavern been any less dim. But the heat wafting from it was every bit as potent as a dragon's breath.

Kael donned his scaled armor, careful to imagine that it covered every inch of him, this time. He imagined that it swelled up to stretch over his clothes. He watched through his mind's eye as they draped across him like an oilskin. Once he was certain every thread of his clothes was covered, he went to work.

The craftsman held the armor in place while the warrior bolstered his strength. He crouched and brought his fist down upon the crack, cringing when it split open with a hiss of steam.

Kael held tightly to his concentration as he struck the ground again. When molten red and orange began gushing from the crack, he had to hold on even tighter. It took him several moments to get used to the fact that the fire didn't burn him. Once he was certain his armor would hold, he stopped worrying and focused.

For the first couple of strokes, things were difficult. He didn't seem to be gaining much ground. But he found that if he struck at an egg's base, its girth would crack the floor around it and send it splashing into the fiery lake. Sometimes a lucky hit would cause a large chunk of the floor to break — sending five or six eggs in all at once.

He worked his way around the center of the room quickly: starting a large ring and smashing his way inward. He was nearing the last few feet of crust when a strange sound caught his attention.

One of the eggs he'd freed was beginning to move. At nearly a full head and shoulders longer than a man, it was easily the largest egg he'd seen. While the other eggs bobbed contentedly inside the molten lake, this one had begun to squirm. It flipped from its top, onto its side, and back again — splashing Kael with waves of red and orange.

The egg kept knocking into him. Kael was about to give it a good shove when it started to glow.

Yellow light swelled within it — bursting, growing, fading back. Each time it glowed, the thousands of hairline cracks across its shell turned crimson. The yellow against the red was an astonishing sight. The bursts of light entranced him.

Kael couldn't help himself: he placed his hands against the glowing shell. He couldn't feel its texture through his armor, but he could feel the warmth. And then all at once, he felt something else.

Kael nearly jumped out of his skin when a hazy shadow scratched by his hands. It was a claw — one already the size of his head. A full, winged body had begun to take shape within the egg. It was a shadow suspended in a glowing world, hanging dully while the flames whipped between its horns.

Then all at once, it moved.

The dragon's body twisted; its wings stretched to fill the egg. A light flared up inside its middle — pulsing along with the egg's steady glow. Kael was so busy watching the light that he almost didn't hear it. But when he pressed his ear against the shell, he caught the faintest murmur of a sound:

Thud, thud ... thud, thud ... thud, thud ...

The sound grew louder and more furious by the second. Kael's heart began to race with it in time. He knew it was ridiculous. He shouldn't have been at all excited about the hatching of a creature that could easily kill him, if it turned.

But he couldn't help it.

"Kyleigh!" he gasped, searching through the rippling waves of heat to find her. "Kyleigh — I can hear it! It's moving!"

She grinned at him from her cave. "Why don't you say hello?"

When Kael looked back, the dragon's eyes were open — two orbs that glowed inside the shadow, two spots of yellow that burned brighter than the rest. They closed and opened as it stretched.

Kael rapped the egg gently. "Hello?"

The dragon's eyes flicked to where he'd knocked. Its head peeled back and slammed hard into Kael's hand, rolling the egg aside. He braced his shoulder against it and managed to flip the egg back over. He was waist-deep in fire, by now. But he was too focused on the dragon to worry over it.

A web of fresh cracks had appeared where the dragon's head smacked against the shell. Its eyes blinked slowly, began to close ...

432

Kael rapped on the shell again. "No, don't go to sleep. We need you to break open the ceiling, all right? You have to distract the others."

The dragon slammed against his hand again. More cracks bloomed where it struck. Kael led the dragon's charge around the shell, making sure it hit the weakest spots. The shell had begun to give way when he heard Kyleigh yelling at him.

The fire lake had come to life. Its waves knocked against the crusted floor, eggs broke free and dragged their companions down with them. What remained of the stone shores were disappearing at an alarming rate — and the heat swelled fast.

Kael left the dragon behind, hoping it would be able to break the rest of the shell on its own. He sloshed his way across the molten river towards Kyleigh. Bubbles swelled and burst across his face; the heat made the whole world ripple madly. It filled the cavern to its sealed top and packed into any space that would hold it — including the caves.

Kyleigh no longer waited at the entrance. Not being able to see her sent him into a run. He jumped onto the wall and yelled as he climbed: "Head for the outside! I'm right behind you!"

His hands moved surely and his arms carried him swiftly to the cave's mouth. The tunnel was so narrow he had to crawl on his hands and knees just to fit inside. Its walls choked him worse than the heat ever could. He hated the way they pressed against him, how they seemed insistent on crushing his limbs. Their coiling grip was closing around his throat —

"Kyleigh!"

He could see her body through the light of the fire lake. She was a little ways ahead of him, collapsed upon the tunnel floor. He yelled again, and she twisted her head around to look at him.

It was too small a space for her dragon shape — and without scales to protect her, the building heat was taking its toll.

Sweat poured from her face and her eyes were glassy with exhaustion. Wheezing breaths slid from between her swollen lips. "Go," she gasped.

"No, you're going to move!"

"I can't —"

"You can." It was only the knowing that one of them had to stay calm that kept him from screaming. Kyleigh was never weakened,

433

never hurting. When he saw her shriveled upon the floor, he wanted nothing more than to panic. But instead, he forced himself to breathe.

She'd gotten them through the mountain — and he was going to get them out.

Kael wedged his arms around her middle and hauled her onto her knees. He braced his shoulder against the backs of her legs and started to push.

He shoved her up the tunnel's floor, through the thick cloud of steam that billowed up as the heat struck its dampened flesh. Even as the walls closed in and the ceiling scraped across his back, he didn't panic. He wouldn't let his fears stop him.

Soon the tunnel came so close that they had to crawl upon their bellies. Kael moved along on one elbow and shoved Kyleigh with the other, forcing her up. Her pace slowed and her breathing grew more ragged.

"Kael ..."

"Keep going! We're nearly there."

"Kael, please —"

"No!"

A swell of anger filled his limbs the moment Kyleigh's gave out. He wasn't giving up. He wasn't going to let her die. Even if he had to give every last bit of his strength, he would do it. So he braced her boots against his shoulders and with a roar, he started to shove.

He inched his way up the tunnel, his feet scrabbling behind him. As his warrior half grew fiercer, the craftsman lost its grip. Cracks split all down his armor. Kael bared his teeth against the singeing heat and stubbornly forced air into his lungs.

They were nearly out. He thought he could feel a wind across his back. He fought on — shoving, scrambling, every toe digging into the rock to give him even an ounce more leverage. The walls were closing in; the heat had a strangling grip upon his chest.

They were nearly there. Nearly ...

He gasped when Kyleigh suddenly disappeared. For the half second it took him to scramble to the tunnel's end, he had no breath. But when he crawled out, he saw that she lay safely upon the ground.

Her chest heaved as she sucked in the cool evening air. Color sprang back into her cheeks. She swiped the dampened hair from her face as he helped her sit up.

"Are you all right?"

"I think so. I'll be better once I have this blasted thing off my neck." She pulled Daybreak from around her shoulders and handed it to him.

He threw it aside. "Just breathe."

"I *am* breathing."

"Well, you aren't breathing enough!"

"Kael," she wrapped her arms around his shoulders and buried her head against his neck, "it's over, now. We're out. I'm all right."

He held her tightly. "Do you swear?"

Her nose scraped up and down his neck with her nod. "I was just a little short of breath, is all. I'm sure the worst is … *move!*"

It happened quickly. One minute they were together and the next, she'd thrown him aside. Roars filled the air as Kael landed: Kyleigh's threat, a sharp reply — and a voice that shook the mountain.

Kael ripped his body around and his stomach lurched when he saw two white dragons go skittering down the mountain's side — claws flailing and their pointed fangs bared.

Kael forgot his pain. He leapt to his feet and his eyes found Daybreak. But before he could reach it, Rua's claw slammed into his chest.

Had his warrior half not already been coiled for the jump, the shock might've crushed him. Instead, Kael blinked the little black spots from his eyes to find that his body had been pinned to the mountain's side.

Rua's furious, blazing glare filled his vision; the crackling of his song matched the heated breath that spewed from his nostrils. Kael's arms were pinned at his sides. His entire body was stuck between a single wedge of Rua's claw.

And Daybreak lay far beneath him.

The red dragon bared his glistening teeth and for a moment, Kael thought he was about to snap off his head. But then a strangled growl from below twisted him away.

Kyleigh had won the fight. She crouched over His-Rua, the white dragon's serpent neck clamped between her jaws. She hadn't crushed down, yet. But by the way she growled around His-Rua's throat, Kael knew she meant to.

Rua's grip loosened and Kael nearly slipped out. But a strangled roar from His-Rua brought the pressure back. The white dragon's eyes blazed defiantly as they locked onto Kael's. She twisted in Kyleigh's grip and her song came out sharp.

Rua's head swung back. His voice shook Kael's innards; he pressed him more forcefully against the mountain, and it was all he could do to keep his ribs from snapping into halves.

But Kyleigh's grip had tightened, too.

Her fangs dug in so sharply now that His-Rua couldn't even sing. She clawed helplessly at the ground while her eyes rolled back.

Kael knew what she wanted, what she begged for with every strangled breath: His-Rua wanted them dead. It was what she'd always wanted, what she asked for even now as Kyleigh held her around the throat — and Rua would have done anything for her.

But if he harmed Kael, Kyleigh would rip His-Rua's throat from her scales.

"You know it isn't really what she wants — her fire's gotten the better of her." The dragon's ear cut towards Kael, but his eyes stayed locked upon his mate. "She's *angry*, Rua. You have to be strong for her. You have to carry her anger wisely, remember?"

The black slits in the middle of Rua's eyes went almost round with thought. But even then, his claw crushed down. It strangled Kael's words, pressed him to his limits. His legs went numb. None of his blood seemed to reach his head ...

All at once, a bright light cut through the dusk. It cast every shadow from Rua's spines and sent his head whirling around. Beneath them, His-Rua had frozen in Kyleigh's jaws. She seemed to hardly feel the pressure of her teeth.

When Kyleigh released her, she scrambled up the mountain to Rua's side.

Kael craned his neck back and saw a blast of fire spew from the mountain's top. Hardly a second after the fire abated, the land erupted in song. Voices of every note filled the air as a swarm of dragons came from Rua's lands. Even from miles away, Kael could see their wings were beating furiously, desperately. He imagined each burning stare was fixed upon the mountain's top, waiting breathlessly for the next wisp of fire.

And when it came, their voices swelled to match the fury of its light.

Shock lined the edges of Rua's face. His claw slid down the stone and to the cliff below. Kael barely managed to escape being crushed beneath it. No sooner had he gotten away from Rua than Kyleigh crashed into the rock beside him. He held onto her horns as she lifted him to where they'd been standing before.

Kael grabbed Daybreak from the ground and fastened the buckle around his waist. "We ought to get moving while they're distracted. If we hurry, we might be able to make it to the Kingdom by dawn."

Kyleigh wasn't listening. Her eyes were every bit as focused as the other dragons. Even after she'd slid back into her human skin, she stayed staring at the mountain.

Dragons landed all around them. They crashed into the cliffs as Kyleigh had done and dug in their claws, each beside his mate — every eye unblinking. Kael grabbed her around the arm. "We really ought to go."

"Please, just a moment."

"We don't have a moment! This could very well be our only chance ..."

Kael's words trailed away at the note of a tiny song. A faint hum trilled from the mountain's top, so small that it could've been lost inside a murmur of the wind. But the dragons answered it with such a burst of noise that there could be no mistaking what it was.

A little fledging clawed its way from the mountain's fire. Its wings were so thin that Kael could see through them; they flapped like sails in the breeze. The dragon raised its wings tentatively at first. But when it felt how the wind filled them, they burst open with another delighted trill of its song.

"A male," Kyleigh said, pointing to the dull gray of his scales. "When he sheds that first batch, he'll get his color."

The little dragon's wings rose and fell boldly, now. Kael had a difficult time looking away. "Well, I still think we're pushing our —"

"We're safer than we've ever been. A hatching is a time of peace. Come here." Kyleigh dragged him to a ledge of rock and made him sit. Then she sat behind him. She wrapped her arms around his middle and set her chin atop his shoulder. She sat so there wasn't so much as a breath of space between them.

And when Kael felt how her heart thudded against his back, he knew it would be impossible to pull away. "What happens now?"

"He'll fly to his parents."

"How does he know which ones they are?"

He felt her shrug. "They just ... know. It's an instinct, I suppose."

No sooner had she spoken than the little dragon took a daring leap from the mountain's top. His wings fluttered in the wind, his long tail whipped behind him. But he managed to land safely — directly before the glittering purple dragon and his mate.

"Corcra," Kyleigh whispered at the dragons' delighted song. "What a lucky fellow."

It was hard to ignore how her arms tightened with those words ... and harder still to ignore that brief pause of her heart.

CHAPTER 44
A NEW FIRE

It took less convincing than Kyleigh expected to get Kael to stay in the Motherlands one last night. The dragons clung to their hatching grounds as evening fell. They lay together along the cliffs and their great heads rose hopefully with every sputter of flame — waiting for the next egg to hatch.

"Staring at it isn't going to make them hatch any faster," Kael muttered.

Kyleigh hadn't realized that she'd been watching, as well. But when he spoke, she found her lungs were sore from holding their breath.

They were camped at the base of the mountain, beneath the heavy shelter of the trees. Kyleigh watched through a gap in the branches while Kael sat a few paces away, tending to the charred scabbard of his strange new sword. "I can't help but watch. It's exciting to see a hatching."

He raised his brows, and there was laughter in his eyes as he said: "Is it? I had no idea you were excited."

She threw a twig at him.

He swatted it away.

A swell of song drew her eyes back to the mountain, and her chest filled when a little dragon clawed his way out. His flight was clumsy. He glided for his parents and crashed directly into the middle of his father's orange chest — who didn't seem at all to mind it.

"What are they saying?"

Kael had crept in beside her while she watched. He sat so that their knees touched, his eyes still upon his work. There were dozens of voices drifting through the air, but she tried to concentrate on picking them apart:

"All of the hatchlings have been male so far — which Rua's thrilled about."

"I'll bet he is," Kael said, a trace of a smile in his voice. "He's probably hoping they'll grow up and take his daughters away."

That was *exactly* what he was hoping for. But Kyleigh knew it wouldn't be that simple. "He'll still put up a fight when they try to leave. Their mates will have to steal them away to keep from catching the barbed end of his tail."

"I see. And how will they steal them?"

"Wooing, mostly. They'll fly through Rua's land, perhaps lead him in a chase. The boldest might even breathe fire on his head."

Kael frowned. "That doesn't seem like a very decent way to get his approval."

Kyleigh tried not to roll her eyes. Seeking out approval from fathers was such a human thing to do. "The only one a male has to convince is his chosen. He'll taunt Rua to prove that he can protect her. Once she's convinced, she'll follow him out of her homelands."

"Then what?"

Kyleigh knew she shouldn't tease him, but he left himself so open to it that she couldn't help but prod. She looked away from the mountain and leaned against his side. Then she traced the line of his chin down his throat, across his shoulders, and murmured: "What do you think?"

She wasn't disappointed. The scarlet that spread across his face made her heart beat wildly. She grabbed his hands when he tried to cover his embarrassment and peeled them away.

"Stop it, Kyleigh!"

"Never," she growled.

He could've stopped her if he wanted to. They both knew he was stronger. But though his face burned, laughter muddled his yells. An involuntary grin made his glare much less menacing. He grappled with her for a moment before he shoved her back.

He peeled his breastplate away and hurled it aside; the sword landed with a *thunk* upon the grass. His hands curled into claws. "Don't make me pin you."

Excited bumps rose across Kyleigh's flesh as she threw herself into him. It'd been so long since he'd smiled like this, so long since he'd wanted to play. She wrestled his arms away and shoved into him with all of her strength, but he held.

"Give up, dragoness," he grunted.

This only made her blood run more furiously. "Never," she said again.

When she dragged her teeth across his ear, his surprise hit her like a wave: a swell of shock and warmth that crashed inside her middle and brought them both to the ground. His grip tightened when her lips slid across his chin. The swell that'd tipped them over was drawn back out to sea — replaced swiftly by flames.

They roared when she kissed him. Their fury drove her mad, made her press against him until there wasn't a single part of them that didn't touch. There was a wildness inside Kael that entranced her, made her forget about the rest of the world. It was an all-consuming storm that left her ragged and weak. Still, she couldn't help but be thrilled by its power ...

Slowly, something began to change. Kael's arms slipped from around her waist and fell to the ground beside him. The fires that'd been blazing so desperately before suddenly melted. Their wild tops sank into their bases and spread a strange warmth along the whirring paths of her blood.

There wasn't a place this new fire couldn't reach. When she felt it beginning to slide into the far corners of her soul, she pulled away. "What's wrong?"

"Nothing's wrong," he said. The pale reflection of the night sky fit so effortlessly against his features. She'd already torn his tunic away. The stars' bluish light drifted across his bare chest — not quite strong enough to chase the darkness from its rifts.

She was about to ask him if he was sure when she felt those strange, slow-burning flames again. They ran up her arm, across her shoulder, to her throat ... following the path of Kael's hand. As if he could sense the worry racing up her spine, his other hand was there. He chased her uncertainty away with a gentle touch.

The movement of his eyes was every bit as soothing as his hands. He took her in slowly, watched her face for any small hint of her enjoyment.

And it was difficult not to show it.

But when the fire crept deeper, when it slid to the edge of something she didn't quite understand, she shoved his hands away. She didn't know what this new feeling was — only that it frightened her. It was a new kind of love, one that threatened the borders of a wall she hadn't known was there.

441

Kyleigh couldn't stand it. She kissed him roughly, hoping to bring those familiar fires back ...

It was a mistake.

Kael had her by the lips, now. She could do nothing to stop the flames as they crawled down her chest and soaked into her blood. She moaned against them as they reached the edges of her soul, as they tested the strength of those towering walls. Their power frightened her. But she could do nothing to stop them.

A dragon rose from the depths of her heart. She carried with her all of the things she felt for Kael, all of the things she swore she would never say aloud. He was human, after all. And she was certain humans couldn't love like this.

Her love might overwhelm him. He wouldn't understand — it would be a burden to him, to know how deeply she felt. *That* was the thing that frightened her, the secret hidden behind the walls.

Still, Kael pressed — unaware of the monster he'd woken. The world turned as he rolled her gently onto her back. He lay down beside her. His lips never left. He slid one arm beneath her head and draped the other across her middle.

Kyleigh was defenseless. Her body had already betrayed her. It'd given in to his kisses, his touch ... her strength had melted in his hold a long while ago. Only her heart still beat defiantly. It thudded to life when he reached for her belt.

"Wait — let me." Her voice was every bit as weak as her limbs, and she hated that. Still, she was determined not to say the things she felt aloud.

He pulled her hand away. "Don't you trust me?"

With everything. There's no part of me I wouldn't place in your hands, the dragon in her murmured. But Kyleigh choked it back. "Yes."

It was painful, how slowly he moved. He could've worked the clasp in half a blink, if he wanted to. But Kael seemed insistent on making her wait. His eyes stayed fixed upon his work as he slid the belt free and lay Harbinger aside — and he might as well have been a thousand miles away.

The air felt bitterly cold without his touch, without his lips — without his eyes upon her. It was strange how the world could feel so cold while the fires inside her burned with an agonizing heat. They blazed until she could hardly stand it.

When Kael's lips came back, the world disappeared. Her last defense fell as he coaxed her heart into a hum. It sang for him in a way it'd never sung before ... and for a moment, she worried he might be able to hear it. But he conquered those worries, as well. Soon the only things she felt were his lips.

Beneath her was a nothingness without end.

Her eyes opened when he pulled away. She could see his face hovering just above hers. She wanted to reach for him, but her arms were too weak to move. No, she was totally and completely at his mercy.

And she knew what he wanted her to say.

"Kyleigh ..."

You can't, her fear moaned. But its cries faded into the darkness beyond, and Kyleigh lay suspended.

He said her name again, whispered it roughly in her ear. She could tell by how his voice broke that he wanted her to say it badly ... and she wanted that, too. Finally, she pushed her fears aside.

"I love you, Kael."

His face came closer. "How much?"

The words were out before she could stop them, bursting free with all the force of the dragon's wings: "More than the sun loves the dawn. You are my sky — my whole horizon."

The earth fell silent with a *whoosh*. Though Kyleigh felt her heart thudding inside her ears, all she could hear was the echo of the words that hung in the air between them. They held bits of her soul inside their letters, between their pauses and breaks. She felt as if she'd been pulled from her flesh and now lay trembling, exposed before Kael.

Once, she'd worried that her second shape would be the monster that drove him away. But now she feared it was this — these inhuman things she'd cried that probably sounded foolish to him. She knew they'd sounded foolish.

It was impossible to put the *valtas* into words.

The silence seemed to last an age. Kael's face twisted into a glare; his lips pulled back from his teeth. But just when she thought he was about to scold her, he gasped.

His head sank to her chest for a moment and he breathed like he'd been stabbed. Kyleigh reached for his face, her heart screaming about what a fool she'd been. "I'm sorry — I shouldn't have said it like that! Dragons feel differently about love, Kael. I don't expect you to ..."

Her words died. She'd managed to pry his head from her chest only to be frozen by his eyes:

Their walls were gone. They'd been stripped of their spines and all of the little lights within them shone unfettered. She'd caught glimpses of them before, flickering with his laugh, his thoughts. She loved the fact that they were hidden. She loved to guess the sort of things that might draw them out. But that was before she'd seen them like this.

His brows fell and his lips pulled back not in anger, but in desperation. Though the lights had broken free, he was still desperate to protect them. He guarded them as fiercely as she'd guarded her words — she understood this, now.

Kael had bared his soul to her, as well.

"No, dragons aren't the only ones who feel differently," he muttered, pressing against her hands. "I just can't say it as well as you."

Kyleigh knew it was time to give up another secret — one she'd planned to hold forever. "You say it well enough. You tell me every night when you think I've fallen asleep, even when you're cross with me. I listen for it," she added, smiling when his brows rose in surprise. "I can't sleep until I've heard you say you love me."

She kissed the red before it could stretch too far across his face ... and for a while, they spoke no more. The sky churned above them and the breeze stirred the forests' roof, but Kyleigh was oblivious to it all.

CHAPTER 45
BAIRD'S CURSED LETTER

There was no longer any doubting it. Kael woke the next morning with his heart already steeled against what needed to be done, against the fact that he stood upon the threshold of a final battle with Midlan — and aside from Kyleigh, he stood there alone.

A few weeks ago, this realization would've crushed him. He would've been a mass of nerves, a tangle of worry. But now ... well, he wasn't sure if it was the power of Daybreak, or the sheer ridiculousness of every dragon he'd encountered thus far. But for some reason, he couldn't bring himself to worry.

Kael was certain they would win.

He struggled out from beneath Kyleigh's iron grip and fumbled in the pale morning light for his clothes. The trousers went on stiffly. He tried to be quiet, but something in them kept crinkling each time he slid them an inch. He'd reached down to pull whatever it was out of his pocket when he suddenly remembered that it was the letter Baird had given him — and his hand froze.

He decided not to touch it. He couldn't risk falling to its whispercraft. The moment he had the chance to make a new set of trousers, he'd burn the old pair — and Baird's cursed letter along with it.

Kael's eyes were still too heavy to even think about donning his armor. It simply wasn't going to happen. Even after a couple of washings, his tunic was still covered in brownish spatter stains from the fight in the Valley. But it was the closest thing to a blanket he had to offer.

He stepped very lightly over to where Kyleigh slept — well, he supposed it was more like a *hobble* than steps. He had to hold his right leg out at such a ridiculous angle that he didn't think anybody could've possibly mistaken it for a walk.

But somehow, the letter still managed to crinkle.

With the tunic's buttons undone, it draped across her shoulders and past her knees. He moved fractions at a time as he covered her, careful not to breathe too loudly. He'd begun to creep away and had even allowed himself the faintest sigh of relief when Kyleigh muttered:

"What in Fate's name have you got in your pocket?"

"It's nothing — just something Baird gave me."

"Fitting." Kyleigh's eyes cracked open with a soft smile. "How did you sleep, whisperer?"

Like the night watched over them while the world stopped turning — like the stars sang to him while he dreamed. The feeling he'd had as his eyes closed was one of the ultimate calm. Had he never faced another dawn, his heart would've stopped peacefully: content in the knowing that it'd already struck a perfect beat ...

Blast it all. Even in his head, those words sounded completely ridiculous.

"I slept well enough," he said after a moment. "You?"

Her eyes blazed as she murmured: "Very well, indeed."

A pair of hums blasted across his ears, startling his eyes from her smile — otherwise, the morning might well have been lost.

Kael watched through the gap in the canopy above them as the moss-colored dragon fell from the high reaches of the clouds, his body tangled with his mate's. They formed a spiral of green and white, one that twisted with a terrible speed until it became nothing more than a blur.

Even from where he stood, Kael could hear the wind shrieking off their wings. They were falling too quickly; they screamed for the earth with a force that not even a dragon's scales could withstand. And for half a moment, he was certain they would be crushed.

Their wings opened and they blasted apart with mere feet to spare them from the forest's top. Their bodies tore in opposite directions, bending the trees back in their wake. When his mate took off towards the east, the moss-colored dragon followed with a loop and an earth-trembling roar.

Even after they'd gone, Kael's lungs were still frozen in shock. "What in Kingdom's name were they doing?"

"Playing," Kyleigh said.

He didn't understand her smile. "Well, there are safer ways to play. They could've been killed!"

446

She inclined her head. "Perhaps. But I've always thought that *love* is well worth a bit of danger." Her grin only widened at his bewildered look. "In fact, I think you may have … inspired them."

She nodded at the hole in the canopy — and with a horror that nearly made his skin burst into flame, Kael understood.

"Oh, no." He stared up, a part of him hoping she was wrong. But when he saw just how much of the sky was visible, he knew there was no way she could be. "Oh, for mercy's sake! Have they got nothing better to do than stare at us? And *you*," he snapped over Kyleigh's laughter, "you knew they were watching — and you didn't say a blasted thing! You didn't stop me! You just let me keep on —"

"I wouldn't have stopped you for the Kingdom, Kael the Wright," she growled, eyes blazing above her smile. "I don't care how many dragons were watching."

"Well, how many *were*…? Wait," He froze as her words sunk in. "Really?"

"Yes." In one fluid motion, she'd sprung from the ground and began striding towards him. Kyleigh slid the tunic across her shoulders — doing a button up for every step. When she stood before him, she brought her lips to his ear and whispered: "I didn't care if the skies fell or the earth split beneath us. If Fate herself had drifted down from the clouds, I would've told her to clear off. What do you think of that?"

"I think you're about to force me to ruin my own tunic," he managed to gasp.

When she kissed him, he felt her smile upon his lips.

Hello, humans.

Kael jumped back and swore when he saw they weren't alone: Rua and His-Rua watched from the edge of the clearing. Their great heads were stuck side-by-side, crammed beneath the branches of a tree.

Rua's eyes went straight to his — and Kael hoped to mercy he hadn't seen … anything. But the yellow flames danced so mischievously within his stare that he knew he'd seen a great deal more than that.

He pulled away from Kyleigh before the red dragon's hum could reach his ears. "Have you told that them we plan to leave?" he said, looking pointedly at the trees beside him.

His-Rua must've protested, because Kyleigh shook her head. "I'm afraid we can't. The Kingdom needs our help."

Rua's voice crackled next — his eyes all but burning a hole through the side of Kael's head.

"Someday, perhaps," Kyleigh answered him. "I think we'd like to come back."

"Provided they *all agree* to quit gawking at us every hour of the day and night," Kael muttered — earning himself one of Rua's tree-shaking chortles. An idea came to him suddenly. He moved his gaze to the branches above Rua's head. "Now that we're friends, I don't supposed they'd follow us into the Kingdom, would they? A swarm of dragons would make short work of Midlan."

They exchanged a long look before they hummed.

"It's too dangerous — the dragons have no defense against the power of the mages. They won't risk the lives they've only just gotten back," Kyleigh said, squinting as she tried to pull their voices apart. "But they've all agreed that you can keep the knight's sword."

"Well, I was going to keep it anyways."

"And Rua wants you to know that it's a *smolder* of dragons, not a swarm."

That couldn't possibly be right. Kael glanced down to say as much and quickly found himself trapped in the dancing fires of Rua's gaze.

The scales around his lips were bent into a smirk — and as Kael watched, one of his eyes closed in what could've only been a knowing wink.

****

They were near the shores of the Kingdom.

Kael couldn't see a thing through the fog, so he had no choice but to trust Kyleigh when she said they were close. The thrill he'd felt as they left the Motherlands was far behind him. It was lost somewhere among the ice of the northern seas — no more present a thing than the white mist beneath him.

Spring had begun to win the fight against the cold. Now the seas and the land sweated against the growing heat, their labor rising in a dense fog. As Kael watched, a thin, grayish line appeared across the horizon. He stared at the sky above that line, but the mountains never appeared.

We're going back a different way, Kyleigh explained when he asked. *I've been giving it some thought, and I think it's best if we cross over somewhere we haven't crossed before. And besides ... there's something I wish you to see.*

"What sort of something?" Kael said, not even bothering to hold his curiosity back.

A place that's always been very dear to me.

He was excited — until she dipped a little lower and he caught the unmistakable reek of a bog. When the tops of wide, drooping trees began to sprout above the mist, he knew exactly where they were headed.

"No, we've talked about this, Kyleigh. You aren't dumping me off at the swamps."

You're right. I'm not.

"Then why are we coming this way?"

I've already said it: because there's a place here I wish you to see. You're always wanting to know more about me, and this might be as good a time as —

Her words stopped abruptly. Every inch of her body tightened and her wings froze mid-beat. It happened before Kael even had a chance to breathe, a chance to blink: a furious red bolt shot out from among the drooping trees and struck Kyleigh hard.

Her head snapped back. She flung her neck and her body twisted as she roared — her voice sharp with pain.

Kael only caught a glimpse between her flailing wings: a red spell was wrapped around her throat, cooling into an iron collar. He flung himself over her shoulder with a howl, his eyes set upon the collar.

He'd managed to grab it when she ripped violently onto her back. In a half second he was hanging over the earth by the collar ...

Watching as the black dragon fell upon them.

His body struck Kyleigh's upraised claws with a noise like the sky splitting into two. Though Kael steeled himself the best he could, nothing could've prepared him for the force of the black dragon's strength. He jarred Kyleigh from his grasp and in a half-second more, Kael was falling.

There was nothing to save him, this time. Kyleigh grappled desperately against the black dragon's grip, against his jaws. He wrapped around her as if he meant to drive her back-first into the ground — and it woke Kael's strength with a roar.

The earth was rising; the wind screamed past his ears. But Kael shoved everything he saw aside and scrambled through his memories. His eyes fell upon something at last: the Scepter Stone of the giants. His hands remembered its unbreakable flesh. His mind swelled along the words of Declan's story, about how not even the mage's spells could break it.

And as he plummeted towards the earth, he convinced himself that it was the one thing in the Kingdom that might be able to withstand this fall.

His flesh hardened and the weight shot him to blurring speed. The wind's scream grew to a whistle; the armor snapped from his chest. Kael shut his eyes tightly as he neared the trees. He knew that if he looked, he might lose his grip — and he couldn't afford to doubt even for a breath.

Limbs snapped as he tore between them. He passed through the forest in an instant. An instant later, he struck the ground.

Black mud spewed up around him. It seeped into his mouth and nose. He sunk so deeply beneath its stinking folds that the swamp began to swallow him. He couldn't move, he couldn't breathe. In his panic, the craftsman lost its hold and the Stone broke from his flesh.

The warrior crawled blindly through the mud, casting it aside — scraping its way calmly to the surface even as his lungs screamed for air. Just when he thought he might be swallowed whole, his hands burst out into the open. With a final surge, he pulled himself free.

The air was so thick that it took him several moments to catch his breath. Kael pulled himself to his feet and sprinted through the stringy woods. His eyes were fixed upon the path ahead. He was certain Kyleigh and the black dragon had fallen that way.

He didn't have to go far.

A figure rose from the mist before him. He recognized its skull-like grin the moment the fog parted around its head. "Let her go, Ulric!" Kael roared, his fury carrying him to a greater speed. "If you want to die quickly, you'll bloody well *let her go!*"

Ulric only laughed.

Kael ripped Daybreak from its sheath and raised it overhead. Its heat roared dangerously through the air above him. He could feel it burning his scalp. But he never broke his stride. One blast of the sword's white-hot fire, and the archmage would be —

Gone.

Ulric was gone — lost in a blur that smeared the swamp aside. Kael's chest tightened as something tore the breath from his lungs. His neck might've snapped from his shoulders, had he not caught himself against the base of a tree.

In the second it took his body to strike the ground, he wished his head *had* snapped off. It would've been a mercy — it would've been better to die straight away than have his ribs shatter down one side. It would've been better to drown in the muck than to feel the warmth spilling down his chest, his leg, his middle.

Three gashes split him. They tore through his clothes and churned thick layers of his flesh aside. Blood wept from their maws in miserable, stinging lines. Through the haze that filmed his eyes and the pools inside his ears, Kael heard the rumble of a creature leaning towards him — and saw the merciless fires of its yellow glare.

Daybreak lay out of his reach, having been flung from his hand by the force of the black dragon's tail. He wasn't sure how he'd survived it, now that he could see the size of the claw falling towards him.

He bit his lip hard when the pressure of the dragon's claw woke his wounds with a scream. All the little bits of his ribs dug into his flesh. Blood rushed from the gashes in an alarming swell.

The muck was creeping in. His scales would do no good: the black dragon had already torn through them once. If Kael turned his flesh to stone, he knew he would drown — and judging by how the dragon watched him, that was *precisely* what he wanted.

For some reason, the fury in the dragon's eyes woke him. He forgot his pain and shoved back on the claw, meeting his roar with one of his own. There was nothing he could do to keep his body from sinking. But he would fight for as long as he had the breath.

With the mud rising and the darkness rushing in, Kael had one final thought — one crazed feeling that rose above the rest and made him grin against the dragon's rage:

He knew why Dorcha was angry.

"She isn't yours anymore." He gasped as he drew another breath, and his ribs stabbed his lungs. "In fact, she was *never* ... yours. She ... will always ... be *mine*."

It worked.

The dragon's eyes tightened. His claw curled as his limbs shook with fury — and the pressure rose from Kael's chest.

But just before he could snap it back down, the collar roared to life against his throat.

"Get away from that thing, beast. Go with the others — make sure the Dragongirl remains bound. I'll be close behind."

Dorcha fixed Kael with one final, seething look. As his collar raged, his eyes tightened again. His lips peeled back from his teeth in a taunt.

Kael didn't have to hear the meaning of his booming song to know what he must be thinking: *You can't have her if you're dead.*

Kael shut his eyes against the blast from Dorcha's wings, hoping to mercy that the tree above him would hold. It did ... but a moment after the dragon had gone, Ulric was upon him.

He crouched beside Kael and squinted at the mud coating his face. His dark stare roved across him, but he kept an arm's reach between them. The archmage seemed unwilling to get too close.

"Who are you?" he whispered, as if he spoke to himself. "A man who can survive a fall from the clouds, the bite of a dragon's tail, and who carries such a strange weapon," he added, gaze sliding over to where Daybreak hissed in the mud, "must surely be a man worth noting."

Kael said nothing. Even if his ribs *hadn't* been gouging him with every breath, even if he the world wasn't spinning from the loss of blood, he still wouldn't have replied.

Ulric deserved no answer.

At last, he sighed. "Very well. Then I suppose you'll die a nameless outlaw."

When he reached his arm out beside him, Kael saw that the mass of silver chains was gone. There were only three links left. Two sat calmly against his wrist.

The other glowed with a raging light.

Kyleigh ...

452

A stone rose from the earth at Ulric's bidding. It squelched as its roots were torn from the mud — revealing it to be thrice the size of a man's head.

Kael didn't know what Ulric meant to do with the stone. Whether he meant to press him slowly into the mud or simply crush his skull, it didn't matter. He knew he had only a precious few moments to think, to live. With his body broken the way it was, he couldn't move. He doubted he could even sit up, let alone run.

Still, he had to try.

Hot tears streamed down his face as he tried to roll aside. Fire burst from his shattered ribs and nearly strangled him with its fury. He tried to reach a vine that hung beside him, hoping he might be able to pull himself onto his feet. But the effort cost him too much. His strength collapsed before he could reach it. His hand fell to his side ...

And touched something that crinkled.

"Yes, I think this one's large enough," Ulric murmured, spinning the stone around in the air. "Which side do you want to strike you first, hmm? The smooth, or the jagged?"

Kael didn't answer. He fought against the darkness, against the shrieking of his gashes and the fire along his ribs. He plunged his hand into his pocket and tore the letter free. He kept his eyes fixed upon the twisting black dragon stamped into its back and turned its front to Ulric.

The archmage squinted at it. "What is ...?"

His voice died as his eyes scrolled across the words. He couldn't help but read them — he *had* to read them. Kael remembered the way they were drawn: with cuts and flourishes designed to entrance the eyes and pound its message into the back of the reader's skull.

Kael knew, as the stone fell and struck the ground beside him, that Ulric's ears must be ringing with a strange little voice:

Open this letter immediately.

He nearly tore the parchment in his rush to snatch it from Kael's grasp. His chest rose and fell with labored breaths and his hands shook as he broke the letter's seal. No sooner had his eyes scraped down the page than Ulric yelped.

"No! *No!* I'm already late!" He spun on his heel and vanished mid-sprint, disappearing into the woods with a *pop*.

Kael lay back in the silence that followed, trying to force his body to calm. He managed to slow his heart and learned to take shallow breaths. Every bit of his mind was focused on the next beat, the next breath. If he could ever conquer the pain, then he would have the strength to heal it.

But for now, he had to find some way to live.

Kael was so lost in his trance that the next time he opened his eyes, evening had begun to fall. The mist was gone and the swamp had come alive with the songs of creatures that loved the night. He tried to match his breathing with the pattern of their chirps and croaks — anything to take his mind from the pain.

He'd only just closed his eyes again when a pressure opened them.

It was a soft pressure: the weight of a shadow upon his head. Something dragged through his curls and he heard a hissing string of sharp breaths. Some creature had found him — no doubt drawn in by the scent of his blood.

No, Kael wasn't going to die like this. He'd managed to store up enough strength for one wild swing behind him.

His hand flung through the empty air, and the motion cost him dearly. A new rush of pain blurred his vision. His arm fell onto the ground above his head as he put everything he had left into staying conscious.

He wasn't ready for the feeling of a hand wrapping around his wrist, or the rumble of a familiar voice behind him:

"I warned you, Marked One," Graymange said, his words a growling whisper. "Did I not tell you that one day you would pay for your meddling? Well, it seems I was right." His grip tightened as he added: "That day has come."

CHAPTER 46
MEDDLING

Black patches covered his opened eyes — the thick gloss of his pain. Still, Kael knew there were voices all around him: he could hear them muttering in the darkness. He didn't understand what they said, and he didn't have the strength to ask them.

Graymange's hand was still wrapped around his wrist. More hands slipped beneath him. His wounds burned against the pressure as they lifted his body from the mud. His chest felt as if it collapsed, dragging him spine-first into a darkened pit. Though it tried to swallow him, Kael held onto its edge.

He wouldn't be dragged down. He wouldn't lose his grip.

Time passed strangely. The voices disappeared and soon the noises of the nighttime creatures were the only sounds he heard. All the while they traveled, the pressure of Graymange's hand kept him anchored to the light.

They tried to be gentle. Kael knew by how slowly the hands lowered him to the ground that they were trying desperately not to hurt him. But when his back touched the earth, it was all he could do to hold on.

A sharp flash of pain struck his chest. It'd swelled to the point that he'd begun to fear for his life when the burning suddenly gave way to a cool relief. The patches left his eyes slowly; they drifted back like frost melting from a window's face as the cold soothed him.

Graymange crouched beside him. He pressed what looked to be a hairy clump of moss into the gash on Kael's chest, muttering as he worked: "You remember him, don't you? Yes, this is the one ... *he* is the one responsible ..."

Responsible for what? Kael wondered. He didn't know what he could've possibly done to anger the wolf shaman — or if he was even angry at all, for that matter. The way Graymange growled through his words made it impossible to tell.

The longer he listened, the more confused he became.

"Yes, you have *him* to thank ... this is good, but I'll need more ... bring more ..."

When another batch of moss cooled the wound on his middle, Kael found the strength to utter a single word: "What ...?"

Graymange's muttering stopped. His head shot over Kael's, followed by a cluster of other faces. They ringed him so tightly that he couldn't see anything but their widened eyes — and their wild manes of red hair.

Mountain folk.

Kael gaped at them for several long moments, and the mountain folk gaped back. None of them uttered a single word. He was certain he'd never seen them before ...

And yet, their faces looked strangely ... familiar.

"Go," Graymange said to them, waving his hands in wild arcs. "Leave us for a moment. He cannot heal if you sit around and breathe all of his air. You will have your chance to meet him," he added, in response to what sounded like a low whine. "But for now, he needs quiet and rest."

The faces drifted away until only Graymange leaned over him. The moonlight paled his skin, but didn't seem able to chase the dark from his eyes. A wooden medallion hung from his chest, the body of a wolf scrawled into its face. Though the moon couldn't have possibly reached it, the medallion still glowed with a faint light.

Graymange stared for such a long, unblinking moment that Kael's skin began to crawl. Perhaps he *did* mean to kill him.

But he didn't care. One thought rose above his worries, blotting out all the rest: "Kyleigh," he whispered, and it was all he had the strength to say.

Graymange never twitched. "We could not reach her in time. She left with the King's shamans — a bargain for your life. Her fury will be great when she hears how you were beaten."

Kael didn't care a whit about his life, and Graymange must've seen it.

"Patience, Marked One. You must heal before you rise. If the shamans meant to kill her, they would not have bothered to chain her, I think," he added, eyes tightening upon Kael's glare. "No, this King is too fond of his prisons to simply destroy such a powerful creature. He will try to wrap her in his curse ... and it will undo him, before the end. Emberfang will vex him greatly."

456

His lips pulled back from his teeth in a gesture that would've been frightening, had Kael not recognized it as one of his peculiar grins.

The noise of trotting steps drew his eyes away. A creature bounded from the shadows and went straight to Graymange's side, a hairy clump of moss hanging from its jaws.

It was a dog — the scruffiest excuse for a dog that Kael had ever seen. His ears stood in points and his tail beat the air with exhausting speed as he dropped the moss into Graymange's hand.

"Thank you, child," he said, ruffling the scraggily fur between the dog's ears. "Go sit with the others."

"Others ...?" Kael twisted to watch as the dog trotted into the clump of mountain folk that waited beneath the branches of a tree. He stretched his paws before him and his leg behind him, growing into the form of a young man.

"Surely you remember them. They have not forgotten *you*," Graymange said when Kael shook his head. "They have not forgotten what you did for them."

Those words stirred something in the back of his mind, something that itched above the throb of his wounds. He'd seen mountain folk in the forest once before, what seemed like an age ago ...

And all at once, Kael remembered.

These were the villagers they'd rescued from Titus's grasp — the ones who'd been cursed and bound by the dragonsbane collars. He still remembered how they'd wailed for mercy. He still remembered how desperately they'd fought.

But he realized that he'd never expected to see them again. He thought they would simply flee into the wilds and become lost among the woods.

"They hid from us for a time," Graymange said quietly. "Newborns are always frightened by the change, at first. But it wasn't long before they began to seek us out. Each was drawn to the spirit of his shaman, lured by our tokens' songs. It felt odd at first, to have so many lives to watch over once more. And they are strange little creatures." His hands pressed down firmly and his voice grew rough as he added: "But they are *our* creatures, our little spirits. They bring such a light to our woods."

Kael lay quietly, trying to piece it all together. "These mountain people, these halfdogs ... you've taken them as your pack?"

"Yes."

"I thought you said they were Abomination?"

Graymange inclined his head. "A great change has come to our forest. These are strange times, the blooms of a summer I've not yet seen — and our world will only grow stranger, before the end. There is no longer any meaning of *Abomination* that I understand. Perhaps there is no Abomination left at all. But I do not fear this change. No," he whispered, "I welcome it."

He looked up when a second dog bounded from the woods: a floppy-eared giant with a thick, drooping face. The moss he dropped into Graymange's hand was quite a bit damper than the batch before.

But that didn't stop the wolf shaman from wrapping a thin arm around the dog's folds. He dragged his great body against his side. "I have never been more pleased to be wrong." He pressed his cheek against the dog's dripping snout, smiling to either ear. "This is not the face of Abomination. No, this is the happy smile of a friend."

"Well, I'm glad it all worked out," Kael said absently. He was feeling well enough that he thought he might be able to start working on his ribs. He felt down the shattered row to his belt — and realized with a jolt that his scabbard was empty. "You have to get my sword. The King can't find it."

"He won't. We've buried it well."

Graymange sounded rather pleased with himself, but Kael couldn't believe it. "You can't bury it! I need that sword — it's going to get lost!"

"We bury things so that they may be *found*, Marked One. A treasure may only be lost if it is left out in the open. Heal yourself," he growled over the top of Kael's protests. "It is important to us that you are healed."

"Why?"

"*Why?*" Graymange stared at him for a moment before he inched around to Kael's head.

The wolf shaman's hands lifted him gently, but Kael still ground his teeth against the pain. His eyes blurred for a moment, smearing the land around him. It was only when his body got used to the angle that his vision cleared.

And what he saw stole his breath.

They were near the banks of a river. He could see its flesh glittering in the moonlight. A small plot of land sat beyond the river — completely shadowed, save for the tree growing atop its middle.

Perhaps it was only a trick of the moon, but Kael swore the tree's bark shone with a stark white light. He hardly had a moment to wonder before his eyes were drawn to something else.

The dogs weren't alone. A horde of shapechangers filled the land between Kael and the tree. He recognized the hulking shoulders and hairy chest of the bear shaman immediately, sitting cross-legged among a gathering of badgers, and the snarling creatures that were a mix between wolf and bear.

The hawk shaman watched him from the trees, her legs dangling over oblivion. Eagles and magpies slept contently in the branches above her. A small clump of owls perched at her side, blinking their enormous eyes.

A lioness was draped atop the rocks to his left, surrounded by cats with mere tufts for tails and others with white, spotted fur. He wasn't sure *what* exactly was hidden inside the maw of a rotted tree: all he could see were dozens of glowing eyes, gathered around a pair that were set a little wider than the rest.

Not a one of them made so much as a sound. They stared at Kael with looks as open and welcoming as stone. He had no idea what they were thinking, or why they watched him so intently.

Then Graymange spoke:

"When our people were taken from us, we knew our stories had reached their ends. The shamans would drift through the forest like shadows, like wraiths. We would never again dwell in the company of our flocks and packs. We would wander and die alone — we were certain of this future, at peace with it, even. And all of these things would've come to pass … had it not been for your *meddling*.

"The Forsaken One changed our story, did he not?" Graymange turned his stare upon the others, listening as their feathers ruffled and their claws scraped through the dirt. "A strange thing happened to us when his shadow crossed our path. Now our flocks are full, our packs are whole. There are little lights in our forest once again."

Kael didn't breathe as the shamans stared him down. The swamps had gone so still that even the frogs stopped their croaking.

"Heal yourself, Marked One," Graymange said again, after a long moment of silence. "You must rise and march upon the King. You must free Emberfang from the curse. And we will stand at your side," he added with a growl. "The shapechangers owe you far more than our lives."

****

The room was growing darker even as the fire closed in. Crevan watched the shadows dance across the charred back of the hearth, his hands clenched against the voice that sputtered from their depths:

I'm going to teach you, Crevan. I'm going to show you how to —

"Your Majesty?"

He spun from the hearth. The air whipped across the cold film of sweat that'd formed upon his brow and sent a chill down his neck. But he forced it away.

There were far greater worries to be dealt with, a problem that kept growing despite his every attempt to quash it — a chill that he feared would quickly swell into a storm.

"What do you mean, they were *melted*?" Crevan snapped.

"I'm only telling you what I've heard." Jacob squinted at the beams across the ceiling for a moment, his head tilted to the side and his eyes distant. "The spy will be here shortly ... he says he's bringing proof."

Crevan didn't want *proof*. He wanted that little whelp dead.

The echo of his steps pounded against the throne room walls, bounced off the bricked-in faces of the windows. The pacing helped steady him. It helped keep the madness at bay, helped his mind to stay sharp.

There was no escaping the tales. The things that'd happened in the Valley resonated inside the ears of every creature trapped beneath Ulric's curse: an army of warriors that magic couldn't touch, led by a man who split bodies with his bare hands — the great and terrible voice that'd been the last sound of the battle.

The cursed seemed unable to forget it. They'd worried over it until their whispering drove Crevan mad. He ordered them all into silence — and for a moment, the castle had been still.

But soon the trouble in the Valley crept across its borders and into the greater realm. There was a force moving across the land that Crevan hadn't been expecting, a strange resistance he hadn't been able to stop: his army burned in Lakeshore, got crushed at the seas. Even the company stationed in Harborville had lost its grip.

Though this new battlemage, *Jacob*, proved strong enough to carry Ulric's chains, he came at a price. Crevan had lost some of his best mages — and a good number of his birds — in the battle to capture him.

But more disturbing than anything else, all of this seemed to happen without the Dragongirl's help. Up until a few days ago, she'd been hiding out of his reach. Then she crossed into the Kingdom precisely where Argon said she would — and her capture had been easy.

But when Ulric returned from the swamps, he brought a new tale with him ... and a letter that made Crevan's blood turn cold.

He'd burned it, of course. He'd ripped it from Ulric's hands and thrown it straight into the hearth. It was hours before the whispercraft wore off, hours before Ulric stopped blubbering about being late and told him of the young man who traveled with the Dragongirl: a mountain man who'd fallen from the clouds, survived a dragon's blow — a warrior who carried a strange, burning sword.

Crevan would not be shaken. He convinced himself that it must've been the *whispercraft* that muddled Ulric's head, that the mages in the Valley had been mistaken. Now that he had the Dragongirl in chains, the Kingdom was his. Nothing could stand in his path.

Still ... one tiny, scraping thought kept him awake.

Ulric seemed convinced that the young man would die from his wounds. But just to be certain, Crevan had sent a northern patrol to find him, to finish him. Once he saw that whelp's severed head, he could rest.

He refused to believe that his patrol had been *melted*.

While Crevan paced, Jacob stood unflinching before the throne. The blues of his eyes were dim and almost always squinched. His thin arms hung limply from his shoulders. There wasn't a thing about him that made Crevan think he was anything more than a sickly, bookish man. But he must've possessed some sort of power, because the chained impetus hadn't destroyed him.

It squirmed contentedly across his wrist; heat flared inside the silver as the creatures bound to its links began to wake. Jacob seemed to be listening intently to their voices. His lips moved along their words ...

Crevan stopped. There was a distinct pattern in the motion of Jacob's mouth. He wasn't *listening* to the cursed — no, he was speaking. He was saying the same thing over and over again. After a moment of watching, Crevan recognized the words:

The burning sword ... the burning sword ... the burning —

"Stop!"

Jacob leapt back at Crevan's shout. The chains burst into an angry, fiery red. He clutched his wrist to his chest, gasping: "He's here."

For one heart-stopping moment, the madness consumed him. It made him fear the worst. Crevan ripped his sword from its sheath and swung it at the man coming through the open door — stopping a mere inch from his throat.

It was a steward. He was short and had a blemish that looked a bit like an inkblot growing just above his upper lip. He kept his hands tucked behind his back as he spoke. "Forgive me, Your Majesty. But you *did* tell me — in the strictest confidence — that I should come straight in the moment your scout arrived."

The steward stepped to the side before Crevan could remember saying any of that, making room for one of the birds to crawl through.

It was half crow and half man — a monster with skin swollen around clumps of glossy black feathers. Sharp bones poked out from its overgrown nose and chin. The growth had so taxed its features that its face seemed lopsided, with one of its shining black eyes perched high above the other. But more unsettling than all of that were the monster's wounds.

Its bare spots were covered in a patchwork of scratches and scrapes — and there were far more bare patches than there'd been before.

The crow monster hobbled by, moving with its wings and talons in a way that reminded Crevan of a spider crawling across the floor. "What happened?" He blanched at a spot between the monster's shoulders, where some of its feathers had been torn away — leaving three weeping holes behind.

The crow went straight to Jacob. It filled the room with its shrieks and caws.

"He'd only just landed in the woods when he was set upon by a pack of animals."

"Wolves?"

"Among other things," Jacob said with a nod. He listened as the crow shrieked again. "Cats ... badgers ... a bear and a fox —"

"I don't need to know about every blasted animal," Crevan said through his teeth. Even as he glared, his fists began to shake. "What about my patrol?"

"He found their bodies in the swamps. Their armor was melted where it'd been hewn, and their bones were charred black," Jacob said flatly, as if it was no more interesting a thing than the passing of a cloud.

The steward stepped forward. "Perhaps seeing it for yourself will help, Your Majesty. The crow was carrying this in his talons, when he returned."

The steward brought his hands out from behind his back and held them towards Crevan. It was the front of a breastplate — and it had indeed been melted. There was an unmistakable weld across its middle, where its bottom half had been cut away.

The oddest thing about it though was the fact that the black dragon was gone from its front. The crest had been smeared into the metal until it resembled nothing more than a blob ... and scrawled through the black was a crest he'd hoped to never see again:

An eye with three interlocking triangles at its base, three triangles fanning from its top, and one triangle directly in the center.

The symbol of the Wright.

CHAPTER 47
THE BATTLE BEGINS

The fortress of Midlan was a beast without equal. Its eight outer walls towered above the trees, each one stretching the full length of a village. They tore from the ground with indisputable might.

Elena led Braver to the crest of a hill, her jaw dropping further with his every plodding step. The falling sun set the western wall aflame. The light that bounced off its unblemished surface made it glow. For now, the land before her was perfectly illuminated by the glint of the wall.

But when the sun rose, she thought the shadow the wall cast might reach back to touch the Grandforest.

"Well, here we are," Aerilyn said weakly. Her hand moved to grasp the top of Elena's arm — as if that was the one thing keeping her from tumbling out of the saddle. "It's quite ... enormous."

Elena had to swallow the panicked lump in her throat before she could mutter: "Well, what did you expect?"

The truth was that she had no idea what to expect. She had no idea what they were doing.

The news of the Countess's death had shocked her for a few days. There'd been so many strange feelings swirling inside her heart that she wasn't sure how to manage them — and it'd made it difficult to pay attention to her companions' many arguments.

Gwen was desperate to find the Wright — for reasons she refused to tell them. Shamus was furious about his village, and the mercenaries they'd brought from the Grandforest were spoiling for a fight. When their stories came together, they realized a good portion of the King's army had already been destroyed.

But they never would've thought of sacking Midlan, had it not been for Captain Lysander.

"The King is weakened. If we part ways now, Midlan will only turn up at our doors again — stronger and more furious than before. We won't get a better chance to stop Crevan. There might not ever be such a force gathered together again. And if you want to find Kael," he'd added, when Gwen started to protest, "I assure you this is the only way to do it. Without the threat of Midlan, Kyleigh will have no reason to run. She'll come back to us, as she always does — and I'll bet my sword that she'll bring the Wright with her."

He'd passed one of his charming smiles around the men, stoking them into cheers. But Aerilyn seemed far from convinced.

"Wait a moment, aren't all of you forgetting something? The King has a *dragon*," she'd said, rolling her eyes in exasperation at their looks. "No matter how many of us there are, we'll still burn just as —"

"You worry about the soldiers," Gwen cut in. She'd raised her golden axe and added with a smirk to the wildmen: "Let *us* handle the dragon."

There'd been so much howling after she spoke that anyone who might've had doubts couldn't squeeze them in edgewise. And so they'd packed their camp and sailed up the coast to Midlan.

"I'm not sure what I expected," Aerilyn said, still gaping at the walls. "I suppose it makes sense that the King would live somewhere so grand —"

"And un-scalable, *and* completely packed with tinheads," Elena added, squinting at the telltale glints of armor coming from the ramparts. They were in a rush to get somewhere — the southwestern wall, by the looks of it. "I'm beginning to doubt all of this. I'm beginning to doubt it very seriously."

"Haven't you been to Midlan before?"

"No. The Countess would never let me. She was afraid Crevan might figure out what I was, and then he would've killed me."

Aerilyn's grip twisted. "At least we have the whisperers."

"The same whisperers who somehow managed to sink one of our boats while playing a *friendly* game of cards? I don't know if they improve our chances."

"I'm sure there's more to the story," Aerilyn insisted.

Elena didn't doubt it, but she also didn't care. All she knew was that the second half of their trip had been considerably more cramped than the first.

Their companions marched nearly half a mile behind them — a strange army made of pirates and mercenaries, with the wildmen and some fishermen from Harborville scattered in between. They'd begun their journey at the shores and seemed to add another few dozen men to their ranks in every village they passed.

But numbers alone wouldn't be enough to win a fight with Midlan. Their army had swelled to the point that no one knew exactly what it was, or who was in charge of it all. Elena had begun to suspect that half of the new men didn't even know what they were fighting for.

"I don't like our chances," she said again.

"Well, there'll be plenty of time to worry about that later." Aerilyn waved a hand at the wall. "How many are there?"

"Too many."

"Lysander sent us ahead to scout," Aerilyn said sharply. "And if we're going to ride out all this way, then we might as well return with something helpful."

"He sent *me* to scout. You just insisted on coming along. There are so many that I bet they could have the walls dressed with our innards by nightfall — if they were to start right away," she added, smiling at Aerilyn's gasp. "If they took the time to *kill* us before they split us open, then it might be closer to midnight."

"If you aren't going to take this seriously —"

"Shhh! Shut it." Elena reached back and clamped a hand over Aerilyn's mouth, listening intently.

There was a noise coming from the forest on their right — the thick crop of trees that faced the southwestern wall. The noise was too distant to make out what it was, but it'd certainly caught Midlan's attention. A large number of soldiers were clustered against the ramparts' edge. Their armor glinted as they began to squirm, jostling for position.

Something was about to happen. Elena could feel it.

She turned Braver and kicked him into a gallop for the trees. They'd just managed to slip beneath a thick canopy of an oak when she heard it: the sound of shrieks and caws, the furious beating of wings.

A cloud of birds erupted from behind Midlan's towers — hideous monsters that twisted the forms of men with hawks and crows. They rose like the crest of a wave and swooped down, sailing in an arrow's head for the trees. Their wave spun into a circle when they reached the forest's heart. They swarmed above its middle, moving steadily towards the open field that led to Midlan.

"Have they seen us?" Aerilyn squeaked.

466

Elena shook her head. "They've got their eyes on something over there. I don't know what it is," she added, before Aerilyn could ask, "but I expect we'll find out in a moment."

Whatever it was would do well to stay in the trees: the branches clumped together so tight and thick that none of the monsters would risk crashing through it. But the second their prey came out into the open ...

Well, that would be a different matter.

They'd been remarkably lucky not to be seen. Elena was about to turn them away when the noises in the woods began to grow. They were coming closer. Soon she could hear the rattle of armor and some deep, panting breaths.

Above all the noise rose a panicked scream: "Open the gates! They're at our heels — we can't last much longer! *Open the bloody gates!*"

But for all the shrieking, the soldiers upon the ramparts never moved. The gates stayed sealed. And soon the man's cry was overcome by something else: an army of footsteps so heavy that they beat thunder from the earth.

The screams grew louder; the thunder swelled. The cloud of birds moved hungrily for the forest's edge. Braver pawed at the earth and his breath blew from his nostrils in a heated stream. Elena wasn't sure if it was the noise that froze her, or the ferocity of Aerilyn's grip.

All at once, soldiers burst from the trees.

It was the ragged remains of a Midlan patrol — a handful of tinheads with holes in their armor and brambles stuck to their trousers. The men who trailed at the rear bore heavy gashes upon their backs. Elena could practically smell the blood wafting from their wounds.

The soldiers at the head shoved each other as they ran, each one desperate to reach the gates; the men at the rear hobbled with their helmets twisted behind them. But it was too late.

Their hunters had already closed the gap.

A man burst from the thicket hardly a pace behind the last soldier. The bellow that tore from his chest matched the thunder of his legs. His thick limbs shone with a layer of blood.

The monstrous scythe he carried made short work of the trailing soldiers. His steps were heavy and sure, his blade hissed through their blood and bones in a deadly stream of attacks. Their bodies had barely crumpled into the grass before he took off after the rest.

"Declan!" When more giants erupted from the forest, Aerilyn's voice rose to a scream. "No, stop — go back! There are birds! There are *birds*!"

But the giants didn't seem able to hear her over their battle cries. The monsters waited until the first few ranks had charged out from the trees before they descended.

Crows swarmed, tearing with their beaks and claws. The hawks fell in streaks from the clouds. Some of the giants managed to raise their scythes in time to skewer them. Others were crushed.

Aerilyn shook Elena hard by the shoulders. "We have to help them!"

"We'd be flattened before we could do any good. Once they turn back for the forest, they'll be safe. I'm sure they'll turn at any moment."

A moment passed, and the giants still hadn't turned. Some of the crows landed at the edge of the trees, using their massive bodies to cut the giants off from safety. They moved in blinks — darting away from the scythes while lashing out with their taloned feet. Above them, the hawks swooped down upon the giants and batted them mercilessly with their wings.

One of the crows struck with such force that its claws punched through a giant's breastplate. It panicked for a moment, thrashing its wings and stumbling the poor giant in every direction. The fall of a scythe put an end to its flails.

A giant who was a little slighter than the rest ripped its talons free and pulled his rattled companion onto his feet. "Fall back, you clods! Into the trees!" Brend bellowed.

The giants swarmed in around him and tried to shove the crows aside, but the moment their attention was turned elsewhere, the hawks gathered for a plunge. Aerilyn screamed again; the giants didn't hear her. Just when it looked as if they would be crushed, a line of spear-toting warriors lunged from the woods.

They were clad in blood-red silk adorned with silver mail, and stood at the height of children. The warriors darted forward in a perfect line and thrust their spears as high as they could reach — jabbing the crows in the feathery smalls of their backs.

They screeched in pain, and the giants fell upon them. Their weapons swept across the monsters' necks and split their twisted heads down their middles. The hawks pulled out of their dives with terrified screams.

Though nearly all of the little warriors fell in with the giants' retreat, one woman fought against the tide to the open field. Elena recognized her singsong voice immediately:

"No, you must turn back! You are going too near to the castle! They will — let me go!" Nadine cried when Brend scooped her over his shoulder. "He must be stopped!"

"Let me handle the stopping, wee thing," he grunted.

Nadine flailed madly, cursing in her strange tongue. But she couldn't escape. Brend handed her off to one of the giants and set out towards the field.

The hawks had given up on their prey and had instead turned their wicked yellow eyes upon Declan. He slashed his way through the patrol's remains, oblivious to the screeching of the swarm about to fall upon him.

"Don't just stand there — *move!*"

Aerilyn kicked her heels into Braver's side, shooting them out from under the trees and in the open field. His stocky legs beat the ground as he charged for the soldiers' flank. Elena felt the weight of eyes upon them and knew they'd caught the hawks' attention. When one of their shadows darkened the sky, she gripped the reins tightly.

"Hold on!"

Braver's powerful legs turned at her command. His hooves left gashes in the earth as he cut to the side — narrowly escaping the grasp of an enormous set of claws. Elena's eyes blurred and her hair whipped back from her face as the hawk *whoosh*ed past them.

Another came at them from the front. She watched its horrible, blackened eyes grow closer. One of her hands went to her bandolier while the other gripped the reins. She held their charge until the last possible moment.

When Braver tore to the right, Elena made her throw. Dirt lashed them in a stinging wave as the hawk's enormous body crashed into the ground beside them, a knife hanging from its throat.

They wove through the hawks' attack, moving ever closer to Declan. He'd finished the last of the soldiers and was now charging towards the castle walls. Braver turned and went into a straight sprint. If they didn't break pace, they might be able to cut him off before he came within range of Midlan's bows.

They were still several yards away when Elena caught something out of the corner of her eye: a flare of purple light growing upon the ramparts. Strange words filled the air, stoking the light to a blaze.

"Mage!" Elena gasped behind her. She wrenched Braver to the left, cutting him steeply towards the castle wall. "Get ready," she roared.

Aerilyn had already begun to move. She leaned forward and lodged her heels across Elena's ankles, wedging them in to keep from being jostled off the saddle. There was some rattling as she freed her bow and pulled an arrow from its quiver.

Midlan's archers stepped eagerly up to the walls, every bow drawn and waiting for Braver to come within their range. Elena knew they would only be able to survive for a moment. Once they crossed that line, a hail of arrows would fall upon their heads.

At the ramparts, the light was about to burst free.

"I'm ready!"

"You've got one shot —"

"I know!"

"Then don't bloody miss!"

"I'm *not!*"

Elena flinched as the bow's string twanged beside her ear and the arrow shot away. She ripped Braver to the side when Midlan's archers fired, and sent him into a headlong sprint for Declan — her teeth bared against the hissing swarm of bolts that thudded into the ground behind them.

Aerilyn missed.

Elena turned in time to see the arrow strike the wall beneath the mage's feet. The force of the explosion knocked him backwards. It shattered the wall and set his robes aflame. The mage toppled into the courtyard, screaming as the fire engulfed his body. He managed to hold onto the purple spell as he plummeted down.

But when he reached the bottom, he must've lost his grip.

A second explosion cracked through the air behind them — a purple burst that shook the ground and sent the archers upon the ramparts soaring into the field. Their bodies sprayed out like foam across a ship's bow and crunched into the grass. The walls swelled outwards beneath the force of the spell. A web of fissures raced across the stone and mortar. But remarkably, it held.

The noise terrified the hawks. They stopped their attack and scrambled off in every direction, like ducks from a stone. Braver's eyes rolled back and Elena held on tightly as he broke into a jagged run for the trees. But at least they'd managed to stop Declan.

His crazed roaring ceased as the earth shook. The black seemed about to leave his eyes when Brend tackled him from behind.

"Calm yourself, you great silly midget!"

When Declan continued to struggle, Brend grabbed a fistful of dirt off the ground and flung it into his face. The black left his eyes immediately, widening into confused portals of stony gray.

"What —?"

"No, never you mind about what's happening behind us," Brend said as he dragged Declan to his feet. "Just keep your eyes straight and your feet facing the trees. Go on, now — don't make me tie you up!"

Brend shoved Declan ahead of him, using his shoulders to block Midlan's walls from his sight. Elena kept Braver trotting behind the giants' jog.

They were near the forest when Brend twisted to look back at them. A grin split his wide face when Aerilyn waved. "That was a good shot, wee lass — a *mightily* good shot."

Elena could practically feel the heat from her blush as she replied: "Yes, well, I have my moments."

"And what a grand moment it was."

They found the giants and the mots a little ways into a thicket. It wasn't difficult: all they had to do was follow the crushed earth and the noise of Nadine's indignant yells.

"Put me on my feet! I cannot help if I am dangling off the ground."

"You couldn't help with your feet *on* the ground, wee mote," Declan grunted.

She cried out at the sight of him. Her legs were already spinning when the giant set her down. Nadine charged up to Declan so zealously that it looked as if she might fling herself into his chest. But at the last moment, she pulled to a stop.

"You are filthy."

"Yeh, I know it. I'll go wash."

She touched his arm as he passed and watched as he thudded away — which made it easy for Elena to slip up behind her. "What in Kingdom's name are you doing in Midlan?"

Nadine didn't hesitate for a moment to throw herself into Elena's chest. "Where have you come from? You are always turning up to surprise me."

Most people annoyed her with their touch. But Nadine's embrace was always warm, her arms wrapped in a way that was more comforting than tight. She seemed to understand that Elena didn't like to be touched — but she also didn't care.

It was a strangely ... endearing, trait.

"I can't help that our paths keep crossing. It seems as if we've had the same ridiculous idea." Elena looked over the top of Nadine's head. Her heart searched hopefully and her eyes strained to see, even as her stomach twisted with dread. The moment she thought of asking, her lips sealed tight.

Luckily, Aerilyn asked it for her. "Is Jake not with you? I expected to see Midlan burst into flame at any moment."

Nadine's dark eyes lost their light suddenly, and her smile faded back. "No. I thought ... I thought your coming here meant that you had heard."

"Heard what?" Aerilyn said.

Elena froze. Every drop of her blood ground to a halt inside her veins. She read the answer in Nadine's eyes long before she spoke, long before she pulled the cracked spectacles from her pocket and placed them in her hand.

But she held on desperately to the moment. It wasn't until her words struck that the world came crashing down.

"Jake has been taken from us. He is being held in Midlan."

CHAPTER 48
ANOTHER HORIZON

There were windows set high into the walls above her. The warmth spilling in through their faces was a welcome relief from the cold stone on her back. Kyleigh kept her eyes shut tightly as the last of the fire left her bones — her mind fixed upon a single, steadying thought:

Kael was all right. There'd been a few hours when the Kingdom had shaken, when the colors of the world began to fade. But Kyleigh had never doubted for a moment that he would survive.

Now when her eyes opened, they sharpened upon colors that were warm and fierce. The evening sun poured down upon her through a strain of glass. It cloaked the grand room, washing the vaults of the ceiling and the flattened tops of the cobblestone in gold. Even the mortar lines were stirred to brilliance beneath its light: they seemed to glow and pulse when the colors touched them — the veins of some quiet, unshakeable beast.

Kyleigh's chest swelled along with the colors. Her strength came storming back. There would be a moment when her captors blinked, when they lowered their guard. Several days had passed while she waited to find a crack in Midlan's armor. At most, she thought she might only have to wait a few days more.

But it was taking everything she had to stay patient.

"How do you feel, Dragongirl? Are you feeling more obedient?"

Ulric's voice swam up to her through a haze of pain. Every bone in her body had been snapped from its place, her muscles stretched to breaking. She'd bared her teeth as her skin split against the rise of her scales — but she never once cried out.

She refused to give him anything to grin about. No matter how many times Ulric forced her body between its shapes, she would never make a sound.

"I'm feeling a bit bored, to be honest," Kyleigh said the moment she caught her breath. Her limbs shook so badly that she knew trying to stand would give her away. Instead, she sprawled out where she'd collapsed upon the floor and tucked her hands behind her head. "You'd think the King's archmage would be able to come up with something a little more exciting than changing shapes."

"Is having your every bone crushed not exciting enough?" Ulric said.

Kyleigh shrugged. "I suppose I was just looking forward to the freezing and the singeing — you know, the more *complicated* spells."

There was nothing Ulric hated more than having his spells insulted. She supposed that was why he'd gone crawling to Crevan in the first place: as long as all the mages in the realm were bound, there would be no one left to laugh at him.

So Kyleigh resolved to laugh as much as she could. "It's my own blasted fault, really. I came in expecting so much from the *arch*mage that I forgot about the fact that he's never been anything more than a potion vendor —"

"I've become far more than that," Ulric said sharply.

She studied him for a moment — which gave her the breath she needed to stop her legs from twitching. "You had one brilliant idea a long while ago. But the curse itself leaves a lot to be desired, doesn't it?" She tugged pensively on her collar and had to fight to keep her face smooth as the magic bit her. "I'd say it's rather shoddy, at best."

"Shoddy?"

"At *best*," Kyleigh corrected him. "At worst, I think it does more harm than good. Look at you," she forced herself to grin, "you're sweating more than I am."

That seemed to push him over the edge.

Ulric's eyes bulged and the tips of his overgrown ears turned red. She swore the beads of sweat that rolled off his chin hissed as they struck the already-darkened ring around his collar. When he spoke, his words sounded as if he'd strained them through his jutting teeth:

"Well, perhaps I ought to make this a little more ... *challenging*."

Kyleigh held her grin as he stomped towards her. She had to force herself not to look at the spell that flared upon the tips of his fingers, not to think about what sort of horror was coming for her next.

Ulric's dark eyes shone mercilessly from the deep pits of his skull. The light of the spell struck his face and gave his skin a burning sheen. He fixed the spell between her eyes, nearly blinding her with its glow. But just before he could loose it, one of his bat-like ears began to twitch.

The spell shrank back. Ulric glared and ground his teeth until the twitching stopped. He brought the spell back to life — just as his ear twitched again. "What?" he snapped, spinning to glare at the wall. "Figure it out for yourself. I'm in the middle of —"

Something like a roll of thunder boomed over his words. It shook the grand room and blasted the glass from its windows. Kyleigh threw an arm over her head as a storm of razor shards fell down upon them. When the storm ended and the thunder's echo faded, she looked up and saw a thick cloud of purple smoke rolling through a row of shattered windows.

Ulric scrambled back from the smoke, nearly tripping over Kyleigh in his rush to get away. But it evaporated quickly — disappearing before it struck the ground.

"Take the Dragongirl to the northern tower. Do not let her out of your sight," Ulric screamed, jabbing his finger into a darkened corner of the room. Then he grabbed Kyleigh by the front of her jerkin.

There were little bits of glass stuck into his face and neck. It was obvious by how many veins bulged from his head that he was trying to lift her. But his feeble arms had no chance against her bones. "Should I come up a bit?"

"I don't care what the King says," Ulric growled, bringing his sopping, bloody face a mere inch from hers. "When I get back, I'm going to send you to the under-realm — *in pieces*."

"As long as you promise to make the journey interesting."

Ulric's roar faded into swears as he stormed from the grand room. The spell that burst from his hand knocked the door off its hinges — and sent the guards on the other side sprinting from his path.

Kyleigh grinned when she heard the clattering of more doors being blasted away, as Ulric's swears became more potent and inventive. She didn't know what had caused the explosion, but it was obvious that Ulric was rattled by it. Perhaps her moment had finally come.

She was so busy listening that she didn't hear the slight noise of the man from the shadowed corner padding to her side. "You're brave, Kyleigh."

She looked up and saw that Devin stood over her, watching intently. "No, I'm simply annoyed. Ulric's such a twit that I feel bad if I *don't* heckle him."

"He's going to find out, you know. He'll hurt you until you let him in." Devin scratched at the spines that'd begun to sprout from the dark crop of his hair. He looked away, and a shadow crossed his eyes as he added: "He'll figure out what hurts you the most ... and then it'll get worse. The curse will tighten, you won't be able to fight it off so easily. Not even the pain will clear your head. You'll just be trapped ... trapped forever. Hold on for as long as you can."

Kyleigh knew what he meant. In the moments her pain was fiercest, she'd been able to hear it: the noise of hundreds of voices filling her ears at once. They wrapped her in a cloud of their worries, their fears. They drained her of all hope. She felt as if she sat upon the edge of sleep, while the voices tried to drag her under.

But she knew there would be no rest in the world that waited beyond — only torment.

"He can't kill you, just so you know. He's as trapped as we are." Devin crouched at her head. Though his gaze was soft, there seemed to be about a thousand little thoughts swirling inside the stark blues. "I'll never understand why someone so powerful would choose to be bound."

"Is that what he told you? I've known Ulric for quite some time," Kyleigh said when he nodded. "And I can assure you it's far more likely that he sold himself on *accident* than on purpose."

"Really?"

"His potions certainly never worked."

Devin was quiet for a moment. He grimaced when his collar flared red — the jab of Ulric's command. "Come on. Let's get you to the tower."

He pulled her onto her feet with ease. The curse had stretched him so tall that Kyleigh's head didn't quite reach the bottom of his chest. As they made their way through Midlan's winding halls, Devin had to walk half-bent most of the way — and at a full duck for the rest of it.

Midlan had been built for warriors. Its halls were wide enough for armored men to walk side-by-side, and so long that they felt more like roadways than anything. Well, she supposed they *were* roadways: the entire region of Midlan fit within three layers of walls, and there were passages connecting everything from the ramparts to the throne room.

It'd been a long while since Kyleigh had walked through Midlan, but she never remembered it being quite so jammed.

Stewards darted from room to room, moving at a brisk, shuffling pace. Soldiers charged through, bellowing for clear passage. The servants plastered themselves against the walls so frequently to make way that she thought it might be days before they reached the kitchens.

An intoxicating scent filled every stretch of the air — a potent mix of excitement and fear. Kyleigh breathed it in, and the dragon woke with an exhilarated hum. There was no better place to start a little mischief than in the midst of chaos.

Though all of Midlan was clearly in an uproar, no one seemed willing to come too close to Devin. Servants balked at the sight of him and bolted behind the nearest door. The soldiers edged past him warily, their necks turned out of his reach. They came around a corner and nearly ran smack into a steward coming from the other side.

The poor man had to shuffle backwards for several feet before he found a door to jump through.

At last, Devin stopped at the base of some winding stairs. They were tight, with just enough room for a man to walk through comfortably — which meant the climb would be far from comfortable for Devin.

"I can't let you out of my sight, remember?" he grunted as he squeezed in behind her. "This'll have to do."

"All right. Just watch your horns."

He smiled uncertainly at her wink.

The tower was a small, rounded room filled with all sorts of books and instruments. There were char marks on the walls and large chips in the stone floor. What little remained of the curtains were tattered — and heavily singed on their bottoms.

But at least there were windows.

From where she stood, Kyleigh had a good look at the northern reaches of Midlan. Its outermost walls stretched to nearly touch the swamps. The falling sun drifted through the trees and brightened them. They seemed far less like drooping, pitiful things with the evening set beside them.

Rows of barracks filled the land between Midlan's walls like houses. Tiny dots of soldiers rushed from their doorways as Kyleigh watched. She expected them to climb the towers, man the ramparts. But only a few stayed behind.

The rest moved as fast as their legs would carry them for the western walls. How quickly the sunlight blinked off their armor told her most were moving at a sprint. She stuck her head out to follow them, just to see if she could catch a glimpse of the west.

But her collar bit down with a burning force the second her head crossed the window's ledge. She stepped back with a gasp.

"What is it?" Devin said as he crouched in beside her.

Kyleigh shook her head. "It's nothing. I like this hour of the day, is all."

"You always have."

She stiffened the moment his voice went deep. Hairs rose down the back of her neck when his arms curled around her waist. He pulled her onto his knee and rested his spiny chin atop her head.

Kyleigh knew she would have to be careful. The man who held her now wasn't Devin — it wasn't a *man* at all.

It was Dorcha.

"How many ages has it been since we watched the coming of the night? For how many journeys of the sun have we stood apart? The stars must've danced above me countless times ... but I saw not a one." His lips moved to her ear as he growled: "The night has no meaning without my heart."

When his arms tightened, Kyleigh swallowed hard. "Dorcha, please —"

"You must remember them. Surely, you remember." He turned her around. The yellow heat of his gaze dug into her, searching. "I haven't forgotten a single night you lay by my side."

"She's gone," Kyleigh said quietly. She was prepared for the fires to rage, but had to brace herself when they suddenly faded back. "Your mate is gone, Dorcha. She left the moment the Tree called her soul away. We've become a new creature, she and I — a halfdragon with new memories, and a new heart."

"That ... *human*?" Dorcha hissed. His glare roared to life at her nod. "You cannot possibly feel anything for him. He's weak, and a fool."

"He isn't weak," Kyleigh said back. "He can be a bit of a fool sometimes, but so can I."

"You are never foolish."

"Yes, I am. It's the human in me — I like to think it keeps things interesting."

Dorcha shoved her off his knee with a snarl. "Your human is dead. I crushed his body in the swamps."

Kyleigh met his glare with one of her own. She didn't care a whit for Dorcha. He was an angry creature who clung to his past like a drunkard to grog: it would kill him slowly, poison him from the center of his heart. She could see the darkness growing in his eyes even now. The curse would eventually snuff his fire out.

If Dorcha's soul were to dry up and blow away, the Kingdom wouldn't have lost a blasted thing. But Devin was a different matter.

Though he had every right to be angry, he didn't give in. The darkness had no hold upon his eyes. There was so much good in him — an almost childlike yearning in his stare. She truly believed that he wanted nothing more than to be at peace with those around him.

He would even give in to Dorcha, in the end. He would step back rather than battle through the dragon's rage. And the moment he refused to fight, Dorcha would trounce him with his stronger will.

So Kyleigh decided to fight for him.

"You didn't kill my mate. I would've felt it the moment he passed. His death would've crushed me, stolen all the light from my world —"

Dorcha grabbed her around the throat, every line of his face alive with fury. "Do not insult the valtas! You could not possibly share such a powerful bond with so small a creature."

"I do."

Red bloomed across Dorcha's flesh as he hissed: "You *lie*. The valtas cannot be broken."

"And it never was. Your-Dorcha loved you to her end. But she's gone," Kyleigh said quietly. She tried not to squirm when Dorcha tightened his hold. "Whatever there was between you passed away the moment her spirit fled her bones —"

"No! It hasn't passed! You may try to keep her from me, but the valtas cannot be stopped." He ripped his hand from her throat and slammed his fist into the wall beside her, rattling the stone. His eyes slipped closer to the edge of darkness — to the maddened, shining black of the curse as he screamed: "I will meet her again in my death!"

Kyleigh didn't flinch. Seeing the black in his eyes so clearly meant that Devin was running out of time. She couldn't afford to take a moment to be frightened.

Instead, she reached out and touched Dorcha's fist. Her fingers brushed across the scars that lined his knuckles — the shining marks left by the trail of her blood. "If Your-Dorcha was still here, wouldn't she fight for you? Wouldn't her heart speak the truth?"

Kyleigh slid her fingers down the scars to the edge of the wall. Blood welled inside the crack where his fingers met the stone. She stopped at its edge and steadied herself with a breath. "If you won't believe me ... then at least believe the valtas."

Though she knew the pain was coming, the fires of his blood still shocked her.

Thousands of white-hot needles stung her flesh. They bit down upon her fingertips with such force that for a moment, she thought they'd been severed. But then the pain spread: it leaked up her bones until her hand shook with the throb.

When she cried out, Dorcha grabbed her wrist and brought her close. He used the ragged hem of his tunic to wipe the blood away. His lips pulled back from his teeth and agony stung his eyes, but at least the darkness was gone.

He stared dully at the blisters that rose across her fingers. "It's true," he whispered finally. "I would've fought for My-Dorcha with every breath of my lungs, every beat of my heart. The valtas' promise would've given me the strength I needed to endure any span of time, any edge of torment. But it's ... left me, hasn't it?"

"No," Kyleigh said quietly. "No, the valtas will never leave — you'll always carry it in your soul. And one day you'll find a creature to share it with. But you can't keep pushing Devin aside. He belongs to this body as much as you do. His heart is equally important. You'll never find your purpose without him."

Kyleigh smiled when Dorcha looked away. The pain sharpened her eyes, cleared her head. For the first time in days, she could no longer feel the collar ...

And she planned to make the most of it.

"What purpose?" Dorcha whispered. His hand trembled as it hovered above the iron around his throat; his brows cinched tightly. "I have no purpose, now. There is no longer any need for my fire, no reason left to fight —"

"Fight for Devin." Kyleigh pressed a fist against his heart and held his eyes tightly. "Fight for each other. No curse can last forever — it's going to be over sooner than you think. And once you're free, you'll have to set your eyes on another horizon."

"What horizon?" he moaned.

Kyleigh shrugged. "I'm not sure ... but I suppose the two of you can discuss it when you wake."

Dorcha must've been too lost in a vat of self-pity to see Kyleigh's fist. He didn't fight her. His body hung limply and he let himself wither beneath her blows. The first staggered him, the second dropped him to his knees. A third caught him under the chin and sent him into a reeling sleep.

"Hold on for a little while longer," she whispered as she laid his head upon the floor. "I promise you ... it'll be over sooner than you think."

CHAPTER 49
A SMALL WAY

Eveningwing had never seen such a flock gathered together. There were humans of every feather: pirates and giants, little mots and the wild ones. He remembered some of their faces, but most were new. He'd spent so long trying to learn them all that his eyes began to throb from the effort.

But he was too excited to blink.

While most of the humans slept or ate, the leaders gathered together. They filled the night with the different noises of their talking. The pirates' voices hardly ever slowed. They were as quick and constant as bluebirds. The giants spoke in booms and bursts: their calls were far between, but powerful enough to silence the others — well, *almost* all of the others.

No matter how the giants boomed, the wild ones would not be quiet. They carried on with a squabble so fierce that it would've shamed the crows into silence. Their voices forced the others to speak louder, and soon Eveningwing's ears were ringing with the noise. It didn't stop until their Gwen finally smacked the loudest one with the flat of her hand.

He yelped and tumbled from his seat. She raised her fist at the others. "I've got one ready for each of you. I promise you'll tire of having your ears rattled long before I tire of slapping them."

They went straight-backed and quiet.

"Thank you," Lysander said. He turned his glare from the wildmen and onto the giants. "So you're telling me you have no idea at all where they're keeping Jake?"

"No, I ... wait a moment." Brend raised his brows and swatted Declan across the arm. "Didn't one of those mages stop to tell you where they planned to stash him?"

"Yeh, floor *and* cell. We had a nice long chat about it, and then I told him we were planning on coming up to Midlan for a visit —"

"All right, that's enough," Lysander said testily.

Eveningwing didn't understand why he stopped them, or why the giants laughed. But even though it sounded as if they were about to find out where Jake was, the giants didn't finish their tale. And Lysander never asked about it again.

Maybe Eveningwing had missed the answer.

"Enough with your teasing," Nadine said, prodding Brend with the shaft of her spear. "This is no time for jokes. Our friend is in danger!"

He flicked the weapon aside. "Calm yourself, wee mot. We're getting to it."

"Yeh, and you'll only make yourself sick if you worry over it," Declan added. When she still fought, he picked her up by the shoulders and set her aside. "Why don't you take your folk and go for a walk about camp, eh? See what's out there."

"It is dark — there is nothing to see!" Nadine insisted.

But the giants shooed her to the edge of the trees until she finally led her warriors away. The poor mots had voices that were smaller than the rest. Their words were no less important to Eveningwing, but they often got swallowed up.

"It's this *Ulric* we ought to worry about," Brend said, dragging a hand through his spikey mass of hair. "From what I've heard, it sounds as if he's the one controlling all the mages."

"He's got them collared up like Titus had his beasts," Declan said with a nod.

Lysander tapped his chin. "So if we manage to kill Ulric, it'll free the others?"

"It should —"

"*Why* are we still talking about this?" Gwen cut in, dragging a hand down her face. "Talking will get us nothing. My warriors could have the King's walls beaten flat by dawn. My craftsmen will chop his army into pieces and scatter his mages to the wind. By the time the sun sets, we'll be using his monsters' hides for cloaks!"

"We're not going to give you the run of things," Aerilyn said, stomping up to her. "You've got no order and no self-control. What if one of the mages you *scatter* is Jake? I won't let you go crashing through those gates if there's even the slightest chance that you'll hurt my friend."

483

"Perhaps the King has already killed him," Silas murmured. "We sit at the threshold of his great den — and yet, there hasn't been a spell sent after us. His swordbearers have been strangely quiet."

He slid into Aerilyn, his glowing eyes upon the shade of Midlan in the distance.

She stepped back uncomfortably. "He's probably only waiting for dawn. No one wants to start a fight in the middle of the — would you stop that?"

Silas had been stepping close to her every time she gave him an inch: touching his chest to her crossed arms, silently pushing her back until she stood several paces from Gwen. He smiled at Aerilyn's scowl. "Mmm, no. I will not stop."

"Fine." She bowed her chest out and shoved against him. "Then I suppose we'll just stand here all night."

"Yes, I suppose we will."

"No." Lysander grabbed his Aerilyn by the belt and pulled her away. "We don't have time for all that."

"What we need is a rescue," Shamus said. He sat close to the fire, hunched on the back of a log and tugging on the bushy hairs that grew from his face. "If we could manage to dig Jake out of there before things get thick, then we could set the whole lot of them loose on Midlan and never have to worry about who they scatter."

"We'll scatter them all!" Gwen cried, stirring her wild ones into howls.

Thelred had been watching silently while the others spoke. He leaned cross-armed against the front of a tree, a wild one named Lydia stuck to his shoulder. It seemed as if she was always stuck to him. Eveningwing couldn't tell if Thelred liked having her close or not, but he thought the pirate's face might've been a little less frightening than usual.

"The only way into Midlan is through its gates. If there'd been any cracks in its walls, then it would've gotten sacked years ago," Thelred growled.

He silenced the leaders. Their faces fell and their stares turned to the fire. Hard lines creased their brows.

But there *was* another way in. Eveningwing knew it! He wasn't sure if his voice would be welcome among the others, but he couldn't stop himself. "There's one way — a small way."

All of their gazes rose from the fire. They stared into the branches where Eveningwing crouched, and their silence made him uncomfortable. He slid deeper into the shadows.

Still, Lysander squinted until he found him. "Is that you, Eveningwing? What's this about another way?"

A knot bunched up in his throat. He swallowed it down. "It's the passage the shapechangers use to leave the castle. The King never wanted us in his halls — he dug us a tunnel out."

"Is it too small for a giant?" Brend called.

"No but it's ... tricky. And you would have to keep your steps quiet."

The giants grumbled loudly at this.

"The wildmen will go," Gwen said, pounding a fist against her chest.

Aerilyn threw her hands up with an exasperated sigh. "Then we'll be right back where we started — with you *scattering* everything that moves and giving no thought at all to Jake!"

"Aye, but things would be much easier if the wildmen went through first. Could you just promise to keep your folk in line, lass?" Shamus said.

Gwen frowned at the fire for a moment, her brows tight with thought. "No," she grunted finally.

Lysander drew his sword. "Then the pirates will go!"

"Wait a moment."

Thelred stepped away from the tree. The wild ones had made him a new wooden leg. It was much quieter than the old one. His trousers covered it well and the end fit easily into his boot. But Eveningwing had seen it uncovered, once — and there were so many little metal pieces stuck into the wood that he wasn't sure how it all fit together.

"What's on the other side of this tunnel?" Thelred said when he stood beneath Eveningwing's perch.

He thought that was an odd thing to ask. "It's the nest where the shapechangers stay — the four-legged ones," he said quickly when the camp beneath him let out a collective groan. "The birds stay in the atrium. But they will all be asleep right now. So if we move without a sound —"

"And what if they make a sound?" Silas purred, his eyes sliding over to the pirates. "Humans are notoriously clumsy. They cannot be expected to move with grace and guile."

Eveningwing had a feeling they wouldn't like his answer. "The shapechangers will send their thoughts to the King if they see you — or hear your footsteps or smell your scent. They don't like having strangers in their nest. Then he will probably open their cages on you."

"So if we go in that way, we can't be seen, heard, *or* smelled?" When Eveningwing nodded, Lysander's sword fell to his side. "All right then, let's get back to it."

All of their faces turned away and their voices started up again. He thought they might still be thinking about it until the forest cook lumbered in with a platter between his arms.

There was a tower of bowls stacked on top of it, and it leaned dangerously with his every step. "Dinner!" he gasped, his face red from the effort. "Come have a bite while it's hot."

The leaders gathered around him quickly, but Eveningwing didn't feel like dinner. Perhaps he would join the mots on their walk. He climbed down from the branches and made his way through camp.

The wild ones had built shelters from the things they found in the woods: there were tents made of deadened limbs, hollows molded into the rocks. They'd even stretched some of the lowest branches downwards — pulling them into arches that leaned against the trunks of the trees.

It'd only taken them a few hours to change the forest. He thought the wildmen could've shaped a nest out of anything.

Eveningwing had just made it beyond the light of the lanterns and fires when he felt a pair of eyes upon him. They stabbed against his back, watching from a knot of shrubs.

He crept over to them carefully. His vision adjusted until he saw the shadow of a woman crouched beneath the leaves. "Elena?" he whispered. "Why are you hiding?"

"I wasn't hiding — I was following you." She rose from the shrubs and took him under the chin. Her dark eyes never blinked. "You know of another way into the castle."

"I do. But the others didn't seem to think it was a good —"

"I don't care what the others thought. Show me the way in."

486

Eveningwing liked Elena. The forest woman was patient and calm, and she had a hunter's stare. Not only that, but she seemed to enjoy the thrill of cornering her prey as much as he did.

They could've had such fun together, if only she'd had wings.

"All right. I'll lead you. But we should —"

"No, wait!"

Eveningwing had been so focused on Elena that he hadn't heard the loping steps coming up behind them. The fiddler tumbled from the shrubs with his tunic unbuttoned and his belt half-done, whispering loudly:

"Did I hear the murmurings of adventure coming from over —? Oof!"

He was so tangled in his clothes that he must've forgotten to watch his steps: he tripped over a root and flopped onto the ground. When he peeled himself up, one whole side of his face was covered in dirt.

"I'm coming with you," he whispered.

When he grinned, Eveningwing saw there was more dirt in his teeth.

He liked the fiddler, too — but he was no hunter. And he was easily the noisiest human in the flock. "I don't think that's a good idea."

"No, you're wrong. It's a horrible idea," Elena growled.

Jonathan scrambled to his feet and sauntered until his toes touched Elena's. "If you don't take me along, I'm going to start singing. And you know how loudly I sing." He drew the fiddle from his belt and placed the bow menacingly atop its front. "I'll have the whole camp wide awake and swearing murder before I even hit the chorus — and the chorus, I warn you, is *dreadful.*"

Elena stared at him for a moment before she shrugged. "All right, you can come along."

Eveningwing wasn't sure he'd heard her. "He can?"

"Of course." Elena's eyes brightened considerably as she watched the fiddler whoop and dance around. "If we're going to be in there with all of Crevan's beasts, we ought to bring someone we can outrun."

****

487

The tunnel Eveningwing led them to was cramped and dark. Its mouth was hardly anything more than a crack at the base of the southern wall — hidden so well behind a clump of foliage that Elena doubted if she would've ever seen it.

"It's slippery," Eveningwing warned as he crawled inside.

Elena didn't care about it being slippery. Her heart was still pounding from their trip around the wall.

Something strange was happening in Midlan. A mass of black clouds gathered above its western wall and grew steadily larger as they traveled, until the storm stood out like a blot against the stars.

Moisture poured from its edges so thickly that it sounded more like a waterfall than rain. Elena knew the King's mages must have summoned it — the clouds stayed fixed tightly above the western wall and the rain fell nowhere else. It was too strange *not* to be magic.

But she couldn't understand why the King would want rain falling in his courtyard. Wouldn't it have been better to send the storm to drench their camp?

At least the clouds had given them the shadows they needed to slip up to the walls unnoticed. The southern wall was much trickier to navigate. It was alive with soldiers: they packed the ramparts and filled the courtyard to its edges. She could hear hundreds of voices, hundreds of steps. There was the groan of ropes and the steady beat of blacksmiths at the forge. The soldiers marched tirelessly about their work — and she could only imagine what Crevan had planned.

As they picked their way across to the tunnel, Elena kept her shoulders pressed against the wall. The rampart's lip protruded just far enough to shadow them. She kept a tight hold on Jonathan while Eveningwing led the way. The fiddler couldn't see very well and kept stumbling over every little rock — and the absolute last thing they needed was to have him go rolling out into the open for all of Midlan to see.

There'd been a few close calls, and she'd all but carried him through the toughest stretch. But they'd finally made it to the tunnel.

"Are you sure you're supposed to go in with your head first, mate?" Jonathan whispered as Eveningwing's legs disappeared. "I think I'd rather start with my feet — they're less important and much easier to replace."

"I'm not sure it would make *you* any difference," Elena hissed.

She slid into the hole foot-first and braced her heels against the slippery floor. The tunnel was dank and so covered in moss that she had to dig her fingers through an inch of slime just to grip the stone.

Things went well for a few moments. Eveningwing clawed his way down on his belly while Jonathan and Elena slid forward by the inch. They'd gone so long without anything foolish happening that she'd actually begun to forget about the fiddler.

But he reminded her quickly.

Elena was between holds when Jonathan suddenly lost his footing. His knees slammed into her back and jolted her forward — driving her heels directly into the flats of Eveningwing's feet.

He shot forward like an arrow, arms wrapped protectively over his face. Elena's fingers clawed through filth and moss, but she could find nothing to slow her fall. In the end, all she could do was drag Jonathan down beside her and clamp a hand over his mouth.

If they fell to their deaths, she didn't want his yelling to be the last thing she heard.

Fortunately, the tunnel came to an end before they could reach a skull-splitting speed, and the moss muffled their slide down. They wound up flopping out of the tunnel's back — filthy and scraped, but otherwise unharmed.

"Ugh." Jonathan wiped at the muddy print Elena had left over his mouth, grimacing. "What sort of stink is this? Did we just come through a lat —?"

Eveningwing slapped a hand over his mouth, leaving another filthy print behind. He motioned for silence and waved them between the arches of some narrow, slime-covered passage.

They were deep beneath the fortress. Elena knew by how wetly the air clung to her skin that the earth was well above them. Hairs rose down the back of her neck and her lungs tightened against the pressure of the walls, but she forced herself to stay calm.

She'd listened to the others talk long enough to know that they had no idea what they were doing. Jake was somewhere inside Midlan. He was depending on her. If she didn't find him quickly, the wildmen would come bursting in on the wings of whatever half-finished plan Lysander came up with and tear him limb from bloody limb.

Elena wasn't going to let that happen. She would crawl through a crack to the center of the earth, if she had to. But she would see to it that Jake didn't come to harm.

There was far too much she had left to say.

The narrow passage never seemed to end. It wound its way through the dank stone in inexplicable patterns. Torches hung sparsely down its length. Every once in a while, they would pass some hissing, sickly excuse for a light. But for the most part, the darkness reigned.

They were coming around one particularly sharp bend when Eveningwing reached back. Elena looked up at his touch and followed the line of his eyes to a section of wall on their left.

A door of iron rods had been fitted into the wall, blocking the entrance to a tiny stone chamber. There was a lumpy shadow curled upon the floor. Elena's breath caught in her throat when her eyes adjusted and the shadow took shape.

It was one of the King's monsters — a man twisted around the body of a lion. The lion's foreclaws were as wide as shovels with daggers sticking out from their ends. Its warped head rested atop them: a man's face split nearly in half around a set of deadly, shining teeth.

The lion's eyes were closed. Its lumpy back rose and fell with sleep. Elena hoped that Jonathan wouldn't see. But when he started gripping the life out of her shoulders, she knew it was too late.

Elena twisted to glare at him. If he so much as *thought* about gasping, she would murder him where he stood.

Jonathan must've read the warning in her eyes, because his grip loosened immediately.

There were hundreds of creatures trapped beneath the fortress. They passed many cages of lions, each sleeping alone. There were chambers filled to their ends with wolves, and several with creatures who kept their heads tucked beneath blood-red tails. But the ones that frightened her most were the bears.

They were monsters among monsters — beasts with heads larger than a man's chest and claws that looked as if they could tear through steel. The growling snores that rumbled from between their fangs shook the slime off the passageways.

Elena began to fear that the walls would split beneath the noise. She stopped at the next chamber they came to: a bear slept heavily against the door, its hideous face pressed into the bars. Drool spilled out from between its teeth and drenched the cobblestone at her boots in a sticky puddle.

Eveningwing took several paces before he seemed to notice that Jonathan and Elena were frozen behind him. He crept back and dragged Elena forward by the arm, a finger pressed tightly against his lips.

They'd just managed to slip past the bear when Elena heard a noise that froze her again:

Thump ... thump ... thump ...

They were heavy footfalls, the sound of something monstrous moving about the chambers. The thumping echoed so badly off the stone that Elena couldn't tell which direction they were coming from.

Eveningwing picked up the pace. He was tearing them through the passageways, now. His hand tightened around Elena's wrist. Jonathan's feet splattered so loudly through every puddle that she knew it was only a matter of time before whatever monster this was found them.

She ripped Slight from his sheath and focused on the dark turn ahead. Her eyes peeled through the shadows, trying to catch a glimpse of the creature's warped flesh.

Eveningwing sped around the next corner and collided with something hard. It jolted Elena backwards and sent Jonathan onto his rump. The creature had its thick, scarred limbs wrapped around Eveningwing. Elena drew Shadow and coiled to spring for its throat.

But when the creature raised its head, surprise stole her breath. It wasn't a *monster* they'd run into.

It was a man.

The man looked as if he'd once been a giant: the thickness of his bruised arms and the tufts of white hair that sprouted from the scars atop his head made him look like a giant. But his face had been so ravaged by tooth and claw that it was impossible to tell.

As he held Eveningwing, his crack of a mouth split in what could've easily been a snarl or a grin.

"Our beastkeeper," Eveningwing whispered, patting the man's ruined chest.

Jonathan had pulled himself from the ground and was bent nearly double in an effort to hide behind Elena's shoulders. "What's a beastkeeper?"

"He's good to us. He feeds us," Eveningwing said simply.

491

The beastkeeper didn't *seem* interested in harming them. Still, Elena couldn't help but keep an eye upon the curved dagger clutched in his meaty hand.

"We need to get into the castle. One of our friends is in danger. I promise we'll be careful," Eveningwing said when the lump above the beastkeeper's one remaining eye slid low. "We'll be gone before the King finds out."

The beastkeeper's mangled face swung over to Jonathan and Elena. His scars made him impossible to read. After a moment, he stepped backwards and beckoned them with a finger — one that was quite noticeably missing its tip.

Elena gripped her daggers tightly as they followed in the beastkeeper's thumping wake. There was a heavy ring of keys swinging from his belt. He stopped at the next chamber and slid one of the keys into its lock.

Elena stepped back against the wall, flattening Jonathan behind her. "What's he doing?" she hissed.

Eveningwing swatted a hand at her. He had his face pressed against the bars and one arm stuck through them, waving excitedly at whatever it was trapped on the other side.

Jonathan let out a moaning curse when the door swung open. "Please don't let it be a monster. *Please*, for Fate's sake, don't let it be —"

"Are they here?" a voice rasped from within the chamber. "Have they come for me?"

The beastkeeper's head bobbed up and down. Eveningwing tried to rush inside, but the beastkeeper grabbed him mid-dart. There was some grunting and a good deal of waving the curved knife about. Then Eveningwing nodded.

"All right. I understand. Of course we'll take him," he said, grinning into the chamber. "Come help me, Jonathan."

The fiddler edged out from behind Elena and stepped up to the door — careful not to brush shoulders with the beastkeeper. He leaned his head around the arch and let out a sigh of relief.

"You had me worried for a second, mate," he whispered as he followed Eveningwing inside. "I expected there to be an eight-legged terror asleep in here. But it's just some wrinkly old fellow with a moppy beard."

"I can hear you," the voice rasped testily.

492

Elena swore under her breath when Jonathan and Eveningwing emerged, toting a frail man between them. His beard stretched down to his chest and had gone silver with age.

"Where are we taking him, exactly? We won't make it far dragging an old man around," she warned, ignoring Eveningwing's frown. "We'll be spotted for sure."

"We cannot leave him here. The King has ordered him to be dealt with — but he didn't say *when*," Eveningwing added, grinning at the beastkeeper. "So we can bring him along with us."

"I won't be much trouble," the old man insisted. His gaze was clear and incredibly deep. Elena felt as if he could see through the windows of her soul — and she didn't like it.

"Who are you?"

"Argon."

"Well, *Argon*, you'd better find your feet. I'm not slowing down for anybody."

Elena stepped past them, following the beastkeeper as he led them towards a door she hoped would take them into the castle. While they traveled, she couldn't help but hear Jonathan and Eveningwing whispering behind her:

"What's that mean, *the King wanted him dealt with*?" Jonathan wondered.

"I'm not sure," Eveningwing said. Then he jerked his chin to the blade gripped in the beastkeeper's hand. "But that's the knife he uses for cutting up our dinner."

CHAPTER 50
A FIGHT FOR THE NORTH

"There it is," Graymange whispered, his teeth bared into the pale light of the coming dawn. "The King's great den."

Kael barely heard him. Midlan's northern wall leered at him from behind a shroud of mist. A rain cloud swelled above its onyx towers and spat thick curtains of moisture down upon the stone. The soldiers that paced across the wall were too distant to hear; the black creatures that swarmed above the courtyards too numerous to count.

There was nearly half a mile of empty land between the shapechangers and the edge of the wall. Midlan would see them the moment they stepped out from beneath the trees. It would be ready for them. The King had every advantage.

But none of that could stop Kael from grinning.

"I'm going for the wall. Don't follow until I've opened the gate, all right? There's no point in getting shot at before you have to."

A thick hand slapped across his shoulder. The bear shaman dropped his voice to a whispered boom: "We will wait for your call."

The other shamans wished him well. They reached out to touch him as he stood. The hawk shaman ruffled his hair, an excited glint in the bed of her strange, yellow eyes.

"Fight well," she said.

Kael promised that he would.

He stepped out from beneath the shadows of the trees and into the field beyond. His armor had been ripped away during his plummet into the swamps, and his clothes badly torn by Dorcha's tail.

Fortunately, a Midlan patrol came looking for him not long after he'd healed — and they'd proven rather useful. Now Kael wore armor made from a patchwork of their leather jerkins: he'd stitched together the pieces that weren't too badly burnt or torn, until they resembled another worn set of armor he'd once seen.

He kept Daybreak sheathed at his hip as he walked. A shield hung from his other arm — a meld of some of the breastplates he'd scavenged, beaten into shape. He didn't exactly need a shield. He didn't need the armor, either. But he thought Crevan needed to see them. He needed to stare into the eye carved across Kael's shield and know that his death was marching into Midlan. He needed to understand that his time as King had ended.

For some reason, wearing the armor and carrying the Wright's crest made him feel as if this was the end of something else: a War started long ago, a life bought with blood.

Kael had sworn that he would try to forget what Setheran and Amelia had done. He'd promised himself that he wouldn't let the weight of his past destroy him — and it was a promise he intended to keep. But he could remember them like this.

He could walk through the gates of Midlan not as a nameless boy from the mountains, but as a Wright. He could make sure the whisperers dealt the final blow, ended the War.

He could finish what they'd started.

Kael had hardly gone twenty paces from the trees when the soldiers on the ramparts spotted him. One of them went charging down the stairs while the rest gathered in a tight line, readying their arrows.

When the soldier returned, he brought Ulric with him. The archmage held a spell above him that blocked the rain like a shield. His skull-like head twisted upon his neck as he struggled to see Kael through the storm. Finally, he seemed to give up. He thrust his arm out beside him, towards the western wall, and one of the links on his arm woke with a burst of red.

Moments later, red lights began appearing in the clouds. Kael hadn't realized how many winged creatures had been hovering around the towers until their shackles gave them away. They pulled together in a swarm above the western wall and circled as a voice beneath them bellowed orders in strange, muffled words.

Then all at once, they turned for Kael.

His muscles tensed as the creatures fell in a wave towards the field. When they crossed out from beneath the line of rain, he saw their twisted faces: the beaks of hawks and crows bursting through the flesh of men, their great wings little more than drooping folds of skin covered in feathers.

He saw his reflection shining in each of their black, pitiless eyes. Scales coated their talons and their grayish tongues stabbed out from between their jaws. They might've been able to shatter the clouds with the noise of their screams.

But Kael never broke his stride.

Dragonscales popped up across his skin, sharpened to edges down his arm and into points at the tips of his fingers. They swelled to cover his armor and stretched to the top of his head. By the time the first crow fell upon him, he was ready.

Its flesh split around his arm and the scream died inside its throat. The birds swarmed around him madly for a few moments longer: their talons glanced off his armor and their drooping skin parted beneath his blows. Kael's steps wove themselves into a deadly attack inside the swarm. He moved from one enemy to the next, hacking their talons aside before they could wrap around him — he wouldn't let them try to lift him away.

A screech sounded above him and the crows peeled to the side. They circled out of his reach as a massive hawk fell from the sky — its talons curled and its shining black eyes locked hungrily upon Kael's throat.

Though he could hear the wind screaming off the hawk's massive wings, though its fall quickly swallowed the sky between them, Kael didn't budge. He didn't even raise his arm, but stood his ground as the hawk fell — watched his reflection smile inside the pits of the monster's eyes.

The hawk's body split against his armor. Its shattering bones felt like leaves as they rolled down his shoulders; its blood nothing more than a spatter of rain upon his cloak. Kael didn't look down to see the mess it'd made. He didn't turn to watch the crows as they bolted away from him in a panicked rush. No, he kept his gaze on the ramparts, on Ulric.

He watched as the archmage's eyes widened in recognition, as his jaw snapped open and he stumbled back. Words raced across his lips as he thrust his arm skyward. Soon his voice had risen above the clouds:

"Stop the whisperer! *Move*, beasts — you have been summoned!"

Beasts?

Kael picked up his pace when he realized what that meant. He crossed into the line of rain at a jog, searching the onyx towers for the first glimpse of white. But though Ulric shrieked her name, Kyleigh never appeared — and after a moment, his cries grew desperate.

When he thrust the chain higher, its links turned from red to white-hot. He held it up, his arm shaking with the effort — until the chain erupted with one final burst of blinding light.

The tower behind Ulric began to tremble. Soldiers scrambled from the ramparts as blocks of stone rolled down its side. No sooner had they disappeared than the spire ruptured beneath the force of a monstrous set of wings.

Dorcha tore himself from the tower, casting man-sized chunks of stone in every direction as he rose. A spout of yellow flame erupted from between his jaws. It shot into the storm clouds and turned its wet to steam, came down in a rain of fire.

"Kill the whisperer!" Ulric screamed.

Dorcha's chin shot away from the clouds and followed the line of Ulric's trembling arm — to where Kael sprinted for the castle. Even from a distance, he could see that the scales along Dorcha's left brow were slightly swollen. But he didn't have time to wonder what had happened. He was too taken aback to give the dragon's wounds a second thought.

All of the yellow was gone from Dorcha's eyes ... replaced by a maddened, shining black.

"Stop him! Kill him!"

The force of Dorcha's wings flattened Ulric against the rampart's ledge, but he still managed to hold onto his unsettling grin as the black dragon swooped out into the field. He seemed all but certain that Kael would meet a grisly end.

Dorcha flew low to the ground: claws tucked beneath him and a storm of flame brewing between his jaws.

Kael never slowed. He held his shield out beside him as he ran and balled his other hand into a fist. It would do him no good if Dorcha turned away before he had a chance to strike. He had to stay patient just a moment more.

In half a blink, Dorcha loosed his flame. The shield was gone in an instant: it melted from his hand and rolled in warm lines down his wrist. But the rest of his armor was covered in scales. Kael picked up speed. His legs pounded against the earth as he charged for the core of the flame — towards the patch that shone the brightest. He waited until he was certain that Dorcha was within his range.

Then he tore Daybreak from its sheath.

Though he'd drawn it once before, the sword's power still shocked him. The heat radiating from its edges tested his armor: it slipped between the scales and burned the flesh beneath. But Kael hardly noticed.

He slung Daybreak towards the center of the flame and a white-hot arc of fire spewed from its molten edges. Kael fell onto his back at the noise of Dorcha's anguished roar — and narrowly avoided getting crushed to death as the dragon soared over his head.

Boulders rolled away and the earth churned aside as Dorcha fell. His great claws dragged ruts into the ground as he tried to stop his body from flipping; his wings scraped all the grass from its top.

For a moment, Kael thought the battle was over. He leapt to his feet and had taken a step closer when Dorcha's head whipped around. There was a long, smooth cut down the middle of his face — one that stretched from the crook of his right eye, across his spiny muzzle, and down to his chin.

The wound steamed as hot blood wept from its edges, and the pain must've shocked him: the black broke from his eyes. He watched Kael through portals of flaming yellow, now. The blackened slits narrowed upon Daybreak for half a blink before his great body shot into the air.

Kael swore as Dorcha headed west. He would never be able to chase the dragon on foot, and Kyleigh was still somewhere inside Midlan.

Ulric must've been able to read the murder in his eyes. The archmage hiked up his robes and went sprinting down the stairs the moment Kael turned, rushing for the safety of the courtyard.

The front gates were sealed tightly shut. Footsteps tromped behind them as the soldiers braced themselves against the doors. Metal strips covered the wood from top to bottom, hammered into the planks by fist-sized bolts. A series of iron beams were clamped across the doors' backs, holding them together tightly. Kael could just make them out through the slight gap between doors.

When he stepped closer, the wood groaned. The soldiers pressed their bodies tighter against the gates. They likely watched his shadow move along the crack at the doors' bottoms, cringed against Daybreak's blinding light. The gates were far more thick than tall — almost insignificant in size, compared to the wall they sat in. They were designed to foil the ram and make burning through almost impossible.

But most importantly, the gates opened *out*ward instead of in.

This would've certainly slowed a battering ram, and it'd likely kept Midlan's enemies out for ages. But today, it would do them no good.

Kael kicked the gates hard and waited as the soldiers threw themselves against it. Then he drew Daybreak over his head and brought it down between the doors.

The iron bolts melted helplessly against the sword's blinding flame. They *click*ed as they snapped into two — and the instant the bolts were gone, the soldiers' weight did the rest.

They tumbled out the doors in a rush, parting around a sweep of Daybreak's fire. The soldiers who weren't hewed flopped onto their bellies beside him. They rolled away, trying desperately to escape his reach.

But Kael would not be stopped.

****

"Dragon!"

Half of the camp woke to the noise of Gwen's shout — the wildmen's excited howling woke the rest.

Captain Lysander stumbled from his bedroll, the waves of his hair standing on end. "What in high tide are you all yelling ab —?"

A roar cut over his words. It whipped across the tops of the trees and shook the pebbles at his feet. Lysander had only just regained his footing when Gwen snatched him by the hair.

"Ow! What are you—?"

"Hold *still*, lowlander!" In one swift motion, she pulled herself onto his shoulders and vaulted into the tree behind him — sending Lysander directly onto his face. He'd only just started to pull himself up when Silas came charging after her.

He lay flat as the mountain lion sprang over his head and into the tree. Silas's powerful claws split the bark as he scrambled after Gwen.

The wildmen raced to the edge of camp, all of their painted faces turned north. The warriors dropped their heavy rucksacks on the ground and the craftsmen began digging through them. They drew out handfuls of rounded orbs, marbles made of dragonsbane. The craftsmen molded sharp points into the orbs until they resembled the spiked head of a mace. Then they tossed them back to the warriors.

"Get ready!" Gwen called. She was perched high atop the tree, her golden axe lifted over her head. When a second roar shook the earth, she laughed. "He sees me — he's turning this way."

"No, my Thane!" Silas pawed anxiously at her boots. "Come down, his fires will harm you!"

"He won't get the chance to breathe. Are you ready, warriors?"

They howled, waving the spiked orbs.

"At my signal!"

"No, please —"

"*Now!*"

Gwen slung her axe downward and the warriors let loose a volley of orbs. Another roar shook the air and a moment later, an enormous shadow darkened the trees.

"Move!" Lysander cried. He waved his sword about him wildly, and the camp scattered in every direction. Still, the dragon's shadow covered them.

The wildmen's volleys didn't slow the dragon down. In fact, his wings picked up speed. Soon his monstrous body hung over the camp. Golden spikes peppered his blackened scales, thickest at his face and chest. His eyes burned and a storm of yellow flame brewed behind his teeth.

"Stop throwing things at him, you clodders! Can't you see you're only making it worse?" Brend bellowed.

He was sprawled out atop a pile of giants — all of whom appeared to be struggling to hold Declan down. The general's eyes were black with madness; he dug into the ground with his boots and a thrust of his thick legs lurched the pile forward.

Brend swore as he fought through the tangle of their limbs. He grabbed one of Declan's arms and wrapped a thick coil of rope around it. "I'm sorry, but I warned you. I can't have you running off — no! Get back here, wee mites!"

"*Mots!*" Nadine shouted. She led her warriors in behind the wildmen. They crouched and raised their spears in a protective wall as the dragon came closer.

Brend swore again. He finished tying Declan and rolled his hobbled body towards a waiting line of giants. "Take him somewhere safe," he barked. Then he turned his glare upon the mots. "The rest of you grab an armful of those wee little terrors and get *running*!"

The dragon came closer. He spread his wings and began a slow, taunting descent towards the trees. There was no mercy in the shining black pits of his eyes. The collar around his throat put off a blistering light — but it was nothing compared to the fire waiting upon his tongue.

Pirates, fishermen, and mercenaries went sprinting as the ferocity of its heat touched the woods. Sweat poured down Thelred's face and Shamus's bushy sideburns hung flat. They grabbed Lysander around his arm and began dragging him away.

"Where's Aerilyn? I don't see her!"

"I'm sure she's fine, Captain," Thelred said.

"Aye," Shamus grunted. "She probably had the good sense to — "

A thunder of hooves cut over his words and a dapple-gray blur spun them around. Aerilyn spurred Braver to the front of the wildmen's line, screaming into the trees as she went: "I thought you were going to *handle* the dragon!"

"We are!" Gwen hollered back.

"Oh really? Then why is there a great," she nocked an arrow, "bloody," aimed its point high, "ball of flame about to —? Ah!"

She squealed and shut her eyes as the arrow flew from its string. An explosion sounded overhead. The dragon roared as the arrow burst against his chest — leaving a raw, bleeding burn just above his heart. He sucked the flames back down his throat and spun away from Aerilyn's next shot in a panic.

A hail of branches rained down upon them as the dragon's wings slapped across the trees. Silas came tumbling from his perch, twisting into a man the moment his paws touched the ground. His glowing eyes went stark upon the ravaged top of the tree.

Gwen was gone.

"You will get yourself killed, you foolish human!" he roared.

Shamus gaped up at the shattered branches. "Is she not already dead?"

"No, she jumped onto his wing," Lydia called. She was nearly doubled over, her face red with laughter. "Oh, Fate — that dragon's going to get the beating of his life!"

"I'm sorry, but what about this is funny, exactly?" Aerilyn snapped. A red line singed her cheeks and she kept a tight grip on Braver — who didn't look particularly thrilled about having been led so close to a dragon. "You're lucky he startles easily. Otherwise we'd all be in ashes!"

Silas didn't appear at all concerned about becoming ashes. He sprinted to the edge of the woods, following the dragon's path. "He's taken her across the walls, into the King's den. Move, wild ones!" He waved his arms around him madly. "Get yourselves to the gates, peel the doors aside. Your Warchief needs you!"

They followed him with whistles and howls.

"I suppose we'd better make sure they don't do anything ridiculous," Aerilyn muttered, pursing her lips after them. She turned and arched a brow at Lysander, who seemed frozen to the ground. "What?"

He stared at her a moment longer before he blinked and shook his head. "That was ... you were ..." He didn't seem able to get the words out.

Red crossed her face again — though this time, it was from an entirely different sort of burn. "Close your mouth, Captain. We've got work to do."

He stared after her as she galloped away, and it was Thelred who finally had to call the pirates to order:

"To the gates! On your feet, dogs."

"Giants," Brend barked with a wave of his scythe. "Ready yourselves. We've got some battling to do."

They fell in behind the pirates, adding their thudding steps to the march.

The mots tried to go along, but Brend stepped into their path. "No, a skirmish like this is no place for such wee things —"

"You cannot turn us away now," Nadine said vehemently. Even standing on her toes, she hardly came to Brend's waist. But there was fire in her eyes as she spoke: "This fight belongs to us as much as it does to you. We have traveled just as far. We have given just as much. We want to do our part!"

Brend shook his head at the collective *thud* of their spears. "You'll be doing your part — while we're off chopping heads, you'll be here making sure no harm comes to our general. He'll be helpless without you," Brend added, squashing Nadine's protest with a look.

Though her mouth stayed shut, her eyes burned after him. She crossed her arms as the others went towards the wall — and the moment they were gone, she called the mots together.

"We cannot stay here while our companions fight. Go." She waved a handful of warriors towards Declan, who lay hobbled upon a bedroll. "Use your spears. Untie his knots."

While they worked, she dug through the one of the pirates' rucksacks and drew out a bottle of bright green grog.

"Find more of these," she said to the others. "They will be in the packs with salt crusted upon their fronts."

Once they'd gone, Nadine crept over to Declan. He was tied like an animal: his wrists and ankles were bound together so that he could do little more than rock impatiently when she approached. The black had begun to leave his eyes. He stared unblinkingly at the castle until Nadine touched his face.

"I know your giants are only trying to protect you ... but I also know that you do not wish to lie here while the others fight. Once the gates are opened, they will be lost to their battle. We will be able to slip inside unseen. But if you wish to come with us, then you must drink," she said, placing the bottle against his lips. "The mots cannot stop you, if you go mad again."

Declan wrinkled his nose at the scent wafting from the bottle. But in the end, he sighed. "Yeh, all right. Just tip it up quick, will you? I swear this stuff curdles on my tongue."

CHAPTER 51
HEARTBREAK

Midlan was proving more difficult to navigate than Elena had ever thought possible. Its dark, twisting halls wove together in a labyrinth of stone. They crossed paths with other chambers in the most unexpected places; many of the hallways ended without warning. There were so few windows that it might be several minutes before Elena had a chance to check their bearings.

And by then, all she knew for certain was that they were going around in circles.

"How much further? My feet went numb an hour ago," Jonathan moaned from behind her.

Elena wasn't sure. They were crouched in the shadow of a doorway, waiting for a line of soldiers to move down the hall. There was a window set into the wall around the next corner. It'd begun to glow with a pale, grayish light.

Dawn was coming. They'd soon run out of shadows — and Jake would run out of time.

Elena twisted to glare at Argon. "You ought to know your way around the castle. You've lived here long enough."

His frail body slumped between Jonathan and Eveningwing, and his deep stare had grown heavy with exhaustion. Still, he managed to smirk through his beard at her question. "I know my way, child. But until I know *your* way, I'm afraid I won't be much help. I'll provide directions the moment you know where you're going."

That was precisely the problem: Elena had no idea where she was going. They'd checked the mages' chambers, but found them empty. The libraries and the spell rooms were vacant as well. All of the obvious places had turned up cold. Now there was no guessing where Jake might be.

But Elena refused to give up. She waited until the soldiers finally wandered down the hall before she waved the others forward.

"Ah, let's rest here for a moment more," Argon pleaded, his stare roving to the window. "Yes, just a moment more."

"I'm all for that," Jonathan agreed.

Eveningwing resumed his crouch with a shrug.

Elena was about a *moment* from killing them all. "No, we haven't got time to take another rest. The wildmen are going to come bursting in here before too much longer, and if they find Jake ..."

She stopped the moment the window started to rattle. A deep gust of wind nearly shook it off its pane — but it was actually the wall that took the brunt of the damage.

Elena threw an arm over her head when a chunk of the wall exploded, showering them with bits of stone and dust. The heaviest pieces slammed against the chamber door beside them, along with something that wasn't a part of the castle, at all.

A figure dragged itself up from the rubble. There were bits of stone lodged in the wild, red crop of her hair, and a thick layer of grit all but covered the painted swirls across her face. Gwen swore profusely as she pulled herself up from the ruins. Her legs wobbled for only a moment before she steadied — and her eyes sharpened.

When she thrust the golden axe at them, Elena saw that its twin edges hissed with a thin layer of steaming blood. "Which way to the nearest tower?" she growled.

Argon pointed over his thin shoulder to the hallway behind them. "You'll find a set of stairs to your right. Take them all the way to the top."

Gwen replied with something that was halfway between a snarl and a grunt before she shoved past them and went sprinting down the hall.

Jonathan gaped after her. "What —?"

"Dragon!" she barked.

Eveningwing fidgeted excitedly. "Will the wild ones bring him down? I wonder —"

"There's no time to wonder," Elena said hoarsely. If Gwen was already here, the others wouldn't be far behind. She started to pick her way over the ruins when the chamber door beside her swung open.

A guard nearly ran her over. His eyes widened through the slits in his gold-tinged helmet as they scraped across her black and crimson armor. A hoard of other guards packed in behind him, heads craning for the source of all the noise.

Elena swore when the lead guard raised his spear. She snatched the weapon and shoved back hard, using it to knock him off his feet. He stumbled into his companions and once they were off-balance, the weight of their armor did the rest: they collapsed in a flailing pile upon the floor.

There was nothing for it. These guards would have to be dealt with. "Get back to that chamber we passed — the one with the lion pelts, and the extra bolts on the door. Close the window and stay out of sight. I'll meet you as soon as I'm finished here."

Elena didn't wait for her companions' reply: she stepped inside and locked the door behind her.

Most of the guards were still struggling to right themselves when she attacked. Elena drove Slight between the gaps in their armor, leaving deep puncture wounds behind. Shadow slid across their throats the moment they arched back in pain. The cuts her blade carved across their flesh ended them quickly ... and silenced their screams.

All the while she worked, Elena was careful to keep her body between the guards and the door. Not a one of them slipped past her. Slowly, they fell — until each one lay unmoving in a ring of his own gore.

It was only after the battle cleared from her eyes that Elena realized what she'd done. These guards would never speak a word about what they'd seen — but they wouldn't have to. The next man who opened the door would see it for himself ...

Elena stopped breathing. For a moment, she thought she might've heard something. But when a long few seconds passed and the sound didn't come again, she convinced herself that she'd only imagined it.

"Ahem?"

She spun around and pressed Shadow against the throat of the man behind her — a steward who had somehow, inexplicably, managed to slip his way through a locked door unnoticed.

There was a large gap between his two front teeth, and the black space between them was easily his most interesting feature. The rest of his face was about as memorable as a weathered board.

506

"Would you kindly remove your blade? There's no need to chop up the messenger."

His utter indifference caught her off-guard. Elena moved Shadow away — but kept Slight poised at her hip. "What message?"

"The King wishes me to send reinforcements to the western wall. He wants to make absolutely certain his new battlemage will be protected, once the gates fall. But, as these particular guards appear to be …" he leaned around her to pass an unconcerned look across the pile of corpses staining the chamber floors, "*indisposed*, I suppose you'll have to do."

Elena could hardly believe it — no, she *couldn't* believe it. There was no way this odd-looking steward could've possibly mistaken her for a Midlan soldier. But she didn't have the breath to worry. "A new battlemage? Where?" she demanded when the steward nodded.

"At the western wall. I've already said it." He sighed at her glare and started what looked like the rather burdensome process of digging through his coat. "I think I may … ah yes, here it is."

He pulled a neatly folded sheet of parchment from one of his pockets and handed it to her. Elena opened it carefully, and was surprised to find a rather detailed map packed within its edges — a map so detailed that she could count the number of bolts on the door in the lion pelt room.

She found the western wall quickly. It was already marked with an inkblot. "Why would I need to know about the tumblers in the locks?"

The steward's hand dipped into his pocket once more, returning with a small, silver key. "Why, indeed?" he muttered as he passed it to her. Then he glanced around the room a final time. "Don't worry — this sort of thing happens in the fortress far more often than you'd think. The King has a frightful temper. I'll send someone along to mop it up."

He turned on his heel and strode out the door — disappearing before Elena could even think to be baffled.

****

Getting through the castle was only the half of it. There was another courtyard between Elena and the door that led to the western wall — and it was absolutely packed with soldiers.

They stood in unflinching lines while their officers paced about them. Their barking commands echoed against the walls, hardly rising above the noise of the storm. Rain lashed against their armor in warm, gusting waves. It spattered upon the courtyard and turned the ground into a murky swamp.

After a few moments of deliberation, Elena had decided to leave her companions behind. She convinced herself that they would be safe in the lion pelt room — and once she found Jake, she would return for them.

Now that she saw the task ahead of her, she knew she'd chosen right.

The great fortress loomed behind her, and the rising sun struck its back — casting a heavy shadow across the courtyard. Elena felt at home inside the darkness. She wove her way between the soldiers' ranks: drifting along the edges of the flood, sliding around the light of their braziers.

When she passed the main door, she saw it was heavily guarded. There were so many eyes upon it and backs pressed against it that she would've never been able to slip through unnoticed. Fortunately, there was another entrance marked on her map.

Elena ducked into a tower to the right of the main door and wound up its narrow flight of stairs. There was a guard stationed before the window, but he didn't notice her approach ... and by the time Shadow touched his throat, it was too late.

Once she'd dragged the guard's body aside, Elena stepped up to the window. She leaned over the ledge, quickly planning her descent. There were enough holds to carry her safely to the bottom.

Beyond the tower's base stood another line of guards. She didn't take the time to count them all, but wagered there weren't many more than a dozen. They were pressed against the tower, packed together on a slight hill of dry earth.

Everything beyond them was covered in water.

It was like a tempest dropped into the middle of the fortress: thick black clouds swarmed above the western courtyard and beat it mercilessly with a downpour of rain. The rows of barracks were gone, swallowed up by an army of white-capped waves. They pressed the

508

gates and slapped against the walls, rising about a man's height from their tops.

Debris from the soldiers' barracks rode across the wastes — their shattered bits jutting out like the spines of creatures lurking beneath the swells. The hill the soldiers stood upon was the last dry strip of land in sight. Their heads moved up and down, cutting between the sky and the row of people at the waters' edge.

Mages.

Lines of different colored lights arced from the tips of their staffs and into the clouds, where they swirled in a blackened mash. The mages stood in water that came up to their waists. When one of them turned to look down the row, Elena's chest clenched tightly.

He was a ... child. They were all children. Their arms shook as they struggled to hold their spells aloft. The sleeves of their robes slipped back, revealing the iron shackles clamped around their wrists. As the storm raged on, they glanced more frequently down the row — watching the man who stood at their center.

This mage was taller than the rest. The water rose to near the top of his thighs. And instead of a staff, he wore a pair of tight leather gloves.

Jake.

Elena nearly shouted his name. She had to clamp a hand over her mouth to keep from yelling after him. Jake stood with one hand raised towards the storm, an arc of bright green bursting from his fist — while the other held the gates.

He'd conjured one of his blue shields against it, no doubt to keep the water from leaking through the cracks. One of the child-mages said something to him, and Elena nearly jumped out of her skin when Jake's voice boomed across the courtyard.

"No. Hold your spells. Do not stop until our enemies breach the gates."

A red line bloomed across Jake's wrist as he spoke. There was a heavy length of chain wrapped around the base of his glove. When the chain burned, all of the mages' shackles flared up along with it. Their arms straightened and they forced their staffs higher.

Jake controlled them — or rather, that *chain* controlled them. Elena had a feeling that Jake was just as trapped as the child-mages. And she knew there was only one way to set them all free.

She swung over the ledge and climbed hand over foot to its bottom, moving faster than ever before. Her eyes swept across the guards' backs before she ripped Slight and Shadow from their sheaths.

There was no way she could hope to keep them all silent. The guards were spread too far apart to control. All she could do was kill them quickly and make sure none of them escaped into the courtyard behind her. If they alerted the soldiers on the other side, Elena would be overwhelmed before she had a chance to reach Jake.

She couldn't let that happen.

The world slowed as she darted in among the guards. Her blades danced across their throats in calm and deliberate arcs — each one marking the end of a life. Their gold-tinged bodies and the red spurts of their blood were nothing more than shades at the edge of her vision. All the while she fought, Elena kept her eyes on Jake.

She watched as he turned at the noise of the guards' faded screams, watched as his eyes tightened upon her mask, as they widened in recognition ... as his gaze turned dark with a maddened scowl.

No sooner had she cast the last body aside than Jake attacked her. She rolled out of the path of a fiery spell and ducked beneath the roar of the next. The magic wouldn't harm her, but she feared she might go mad if it struck her face. She might wake to find Jake slaughtered beneath her — a victim of the whisperers' curse.

So she forced herself to be patient.

Spells whipped past her on all sides. Jake was impossibly quick: he slung bolt after bolt, singeing the ground her boots left behind. Elena's breath rasped from her lungs and her muscles screamed each time she forced them to twist away, but she was quickly gaining ground.

Finally, she came within reach. When she sprang to tackle him, Jake was ready. He raised his fist and a wall of earth peeled up from the ground at his feet, swelling into a hill.

Elena struck the hill chest-first. Her body sank inside its muddy flesh and the breath *whoosh*ed from her lungs. She could feel the earth gathering beneath her. It tightened along with Jake's stare. He bared his teeth and stretched his hand towards her, preparing to fling her back.

She knew she might not get another chance to save him. She might never be this close again. Elena took a deep breath and, in the moment before he could toss her aside, she lurched forward — throwing a wild punch for his face.

The hill collapsed when her fist struck true. Elena landed in a crouch as the hill gave way beneath her. Tears swelled in her eyes. The scent of magic came through the slits in her mask and tried to cover her sight with darkness.

Across from her, Jake had fallen to his knees. Blood poured down his face, weeping from his broken nose. Though his eyes were clouded with pain and dulled without his spectacles, there was a message carved deep inside his stare:

It's all right ... do it.

Every inch of her wanted to stop his blood. A cool relief flooded her limbs at the very thought of tearing his throat away — it dulled the horrible, aching madness that washed her eyes in red. But there was one thing she wanted more than that. She wanted it more than anything ...

And it made her next decision easy.

Elena brought Slight down quickly — one jab into the top of her leg. The pain jolted her from her fury; the crimson that welled inside her wound overtook the red behind her eyes.

"What —? Are you *mad*?" Jake scrambled over to her. He tried to staunch her bleeding with the hem of his robes, but she knocked his hands away.

Elena pulled her mask aside so furiously that it broke: the leather guard ripped from its binding and fell onto the ground beside her. But she didn't care. How could she possibly care about that, about anything? Jake's lips were pressed against hers once more, his hands dragged warmth across her flesh ... he held her as if he never meant to let her go ...

Those were the only things she cared about.

"I'm sorry," Jake said when she pulled away, eyeing the blood he'd left on her chin. His stare trailed down to her leg. After a moment, he frowned. "You stabbed yourself to keep from killing me."

"I remembered you said that pain weakens the King's curse. I thought it might do the same for a whisperer's madness," Elena said.

"That's ... brilliant." Jake tried to smile, but wound up grimacing against his broken nose, instead. "The pain won't hold the curse back forever, though."

"I know." Elena grabbed the chains around his arm and nearly cried out at the jolt of magic against her skin. But she forced herself to rip them apart.

The chains broke. She went to pull them off his wrist and found they wouldn't budge. In the half-second it'd taken her to adjust her grip, they'd sealed back together. She tried again, but the same thing happened. No sooner did she manage to break them than the chains grew back. When she tried to rip the broken ends away, the chain only cinched tighter around his arm.

"You can't break it. This is a *living* impetus. It will exist for as long as I exist. It feeds off the beating of my heart and the warmth of my blood." Jake's eyes dragged up from the ground and onto hers for a moment. Then he twisted around to the mage-children.

They'd dragged themselves from the water and huddled together upon the shore, all of their stares fixed warily on Elena.

Jake took a deep breath. "The only way to break the curse —"

"I'm not going to kill you." The words burst hotly from her lips, and she expected Jake to meet them with a cry of his own. But instead, he only smiled.

It was a calm smile, a sad smile. His look drowned her anger in a knowing that crushed her chest. "Do you remember what you said to me, when we fought that bandit lord in the Valley? *Someone's going to die today, mage. You can't stop that from happening, but you can make sure that fewer of your friends wind up among the dead.* Now, when the wildmen come through that gate —"

"That isn't what I —"

"— they're going to unleash the full force of the sea: on themselves, on the pirates, the giants, and the entire camp beneath them. It isn't magic," he said, raising his voice over her protests. "These waters are real. I knew it would be the whisperers coming after us. So when I was commanded to find some way to stop them, I came up with this," he waved a hand at the water behind him, "an ocean made of storms summoned from across the realm — a trap with enough power to crush anybody standing at the gates, and deep enough to drown the rest. Those who aren't shattered against the trees will still have the life strangled from their lungs. Being a whisperer won't save them.

"This is what I do, Elena. This is what I've always done. And to die is no less than I deserve. But once I'm gone, you can warn the

512

others. You can make sure they don't try to cross this wall. If someone has to die today, then I'd rather it were me. Please," he added, reaching for her hand, "my life isn't worth all of this."

He was right. Elena knew how many men and women stood behind the western wall — and though she didn't care for most of them, Nadine would be there among them, and Braver … and Aerilyn.

Three lives to Jake's one. She stared down at the chains that wrapped around his wrist and watched its links began to glow. The curse was coming back. If she didn't stop him now, far more than three lives would be lost.

Elena knew what she had to do … though it broke her heart.

She paced back to the guards and drew a sword from one of their belts. What she did to Jake would be done cleanly. It would be over before he had the chance to feel the pain.

He bent his head as she approached, exposing the back of his neck to her blade. "Before I do this, I want you to know that I love you."

"Yes, I —"

"Quiet, mage. Let me speak," she growled, even as her stomach twisted. When his eyes fell back to earth, she forced herself to continue: "I've loved you for a long while, I think. But for all that time, I'd been made to believe that I didn't deserve you. I'd made myself believe it. Now I know for certain that I don't deserve you, and I never will.

"Luckily for me, love's not at all like the rest of life. Love isn't about getting what you deserve: it's about accepting what somebody else chooses to give you. That's what makes love so bloody hard, isn't it? Because in order to accept a thing like that, you have to first come to terms with the fact that you don't deserve it. I understand that, now." She braced the sword against his shoulder. "I just wanted you to know that I've tried to accept it. I will always love you … and I hope that someday you'll be able to forgive me."

"I … wait — what?"

Jake raised his head when she grabbed his arm. She flung him onto the ground and trapped his wrist beneath her heel.

It was the hardest thing she'd ever had to do. There wasn't a single cord of her heart of a shred of her soul that wanted to strike him, but she had no choice. Her sword came down …

And the curse ended.

CHAPTER 52
A MAGE'S REVENGE

Jake let out an inhuman cry when the blade came down. His face paled and his eyes rolled back in shock. Elena threw the sword aside and grabbed his arm.

"Hold still — I have to stop the bleeding!"

"No ... let me." Jake's hand shook horribly as he stretched it over the wound. A blue spell wrapped around its gushing end and hardened, stopping the flow of his blood. "Now ... give me the ..." He gestured, but couldn't seem to get the words out.

Still, Elena knew what he meant.

His other hand lay upon the ground, drenched in a dark puddle that welled from its severed end. The chained impetus was wrapped around it tightly. But the moment Elena reached for it, something odd happened.

A high-pitched whistling stabbed her ears. It grew louder and more insistent by the moment, swelling until she thought her head might burst. The chain's silver links glowed red and enflamed. They bulged out, stretching until their skin could no longer contain them.

Then, they exploded.

A blast shook the ground and peeled waves from the ocean's top. It shattered the storm, sent the clouds rolling in every direction. Red shrouded the world for a moment like a mist of blood. It hung about them so thickly that Elena could feel it clinging to her skin.

She held tightly onto Jake as the sky roared and the mist swirled around them — focused on the pain in her leg to keep from drowning in the magic. Just when she feared she could bear it no longer, the mist ended.

It fell back to earth in a red drizzle, pattering harmlessly onto the tops of the waves.

Elena lay very still in the silence left behind. Her head rose at Jake's deep, shuddering breath. "Well ... I suppose that ends it." She helped him sit up, and watched as his eyes roved blearily to the mage-children. "Is everybody all right?"

They didn't answer. Each of them watched unblinkingly as the shackles around their wrists melted and fell away, sliding into dull pools at their feet. Hesitant smiles stretched across their faces — smiles that quickly grew to laughter.

Elena scooped the severed hand off the ground and handed it to Jake. "Here. I'm sorry about that, by the way."

"Don't be. I'd much rather lose a hand and keep my head." Jake capped its end in blue and slid it into the pocket of his robes. "Who knows? I might be able to patch it back on."

"Knowing how your spells work, you'll probably end up with a set of talons," Elena warned.

His laughter went on for only a moment before he grabbed her beneath the chin. Warmth filled her to the top of her head when his voice dropped to a growl: "That was absolutely brilliant."

Elena's heart stumbled and tripped mid-beat. She'd never heard him speak like that before — never felt such heat in his touch, or seen such an edge in his eyes. The world melted beneath her ...

"Battlemage, look!" one of the children cried.

Jake pulled away and turned to where he pointed. The sky darkened suddenly and the calls of hawks and crows filled the air. They tore off in every direction, their wings beating madly towards the lines of the four horizons.

Jake stared after them, his mouth parted slightly. "It's over, then. It's all truly ended."

Before Elena could answer, a chorus of howls drew their eyes back to the gates. Rocks and weapons and small, spiked orbs flew into the mass of crows, knocking several of them off their wings.

"The wildmen are at the gates," Elena said, leaping to her feet. She had no idea how she would cross the sea before her, but there wasn't time to think. "I'll try to warn them —"

"No. No time," Jake grunted as he stood. He squinted at the sea before he turned to the eastern wall. The mage-children clustered together at his wave. "Does everybody remember how to cast a wind spell? Good. We're going to need wind — lots of wind."

Elena stood back as they walked to the waters' edge. She didn't know what Jake had planned, but knew she likely wouldn't be of any help. No sooner had she backed up against the wall than the main door started to rattle.

Someone was trying to work the lock. The soldiers in the courtyard behind them must've seen the red burst. Now they clustered at the door and shouted after Jake.

"What's happened, battlemage? Why has the storm stopped?"

Elena thrust Slight into the keyhole before it could turn, jamming the door with its point.

"It won't bloody open," the man with the key grunted.

"What do you mean, it won't open?"

"It means the key won't turn, you maggot." He pounded his fist against the door. "Open up, blast you! Open in the name of the King!"

Elena kept Slight pressed inside the lock as the soldiers threw their bodies against the door. There was some swearing, a heated argument, and a few muffled punches — then someone suggested finding a ram.

To the south, the ramparts had come to life. The guards behind the next wall must've noticed the storm breaking, as well. A few of their helmeted heads appeared over the wall for a moment. When they saw the gold-tinged bodies littered at the tower's base, they sprinted back down in a rush — bellowing for the archers.

Elena knew their time was up. She'd turned to warn Jake when a roar of wind cut over her words.

The mage-children stood in a line at the water's edge. Wind blasted from the tips of their staffs and struck the sea before them. It was a monstrous wind, an impossible wind — a gale that lashed the waves so fiercely that it began to churn them aside.

Jake kept his wounded arm pressed against his chest, and with the other, he held a blue shield. The shield was easily as tall as a castle tower, and more than twice as wide. Sweat gathered upon his brow as the force of the wind drove the water against its curved blue sides, but he never flinched.

"Keep pushing! Aim for the edges! Really get it spinning, now," he called.

When the other mages redoubled their efforts, the water rose higher up the shield. As the wind shoved on, it spun the sea like a potter's wheel: trapped against the shield's sides, it had no choice but to grow *upwards* instead of out. Debris got sucked up along with the water. It swirled inside the spout, adding to its height.

Soon the whole sea had been molded into an enormous tower. It leaned dangerously against the shield as the wind lashed on, but Jake held strong. He moved it fractions at a time, edging the spout for the southern wall.

The archers who'd been called to the ramparts paled as its shadow crossed their heads. They spilled from the top in such a rush that Elena thought more of them had likely jumped than used the stairs. But no matter how they screamed, it wouldn't save them.

Her blood rose when Jake let the tower fall. The roar as it tumbled through the air, the thunder as it crashed into the southern courtyard — the flash of gold-tinged bodies launched helplessly skywards as the monstrous waves slapped against their ranks. Elena had always known that Jake was powerful.

But this was, without a doubt, the most fantastic thing she'd ever seen.

Her eyes were so fixed upon Jake that she hardly felt the first *thud* of the ram against the gate behind her. She knew they ought to move ... but for some reason, she couldn't look away.

Jake called the mage-children together again and joined in their cheer. "Yes, well done, lords and ladies. Very well done, indeed."

The wildmen's howling had slowed while the spout towered inside the courtyard. But now that the danger had passed, they were at it again. Even from a distance, Elena swore she could hear the craftsmen scraping against the gates. They would be through in a moment.

"I think it would be best if you all left now. Get as far from Midlan as you can," Jake said, passing a severe look around the mages. "Use the invisibility spells I taught you. Stick together, and do not stop."

Most of the children disappeared with a *pop* — but all one boy managed to do was turn himself and his clothes to the color of stone.

"Just edge around the walls for as long as you can," Jake said, shoving him away. "Somebody help Patrick, will you?"

The boy jerked aside as an invisible hand wrapped around his wrist — and the moment they dragged him against the wall, he disappeared.

"What are we going to do about this?" Jake muttered, glaring at the main door. The guards were nearly through: they'd split the door badly, and were perhaps only a hit or two away from breaking the latch.

"You could blast them to bits," Elena said hopefully.

Jake laughed and wrapped his wounded arm around her waist, dragging her against his side. "I *would* ... but I'm afraid you chopped off my sword hand. Don't worry — I think I'll still be able to get us through. Hold on tightly."

She did. And when the gates burst open, the guards on the other side met the unforgiving front of Jake's shield.

It wrapped over their bodies in a protective orb, churning everything in their path aside. He flattened the guards and knocked the ram askew. Blades shattered all around them and arrows snapped helplessly against their sides.

"Where are we off to?" Jake said as they neared the keep doors. Though the shield was plenty wide enough for both of them, he kept Elena pressed against his side.

And she didn't mind it in the least. "We should probably find Jonathan and Eveningwing. I had them lock themselves into one of the chambers before I left."

"All right, then." Jake dropped his shoulder and sent the keep doors flying backwards. "Lead the way."

The halls twisted by them in a rush. Most of Midlan was smart enough to stand aside — though a large group of soldiers at the end of one passage mounted a brave attack.

They stood with their spears raised and their feet set beneath them ... as if any of that could've possibly stopped Jake.

Elena laughed when the shield smacked into them. Their limbs flailed as their bodies churned like dirt from a plow. One soldier got stuck against their front: they dragged him, his body trapped in a clanging roll, for nearly the full length of the next hall.

By the time Jake managed to scrape him off against a pillar, Elena was out of breath. "I'm always surprised by the things you find amusing," he said with a slight grin. "If I loved you any less, I might accuse you of being odd."

They barreled their way to the lion pelt room. Elena pounded on the door, but didn't get an answer. So she kicked it in.

"I can't believe it," she snarled when she saw the room was empty. "I told them to get here and stay *put*! They've got no business trying to drag that old man all around the castle."

"Old man?" Jake said. He stretched his hand out and the shield swelled to fill the room. It slammed the shattered door closed and held it tightly inside its frame, even as the guards who'd followed in their wake began to beat it with their fists.

Elena told him quickly of the old man they'd found in the dungeons, and how Eveningwing insisted that they bring him along. Jake's smile only got wider as she spoke, and she didn't understand why. When she finished, he laughed and shook his head.

"What's so blasted funny?"

"You have no idea who they've got with them, have you? It's a longer story than I wish to tell," he said when she shook her head. "But I've had the pleasure of meeting Argon once or twice. Trust me when I say that our friends are safe. That *old man* can see trouble coming three years out."

Elena thought the loss of blood might be getting to his head. "Are you all right?"

"Better than I've been in ages. I think we ought to stay here for a while — at least until the wildmen have the battle worked out of them. I'm not eager to step in the middle of their fight."

He cast his gaze around the room slowly, taking in everything from the pelts upon the floor, to the blue-shining walls. When his eyes finally settled back onto hers, Elena realized just how wildly her heart beat.

Her legs shook as she took a step towards him, a tremor that had nothing to do with her wound. "We should probably think of a way to pass the time."

That edge in his eyes clashed against hers. His smile held her to her feet. "Yes, I was just thinking the same thing — ah, but nothing too strenuous."

"No, of course not."

"I *have* lost quite a bit of blood, and my nose is throbbing horribly. Still, it might be nice to ... have a distraction."

"I'm no healer, Jake."

"Well, nevertheless, I think — wait a moment." He clutched her hand and squinted at her face, staring as if he thought she might've been someone else. "You ... you called me by my name."

Elena tried to stay calm, but it was difficult. Everything between her ribs had ground to a sudden, trembling halt. "I suppose I did."

"You hardly ever do that."

"I suppose I don't."

He glanced away for a moment. Red singed his throat as his hand tightened around hers. "I … well, I don't suppose you'd say it again, would you?"

Elena couldn't stop herself. The uncertainty in his touch, the way he reddened so magnificently against those words — it utterly and completely undid her.

"Perhaps," she managed to growl.

Then she shoved him onto the bed.

CHAPTER 53
A LESSON LEARNED

"They've spotted someone near the northern gates, Your Majesty. Ulric's already on his way," the mage said flatly.

"He's probably a spy. They're looking for another way in. See to it that he's dealt with — quickly. I want them to believe that the western gate is their only entrance," Crevan said.

He paced before the dying hearth, his mind spinning along the fall of his steps. The night had passed by in a blink, and now the dawn approached. There'd been not a moment wasted: no sooner had the whisperers appeared than Midlan rallied its strength. They'd woken a monster, when they dared to march upon his walls.

And now, they would face its teeth.

Aside from the mage who sat beneath the bricked windows and the steward who waited beside the door, Crevan was alone in his throne room. Soldiers packed the hallway outside — just to be safe. Though he was confident in his plan, there was one thing that made him uneasy.

The mage beneath the windows shifted suddenly. The shackle upon his wrist burned and he bit down on his lip, as if he was doing everything he could to keep the words from spilling out. But Crevan's command was far stronger — and he'd ordered him to relay everything the archmage said.

"Ulric wants to know why you won't use the dragon. He says if you mean to end the whisperers, it could easily be done —"

"Nothing is ever easy with the whisperers," Crevan said, his mind darkening against the light of a distant memory. "They're worse than serpents. The moment you believe you've got them trapped, they lash out and bite you. Once the battlemage has them weakened, *then* I'll send the dragon to finish the rest. But not a moment before."

When the mage nodded, Crevan went back to his pacing.

The truth was that he wouldn't send Devin away unless he had no other choice. Though he had her bound in magic and had taken

521

away that cursed white sword, the Dragongirl was still dangerous. She could undo everything, if she got loose — she'd managed to slip from his grasp countless times before. No, he wouldn't leave her unwatched for even a moment.

If she *did* manage to escape ... Devin was the only one who could stop her.

"Your Majesty!" The mage nearly fell in his rush to stand. His hands dragged down his ears and his eyes went stark with terror. "The man at the northern gates ... it's the Wright! The birds see the emblem on his shield. He ... oh, he's tearing them apart! He's slicing them to pieces with ... with his *hand*. He's killing them with his bare hand!"

Crevan's boots froze to the floor.

It wasn't possible. The birds must've been mistaken. He'd driven a sword through Setheran's chest, himself — had his body tied up and burned. There wasn't a trace of the Wright left within the Kingdom's borders.

But if there was a chance, if there was any chance at all ...

"Send the dragons. Send them both. Do it *now*!" Crevan roared, snatching the mage by his robes. "Kill him! Do not let him near the gates!"

He listened as Ulric's voice boomed above the fortress, relaying his orders —bolstered by the fury of his command. Several long moments passed before he heard Devin's roar. A rumbling sound echoed his voice, and the slightest tremor raced across the throne room floor.

"He toppled one of the northern towers, Your Majesty," the mage said at Crevan's look. Then he crouched and cupped his hands against his ears. His eyes tightened as he listened. "Devin's going after him. He sees the Wright —"

"What about the Dragongirl?"

"I'm trying, Your Majesty!" the mage whimpered when his shackle flared hot. "I'm trying to listen for her, but Devin's voice is too strong — he covers everything else."

"Burn the Wright!" Crevan demanded, his blood boiling hot. "Destroy him, leave his bones in ashes!"

He watched as the mage's lips moved with his command. They flew furiously across the words, forcing them through the walls and beyond the courtyard. But then all at once, he stopped.

The mage's hands crept from his ears to grip the top of his head. He rocked in his crouch, moaning nonsense under his breath. His eyes went stark again.

Crevan leaned down and wrenched the mage's head from where it'd fallen. "What is it?"

"The burning sword," he moaned, clawing at his face. "The burning ... no, I've lost him. I — I can't hear him anymore."

"The Wright?"

"No ... Devin. He's gone. I can't hear —"

"Send them to the northern gates!" Crevan shouted at the steward beside the door. "Send every man in the hall, pack the entrance with swords — do not let him through. Then go to the western corridor and make certain the battlemage is protected. Give him whatever he needs. Move!"

The steward rushed out the door and a moment later, the noise of tromping footsteps covered over everything else. While the soldiers in the hallway rushed to their posts, Crevan tried to steady himself. But his hands still shook when he grabbed the mage around the throat and growled:

"Send me Ulric."

In the few minutes they waited for the archmage, chaos erupted.

It was all falling apart. Everything was falling apart. Footsteps rattled the walls; voices packed the throne room to its edges. Stewards and guards poured into the chamber in a near constant stream:

"The Wright's just come through the doors — he's melted the gates!"

"Set the beasts on him. Tear him to pieces," Crevan said. Though the mage's shackle already glowed hot, he spurred him on with the edge of his boot.

"Y — yes, Your ... the dragon's returned, Your Majesty! I hear him!" the mage said suddenly.

Crevan dragged him up by his robes. He didn't know what power of the Wright had caused Devin to flee, but he wouldn't risk it again. His hold on the battle was slipping — and he meant to get it back. "Send the dragon after the whisperers. Burn them alive."

The mage's face paled, but he did what he was told. A moment later, he moaned again. "They have magic ..."

A frozen hand clenched around his gut. The whisperers didn't carry magic. They *never* carried magic. It was impossible — *impossible!*

"They struck Devin with a spell. He's fled from their reach."

Crevan was about an inch from tearing the mage down the middle when a pale-faced steward collapsed in the doorway. "Our enemies have slipped into the fortress, Your Majesty! There's a stack of bodies in one of the western corridors. They've all been cut to ..."

The steward was violently sick on the throne room floor.

Crevan had him hauled away by his throat.

Once the steward was gone, he bolted the doors. There were so many voices bouncing off the halls that he couldn't think to give orders. He needed silence. "Where's Ulric?" he snapped as he slammed the latches into place.

"I don't know, Your Majesty," the mage replied.

"Tell him to hurry up, or I swear I'll tear the cords from your throat. Do you hear me, mage?" Crevan snatched him up again. He shook his body hard, trying to fight the urge to crush him against the floor. Red swarmed at the edge of his vision. The madness circled hungrily as his panic rose, waiting to overtake him. "Send Ulric *now!*"

"I ... can't," the mage whispered. All of the flatness was gone from his voice. As he spoke, it rose across the shocked lines upon his face. "I can no longer hear him, Your Majesty. The beasts, the other mages, I can't hear any of them."

"What do you ...?"

Crevan's words trailed away when the mage raised his arm. The shackle upon his wrist was ... *melting.* Iron dripped from his fingers in molten lines, falling to cool across the front of his robes.

"I can't feel them anymore. The curse, it's — no! No, Your Majesty! Please!"

But Crevan didn't stop. He couldn't chance it.

He drove his sword through the mage's chest and tore it free. The moment his knees touched the stone, Crevan lopped off his head.

His lungs tightened even as the mage's blood spilled across the floor. His ears sharpened upon every sound, his eyes scraped against the shadows. Screams echoed down the hallway — a terror mixed with roars and wild, bloodthirsty howls.

The beasts were free. The mages were free. If Ulric had fallen ... then *she* would be free, as well ...

Madness gripped Crevan with this thought. It burst from the corners of his eyes and drowned his ears. He'd taken a step towards the door when the latch suddenly began to shake.

Crevan charged it with a bellow. The surge of his fury outweighed all thought. It covered the world in a mask of red. His sword fell upon the man who'd stepped through the door — and shattered against his upraised spell.

So Crevan grabbed him around the throat.

"Your Majesty!" Ulric gasped, holding up his arm.

Slowly, the red mist faded from his eyes and Crevan could see the silver links wrapped around Ulric's wrist. Only two remained.

"Something's happened to the battlemage," Ulric said the moment Crevan released him. His face had gone ashen; he strained air between his jutting teeth. "His link melted from my arm. The whisperers have taken the western wall. They must've slain him —"

"Help! The battlemage has gone mad!" a steward cried. He leapt through the open doorway and grabbed Ulric by the robes. "The army in the southern courtyard — he's drowned them! The whole lot of them! He dumped the ocean on their heads and broke into the keep. He flattened everybody who tried to stop him. Now he's got himself locked up with some forest woman. Kingdom knows what new terror he'll unleash upon us next. We can't get in to stop him — he's magicked the door shut!"

Ulric's face went dark. He knocked the steward aside with a spell. "I'll get him out —"

"No. Leave him," Crevan snapped.

He couldn't have cared less about the battlemage or the whisperers. At the moment, one fear rose above everything else. He looked down at the chains on Ulric's wrist and saw that one of them glowed red ...

But the other was dull.

"Where's the Dragongirl?"

Ulric's face turned the color of sand when Crevan spun on him. Only when his chains burned white-hot did he finally admit with a yelp: "I don't know! I can't hear her — but she's still bound, Your Majesty. I swear she's bound!"

Crevan didn't care. He didn't care what Ulric's excuse was. He'd entrusted the archmage with everything ... and he'd failed.

Ulric cried out when Crevan grabbed him by his face. Red seared the edge of his vision and madness swelled inside his veins. He was going to crush Ulric between his fingers, snap his skull into pieces and grind all of the little bits of bone into the mortar beneath his feet ...

"... the Dragongirl!"

A cry swam through his ears, followed by a pressure on his arm. Someone grabbed his wrist. A man's full weight dragged him down, pulling his hand away from Ulric ... stopping him, slowing the pressure ...

Crevan swung out against the force that held him back and struck a steward across the face.

His slight body flopped onto the ground. Crevan's blow had broken his nose, busted his lips, and must've knocked out at least one of his teeth: there was a large, black gap at their front. The steward's mouth parted around his swollen lips and he moaned: "The Dragongirl ... *escaped*, Your Majesty. Have to move ... had to warn ... coming ..." Blood poured in a renewed trickled from his nose as he raised himself up. "She's coming for ... the throne room!"

The madness fled Crevan's eyes in a blast of cold. Shouts filled the hallway, shadows scraped across the walls. Ulric lay curled upon the ground at his feet, clutching piteously at his face.

"Get up and follow me. *Now!*"

But no matter how Crevan barked, Ulric wouldn't move. Bruises welled across his head and gashes marred his face. In his rage, Crevan had wounded him: the archmage could no longer feel the shackle's curse above his pain. Now the madness was gone ... and his sword was broken.

He feared what would happen if Ulric realized he was free.

"Seal the doors," Crevan managed to gasp as he backed away. He kept a wary eye on Ulric while the stewards rushed to do as they were told. The moment they'd turned their backs, he bolted for the passageway.

The tunnels through Midlan were his only escape, now. There was a tapestry hanging at the back of the throne room. He ripped it aside and slid through the door behind it. Crevan stumbled for a moment, feeling along the wall until he touched a familiar track of stone.

526

He'd traveled this path so many times before that the darkness hardly slowed him. The stairs and passages twisted beneath his feet. They would carry him away from Midlan. He would escape with his life. But before he left, he had to retrieve the sword.

He couldn't let her have it. He couldn't let her carry it again.

I'm going to teach you, Crevan. Let me show you —

No! He shoved her voice away and clawed the stone door aside. Crevan tumbled out into a well-lit passage and staggered to his chambers. His fingers numbed against the door's handle. When he finally managed to get it open, he fell inside.

The room beyond was dark. All of the windows had been sealed with stone and mortar; the hearth fire burned out days ago. Crevan rushed to the table beside the hearth and gasped in relief when he saw that the sword still lay upon it.

He snatched it up and had gone to turn when he noticed the scabbard was strangely ... light.

An orange glow flickered from beyond the opened door — one thin beam to see by. He turned the scabbard's mouth into the light, hands shaking. It was empty. The sword was gone.

All of the blood plummeted from his body and gathered in the bottoms of his feet. The line of orange light thinned considerably as Crevan stared down at the scabbard. He watched it shrink into a thread, a scratch ... until it finally disappeared with a *click* of the closed door.

"It's been a long while, Crevan."

Her voice scraped down his spine with a dagger's edge, deepening to a growl at his name. The scabbard slipped from his hand. He stumbled in the pitch black of the room until his back struck a wall. Crevan was pinned inside the darkness, blind and helpless as her words filled the chamber with cold:

"I had a feeling I'd find you here. This is where it all began, isn't it? This is precisely where I found you the last time we ... *talked*."

Crevan's tongue swelled inside his mouth, drying even as a cold sweat drenched his face. "Please ..." he managed to gasp.

A hum started in the darkness before him. It was the moan of a vengeful spirit, a sound that crushed his bones: the whispering of that cursed white sword.

"No."

There was a hiss through the air before him and Crevan went blind against a flash of pain. His head slammed back against the wall. Warm lines of blood poured down his face, weeping from the fresh tear though his scar. Her blade split that line a second time. She'd carved him exactly where she'd carved before.

His blood spilled with such a resigning weight that it dragged him to his knees. Crevan barely heard it when she drove her fist into the bricked window beside him. He moaned and shut his eyes when she began to claw the stone aside, as the gray dawn came spilling in through the window behind it.

The madness was gone. He would've given anything to have it consume him, to have its red fury cover the world. But she'd taken it from him. She'd taken everything from him. Crevan had never been made to cower before she struck him. He'd never known fear. He'd never lost. But the Dragongirl stripped him of his blood, his pride.

The day she'd split his face was the day he'd first tasted death … and now, it was all happening again.

"Please, I'll give you anything you want."

"Can you give me the lives of my wolves, the lives of their pups?"

"The curse is broken! They're free to go," Crevan said. He pressed a sleeve against his wound and dragged himself to his feet. "Your wolves can leave this very —"

"Those aren't *my* wolves, Crevan. Not anymore. You've taken all the life from them, destroyed their souls with your hate. Had you released them when I first asked — when I first *begged* you to — they might've gone on to live happy lives. But now their only happiness will be in the peace of the eternal woods."

She ripped the last chunk of stone from the window and glared out into the coming dawn. Her eyes raged against its light. Their fires clenched his chest in a pitiless, aching cold.

"Please …"

"Do you remember the day I asked you for them?" she said quietly, her eyes distant. "Do you remember what you said to me?"

"No — I don't," he said when her hand curled into a fist. "I don't remember!"

"You said …"

Her voice trailed into a groan. Red bloomed across her throat for a moment as her collar flared — and Crevan saw his chance.

"End yourself, beast," he said as he sprang to his feet. Her face twisted against the pain of the blazing collar; sweat filmed her brow. "Yes, drag the blade across your throat. Do not stop. Coat the floors with your blood."

The curved white sword rose against the shaking of her arm. It came to within a mere inch of her neck. The Dragongirl growled and her glare tightened as she clenched her fist again.

There were raw, red blisters across her fingers. She pressured them, her face paling against the pain even as her burning stare stayed locked onto Crevan. Slowly, the red began to fade from her collar.

He bolted for the door.

She caught him around the throat.

The world shook as she slammed his body against the wall. Crevan fought to stay conscious. "Don't run from me, coward. You were always so brave, as long as you had someone else around to fight for you. Midlan, the mages, the Sovereign Five — they were only too happy to do your bidding. But they aren't here anymore, are they? No ... it's just you and I."

Crevan couldn't breathe. It was happening again. It was all happening again. This room, those words, the blood pouring down his face — the unforgiving strength of the hand wrapped about his throat.

"You said you'd never understand it," the Dragongirl whispered. "When I asked you to set my wolves free, you said you'd never understand why I would possibly waste my time on them. You said it was baffling, the idea that any man could choose to become *less* than human — and that being chained to your service was a far greater honor than they deserved.

"You said you'd never understand how so lovely a woman could possibly care about such a mindless pack of barbarians. You didn't know my secret, then. You didn't know that I *was* one of those barbarians."

No, Crevan hadn't known what she was — but he knew what would happen next. He clawed furiously at her hand, though there was no hope of breaking her grip. "Take the shapechangers, if you want them. Take the Kingdom!"

"No, it's too late for that."

She dragged him to the window and pressed his face hard against the glass. From where he stood, Crevan could see the entire northwestern reach of Midlan stretched out before him. His army scattered like ants from the force that burst through the western walls: an ocean that writhed with swords carried by men of every region. They tore through his soldiers and swarmed into the keep.

To the north, monsters reigned. His beasts had broken free of their chains and now set upon the soldiers trapped beside them. A mob of animals crushed through the melted gates, led by a light that made Crevan's eyes ache against its fury.

A man moved beneath the light, his figure turned to shadow. Weapons and armor broke beneath its power; soldiers fell helplessly before it, their bodies engulfed in flame ...

"The burning sword," Crevan moaned in disbelief. He twisted against the Dragongirl's hold. "Please, I'll give you anything!"

She leaned to whisper in his ear: "There's only one thing I want from you ... I want you to understand."

"No!"

"I want you to know what it feels like to have the world ripped out from under you, what it's like to be made to watch as everything you know and love goes flashing by — what it's like to be utterly, and completely helpless."

The window groaned as she pressed him tighter against it. A hairline crack webbed across the glass. Crevan's eyes twisted to the chamber behind him.

"Ulric ... *Ulric!*" he cried, but there was no answer.

Crevan begged for the door to open, begged for the Dragongirl to be stopped. But there would be no stopping her, this time. Ulric couldn't hear him over the pain of his wounds — wounds left by Crevan's fury. And the man who'd burst through the door nearly twenty years ago wouldn't be able to save him again ...

Crevan had ordered the beastkeeper to skin him alive the night before.

As the Dragongirl pressed him against the shrieking glass, he could do no more but stare out at the ruins beneath him. The fortress of Midlan had fallen: its walls had given way and its enemies stormed into its keep. Never mind the catapults or the archers — this army didn't need them. All of the wards upon his tower were useless.

From this highest, insurmountable point, King Crevan paled against the view of a man who'd lost everything.

"I think it's time you understand what you did to the shapechangers, to the whisperers ... to me. And I can think of no better way to explain it than this." She jerked him back and slammed his head through the glass, forcing him to look at the world below. "I'm going to teach you, Crevan. Let me show you how to fly."

CHAPTER 54
A STRANGE LOT

A monstrous army crushed its way across the northern courtyard.

Kael could hardly focus on the soldiers when he saw the horde of beasts pushing in behind them: wolves, lions, bears, and foxes — all twisted into hideous giants beneath the King's curse. They towered above men on two legs, and hefted claws that looked capable of snapping entire cages of ribs.

No sooner had the monsters come pouring from the keep than the shapechangers arrived. Graymange howled at the sight of them, and the other shamans added their cries to his.

They tore off before Kael could stop them, weaving their way through the soldiers. Most of them were slight enough to slip between the ranks unnoticed — though the bear shaman left a considerable mess in his wake.

Kael knew he couldn't keep up with them. So instead, he struck the soldiers hard. He fought to keep their eyes turned upon him and away from the shapechangers.

Daybreak roared through the air in a storm of flame and sparks. It devoured every last drop of moisture in the air above him. Against its power, the heavy flow of rain was reduced to nothing more than a thick, damp cloud.

The blade's heat slid between the scales of Kael's armor and bit his skin with all the unforgiving force of the sun. Though he could feel himself turning raw, he never once slowed his pace. Each new wave of soldiers staggered back from the white-hot blade in surprise — and the moment they were off balance, Kael melted them through their armor.

The monsters bellowed with fresh life when the shapechangers reached them. Though their bodies were massive, they didn't move as one. All it took was a dog's bite or the swipe of a badger to anger them. Kael watched a lion charge away from its companions, only to get dragged down by a horde of the strange, striped creatures who followed the fox shaman.

"Abominations!"

Kael swiped a cluster of soldiers out of his path and saw the bear shaman standing at a corner of the fray. He held the wooden medallion from his chest and it burst with a strange white light.

Three more bursts answered it, each rising from a corner of the fight. The lights swelled into pillars as they rose and fell back to earth in something that looked like a blinding white net.

The net's cords draped over the monsters' heads and for a moment, they clawed desperately against the trap. Then all at once, they fell silent.

The rain stopped. Kael watched in shock as the clouds above them broke, shattering like a clay pot against the stone floor, evaporating into the pale sky beyond. A red shadow crossed his boots. He turned in time to see something that looked like a mist of blood spray above the western wall.

It hung for only a moment, all of the crimson droplets trembling in the light of the coming dawn. Then it dropped back behind the wall with a hiss.

Another surge of red light drew Kael's eyes back to the battle. The King's monsters had fallen silent the moment the clouds broke. Now they watched with black, deadened eyes as the collars around their throats turned molten. Their shackles slid away in an iron rush, matting into their fur and cooling against their skin in ripples.

The silence lasted only a moment before the monsters attacked.

They scattered in every direction, bursting out from beneath the shaman's white net and onto the throats of Midlan. Gold-tinged bodies flew through the air; screams racked the walls. A large group of soldiers shoved past Kael and sprinted for the gate — braving the light of Daybreak to avoid the monsters' jaws.

It happened so quickly that Kael hardly had a chance to breathe. The mass of bodies that crushed for the gate parted against an arc of Daybreak's molten edge, but there were still too many soldiers in the way. The tide of monsters was coming closer: drool trailed their fangs and their blackened eyes shone with fury. The shamans' spell flickered as more of the monsters escaped the net.

Then with a pained howl, the light went out.

A wolf monster had Graymange around the throat. Panic shoved Kael forward the moment he saw the wolf shaman's thin figure hefted above the fray. Daybreak slung through the crowd, devouring flesh and steel. Its fire seemed to burst with renewed fury as Kael's panic rose. But there were simply too many bodies in the way.

He would never reach Graymange in time.

The wolf monster almost lost its grip when the shaman twisted into his second shape, but managed to catch him by the scruff of his neck. Kael watched them between blinding flashes of Daybreak's light, bellowing at the tops of his lungs.

A scruffy pack of dogs tried to free their shaman, but a line of monsters kept them back. They weren't fooled by the shapechangers' speed: their black, pitted stares wrapped around the entire courtyard, and their warped ears twitched to follow every sound. It seemed to be taking all of the dogs' focus just to avoid the sweep of their claws.

Graymange and the wolf monster had their faces hardly an inch apart. The shaman snarled viciously, his lips peeled back from his jagged teeth — while the monster's jaw cracked open for the kill.

Kael was still too far. The shapechangers beat helplessly against the monsters' line. There were too many bodies in his way, his glimpses between them too brief to line up a throw. An arc from Daybreak would devour them both. He'd spun for the ramparts, hoping the height would give him a decent shot, when something high atop Midlan caught his attention.

He thought it was one of the King's birds, at first: an object the size of a man plummeted from the mouth of an opened window. It twisted and flailed against the pull of the earth. But it wasn't until the object crossed out from beneath the shadow of the onyx towers that he saw what it was.

A man — a man in a gold-spun tunic with a black dragon etched across its front. His hands scraped helplessly at the air beneath him; his legs kicked in wild arcs. Kael only caught a glimpse of the terror upon his face, and the deep gouge that ran across his jaw.

The man's eyes seemed to widen with every second his body fell, until he finally struck the ground.

His death sent tremors across the battlefield. The monsters staggered backwards in the silence it left behind, and Kael saw his chance. He sheathed Daybreak and grabbed a dagger off one of the fallen soldiers. Though its hilt was slightly melted, he thought it still ought to fly.

By the time he made it up to the ramparts, everything had changed.

The wolf monster held Graymange tightly, but its snarl had fallen slack. All of the black pulled from the edges of its stare, swirling away like foam swept out by the tide. The black drained into the monster's pupils slowly — leaving its eyes a deep, intelligent brown.

Kael's arm froze above him, and the dagger slipped from his hand. Those eyes ... they were the same as Bloodfang's — the mark of a shapechanger with its mind still intact. Though its body stayed twisted, all of the fury left its gaze. The monster sat Graymange gently upon the ground and called to him with a low whine.

The other monsters stumbled like drunkards as the darkness left their eyes. They blinked around them, their faces bent in shock. The shamans watched unblinkingly from the four corners of the courtyard. With all of the soldiers either dead or scattered, the battlefield seemed frozen in time.

Graymange stared the wolf monster down. His furry head tilted at the noise of its whines and his ears pricked tall. Then all at once, his chest swelled — and a sky-rending howl burst from his lungs.

It was so sharp and terrible a sound that Kael expected the battle to start all over again. But it didn't. Instead, wolf monsters came pouring from every direction to cluster around him, adding their own voices to Graymange's song. The dogs barked and leapt around the monsters, tails beating furiously against the air.

One by one, the shamans called out — and the monsters answered: the bears bellowed, the lions roared. Foxes yipped and sprung from the crowd, their bright red tails bristled with excitement. When the hawk shaman took to her wings, the screech she let out drew all of her birds in a swarm around her.

She took off towards the swamp — and as she went, crow and hawk monsters drifted from every corner of the sky to follow.

There were so many strange creatures gathered together that Kael could hardly take it in. But the strangest among them wasn't a *creature* at all: it was a man. He lumbered out from between the keep's shattered doors, his heavy steps thumping against the earth. Though his face was badly mangled with bruises and scars, it was difficult not to notice the upward tilt of his crooked mouth ...

Or the gleam in his one good eye.

The wolf monsters howled again at the sight of the scarred man. They leapt around him and threw their great bodies against his ravaged chest. Deep growls split their twisted throats as he scratched their ears.

Graymange bared his teeth as he reached up in welcome. His hand hardly came to the small of the scarred man's back. It was only when the wolf shaman turned to Kael that he realized all eyes had fallen upon his.

The hawk shaman was already gone, having winged off into the swamps with her strange flock in tow. Kael stared at the courtyard around him — empty, save for the shapechangers and the mass of gold-tinged bodies. The fact that all the darkness was gone from the monsters' stares could've only meant that the curse was broken.

He saw no need to keep them in the fortress a moment longer. "Go," he said, fighting against a smile. "Your debt is more than settled."

Graymange touched his chest. "We will be forever grateful, Marked One."

Though he'd done nothing to deserve it, the thunder of their thanks broke his smile free. He was grinning by the time the last fox slipped out the of the gates, into the field beyond — and perhaps it was because he was so focused on their march that he didn't notice the growing shadow above him until it'd already struck.

The wind screamed past his ears as he fell from the ramparts, but the warrior in him steeled its legs. He caught himself in a roll and flopped onto his back — just in time to bear the weight of a familiar iron grip.

"Kyleigh!"

She sat on top of him, eyes blazing beneath her scowl. Sweat covered her face and ran down her neck in molten lines. Her arms trembled as her hands scraped up his chest ... and curled tightly around his throat.

Her grip shortened his breath. She was pushing down upon him, strangling him. "Kael," she growled as her fingers tightened.

Red crossed her skin in a furious rush, and that was when he noticed the collar around her throat. Though the monsters' collars had melted away, Kyleigh's still burned brightly. She bared her teeth against its growing light; her fingers tightened again.

"*Kael.*"

He worked quickly, peeling the spell away and tearing the iron collar into two. Only once it'd fallen did she collapse upon his chest.

"Kael ..." she breathed as her hands slipped away. "Blazes. For a moment there, I thought Ulric was actually going to make me kill you."

He wrapped his arms around her middle and crushed her in against him, holding on as tightly as he could. Relief filled his limbs in a rush of cool, filled his heart to its brim. "Well, I'm glad you didn't kill me."

She laughed as she kissed him. "Me too. I hate to admit it, but I've grown rather fond of you."

His reply was swept away, drowned out by a familiar, earth-trembling roar. Kyleigh twisted to glare at the monstrous black shadow that rose above Midlan's onyx towers.

A flash of gold shone on Dorcha's spiny back. His great neck twisted and with a heave, he managed to knock a tiny figure off his spines. She caught herself on the jagged ledge of a tower and held on with one hand as Dorcha tore past her — waving a golden axe at his tail with the other.

"Gwen," Kael said, when he recognized her curses. "What's she —?"

"They're all here. Everybody. They stormed the western wall and broke Midlan to pieces. I've taken care of Crevan, but Ulric's still alive. And he's got a hold on Devin." Kyleigh sprang to her feet and pulled Kael up beside her. "I'll keep him busy —"

"No, I don't want you anywhere near that monster. He'll kill you!"

She grabbed him around the face, and her eyes blazed as she growled: "He's not a monster. Devin is a decent creature, but he'll be dangerous for as long as he's cursed. That's why I need you to go into the fortress. Find Ulric. Kill him. Put a stop to this madness. I'm depending on you, Kael," she added at a whisper. "Please — trust me one more time. I promise I'll fly safely."

She took off before he had a second to protest, tearing into the skies with a roar and a burst of grit. Her body was little more than a white bolt as she shot past Dorcha. His mad, blackened eyes traced her flight — and his enormous body twisted to follow.

Kael knew there was only one way to stop him. So he drew Daybreak and charged into the keep, his mind set on what had to be done.

****

"Are you sure we're headed the right way?" Declan grunted as he squeezed through another narrow portal. His head thumped hard against a low jut of stone, but he hardly felt it: the pirates' grog had numbed him to the point that he hardly felt anything.

"I do not know what the *right* way is. But I know we are going north. Keep up, giant," Nadine said, reaching back to prod him with her spear. "And watch your great stone head."

They were deep inside the tunnels of Midlan. Declan hadn't even known that Midlan *had* tunnels. They'd slipped through the gates not long after the wildmen had busted them open, and planned to hide out inside one of the towers until the rest of the army went on.

But no sooner did Declan turn his back than one of the little mots found a passage hidden behind a stack of crates — and off they'd gone.

"Leave it to the wee sandbeaters to find the cracks in everything. You probably live under rocks and swim in puddles," he grunted.

Nadine frowned at him from over her shoulder. The torch she carried brightened her eyes and brought a warm glow to her skin. It set such a fire in Declan's chest that he had to smile to keep from roasting.

"You are a fool," Nadine muttered — but not before she'd smiled back.

They lagged at the rear of the mots' line. All of the little desert people flitted through the tunnels ahead: they'd pop in and out of chambers, torches spitting behind them — chattering to each other in their strange, musical tongue. Every once in a while, they'd give Nadine some sort of direction, and she'd turn them down a different path.

"How can they keep up with it, eh? How do they know where we're headed?" Declan wondered. The way the grog had his head spinning, it was a struggle to keep track of his *feet* — let alone which paths they'd already taken. They might very well be going around in circles.

When he said as much, Nadine prodded him again. "Do not worry yourself over it, giant. This is a *mot's* business."

538

He was thinking of a retort when one of the mots called to Nadine. He spoke in a rush and, after a moment of listening, she sent the others after him with a wave of her spear.

"What is it?" Declan said as they peeled away.

"There is a strange voice coming from up ahead — a voice that says he is in trouble."

She rushed off, and Declan thumped after her. "Well, just be careful about it. You never know what you're going to find in these dark, twisty sorts of places."

A few steps more, and he heard the voice for himself. It was coming from the other side of the wall, muffled by several inches of mortar and stone:

"Hello? Is someone there? Oh, you have to help me! The King's got me locked away, and I can't work the latch. Come quickly — ah, unless you're one of those foul mages, in which case I'd rather just be left alone to rot."

There was a thick wooden panel set inside one of the walls. The mots swarmed around it, running their fingers across its edges. They traced as high as their hands could reach, then they searched with their eyes.

"Ah, there!" one of them called.

There was a short coil of rope hanging from the ceiling. The mots had no hope of reaching it, but Declan could. He gave it a sharp tug, and the panel swung open with a *thwap*.

Nadine slapped him across the arm. "Shhh!"

"Well, how was I to know it'd open like that?" Declan grunted.

He had to duck to follow her through the doorway. They stood inside some sort of clutter room. There were bits of things scattered everywhere — so coated in dust that it made Declan's eyes water just to look at it.

The mots spread out across the chamber, poking their spears through the mess. Though they called out, the voice didn't answer them back.

"Stay close to me," Nadine said, waving Declan forward.

He didn't have to be told twice. Perhaps it was just the grog getting the better of him — but he swore as he watched her move around the dusty chamber that she'd never looked so ... beautiful. The way she smiled, the way she fought — the way her people followed her lead. She was a wonder.

And Declan knew he couldn't live with himself if he didn't give it one last try.

When she stepped inside a broom closet, he blocked the doorway.

"What are you —?"

"Why won't you marry me? And don't say I wouldn't understand, because you haven't even tried to tell me. I might understand it," Declan said roughly. Though the liquor steeled his nerves, he had to press his fists against the doorframe to keep from toppling over.

But even as the closet spun, he could see the surprise on Nadine's face. Her dark eyes flicked beneath his arm. "No, not here."

"Yeh, *exactly* here. Right now, before you have a chance to run off again."

"But everybody is watching!"

"I don't care! They can watch all they want to. Tell me why you won't have me, Nadine. Is it because I'm not one of your kind?"

"No —"

"Is it because I haven't got much to give you? I know my house is small, but —"

"*No!* It is nothing to do with you. It is all my doing." She looked away and said with a glare: "I am barren. I cannot have your children, and so it would not be right to let you tie yourself to me. You would only be disappointed."

Declan stared at her for nearly a full minute, sifting through the shock, before he was finally able to work out exactly how he felt. "That's the stupidest thing I've ever heard. Haven't we got enough of them? What could we *possibly* need another child for? We've got so many little mice running around the fields that I've got to look twice before I put my feet down!"

Her glare shone fiercely in the torchlight. "You have been very kind to take us in. I will never be able to repay your kindness. But one day, you will want your own family — what are you doing?"

Declan didn't trust himself to grab her around the arms. His balance was bad enough that he thought he might accidentally crush her, if he tried. So instead, he fell to his knees.

From this angle, he had to look up at her. It was more than a little frightening — it would hurt badly, if she stomped him while he sat like this. But he swallowed his fear and forced himself to say it:

540

"Is that what you think of me? Do you think I'm just putting a roof over your head while I wait around for a family? You *are* my family," he grunted, his chest tightening against the words. He hadn't expected them to come out so strongly. They practically burst him, pushing through. "We're a strange lot, I'll give you that. But I love those little mountain mice. I don't care that they aren't giants. I don't care that they don't look like me. They're mine in every way that counts. If you ever took them away ... it'd break my heart."

The mots were crowded in tightly behind Declan, watching. He could feel their little shadows across his back. But he didn't care: he kept his eyes on Nadine.

For a moment, she didn't budge. Then all at once, something twisted across her face. She dropped her spear and, as it clattered to the floor, pressed a hand against her eyes.

Declan pulled it away. "If you don't want me, I'll understand it. And I'll never ask again. But if *this* is all it is ... well, that's not good enough. You'll have to try harder than that to —"

"Yes," Nadine said suddenly. She pulled her hand from his and dashed the wet from her eyes, smiling as she said again: "Yes, you foolish giant."

Declan was about to smile back when a thought struck him. "Wait — *yes*, you'll have me? Or *yes* you don't —?"

She kissed him firmly, leaving absolutely no doubt.

The floor shook as the mots cheered and thumped their spears hard against the planks. All of the pounding knocked something loose in the broom closet — a hefty chunk of wood that'd been leaning against its side.

The wood thumped hard into Declan, and he nearly leapt out of his skin when he felt a blast of hot breath against his shoulder: "Sorry about that. I was going to be polite for once and wait till you'd all finished talking, but the floor had other ideas," a voice mumbled into Declan's shoulder.

He shoved the chunk of wood back into the depths of the closet, his heart pounding in shock. There was a knot in the wood about halfway up. He groaned when a lopsided face appeared inside its center.

"Clodded pirate grog," he swore.

But Nadine gasped beside him. "No, I see him as well! It is magic."

"It's *Knotter*, actually," the wood replied. "And I'd very much like to go home."

CHAPTER 55
THE EDGE OF VILLAINY

"Are we out yet? Are we free?" Knotter hissed.

"Can't you see we're still in a tunnel, you clodded thing?" Declan grunted.

As he was the only one strong enough to carry Knotter, he'd been given the task of toting the door across his back. Now the tunnels were much tighter than they'd been before, he was sweating through his tunic — and Knotter's moaning showed no signs of ending.

"I don't know — all I see are miles and miles of dank, moldy rock."

"Yeh, and it matches well with your breath."

"I spent almost a week fully sunk inside a vat of water, a stone sitting atop my middle," Knotter said evenly. "Yes, I contracted a nasty rash of mold, and I'm afraid being locked inside that closet didn't help things. But once I spend a few days in the sun, it ought to dry up nicely ... *if* we ever get out of here, that is."

Declan couldn't help but feel a bit sorry for him. From what he could remember through the cloud of grog, Knotter said that he used to be a part of the front gate at the Wright's castle. When the castle burned, the King's mages found him out. They'd ripped him from his frame and taken him to Midlan — where he'd been tortured for weeks.

"They tried magic, but of course that didn't work. No spell can touch me. The termites weren't at all interested. So after that, the mages had no choice but to try and drown me." Knotter's laugh bounced off the passageway suddenly, causing several of the mots ahead of them to jump. "But no matter what they did, I wouldn't give them so much as a *murmur* of what I knew. A gate must be loyal to everybody inside his walls — even if they threaten to burn him alive nearly every other day. Such is my burden and my solemn oath."

"Yeh, well, when you start to smell fresh air, you'll know we're almost out. I can't give you anymore a clue than that," Declan said.

Ahead of them, Nadine spun around. "*Can* you smell?"

"Yes, I can smell. I can hear and I can taste ... and just recently, I've learned to love, as well."

"Plains Mother," Declan grumbled.

Knotter didn't seem to hear him. "Yes, it's true — though I didn't realize that I loved her until after we'd already been torn apart. She's always been there for me, always by my side. She is, without a doubt, my other half."

"Nadine!" One of the mots stuck her head from a passage and swung her spear in a wild, frantic arc. "Come quickly — I hear another voice!"

"Please don't let it be someone else who needs saving," Declan muttered as he followed them. "I've got my hands full enough, as it is."

The mots crowded around a small wooden door. Several of them had their ears pressed against it. As Nadine listened to the muffled voice on the other side, her mouth parted slightly — and her brows dropped low.

She only got that look when she was troubled about something. Declan sat Knotter face-first against a wall and eased his way to her side. "What is it, wee thing?"

"They are strange words ... the words of a spellweaver."

Declan pressed an ear against the door above her. "Is it Jake?"

"I do not think so."

"That's Ulric," Knotter called. With his lopsided face crammed so tightly against the wall, his words sounded as if they came out of his nose. "Yes, that's *definitely* Ulric. I'd know that sniveling, whistle-breathing spell-flinger anywhere."

Even through the power of the grog, Declan felt a twinge of fury. No sooner had he reached for the door's latch than Nadine grabbed him around the wrist.

"No, keep yourself calm. We have no power against the mages."

"I'm not going to attack him," Declan promised. "I only want to see what we're up against. I'll just open it a crack."

After a moment of glaring, she relented. "Be careful."

"I will." Declan eased the door from its frame an inch. "There's a tapestry on the other side. I can't get a good look at ... wait a moment. Here's a worn bit."

544

He peered through a bare section of thread and a large, dark room came into focus. Light spilled from the hearth, but that was it. There didn't appear to be any windows in the chamber.

A man paced back and forth across the flickering trail left by the hearth fires. There were scratches and bruises across his face. He wore gold robes — the same as the mages who'd attacked them in the plains. There was a shackle glowing red upon his wrist. As he stalked, he whispered loudly into the silent room:

"Get her, beast … grab her around the throat … yes!" he cried suddenly, clenching his fists before him. "*Yes*! Drag her down, send her body through the fortress! Crush her! *Crush* —"

A blast stumbled Declan backwards, and a flare of light blinded him for a moment. Nadine grabbed onto his belt to keep from being rolled away by the force of the blast. When Declan finally steadied himself, a new voice filled the chamber:

"Enough, Ulric! The battle is lost, Midlan has fallen. Let the boy go … or I'll put a stop to you, myself."

Ulric responded with a roar and an arc of red flame. It flew towards the three darkened figures standing in the doorway: the two on either side leapt out of its path, but the man in the middle caught the flames against a spell of his own.

The noise as the two spells collided stabbed Declan's ears. He held on tightly to Nadine as the mages tried to blast each other into the under-realm. Back and forth they fought, moving around the room in a dueler's dance.

Though the mage with the green spells held his own for a moment, he was quickly driven back against a wall. His many wrinkles deepened against the fury of the red light, and his gray beard seemed close to catching flame.

"We must do something!" Nadine cried, her hands twisting into his tunic.

The mages' battle had carried them close to the tapestry. Ulric was only a few paces away. When he tried to outflank the older mage, it left his back exposed. Now he faced the wall and kept all of his focus on the battle. He paid no mind to anything behind him …

Declan had an idea. "Pass me the door."

"I — what? No, what are you doing with me? Put me down!" Knotter cried.

But the mots paid him no heed. They wedged their tiny fingers beneath him and passed him in an ant's line to Declan — who grabbed him firmly around the wooden sides.

"No spell can touch you, right?"

Knotter replied with an unintelligible groan.

Nadine seemed to realize what Declan had planned. She slid her spear against the tapestry's edge. "When you are ready, I will cast it aside. The mots will be right behind you."

"Yeh, and stay close together, wee things. It's about to get thick —"

"No, wait!" Knotter's lopsided face twisted with a sigh. "If you're going to do this, at least turn me around. I'd like to be able see what's coming."

Declan flipped him so that his knot faced out. "All right, then. Here we go!"

Nadine slung the tapestry aside — and Declan charged through the door. The chamber shrank quickly beneath his sprint. Ulric twisted around at the sound of his roar and only managed to fire one spell.

It struck Knotter hard, and the door let loose with a battle cry when the fires shook him. Declan's muscles swelled as he struggled to hold his course. But hold it, he did. He picked up speed the second they struck flesh — and he didn't stop until he'd crushed Ulric against the wall.

"Is that it? Is he dead?"

"No, not yet," Knotter grunted.

Declan's next thrust brought with it the unmistakable sound of crunching bones.

"*Blah*! That did it."

Ulric left such a mess against the wall that Declan didn't think the stones would ever recover. To his right, the mots gathered around the old mage. He thanked them quietly as they helped him to his feet.

"Much appreciated, little ones. You were a bit late, but not *too* late. That's the main thing."

Nadine stared him in the eyes for a moment, mouth agape. Then all at once, she grinned. "You have the Sight."

"I do, yes. How wise of you to notice." The old mage cast his stare around the room, and his mouth went sharp. "We really must be going, now. There's something —"

"Ahoy there, mates!" Jonathan called. He jogged through the door, arm slinging before him in a wave. Eveningwing darted in close behind.

Declan had to squint just to make sure it wasn't the grog playing tricks on him. "Is that you, wee fiddler?"

"Sure. Who else would it be?" he said with a grin.

Jonathan slung one of the old mage's arms across his shoulder, and Eveningwing propped him up on the other side. No sooner had they gotten settled than something like thunder shook the stone beneath their feet. A pair of furious roars filled the hallways.

The old mage's eyes widened, and he cried out. "No! Oh, we're too late! Move me quickly — please, we must hurry!"

"What is wrong?" Nadine said.

The old mage shook his head. "Devin was supposed to stay out of reach. He wasn't supposed to come down. If the Forsaken One finds him ... oh, I groan to think of it! Please, *please* we must hurry!"

****

Kael knew he had to find Ulric — but he had no idea where the archmage might be.

Most of Midlan was deserted. He'd come across a band of soldiers every once in a while. But the moment he drew Daybreak, they'd tear off in the other direction. The hallways twisted and turned in unreliable patterns. He listened at every bend for the sound of a mage's spell. He scanned the chambers as he jogged past, hoping for any sign that the archmage might be hiding within them.

He was halfway up a tower's steps when the floor shook violently. Roars billowed up throughout the halls — and they were unmistakably familiar.

Kael forgot his task. He tore down the steps and sprinted in the direction he thought the roars had come from. No matter what Kyleigh said, he couldn't leave her on her own. She was no match for Dorcha — and if the black dragon had fallen back to earth, he wouldn't need to find Ulric.

Kael could end the battle, himself.

By the time he reached the end of the next hall, the roaring had stopped. His heart pounded inside his chest as several long, silent moments passed. Worry clenched his knees, but he forced himself to move. At last, he found a promising chamber.

What looked to be the last remaining company of Midlan stood before it. They slammed themselves against the towering doors, trying to force their way inside. Kael ripped Daybreak from its sheath and charged into their backs. A spout of white-hot flame cut the nearest men across their middles — the rest fled his path.

The door's bolt melted beneath Daybreak's flaming edge. Kael kicked them open — and marched straight for Dorcha.

The black dragon was crouched in the middle of an enormous chamber. The roof lay in a shattered mess all across the floor. Dawn light poured in from above. Dorcha had his back turned to the door. His deep, booming hum rattled the grit across the stone. His wings bent open slightly, and Kael thought he might be about to take off again.

He couldn't let Dorcha leave. He couldn't let him go after Kyleigh.

A storm of anger and fear erupted in Kael's veins. The world blurred as he pounded for Dorcha with a cry.

An arc from Daybreak slapped against Dorcha's back. When he flung his great body aside, Kael struck him across the chest. The shock of his wounds must've knocked him from his scales: Dorcha twisted in pain, roaring as he slid back into his human skin.

And Kael saw his chance.

He stepped over to where Dorcha lay and pressed a boot across his throat. He held Daybreak's point above his chest, aiming over his heart. It was difficult not to notice the scales that burst through his human skin: they were raised taut, swollen painfully around fresh pools of blood. The collar around his neck was gone, melted. Its iron trail left shining lines across his shoulders. Ulric must already be dead. If that were true, then there was no need ...

No. No, this is different, Kael reminded himself. *Dorcha can't be allowed to go free. He's far too powerful. He's far too dangerous.*

He met the halfdragon's burning yellow eyes, hoping to find some proof within them. He wanted to find the cruelty he'd seen in Finks, or the wickedness of Earl Titus — some raging, unrepentant line of evil strong enough to send Daybreak through his chest ...

But there was none.

Without the collar to madden his gaze, Dorcha stared up at him, defeated. His arms lay limply by his sides. A burning wound hissed across his chest — a mark of Daybreak's fury. But though he must've been in pain, he didn't show it. The look he wore was of a man who knew all of the horrible things he'd done, and who expected to pay for them.

Kael could've paid him back. He was an inch from ending him.

But at the last moment, a truth he'd once spoken struck him hard: Dorcha deserved a chance. Every creature deserved a chance. The fact that he was powerful shouldn't have meant a blasted thing. At his heart, the halfdragon was no different than the mountain folk, or the King's monsters. That's what Kyleigh had been trying to tell him all along — Kael had just been too stubborn to listen.

If he killed Dorcha now, it would only be because he feared him ... and that was no better than what Titus had done to the wildmen, or what Crevan had done to the whisperers. There was absolutely no good in it.

Kael stood upon the edge of villainy — and it was that bitter realization that drew his boot away, that sent Daybreak back into its sheath. Perhaps he was a fool for letting Dorcha live. Only time would tell.

But for now, he was giving him a chance.

"Where's Kyleigh?" he said, turning his glare upon the hole in the ceiling. He nearly jumped out of his skin when Dorcha grabbed his leg ...

No, it wasn't Dorcha. The eyes that widened upon his were a pure, stark blue — the eyes of a draega. When he spoke, the panicked voice belonged to a young man:

"Please, help her! You have to help her!"

The world fell out from beneath him. He didn't remember moving. He didn't remember breathing. His eyes stayed glued to the back of the halfdragon's head as he sprinted for the rubble in the middle of the room.

Tears streamed from the boy's eyes as he crouched beside something in the ruins —

"Kyleigh!"

Kael fell down beside her and placed his hands against her wound: a horrible gash that tore down her side, shattered her armor, and ripped across her middle. Blood poured from it in a terrifying rush. The things beneath her flesh were traumatized, ravaged into splits.

It took everything in his power, every ounce of his will — but somehow, he managed to keep his hands from shaking. "Hold on, Kyleigh — I can fix this. Just breathe. Breathe for me, will you? Try to stay calm ..."

Her hand gripped his, jarring him from his trance. He glanced up to tell her to be still, and instead ... he saw something that crushed him.

The fires in her eyes were ... fading. Already, they'd shrunk to a single spark — a frail, sputtering hiss of flame. They were so glassed in agony that he didn't think she could see beyond her pain. But her fingers wrapped around him gently, calmly. There was an assurance in her touch that somehow carried the weight of a thousand mountains with it:

She was telling him she was ready. She was at peace ...

"No, I don't want to hear it. Don't let go, Kyleigh — don't you *dare* let go!"

Her mouth twitched slightly at his words — whether in a smile or a grimace, he would never know. Kael clung to the last remaining shred of light in her eyes.

It was a tiny, miserable thing — a flake of ash batted by the wind. But every piece of his flesh and every thread of his soul was bent upon it. The tiny ember seemed to call out to him as it fluttered off into the distance, into whatever cold, immeasurable depth of silence waited beyond the light ...

And Kael plunged after it.

CHAPTER 56
KAEL THE FOOL

The strange trinkets shattered into pieces, all of the tapestries ripped from the walls. A horrible, monstrous windstorm blasted through the hall of Kyleigh's mind — and at its end, a bright light awaited.

Kael stood untouched by the wind. All of the debris of her memories tore through him, as if he were made of smoke. The light at the end of the passage began to dim: a darkness dragged behind its fading reach, plunging the hallway into nothing.

He broke into a sprint — pounding his way across the cold stone floors, desperate to stay at the edge of the light. Kael sensed that if he fell behind and the darkness overtook him, he would lose his grip. He'd be spat into reality ... and Kyleigh would slip beyond his reach.

No. He wasn't going to let that happen.

The warrior in him spurred his legs to a new, furious speed. His lungs burned, his body ached. Sweat drenched his back even as the light grew dimmer. The darkness was an ever-present force: it lunged for him, snapped at his heels. All of its grasping tendrils shrieked as they tried to drag him under.

But Kael would not be stopped.

He threw himself into the last remaining shred of light and shut his eyes against the world that awaited him beyond.

For a moment, he was weightless. Kael's body hung inside the grip of a boundless, clear blue sky. There was a large track of barren land several miles beneath him, scorched brown by the fury of the sun.

All of the pieces of Kyleigh's mind whipped away from him. They rode like leaves along the path of the wind. The storm gales carried them across the sky, over the barren land.

But Kael couldn't feel the wind. Its power couldn't touch him. Instead of following after Kyleigh, he began to fall.

He wasn't sure how far he fell. The whole time his body plummeted through the sky, he kept his eyes on Kyleigh's memories. They danced away until they finally disappeared into the line of the horizon — just as Kael struck the ground.

All of the wind left his lungs and his head snapped hard against the earth. A cloud of dust stung his eyes. He should've been dead. There was no way his body could've possibly stayed in one piece. But somehow, it had.

The sun hung high above him — an unblinking eye of the purest, most draining heat he'd ever felt. Not even the warmth inside the dragons' mountain had tested him so fiercely.

When Kael tried to don his scales, his mind struck a wall. It was as if his powers had been swept away by the wind. He couldn't remember how to conjure his armor. Where the memories ought to have been, there was nothing but a ragged, gaping hole.

He didn't have time to worry over it. He couldn't have cared less about having his powers. At that moment, there was only one task he could remember — and it consumed his every thought:

He had to find Kyleigh.

A range of mountains loomed behind him. They stretched from one end of the world to the next — impenetrable, save for a jagged pass that split the rock at his back. Kael stood so close to the mountains that he might've been able to touch them, had he reached out. But Kyleigh's soul hadn't gone into the mountains.

The land before him was as endless as the seas. Countless miles of cracked, sandy earth awaited him. But there, just along the edge of the far horizon, he saw a line of green.

There must've been a land beyond this one, a place where all the souls of men found their rest: the under-realm, the eternal woods — whatever world it was that stood along that line, Kael was determined to reach it. He was certain he'd find Kyleigh there.

So he set out.

The barren land was silent and still; the rhythm of Kael's boots against the earth was the only noise for miles. His panting breaths scraped loudly across his ears. The sun's fire beat him mercilessly. Without his warrior's strength, his legs began to shake. Soon, torrents of sweat stung his eyes, and his lungs screamed for air.

But though he could hardly see through the pain, he kept his gaze bent upon the far horizon — on that thin, wavering line of green.

The sun never moved. It was as if this entire world were frozen into a single moment of time. There was an unshakeable spirit about it, one that draped itself in relentless folds across his shoulders. Every breath he took singed the insides of his chest: the air seemed to drain him, rather than give his body strength. He found no reprieve in slowing his pace.

It wasn't long before he fell into a dogged march.

Though he must've run for hours, the horizon seemed no closer. Surely it was only a trick of his eyes. Kael turned to see how far he'd gone from the mountains ... and saw that he hadn't moved an inch. They were still right behind him — an arm's reach away.

It ... it wasn't possible. It simply wasn't possible.

Kael twisted back to the horizon and nearly jumped out of his skin when he saw he wasn't alone: a man had appeared before him. He was dressed all in white, clothed in a plain tunic and breeches. There was a great sword propped over his shoulder — one so large that he didn't think anyone but a whisperer could've carried it, in life.

The man's slight frame, thin features, and flaming red hair were undeniably familiar. Kael recognized him immediately:

"Setheran?"

The man didn't reply. Though his body certainly belonged to Setheran, the eyes did not. Where the Wright's calm stare should've been, there were two pale orbs — a dead man's eyes that shone with a soft light.

When the man stepped closer, he didn't move with Setheran's commanding gait. Instead, his feet seemed to drift across the top of the earth — still and silent as the barren lands, not a trace of dust churned up behind him.

Though this man wore Setheran's skin, Kael had a feeling he was ... someone else. Some*thing* else, perhaps. His body didn't even cast a shadow behind him.

"Who are you?" he whispered.

The man's white eyes pierced him as he replied: "Death."

For a moment, Kael froze. All of the sun's heat evaporated against the chill that coursed down his spine — peeled aside by a set of horrible, dagger claws. But behind his fear rose something else: an armor that didn't give in to the cold, a resolve that melted his worries.

It made even *Death* seem small. "If you've come to kill me, then get on with it. Otherwise, let me pass."

Death studied him calmly. "I haven't come to kill you. Your mortal soul has fallen here while your body lives on in the realm of light — and since you are not truly dead, your spirit isn't weak enough to cross these lands." His head turned slightly, and his stark eyes fell upon the green horizon. "I can offer you no passage."

The sun burned so fiercely now that Kael swore he could feel his skin shriveling beneath its light. His sweat turned molten and stung him along every hair's breadth of its trickling path. His legs shook too badly to run. Though he hadn't moved in minutes, his lungs still screamed for air.

"There is relief beyond the mountains," Death murmured. His chin rose to point at the crack inside the rock. "The journey back into life is a short one. The way is easy, a simple river's crossing. Here ... there is only pain."

Kael was aware of this: already, he was struggling to keep his feet.

An endless, burning land stretched before him — beyond it, the thinnest line of peace. Death, himself, warned that he would never be able to reach it. But when he thought of what it would mean to turn back, when he thought of the emptiness that waited in a life without Kyleigh ...

Well, it gave him all the strength he needed to try again.

"Fool," Death whispered as Kael stepped forward.

He fell back into a dogged march, staring straight over Death's shoulder at the wavering horizon. Though he tried to keep all of his concentration bent on walking, it was difficult not to listen to Death speak.

"I suppose I shouldn't be surprised. You have always been a fool. It's your heart that makes you foolish: you've allowed it to rule you completely. When your heart is whole, you speak like a wiseman. But when it is broken, you behave like a fool. It's Kael the Fool who stands before me, now — a jester and child."

He couldn't have cared less what Death thought of him. In fact, his taunts only brought another surge of fire into his blood.

Kael broke into a sprint, every cord of his muscle bent upon the green horizon. He forced himself to run even after his lungs seized up and his legs went numb, even after the heat sent a torrent of blood rushing from his nose.

But though his mind was bathed in steel and sharpened upon its task, his body lacked the strength to move another step. His legs collapsed beneath him and his chin struck the ground hard.

Blackness swarmed at the edges of his vision. Every inch of him burned: he felt as if he wore a cloak of flame. But though the darkness teased him with the promise of relief, his eyes stayed open. The pain never faded.

"You are not dead," Death whispered. He inhaled deeply, the light of his stark eyes flaring brightly. "But whenever I hear the cries of an aching spirit, it is my task to cut its bonds and set it free. I must break it from its mortal shell — otherwise, it cannot escape its torment. I will break your shell now, Kael the Fool, as is my task to do so. But be warned: you will never escape your torment. You will wake in the same fires that devour you now."

Death drew the sword from across his shoulder and advanced.

Kael reached for Daybreak … but the blade was gone. When he tried to imagine a weapon in his hand, he found only another gaping, ragged hole. He had no power. He had no strength.

And all too soon, Death stood above him.

The great sword pressed into his back, just below his left shoulder. "I feel it … that meddlesome, stubborn heart. You would be so much better without it. You could be so much more …"

The sword came down.

Kael cried out when it first bit his flesh. Death drove it in a fraction at a time: he felt it break through every layer of skin, every wire of muscle. They snapped one after the next against the sword's merciless point — each burst wracked him with a wave of pain more terrible than the one before.

Then at last, it struck his heart.

Agony shook Kael's body as his heart split against the sword. It was a torment no man could've survived. He begged for the darkness, begged for the shadows to cover his eyes. Even if all that awaited in the world beyond was a fathomless, burning pool, he would've accepted it gratefully. He would've thrown himself into the fires rather than have to be awake when Death's sword struck the middle of his heart.

But he *was* awake. He swore he was awake for half an age as the sword ground into the inside edges of his heart. The darkness hung at the corners of his eyes for an eternity, taunting him.

When at last the shadows came, they shuttered his vision for only a blink. There wasn't any peace inside that flash of darkness. There wasn't a moment's rest. Kael woke exhausted and sore, still trapped inside the barren lands.

He should've cried out at the loss of his strength, at the fact that he was weaker now than he'd been before. But instead, he smiled.

It'd given him an idea ... a mad, impossible idea.

Death crouched before him — except now, he wore Roland's skin. It was Roland's swollen fingers that wrapped around the great sword, Roland's mouth that fell into a saddened frown.

"Go back into the mountains, Kael the Fool. Do not linger here ... or I'll have to break your shell again."

The thought of having his heart split open a second time was enough to make Kael consider turning back. But his worry faded quickly. In order for his plan to work, he had to survive a little longer; he had to suffer the sword again.

His bones cried out in protest as he dragged himself to his feet. His legs trembled at first — but it wasn't long before he'd found his dogged pace.

Death stood from his crouch and twisted the wires of Roland's beard between his fingers, watching. "I don't understand it. He usually listens so well to these faces."

Though it sounded as if he spoke to himself, Kael couldn't help but be interested. "You've spoken to me before? When?" he said at Death's nod.

"As you slept. Fate keeps a tight hold upon the Veil, and the fall of her die decides the future — while I am banished to the past. But sleep is a curious thing ... it brings you close to me. The hours in which the body seals its eyes are precisely the hours in which the spirit is free to roam. You have no idea the thousands of miles you've traveled as you slept, or the many haunted realms your soul has crossed. And occasionally, I would join you on your walks."

Kael was so surprised that he nearly stopped. He'd dreamt of Roland before, of Amos and Morris. At the time, he'd thought the dreams were just a part of his worry.

But now ... chills ran up his spine.

"Yes, you've been a great ally, Kael the Fool — the single stone that topples my sister's plans, the pawn who wreaks havoc across the board." Death's face twisted into a smile. "She's tried so many times to kill you ... but she cannot cast for your life. No, you will live on until your body finally withers and I come to answer the weeping of your soul. That's what it means to belong to Death."

"I don't belong to anybody," Kael said shortly. He fought to catch his breath. But each time he tried to breathe in, the sun snatched it away. The horizon was no closer than it'd been the first moment he'd fallen into the barren lands.

When his legs began to go numb and the darkness drifted to the edge of his eyes, he knew what was about to happen. Though he feared the fall of Death's sword with every ounce of his soul, his chest ached to think of the emptiness that waited beyond the mountains.

It was worth the pain, worth the centuries of torment. As long as he could survive the sword, he would be close to Kyleigh. They would exist in the same world, at least — just an ocean apart.

Kael kept his eyes on the horizon as he collapsed again, and imagined that he could see her standing there upon its shores. She shook her head at him. She called him a stubborn mountain boy, and the playful fires in her eyes set his heart ablaze. Soon, he could no longer feel the ache in his legs or the wrath of the sun.

When he imagined Kyleigh smiling at him, he couldn't feel anything.

But then Death's sword fell again and the world was wrought in pain. When the darkness finally crashed over his eyes, it hung for less than a moment. Kael woke more exhausted and sore than ever.

He wished he had the strength to laugh, but he settled for a grin.

Death crouched before him, wearing Amos's frail shape. But the hand that gripped Kael's hair was strong. "You must leave here, Kael the Fool. Your spirit is weakening."

"Yes, that's the idea," he muttered.

He swore he could almost feel the desperation in Death's grip as it tightened. "If you continue this defiance, I'll have to strike your soul again. I *must* strike it — it's against my nature to let a spirit suffer. But your soul can only bear so much. I fear another blow will send you on —"

"Good. That's precisely what I was hoping for."

"I'm not ready to send you, Kael the Fool!" Death snarled, glaring. "You are far too valuable a weapon. I'll give you whatever you wish: any strength, any power, any throne of men. It's all yours for the taking — it's always been yours."

Kael didn't care about any of that. "I want Kyleigh."

Death shoved him away with a growl. "No. Her soul belongs to Fate. Every soul across the earth belongs to Fate, save for yours. *She* commands them. She casts for them." Death clenched a fist at his head; his stark eyes twisted back to the horizon. "She knows you want that woman ... *that's* why she's holding her soul at the edge, why she hasn't sent her on. She means to lure you there. And once you're inside her realm, I won't be able to help you. The torment you suffer here will be nothing compared to what you will suffer at the hands of Fate."

It took all of his strength, more than he thought he had in him. But somehow, Kael managed to drag himself to his feet. "I don't care. As long as I'm with Kyleigh—"

"Fool!"

Death turned and slung his sword into the earth behind him. It split open with a roar. A canyon ripped across the barren lands, all the way to edge of the green horizon. The earth shook for a moment. Kael fought to keep his feet. But half a moment later, the canyon sealed itself shut. The air went silent once more.

And he set out.

"You're a wastrel," Death growled as he collapsed again. "If any other man had been given half your powers, he could've done twice as much."

"Crevan is dead. The Kingdom is free. My companions are safe. I've done all I meant to do," Kael muttered into the dusty ground. "Maybe I haven't done it as well as you'd like, but I've done it well enough. Now ... let's get on with it."

The sword came down.

An eternity of pain, a flash of darkness, and Kael woke once more.

Back and forth they went: Death shrieking while Kael fought on. Every bite of the sword weakened him further. After the sixth time it fell, he could do no more than crawl.

Kael dug his fingers into the cracked earth and dragged himself along on his belly. The grit scraped his flesh, left blisters across the pads of his fingers. The sun spat its fire upon his head.

All the while he fought, Death sat upon the ground before him. He wore Noah's skin, now — the body of the sandy-haired boy who'd been killed in the Endless Plains. Though he knew it was only Death, Kael's heart still lurched when Noah's head fell into his hands.

And Death must've heard it. "Oh, that heart! That cursed heart! I used to laugh when it drove you into battle, when it scattered all of my sister's plans to the winds. Fate thought that *she* would be the one to bring about the Kingdom's reckoning. But you left her nothing to cast for."

"What do you mean?" Kael grunted as he dragged himself an inch.

"There was supposed to be another war — a second great wave of strife in the Kingdom that would turn all eyes upon Fate. But that didn't happen did it?" Here, Death gave him the faintest smile. "No, every time Fate went to move her pieces, *you* were there to scatter them across the board. It didn't matter how many armies or rulers she controlled, or how she tried to hurt you — on you went, marching to the stubborn beat of your heart.

"I don't know what exactly my sister had planned. She guards her secrets jealously. Still, I know that Midlan wasn't supposed to fall today ... I doubt if it was ever meant to fall. But because of you, because of the paths you chose, Fate found herself pitted against a force she simply could not defeat."

Kael slowed as his limbs began to tremble against the heat. Blood coated the tips of his fingers. "What ... force?"

Death smiled again. "The rise of a new Kingdom. Wildmen who'd had their powers awoken, giants who'd been given hope, shamans with their families made whole, pirates with a strong captain to lead them, a halfhawk who'd been set free, a battlemage given a second chance — and a whole host of mercenaries snared by an apple sauce," he added, with a roll of his eyes.

"All this came to pass because a boy from the Unforgivable Mountains climbed down to meet them. He saw them at their lowest points, and he lifted them up. Never mind that he was powerful, because his *power* didn't bring them to the fortress today. It was his heart ..." Death shook his head, his stare turning upon the clear blue sky. "And now, his heart will end him."

Kael wasn't sure if he believed all of that. He didn't think he'd done much of anything to save the Kingdom. In fact, he could think of several times when his companions had saved *him*.

But he supposed none of that mattered, now. He closed his eyes as he felt Death's sword against his back. He hoped this would be the last time it fell.

"Your soul cries out to me, Kael the Fool. I have to end its weeping. But if my sister shows you mercy, if she sends you back into the living realm, you would do well to remember the day you were born. Remember that you belong to me." His hands twisted about the sword. "In time ... perhaps you will see it for the gift it was meant to be."

CHAPTER 57
THE ETERNAL WOODS

"Kael!"

Tears poured down his face the moment he felt Kyleigh's arms around him. His eyes were still black with pain, but he would've known her voice no matter how badly he ached.

There was a bed of soft, cool grass beneath him. It eased his burning skin. By the time Kyleigh pulled him into her lap, his pain had all but vanished. "I never thought I'd see you again," he murmured, pressing his face against her neck. He was afraid to open his eyes — afraid that if he did, the dream would end.

Kyleigh laughed and held him tighter. "Is that so? Well, I always knew you'd come for us."

"As did I," another voice whispered.

He opened his eyes when he felt something heavy scrape across his legs. It was a dragon's white tail — one that wrapped Kyleigh and Kael in its embrace and dragged them in against a warm, scaly chest.

He looked up and smiled at the dragon's familiar, green-blazing stare. "Hello again."

"Hello, my love." The dragon held them between her foreclaws and rested her head atop Kyleigh's shoulder. Her eyes closed with a contented sigh. "All of the little pieces of my soul are together again."

"We've missed you, in case you haven't noticed," Kyleigh said. She kissed him on the top of his head before she called to someone beside them. "Well, what do you think? He's a marvel, isn't he?"

Kael groaned when an old woman's voice replied: "He is, indeed."

Fate looked exactly the way he'd expected her to: a crone with shriveled fingers clad in a tattered robe. She leaned heavily against a twisted cane and leered at him with a set of bottomless eyes. They were as dull as her brother's were bright, as black as his were white.

Something *clink*ed against her long nails: a many-faced die that rolled inside the spidery cage of her fingers. As he watched, Fate let the die fall. It bounced across the ground and came to rest before his boots.

There were symbols painted across its sides, each appeared to have been scrawled in blood. But the die didn't land on any of its faces. Somehow, it landed on its edge.

"Remarkable," Fate said, smacking her gums against the word. "Even in my presence, you have no discernable future. My brother always knows just how to vex me."

She snapped her fingers, and the die shot back into her hand.

Kael looked away and saw they were gathered on the edge of a forest. Dawn light spilled between the trees and the birds woke with song. Creatures of every shape and size ran wild beneath the canopy, their figures turned to shadow against the sun.

"The eternal woods," Kael breathed.

Kyleigh held him tighter. "What do you think?"

"It's ... beautiful."

"And it goes on forever." Kyleigh's voice dropped to a playful growl. "Think of all the trouble we'll get into — an eternity's worth of mischief."

Kael groaned, half-laughing.

"Think of all the lands to cross, all of the winds to chase," the dragon added with another happy sigh. "My wings long to take flight."

Kael smiled out at the woods for a moment, listening to all of the creatures at play inside its heart. But it wasn't long before a strange feeling drew his eyes away.

A thick cloud of haze covered the whole earth behind him. It stretched into the sky and ran in a perfect wall to either end of the horizon. Muffled voices drifted from inside the haze, their words lost behind the wall. Colors swirled into the blurry shapes of beasts and men. A few of them looked ... familiar.

"This is the Veil," Fate said when he asked. She hobbled to the wall's edge and brushed her cane against it. The shapes stirred beneath her touch like the wind across a curtain. "A realm of chaos and strife, where all the desires of men war against their faults. It is an imperfect, desolate, and unjust span of time. All those who cross its shores in triumph have truly earned their eternal rest."

562

Something about Fate's toothless smirk made Kael uneasy. He remembered what Death had said — that Fate was angry with him for destroying her plans, that the torment he suffered in the barren lands was nothing compared to what awaited him in the realm beyond.

Now he stood inside that very realm ... and when Fate spoke again, he knew he should've listened.

"I've waited a long while for this day. I tried to cast for Kyleigh's life several times before, knowing that you would follow. But the future was always against me. This time, though," she turned, and her bottomless stare scraped across him, "this time, the die landed in my favor. Her soul slipped beyond the Veil ... and you followed. I've got you, now."

Kyleigh's arm clamped across his chest and the dragon snarled in warning.

But Kael wasn't the least bit afraid. "Torture me however you like. Just make it quick, will you?" He wrapped his hands around Kyleigh's arm. "I don't want to waste another moment of our time."

Fate cackled, leaning all the more heavily against her cane — as if the force of her mirth might very well knock her over. "Oh, my brother was right about you! You truly are Kael the *Fool*. What I had planned isn't as simple as having your heart sliced out. No," her dark eyes slid over to Kyleigh, "I was going to throw your love into the river and make you watch while she drowned ... over and over again, for all e —"

Fury tore Kael into a sprint. He charged for Fate, his fist raised to put a dent through he middle of her face. But she stopped him with a wave of her hand.

His body fell as if he'd been kicked in the middle. His back struck the ground hard. Kyleigh and the dragon gathered him up again before he could stand and held him in a vice.

"You're in my realm now, Forsaken One," Fate hissed. The die clinked between her fingers as she watched him. "The more you vex me, the worse it gets."

"If you hurt her —"

"You'll do nothing. You'll stand there like a root and watch. Don't test me," she added with a glare.

She stepped forward, and Kael held on tightly to Kyleigh's arm. He wasn't going to let her go. He wouldn't let Fate harm her. He would do whatever had to be done, no matter how it stung him.

So he took a deep breath and whispered: "Please."

Fate stopped. Countless more wrinkles popped up across her forehead as she raised her brows. "What was that?"

"Please don't hurt Kyleigh."

"Are you ... *begging* me, defiant one? The one who laughs at Fate? Who's cheated Death? Clever of you to force my brother's hand, by the way," she added with a smirk. "There aren't many men who'd brave his sword a second time — let alone brave it *seven*."

"I'd do it all again —"

"No, Kael," the dragon said sharply.

Kyleigh looked to Fate. "I don't want to lose him. But if it means he won't be hurt, I'll follow you to the river."

"No, I'd rather die a thousand times —!"

"So would I!" the dragon roared over the top of him. "You've already done more for me than I could ever —"

"Enough." Fate sealed their lips with a second wave of her hand. She regarded them for a moment with an inscrutable look. "Usually, souls beg me *not* to die. I've never come across a group of spirits fighting over the first to be drowned. No one's dying today."

Kael couldn't believe it. Even when Fate released him, all he could think to say was: "You aren't angry with me?"

"Well, I wouldn't say that I'm *thrilled*. But though you certainly ruined all of the little things I had planned, you saved the thing that mattered most — a reckoning a thousand years in the making." Fate's lips twisted around her next words, as if it pained her to speak them: "When you had the chance to slay my King, you didn't. I watched you stand over him with your sword drawn, helpless to stop its fall. The last threads of my great plan lay tattered beneath your foot. But ... you never cut them. You spared his life —"

"Wait a moment — *Devin?*" Kael said, his head spinning. "Devin is your King?"

Fate smiled wryly. "Yes, the shaman's son. The last of his mother's brood, the last of the halfdragons — my last chance to right an egregious wrong. I always regretted the roll of the die that brought the mages into the Wildlands. They will never be as grand a thing as they were before ... but with a draega upon the throne, they will heal. No one among men will be fool enough to challenge him," she added with a laugh. "His rule will stretch as long as his life — a truly eternal crown. And in time, my shamans will have their honor back. All will be as it was before."

Kael was still trying desperately to make sense of what she'd said when he heard Kyleigh whisper: "That's brilliant."

"A great trick, isn't it?" Fate agreed. "But how unlucky for me that my King's life crossed paths with the Forsaken One. My sly, meddling brother never lets me have a moment's peace!"

Kael thought it was rather bold of Fate to accuse someone else of being *sly* and *meddling*. But he also thought better of saying it aloud.

After a few moments of cursing under her breath, Fate's wrinkled fingers twisted about her cane. "Yes, an unlucky thing, that the Forsaken One had a chance to do me a kindness. Now, instead of having the pleasure of torturing his spirit forever, I find myself in his debt. So, what's it to be, mortal? What gift do you ask of Fate?"

Before he could open his mouth to say it, she rolled her bottomless eyes.

"Yes, yes — you can keep your love. No need to waste your breath. But I can't have you sitting here at the edge. Your souls must move on. So, would you rather love her in the Veil ... or in the woods?"

For Kael, there was only one obvious answer. He turned to face Kyleigh and the dragon. "If we stay here, we'll never be apart. You'll never have to suffer the way Dorcha did."

When he turned to answer Fate, Kyleigh clamped a hand over his mouth.

"Death is an eternity, but life is merely a season," the dragon said. "You are so young, my love. It would be a tragic thing to have it taken from you."

Kyleigh nodded. "Yes, and the woods will still be here when our lives end ... provided we behave."

Kael didn't return her smile. He remembered all too well how the valtas cursed the dragons. He wouldn't leave her to mourn for hundreds of years after he'd gone.

But before he could say as much, Kyleigh blurted out: "We want to return to the Veil."

Fate bent her wrinkly head. "All right —"

"No, it isn't *all right*! This was supposed to be my choice!" Kael fought his way out from under Kyleigh's grip and stormed up to Fate. "You can't let her do this — you can't just change the rules!"

She cackled in his face. "I'm *Fate*, mortal! I'll do whatever I please. Though I can't cast for your soul, I can always cast for the ones you love. You'd do well to remember that," she added, when Kael began to argue. Her eyes wandered over to Kyleigh, and her mouth bent in an unsettling grin. "Perhaps I ought to send you a little ... *reminder.*"

Kael's stomach twisted into a knot. He knew he had no choice. "Fine, we'll go back to the Veil. I won't say another word about it. But I'm still furious with you," he snapped at Kyleigh, who only grinned in return.

Fate threw a frail arm about his waist. "It'll do you no good to be angry with her — her soul traveled here the *right* way. She won't remember any of this ... but you will."

Kael didn't like her words — and he liked her smirk even less.

But before he had a chance to worry, Fate reached for the Veil. "I'll hold onto her spirit from this side and make sure she doesn't slip away. But you must work quickly, mortal," she added with a glare. "Do not test my patience."

****

"No ... *no.*"

Kael pulled himself from the darkness, following along the path of a sobbing voice. For a moment, the world seemed upside down. He had no idea where he was, or which direction his head was turned.

Everything wavered beneath the pressure of sleep. But there was an echo in the back of his mind — words that stung him with their urgent message: *Work quickly, mortal.*

He blinked the sleep from his eyes, and the shattered room came into focus.

Devin crouched beside him, rocking on his heels. He sobbed thickly into the crook of one arm and reached out with the other. His fingers brushed across Kyleigh's face — so horribly pale and transfixed by death that for a moment, Kael thought he'd been tricked.

Then all at once, she woke with a gasp.

"Hold on!" Kael cried, nearly choking on his heart. "Hold on, Kyleigh!"

His hands shook as he placed them against her wounds. There were tears across her innards, through every layer of her muscle and flesh. She shook badly as the pain seized her limbs. Kael nearly lost his grip a few times, but he fought to hold on. He wasn't going to lose her again.

They were the most agonizing moments of his life. Each second that slid through the glass carried with it the weight of everything — every cord of his heart, spread out and bound across the grains of time. Every breath that passed between them had the power to tear the Kingdom from its roots. And if he was even a moment too slow, they would.

By the time Kael had sealed the last bit of her skin together, Kyleigh stopped moving. He was afraid to look up at her, afraid of what he might see. He clung to this final moment of uncertainty with the knowledge that it might very well be his last chance to feel hope. Once he looked up, all of the light could leave his world forever.

But that didn't happen.

Kyleigh's chest rose with a shuddering breath. Her hand ran up his arm, grasped him around the neck — and the next thing Kael knew, he'd been dragged to the ground.

She kissed him savagely, laughing at the fall of his tears. "Don't cry, you silly whisperer. You haven't lost me, yet."

But he *had* lost her. He'd lost her for a thousand years, while Death gouged his heart inside the barren lands. It was only by the mercy of Fate that he held her now.

And though he might wish to, Kael would never forget it.

They stayed tangled for a few moments more — Kyleigh smothering him with kisses while he tried desperately to hold on. A slight cough finally reminded them that they weren't alone.

"Are you all right, Devin?" Kyleigh said as Kael helped her to her feet.

He nodded, and his face turned red as his stark blue eyes flicked between them. "I suppose this must be your mate?"

He smiled at her nod — and that's when Kael realized just how badly wounded Devin was. There were little punctures across his shoulders and above his brows. When he turned, he saw there were a number of shallow cuts down his back. The burn lines that split his face and the scales across his chest belonged to Daybreak.

And Kael immediately felt guilty for it. "Come here, and I'll seal you up."

"It's all right," Kyleigh said when he hesitated. "Kael doesn't bite often."

After an uncertain moment, Devin smiled. "You're joking."

"Yes, and more often than not," Kael said, shooting her a look.

It didn't take him long to patch up Devin. No sooner had he sealed the last gash than a voice boomed from the door:

"Stop, Forsaken One! Don't hurt him!"

Kael jumped. Harbinger shrilled as Kyleigh tore him from his sheath.

An old mage hobbled through the shattered doorway. His stare was deep and his gray beard stretched almost to his middle. But it was the men on either side of him that caught Kael's attention.

"Oh, for mercy's sake," he managed to grumble — just before Eveningwing slammed into his chest.

"Kael!" The halfhawk wrapped his arms and legs about him, grinning to either ear.

Jonathan joined in — crushing them both to a mash. "Oh come on, mate! You know you've missed us."

Kael hadn't missed them *that* much. But before he could say it, there was a loud clattering sound at the doorway, followed by some thumping steps — and then another thick set of arms lifted them all off their feet. "Oh, this is almost as good as the last time!"

"No it isn't," Kael grunted into his chest. "In fact, neither time was good."

Declan dropped them suddenly, spilling them into a pile. He snatched Kael up before the world stopped spinning and fixed him with a gaping look.

His eyes were more than a little bloodshot, and the giant's breath reeked of what smelled suspiciously like pirate grog. "Did you not hear the good news, wee rat?"

"How could he have heard it? We have only just found him!" Nadine called from the doorway.

An army of mots spilled in behind her. Several of them rushed forward to grab at a large chunk of wood that'd fallen just inside the room. When they flipped it over, a familiar voice cried out in relief:

"Well, it's about time! If that giant tosses me again, I'll —"

"Is that you, Knotter?"

"Ah! Lady Kyleigh! Thank the stars you're here," Knotter moaned. "Take me back to my gate. I don't think I'll last another moment in the hands of that brutish oaf."

Declan didn't look at all concerned about having been called an oaf. He grabbed Kael hard by the shoulders and said: "We're going to be married! That wee mote has finally come to her senses. Look at her," Declan added, spinning him around, "look at how she smiles at me, will you?"

Nadine *was* smiling — but only because she seemed completely unable to stop herself. "You are drunk," she muttered, waving a hand at him.

"Yeh? Well, I'll just have to say it again when my head's cleared up," he said back.

While everyone clustered around to congratulate them, the old mage went after Devin. He was so incredibly frail that Kael thought he might break, when Devin grabbed him by the arm. But he didn't.

"Are you well, child?"

"I'm fine, Argon. I'm happy to see you again," Devin added with a grin — one that made him look at once less monstrous.

Kyleigh stared at them, her mouth agape. Harbinger hung loosely in her hand for a moment. But all at once, she swung it up at Argon's face. "You ... I know you."

He nodded, tucking his hands into his sleeves. "The last time we met, I believe I sent you to do something for me ... something very —"

"Important." She spoke as if the word was some sort of accusation. Her hand twisted tighter about her sword. "You hexed me, didn't you? You made me forget Kael's name. You stopped me from killing Crevan. I could've ended all this years ago —!"

"No," Argon said calmly. "No, child. Had you killed Crevan that day, you still would've been run out of Midlan for your crimes. Another King would've assumed the throne — one not so easily maddened by your tricks. In order for our plans to work, we needed a weak-minded King behind these walls."

Kyleigh glared at him. "Who's *we?*"

Argon didn't reply. His eyes slid over to Kael, and he couldn't help but be reminded of another dark, bottomless gaze.

He thought he might've figured out exactly who *we* was.

"Devin? Why don't we visit your garden? I know you've missed it terribly. I'm sure Kyleigh will be happy to go with you," Argon said lightly, when the boy hesitated.

Devin turned his eyes upon her, and she sighed beneath his look. "All right, then. But this isn't over. You've got plenty to answer for," Kyleigh said severely.

"Yes, we'll be right behind you," Argon called as they strode away.

Though Devin towered over Kyleigh, he walked a pace behind her — hands clasped against his chest. His pointed ears bent to catch her every word. The mots waved to them as they passed, and Devin smiled uncertainly.

Kyleigh grabbed him around the wrist. "Move your hand back and forth — no, open it up! Don't go waving your fists at people, or they'll think you haven't got fingers."

Under her instructions, Devin wound up hailing the mots with a grimace and a panicked, spread-fingered wave. It looked as if he was trying to sling hot coals off his hand — and Kyleigh lost her grip.

She stumbled out into the hallway, laughing like a madwoman.

Devin hurried after her. "Are you all right? Did I do something wrong?"

"I don't know! What in *blazes* were you even doing?"

"He has a child's heart," Argon murmured as he watched them go. "Devin will be more a *caretaker* than a King, which I think suits the Wildlands rather well."

Kael wasn't so sure. He knew the sort of greed that'd consumed the King's rulers. "What if someone comes after him? What if they try to take the throne?"

"Then it won't be *Devin* they meet — it'll be Dorcha. And I daresay he'll staunch any battle before it begins."

"The wildmen aren't going to be pleased," Kael said, and just the thought of the argument ahead made him groan.

"True … but I'm sure you'll think of something. In my experience, these things have a way of working themselves out." Argon regarded him with a deep-pitted stare. "You have the look of a man who's seen the one I serve."

"Yes, though I wish I hadn't."

"And you know what it is you've done?"

"Well enough," Kael muttered, though he didn't much care about what he'd done: he was just glad to have it all finally ended.

"You'll understand, then, that Fate wishes you to help convince the others that Devin should be King. Since your choices led them here, they are your responsibility — and Fate will hold you accountable for their actions," Argon added with a weighted look.

More than anything, Kael didn't want to spend the rest of his days running Fate's errands. But when he remembered how she'd threatened Kyleigh, he knew he had little choice. "All right, I'll convince the others."

"Very good. This is your final task," Argon promised. "Fate won't trouble you again."

Kael wanted to believe him ... but for some reason, he doubted it.

They stood in silence for a moment. Just before them, their companions were locked in a heated argument over whether or not Jonathan should be allowed to play his fiddle at the wedding. But here, the world was cold.

"Did you really make Kyleigh forget my name?" he wondered aloud.

"In a way, I suppose. Though all I really did was *hide* it from her. Just a simple muddling spell."

"Because Fate wanted us apart?" he guessed.

Argon shook his head. "No, Fate wanted you to stay trapped atop those cursed mountains, where you could never interfere with her plans. A man with all the powers of a Wright, completely freed of her will? She was terrified of you, child. She was afraid to set you loose.

"But I thought the Kingdom needed its Wright — and hiding your name from Kyleigh was my one great defiance. Though you were only an infant at the time, she spoke as if she'd known you for ages. I suspected then that she might have a dragon's love for you. A fascinating bond," he added with a slight smile. "I thought you might find her peculiar healing abilities to be rather useful."

He had. She'd pulled him from the edge on more than one occasion. But there was still something he didn't understand. "If you wanted us to find each other, why did you make her forget my name?"

"Timing is everything, when you intend to change the future. Yes, I wanted you together — but only once you'd grown strong

571

enough to contend against her will. Had she found you when you were an infant ..."

"She would've stashed me away somewhere," Kael whispered, shaking his head in disbelief. "She would've sacrificed the whole blasted realm, just to keep me safe."

Argon smiled slightly. "Yes, and you would've been happy in the glow of her love — unaware that the Kingdom suffered beneath the chaos of another one of Fate's wars. It was a terrible gamble, letting a Wright with no future loose upon the realm. And one way or another, the Kingdom would've been set free. Perhaps, in the end, my defiance didn't make much of a difference."

Argon turned to smile at their companions: Jonathan screeched across his fiddle, Eveningwing danced an odd jig with the mots — Nadine laughed at them from within the gentle hold of Declan's arms.

"But though they're never sewn with the grandest strokes, small things *can* make a difference. If there are enough of them, the whole tapestry can be changed — and in the end, when you step back to see it, you find that all of those little threads matter very much."

CHAPTER 58
A NEW KING

They didn't make it far beyond the shattered room. No sooner had they gone down the next hall than Argon and Kael ran smack into the pirates.

They'd filled the passage from its edges to its end, staring with wide eyes at Kyleigh and Devin. More than a few of them had their cutlasses drawn.

Captain Lysander paced at their head. His wavy hair was a mad tangle of sweat and gore. His white tunic was stained beyond repair. Still, he barked as if he stood aboard his ship: "No, I've seen what's he's capable of, and I can't in good conscience allow him to —"

"He isn't dangerous anymore. The King's curse is broken. So there's no need to get your skirts in a bunch, Sandy," Kyleigh added, earning herself a rather potent glare.

But before Lysander could retort, Kael stepped in. "Yes, and that's no way to speak to your new King."

Lysander's chin nearly touched his chest.

Devin whirled around like he'd taken a shock. "A King?"

"I'll explain it to you later, child," Argon assured him. "For now, we must simply —"

"No, *no!*" Thelred shoved his way to the front of the crowd and fixed his burning scowl directly onto Kael. "There's no way you're going to make him King. In a long list of ridiculous things you've done, this is by far the most ridiculous. We won't let it happen."

"Then you're welcome to fight him for it. One quick blast of flame, and I think you'll all know who the King is," Kael said. He struggled not to laugh when Thelred took a step back.

Lysander, who'd been quietly watching Devin for a long moment, waved his cousin aside. "There's no need to get all testy about this, Red. We haven't even given the boy a chance."

The pirates leaned forward when Lysander marched up to Devin. It was clear that they didn't want him to get any closer — but it was also clear that none of them were eager to follow.

Devin bent nearly double at Lysander's gesture, until they stood face to face. The Captain regarded him with a stony-eyed look. "Before we agree to make you King, there's something I need to know."

"What is it?"

"How will you handle the taxes?"

"I'm not sure. I don't know what a *taxes* is."

"They're horrible, nasty little rules used to chain decent men beneath an unjust burden of gold."

Devin's dark brows snapped low at this. "Then the taxes will be destroyed. I don't want anyone in chains."

"Well, he's got my vote," Lysander said with a grin.

Thelred dragged his hands down either side of his face. "You don't *vote* for a King," he grumbled.

But the pirates' cheers quickly drowned out his protests.

Once they'd picked their way through the crowded hall, they got a few moments' peace. Then they found the giants.

"Ho there, you scrawny wee mountain rat! Don't think you're getting by without giving the Prince a proper greeting."

Kael didn't have much of a choice. The moment he turned the corner, the damp stains of Brend's tunic were right at his eyes' level — and the giant pressed him tightly against their reeking folds.

"And who's this? Not the great black terror who was chasing us around the forest, eh?" Brend glanced at the streaks of iron that crusted across Devin's chest before he reached over and ruffled him on the top of his spiny head. "Giants don't like to be chased. We're likely to trip, if you force us to move our legs like that."

"I won't chase you again," Devin swore.

At Argon's sharp nudge, Kael gave the giants the news. He was expecting Brend to snort and say *never*. But surprisingly, he only shrugged.

"What you manfolk decide to do with Midlan's throne is your own business. The giants already have their Prince," he said, to a collective grunt from the soldiers behind him. "As long as your King stays away from our crops and out of our lands, you'll have no trouble from us."

"That seems fair enough." Kyleigh looked up at Devin. "What do you say?"

The boy frowned at Brend. "What are *crops*?"

His question brought on a roar of laughter from the giants — while Brend looked as if he'd just been slapped. "What are ...? *Crops* are the lifeblood of your clodded Kingdom, I'll have you know. If it weren't for the giants growing all of your food, you'd have not a thing to eat."

"I have a garden," Devin offered. "Would you like to see it?"

"Oh, a *garden*, he says." Brend snorted and rolled his eyes. But after a moment, his scowl softened a bit. "I hope you've got some barley growing in there. Well, it's a shame if you haven't — the soil's perfect for it!" he said when Devin shook his head.

"Have you at least got some rosemary, or sage?" one of the giants called.

"I have a lemon tree," Devin replied — and drew such a round of indignant cries from the giants that Kael expected the floors to start shaking.

Brend threw an arm around Devin's shoulders, careful of the short spines that sprouted from their tops. "You'd better show us that garden, wee dragon — quickly, now. The giants will do whatever we can to save it."

Devin led them down another branch of hallway, smiling at their grunts and the occasional burst of rowdy laughter. The last thing Kael heard before they thumped out of earshot was Brend loudly declaring what a *mightily grand* thing it was to have a King who stood at a *proper* height.

"Let's go this way, shall we?" Argon said, nudging Kael down the opposite hall.

It was absolutely littered with the ruins of the giants' march: gold-tinged bodies hewed by their great scythes and crammed against either wall. Kyleigh walked a little ways ahead of them. She opened every door they passed and glanced inside the chambers.

There were several doors she left ajar, and Kael looked inside to find the chambers empty. But there was one door she shut with a grimace. "Blazes, I almost feel sorry for them."

The way she wrinkled her nose would've made Kael smile, had there not been such a weight upon his heart. Kyleigh's hand trailed softly across the wall as she neared the next corner. A large chunk of armor was missing at her waist, torn away by Dorcha's claws. It left her pale skin exposed — a gap of smooth and perfect flesh. But even though she was healed, Kael's heart still twisted to think of how she'd been wounded. He could feel the agonized tremors of her body when he clenched his hands.

As she reached the end of the wall, Kyleigh grinned at him from over her shoulder — as if she'd been able to sense him watching. Her eyes burned furiously onto his, holding his gaze until she'd disappeared around the corner.

"This had better be it, Argon," Kael said hoarsely. "I don't want Fate to come within a thousand miles of her again."

The mage closed his eyes for a moment. "She swears she won't trouble Kyleigh. There's no sport in it — you care far too much for her life."

Kael wasn't sure that was even possible. But before he could say as much, they rounded the next corner — and had their ears accosted by a familiar, high-pitched squeal.

Aerilyn already had her arms wrapped about Kyleigh. Behind her, Jake and a smiling forest woman walked hand in hand. It took several moments of staring for Kael to realize that the forest woman was Elena. He swore he'd never seen her smile, let alone beam as if the sun wouldn't stop shining.

Kael was still gaping at her when Aerilyn smacked against his chest. "Oh, Kael! I'm so glad you're here. I've had it up to my ears with these two. They're wounded — and they won't do anything at all about it!" She passed a glare between Elena and Jake. "They've done nothing but smile since the moment I found them, and neither one will tell me what's so blasted funny."

Kyleigh fixed them with a wicked grin. "I have a guess."

"And you'll keep it to yourself," Elena warned.

"It really isn't all that serious," Jake insisted, his voice thickened beneath the swollen hump of his nose.

Aerilyn made a frustrated sound. "You have a hand in your pocket — and it's *not* attached to your wrist!"

"Well, I'm sure it's nothing the Wright can't fix."

"Oh, for mercy's sake," Kael grumbled, when Jake held up his blue-capped nub. "Bring it here."

He'd never sealed a hand back onto its wrist before. But luckily for Jake, the cut was so clean that none of the pieces were missing. It

576

only took him a few tries to get it attached correctly. When Jake was able to move all of his fingers, they considered it a success.

"Remarkable," he said, grinning as he twisted his hand about. "Absolutely remarkable."

The gash in Elena's leg was much easier to seal. Once he had it closed, Kael told them about Devin.

Jake looked immediately to Argon. "Your ward? Really? Well, he's a bit simple, but I'm sure most of the Kingdom will be all right with that."

"Lysander's already thrilled about the fact that there won't be any taxes," Kyleigh said with a nod.

Aerilyn rolled her eyes. "I'm sure he is. And I suppose as long as this *Devin* doesn't try to enslave or starve anybody, he'll already be three steps ahead of Midlan's last King." After a moment, she raised her brows. "He wouldn't happen to need a cook, would he? I know of a rather good one — an entire household, really. They'll be happy to help him manage things."

Argon inclined his head. "I'm sure Devin would be most appreciative."

Aerilyn let out an excited squeal. "Wonderful! I'll go tell Horatio straight away." She spun and took off down the hall, her quiver clattering with her jog.

"And what do you think about all this, Elena?" Kyleigh said.

"I couldn't care less. In fact, I doubt if I'll ever set foot in Midlan again. Jake and I have decided to live peacefully."

"Our fighting days are over," he agreed, smiling as he took her hand. "We'll travel around a bit until we find a nice, quiet place to settle. Our journey begins first thing tomorrow."

"There could be trouble along the way, though. The Kingdom's still crawling with thieves and bandits." Elena's dark eyes roved thoughtfully. "I mean, we ought to at least be *prepared* to fight, if need be."

Jake nodded. "Absolutely. It seems as if one can hardly step outside one's door without running into some sort of trouble. But we'll only fight to defend ourselves."

"Of course."

"And if a few bandits happen to get their throats cut —"

"Or their legs blasted out from under them."

"— so be it."

They grinned at each other as they wandered down the hall, chattering about all the many ways they were determined to be *peaceful*. Kael was still shaking his head at them when Argon prodded him in the side.

"We're nearly there. The last step is always the most difficult."

And he wasn't wrong.

They found the wildmen inside the western courtyard. Mud matted their furs and there were dark red spatters across many of their painted faces. The craftsmen were drenched up to their elbows in gore. But it looked as if they'd fought well.

The warriors hefted gold-tinged bodies across their shoulders and moved in a steady line. Silas waited at the gates' edge, waving them towards a towering mound of soldiers.

"Pile them up outside the walls. We'll set fire to them later," Gwen barked. She snapped her fingers at a group of craftsman standing beside her. "Drain the southern wall, let the bodies wash into the forest. Then start digging a grave. We'll have to bury that lot — it'll be ages before they dry enough to burn, and I don't care to wait."

"Yes, Warchief!"

"Warchief?" Kyleigh said as the craftsmen scattered off. "Has your brother finally kicked you off the frozen throne, then?"

"It was always my father's wish to have Griffith rule. He's patient. He sees things that I do not. Now that he's grown into his wisdom, I've stepped aside." Gwen half-turned to scowl at Kyleigh. There were scrapes across her face and bits of debris lodged in her wild tangle of hair. Her armor was coated in a thick layer of grit.

Kael had to wonder just how many times Devin had thrown her through the walls. But before he could ask, she saw him. And she stomped over immediately.

"I've got a lot to say to you, mutt."

Kael braced himself against her snarl. "Well, it'd better start with an apology —"

"It will. You were right: I *am* a fool," she said through her teeth. As she spoke, a film of glass coated her eyes ... and it made Kael nervous. "I was so blinded by my pride that I nearly got my people destroyed. They would've all been killed, had it not been for the bard."

Kael's nerves grew sharper, stretched into a cold worry. "What happened?"

Gwen glared up at the sky, as if it was all she could do to keep the glass from breaking. "He got a whisperer's headache, and he's fallen into a deathly sleep. Griffith sent me to find you. He told me to do whatever it took to bring you back. Baird needs healing." Her glare fell onto his, but it wasn't entirely sharp: there was a pain behind the glass that softened her anger. "Please help him."

She didn't have to ask. Kael had already taken a step towards Kyleigh when Argon snatched him around the shoulder — reminding him of his task.

Kael thought quickly. "If I do this for you, you'll have to promise me something," he said, fighting not to let his worry show through.

Gwen dashed the wet from her eyes. "Yes, I expected as much. Griffith's allowed me to grant you any favor in return. Name it."

"We're going to make Devin the next King of Midlan — the black dragon," he said at her confused look.

Gwen bared her teeth, and her face turned a furious red. "The *dragon*?"

"Yes. And I need you to swear on all of your ancestors that you'll leave him alone —"

"I can't serve a dragon! I won't do it!"

"Think of Baird," Kyleigh reminded her with a growl.

A rather tense moment passed — one in which Kael thought she would either punch him in the throat, or burst into flame. But finally, Gwen gave him the stiffest, slightest of nods.

"No, I'm afraid I'm going to need to hear you say it."

"Fine. I'll never bow to him, but I swear I won't lop off the dragon's head and hang it on my walls. I swear it for all the wildmen. That's the most I can promise." Then she grabbed him by the shoulders and shoved him away. "Now *go*, mutt!"

****

"I knew you'd come back for me, young man," Baird whispered the moment he woke.

It'd been a trying number of hours: there was a knot inside Baird's skull, an inflamed patch of gray that Kael had to figure out some way to soothe. He'd never worked on that part of the body before, and it frightened him to see how complex all of its many little ridges were.

Even after he'd drained the knot and sealed it closed, Baird still hadn't stirred. Though the wildmen had done their best to feed him, his limbs had grown terribly thin and frail. His knobby hands shook a bit when Kael grasped them.

He couldn't help but feel responsible. "I'm sorry, Baird. I should've listened to you — I should've stopped the mages first thing."

"It does him no good to dwell upon the past. I thought he'd already learned," Baird replied, brows creasing over the top of his bandages. "Still, I suppose the young ones must be reminded. Knowledge runs like water off their backs — but it sticks tightly in wrinkles and folds. That's how the old ones are able to carry so much wisdom."

"Is that it?" Kyleigh called from the balcony, her voice tinged with amusement. "And here I thought wisdom came from age and experience."

Baird smiled widely. "A common mistake, to be sure. Come here, Swordmaiden. Kael the Wright has much to tell me, I sense — and I know he cannot possibly do the story justice without your help."

They stayed in Thanehold for several weeks, spending nearly every hour of the days with Baird. He seemed to brighten considerably as they told them of their adventures in the Motherlands, and laughed outright when he discovered how his letter had tricked Ulric into running back to Midlan.

"A weapon of the King used to foil him? A fitting end!" Baird said. Then he twisted around to Griffith. "Mark that down, young man. Are you getting it all?"

"Yes," he replied, grinning as his quill rushed across the page. "What happened to Crevan, then? How'd you gut him?"

Kael realized that he had no idea: Kyleigh had never told him.

"I tried to teach him to fly," she said when they asked. The fires in her eyes took on a dangerous edge as she smirked. "Though as it turned out, he wasn't very good at flying. I suppose you really *do* need wings."

"An age-old question finally answered!" Baird cried.

Kael couldn't believe it. "Wait a moment — the man I saw fall from the tower ... that was *Crevan*?" Even when she nodded, it still felt strange. His only glimpse of the King had been as he plummeted to his death. He'd always expected a ... grander end, to his rule.

Though when he thought about it, he supposed being thrown from a window was about as grand a death as Crevan deserved.

"How high was the tower?" Griffith pressed.

"High enough that he had plenty of time to think about what an evil rash he's been the whole way down," Kyleigh said.

"He left a horrible mess at the bottom," Kael added — which made Griffith laugh.

Baird had them tell the whole story five times through before he felt *well enough* to start walking on his own. Then for a few days more, Griffith led him patiently around Thanehold — Baird's knobby hands clenched around his arm.

"I think he's going to pull through," Kyleigh mused, at the dusk of one particularly entertaining day.

Not only had the beggar-bard decided that he felt well enough to start whistling at the birds again, but Gwen had returned from Midlan that afternoon — her army reduced to a mere handful of what it'd been before.

It turned out that the wildmen were rather taken with their adventure across the Kingdom — so taken, in fact, that they'd scattered off in every direction the moment the battle ended. A few stayed in Midlan to help with the repairs, and a handful or so had joined up with the mercenaries in the forest.

Kael wasn't at all surprised that a good number of them had decided to become pirates. But what *did* surprise him was the fact that Brend had allowed a small group of craftsmen to follow the giants into the Endless Plains.

"There'll be whisperers in every region again, just like there was before," Kyleigh said with a smile. "It's all coming back."

Griffith had taken the news rather well, but Gwen was clearly heartbroken — though she mourned in a way that made it difficult to pity her.

She'd stormed and stomped all afternoon, yelling about how she meant to tan their traitorous hides. Nothing Griffith did seemed to calm her. Not even Silas could think of anything to say to stop her rants. He did finally manage to corner her in an empty part of the castle — but even then, she put a boot through the wall.

Though Kael certainly understood her anger, he knew how the wildmen felt. And he couldn't bring himself to leave Thanehold without at least trying to explain it to Gwen. "The mountains will always be their home. Nothing will ever change that," he said, once he'd managed to pin her against the floor.

He knew full well that Gwen would rage unless he held her down. But Silas wouldn't have it: he'd lunged for Kael the moment he touched her, so Kyleigh tossed him out by the scruff of his neck.

Now he yowled and scratched against the door while Kyleigh stood guard — and taunted him mercilessly through the keyhole.

"They're traitors!" Gwen snarled.

When she tried to squirm out from beneath him, Kael pressed harder against her back. "You know that isn't true. They're not traitors — and they won't forget you, by the way."

"You don't know that," she said, her voice breaking slightly. All the coil went out of her muscles as she finally collapsed. "You don't know that."

"I haven't forgotten you yet, and we haven't known each other half as long. Just because there's some distance between you now doesn't mean they no longer care. There's a whole Kingdom out there, Gwen," he said, rolling to lie beside her. "As someone who's just come off the mountains, himself, I can tell you that it's an exciting thing. But Thanehold will always be their home, and the wildmen will always be their people. They might even come back someday."

"Do you think so?"

"*I* certainly plan on coming back — I miss the cold. But you're going to have to welcome them."

"I will."

"And you understand that threatening to ram your axe down their throats blades-first isn't at all welcoming, don't you?"

"Yes," she moaned.

Though she'd been ordered not to come within punching distance, Kyleigh wandered over to them. She crouched on Gwen's other side, her brows raised at the sight of them sprawled out upon the floor. "How's it coming, over here?"

"I think we've got it all managed," Kael said, glaring until Gwen agreed with a somber nod.

Kyleigh smiled. "Brilliant. Well, if we're all through moping, I think it's time to say goodbye."

She smacked Gwen hard on the rump — Kael thought the ensuing brawl might've cheered her more than anything.

CHAPTER 59
A DOSE OF TONIC

When they finally returned to Copperdock, they discovered that Shamus had managed to convince a few of the wildmen to become shipbuilders — and they were already hard at work on Roost.

"Grab a handful of rubble and let's get her looking decent again," Shamus called when he spotted Kael. Though his bushy sideburns were nearly flattened with sweat, he still managed to grin. "Lady Kyleigh? I'd love to have my shipbuilders come back to their homes, if you wouldn't mind spreading the word."

"I think I can manage that," she said with a nod. Then she grabbed Kael under the chin and growled: "Be good while I'm away."

"Never."

"You'll pay for your insolence, whisperer," she warned as she kissed him. "Mark my words."

The days they spent repairing Copperdock passed in a wave of exhaustion and heat. Dampness hung from every thread of air, and the summer winds did nothing but swirl the discomfort around. Though the wildmen had to strip down to their underthings just to keep from melting, they never relinquished their grins — and the moment Shamus announced the end of the day, they'd tear off to cool themselves in the sea.

After a few hours' practice, the warriors swam as well as fish. The craftsmen, on the other hand, spent most of their time being rolled around by the waves. It seemed like hardly an evening passed that one of them didn't have to be rescued from the pull of the tide. But for whatever mad reason, they kept splashing right back in.

Ships began arriving a few days after Kyleigh left, their decks packed with villagers. They poured into their homes and went straight back to their chores. Soon, Copperdock bustled as if its people had never been gone.

Once they'd put Roost back together, they fixed its shattered gate. "Finally!" Knotter cried as the craftsmen hung him into place. "I never thought I'd escape that awful closet. My rash has only just cleared up. Hello, my beauty." His lopsided eyes twisted to the other door. "I hope you've missed me as much as I've missed *you*."

Kael didn't have the heart to tell him that they'd had to replace the other door, not when he saw how Knotter's crack of a mouth bent so happily.

"Eh, what he doesn't know won't hurt him," Shamus said with a shrug. "That, and I don't want to give him a reason to jam the latches."

Gerald and Mandy returned not a day after Kael had settled back into his chambers. He came down the next morning to find Gerald at his post, armor clattering with an enthusiastic wave. No sooner had he stepped into the kitchens than Mandy handed him a plate piled high with breakfast.

"Isn't it nice to be home, Master Kael?" she called as she bustled past him.

It was, indeed. Though they'd put the walls and ceilings back together, Roost had still felt empty without its people.

Geist showed up later that afternoon — clad all in black and with the remnants of a nasty bruise shadowing his eye. "I tried to find a position elsewhere, but my last employer was not so kind," he droned, touching his faded wound. "A flaw, I fear, that was his ultimate undoing. Would you have any need for a butler?"

"Of course. Someone's got to keep Kyleigh in line," Kael said.

Geist nodded slowly. His expression never once changed as he mumbled: "Ah. That reminds me."

He stepped to the side, and the force that charged through the door behind him very nearly knocked Kael flat. The world spun as Kyleigh grabbed him around the waist and tossed him over her shoulder.

"Come on, you," she growled.

"Mind the steps," Geist muttered after them. "And try to keep the disaster *small*."

****

"I've missed you," Kyleigh murmured into his chest. Her arm lay heavily across his middle, and her eyes had fallen closed. "Why do the days we're apart seem so much longer than the rest?"

Because we haven't got much time, Kael thought dully.

It was easy to forget his troubles, while he loved her. But the truth spoke loudly in the following quiet. It was a truth that pressed against him, an ever-present smog in the back of his mind — a problem he just couldn't figure out how to solve.

Kael traced the mark on Kyleigh's back as he thought: it was the crest of Midlan, branded into her flesh. She'd refused to let him erase it. No matter how he begged, and no matter how she seemed to loathe it, Kyleigh wouldn't budge.

It made no sense to keep the mark — just as her deciding to send them back to the Kingdom made no sense. He didn't understand why she would choose anguish over the eternal woods ... and though he was furious about the whole thing, he knew it would do him no good to be angry.

Kyleigh had no idea that she'd chosen to suffer.

"What are you thinking about?"

"Nothing," Kael said quickly. He tried to clear his mind, tried not to let Kyleigh feel his worry. He didn't want to ruin the few seasons they *would* have together.

"I stopped in to see Devin, while I traveled."

"Oh? How's he taken to being King?" Kael asked, grateful to have a distraction.

"He *loathes* it. Argon's trying to shake all of the wildness out of him before the nobles start turning up. He says that having spines is no excuse to not have manners. Honestly, it's nothing compared to what Crumfeld put me through." Kyleigh grinned sleepily. "I think the molting's just making him grumpy."

Kael ran his finger down the branded dragon's throat — and tried not to imagine that it taunted him. "Devin's molting?"

"Yes. I built him a forge and taught him how to save his scales in the fire. Once they fall, I'll make him some armor. It'll be our coronation gift."

"Coronation?" Kael said absently.

Kyleigh replied, but he didn't hear her answer. Something she'd said struck him hard across the front of his mind: *gift*. Something about a *gift* ... something he'd heard an age ago ...

Kael traced the curved edges of the branded dragon's wing, all of his thought bent upon that word. It was a loose thread — he was certain of it. He didn't know where it might lead, but he was determined to reach its end.

586

Gift ...

Something that was *meant* to be a gift ...

... the gift it was meant to be ...

... you would do well to remember the day you were born. Remember that you belong to me. In time ... perhaps you will see it for the gift it was meant to be.

Kael stopped. He didn't move, he didn't breathe. It wasn't the thought of Death that froze him: it was where Death's words had led him. It was at the thread's end, at the idea that waited in a knot before him ...

A mad, impossible idea.

"The first snow," Kael said quietly. He braced himself, convinced a wall of doubt would come to crush him, but it didn't.

Kyleigh rose up to frown at him. "Are you all right?"

Kael couldn't think to reply. He was afraid that if his mind so much as twitched from this thought, it would be lost to him forever. "Will you stay here with me?"

"Of course. We can stay anywhere you like —"

"No, it has to be here." He grabbed her around the shoulders, his heart racing. "I was born on the day of the first snow. But it never snows in this part of the Kingdom. So as long as I stay here, I'll never age."

It was a ridiculous thought — in the same way that turning flesh to clay or skin to stone was ridiculous. But all Kael had ever needed to do anything ridiculous was a reason to believe he could. And the thought of living someplace where the snows never came gave him the reason he needed to convince himself that it could be done.

His heart calmed immediately. He was no longer mindful of its every beat, that each throb carried him closer to his death. Instead, he imagined that it more whirred than pounded — as if it would sing on for ages in a relentless hum.

Kyleigh stared down at him, her brows arced in confusion. "Kael, I don't think —"

"Good. Don't think." He pressed his fingers softly against her lips, letting all of the relief he felt rise to their ends, where he knew she could feel it. "Just trust me."

He held her tightly as the night drifted on, listening to the strange new hum inside his chest.

587

Death had given him the answer he needed, told him exactly how to convince his heart. Kael realized that, now. And though he was fairly certain it'd been more about meddling with Fate than anything, he didn't mind it.

If being stuck in the middle of their war meant he'd get to spend an age with Kyleigh, that she would never have to feel the valtas' sting ... well, he would take it gladly.

****

One morning, and after a particularly rowdy night, they dragged themselves from their chambers and stumbled into the kitchens — bedraggled and grinning to either ear.

"Good morning, Master Kael," Mandy said cheerily, pressing a plate of breakfast into his hands.

"Guff mornin," he replied — around a mouthful of toasted bread.

She shook her head at him before holding a plate out to Kyleigh. "And how are you today, Miss ...? Oh, Miss Kyleigh!" Mandy gasped — so suddenly that Kael nearly choked on his eggs.

"Waff?"

"It's my hair, isn't it?" Kyleigh said, tugging at her wreck of a pony's tail. "I promise I'll try to fix it before Crumfeld sees."

Even when she took her plate, Mandy still gaped at her. The maid's eyes roved across her every feature ... and her shock slowly bent into an open-mouthed smile. She waved Kyleigh to her chair. "You have a seat, Miss. I'll fetch your tonic."

Kyleigh frowned as she sat. "Tonic? What tonic?"

"You don't have a fever," Kael said. He slapped a hand against the back of her head to prove it.

She punched him hard in the shoulder.

Kael was about to flick a bit of toast at her when Mandy grabbed his wrist. "No, there'll be no more of that. From now on, you're going to have to be gentle with her."

"Hmm, I'd rather he weren't," Kyleigh growled, with a look that not even a blind man could've possibly misread.

But before things could get out of hand, Mandy slammed an earthen cup on the table between them. "No. There'll be no more punching or shoving or tearing the room to pieces. You need to drink

588

your tonic and be *careful*, Miss. These first few weeks are always the trickiest."

"The first few weeks of what?" Kael said.

No one answered him.

Mandy stood cross-armed and silent, while Kyleigh stared at her as if she'd just sprouted wings.

"It's not possible."

"It's *quite* possible, Miss. In fact, it was bound to happen."

"What's not possible?"

"It's not possible!" Kyleigh said sharply. She pushed the tonic away and stood. Before Kael even had a chance to turn, she'd marched out the door.

Mandy scowled after her. "She's cross already ... and it's only going to get worse. But I wager she'll come around in another month, once the sickness sets in. You keep a close eye on her, Master Kael," she added with a sharp look. "Make sure she's careful — for the baby's sake."

That time, Kael really *did* choke on his breakfast.

****

Kyleigh was right: it wasn't possible.

Kael told himself this over and over again. He remembered what Gwen had said about them being two completely different creatures — about how they were far too opposite to fit. Even Kyleigh had warned him that they would never have children of their own.

It made perfect sense. They *were* far too different. It simply wasn't possible. And he'd always accepted this — welcomed it, even. Kael had always been entirely certain that he never wanted children ... or at least, that's what he tried to tell himself.

But as the weeks went on, a tiny hope crowded its way into his heart. He held it down tightly and refused to let it grow. He was careful to keep it away from the center, where he knew it would quickly take root. Instead, he pressed it into a corner and tried not to think about it. There was no point in thinking about something that simply wasn't possible.

Still, as another month stretched on, he found himself watching Kyleigh more and more often ... looking for a sign.

She always ignored the tonic Mandy served her at breakfast. Geist would bring her another dose in the evenings — which she'd promptly toss out the nearest window. Any man who looked at her strangely could expect to have his head bit off, and Kael was no exception.

He'd been playing chess with Shamus in the library one evening when he made the mistake of glancing over at her.

Kyleigh was sprawled between the arms of a cushioned chair, running a cloth down the edge of Harbinger's deadly, curved blade. Her eyes never left her work as she growled: "Keep staring at my middle, whisperer, and I swear I'll rip your eyes out and stomp them flat."

She went to bed in a foul mood — and woke up in an even fouler one.

Kael tried to lie very still as Kyleigh dragged herself from the covers. Her heels slapped the floor hard and she cursed under her breath. He cringed when he heard the window's shutters slam open against the wall, half-expecting her to tear them from their hinges.

Instead, she was violently ill.

"Kyleigh?"

"I'm fine," she said shortly. "It was probably just that deer I had for dinner. I knew he had a strange look in his eye ..."

She was ill again — out the window and straight into the courtyard below. After the third time, a few of the guards jogged over to watch. "Somebody go get Mandy," Kael bellowed at them.

One guard peeled away. The rest stayed behind to bet on how many stones Kyleigh would hit on her next attempt.

The man who guessed *six* won it.

Mandy rushed in a few minutes later. She grabbed Kyleigh by the hand and led her back to bed, ordering her to lie still. No sooner had she gotten her settled than Geist turned up at the door.

He carried a large tray between his hands. There was a cup of water and a plate of bread settled atop it — along with a second cup that smelled suspiciously of tonic.

"For the last bloody time, I'm not pregnant. It's not possible," Kyleigh said hoarsely.

"All right, then." Mandy passed the tonic behind her back and held it out with the other hand. "I've worked my magic on it. Now it's *not* a tonic for pregnancy — just a little something to settle your stomach."

Kyleigh glared at her teasing. But in the end, she was just pale enough to take a drink. "It tastes like you've scraped it out of a goat's belly."

"Perhaps I have. But you're still going to finish it," Mandy said tersely. "You'll have another dose this evening — and when you get to feeling ill at breakfast tomorrow, you'll drink it again."

"No, I'll be *better* by tomorrow. It was only a bad deer."

Mandy laughed as she walked out the door. Geist watched her go before he followed with a slight bow. "I'll see you this evening, Lady Kyleigh."

"No, you blasted won't," she muttered into her cup.

Kael sat beside her while she drank and tried not to say anything upsetting. But deep inside his chest, that tiny hope had begun to grow. It stretched tentatively for the middle of his heart. He finally managed to push it back ... but not before it'd gained considerable ground.

The tonic seemed to make Kyleigh feel better. She was back to her usual self by the early afternoon. When Geist brought her another dose of tonic that evening, she threw it into the hearth — insisting that she'd been cured.

Kael hardly slept a wink that night. He kept thinking about what it would be like if Kyleigh *were* pregnant. He kept imagining how their lives would change, tried to convince himself that it would be frightening beyond belief.

But the only word that came to him was *wonderful* — and it tinged all of his dreams in sunlight.

When Kyleigh woke, he thought she might've looked slightly pale. She leaned heavily against the wall as they made their way downstairs and bit down hard upon her lip.

But though he strongly suspected that she wasn't feeling well, she managed to keep herself together — until Mandy set a full plate of rather wobbly eggs before her.

Then she got sick into the mouth of the nearest cauldron.

Kyleigh put up a brave fight. But after nearly a week of disasters, she finally gave in: the tonic went down begrudgingly in the evenings, gratefully in the mornings — and if anyone so much as thought the word *pregnancy*, they'd get a sharp slap. So they all agreed not to mention it.

Kael was slightly proud of how well he was able to keep quiet. When Kyleigh went without her armor one day because it felt *too tight*, he said nothing. As that single day stretched into a couple of weeks, he still managed to keep his mouth shut. But the day she decided to try to put it back on again proved to be his greatest test.

"It won't clasp," she grunted, trying to stretch the buckles of her jerkin together. "It's never not clasped before."

"That's odd," Kael said calmly — though just beneath the skin, his heart screamed and danced a maddened jig.

A small bump had begun to take shape at the base of her stomach. Its gentle slope flattened the hard lines across her middle and poked out just over the top of her breeches.

"The cook's been feeding me far too well. That's probably what it ... Kael?"

He glanced up — and found himself snared in the fires of her glare. "What?"

"You know very well *what*. Stop it."

"But —"

"You'll be dead before you strike the ground," she said sharply.

He shut his mouth, but only because he swore he'd seen something in her eyes as she snapped at him: a tiny, hairline crack in her resolve ...

The faintest admission that it might possibly be something more.

****

One week later, she finally gave in.

It happened as they were sitting at dinner. Shamus set off on an ale-fueled account of how he'd once seen a goblin trotting along a beach outside the castle, and the guards egged him on.

"Oh? How many legs did it have?" Gerald called around a mouthful of his dinner.

"Five," Shamus said firmly. Then he squinted at the wall. "No ... seven. It was seven, I'm sure of it."

"Well, as long as it was an odd number. I'm not sure I could believe a story about a *balanced* goblin," Kyleigh said with a grin.

While the rest of them had potatoes to go along with their lamb, Kyleigh had nothing but an entire rack of red meat. She fought her way through it at a steady pace — glancing up every once in a while to heckle Shamus.

"What color was the goblin's skin?" Kael said.

Shamus snorted loudly. "Goblins don't have skin. They've got scales. And they were yellow — a bright, weedy sort of yellow."

"*Weedy* isn't a sort of yellow," Kyleigh said, laughing.

Kael was about to add on when he saw Kyleigh reaching for his plate out of the corner of his eye. She stole something and popped it into her mouth ... and he was almost entirely certain it wasn't a piece of lamb.

The others went on with their story, but Kael wasn't listening. He tried to keep eating as if nothing had happened. When he saw Kyleigh move again, he caught her around the wrist.

"Are you nicking my potatoes?"

She froze, staring at the roasted bite stuck to the end of her fork as if she'd only just discovered it. "I ... thought it looked good."

Nothing Kyleigh had to say about vegetables had ever involved the word *good* — and it might as well have been a filthy swear.

The whole table fell silent. Eyes went wide and forks paused upon their plates. For a long moment, no one so much as chewed. They watched Kyleigh stare at the potato as if they were about to witness the start of a battle.

Instead, she burst into tears.

The table cleared immediately: the guards snatched up their plates and scattered, running as fast as they could without sloshing the ale from their cups.

"It isn't ... *possible*," Kyleigh sobbed. She threw the fork down upon the table and buried her head in her hands.

It took everything Kael had not to laugh as he gathered her up. "I thought you wanted a child?"

"I do ..."

"Then what are you so weepy about?"

"We can't ... we *can't.*"

"Well, it looks as if we have."

"Aye, you certainly have. Did she not know it?" Shamus blustered from across the table. "How could you not have known it, lass? We all blasted well knew it."

"I didn't want to think it. I didn't want to hope. But I suppose it's true." When she finally lifted her head from his chest, a smile glowed through her tears. "I'm pregnant, aren't I?"

"Very much so," Kael said with a grin.

Shamus raised his tankard high. "Cheers to you both — and cheers especially to *you*, Sir Wright," he added with a wink.

CHAPTER 60
A LITTLE REMINDER

"She's beautiful," Aerilyn whispered.

She was, indeed.

Kael had gotten to hold her every day for all of her three months of life. He'd talked to her, read to her, and told her all manner of stories. He'd stared at her far more than she probably would've liked. But he still hadn't quite gotten used to how stunning she was.

Aerilyn held her gently, smiling down. "What have you named her?"

"Ryane. It was Kael's idea, and I thought it was perfect," Kyleigh said.

As protective as Kael was, Kyleigh was far worse: she hovered at Aerilyn's elbow and kept one hand beneath Ryane's head, as if she was preparing to catch her at any moment. A whole cluster of people waited to hold her — and as Ryane went around the room, Kyleigh followed closely.

"She has got her mother's eyes," Nadine said when it was her turn.

Declan leaned over her, one thick hand resting gently atop her shoulder. "Yeh, *and* her mother's looks."

"A mightily grand thing! Can you imagine how mad she'd be if she came out looking like a mountain ra —? Ah, *mouse*?" Brend amended quickly, when he saw Declan's glare.

They stood inside what had once been the King's throne room. Now the chamber looked more like a gathering place: thick rugs adorned the floor, and a few small tables sat between the cushioned chairs. The hearth warmed their skin while the night poured coolly through the window.

Fortunately, Declan and Nadine's horde of redheaded children were well out of range of Brend's voice. They sat before the hearth, listening patiently to Baird.

With Griffith's help, the beggar-bard had finally finished his book. Now the whole massive tome sat open across his lap. He dragged his knobby fingers along the quill's marks and read the words aloud:

"By this point, my satchel was practically bursting with letters. Every corner of the realm seemed to be in some sort of peril — and I was determined to deliver them from harm. But a full satchel is both a courier's joy and bane. You're bound to find out the truth eventually, dear reader, so I might as well warn you now: there isn't much that can be done for a parchment cut ..."

Baird told his stories with whispers and shouts. Sometimes, he even forgot to read it: he'd take his hands from the pages and wave them in frantic arcs, going on about whatever parchment cut he'd gotten next.

The moment he took his hands away, Griffith would lean around him and quickly flip a few pages ahead — getting them back to the exciting bits.

"Where was I?" Baird frowned as he dragged his hands across the page. *"The Battle of the Tide Winds*? That can't be ... ah, well. I suppose I must've forgotten where I ended up ..."

Things were getting a bit tight where Kael stood. Kyleigh hovered so watchfully over Ryane that he knew nothing short of the Kingdom's end could tear them apart. So he slipped away from the crowd and went in search of a quiet place to sit.

One corner looked promising. But as he neared it, Thelred stomped by — followed closely by Uncle Martin.

"So, where's this *Lydia* I've been hearing so much about?" Uncle Martin said.

"I don't know. You certainly didn't hear it from me," Thelred grumped.

"Well, I never hear a blasted thing from you! I've got to get it all from Lysander —"

"Who greatly embellishes everything to the point that there's not a shred of truth left in it. Lydia is nothing more than a friend. We play music together."

"It doesn't matter what you call it. I think I've got a right to meet the woman my son keeps traveling into the Valley to *play music* with. She must be one fantastic *musician*," Uncle Martin added, wagging his brows.

Thelred spun around. "Oh, she is."

As far as Kael could remember, that was the first time he'd ever seen Thelred grin — and it was every bit as terrifying a look as he'd expected it to be.

Uncle Martin stood frozen nearly a full minute after Thelred stomped off, his mouth agape beneath his mustache. "Well, now I've *got* to meet her!" he finally said, hobbling away.

Kael managed to take one more step towards the corner before Lysander ran into him.

"No, no, Dante! Leave that alone."

When Kael looked down, he was surprised to see that little Dante had snuck in beside him. The child stared up with big blue eyes, a wide smile upon his face — and with his little hand clenched firmly around the hilt of Kael's hunting knife.

He'd managed to lift it halfway out of its sheath before Lysander pried his fingers away. "No, young man. You aren't old enough to be handling sharp things. Your mother would absolutely kill me if she found out. She's already mad enough about the jam."

That's when Kael noticed the many purple handprints that dirtied the captain's white tunic — and matted the waves of his hair.

"Infants are trying enough. But just wait until they start to walk," Lysander warned as he watched Dante toddle away. "That's when the *real* trials begin. I keep telling people not to try to hold him, warning that he'll only rob them blind. But no one believes me. Here ..."

There was an odd assortment of rings on Lysander's fingers and a tangle of necklaces upon his arm. He dug through them until he found one with a blood red jewel hanging from its middle.

"I don't know who half of these belong to — he nicks them before I have a chance to see, most times. But I know for certain that this one belongs to Gwen. Make sure she gets it back, will you?"

Lysander rushed off before he could reply, already yelling at Dante for rubbing jam into the curtains.

Kael turned to search the room — and nearly skewered himself on the tip of Elena's black dagger. "I thought you were never coming back to Midlan?" he said.

"Well obviously, I've changed my mind." She slid the dagger upwards to press it against his chin. "Congratulations on becoming a father."

597

"Thanks," Kael said warily. "I hear you run an inn?"

"*The Mage and Blade,*" Jake said as he came up beside her. There was a rather potent scent wafting in behind him: the stink of the skunk oil he used to cover his magic.

Elena didn't seem at all to mind it. She smiled as she nudged him with an elbow. "I'd rather missed having an inn."

"Yes, and we felt it only right to help rebuild Crow's Cross, after the … incident with the lantern. It turns out that the Valley is a very peaceful place to settle."

"Jake does his own brewing," Elena said, sliding the dagger back into its sheath. "It's made things rather … exciting."

Though Jake tried to wave her off, it was too late: Kael was already interested.

"I don't know what it is. The spells I use *should* work," Jake groaned when he asked. "But for whatever reason, my patrons keep turning purple. One in eleven of them, to be exact."

"They come in groups, and the man who turns has to pay for everybody else's drinks. Word's started to spread. We've got travelers from all over the Kingdom coming to give it a try. I doubt we'll be able to make it out the door, before too much longer," Elena said.

Jake nodded in agreement. "Yes, the inn's doing well. We're rather enjoying the quiet life."

They fell silent for a moment. Elena fidgeted with her bandolier while Jake stared into the hearth. Something hung between them — a thick, uncertain air. Both seemed to be just at the edge of speaking.

But it was Jake who spoke first: "Although …"

"Yes?" Elena stepped closer to him, her dark eyes searching.

"It's nothing, really. I've certainly enjoyed every peaceful moment we've spent in the Valley. But I was thinking about the minceworms the other day. Now that their queen is, ah … *deceased,*" he smiled at Elena's grin, "I've realized that there might not be much time left to study them."

"You ought to go back to the desert, then."

He shoved his spectacles up his nose thoughtfully. "Yes, I've considered it. Though there are outlaws in the desert. So I'd probably need some sort of protection."

A glint crossed Elena's eyes. "I think I can help with that. I'm sure the girls can run things on their own for a bit."

"But we can't do anything too dangerous. We have an inn to manage, after all."

"Of course not. And once we've finished your research, we'll come straight home."

"Yes, I'm sure we'll be more than ready to get back to something peaceful, by then," Jake agreed.

While they discussed their plans, Kael slipped away quietly — shaking his head as he went.

The crowd that'd been gathered around Ryane slowly spread out across the room. Kael thought he saw a patch of flaming red hair in the far corner, but he wasn't at all eager to go fighting through the bodies to get to it. Fortunately, Jonathan came bursting through the doors at that very moment — and his announcement drew the crowd away.

"Prepare yourselves, gents!" he cried.

Kael cringed, expecting an atrocious note to go screeching off his fiddle. But instead, Jonathan merely swept aside to let Clairy through.

Crimson stained her cheeks when she saw everybody watching her. She wore a deep blue dress and had her hair braided softly over her shoulder. There was a light in her eyes, a smile upon her lips ...

And an unmistakable bump on her belly.

Most of the room erupted in cheers — though Aerilyn swore loudly.

"That's exactly what I said when I found out," Brend grunted, shaking his head.

"Oh, and there's going to be more of them!" Aerilyn pressed her hands against her face, as if it was all she could do to keep from fainting. "I don't think the Kingdom's prepared."

"For what? Wee giantlings with the fiddler's gift for mischief? No." Brend laughed through his grin. "No, but the Kingdom'll *never* be ready for that!"

With the crowd moving to congratulate Jonathan and Clairy, Kael finally got a decent look at the other side of the room.

Gwen leaned against the far wall, staring listlessly out the window. Several of the wildmen had turned up in Midlan for the King's coronation feast. They'd spent the evening telling her all about their adventures in other parts of the realm — and instead of gutting them, she'd actually listened. She'd been reasonably pleasant and had even managed to smile at a few of their stories.

But once the wildmen drifted to other parts of the room, her misery returned.

She slumped against the wall, arms crossed over her chest. Her paint was gone. She wore a soft linen tunic and breeches. The wide belt around her middle revealed a surprisingly graceful figure. Aerilyn had even convinced her to run a brush through her hair, which beat the mad, red tangles into waves.

Gwen was lovelier than Kael had ever seen her ... and he thought it would be a shame if she wasted the whole night moping about the wildmen. So he came up with a plan.

He made a great show of straightening his collar before he stepped towards her, hoping it would draw the attention of a certain glowing set of eyes. And he wasn't disappointed.

"Where do you think you're going, Marked One?" Silas hissed as he stepped into his path.

Kael held out the necklace. "I was just going to return this."

"*I'll* return it. Go back to your side of the room."

Silas snatched the necklace from his hand, but Kael didn't flinch. Instead, he stared unblinkingly at Gwen.

"What are you ...? No, stop looking at her! She isn't yours to look at!"

"She's not *yours*, either," Kael retorted. "And it isn't against the law to look. She's beautiful, isn't she? But she seems so ... upset."

Silas's brows bent into pained arcs as he glanced at her. "My Thane misses her people. She does not live as wildly as she used to. That's all it is. Looking at her won't make her feel any better," he added with a growl. "So go away."

"No ... in fact, I think I'm going to kiss her."

"What? No!" Silas dropped the necklace and grabbed Kael roughly by the tunic. "You can't kiss her!"

"Sure I can."

"She won't like it!"

"She liked it well enough, the last time." Kael bent to whisper menacingly into his ear. "And I've learned an awful lot since then."

When he tried to step past, Silas held desperately onto his shirt. "But — but you already have a mate! The dragoness will be furious with you if you kiss someone else."

600

"Oh, I don't think she minds it. Do you, Kyleigh?"

She stood beside the hearth, bouncing Ryane gently in her arms. "Do I what?"

"Do you mind if I give Gwen one of my deepest, most passionate kisses?"

"Of course not. And give her one from me, as well," she added with a wink.

By now, Silas's eyes had grown so wild with terror that they looked as if they were about to burst from their sockets. "Please, Marked One! *Please* don't kiss her!"

Kael grabbed him around the collar. "Someone's going to kiss Gwen tonight. Either you do it ... or I will."

"But it's abomination," he moaned.

"There's no such thing as abomination. I've seen how you protect her, how you follow along in her shadow. You obviously care for her, and you have a chance to make her happy. So quit twiddling your thumbs and get on with it."

Kael didn't like shoving Silas around, but that seemed to be the only way to get through to him. The halfcat took an eternity to slink across the room, hands twisting nervously before his chest. When he finally reached Gwen, he froze.

She turned from the window and looked him up and down. "What is it, cat? And why are you ... *sweating*?"

Silas said nothing for such a long moment that Kael feared he might faint. Then all at once, he grabbed Gwen by the face and slammed his mouth against hers.

It was easily the worst kiss Kael had ever seen. No woman could've possibly enjoyed it — unless that woman's name happened to be *Gwen*.

After a brief moment of shock, she grabbed Silas by the hair and pressed against him so roughly that Kael thought for certain one of them would break. But they didn't. And several seconds later, the kiss still hadn't ended.

"Ugh, it's like watching a lion tear into a goat," Kyleigh muttered as she slipped in beside him.

"Well, I'm sure he hasn't had much practice," Kael said with a grimace.

She smirked. "I wasn't talking about *Silas*."

He supposed he could see her point.

When the doors opened again, it was Eveningwing who stepped through — followed closely by the shamans.

From what Kael could make of the rumors, the shapechangers had begun wandering up to the castle not long after Devin was made King. They came in flocks and packs to greet him. Many of them roamed for days around the fields, leery of stepping inside the fortress walls.

So Devin removed the outer gates, which allowed them to come and go as they pleased.

It was nothing any other ruler would've done. Crevan's fortress, Reginald's island, and Gilderick's thick reddened walls — each of their castles had been designed to keep people out, to keep a barrier between their subjects and their thrones. But Devin wasn't like any other ruler, and what he'd done for the shapechangers was only the beginning.

The giants had sent him a caravan's worth of saplings and seed as a coronation gift. According to what the merchants in Copperdock had said, Devin spent weeks planting them all by hand — packing the courtyards and the fields around the castle with green. Several of them exclaimed that they'd been shocked to find their new King kneeling in the mud.

But though Kael had heard the rumors, he didn't quite believe them until he saw the castle grounds for himself. Now he thought that if Devin cared for his people even a fraction as much as he cared for his garden, the Kingdom would thrive.

It took quite a bit of convincing, but Devin had finally managed to get the shamans to come inside long enough to join the coronation feast. Though they wore far more clothing than usual, their feet were still bare.

Graymange's sharp eyes roved until they found Kael — and he bared all of his teeth into a wolfish greeting.

The shamans stood quietly while Eveningwing spread his arms and blurted:

"Dinner's ready!"

"No, it's *dinner is served*," Horatio hissed loudly from behind the door.

"Oh. There's a dinner served and the King wants to see you!"

"Remember to thank them, now."

"And thank you!"

"Gah!" Horatio bustled out from behind the door and shooed Eveningwing to the side. "Dinner is served, and His Majesty eagerly awaits his guests of honor. On behalf of his shamans and his court, he thanks you all for your gifts. Now, please follow me."

The crowd spilled from the room in an excited, chattering rush — eager to see Devin.

Their new King had spent his first few months of rule soaring around the realm, learning everything he could about his Kingdom. There wasn't a region he didn't visit or a village he overlooked. People were certainly leery of him, at first: not only because he rode in on monstrous wings, but because even his human body was twisted with spines and scales.

Still, Devin managed to win them over — if not with his kindness, then with his complete disinterest in trying to tell anybody how to live. Every region was left to its own devices, governed by its own chosen form of rule.

In the end, Kael supposed Argon had been right: Devin truly *was* more a caretaker than a King. After having been ruled over for so long, he thought a *caretaker* was exactly what the Kingdom needed.

"I suppose we should follow," Kyleigh said quietly.

They were the last ones left — even Silas and Gwen had managed to pull apart long enough to go to dinner. "Fine," Kael said with a sigh. Then he held out his hands. "But it's my turn to hold her."

Kyleigh laughed as she handed her over. Ryane stared up at him through a pair of wide, green eyes, her lips a bright pink against her pale skin. She looked like her mother in every way, save one.

Flaming red curls had begun to sprout up across her head. He loved how they seemed to war against the green of her gaze: two separate colors, each shining equally as bright. But there was something odd about it.

Only children born in the Unforgivable Mountains had red hair. It was their crown and curse. He'd never heard of a redheaded child being born any other way ... and yet, Ryane had been born in Copperdock.

Kyleigh insisted that her hair was just a bit of mountain blood showing through. But Kael knew differently. He'd known from the moment her first curl appeared that the red was a message, and a taunt. It was a final jab from the world beyond, a weighted roll of the die:

Ryane was the *little reminder* that Fate had promised him — a warning that she could always cast for the ones he loved. But though it had clearly been meant to keep him from interfering with her plans, Kael didn't mind it.

He would've given up far more than a bit of freedom, for Ryane.

"I know what you're doing, whisperer," Kyleigh said when he turned Ryane towards the hearth. She stepped in behind him and wrapped her arms around his waist. He could feel her smile against his shoulder. "No matter how many times you look, it's going to be the same."

Kael knew this. Still, he couldn't help but look. When the hearth light brushed across Ryane's eyes, there was a symbol carved into their middles — a pair of diamonds that wreathed the blacks in gold.

They were a whisperer's eyes ...

They were the eyes of a healer.

ACKNOWLEDGEMENTS

Well, this has been quite a journey for me, and I'm sad to have it end.

I want to begin by thanking everyone who made this series a possibility. Thank you to my wonderful beta-readers: Prudence, Fran Mason, and Ms. Carmichael. You guys see all the things I can't, and I couldn't have done it without you!

I also want to thank Miguel Coimbra, who did such an absolutely fantastic job on the new cover art. You truly brought the characters to life, and gave them a place to shine. Now the story begins before the first page has turned — and that's a wonderful thing.

Thank you to my family, who has helped in every conceivable way: you read my roughest drafts, encouraged me, pushed me through the low points. You've lifted me up in more ways than I can count. Never once was I handed anything but love from you, and I will be forever grateful.

Thank you to my readers, who supported me not only in buying copies of the books, but through their kindness as well. It is a kindness I never expected — a kindness that seems to permeate the world. You brought these stories into your homes and made a place for the characters inside your hearts. If I've been able to make you smile or laugh, if I've lifted your spirits even once over the years, then make no mistake: these stories belong to you.

My own story is a relatively short one.

Way back in 2010, I was a grad student working towards a business degree, and writing was nothing more than an escape from coursework. But somewhere along the way, I accidentally fell in love with it.

I wound up publishing *Harbinger* in 2012 at the age of 23 — with crossed fingers and a good deal of *misguided courage*. The last three years have taken me on a journey that I will forever cherish as the adventure of a lifetime. I am beyond grateful to have had the opportunity to earn a living doing something I love, and it's an opportunity *you* have given me.

I say all of that to say this:

Some of you may have read these books and thought, "*Pshh*, I could do that!" And if you're one of those people, I want to be the first to tell you to *Go for it.* Don't hold off until you're "old enough" or have an MFA. Don't wait around for an agent to accept you.

We just happen to live in an age where anybody with a story to tell can share it with the world — and I consider it a golden age. For the first time in the history of storytelling, the writers will decide what is written, and the readers will decide what is read.

So to all of you aspiring authors out there, dust off that notebook and give it a try. There's never been a better time to write.

And to all of you who are readers, as requested, I'll leave you with this:

One thing I have learned throughout this journey is that my intentions as a writer are not nearly as important as my readers' interpretations. Words can be written, words can be spoken. But, like any other wave of light or sound, unless they hit some sort of receptor, they might as well not have existed.

It's in the hearing and in the reading that words take on their meaning — and there are as many meanings as there are ears to hear them, eyes to read them, minds to perceive them. It's a mosaic that began at the first moment of imagination, and it continues on even now.

Your journey isn't over, dear Reader. There are many characters you have yet to meet, countless worlds left to be explored — and explore them you must, for it's the eyes upon the page that raise these worlds from the dust, the imagination of the reader that brings these characters to life. A book left unopened has no meaning at all. You make the story what it is.

So stride on, dear Reader. Stride on, and add your colors to the picture.

CPSIA information can be obtained at www.ICGtesting.com
Printed in the USA
BVOW02*1323030516

446576BV00002B/6/P